Library of America, a nonprofit organization,
champions our nation's cultural heritage
by publishing America's greatest writing in
authoritative new editions and providing resources
for readers to explore this rich, living legacy.

JOAN DIDION

JOAN DIDION

THE 1960s & 70s

Run River
Slouching Towards Bethlehem
Play It As It Lays
A Book of Common Prayer
The White Album

David L. Ulin, *editor*

THE LIBRARY OF AMERICA

JOAN DIDION: THE 1960s & 70s

Published in the United States by Library of America.
Visit our website at www.loa.org.

This paper exceeds the requirements of
ANSI/NISO Z39.48–1992 (Permanence of Paper).

Distributed to the trade in the United States
by Penguin Random House Inc.
and in Canada by Penguin Random House Canada Ltd.

Library of Congress Control Number: 2019936184
ISBN 978-1-59853-645-4

Fourth Printing
The Library of America—325

Manufactured in the United States of America

Joan Didion: The 1960s & 70s
is published with support from

Harrison Ford, ***in memory of***
Melissa Mathison and Earl McGrath
Alan Alda
Big Beach
Boaty Boatwright
Susan L. Brody
Lucy Fisher and Douglas Z. Wick
Louise Grunwald
Penelope C. Hall
David Hare
ICM Partners
Kathleen Kennedy
Lyn and Norman Lear
Carey Lowell
Liam Neeson
Wyndham Robertson
Richard Roth
Meryl Streep
Jann Wenner

Contents

RUN RIVER

For my family and for N

"All night I've held your hand,
as if you had
a fourth time faced the kingdom of the mad—
its hackneyed speech, its homicidal eye—
and dragged me home alive . . ."

—Robert Lowell

". . . the real Eldorado is still further on."

—Peck's 1837 New Guide to the West

August 1959

I

LILY HEARD the shot at seventeen minutes to one. She knew the time precisely because, without looking out the window into the dark where the shot reverberated, she continued fastening the clasp on the diamond wrist watch Everett had given her two years before on their seventeenth anniversary, looked at it on her wrist for a long time, and then, sitting on the edge of the bed, began winding it.

When she could wind the watch no further she stood up, still barefoot from the shower, picked up from her dressing table a bottle of *Joy*, splashed a large amount of it onto her hand, and reached down the neckline of her dress to spread it, a kind of amulet, across her small bare breasts: on the untroubled pages of those magazines where *Joy* was periodically proclaimed The Costliest Perfume in the World, nobody sat in her bedroom and heard shots on her dock.

Her eyes fixed not on the windows but upon the framed snapshots of the children which hung above her dressing table (Knight at eight, standing very straight in a Cub Scout uniform; Julie at seven, the same summer), Lily held her hand inside her dress until all the *Joy* had evaporated and there was nothing left to do but open the drawer where the .38 had been since the day Everett killed the rattlesnake on the lawn: the drawer in the table by their bed where the .38 should be still and where it was not. She had known it would not be.

Nine hours before, at four o'clock that afternoon, Lily had decided that she would not go at all to the Templetons' party. It was entirely too hot. She had been upstairs all afternoon, lying on the bed in her slip, the shutters closed and the electric fan on. Everett was out in the hops, showing the new irrigation system to a grower from down the river; Knight had driven into town; Julie, she supposed, was somewhere with one of the Templeton twins. She did not really know.

The afternoons always settled down this way. Late in June, after all the trouble, she had begun insisting that everyone lie down after lunch. Although on three afternoons everyone had gone upstairs, on the fourth she had heard Julie talking on the telephone downstairs ("You couldn't *mean* it. He swore they broke up *months* ago"), and on the fifth she was, as usual, alone in the house. Everett and the children had been, nonetheless, extravagantly agreeable about the plan: if there was one word to describe what everyone had been about everything since June, that word was agreeable. It had been all summer as if a single difference among them might tear it apart again; as if one unpremeditated word could bring the house down around them for good.

She got up and opened a shutter. The heat still shimmered in the air, so concentrated as to seem incendiary. After dinner she would take another shower and throw the windows open and read one of Knight's books. The floor of his room was stacked with books. It seemed to her that Knight had spent the entire summer packing, unpacking, arranging and rearranging the things he planned to take East to Princeton: he had already packed so many books to ship East that Everett had finally asked if he had reason to believe the Princeton library off-limits to freshmen. "Why leave them here," Knight had shrugged, and for a few seconds Lily had hated him, had read malice into his bland voice as she watched Everett's face take on that look of elaborate unconcern.

At any rate, she would try to read tonight, although she found concentration increasingly difficult; lately she had been able to read only books about Chicago gangsters or by oceanographers. The Saint Valentine's Day Massacre and the Mindanao Deep seemed, in their equidistance from her, equally absorbing. She had asked Knight, last week when he was driving to Berkeley, to pick up some new books in one of the paperback bookstores along Telegraph Avenue. The books could no doubt be found, Knight had informed her, right downtown in Sacramento. She did not seem to realize that there were now paperback bookstores in Sacramento. She and his father would never seem to get it through their heads that things were changing in Sacramento, that Aerojet General and Douglas Aircraft and even the State College were bringing in a whole new class of people, people who had lived back East, people who read things. She and his father were going to be pretty surprised if and when they ever woke up to the fact that nobody in Sacramento any more had even heard of the McClellans. Or the Knights. Not that he thought they ever would wake up. They'd just go right along dedicating their grubby goddamn camellia trees in Capitol Park to the memory of their grubby goddamn pioneers.

Although she did not suppose that Knight would have brought any new books about either Columbus Iselin or Mad Dog Coll, even to simply sit in the dark and watch the lights on the levee road would be better than going to Francie Templeton's, where everyone would be hot and someone would drink too much and say something with a familiar edge to it; going to river parties had become unpleasantly like watching reel after reel of badly focused home movies, the prints a little frayed by wear. *Here's the kitchen and there's Joe Templeton, trying to pour Francie's drink down the sink; look, Francie's stamping her foot and it's not even midnight yet; watch now, here comes little Jennie Mason, looking in the garden for Bud Mason; remember that, because next you'll see Jennie Mason (who, in a sequence spliced out of this reel, unfortunately but naturally misinterpreted Bud Mason's presence in the garden with Lily McClellan) being comforted by Everett McClellan; that's Everett, there in the long-suffering suit.* You did not even need audio. You could count on little Jennie somebody, could count on all the same faces, all the same games; at one of Francie's parties last year, when Ryder Channing had announced belligerently that he owed money to five of the ten men in the room, it had occurred to Lily that she had been to bed with seven, and in four cases could not remember exactly when or where. They were all, now, one error in taste. Although she had not been to a river party since June, she could remember what had happened after that one with the same distorted clarity that hung about the whole of June: it had not been the first party she had deserted for a hotel room, but it had been the first party she had deserted for a room at the Senator, which she thought of, still, as her father's hotel. Her father had liked the Senator bar, and several times when she was small he had taken her there for lemonade with grenadine. (The morning after that party, clutching Everett's pillow to her stomach, she had dug her fingernails into her arm until the skin bruised, but by noon, driving to the lake by herself, she had begun again to see it all as

Everett's fault. It would not have happened had Everett been at the party instead of home brooding about his sister; none of it would ever have happened had Everett been there.)

You better cut it out, Ryder Channing had said in June, that day at the lake which had been part of the trouble, and although Ryder was the last one to have said it, Ryder was right. A party could begin it all again—two drinks, someone from out of town, Everett ignoring her, that was all it would take—and when Everett came upstairs at four-thirty she told him that she did not want to go to Francie Templeton's.

"It's too hot. You go if you want."

She was brushing her hair, pulling it down over her face, trying to find the gray Julie had claimed to see among the dark. Lily could not imagine herself with gray hair: in the first place she was not yet thirty-seven and in the second place she had always imagined her style to be striking frailty. You could not, with graying hair, look strikingly frail; you could only look frail.

"Knight and Julie are going," she added.

Everett sat down by the window. Both his face and his khaki shirt were splotched with dust and sweat. "I think you should go. They're expecting you."

"I have a headache," she said mildly. "I can't help that, can I. I mean that's what anybody'd have to call an act of God, isn't it. Even Francie Templeton. You'll catch cold if you sit by the fan in a wet shirt."

"You and your mother."

"It's congenital. I read it in the *Reader's Digest.* Five New York doctors. How to Make Headaches Work for You. Anyway. You go."

"All right," he said without interest. "All right."

Everett began whistling tunelessly through his teeth. Only that and the whine of the electric fan broke the silence. Lily was aware that he did not take his eyes from her bare arms as she brushed her hair.

"We could go away this winter," he said abruptly.

"Go away," she repeated. "Go away where?"

"We could take a trip. We could take one of those boats that keeps going for forty-one days or something. We could go to Alaska or Australia or Europe or someplace."

"Not Alaska, baby. I mean it couldn't be much fun to go to Alaska in the winter."

"Somewhere," he insisted.

"Australia. Imagine."

"Listen," Everett said. "I'd like it. We've never done that, gone away together. For a long trip. It'll be good for you."

It was unlike Everett to want to go away. Since the war he had left the ranches only for occasional weekends, growers' meetings, funerals down the Valley; one might have thought him some agrarian Ivar Kreuger, guardian of an ephemeral empire in need of constant control, split-second manipulation. Although she had wanted him to go abroad with her and the children when they went the summer of 1957 (*There's no point if you don't go, Everett, baby, there's no use in sending me off alone, it'll only be the same when I come back, please, Everett*), he had refused.

"Could you get away?" she asked now.

"I think so." He stood up and opened a shutter. "Anyway," he added. "You and Julie could go."

"She can't leave school. She has to study for her College Boards and besides she thinks she's in love. She thinks she's going to get pinned to that Beta from Berkeley. I doubt that she could tear herself away long enough to see us off at the boat."

"You don't mean that boy she had up here."

"That's right. That very one."

"I didn't like him. You know I didn't like him." Everett paused. "He looked like a little wop in that jacket he wore up here."

Lily said nothing. The boy was six foot two, an inch taller than Everett; was almost as blond as Everett had been at his age and as Knight was now; and had worn, one day in July when he drove up to see Julie, a madras jacket identical to one hanging in Knight's closet. Everett had not liked him because he had made a drink for himself and offered one to Julie.

"Anyway," Lily said finally. "That's not the point, for me to go with Julie. I mean is it?"

"A trip would be good for you," Everett repeated without looking at her.

"It would be just like before."

"We'll see," he said. "A long vacation."

She leaned back against the walnut headboard of the bed until the carved leaves cut into her back. *A long vacation.*

Sitting down beside her, Everett took the hairbrush from her hand and began to brush her hair. When she let her head drop against his arm he put the brush down and began massaging her shoulders.

"Julie said she saw gray," Lily said.

"That's not so bad, is it?"

"She thinks it would be distinguished. She thinks it's very distinguished of you to be getting gray. Very distinguished and about time. I told her forty was not generally considered the other side of the mountain, and she just looked at me."

Everett kneaded the muscles in her neck. "There's nothing wrong with Julie."

"I never said there was. That helps my headache."

"Get in bed," he said, still holding her shoulders.

She pulled back the sheet with one hand, slid the straps of her slip down with the other, and kicked off her straw sandals. Lying on the sheet, she watched Everett close the shutters again and take off his clothes. She had always liked the rangy way he looked without his clothes. He was the only man she had ever seen whose bones looked right to her.

"Oh, Christ," she whispered as she reached for him. "Everett, baby, we're so tired."

Before he was finished she began to cry, a tearless weeping compounded in part of pleasure, in part of weariness, and long after it was over she still clung to him, her shoulders moving in faint convulsive sobs, her legs caught around him. (They could lie together now only in the afternoons or in the middle of the night, after both had been asleep; not since the first years of their marriage had they been able to turn out the lights and turn to each other. Some pride overcame them instead, some reticence or aversion. Each, over the years, had read a great deal.) Nerveless, Lily lay listening to the fan, to the mosquitoes, to Knight's car outside the house; listening without moving to the persistent ring of the telephone and finally to the knocking on the bedroom door.

"Your ma's sleeping, Knight," China Mary called up from the kitchen; "she don't want no telephone callers now. You tell him he can call back."

"Call back, hell," Everett murmured, half asleep. "Why'd they answer it at all. Why don't they turn it down so they don't hear it ring."

"Why don't you go to sleep," Lily whispered, kissing his cheek. Everett's aversion to answering the telephone had seemed, when they were first married, a great compliment: *we won't have it known, dear, that we own a tel-e-pho-own.* It had taken her almost two years to see that it had nothing to do with her, that Everett was about the telephone exactly the way he was about the mail, as wary as if he were investigating night noises at the basement door.

"You lie still a minute," she added, "and I'll get you a drink."

Although she would just as soon have sat on the bed whispering with Everett and drinking bourbon for another hour (the telephone rang twice again), they did, eventually, go downstairs for dinner. Julie was late, coming in some time after the artichokes with her face flushed and her eyes bright, a cotton shirt pulled over her swimming suit and a faded pink grosgrain ribbon tied around her wet blond hair (she had driven Mrs. Templeton's T-Bird and talk about *power* on the *pull*out—*not* automatic, *a straight-stick T-Bird* if you can imagine), and somewhere between the artichokes and Julie's arrival Lily took the telephone call, told Ryder Channing that she could be home, later on, which could have been easy enough but *count on her.* Everett did not ask who had called (he knew, he always knew) and as she saw the heat and tension tightening the vein on his forehead she knew that she had to say something. What she said, elaborately casual in that rush of confused guilt and love, was that she might go to the Templetons' after all. *Count on her.* Never mind. Some of the tension left Everett's face and it would be all right. She could take her own car, leave early (she did, Everett knew, have the headache), meet Ryder on the dock but only for a few minutes; figure out, later, some way to make it all right, make everyone happy. Dinner, at least, had been saved. Nonetheless, she began to wish immediately that she had never answered the telephone at all, began to wish that she and Everett could have stayed in bed while the sun gradually left the room and the crickets began and the night wind came up off the river (they had done that sometimes the first year they were married, stayed in bed in the falling dark, not talking, drinking a little now and then from the bottle of bourbon Everett always kept by the bed); began to regret that they could not have lain inviolable on that walnut bed from five o'clock until the following morning.

2

EVERETT SAT on the dock fifteen minutes before Lily came. He heard her long before he saw her, because now at one o'clock the moon was entirely down. Although house lights flickered on the water downriver, the mile and a half of McClellan riverfront showed only the even flash of the Coast Guard channel markers; the light on the dock was gone, burned out he didn't know when. *Remind Liggett*, he thought, abruptly alarmed about the dock light. (A dock light first, a torn fence next, maybe the pump goes off and loses its prime: before long the whole place would come crumbling down, would vanish before his eyes, revert to whatever it had been when his great-great-grandfather first came to the Valley.) Through the growth of oak and cottonwood Everett could see a single light on the third floor of the house; the lower stories were blocked out by the levee.

During those fifteen minutes Everett thought only of the dock light (*Liggett should watch these things*) and of the hops. Although he still held his father's .38-caliber revolver in one hand, he did not think about that, any more than he thought about Ryder Channing's flashlight, still burning, its thin light filtering through three inches of muddy water, caught there in the tangle of roots that showed where the current had undercut the bank. Next week they would be taking the hops down, stripping the vines from the strings. Each August, just before picking, Everett was suffused with a single fear, an apprehension specific in exactly the sense that nightmares are specific: the unshakable conviction that his kiln would explode as the hops dried. He could never sleep during the week the hops were drying. Sometimes he would go downstairs and sit all night in the kitchen, because he could see the kiln from the kitchen window. It was not, this or any year, that the loss of the crop could ruin him: he had fewer acres in hops this summer than any since his father's death, fifteen years before. There was no longer any money in hops: everyone on the river was getting out of them. *"It's a combination of factors," he had tried to explain, repeating by rote what the buyers told him, to his sister*

Sarah and her third husband when they came through in June on their way from Philadelphia to the Islands. (*"Not Honolulu, Everett," Sarah had corrected him. "Maui. Oahu's been ruined for years."*) *"Your shares aren't paying what they used to pay because we aren't making what we used to make. For one thing people aren't drinking as much beer as they used to drink. For another the brewers are making what they call a lighter beer, using fewer hops."*

The loss of the hops would not matter to Sarah. Nothing about the ranch had ever mattered to Sarah. But Everett had seen little all week but that familiar image: his drying kiln burning, the flames breaking out against a night sky and still (impossibly, as in a nightmare) throwing no light into the dark. *It would happen this year for certain*, he thought now.

When he heard Lily he sat perfectly still, aware suddenly of the .38 in his hand, the blood on the sleeve of the Dacron suit Lily had bought for him at Brooks Brothers in San Francisco. He heard her high heels on the wooden steps down the river side of the levee (*Jesus Christ*, he thought with abstract tenderness, *high-heeled shoes to get screwed on the beach*), heard her pushing aside the oak branches, heard her call his name.

Everett, she called, long before she could have seen him on the dock. She called him, not Channing, answering the question he had never asked: would she hear the shot and come to him or would she come as usual to meet Channing; would she come to him, knowing, or would she come to Channing, come clean and unaware from the shower where she had been maybe twenty minutes before, come intending to take the boat downriver half a mile, meaning to lie there with Channing on the stretch of sand where Knight and Julie gave beach parties. (He had heard the shower when he went into the house to get the gun. Standing in their bedroom after he had taken the gun from the drawer, he had watched the steam through the open bathroom door, had listened to her humming a song to which she could never remember the words, *we will thrive on keep alive on/just nothing but kisses.*) Well, she had heard the shot and come to him: she had called *Everett*.

Still holding the gun, he got to his feet. Lily stood in the clearing by the dock, looking first at him and then at Channing's body where it lay sprawled over a rotting log. In that moment before either of them spoke, it occurred to Everett that Lily was not as pretty as she had once been. No one had ever called her beautiful, but there had been about her a compelling fragility, the illusion not only of her bones but of her eyes. It was not that her eyes were any memorable color (hazel, her driver's license must say), any extraordinary shape. It was simply that they seemed larger than anything else about her, making her very presence, like that of someone on a hunger strike, a kind of emotional claim. It exhausted him to look at her now: her eyes were too large.

"I guess he came here to meet you," Everett said, swiping at a mosquito with his free hand. He did not look at Channing's body.

She did not speak.

Unable to think, Everett wished that they could go back to the house and to bed; he wanted to make her a drink, bourbon with crushed ice the way she liked it, sit with her in the dark calm beneath the mosquito netting.

"There was no need," she said finally, her voice barely audible. "No need."

She began crying then. Everett stood watching until her sobs took on the helpless, automatic quality which meant that she was losing control, crossing an invisible border into some unmapped private terror. Sudden or expected death, the sight of a stranger planting daffodil bulbs, or the recollection of some commonplace, forgotten afternoon (say when they had taken the children to look at the seahorses in Golden Gate Park and the seahorses had been gone) could tap Lily's reserve of hysteria. ("That's how people should live," she had said about the planter of daffodils; he had suggested that she set out some daffodils around the house.) He wondered without interest if Channing had ever seen Lily cry. He supposed he had. He supposed every son of a bitch on the river had.

He laid the gun on the dock and walked over to her. Her sweater had fallen from her shoulders, and he stooped to pick it up from the dirt. It was a pink cashmere sweater that belonged to Julie; one of the name tapes Lily had bought when they sent her down to school at Dominican was sewn in the neck. *Julia Knight McClellan.* Julie was as pretty now as Lily had once been. Although her fine, almost white blond hair had always reminded Everett of his sisters ("She may look like Sarah but she looks nothing *like* the way Martha looked," Lily had said this summer, nearly screaming. "I don't know how you can even *say* that"), Julie looked, on the whole, more and more like Lily: she moved the way Lily moved, had even the shy, hesitant smile which by now was only a mannerism for Lily. (Only about an hour ago, at the Templetons' party, had he not looked across the room to see Julie brush a strand of hair from her face with Lily's own rapid, tentative gesture? *Lily*, he had thought, his face suddenly cold with relief and shame, in that instant between seeing the gesture and realizing that it was not Lily at all, but Julie. Until that moment when he thought he knew he had refused to ask himself where Lily was. Only then did he realize that he had not moved from the room in half an hour, had stayed there deliberately so that he might believe Lily to be on the terrace, or downstairs in the room with the piano. *We will thrive on keep alive on/just nothing but kisses.* Julie had been wearing a white dress cut low in back, and he had stared at her sunburned back as if he had never seen it. What he had never before noticed was that her back was exactly like Lily's. You could see the small bones. Both Lily and Julie stood very straight, holding their narrow shoulders back as if to hide the bones. He had been staring at Julie's back as if in trance, wondering with intense irritation why she had not worn a dress which covered her bones, when he felt someone's hand on his shoulder. In his irritation, he jerked away; it was Francie Templeton. "You need a drink, Everett," she had laughed; he smiled and put his arm around her bare shoulders. "Sure, Francie," he had said. "Sure I do.") *She was already gone then*, he thought now, trying for the first time to make chronology of it.

The wind was rising off the river, breaking both the quiet and the still heat, disturbing the dry leaves and splashing water against the dock, rocking the little cruiser in its mooring, knocking Channing's flashlight free from the tangled roots and into the drift of the water. *Willows whiten, aspen quiver.* It was the only line of verse Everett knew: he had learned it maybe thirty years before and he did not remember who had written it or what followed it, but often when the wind came up on the river he found himself repeating it in his mind. Once in

Colorado he had seen aspen trembling, miles of them, and had wanted them for the ranch.

He brushed the leaves and dust from Julie's sweater and wrapped it again around Lily's shoulders. *If a wind comes up when the kiln burns*, he thought distantly, *the house could go.* He stroked Lily's hair, imagining the flames flashing down through the windbreak of eucalyptus, catching the immense dusty growth of ivy on the north walls, smoldering, then flaring up irrevocably through the entire wooden frame of the house. He could not get it out of his mind that Lily would be trapped in the fire, and he shut his eyes in vain against the ugly image of her fragile bones outlined in the incandescent ruin.

"You knew," she said finally, her dry sobs mixed with coughs now. "You knew there wasn't any need."

He recognized her plea and could not answer it. He wished that he could comfort her (*there was no need, Lily, no need, you weren't involved, Lily, count yourself out*), because she had not, in fact, been involved. Now that it was done, now that Channing lay dead between the river and where they stood, it seemed to Everett that none of them, least of all Lily, could have been involved; that all of them, he, Lily, and Channing, had simply been spectators at something that happened a long time ago to several other people.

"You shot him," Lily whispered.

Everett nodded, abruptly exhausted. *Maybe she didn't realize*, he thought, inert with the new possibility that he would, after all, have to explain it to her. (He had thought they were at least done with that, had thought she realized that for once she had something worth crying about.) *Maybe she just now figured it.* Then he saw that she was looking beyond him at the dock where his gun now lay, and realized that she was doing no more than framing a question: *what would he do now.*

He had not thought of there being alternatives, solutions, next steps. Although he could not now focus upon how it had happened or what would happen next, he seemed to have known all along, as surely as he knew about the kiln fire, not only that it would happen but that everything he knew would be obliterated by it. Lily meant something else: *you shot him*, she meant. *Now what.*

It occurred to him that Lily had always been keyed to picking up pieces, peculiarly tuned for emergency. What eluded her was the day-to-day action. She would not buy a dress without his approval, but she had driven into the hospital without waking him the night last Christmas when they called to say that Julie had been in an accident after a dance. She had gotten a respirator down on the dock in ten minutes the night his sister Martha drowned. And once, years and years before, she had literally saved Knight's life: he had been playing with Knight on the grass when Knight crawled away and tore his foot open on a broken Coca-Cola bottle. He had knelt there for whole minutes with Knight in his arms, helplessly watching the blood spurt clear red on the grass. Then as now, he could not think. (That time it had been Lily who had seen them from the house, had come running with a dishtowel and had known how to make the blood stop, and finally shoved Everett and the baby into the pickup and had driven twenty-five miles in to the emergency hospital in Sacramento, her foot down on the accelerator all the way in along that twisting river road. Knight nearly died and he might have died anyway, there in the waiting room of the hospital, if Lily had not slapped the attendant and screamed *I don't give a goddamn what the rules are you're going to help my baby whether he's a resident of the city of Sacramento or whether he's not and you'd better get to it or my father's going to have every one of you on trial for manslaughter.* On the way home, with Knight in her lap, she had begun crying for the first time: she had forgotten, she said, that her father was dead.)

Lily's hands were on his arm.

"Did Ryder have a gun?" she whispered.

"I can't hear you," Everett said harshly. Why did she whisper, knowing full well that there was only one person for miles around (Julie and Knight would still be at the Templetons', and Liggett and the Mexicans in town; it was Saturday night) and that this one person, this single listener, the topic at hand, was dead.

Lily had stepped back and was staring at him.

"I mean you don't have to whisper," he said, brushing a mosquito from his face.

"I said did he have a gun."

"What do you think? You think he had a gun? He wasn't out here for the goddamn pheasant, was he?"

"He threatened you."

Everett looked down the river. "No," he said. "He did not have a gun and he did not exactly threaten me."

"He might have, you see." Lily spoke slowly and clearly, as if to the children when they were small. "He could have threatened you."

Running for her life, Everett thought. He did not say anything.

"He'd been drinking and he might have come out here and tried to—" She broke off and looked away. "Tried to hurt me."

"Sure thing," Everett said. "That's a nice one. You think the smartest Jew lawyer in California could find twelve friends and neighbors between here and Stockton who'd believe you hadn't asked for it?"

"We could make the reasons."

"Listen," he said. "You listen to me now, this once, and mind what I say. It's not as easy as that. There aren't any reasons. I don't want that."

"It's a little late for choosing."

"You don't see. I don't want that."

"What is it you want," she said without inflection.

He looked down the river. *What is it you want.* He had wanted to go away with her, for one thing. The idea of *going away* had been weaving itself into the fabric of his daily life for months. He had not in the beginning (say in April) thought of it as a trip, a possibility, something which might easily be arranged by travel agents, steamship pursers, airline clerks; even by July, his desire had acquired neither the brilliantly attainable colorings of travel posters and *Holiday* magazine nor the subtler, more exotic pastels of Rand-McNally cartography. The want would strike him briefly, and at odd moments: while he talked price to the hop broker, or waited for someone to answer the telephone. Even before the idea took real shape, he had begun to count on it: *when we're gone*, he would think without perceiving that he had thought it.

But a trip was not much to want. More than that, he had wanted this summer to do something with the children; he had not. In a few weeks Julie would be going back down to Dominican, and all he could remember of the summer was the heat. That was all he could make of it now: the heat, and Lily lying upstairs with the shutters closed against it, and Julie coming in jumpy from it, and how it had bothered Sarah when she came through in June, and how the coolest place was down in the dust among the hops. The house had seemed too small all summer. Three floors, seventeen large dark rooms, room enough for three generations of his family before him: the house had not seemed, this summer, big enough for the four of them. It had been the heat. (*"I didn't remember the heat this way," Sarah had apologized breathlessly to her husband. "When you've lived where it's green you forget how it is out here. You realize it hasn't rained since April and it won't until September? You realize that?" As disturbed still as he had been when Sarah first went away, Everett had said that if she wanted to see green, she had only to look out into the hops. Counting the new system they were spending maybe ten thousand dollars this summer keeping those hops green. "That's exactly my point," Sarah had said.*)

It had been the heat, and Sarah, and the way the summer had begun. Everett had wanted to find some way to talk to Julie, to tell her that he would take care of her, that she need not be frightened of anything. He had not even found a way to tell her that she drove too fast. He had once seen her doing eighty in the Lincoln on the river road. And Knight would be going East, alone. It was not that Everett minded. Although Princeton had not been his idea he thought it a good idea; he even thought that he might have liked, himself, a year somewhere other than Stanford. But he knew that Knight considered the trip back East less an interlude than a beginning. No matter what Knight said, he was not thinking of coming home to the ranch. *What is it you want.* Whatever he had wanted, none of the rest of them did. Before his grandfather had died, he had told Everett's father that the riverfront and the other ranches, some seven thousand acres in all, were to be divided equally among his three grandchildren: Sarah, Everett, Martha. Although they had sold off some here and picked up some there, they still had the riverfront and they still had about seven thousand acres, all controlled by the corporation, the McClellan Company. (There was even a corporate seal, although Julie had broken the stamp years ago, trying to make an imprint on a leather suitcase.) Since Martha's death, Everett and Sarah had each owned half of the McClellan Company, and Everett had managed all of it. Knight would hold even more land than that. All the old Knight orchards would come to him through Lily, and he would probably have everything up for sale before the ink was dry on the papers. (It had been Knight who had first pointed out to Sarah that the piece immediately upriver from the ranch was a tract called Rancho Del Rio No. 1 and the piece immediately downriver, developed a year later, a tract called Rancho Del Rio No. 3. "They're just biding their time," Knight had laughed, "waiting it out for Rancho Del Rio No. 2.")

What is it you want. He had said it to Martha (*what do you want, baby*, he had said, *what did you want*) the night she drowned off the dock where his gun now lay. He had wanted to say it to Sarah, every time she came home (only she did not now call it home). He had wanted to say it to Knight and he had wanted to say it to Julie. He looked at Lily again. She had the blank, frightened look that she had some nights when he woke her from bad dreams. She had always been afraid of the dark. *Sweet Jesus, what had she wanted?*

"I want to go up to the house," he said.

3

We could make the reasons. Everett's mind began to function now for the first time since he had left the Templeton house (it must have been about midnight, because someone had shouted "no dancing on Sundays," and then Francie Templeton had gone to get him a drink he did not need, Joe Templeton had asked him where Lily was, and he had walked out of the house, across the lawn and down the graveled drive to the car; he had seen Knight kissing Francie's niece from Santa Barbara down on the stone bench by the swimming pool, had discerned Francie's laugh among the voices and music from the house, and had seen then that Lily's car was gone); began to weigh the potentialities now as he stood on the levee waiting for the headlights to pass so that he and Lily could cross the road to the house. (Oh God remember how it was to drive the river road late on hot summer nights with Lily asleep, her head dropped on his shoulder, to hear the mosquitoes above the sound of the motor and to know that ahead was the cool white room, the walnut bed with the mosquito netting, Lily's room and his, his grandfather's before him. Lost in the night fields, his body, Lily's body, the house ahead: all one, some indivisible trinity. But maybe it had never been that way except late at night, never except when Lily was asleep. He knew this road so well that he could drive it with his eyes closed, could have plotted every curve in his sleep, knew exactly when to expect the jolt where the roadbed changed at the county line. Remember how it was. Asleep, Lily was any way he willed her.)

"Don't be afraid now," Lily said, her voice harsh. She put her hand on his arm as if to pull him along.

He realized then that the headlights were long past, that he still stood in the gravel with his head dropped forward. He had remembered, while they waited for the car to pass, what had happened between the time Joe Templeton asked him where Lily was and the time he walked out of the house. He had taken a swing at Joe, grazing his jaw and causing Francie, Everett's drink in her hand, to step between them, almost sober for a change. *What happened*, she kept saying. Everett had not known what had happened but it had something to do with Joe. *You've really got it made, haven't you, Templeton*, he had snarled. *Swimming pools. New Thunderbirds. For a lousy dirt farmer you really got the world by the tail.* As he walked out Francie was laughing: *I don't notice you driving any Model T, Everett McClellan. I don't notice your kids swimming in the river. Between semesters at Princeton.*

Straightening his shoulders, Everett pulled his arm from Lily's touch.

"When's Julie coming home," he said.

"I don't know." She dropped her hand. "I don't know about Knight or Julie. She was with one of the twins again."

He looked toward the house. "The lights are on downstairs."

"I left them."

"I just don't want to see Julie."

"Listen," she said. "We can make it all right."

"Not Julie," he said.

She put her fingers against his cheek and he caught them there with his hand. Her skin was soft and in the darkness she looked about twenty again, and vulnerable. Well, vulnerable she was. *Pity her simplicity and suffer her to come to Thee.* It could be easy enough. He could go back to the river now, lift Channing's body off that rotten log, weight it, and roll it into the river. It would lie there three, maybe four months, anyway until the river picked up a little water, began running fast enough to move the body downstream. Then it might be found: might catch on a piling or wash into a slough, be dragged up. How much could they discover by probing that disfigured, disintegrating mass of flesh? He tried to recall detective novels, but could think only of the kind in which the room blacks out an instant and the victim, when the lights go on again, is discovered slumped across the chemin de fer table. At any rate, he need deal here with neither the C.I.D. nor the Sureté, but only the incalculable expertise of the county coroner's office, an unknown quantity. This was less the stuff of detective novels than of newspaper murder accounts, which he had read throughout his life with a disinterest born of disbelief. They had never seemed probable. *Father Kills Daughter's Swain, Argument over Car Keys. Wife Kills Mate, Wounds Child, Did Not Mean to*

Fire. Carhop Slain, Assailant Unknown. He could dredge from all those years of reading only the impression that dentists were frequently key witnesses when it came to identification; he had a further notion, even more dim, that no matter how advanced the decomposition an autopsy would show whether or not the cause of death had been drowning. The lungs either did or did not contain water, he could not remember which. Even if the body did not turn up for months, in that case, there would be inquiries, questions asked of all Channing's acquaintances and particularly of him, particularly of him and of Lily. Everyone knew, everyone must know, about Lily and Channing, about Martha and Channing. Fifteen years.

Anyway, it might be discovered tomorrow, next week. Nancy Channing would miss him, if nobody else did: she was suing for back alimony and had her father's lawyers after him all the time. For all Everett knew a hearing was scheduled for Monday. Were Channing reported missing, they might think —would certainly think, in a summer when there had been three or four drownings a month—to drag the river; might drag up the weighted body, leaving no question of accident, no possibility that the generally disorganized details of Ryder Channing's life had led him to drown himself. There were altogether too many variables.

"Where's his car?" Everett asked suddenly, and as he said it the variables began crowding in, the elements he could never calculate, the other factors overlooked. Channing's car still on the ranch; China Mary, not at her sister's as she usually was on Saturday night but maybe in her own cottage beyond the house, hearing the shot, knowing; the possible appointments set up for Monday. Not that suicides didn't set up appointments; not that Channing, in any case, had made much of a practice of keeping appointments the past few years. But still.

"Down the back road to the dock," Lily said, calm, and the old resentment flared briefly, obscuring everything. (Parked just off the levee road, hidden in the trees and darkness along the old dock road; the black Mercedes still unpaid for. "I was down on the dock, baby," she would have said in the same calm voice had none of it happened, had he simply come home from the party and found the house empty, simply waited upstairs as he had waited other evenings, listening for her high heels on the wooden verandah, listening for the screen door, for her humming. *We will thrive on keep alive on/just nothing but kisses.* "I was down watching the water. Didn't Francie tell you I'd gone on home? Didn't she tell you I had a headache?")

He could get rid of the Mercedes, all right, but it would be like sandbagging a levee already breached. Something else would keep turning up. There was still, however, Lily's way, the almost straight way, the way which would still give them something to talk about but the way which would be, in the end, the easy way: he could call the sheriff's office now —he could call Ed McGrath at home, they had gotten him at home the night Martha drowned—and tell him that he had shot Ryder Channing in self-defense. Or protection of property. Or whatever they wanted to call it. He had come home, heard Lily screaming on the dock, had picked up his gun and run down to investigate. When he found Lily struggling with Channing he had tried to break it up; Channing had gone for him and he had shot him. *Rancher Shoots Friend in Row over Wife, Did Not Mean to Kill.*

It was plausible only if you accepted as given Lily's alleged resistance. Get some hotshot District Attorney in there—who would it be? Everett no longer knew—he could make something of that, make it clear how many times Lily had heard the song before. Although they could probably prove nothing about Lily and Channing (Nancy Channing, he thought, would not have bothered to get whatever evidence there had then been; she had divorced him a long time ago and simply said mental cruelty but of course she might have had the evidence anyway—more variables, incalculable again), they could imply plenty, maybe prove something else, possibly even drag Martha's name into it once they talked to Nancy Channing (he did not know how much if anything Nancy Channing had known about Martha), sink the knife in Lily, make it hard for a jury to believe she would have drawn a line, started screaming after that many times around.

But it was possible: Lily could probably make it work. They would drag it all out in the newspapers (give Francie Templeton two drinks, she'd probably testify herself) but Lily could make it work. She would say anything now, not particularly to save him but to save them all, him, Knight, Julie, herself.

It would be a sweet trial, all right; a sweet trial for Julie. Well, he wanted to save them too. (Never had Julie seemed more precious to him than she had tonight: he would consider the world well lost to keep her intact, her small bones, her sunburn, her white dress, her hair so like Martha's, her longing for a straight-stick Thunderbird. And his entire commitment to Lily had become an unbreakable promise to protect her from the mortal frailties which were, since they were hers, his own.) He wanted to save them and he would. It was only that he was not sure how. He could sort out no clear reason, no starting point. It was the kind of letters he got from Sarah and it was Martha buried there by the levee and it was the way Knight had talked in June; it was the way he had always felt about the kiln burning, only that no longer mattered. It was as if the kiln had burned already. Everything seemed to have passed from his reach way back somewhere; he had been loading the gun to shoot the nameless fury which pursued him ten, twenty, a good many years before. All that had happened now was that the wraith had taken a name, and the name was Ryder Channing.

1938–1959

4

A little late for choosing, she had said to Everett, quite as if it hadn't always been. Was there ever in anyone's life span a point free in time, devoid of memory, a point when choice was any more than the sum of all the choices gone before? A little late for choosing: her father had known it, even as he denied it. But deny it he had. *You say what you want and strike out for it,* he told Lily on the morning of her sixteenth birthday: it was one of their rare attempts to grope through a conversation with each other, deafened as always by the roar of the blood between them. (Neither Walter Knight nor his only child ever forgot that blood: dumbly, they exchanged deliberate commonplaces, phrases perhaps dry and hard enough to carry the weight of something for which there was no phrase at all. Take care of yourself. Do you need any money. Write.) *You say what you want and then go after it, and if you decide to be the prettiest and the smartest and the happiest, you can be.*

"Just you remember that everybody gets what he asks for in this world," Walter Knight repeated, making two stacks of the sixteen silver dollars he had dropped on her bed.

"Maybe that's not such a prize," she said. "Getting what you ask for."

She was aware that the attainment of her own most inadmissible wish, to be asked to play Scarlett O'Hara in the movie version of *Gone With the Wind*, was not only outside the range of probability but not, over the long stretch, in her best interests. It would not, *per se*, build character. On the other hand her father was not talking about her character, which was one of the things that distinguished him from other people's fathers. Another was that he was good-looking enough, despite what was called in her mother's family "a weak mouth," to play Rhett Butler.

"I didn't say it was any prize." Walter Knight took a fruit knife from his pocket and began cutting up the apple he had brought for Lily's breakfast. "I didn't say that at all. I said it's nobody's fault but your own. My own. Anybody's own."

He paused, dropping the core of the apple in a wastebasket.

"Eat this apple and we'll get some waffles. You're too thin. I said you play the game, you make the rules. I said if a lot of people a long time back hadn't said what they wanted and struck out for it you wouldn't have been born in California. You'd have been born in Missouri maybe. Or Kentucky. Or Virginia."

"Or abroad," Lily suggested.

Walter Knight paused. To have been born abroad was not, even within the range of his own rhetoric, quite conceivable.

"Or abroad," he conceded finally, seeing that the point was his own. "What I mean is you come from people who've wanted things and got them. Don't forget it."

"Maybe I don't know what I want. Sometimes I worry about it."

"I'll do the worrying," Walter Knight said. "You know that."

With a faith that troubled Walter Knight even as he encouraged it, Lily believed at sixteen, as firmly as she believed that it was America's mission to make manifest to the world the wishes of an Episcopal God, that her father would one day be Governor of California. It was only a matter of time before he could be rightfully installed in Sacramento in the white Victorian house he still called, in an excess of nonchalance (it had been since 1903 the Governor's Mansion), "the old Gallatin place." Any time Walter Knight spent in town could be explained in view of this end, and he spent, the year Lily was sixteen, a great deal of time in town: more time than he would ever spend again, for 1938 was to be, although they did not then know it, his last year in the Legislature.

Gomez ran the ranch, even bargained with the fruit buyers, while Walter Knight sat in the familiar gloom of the Senator Hotel bar and called at the white frame house on Thirty-eighth Street where Miss Rita Blanchard lived. (Miss Rita Blanchard was, as he so often said, his closest friend in town, a good friend, a loyal friend, a friend whose name could be mentioned in the Senator Hotel bar in the presence of Walter Knight only by Walter Knight.) Gomez was the most dolorous of men; one might have thought him intent only upon disproving the notion that our neighbors from south of the border were so *muy simpatico*. Patiently, he illustrated Walter Knight's contention that honesty could be expected only of native northern Californians. "I pay that bastard more than any Mexican in the Valley gets paid," Walter Knight would say periodically. "Yet he cheats me, finds it necessary to steal me blind. Add that one up if you will. Rationalize that one for me." The challenge, although rhetorical, was calculated to lend everyone present a pleasant sense of *noblesse oblige*; as Walter Knight was the first to say, he had never hired a Mexican foreman expecting that they would operate under the Stanford Honor Code. Once Edith Knight had taken up the challenge, but the rationale she offered had little to do with Gomez. "Maybe that wouldn't happen," she said one night at dinner, her hands flat on the heavy white linen cloth and her eyes focused at some point away from her husband and daughter, "just possibly that wouldn't happen if you were to spend, say, one-half the time on this ranch that you spend on Thirty-eighth Street."

Walter Knight demanded that Lily observe the delicacy of the asparagus, grown, despite an extraordinarily poor season for asparagus growers in the southern part of the state, not three miles away on the Pierson place.

"Walter," Edith Knight whispered finally, flushed and rigid with regret as if with fever. Without looking at her, Walter Knight reached across the table and touched her hand. "Sarcasm," he said, "has never been your *forté*." Edith Knight stiffened her shoulders and picked up her water goblet. "The word is *forte*, Walter," she said after a moment, entirely herself again. "Quite unaccented."

Such lapses were rare for Edith Knight: a change for the better was among the prime tenets of her faith. That was the year, Lily's sixteenth, when she tried parties. Through the holidays and late into spring, she entertained as no one on the river had entertained in years, confident that the next party would reveal to her the just-around-the-corner country where the green grass grew. *I thought of floating camellias in the silver bowls*, she would write to Lily at Dominican, *or do you think all violets, masses and masses of violets? p.s. bring someone home if you want but don't come if it's an Assembly weekend, you'll miss meeting a great many nice people if you keep on missing those dances.* Because Lily would have gone to extraordinary lengths to avoid an Assembly (the sight of the inexorable square envelopes in her mail slot at school turned her faint, chilled her with a vision of herself stranded on a gilt chair at the St. Francis Hotel, her organdy dress wilting and her hands wet in kid gloves), she always came home for her mother's parties.

She would arrive on the Saturday morning train, and Gomez would meet her in Sacramento. ("*Como esta usted, Señor Gomez?*" she called one morning as she stepped off the train. "I don't get you," he said, picking up her two bags and handing her the heavier one.) Although Gomez would sometimes agree to stop at a place in the West End where she could eat tacos with her fingers, he never spoke on those occasions unless Crystal was along. Crystal was his common-law wife by virtue of mutual endurance, and if Gomez brought her into town on Saturday morning it was only to confront her with the scenes of her Friday-night defections. In a moment of misdirected intimacy, Crystal once told Lily that she had worked the whole goddamn Valley in season before Gomez latched on to her in Fresno. "I don't mean picking, honey, you get that," she added, producing as evidence her white hands, each nail filed to a point and lacquered jade green. Ignoring Lily, Gomez would vent his monotonous fury in Spanish, which Crystal pretended not to understand. "You're a nutsy son of a bitch," she would drawl from time to time by way of reply, nudging Lily hilariously and inspecting the dark roots of her Jean Harlow hair in a pocket mirror. (Although Crystal had lived with Gomez three months before Walter Knight noticed her presence on the ranch, she had become, the moment he did notice her, one of his favorite figures, referred to alternately as "Iseult the Fair" and "that sweetheart.")

About seven o'clock, when the house was full of the faint sweet smell of wax and the almost palpable substance of Edith Knight's anticipation, Lily, dressed in the pale blue crêpe de Chine her mother thought most set off her hair, would take a glass of champagne up to the third floor and sit by a front window, watching the cars swing off the bridge and up the road to the ranch. Everyone came to those parties: river people, town people, and, when the Legislature was in session, people from Red Bluff, Stockton, Placerville, Sonora, Salinas, everywhere. Even the people from down South came, proof to the doubtful that Walter Knight was more interested in California than in water rights, than in small disagreements, than in a bill he had once introduced proposing the establishment of two distinct states, the border to fall somewhere in the Tehachapi. "I'll tell the world," a lobbyist from down South once said to Lily, "L.A. is God's own little orchard." His wife echoed him: God's own little orchard. Neither was actually from California; he had met the little lady in a band contest, an all-state high-school competition held in the Iowa State football stadium. His band won first prize, her band won third; and the three winning bands were awarded all-expenses-paid trips to the Palmer House in Chicago, where he and the little lady had decided, he said, to make it legal. "Came to L.A. with a bride on my arm and a dime in my pocket," he added, "but baby won't you look at us now. God's own orchard." "I've got a few of your compatriots in my orchard," Walter Knight said; the Okies were still pitching tents at the far end of the ranch, near the main highway south. Although he said it pleasantly enough, Edith Knight looked at him, reproof in her eyes. That wasn't the way to the green grass.

No matter who else came, Rita Blanchard always came. As if she had lain in a dark room for days, conserving all of her animation for this one evening, she smiled constantly, watching Edith and Walter Knight even as she talked to someone else. Her apologetic inattention was part of her face to the world, vital to that air of being irrevocably miscast, fatally unfitted, the kind of woman who appears for dinner a day before or a day after the day appointed, who inevitably arrives dressed for tennis when the game underway is bridge. Her mooring in the world seemed so tenuous that every spring when she went away (to Carmel for the month of April, abroad for the month of May), there were those who said that she had in truth been committed. In spite of what she knew, Lily felt a guilty love for Rita Blanchard: even at thirty-five, Rita seemed always to be sitting on those gilt chairs at the St. Francis. Although she must have known that she was considered something of a beauty in the Valley, the very way she walked into a room belied that knowledge, announced her certain faith in her inability to please. She dropped her head forward, brushing her long hair back from her face with nervous fingers; should someone startle her by speaking suddenly, she would begin to stutter. Each tale in the folklore of spinsterhood had at one time or another been suggested in explanation of her official celibacy: the secret demonic marriage and subsequent annulment; the dead lover, struck down on the eve of their public betrothal; the father who would allow no suitor close enough. Not even the fact that Rita's father, the gentlest of men when alive, had been dead since Rita's twelfth birthday could abate the popularity of the last theory. The truth was simply that Walter Knight had kept her company for twelve years, and if Rita had once expected something else, her diffidence and Walter Knight's lack of it had combined to dispel those shadows. Although it was rumored that there was not the money there had once been, enough remained of the Blanchard estate to enable Rita to give Lily expensive presents every Christmas ("You be sure now you *thank* poor Rita," Edith Knight always ordered—the adjective "poor" was for her a part of Rita's Christian name—"but French perfume is not what I would call a suitable gift for a *jeune fille*"), to bring home all her clothes from Jean Patou in Paris, and to ask favors of no one but Walter Knight.

So Rita came, along with everyone else, and if everyone had a good time at those parties, who enjoyed them more than the Knights? When the evenings grew warm that year they threw open the French doors and set up the bar in the garden, to catch the first cool wind off the river. "Edie says hot nights make better parties," Walter Knight would say, drawing her toward him, "and Edie's right about most things." There seemed a tacit promise between them, lasting the duration of each party: all they had ever seen or heard of affectionate behavior was brought to bear upon those evenings. One might have thought them victims to a twenty-year infatuation. As they said good night at the door, Edith Knight would stand in front of him and lean back on his chest, her face no longer determined but radiant, her manner not dry but almost languorous, her smallness, against Walter Knight's bulk, proof of her helplessness, her dependence, her very love. "Take care now," she would say softly, her eyes nearly closed, "we're so happy you came." All the world could see: there was bride's cake under her pillow upstairs, and upstairs was where she wanted to be.

After everyone had gone, she would hum dance music as she and Lily blew out the candles, closed the glass doors, picked up napkins here and there from the floor. *Of thee I sing, ba-by, da da da da da da-spring, ba-by.* "Do you know," she would break off suddenly and demand of Walter Knight, "how many times Harry Scott's sister saw *Of Thee I Sing* when she was married to that man who did business in New York City?"

"I can't imagine."

"*Fourteen*. She saw it fourteen times. With customers."

"I trust she knows the lyrics better than you do."

"Never mind about that."

Still mesmerized by her own performance, she would go then to sit on the edge of Walter Knight's chair. "You go on up, Edith," he said invariably, kissing her wrist. "I'll be along. I want to finish this drink." Embarrassed, Lily would find more ashtrays to empty, more glasses to pick up: she did not want to follow her mother upstairs, to pass her open door and see her sitting by the window in her violet robe, filing her nails or simply sitting with her hands folded, the room a blaze of light. *Of thee I sing, baby.*

Walter Knight would sit downstairs, looking at the pages of a book until it was time to go to the earliest Mass. He did not, however, go to Mass; only to bed. "I like to watch the sun come up," he explained. "Most people are satisfied to watch it go down," Edith Knight said one morning. "Ah," he answered. "Only in California."

Edith Knight spent the day after every party in her room, the shutters closed. Although the doctor had told her she had migraine headaches, she would not take the medicine he gave her: she did not believe in migraine headaches. What was wrong with her, she told Lily and Walter Knight every Sunday morning, was a touch of the flu complicated by overwork and she never should have taken two drinks; what was really wrong with her, she had decided by the end of May, was a touch of pernicious anemia complicated by the pollen and she needed a change of scene. She would take Lily abroad. She had always wanted to see Paris and London, and the way they were abroad, you could never tell. It was the ideal time to go.

A week later they left for Europe, and it occurred to Lily later that the highlight of the trip for her mother, who kept her watch all summer on Pacific Standard Time, had been neither Paris nor London but the night in New York, before they boarded the *Normandie*, when they met Rita Blanchard for dinner at Luchow's. In New York for a week on her way home from Paris, Rita looked pale and tired; she dropped a napkin, knocked over a glass, apologized, stuttering, for having suggested Luchow's: possibly Lily did not like German food. Lily loved German food, Edith Knight declared firmly, and it had been an excellent choice on Rita's part. She for one did not hold with those who thought that patronizing German places meant you had pro-German sympathies, not at all; at any rate, anyone could see, from Rita's difficulty with the menu, that Rita's sympathies were simply *not* pro-German, and that was that. The night was warm and the air heavy with some exotic mildew—the weather was what Lily always remembered—and after dinner they walked down a street where the sidewalk was lined with fruit for sale. Rita noticed that some of the pears were from the Knight orchards; unwary in her delight, she drew both Lily and Edith Knight over to examine the boxes stamped "CAL-KNIGHT." "Do tell Walter," Edith Knight said to Rita in her dry voice. "Do make a point of ringing him up when you get home. He'll so enjoy hearing."

After Walter Knight left the Legislature that fall they did not have as many parties. Possibly due to his failure to comprehend that three speeches at dinners at the Sutter Club in Sacramento and a large picnic attended mainly by various branches of the candidate's family did not in 1938 constitute an aggressive political campaign, he was defeated in the November general election by the Democratic candidate, a one-time postal clerk named Henry ("Hank") Catlin. Henry Catlin made it clear that the "Gentleman Incumbent" was in the pay of Satan as well as of the Pope, a natural enough *front populaire* since the Vatican was in fact the workshop of the Devil. In neighborhoods of heavy Mexican penetration, however, Henry Catlin would abandon this suggestion in favor of another: that Walter Knight had been excommunicated for marrying out of the Church and other sins, and he could send his Protestant daughter to Catholic schools until hell froze over and it wouldn't make a whit of difference. "I don't know how *you* folks think a family man ought to behave," he was frequently heard to remark at picnics and rallies. Quite aside from Walter Knight's not inconsiderable personal liabilities, he was, as well, the representative of "the robber land barons" and the "sworn foe of the little fellow." Henry Catlin, on the other hand, stood up for the little fellow and for his Human Right to a Place in the Sun, and if he failed to quote *Progress and Poverty*, it was only because he had not heard of Henry George.

On the night of the election, Lily and Edith Knight sat in the living room alone and listened to the returns on the radio. Although the shape of Walter Knight's political future was clear by ten o'clock, Edith Knight waited until the last votes had been reported before she folded her needlepoint and stood up.

"Don't cry," she said to Lily. "It's nothing for you to cry about."

"I'm not."

"I can see you are. It's your age. You're going through that mopey phase."

"He can't be Governor now. He couldn't lose this election and ever get nominated."

Edith Knight looked at Lily a long time.

"He never could have been," she said finally. "Never in this world."

From the stair landing, she added: "But don't you dare pay any mind to what those Okies said about him. You hear?"

Lily nodded, staring intently at the red light on the radio dial.

She was still crying when Henry Catlin came on the radio to accept his sacred burden. He explained in his Midwestern accent how humbling it was to be the choice of the people—of all the people, you folks who really work the land, you folks who know the value of a dollar because you bleed for every one you get—to be the choice of the people to help lead them into California's great tomorrow, the new California, Culbert Olson's California, the California of jobs and benefits and milk and honey and 160 acres for everybody equably distributed, the California that was promised us yessir I mean in Scripture.

"Well," Walter Knight said, taking off his hat. "Lily."

She had meant to be upstairs before he came, and did not know what to say. "I'm sorry," she said finally.

"No call to be sorry, no call for that at all. We're in the era of the medicine men. We're going to have snake oil every Thursday. Dr. Townsend is going to administer it personally, with an unwilling assist from Sheridan Downey."

She could tell that he was a little drunk.

"Snake oil," he repeated with satisfaction. "Right in your Ham and Eggs. According to Mr. Catlin, we are starting up a golden ladder into California's great tomorrow."

"I heard him."

Humming "We Are Climbing Jacob's Ladder," Walter Knight opened the liquor cupboard, took out a bottle, and then, without opening it, lay down on the couch and closed his eyes.

"Different world, Lily. Different rules. But we'll beat them at their own game. You know why?" He opened his eyes and looked at her. "Because you've got in your little finger more brains and more guts than all those Okies got put together."

She tried to smile.

"Now, Lily. Lily-of-the-valley. Don't do that. I'm going to have a lot more time to spend on the ranch. We're going to do things together, read things, go places, do things. I don't want to think you're crying about that."

"That'll be nice," she said finally, crushing the handkerchief he had given her and jamming it into the pocket of her jumper.

"You're still my princess."

She smiled.

"Princess of the whole goddamn world. Nobody can touch you."

He opened the liquor cupboard again, replaced the bottle he had taken out, and picked up instead the squared, corked bottle which held the last of his father's bourbon, clouded and darkened, no ordinary whiskey.

"This is to put you to sleep," he said, handing her a glass. "Now. What you may not have realized is that Henry Catlin happens to be an agent of Divine Will, placed on earth expressly to deliver California from her native sons. He was conceived in order to usher in the New California. An angel came to Mr. Catlin's mother. A Baptist angel, wearing a Mother Hubbard and a hair net." He paused. "Or maybe it was Aimee Semple McPherson. I am not too clear about Scripture on this point."

"He's not at all a nice man," Lily said firmly, encouraged by the bourbon.

"Everything changes, princess. Now you take that drink to bed."

*

Everything changes, everything changed: summer evenings driving downriver to auctions, past the green hops in leaf, blackbirds flying up from the brush in the dry twilight air, red Christmas-tree balls glittering in the firelight, a rush of autumn Sundays, all gone, when you drove through the rain to visit the great-aunts. "Lily is to have the Spode, Edith, the Spode and the Canton platters Alec brought from the Orient, are you hearing me?" And although Aunt Laura dies neither that year nor the next, she does die one morning, fifteen years later: the call comes from the hospital while you sit at breakfast telling Julie that soft-boiled eggs will make her beautiful and good, and the Spode does pass to you, the Spode and the Canton platters Alec brought from the Orient. (You have seen only one yellowed snapshot of Alec, and that was much later, after he had lost his health and mind and all memory of the Orient. But imagine him a young man, a fine figure of a man or so they said, sailing out from San Francisco and Seattle in the waning days of the China trade, touching home once a year with Canton for his sisters and sailing out again.) Things change. Your father no longer tells you when to go to bed, no longer lulls you with his father's bourbon, brought out for comfort at Christmas and funerals. Nobody chooses it but nothing can halt it, once underway: you now share not only that blood but that loss. A long time later you know or anyway decide what your father had been after all: a nice man who never wanted anything quite enough, an uneven success on the public record and a final failure on his own, a man who liked to think that he had lost a brilliant future, a man with the normal ratio of nobility to venality and perhaps an exceptional talent only for deceiving himself (but you never know about that, never know who remains deceived at four o'clock in the morning), a good man but maybe not good enough, often enough, to count for much in the long run. When you know that you know something about yourself, but you did not know it then.

5

"YOU MIGHT marry Everett," Martha McClellan had suggested to Lily, once when they were both children, "if I decide not to." "You aren't allowed to marry your own brother," Lily had said, quite sure of her ground until Martha smiled wisely and predicted, apparently interpreting the regulation as something else initiated during the first hundred days, "Roosevelt won't be president forever, you know."

It seemed in retrospect an amusing story, and Lily wondered, the June afternoon in 1940 when Everett and his father came to the house for a drink, whether or not she should tell it. She decided that she should not: his four years at Stanford and her one at Berkeley had made Everett seem almost a stranger. She could not remember even seeing him for a couple of years, except once that winter when she had gone down to Stanford for a party and had gotten sick on Mission Bell wine at the Deke house. (Everett had gotten her some cold coffee from the kitchen and had made her date stay in another room until she felt better; she had thought herself humiliated, and neither she nor Everett's girl, a blond tennis player from Atherton, had much appreciated his gallantry.) He looked, now, taller than she remembered, and older. She wondered whether some small tragedy had befallen him and hardened his face, whether perhaps he had thought himself in love with and spurned by the tennis player. He would be, she thought, the type.

"I tell him he ought to go into the law," John McClellan said, taking off his rimless glasses and polishing them on a corner of his jacket. "Into politics. We could use some growers in Sacramento."

"Maybe I better get to be a grower first," Everett said politely. He had been, Lily remembered, a precociously polite child. Her clearest recollections were of him assuming full responsibility for Martha's social errors, gravely apologizing for the spilt strawberry punch, the uprooted azalea, the hysteria when someone other than Martha pinned the tail on the donkey.

"You tell him how they need us," Mr. McClellan said. "You're the one to tell him."

Walter Knight picked up a pair of garden shears from the tiled terrace floor and pruned a branch from a dwarf lemon.

"I'm not sure they do," he said finally, intent upon the lemon. "I'm not at all sure they need us. The San Joaquin still makes itself heard."

"Hah," Mr. McClellan said triumphantly. "The big boys. The corporation boys. There's your point."

Lily did not look at her father. When he spoke at last there was no inflection in his voice.

"This isn't the San Joaquin. They don't run ranches around here from offices in the Russ Building in San Francisco."

"There's your point," Mr. McClellan repeated.

"Here's my point," Walter Knight said. "We're expendable."

Everett smiled at Lily. The sun was setting behind his chair and his blond hair, cut close, looked white in the sunset blaze. Lily extended one bare foot and contemplated it, not smiling back. Neither she nor her mother ever mentioned politics to her father any more: it had been tactless to speak of the Legislature.

Although Everett called her at six-thirty the next morning he did not wake her, because the heat had stayed all night and she had gotten up at five-thirty to lie on the terrace in her nightgown. By six o'clock the sun had been high enough to make the heat shimmer in the air again. Looking to the east and squinting to block out the sun, she could make out the Sierra Nevada swimming clear on the horizon.

She wanted to go somewhere but did not know where. There was a glass of beer on the table, left from the night before, and she flicked a small colorless spider from the rim with her fingernail and let the warm flat beer trickle down her throat. That there was really nowhere to go (she did not like the mountains and had only a week before come home from the coast) made her no less restless, lying almost motionless in the still morning heat and chewing absently on the sash to her nightgown. She wanted to stay here and she wanted something else besides. Her grades had arrived from Berkeley yesterday, neatly and irrevocably recorded on the self-addressed postcards she had left in her bluebooks. One B-minus, in English 1B; a C in History 17A, a C in Psychology 1B, a C-minus in Geology 1 (commonly known as a football players' course in which it was impossible to get below a B), and a D in French 2. Because the single B was in a three-unit course and the D in a four-unit course, she supposed that she was down grade points and therefore on probation. Had the postcards arrived at school, she would have been embarrassed. Here, it did not seem to matter. As her mother had observed, she had read some interesting books and gone to some nice parties; once she was home, that was about the sum of Berkeley. She did not want to go back anyway. She could read books at home; she could have a better time at parties at home. It was not that she had not been asked, at least at first, to the parties which were the parties to go to; she had. On a campus where healthy color and easy smiles were commonplace, her fragile pallor, her uncertainty, had attracted a good deal of attention and speculation. Only when the boys who asked her out discovered how real the uncertainty was did they begin, bewildered and bored, to lose interest. As one of them told Lily's roommate (who, reprovingly, told Lily), taking out Lily Knight was like dating a deaf-mute. "You have to kid around with them, be more fun," the roommate advised. "Be yourself." Although these admonitions seemed to Lily in some sense contradictory, she tried, the next weekend, to be more like the girls who were considered fun. Out with a Sigma Chi who had just been accepted at Princeton Theological Seminary, she had attempted some banter about Reinhold Niebuhr; when that failed, she admired the way he played the ukelele. After several drinks, he told her a couple of *double entendre* stories, and although she neither understood them nor thought he should be telling them to her, she laughed appreciatively. When he asked if she would like to drive up in the Berkeley hills, she smiled with delight and said it sounded like fun; later, she reflected that it had not been entirely his fault that he had misinterpreted her behavior that evening, which had ended in front of an all-night drugstore on Shattuck Avenue where, the prospective theologian told Lily, he could get some rubbers. ("Rubbers?" she had said, and he had looked at her. "Safes. Contraceptives." She had begun shaking her head then, unable to think what to say, and he, sobered, had driven her in silence up the hill to the Pi Phi house.) After that, she had refused all invitations for three weeks. During the spring semester she had gone out briefly with a graduate student who read for her psychology class, a Jewish boy from New York City named Leonard Sachs. He had graduated from the University of Chicago and knew none of the people Lily knew. They had taken long walks in the hills above the stadium, back through Strawberry Canyon; had eaten dinner by candlelight in the small apartment he shared with a friend who did not like Lily and made a point of going to the library whenever she was around; and had sat on Thursday nights in the empty box at the San Francisco Symphony for which the Pi Phis paid every year. He gave her articles clipped from *The New Republic* outlining the intrinsic immorality of an itinerant labor force, hunted up for her an old pamphlet demanding repeal of the California Criminal Syndicalism Law, took her to San Francisco on the F train to hear a tribute to Harry Bridges, and urged her, after he had observed her knitting a sweater for her father, to utilize what slender talents she had by teaching handicrafts in a settlement house. Unable to locate "settlement houses" in the Berkeley Yellow Pages, she finally abandoned that project. He referred to the ranch as "your father's farm," and regarded her with an uneasy blend of the disapproval in which he held defective mechanisms and the craven delight he secretly took in luxury merchandise; she asked him if he would not miss being home at Easter, and regarded him in constant and only occasionally unwilling wonder. What both aggravated and enthralled him was her total freedom from his personal and social furies, and those Eumenides at his back were what attracted and repelled Lily. "You're my haunted lover," she would laugh, although he was, literally, neither; a fact which, in his roommate's eyes, tended to confirm Lily's social uselessness.

She had even invited him up the river for a day during spring week. Once home, she regretted having asked him. But he was delighted by the prospect of observing her in her native decay, and so she drove to Sacramento to meet him one morning. As soon as she saw him standing on the lawn in front of the Southern Pacific station, radiating the same intense concern which had first charmed her in Berkeley, she knew that it would be a difficult day. He was as alien to the Valley as she might have been to the Bronx, and the alienation went deeper than his black turtle-necked sweater, went beyond the copy of *In Dubious Battle* with which he had been briefing himself on the train. By the time she drove him to the station that evening (he had tried throughout dinner to correct the errors in Walter Knight's impression of Upton Sinclair and EPIC), she was too exhausted even to speak. "You'll be glad to get away from all this," he said tentatively, taking a last drag on a cigarette and throwing it out the window. "Get away from all what?" she said, watching the sparks in the rearview mirror. "I meant you'll feel free in New York. You'll develop." Uncomfortably aware that she had at some point agreed to go to New York with him (although she had never had the slightest intention of doing so), she increased her pressure on the accelerator. "I'm not likely to get away from all this," she said, for once safe enough to say what she meant, her hands on the wheel of her father's car, driving the roads for which her father paid. "Any more than you're likely to get away from wherever it is you come from. And we don't throw cigarettes out the window here. It starts fires." She had meant to go to bed with him but because she had still to discover, at seventeen, the possibilities in someone she did not like, she had not.

Abruptly, Lily stood up and lifted the damp hair off her neck. With aimless violence, she threw the beer glass down the slope, then ran after it to where the lawn faded into dirt and dry yellow grass. Kicking a faucet open with her foot, she let the clear water (well water, not the river water they used for irrigation) splash over her arms and face. It was a waste of water early in a dry summer, and its extravagance relieved her. That helped some, that and swinging from an oak branch about to break from the tree, and by the time she reached the house in her wet nightgown the telephone was ringing.

"Sorry if I woke you," Everett McClellan said. "I'm about to take a truck into town for some extra help."

"You didn't wake me." This was more like it. Hoping, although it could not matter, that her mother had not picked up the extension in her bedroom, she tried to smooth her hair with her free hand.

"I mean I thought—" He spoke with some difficulty. "I thought you might like to ride in."

"Right now?"

"You're probably busy."

"Not really." She wondered what he thought she did between six-thirty and seven-thirty in the morning. "I'll get dressed."

As she shook out her wet hair with a towel she hummed softly, and looked in the mirror for the first time in months without regretting the waste of her perfectly good but constantly depreciating body.

"You look younger than Marth," Everett said when she climbed into the truck.

"I'm older. A year." She glanced down at her thin arms, brown against the white of her dress. Martha McClellan was not yet seventeen, a freshman come fall at the University of California at Davis. When Lily's mother, on the behalf of the Pi Beta Phi Alumnae Club, had urged Martha to enroll at Berkeley and participate in rushing, Martha had told her that it was necessary that she go to Davis, which was mainly an agricultural station, because her father wanted her to marry a rich rancher. And as a matter of fact so did she. Martha McClellan, Edith Knight had observed, was "a case."

"I know how old you are," Everett said without looking at her.

Lily pressed her forehead against the window, closed against the heat. Now in June the hops were starting up the strings, miles of them, ready to bear the thick green weight of the August vines. It was said to be a good year for the hops; because her father did not grow them she did not know why. She supposed that it had to do with when the rain had come. Everything else did.

"The hops are pretty," she said.

"You think so?"

"Yes, I do," she said, rather at a loss. When it came to conversation, Everett McClellan was not one to give much away. "I think they're very pretty and I'm glad I'm home."

They did not exchange another word until they reached the Labor Center in the West End, where Everett, getting out of the truck, ordered her to lock both doors from the inside and wait until he came back. As soon as he had entered the office, one of the Mexicans standing on the sidewalk outside made a face at Lily. She smiled, embarrassed, and then pretended to be reading a book in her lap. After Everett had recruited thirteen men, they started back out to the McClellan place; Everett looked once at her, when he had trouble starting the truck, and then neither looked at her nor spoke. Her eyes closed, she listened to the men in the back of the truck, singing Bing Crosby songs and passing around a bottle of dago red, and wondered why Everett had called her at all.

Mr. McClellan met them at the ranch, flagging wildly when he caught sight of the truck, an unnecessary exertion since he was standing where the trucks were habitually parked. Lily could not remember ever having seen him calm: even years before, when he had brought Everett and Martha and Sarah to call, he had given the appearance of a man beset by his own energy, scrawny with tension. He would leap to his feet when Edith Knight entered the room, accidentally knock over a chair, institute a prolonged search for a handkerchief, bound across the room to collar one of the children. He had always spoken to them as if they were puppies. *Down, Martha. Sit, Martha.*

"You should have got in there earlier," he muttered now, leaning over Everett's shoulder as Everett entered the names on the payroll ledger. "Nobody left come seven o'clock but high-school boys and drunken wetbacks. Here's one fact you won't learn in college, Miss Lily Knight: there's nobody in God's green world has less native intelligence than a goddamn wetback." Everett had once explained that his father referred to all Mexicans and to most South Americans—including the President of Brazil, who had once been entertained on the river—as goddamn wetbacks, and to all Orientals as goddamn Filipinos. There was no use telling him that somebody was Chinese, or Malayan, or Madame Chiang Kai-shek; they were goddamn Filipinos to him. Easterners fell into two camps: goddamn pansies and goddamn Jews. On the whole, both categories had to do with attitudes, not facts, and occasionally they overlapped. His daughter Sarah had for example married a goddamn pansy and gone East to live, where she picked up those goddamn Jew ideas.

Lily stood watching Everett, aware of the dust on his Levis and of her incongruously white dress. There was one thing about the McClellans not true of her father: they wouldn't run their ranches out of an office in the Russ Building even if they could afford to.

Everett looked up. "We could ride along the river when I'm finished."

"I don't ride very well."

"Hah," Mr. McClellan said. "I'll say you don't. She used to ride like she was sitting on a barbed-wire fence. I remember that much about Miss Lily Knight. Don't be a fool, Everett. Take her swimming."

"I don't have my swimming suit." Lily remembered that Martha not only jumped horses at the State Fair every year but had twice beaten the Del Paso Country Club junior swimming champion in unofficial competition. "That child sees a bird, she tries to race it," Edith Knight had once observed of Martha. An admirer of competitiveness in all forms, Edith Knight had frequently urged Lily to "take a leaf from Martha McClellan's book"; that Martha was a notoriously poor loser did not bother her, since she did not believe that losing was the point.

"There's one thing Martha has plenty of, that's tank suits," Mr. McClellan declared. "We can suit you fine." Pleased with this play on words, he repeated it, and then bounded up to the house, screaming ahead for China Mary to get Martha on the stick and rustle up some tank suits.

The McClellan house had the peculiarly sentimental look of a house kept by men. There were pictures of Sarah and of Mildred McClellan, who had died at Martha's birth; above the piano ("How's that for a piano?" Mr. McClellan liked to demand affectionately. "Came 'round the Horn in 'forty-eight"), the California Republic Bear Flag hung at what appeared to be half-mast. One wall was covered with framed certificates from the Native Sons of the Golden West and river maps showing channel depths during the summer of 1932; China Mary's efforts toward brightening up ran to crocheted antimacassars on the chairs and orange zinnias crushed haphazardly into Limoges cream-soup bowls. In one corner of the living room, on a table covered with a mantilla, was an assortment of gold nuggets and ivory fans. Although the table had always been there,

there had been, since Lily's last visit to the McClellans, certain additions: over the table hung an old *Vanity Fair* cover, a photograph of Katharine Cornell and her cocker spaniel as Elizabeth Barrett and Flush, and a yellowed front page from the *Sacramento Bee* showing pictures of the Duke of Windsor and the English princesses. The headline read "KING EDWARD ABDICATES! DUKE OF YORK WILL RULE. 'My Mind Is Made Up,' Says King." The words *Sacramento Bee* had been partly obscured with adhesive tape, in deference, Lily assumed, to Mr. McClellan, who had little use for the English but even less for the *Bee*.

"I see you're admiring my memorabilia," Martha said from the stair landing.

Startled, Lily looked up: she had not seen Martha since the Christmas parties, at which Martha had, night after night, in some indefinable way made a spectacle of herself. Although she had not been drinking and had done nothing extraordinary, it had been impossible not to notice her, as it might have been impossible not to notice someone running a high fever, or wearing a cellophane dress. She had the same look about her now: her long straight blond hair hung loose around her thin face, so tanned that her eyebrows looked bleached, and she had on what appeared to be a leotard and a long green silk jersey skirt which trailed after her on the stairs.

"What in the name of sweet Christ is that get-up?" Mr. McClellan said. "You been practicing your ballet dancing?"

"I haven't taken ballet since I was twelve years old, thanks to the fact that nobody in this family except Sarah would ever drive me to my lessons. I've been reading."

"Nobody gives a goddamn what you've been doing. Get Lily Knight here a tank suit."

"Everett," Martha called imperiously. "Guess what I've been reading."

Everett looked up. Throughout this exchange he had seemed to withdraw: Lily had watched him fish in his pocket for a cigarette, inspect the cover of a *Reader's Digest* which lay in a chair, whistle between his teeth.

"What," he said now. "What have you been reading, baby."

"*The Anatomy of Melancholy*. It's number twenty-two on the list."

"She asked me for a reading list," Everett said as Martha started back up the stairs. "I gave her one from Stanford. She's already read about half the books on it."

"Strange little creature," Mr. McClellan said.

"You upset her," Everett said with apparent effort.

Mr. McClellan ignored him. "Melancholia's one study you don't need any lessons in," he shouted up the stairs. "You strange little creature."

"Your brother thinks I upset you," he added as Martha came trailing downstairs again with a swimming suit in one hand.

"Poor old Everett," Martha said indulgently.

"Don't be a fool, Everett. Now let that girl get suited up."

They swam in the river, striking out for the far bank and swimming downstream with the current, still running cold with late melting snow from the mountains. When Everett reached the bank he waded back out to where the shallow ledge dropped off into the channel and pulled Lily, still struggling with the current, across the ledge and up onto the bank.

"You do all right," he said, pulling himself up after her.

"I always think I'll get dragged under." She did not let go his arm.

He moved as if to push her back into the water and then caught her, laughing, his arms low on her back.

"You better not," she laughed.

"Why not."

"You just better not." She was pleased with their dialogue: it had about it the authentic ring of teasing, of inconsequentiality, that had eluded her at Berkeley. She had known all along that she could do it with someone she knew. Delighted, she lay back over Everett's arms and stretched her legs in the hot dry air. By contracting her stomach she could make it concave beneath the wet coolness of Martha's swimming suit. She lifted one leg and saw, besides the water still glistening on it, a long scratch on her left thigh, gradually turning bruised where Everett had pulled her across a submerged root into the shallow water.

"You look good." Everett touched the scratch.

"I feel good."

"You have the prettiest legs," Everett said slowly, "of any small girl I ever saw."

"I guess you like tall girls better." There: she was still doing it.

Everett looked at her, not smiling, and she was struck by anxiety: in her ignorance of how the game was played she had said the wrong thing, broken some rule.

"I like you all right," he said after a while, still looking at her. "I never thought about it until last night."

"Never thought about what?"

Everett said nothing, and she wondered if she had angered or disappointed him, wondered if it was possible that she could lose Everett McClellan, in the sense that you could lose people who were not your father or your brother.

"I wish you would kiss me," she whispered, feeling again that Everett was suddenly not Everett but a stranger, someone to be won.

He kissed her, and she clung to him a long time, watching the oak leaves swimming against the sun and feeling the ends of her hair floating just on the surface of the water and after a while opening her mouth and pulling down the straps of Martha's bathing suit, before his hand tightened over the scratch on her left thigh. *All right*, she whispered over and over, and after a while she began to think it could never happen because it hurt so much. When Everett finally said, again and again in a kind of triumph, *you feel it? baby feel it*, she assumed that it had happened. Later the scratch on her thigh became infected from the river water and left a drawn white scar noticeable whenever her legs got brown, but she did not think of it at the time.

6

Lily, HE WHISPERED every time as he lay spent in the rising morning heat, but she hesitated, equivocated, wondered if she was really obliged to marry him simply because he had wanted and taken her.

That was in June. In July, when she figured that she had been screwed (the word, which she had heard Everett use in reference to someone else, pleased her with its crisp efficiency, its lack of ambiguity) a total of twenty-seven times, they once had an entire morning to spend: coming back from the narrow strip of beach they waded in the irrigation ditches, knee-deep in the soft ditch grass and slow muddy water, the sun hot on their heads. All around them were her father's orchards: the pears hanging warm and heavy, dropping to rot on the ground beneath the trees, going brown and bruised and drawing flies, going to waste in that endless summer as she, *thank God and Everett*, was not. She let her dress trail in the water and ran splashing through the ditch with her eyes closed against the sun. Catching her, Everett rubbed her face and bare sunburned arms with the cloudy river water that bubbled from a supply pipe; they laughed (*Everett you fool my sunglasses I like you for being so brown Everett baby so hard I love you*) and fell down again together, for the pickers were working the far orchards that week, and when she screamed beneath him, remembering that snakes infested the ditches, he neither told her that there was no snake nor told her that the snake (if there was one) was harmless, but picked her up and held her until she was quiet and until the snake (if there was a snake at all) had gone away. Shortly before noon she told Everett that she would marry him, and then she ran up to the house to change her dress for lunch. It seemed as inescapable as the ripening of the pears, as fated as the exile from Eden.

She mentioned it, however, to no one; scarcely thought of it away from Everett. Through day after summer day she moved as if sunstruck, dimly aware that any announcement would disturb the delicately achieved decision which had been, really, no decision at all: only an acquiescence. Was it, after all, so inevitable? The word *why*, once spoken out loud, could bring the pears all tumbling down. She would have to say that she loved him: it was the only incantation which would satisfy them, even as it would dispel her own illusions. Unspoken, it might still be true.

Everett remained the flaw in the grain. His constant and incontrovertible presence intruded upon her, prevented her from contemplating the idea of him, from polishing that idea into some acceptable fact. Sometimes when she came downstairs in the morning Everett would be sitting there, reading the *Chronicle*; he would call her several times during the day, and a suggestion, from Edith Knight, that she and Lily might go to San Francisco for the day could throw him into such despair that he would call every half-hour, all evening, to see when they were going, what they would do, when they would be home. Every scene Lily saw seemed to include Everett; all she heard was Everett's voice, asking when they would be married.

"I don't know," she said finally one morning on the river. "I mean I don't want to think about it right now."

"When do you want to think about it? Next year? The year after?"

"Everett. Stop talking that way. I'm nervous. All brides are nervous." She had read in a magazine that all brides were nervous, and had wondered whether that might not be her only problem: an apprehension which would turn out to be not unique but common to all women.

"If you could just leave me alone a little," she added, hopeful that she might be right.

"Leave you *alone*," Everett repeated. "I want to marry you. I don't know how many times I have to say it."

"Wait until the hops are down," she said finally. "You're too busy now, you know that."

"I'm not too busy to tell people. Don't you want to tell people?"

"No," she said faintly. "I don't."

"You have to. You have to do it now."

"I told them I'm not going back down to Berkeley. So they might have guessed." She had told her parents that she wanted to take a semester off; as far as their guessing the other went, she had invested her faith in the extreme improbability of their guessing anything at all. Putting asunder the delicate balance of dependency among them seemed every day more unthinkable.

"You have to tell them. Your father likes me all right. Although nobody'd know you did, the way you act when they're around."

"I'm not demonstrative." She picked up a white pebble and skimmed it across the surface of the water, angling it downstream to catch the drift. "I don't guess you learned to skip stones like that at Stanford."

"Lily," he pleaded, sitting up and grasping her shoulders. "Listen to me."

She traced an *L* and a *K* and half of *McC* on his chest with her fingernail, not looking at his face.

"There's no use talking to Daddy until he gets the fruit out of the way," she said at last.

But when all the pears had been shipped to the canneries and the hops on the McClellan place had been down six weeks, she still had told no one.

"I don't think you want to," Everett said finally. "I don't believe you want to marry me."

"Ah, sweet." She kissed the back of his neck, ran a finger down his backbone. "It's not you."

"What is it?"

"It's anyone. Sometimes I don't want to marry anyone. Some afternoons I lie on my bed and the light comes through the shutters on the floor and I think I never want to leave my own room."

"You'll have a whole house. Isn't that better?"

She patted his hand and looked away down the river. "It's your father's house," she said finally, grasping at the nearest point although not the one she had in mind.

"We'll build another house if you want. Would you like that?"

"I don't know." She was abruptly weary of trying to talk to Everett at all. "I don't think you understand what I mean."

He turned away from her. "No. I don't think I do."

She felt, as physically as she would a headache, the weight of Everett's vulnerability.

"Of course I want to," she said flatly. "You know I want to."

Although they agreed that she would have told Edith and Walter Knight by the time Everett came by for dessert that night, she had not. Telling them, she whispered to Everett when she opened the door, was impossible. Accepting this as fact, he got up from Walter Knight's table and drove Lily to Reno that October evening, the night the year's first snow settled over the Sierra Nevada, and had her declared his wife in the name of Washoe County and the State of Nevada. The ceremony was witnessed by the wife and son of the justice: the son pulled on blue jeans, the fly open, over his maroon-striped pajamas; the wife, roused unwillingly but dutiful, smiled drowsily and patted Lily's hair. Not quite eighteen, Lily had the distinct impression throughout the ceremony that her lie about her age would render the marriage invalid, nullify the entire affair, no tears, nothing irrevocable, only a polite misunderstanding among good acquaintances. Later, from their hotel room, she called down a telegram reading "MARRIED EVERETT NOW AT RIVERSIDE RENO HOME SOON LOVE LILY"; whatever her extravagances, long telegrams were not among them. Everett called the ranch to tell his father, but Martha answered the telephone.

Covering the receiver, Everett turned to Lily, who sat, still wearing the skirt and sweater she had worn at dinner, on the edge of the bed with *Hotel Riverside* embroidered on the sheets.

"Martha's crying. She says I'm leaving her alone."

"You'll be living right there."

"She says that's not the same thing and I must be a fool to think it is."

Lily lay down on the bed and buried her face in the pillow. She wanted nothing so much as to have her father there, to be downstairs watching him shoot craps, lulled by the action, the play of chips and silver on the green board, the ring of the silver dollars as he stacked them. *Make it the hard way.*

"Maybe she's right," she said, her voice muffled.

They stayed a week in Reno. Lily bought a toothbrush and a pair of stockings in a Rexall drugstore, located some white cotton underwear in a shop specializing in trick holsters and mesh briefs embroidered with the days of the week, and ran into a

Sacramento girl, Janie Powers, in the Riverside lobby. Apprehended by Janie as she stood, that first morning, wondering whether Everett would think himself slighted if she ate breakfast without waking him, Lily could not at first think how to explain her presence in Reno; as it turned out, she did not have to. "I'm getting a div*orce*," Janie caroled across twenty-some feet of lobby. "What are you doing?" Although Lily could not remember knowing that Janie had even been married, she supposed she must have heard and forgotten; she could never keep straight the social details which so absorbed her mother. "I'm going out to buy a sweater," Lily said guiltily. "I'm just up for a few days and I forgot an extra sweater." "Never mind that," Janie said. "I've got dozens. Have breakfast with me." Once they were seated, Janie launched into a monologue about her husband, who was being *très impossible* ("I can't even spend one night on the California side of the *lake* or he'll contest my residency, he's got somebody watching me night and *day*"), and it was not until they had finished a second cup of coffee that she again asked what Lily was doing in Reno. "Nothing special," Lily said, pretending to look for a clock. "Listen. I promised to wake up my mother."

Two days later, Everett saw Janie Powers sitting at a blackjack table in Harold's Club and asked her to have dinner with him and Lily. ("You darlings," Janie kept saying at dinner. "Up here on a honeymoon and this sweet little thing keeping it a secret from Janie." After two whiskey sours and a bottle of wine, Janie was struck by "the *i*rony of it: Lily getting married, me getting—anyway. *Très symbolique.*")

Other than Janie, they saw no one. Everett slept late in the mornings (Lily seemed to have known, always, the way he would look and feel beside her in bed, a comfortable if not particularly electrifying thing) and shot craps a little in the afternoons; Lily got up early, careful not to wake him, and walked by herself up one side of Virginia Street and down the other, stopping always on the bridge to watch the ducks on the Truckee River. She had asked Everett, thinking it might be wifely, if she could get him some toothpaste or shorts or something; he had looked at her a long time, laughed, and said that he could take care of himself. One morning she thought she saw the son of the justice who had performed their marriage, and she turned immediately into a coffee shop and began dropping nickels into a slot machine. Although she did not want him to see her, it seemed important that she see him (had it, after all, happened?), and after he had passed by she ran out and watched until he turned the corner, but could not be certain that he had been the one. All she could remember clearly was his voice, an Okie voice: *Ain't she the prettiest little bride we had all week, now.* One evening they had dinner on the California side of Lake Tahoe; another they drove at twilight over the Geiger grade to Virginia City and found, there in the cemetery on the hill, the grave of someone in Everett's family. *Francis Scott Currier: B. 1830, D. 1859. R.I.P. 2000 miles from home, 1½ miles from the Ophir.* They played tennis twice, and Lily ate lobster, in the dining room at the Riverside, for the first time in her life. It seemed then that the lobster alone lent those few days in Reno a distinct air of celebration, the flavor of a wedding trip.

When Everett took Lily home a week after their marriage, Edith Knight presented him with a kiss on each cheek and Lily with a list of two hundred people who had been invited to the reception. A practiced saver of situations, she had already begun a scrapbook pasted with clippings from the Sacramento and San Francisco papers. Each showed Lily in a white middy blouse, her Dominican graduation picture. There was even one clipping from the *Los Angeles Times*, headlined "Former Solon's Daughter Wed in Nevada."

Everett seemed bemused not only by the clippings but by the prospect of the reception: he took the list from Lily and studied it, asked about a few of the names on it, seemed to forget, and asked again. "This is quite a large party," he said finally.

"You were the one so crazy to get it institutionalized," Lily whispered absently, touching the back of his neck with her fingers. It had just occurred to her that in all the years she had known the McClellans, they had never, except for Sarah's wedding, four years before, given a party. Even Sarah's wedding, or as much of it as Lily could remember, had seemed oddly improvised, an affair which included all the accouterments of other weddings but remained, in some vital way, not entirely a party.

"I just wanted to marry you," Everett whispered.

"Well, you did." Lily raised her voice. "Where's Daddy?"

"It's such an off season," Edith Knight fretted. "It can't be a garden party and it can't be a holiday party. If you'd waited six weeks we could have used Christmas trees. Something festive."

"The bride," Lily said, "is generally considered attraction enough. I said where's Daddy."

Edith Knight shrugged. "In his office, I suppose. I don't believe he's left the house in five days. He's been no help with the arrangements. No help whatsoever."

Lily stood outside her father's office, then opened the door without knocking. He was sitting behind his desk, looking out the window toward the island bridge. Everett's Ford was clearly visible in the driveway; her father had known she was home.

"Well Lily," he said, turning away from the window. "The child bride."

"I see we got a good press."

"Lily McClellan." He gave the dry laugh Lily recognized as forced. "How does that sound?"

The words seemed to hang unnaturally between them. Lily averted her eyes.

Laughing again, Walter Knight walked around the desk and put his hand out, tentatively. "Well," he said.

Although it did not seem likely that he had intended shaking hands with her, his hand was there, and so Lily shook it. He did not seem to know what to do then, and patted her shoulder gingerly.

"Good to have you back," he said finally, as if she had been a long time in a far place, and then, apparently relieved to have hit upon the phrase, he repeated it.

"It's nice to be back," she whispered, able neither to look directly at him nor to speak normally.

"You'll be closer to home than you would have been in Berkeley, actually."

Encouraged by this view of the situation, Lily nodded.

Her father smiled and patted her shoulder again. "The McClellans are old friends."

She said nothing. In view of a fact she had just remembered—that Everett was a second cousin to Rita Blanchard, whose grandmother had been a McClellan—her father's remark seemed obscurely pointed. The issue seemed confused beyond repair, and Lily, blushing, took a silver dollar from the pocket of her polo coat and began to throw it up and catch it.

"It's snowing on the Pass," she said rapidly. "We had a nice time in Reno. I won two twenty-five-dollar jackpots and ate a lobster."

Her father nodded gravely.

She dropped the dollar, which Everett had given her one night when he was winning, and watched it roll across the floor.

"Well, princess, there's no place like Reno." Walter Knight picked up the dollar and dropped it into her pocket. "For all the mortal delights. Now let's see if we can't get a drink before lunch. You could probably use one. Or two."

She tried to smile. Although she had hoped, all week and even this morning, that her father would tell her not to worry and somehow take things in hand, she saw now that it would be more or less up to her.

Whenever she thought later of that week in Reno—and she thought of it quite often that first year, thought of it while she sat at dinner, listening to the clock in the hall and to Everett's father chewing; thought of it in bed, and reached to touch Everett's face in the dark so that she would know she was not alone; thought of it sometimes before Knight was born, when she had been so frightened and Everett so reasonable, bringing her, every morning, the flowers she did not know how to arrange, the words she did not know how to accept—it was with a longing she could never quite place, a nostalgia neither entirely truthful nor entirely imagined. It was as if the week had existed out of time, as if they might happen upon it again one day by accident and find the same limpid air, forever suspended there between autumn and winter; the same faces in the Riverside bar; the same wild ducks lighting down on the same rocks along the Truckee, although even that week they had been on their way south: everything untouched, impervious to erosion, not exactly shining and not exactly innocent but preserved exactly as it had been, absolute proof against further corruption. She had said to her father that morning everything she could have said: *We had a nice time in Reno.*

7

YOUNG MARRIED, river matron, mother of two: on the February morning in 1942 when she learned she was pregnant the second time she knew the rôles she should be playing. It had not seemed as urgent when she had only Knight. Knight's birth had pleased Everett; Knight's birth had pleased her, once it had happened. In the six months since Knight's birth, however, nothing had changed. China Mary took care of him, just as she took care of everything else that needed doing in the house; Martha worried about him, just as she worried about everyone else. She would call up from Davis in the middle of the week. "That fever," she would begin. "What fever?" Lily would ask. "That 104° fever he had a week ago Sunday. What fever. Anyway. You don't think it could have damaged his heart?" "We had Dr. Dubois," Lily would say. "Dr. Dubois. Dr. Dubois has been senile since shortly before he delivered *you*. Let me speak to Everett." As far as Mr. McClellan was concerned, Knight was a small animal still too inert to be entertaining; he largely ignored his presence, pausing by the crib upstairs only when he suspected Everett or Lily to be watching. Nothing about Knight's arrival, in short, had changed the mood of the house: Lily continued to stay upstairs as much as possible, nervous whenever she was downstairs that she was intruding upon the family she continued to think of as the McClellans, a house guest who had stayed on too long; Everett became every day more abstracted, the way, she saw, he had always been around his father. "If you don't stop whistling through your teeth," she had whispered one night after dinner, "I'm going to start screaming." "Everett has always whistled through his teeth," Martha had interrupted; it was impossible to say anything, when Martha was home from school, that Martha did not hear and work into an issue. "Whistling is simply Everett's way," Martha had added, looking directly at the book in Lily's lap, "of pretending to be reading." Everett seemed to Lily to act himself only when they were alone, and Knight did not change that. They could lie in bed in the mornings with

Knight between them and laugh, but that did not quite make, Lily thought, a family.

With two children, however, she would have to make more of an effort. Nothing about her *modus vivendi* was appropriate to a young wife and mother of two: the doctor, quite inadvertently, made that much clear. Examining her, he asked whether any of her friends had told her about Dr. Grantly Dick-Read. "I suppose you mean natural childbirth," she said quickly, uncomfortably convinced, as she lay in ignominy on the table, that both the doctor and his even more disapproving cohort, the nurse, had divined the shameful fact she had only then realized: she had no friends. She had her family, she had the McClellans; she had a neat leather address book respectably if not completely full of names, mostly those of girls with whom she had gone to school, to which she could address Christmas cards. But she had no one with whom she might have sat around over coffee and compared obstetrical notes. It was a failure she had never before fathomed: she did not much enjoy the company of women.

"Natural childbirth," she repeated, stalling. "I'm not sure I'd like that. I was in labor thirty-four hours with Knight."

"That's because you were afraid," the doctor said genially. He was a young obstetrician recommended by Martha; Dr. Dubois had retired.

"I don't know." Lily wondered with some irritation how she had happened to think Martha an authority on obstetricians.

The doctor patted her thigh, affably. "You talk it over with your husband."

The notion that she might talk over natural childbirth with Everett seemed only slightly less ludicrous than the notion that she might have already talked it over with friends, and when Lily left the doctor's office she walked through Capitol Park, distracted by the vistas of social failure opened up by the doctor; sat down on the wet steps of the Capitol Building, and tried to think exactly what it was that young wives and mothers did. For a starter, they did not sit around by themselves on the Capitol steps smoking cigarettes in the rain; she was sure of that. If they found themselves downtown after an appointment in the Medico-Dental Building they would have swatches to match, War Bonds to purchase, friends to meet for lunch. They would have an entire circle of friends with whom they lunched regularly, played bridge, talked about natural childbirth and saddle-block anaesthesia and twilight sleep and the last time the Lunts played Memorial Auditorium.

Deciding as she drove out to the ranch that the first step toward social regularity might well be the proper equipment (she could not think what else it might be), she wrote immediately to Shreve's in San Francisco and ordered six hundred sheets of pale blue letter paper monogrammed L.K.McC., four hundred lined envelopes engraved *McClellan's Landing, California* (an address acceptable to both Everett and the Post Office and one which she thought had a good deal more innate style than the Star Route number Mr. McClellan persisted in using), six hundred folded notes (with matching envelopes) engraved *Mrs. Everett Currier McClellan*, and something she had seen described in *Vogue* as a "hostess-saver," a small book similar to one used by Mrs. Roosevelt's social secretary to record the preferences, disinclinations, and favorite menus of all one's guests.

On the day the package arrived from Shreve's, she set up a card table on the sun porch, filled Everett's fountain pen, arranged a tray with a glass of iced tea and a fresh package of cigarettes, and set about writing some notes. Unable at first to think where to begin, she located the neat leather address book and turned the pages methodically from A (Alice Adamson, an unattractive but popular girl with whom Lily had once shared a room at a Stanford house party and had never seen again), through the heavy concentration of relatives under K, right on to Z (Zenith Jewelry in Berkeley, where she had once left a bracelet to be repaired): there was no one to whom she could reasonably write a letter.

By the end of the afternoon, nonetheless, using rather larger than normal handwriting and in one case asking for a recipe she did not want (Baked Alaska made with cottage cheese would be beyond, she could not help feeling, even her expanding horizons), she had managed to write three: one to her roommate at Dominican, a girl she had not felt one way or another about; one to the rather sententious widow who had been housemother in the Pi Phi house the year she was at Berkeley;

and one to Martha, who had not been home from Davis in eight days and had twice called Everett and urged him to write. Although the box of folded notes remained untouched, she had a definite purpose in mind for them: invitations. Starting with luncheons and afternoon desserts, she would progress to mixed entertainments—cocktail parties, Sunday-night suppers, little dinners so well planned that even Mr. McClellan could not turn them awry; simple but perfectly done, suitable wartime entertaining. "My mother is a *great* hostess," she explained to Everett as they drove to the post office to mail her three letters. "When Daddy was in the Legislature she was possibly *the most noted* hostess on the river. Now. There's no reason why I can't give a simple little party. Is there." Everett, his eyes on the road, could see none. "Let's stop for a drink before we go back," Lily said happily. "Let's have a drink by ourselves in a roadhouse or something. There's time before dinner." All right, Everett agreed drily, kissing her hair at a stop sign, they would have a drink in a roadhouse or something. "To celebrate," she added. To celebrate, he repeated after her, smiling, although she could see that he was not entirely sure what they were celebrating, or why.

Fifteen days later, after drawing up several lists and then abandoning them in periods of retrogression, she opened the box of folded notes and wrote out eighteen invitations for a luncheon one afternoon in May. Everett put up card tables on the verandah for her, Martha called from Davis to encourage her (as well as to suggest that the unprecedented number of people might upset Knight), and for a few hours that afternoon the McClellan place had about it the illusion that someone other than Lily lived there, someone used to casual friendships, at home with the sound of women's voices, luncheon forks, bridge being dealt. But although Edith Knight declared after everyone else had left that it had been the loveliest afternoon possible, Lily knew that it had not quite worked. It was nothing she had done or not done. It was simply that there existed between her and other women a vacuum in which overtures faded out, voices became inaudible, connections broke. With increased apprehension but unalloyed determination, she set about correcting it: if she was incapable of having a circle, she would then direct her efforts toward cementing Everett's circle. But when she discovered that Everett's disinterest in her friends or her lack of them was equaled only by his disinterest in seeing his own friends with any regularity (did he have any friends? she sometimes wondered), she was at a loss as to what to do next, and when her father died in June she had every reason not to do anything. The single luncheon, the handful of letters and telephone calls, the Sunday-night supper to which Everett had finally agreed and at which no one, not even Martha, could think of any conversation that quite caught on: she could repeat none of it. She would become a wife and mother later, for as she said to Everett in the terror of the day she found out, *I'm not myself if my father's dead.*

8

A MAN and woman from Chicago discovered the accident: they had been told at the Texaco station downtown in Sacramento that they might get a breeze that hot June night by taking the river road instead of staying on U.S. 40. They slowed down (the man told the Highway Patrol) because of the curious light rising off the river. Tired and bored and sticky from sitting all day in the car, his wife said at first it was another California trick, and wanted to go on. Five would get you ten there was another Giant Orange drink stand involved in it somewhere, and for her nickel you could take every Giant Orange drink stand between here and San Berdoo and sink them five feet under. He parked the car, however, and got out to stand on the levee. When reconnaissance of the terrain turned up no evidence of a Giant Orange drink stand, his wife became apprehensive (it was eerie, she said, it was so creeping eerie), and would not get out of the car. It took him three or four minutes to apprehend what anyone from the river would have known immediately, for this was a bad curve, frequently miscalculated, or at any rate frequently as that kind of miscalculation goes; to realize that the glow on the water was rising through twenty-five feet of muddy water from the headlights of a car. The light filtered up through layer upon layer of current and cross-current, and flickered all about the channel as the wind disturbed the surface water. *If I told her once I told her twenty times, there was something funny going on here and it was up to us to see what was what*, the man said again and again to the state patrolmen, his curiosity already transmuted into the sense of civic responsibility which would become, in future tellings, the leitmotif of the story about the night they were someplace in California and saw this light Melba claimed was a Giant Orange, which is a kind of drink stand they have out there shaped like a giant orange. It was well after midnight before the river salvage people could get there from Yolo County with a hoist, and nearly five o'clock before they knew enough to call Edith Knight.

She drove into town alone, a silk robe pulled over her nightgown, to identify the bodies. Because the accident had been discovered so quickly, identification was only a formality. Walter Knight's face, unmarked, bore only the featureless look of the recently drowned. Rita had been cut, across her left cheek and down that long Blanchard throat; she had been thrown, they said, against the dashboard before the car hit the water. Her long hair was still wet, and Edith Knight wondered, irrelevantly but obsessively, if it would dry before they buried her. She did not see how it could dry in the grave. Although she asked the coroner's emergency attendant if it could, he did not seem to know. A small man possessed of a large curiosity about people under stress (an interest which relieved the general tedium of his work), the attendant took advantage, however, of this opening: he wondered, probing delicately, if the lady with the beautiful hair had been visiting Mrs. Knight and the late Senator. The late State Senator.

"Miss Rita Blanchard has lived all her life on Thirty-eighth Street," Edith Knight said sharply. "She is from an old, old family in the Valley. A family," she added magnanimously, "which crossed the Great Plains a year before my own."

"A great tragedy, Mrs. Knight," the coroner's assistant said, abandoning the opportunity to pursue Sacramento Valley genealogy further and reaching instead for her hand. "A tragic loss."

"The Lord gives it and takes it, Mr. Paley," she said, turning away from his outstretched hand.

By the time she left the morgue the sun was completely up, and the heat rising. She drove directly to the McClellan place and found Lily in the kitchen. "Oh Christ," Lily whispered. "He'll never have the marmalade." She had gotten up at dawn to make pear marmalade for her father before the heat came up. The marmalade was a kind he especially liked, from a recipe of his mother's, and she had planned it as a surprise. She had gone to the ranch the day before to get the pears from Gomez. "The marmalade would have shown him," she whispered. "Shown him what?" Edith Knight asked, but Lily did not answer because she had put her knuckles against her teeth to keep from screaming and had slipped down beside the sink to the linoleum floor. Shaking but not moving in any other way, she stayed there until Edith Knight pulled her to her feet, untied the apron she was wearing over her nightgown, and led her upstairs to Everett, who was shaving. Later the doctor gave Everett enough pills to keep her quiet for two days and Edith Knight said she had never, never in her entire life, seen anybody react the way that child reacted to a death in the family, she had always been morbidly sensitive and frankly it would have been better if they had gotten the pills before they told her, they might have known it would happen and she of all people should have known Lily was not strong enough to cope with the things other people had to cope with, but when do you think at a time like that.

On the morning of the funeral, Edith Knight and Martha, together, managed to get Lily dressed. She sat on the edge of the bed, staring at the floor while Martha went through her closet. She had nothing which approximated mourning except a black silk suit she had bought in Berkeley; now, six months pregnant, she could not fasten the skirt. "Everett said it didn't matter what I wore," she said again and again, and finally, after her mother and Martha had conceded that it did not, she put on a maternity skirt, a pink and white flowered blouse that her father had once admired, and, an afterthought, a black lace mantilla. She looked, Martha whispered to Everett, like a stray from *The Grapes of Wrath.*

It was another bad day, close to 108° at eleven o'clock. Lily sat between her mother and Everett in the car, her composure so precarious that she could look at neither of them.

"I feel stronger every minute," Edith Knight announced, trying to work her long gloves onto her fingers. "Here," she added, pulling off one of the gloves and twisting a large ring from her finger. "I meant for you to have this some day anyway."

Lily slipped the ring over her wedding ring and closed her eyes again. It was a diamond her father had given her mother the day she was born.

"Thank you," she said.

"I don't know." Edith Knight lifted Lily's left hand and appraised the effect. "You're really too young."

"She's really too skinny," Everett said. "She'll lose it."

"I *want* it," Lily said, opening her eyes; it was the first unequivocal statement she had made in two days.

*

They did not have a Catholic funeral. Because only a handful of the Knights were Catholics in the first place and because even their Catholicism was more an accident of birth or marriage than an act of faith, the family was not troubled by the Episcopal service, the unconsecrated ground: the family graveyard, near the ranch, where no one had been buried since 1892. "I don't care if he was brought up Catholic or brought up Hindu," Edith Knight had declared. "I guess I know where he'd want to lie. I guess I know that much."

From all over the Valley and from the Sierra foothills the family came; everyone from the river came and everyone from town came. Gomez and Crystal came, the Governor came, and the bartender from the Senator Hotel came. As if she were immune to grief, love, all the transient passions, Edith Knight stood throughout the funeral without moving. Lily stood behind her, looking away from the grave toward the distant line of cottonwoods which marked the river. She had thrown the mantilla back from her hair because it seemed to draw the heat; now it lay, fallen from her shoulders, on the ground behind her. She could not stoop to pick it up.

There was a certain comfort in the unkempt graveyard. Dried grass obscured the markers, and the wings had been broken years before from the stone angels guarding the rusted wire gate; there was about the place none of the respect for death implicit in a well-tended plot. Once, a long time before, Walter Knight had brought Lily to see this graveyard. He had made her trace out with her finger the letters on the stones, the names and their dates, until she found the small, rough stone which marked the oldest grave. *Matthew Broderick Knight, January 2, 1847, until December 6, 1848.* The baby had been the first of them to die in California. It was a favorite story, passed on from Knight to Knight and documented periodically in the historical supplements to the *Sacramento Union.* Born in Kentucky, the child had begun to burn with infant fever on the way west. Another child in the party had died of it, and that mother had carried the dead child in her arms for three days, telling no one, afraid they would bury her baby before they came to a station. But Matthew Knight had lived out the crossing; he died instead in a room in Sacramento that first winter, while his father, Lily's great-great-grandfather, was building the first house on the ranch. His mother, twenty years old that winter, was deranged for months, believing herself at home in Bourbon County even as she hauled buckets of Sacramento River silt to cover the hardpan around her raw house. She wanted to grow a garden of forget-me-nots and love-lies-bleeding and the dogwood she remembered from her mother's kitchen stoop, but as summer broke and she began to feel herself again she planted those same alien poppies and lupine that grew on the child's grave. *By the rivers of Babylon, there we sat down*, she had ordered cut into the gravestone, but that had been when she was ill. The symbolic nature of Amanda Broderick Knight's first garden on the ranch was, for the Knights, this story's *raison-d'être*. "I think nobody owns land until their dead are in it," Walter Knight had said to Lily, playing a familiar variation on a familiar motif. Even as she recognized that all he was giving her was the official family line, Lily could not help but be disarmed. She answered in the same rich vein: "Sometimes I think this whole valley belongs to me." "It does, you hear me?" Walter Knight said sharply. "We made it." She had never doubted that.

The grave was covered by noon. Her arm through Everett's, Lily sat in the car, twisting the diamond on her finger and watching her mother. Edith Knight stood in the dry grass by the wire gate and received: accepted as her due the certified recollections, the ritual testimonials which serve as visas into that comfortable territory where no dead man is less than noble. *You remember when Walter came up that summer, 'thirty-three, we were in the middle of a crop and there was all the trouble and Walter sent in his own men and cleaned up the crop. You remember how Walter held the note on the Hawkes place all those years after it was due until the son could pay it off. Remember now. Remember.* The litany of Walter Knight's shining hours continued until one o'clock, long after most of the mourners, including Mr. McClellan and Martha, had left for Rita Blanchard's funeral in town; Edith Knight stood impassive and triumphant throughout. Were they not attesting, after all, that he now belonged to God alone and that she, Edith, had sole rights to his relics in this world?

Two weeks later, the lawyers notarized her victory. In 1933, Rita Blanchard, needing cash, had sold to Walter Knight 120 frontage feet of a downtown block which had been in her family for eighty years. Although his will provided that this parcel be returned to Rita, their simultaneous deaths meant that it now belonged to Edith. To the lawyers, the family, and to the reporter who was writing up the disposition of the estate, she announced that she wanted the sizable income from that property placed annually in a University of California scholarship fund to be administered by the Department of English and to bear Rita's name. "If there is one thing I will remember about poor Rita to my dying day," Edith Knight explained, "it's that Rita was a *reader*." Because the entire estate went to Edith (passing to Lily at her death and held throughout both their lifetimes in a loose trust which would vest in Knight at some point after his twenty-first birthday), she could now afford, in every sense, to dispose of Rita with that grand gesture. (The impact of the Rita Blanchard Scholarships was somewhat weakened, however, when it became apparent a month later that Rita had left half the Blanchard estate to Lily, the other half to be divided among sixteen cousins, including Everett, Martha, and Sarah McClellan. As Martha said to Everett in the Blanchard lawyer's office, you really had to grant that round to Rita.)

9

THERE WERE roses (so many for September) and late poppies: the room was full of them. Everett must have brought them in from the ranch. No matter what way Lily turned her head on the pillow she saw roses, dropping their petals in the closed gray room which looked exactly like the room they had given her when Knight was born. Somewhere among the roses were jasmine gardenias, sweet and heavy as the drugs. The nuns would not open the windows in the storm. The rain had begun the night before she started labor and was still falling; she watched it washing down the narrow windows all that morning. When she closed her eyes she saw rain beating the leaves from the camellias around the house. It must be raining in every part of the world, flooding all the valleys: she was certain that her baby had died in the night, that the nuns were concealing the death from her, and she knew as well that before long she would begin to hemorrhage and die herself. She had recently read *A Farewell to Arms* and now she cried to think of Everett walking out of the hospital into the rain like Lieutenant Henry.

Everett had come yesterday. When she woke from the drugs he had been sitting by the window, and she had watched him for several minutes without speaking. The San Francisco papers were spread on the floor around his chair. He had been reading three or four papers all that year, since before Pearl Harbor. Although she tried every few days to read a paper through, she seemed always to have come in too late on any given action to understand that day's plays. After a while she had tried concentrating only on the war in the Pacific, which as far as she could gather America seemed to be losing. Although this did not seem entirely credible, it seemed, winning or losing, more credible than anything about the war in Europe; what the war in Europe so notably lacked, for Lily, was a Pearl Harbor. As Mr. McClellan had said the morning of Pearl Harbor, when Martha ran downstairs wrapped in a towel to tell them, "That tears it." (That was all he said, and he did not say that until he had shouted at Martha "You keep on listening to the radio in the bathtub, Missy, you're going to fry yourself," but he spent the rest of the day pacing up and down in front of the house, scanning the sky and muttering to himself.) Until Everett had explained to her that the Germans and the Japanese were pledged to defend one another, a point which had eluded her for the first two weeks of the war, Lily had been at a loss to understand what the United States was doing in Europe at all. The Pacific, of course, was another case. It did not please her to think, as she had thought, that this baby might have been conceived the morning of Pearl Harbor. It was not propitious.

Everett, yesterday, had been looking out the hospital window into the rain. The lights seemed to be just coming on outside. It would be about five o'clock, she supposed, and there would be lights in all the windows down Thirty-eighth Street. Only Rita Blanchard's house would be dark; the house had been empty since the accident. She could never remember that the house now belonged to her, to her and Everett and Martha and Sarah and thirteen other people, but mostly to her. Everett had talked a few weeks ago to a man who wanted to buy the place and have it rezoned for a day nursery. That would be the day. Painted wooden rabbits on Rita Blanchard's lawn.

"Tell me what's in the newspaper," she said finally. Everett was always trying to tell his father what was in the newspaper. Because Mr. McClellan neither read the papers (none of them, he said, carried anything but pictures of that crew in Washington) nor listened to the radio, his many ideas about how the war should be conducted were based almost entirely upon information given him by Everett. Once he had absorbed two or three facts, usually tangential, he would cut Everett off by saying that it was no news to him, he knew those yellowbellies and all their tricks like the back of his hand.

Everett folded the newspaper and smiled. "How long you been awake?"

She laughed and put her hands to her stomach. It was still swollen. "You needn't whisper. Where's the baby?"

He came back in a few minutes with one of the nuns, who held the baby wrapped in pink flannel.

"A girl," she said. "That would have pleased Daddy."

"It pleases me."

Lily turned her head on the pillow so that she could see Everett's face.

"Listen," she said. "I was all right this time, wasn't I."

"You were fine."

She lay back. "I can't feed it, you know."

"They'll feed her."

"It's funny to hear you say *her*. I don't even know what we'll call it."

"You said Julia. Julia Knight McClellan. I thought we decided that."

"I just said that because of my grandmother. I never really thought it would be a girl. I was thinking of Walter." She laughed. "It's entirely too small to call something like Julia Knight McClellan. It sounds like a suffragette."

"She's big for a baby." Everett turned to the nun. "Didn't you say she was big for a baby?"

"Everett, I *know*. She's a regular King Kong of a baby."

"Listen," she added after the nun had left the room. "We'll have more. We'll have about six. And Martha can have about six. And they'll have these terrible fights because there won't be enough land to go around."

"And Sarah. Don't forget Sarah."

"That's right, and Sarah." She had in fact forgotten Sarah. "Anyway. There'll be this one runt. Likable but you know, a loser. He'll be conned out of everything but some little back piece with no water. Then one day while the rest of them are playing golf—they'll be forever hanging around the country club, that type—and he's scratching around his place, you know what happens then?"

"Gold."

"Everett, baby. You live so in the past. It turns out his piece is the only exit for one hundred miles on a proposed transcontinental freeway."

"A freeway?"

"An *exit*, Everett. Standard Stations. Motels. Piggly Wiggly Markets. Long-term leases."

Everett smiled.

"Listen," she said. "I behaved this time, didn't I."

Everett sat down by the bed and took her hand. "Yes."

"I didn't get scared and make a lot of trouble. I mean all the way through it was all right this time."

"You didn't make a lot of trouble before."

"I did. Your father told Martha he hoped I never got pregnant again because I was impossible."

"Who told you that?"

"Never mind. I was, that's the point."

"Martha didn't mean it if she told you that."

"Never mind. It was better this time, you saw."

"It was fine."

"You have to take care of me," she whispered.

He held her hand and looked out the window a long while. "I will," he said. "I do. Don't I."

Although she had thought for a moment that she had never been so happy, Everett had left when her mother came ("I meant to come earlier but I was downtown," Edith Knight said, remotely bewildered, the way she had been since a few weeks after the funeral; despite a new vicuña coat and an absolute lack of any visible defect in her grooming, she presented a curious impression of disarray, twisting her rings, smoothing her hair; straightening the sheet as she kissed Lily goodbye), and after her mother left Lily was alone. The nuns had begun their evening visits, walking the corridor in pairs. When one paused outside the door, the light blinking off her thick glasses, Lily turned away from the door, pretending to be asleep, and as she watched the street lights blur through the blown branches outside the window she wondered how the nuns had known, and if they had once been as she was now. She thought of her mother, who by now would be sitting alone with a tray in the living room at home, picking at her inevitable lamb chop and watching the same rain. Rain seldom fell so long so early; if it kept up there could be floods before Christmas. Once when she was a child a levee had broken on Christmas Eve, and the churches were filled with tired women in raincoats and children in blue bathrobes. At Edith Knight's insistence she had given all but one of her unopened Christmas presents to the evacuated children, whose own, Edith Knight had explained, were floating over to the poor Chinese children. Put that way, it had seemed an ideal situation, one in which only Lily came out behind.

Although Everett should have eaten with her mother tonight, eaten with her or taken her down to the ranch, he would not have thought of it. And her mother was so lonely that she seemed to have lost even the idea of communication. "Some nights when the wind comes up I think I'm the only person alive on the river," she had said a few weeks ago. "Why don't you call me?" Lily said. "Why don't you call me or one of the Randalls?" "I could, of course," her mother said without interest, as if Lily had introduced a quite irrelevant topic. In a sense she had: there was little that Lily or the Randalls or anyone else could do to mend the web of concern which Walter Knight and Rita Blanchard had woven around Edith Knight for a dozen years and had torn apart in June. It had once occurred to Lily that her mother missed Rita more than she missed Walter Knight; it had been Rita, after all, who provided her with her rôle, who might well have gone on providing it, walking proof not only of Walter Knight's failure (dead or alive) but of Edith Knight's strength in the face of it.

Well, her mother had chosen her rôle, the nuns theirs. But how did they know. How had Mary Knight known. Mary Knight Randall had entered the Sisters of Mercy the summer she was eighteen. She had gone to Europe with her father, Walter Knight's cousin, and when they got off the boat in New York that August she told him that she did not intend to go to Berkeley in September. Although he tried to reason with her all the way across the country on the train, even promised that she could have a new robin's-egg blue Ford convertible and spend the entire month of January skiing at Aspen, Mary Knight entered the convent the same week Lily went down to Berkeley. It was the week of rushing, and because Mary Knight had planned to be with her, Lily had a double room alone at the Durant Hotel. She lay awake every night, listening to the Campanile strike in the coastal fog and feeling intensely sorry for herself, partly because she did not know how to talk to the golden girls from San Francisco and Pasadena but mostly because she had been deprived of Mary Knight, who was older than she was but had never known anything at all, had moved through adolescence in an untroubled innocence which had obscurely reassured Lily, made her want to have Mary Knight with her always, a talisman. (Once at a beach party, Joe Templeton's younger brother, Pete, had tried to get Mary Knight up on the bluff in a car with him. "Why do they want to do that?" she whispered later to Lily. "Never you mind," Lily said, throwing sand on the fire. She had disliked Pete Templeton for trying and loved Mary Knight for not knowing.) Even the Catholics mourned Mary Knight; Helen Randall, who had refused to go to Europe with them because she wanted to go to Banff, still put the blame on Mary Knight's father. Mary Knight was an impressionable girl and if he had not exposed her day after day to those morbid European cathedrals it simply would not have happened. He should have taken her, as she, Helen, had suggested in the first place, to the Calgary Stampede. Now there was a portrait in the dining room of the Randalls' house, hung as prominently as if it were of someone dead, Mary Knight at sixteen, absurd but oddly indomitable in a pink tulle dress.

Mary Knight, her mother, the nuns in the corridor: they all seemed to know something she did not. Well, she had at least given Everett what he wanted. Even Martha could scarcely have given him two children. But she could not escape the uneasy certainty that she had done so herself only by way of some intricate deception, that her entire life with Everett was an improvisation dependent upon cues she might one day fail to hear, characterizations she might at any time forget. Except when she was in trouble (when her father died, or when she was pregnant with Knight), she could think of little to say to Everett: she was not, nor was he, a teller of anecdotes or gossip, and sometimes whole weeks passed without their having what could be called, in even the crudest sense, a conversation. Usually in bed she pretended that she was someone else, a stranger, and she supposed that Everett did too; when she did not pretend that she was someone else, she pretended that Everett was. The only times she did not pretend that either or both of them were someone else, she pretended that it had never happened before, that it was again that first time on the river. There had been about that first time a sharpness, a finality absent since. For a long time, even after she had done it hundreds of times, the fact that it had happened at all would come to her with a shock; it had seemed improbable that anyone else could do it, and the hearsay knowledge that not just anyone but almost everyone had done it remained a persistent flaw in her satisfaction with her own performance. It was as if she had stumbled alone across the plains and found that everyone else had already arrived, by TWA. Even now, two years later, those few minutes were more vivid than any since: she had lost neither the sense of wonder nor the sense of deprivation that the experience had not been uniquely hers. The summer smell of that morning, river water and sweat and the acrid sting of weeds breaking under them (and that would always be summer's smell), was stronger still than all the roses and jasmine gardenias in the whole of Mercy Hospital.

I should have taken the Holy Ghost not Everett, she had thought when she woke this morning, and she had snapped at the nun who was trying to take her temperature. A pillow over her head, she had lain still all morning, lifting the pillow only to watch the rain outside. She should sit up and comb her hair, wash her face, put on the silk bed-jacket her mother had brought. Everett would come again this morning, and she did not want to see him. She was not sure that it would be all right even if they could go back to that morning on the river and start over again; because she could not put her finger on what was wrong it would only go wrong a second time. She wanted now only to see her father, to go back to that country in time where no one made mistakes. *For a thousand years in thy sight are but as yesterday when it is past, and as a watch in the night.* She had memorized those words at the time of her father's death, had repeated them as she walked down streets and brushed her hair, as she lay in bed and as she drove the river road, and she repeated them now against Everett's arrival.

10

"YOU'LL GET along fine," Everett said, the morning he left for Fort Lewis. "You're a big girl now. You wait. You'll be all right here. Wait and see."

He spoke very low; both Knight and Julie were asleep in the next room.

"You didn't have to go," Lily repeated. She could not view Everett's enlistment as anything other than personal and possibly deserved retribution. Bataan might fall, Corregidor might fall, and the Japanese might occupy Attu and Kiska, but Everett could not have gone had she not failed him somewhere. "You have a son. You have a two-month-old daughter. Your father needs you."

Everett sat up on the edge of the bed and lit a cigarette. Although light now filtered through the shutters, they had not slept. After Mr. McClellan went to bed they had, between them, drunk most of a bottle of bourbon, and then Lily had cried (partly the bourbon) and they had lain in the dark awake, oppressed less by the parting than by some uneasy apprehension of how the parting should be affecting them.

"Lily," he said. "You keep saying the same things. I want to go."

"I don't see why."

"I waited a year. Almost a year. Now I have to go."

"You don't have to. You want to. You said you wanted to."

"All right. I want to. I don't see any difference."

Lily lay without moving, her head aching dully.

"I believe you want to die," she said after a while.

"All right. I want to die. Now I have to get up."

While Everett shaved she finished packing his bag, trying dutifully to memorize the way his shorts felt to the touch, the particular color and translucency of his toothbrush. They seemed things that she might want, at some future point, to remember. Although she considered putting on the same plaid skirt and paint-stained sweater she wore most mornings, she thought then of ships going out under the Golden Gate in fog, of Wake Island, of that hot golden summer before they were married, and pulled on instead the white cashmere sweater that Everett had given her on her nineteenth birthday.

He was to take the Shasta Daylight from Davis station at seven o'clock. It would take them close to an hour to drive there. Although Lily wished now that someone would drive over with them, all the goodbyes had been said already: Martha had come over from Davis for dinner, and had driven back before midnight to study for a midterm. ("Daddy is of the opinion I'm meeting all kinds of rich citrus growers from down South," she had said at dinner. "When all I'm doing is taking midterms and lending my clothes to rich citrus growers' daughters so they can go out with rich citrus growers' sons." Everett had seemed puzzled. "What do you want to run around with people from down South for?" he had wanted to know. "Oh you know me, Everett," Martha had said. "An old One-Worlder.")

The house was perfectly still, and cold from the November night. Chilled through, Lily stood in the hallway and ran her fingers along the grain of the stair railing. When she heard Everett on the stairs she began, nervously, straightening some letters left on the hall table.

"Now listen," he said. "I'll write you tomorrow. Then will you please write me and tell me how you're getting along?"

"Yes," she said, her eyes fixed on the fireplace in the living room. The house downstairs had the same curious appearance it always had in the early morning, the look of a house abandoned in an emergency years before. It was hard to believe there were not really dusty sheets thrown over the faded slipcovers, impossible to think that the magazines thrown on the tables were actually dated 1942. "I'll write you," she added. "Every day."

"And try to get my father to slow down."

"Yes."

"And see people and get some sleep. Gain some weight."

"Yes," she said. "I'll knit you some khaki socks."

"Well." He held out her coat. "The home front."

"That's right," she said. "The home front."

*

She drove to Davis; they scarcely spoke. She watched the road and he stared out the window. A light fog hung low on the river and the knotted, broken strings fluttered among the fields of bare hop poles. There had been frost in the night; it would warm toward noon.

Although the train was due in fifteen minutes, there were only a few other cars at the station. They sat in the station wagon, the heater on and the windows steamed, and Everett put his arm around her shoulders. She said that the sweater made her feel pretty; he said that she was pretty, pretty hair, pretty eyes, pretty arms. Be quiet, she said, pressing his arm. There was little now that she wanted to say, and in the end she did not say anything, because Martha came to the station. They saw her running down the platform, clutching a book and a bunch of yellow chrysanthemums, a dirty poplin raincoat over her nightgown.

"You look like a goddamn refugee," Everett said, opening the door of the station wagon.

"I was afraid I'd miss you if I stopped to get dressed. So I just came."

"Lucky you didn't run across any rich citrus growers," Everett said.

Martha pushed the book and the chrysanthemums into Everett's arms. Embarrassed then, she stood outside the car, looking off toward the station, her hands shoved down into the pockets of her raincoat.

Everett opened the book and looked up at Martha.

"It's my copy," she said. "I knew you didn't have one."

"What is it?" Lily asked.

Martha did not look at her. "A family book."

"*The McClellan Journal*," Everett read. "*An Account of An Overland Journey to California in the Year 1848.*"

"Privately printed," Martha added.

"Imagine," Lily said.

Everett and Martha, she thought. *Forward into battle with the Cross before*. She remembered her surprise at finding on the walls of Martha's room, when they had been children and she had been sent to play at the McClellan place, neither Degas ballet dancers nor scenes from *Alice in Wonderland* but a framed deed signed by John Sutter in 1847, a matted list of the provisions carried on an obscure crossing in 1852, a detailed relief map of the Humboldt Sink, and a large lithograph of Donner Pass on which Martha had printed, in two neat columns, the names of the casualties and the survivors of the Donner-Reed crossing. Martha's favorite game as a child had in fact been "Donner Party," a ritual drama in which she, as its originator, always played Tamsen Donner and was left, day after day, to perish by the side of the husband whose foolish miscalculations had brought them all to grief. (In Martha's re-enactments, the Winning of the West invariably took on this unobtrusively feminist slant; in another game, "Central Pacific," the power behind the transcontinental railroad turned out to be not Collis Potter Huntington at all, but Leland Stanford's wife Jane, and Lily grew up with the distinct impression, planted by Martha and uncorrected for years, that the *éminence grise* behind the California Republic had been Jessie Benton Frémont.) It seemed to have been an ineradicable mote in Martha's eye that everyone from whom she was descended had, unlike Tamsen Donner, gotten through, and when Lily told her that someone in her father's family had traveled with the Donner-Reed Party as far as the Applegate Cut-off, Martha had been despondent for several days. As a matter of fact she had mentioned it querulously only a few weeks before.

"You could lend it to people," Martha suggested, her hands still in her pockets. "I mean it might be very inspiring."

"It's the nicest present you've ever given me," Everett said, getting out of the car and putting his arms around her shoulders. "The nicest anybody's ever given me."

After they had put Everett on the train ("The *train*," Martha screamed, and the three of them ran, Everett trying to take his other bag from Martha and Martha wrenching it away, to the platform, where Everett kissed first Lily, then Martha, and then a small girl who had wandered, carrying an American flag on a stick, from a family at the far end of the platform), Lily and Martha sat in the car, not speaking, until the train began to roll. Tapping an unlighted cigarette on the dashboard and humming "The Battle Hymn of the Republic," Martha had seemed, until then, in trance. When the train whistled, however, she jumped out of the car and ran again to the platform, calling Everett's name, looking in all the windows as the cars gathered speed, and then she walked slowly back to the station wagon, her raincoat fallen open and her pale blue nightgown trailing through the leaves that blew across the concrete parking lot.

"Get in," Lily said. "We'll get some breakfast."

"He left the flowers."

"He's got *The McClellan Journal*. That's what counts."

Martha looked away. Lily saw that she was crying.

"They'd only have died on the train," Lily said. "You put them in your room."

Martha slammed the door closed. "I think I'll go over home with you."

"I thought you had a midterm."

"I do."

"We'll get some breakfast," Lily repeated, turning the ignition key.

They stopped at a drive-in near the Davis campus. Martha talked animatedly for a few minutes about the rôle played by Alice Lee Grosjean in the Long Administration in Louisiana (it seemed she was writing a paper about the Longs) and about someone at Berkeley who had invited her down for the Miami Triad dance. (It was to be at the Fairmont and she really wanted to go, except this boy had an unfortunate predilection for saying things like you're the most terrific girl I've ever known, and she really wasn't up to that kind of thing, not these days, not any more.) Then, abruptly, she stopped talking and began examining her fingernails, three of which were enameled a brilliant American Beauty red.

"Everett said last night I shouldn't wear fingernail polish," she said after a while. "So I started to take it off this morning but I was in a hurry and spilled the whole bottle of remover. All over Betty Jean's V-Mail." Martha giggled. Betty Jean, who was engaged to a Marine, was her roommate and current *bête noire*. According to Martha, Betty Jean saved on board money by eating cheese and crackers in their room instead of lunch downstairs; the further economy was that she then saved the cheese glasses for her hope chest. Martha claimed that Betty Jean had twenty-seven cheese glasses, fifteen with red tulips and twelve with blue cornflowers.

"It's a pretty color," Lily said.

"Everett doesn't like it. I told you." Martha began drumming her fingernails on the metal tray.

Lily did not say anything.

"You'll miss Everett," Martha said finally.

"Yes."

"A whole lot?"

"Of course."

Martha looked out the window. "How much?"

"A whole lot," Lily said, faintly irritated. "What did you mean about the boy who asked you to the Miami Triad? Why don't you go?"

"Daddy thinks I should get married."

"What's that got to do with the Miami Triad?"

Martha did not answer.

"Who do you want to marry?" Lily said.

"I don't know. Somebody." Elaborately, Martha lit a cigarette. "It doesn't much matter who, does it?"

Lily shrugged, and after a while Martha reached in front of her and flicked on the lights to call the carhop.

"I better take my midterm."

When Lily stopped in front of the dormitory, Martha opened the door but did not get out. "Listen," she said. "Do you think I should?"

"Not unless you want to. Not unless you love someone."

"Come off it, Lily. I didn't expect you to talk like such a fool. Whoever loved anybody for more than two weeks. Except your own family. Or maybe somebody you've lived with for years and years, I don't know about that."

"There's a lot of time."

"'There's a lot of time,'" Martha mimicked. "There's no time at all. That's exactly the point. Everybody's going away, and half of everybody's going to die, and the war may go on twenty years, and Everett's gone away—"

"Anyway," she added. "I'm sure I don't know who I'd marry. I'm sure I don't know anyone who could take care of me."

"Maybe," Lily said after a while, "you could marry someone you could take care of. Maybe that's the same thing in the end." As she said it, it occurred to her that she might well have happened, while fumbling through platitudes for Martha's benefit, upon an actual fact, a profound truth: someone could take care of you or you could take care of someone; you could be told or you could tell the comfortable loving fictions (*If you loved me you would steal for me, and tell me fairy tales of a happy land*, it was, she thought, a German song), and in either case what was involved—all that was involved—was a commitment. Perhaps it did not matter much who made it, or how or why: it might very well be the same thing in the end. *It doesn't much matter who does it.*

Martha picked up one of the chrysanthemums and began rolling and shredding the petals into small balls.

"Maybe it would be the same for you," she said finally. "You're so strong."

"I am not," Lily said, jarred by Martha's moodiness and by the note in her voice. "I'm not a bit strong."

Martha shrugged and got out of the car. "All right, you're not a bit strong. It's your act, Lily baby, you play it any way you want. Anyway," she added, "you're strong enough to make people take care of you."

Even if Lily had been able to think what to say it would have been too late: Martha was already running up the walk, her hands over her face, running and stumbling on the lace hem of the pale blue nightgown, last year's Christmas present from Everett, picked out by Lily, extravagantly expensive, handmade at Maison Mendessolle in the St. Francis Hotel.

"We saw Martha this morning," Lily said to Mr. McClellan at dinner. Although she had intended to stop by her mother's on the way back from Davis, she had driven instead directly to the ranch, and had spent the rest of the day upstairs, aimlessly taking things from drawers and putting them in other drawers, sleeplessly lying on her back in their bed, still unmade, the sprigged lawn spread her great-grandmother had quilted thrown down on the floor along with Everett's worn sneakers, the November *Fortune*, and the bottle of bourbon they had almost finished the night before. Not until five o'clock did she go downstairs to see China Mary and the babies; then she kissed Knight absently and carried Julie upstairs in order to feed her in the bedroom. Finishing the bottle of bourbon as she spooned Julie's puréed carrots, she avoided Mr. McClellan for as long as she could and then felt guilty about even that: there she was, pointlessly depriving him of a small pleasure, the opportunity to watch Julie eating, one of the few activities on her schedule animated enough to interest him.

"I said we saw Martha," she repeated. "She came to the station."

Mr. McClellan did not answer.

They were alone in the dining room, absurdly cavernous, oppressively lined with glassed cabinets of crystal and china; the shelves held two complete services of Limoges, each for forty-eight, although in two generations the McClellans had not, to the best of Lily's knowledge, entertained more than three guests at dinner on any given evening.

Mr. McClellan had not spoken since the fruit cup, during which Lily had said that she did not agree that the International Workers of the World were the principal threat facing the United States in 1942. Apparently because he had seen mention of Tom Mooney's name in an unprecedentedly thorough reading of the *San Francisco Chronicle*, Mr. McClellan had been brooding all day upon causes and effects. He guessed Miss Lily Knight, since she was so smart, knew every detail behind the 1916 Preparedness Day Parade bombing in San Francisco. No, of course not. Well here it was: ten people in their graves, thanks to anarchists and Wobblies. He guessed Miss Lily Knight knew all about the 1913 Wheatland Riot, three thousand hop pickers running amok, a tragedy so close to home it might as well have taken place on the kitchen stoop. No, of course not. Possibly Miss Lily Knight still had a few things to learn about Wobblies. He, on the other hand, knew the details behind such events, and was therefore in a position to know that wherever you found trouble in California today you had those boys to thank for it. *Cherchez le Wobbly*, Lily had suggested, and Mr. McClellan had withdrawn into injured silence, broken only when he was moved to place his knife and fork side by side on his plate, wipe his mouth with his napkin, slap both hands palms down on the table and demand loudly: "*What are laws for?*"

Lily raised her voice now. "I said Martha came to the station. She's upset about Everett."

Mr. McClellan cocked his head to one side, apparently to get a different light on the picture which hung on the wall opposite him, a large oil painting of a cornucopia.

"What about Everett?" he said finally.

"His going away."

"She's not a gold-star sister yet," Mr. McClellan said, his voice flat.

II

THEIR COMMUNICATION did not improve noticeably during evenings to come, that winter when the rain fell for what seemed weeks on end. Quite often Mr. McClellan would not speak at all, not out of any hostility but simply because the capacity for random conversation seemed to him less a grace than the certain expression of a weak mind; other nights he would become quite voluble, usually on the subject of the county supervisor (who was, he had come to believe, a paid agent of Franklin Delano Roosevelt), and then he would settle down after dinner with a copy of the California Penal Code, pouncing with intense delight upon certain loopholes and inconsistencies. He had first hit upon this diversion some years before, not long after Mildred McClellan's death, and had regretted ever since, he told Lily, that he had not read for the law. Aside from the evenings when he read aloud from the Penal Code, their liveliest times together were spent playing hearts, for small amounts of money which Mr. McClellan almost inflexibly won. If, after querying China Mary and checking the pockets of all the coats in all the closets, they could still find no change in the house, they played for toothpicks, redeemable no later than the next evening in cash.

Nonetheless, they had between them a curious companionableness, a real, if not exactly infectious, rapport, most apparent to Lily on the occasional evenings when Martha came over from school and upset it. It did not seem to matter if Martha were calm or nervous, buoyant or depressed (although in practice she seemed to come home only in states of aimless crisis): she invariably shattered the balance of reserve and aggressiveness which existed in the house when Mr. McClellan and Lily were alone with the children. Lily did not know what it was about Martha. She thought probably it was that neither she nor Mr. McClellan were what her father would have called "good company," and that possibly Martha was.

But in spite of the unexpected comfort Lily took in Everett's father, it was still the sad season: Everett gone from the McClellan house, her father gone from her own house. All that month before Christmas the house was cold and dark, and Knight could not play outside. In the afternoons Lily wrapped the children up and drove through the rain, past the eroded gullies where muddy run-off swirled along the ranch road, to see her mother; in the evenings, no matter if dinner had been silent or combative or comparatively festive with the promise of hearts or the Penal Code, Mr. McClellan went to his room at ten-thirty, and Lily sat on downstairs alone, listening to the rain and night noises. At first she had tried turning on the radio, and had learned the lyrics to a great many songs including one called "I Spoke to Jefferson at Guadalcanal," but after a while the radio seemed only to intensify, with its impenetrable cheerfulness, whatever was ominous in the noises outside.

Again during those first few weeks after Everett went away, she began to think of little but her father's death. During the five months since it had happened, she had been distracted first by Julie's birth, then by Everett's desertion; now, it was with her every night. Sitting downstairs alone after Mr. McClellan had gone to bed she would take first her father's point of view, then her mother's; then, more and more often, once Rita had been revealed to her in the rôle of victim, Rita Blanchard's. It was not that there had not been something about Rita Blanchard from the beginning, some inability, some failure in her eyes, that marked her for Walter Knight. It was only that if he had wanted to love all of them and been capable of loving none of them, only Rita had really been deceived. Only Rita had put all her chips on that board.

Although Lily wrote to Everett at Fort Lewis every night, there was little to say. She could not write to him about Rita Blanchard; she had never even talked to him about Rita Blanchard. *The babies and I miss you*: that was what she could write to Everett. *China Mary sings Knight a song about how you're off to get a rabbit skin to wrap your baby bunny in, which delights him no end. Julie has a cold from the rain. You must please write your father to do something about the furnace. I do not mind eating breakfast in two sweaters but it is the last straw when he declares the cold is good for the children because look what it does for a collie dog's coat. Last night we played hearts and I won for the first time, although as it turned out I was sorry. The thing is we played with toothpicks again, and because I won thirty-three cents I ended up with thirty-three toothpicks. Well. Tonight before dinner he appeared with a quarter and eight pennies and demanded the toothpicks. I couldn't think what I'd done with them and he said in that case he could hardly be expected to turn over the thirty-three cents. I said all right, don't, we'd forget it, but he held up dinner an hour and fifteen minutes while we enlisted China Mary in a search for the toothpicks. Finally she found them in my apron pocket, but unfortunately there only seemed to be twenty-eight left. He finally gave me the full thirty-three cents in exchange for the twenty-eight toothpicks, but said he was setting a bad example and lectured me all through dinner on the importance of property rights and keeping one's accounts in order. It was, he said, the American way and we could not begin too soon setting an example for Knight and Julie. It seems funny now that I tell you about it but it was nerve-racking at the time. I love you and miss you especially at night.*

The first week in January, there was at least some news: *Joe Templeton came by after dinner and spoke to your father about buying the Braden place at Auburn. He'll write you but your father hopes you won't sell.*

"Joe Templeton wants the Braden place," she said to her mother the next afternoon. Their afternoons together had taken on an unvaried pattern: after Lily had put the children down, she and her mother would knit; Lily for Everett, her mother for the Episcopal Guild bazaar. While they knitted, Edith Knight would resume a monologue about things which had happened some years before; the details, for example, of how the Blanchards lost their river place on a note to a man named C.T. Godey in 1927, or an analysis of a rumor, current in 1931, that one of Lily's second cousins (once removed) had been carrying on with a clarinet player in the orchestra at the St. Francis Hotel. (It was an untruth, according to Edith Knight, although it was no surprise it got started because Elizabeth was practically mental about jazz musicians and had once stood up in a speakeasy on Sutter Street with everybody on the river looking on and sung "Big Noise Blew in from Winnetka" with her arm around a colored drummer.) Once she had become familiar with the names and the chronology, Lily found these accounts generally interesting; she had never felt so close to her mother.

Edith Knight put down the Peruvian face mask she was knitting for the bazaar. "You saw poor Joe?"

"He came by last night. He didn't realize the piece was in Everett's name."

"If the McClellans have the sense God gave them they'll hang on to the Braden place. I used to go on picnics there." Edith Knight paused. "Francie wasn't with Joe?"

"No. He came alone."

"Alone," Edith Knight repeated with satisfaction. "Of course he would have."

Lily did not say anything. Her mother began to hum tunelessly, tapping one knitting needle against the arm of her chair. Her eyes were closed.

"Francie may have been outside in the car," Lily said. "Actually he only stayed a few minutes."

"Oh no." Edith Knight opened her eyes and started to work with fresh vigor on the face mask, intended for use whenever there was danger of frostbite. "I wouldn't think so. He was no doubt quite alone."

Lily did not know what she could say that might not in some way corroborate her mother's fairly opaque conclusions. She rather wished that she had never mentioned Joe Templeton, and tried to think of some way to turn the conversation back a decade or two.

"Didn't Francie Templeton have a sister who wasn't quite bright?" she asked finally.

"That's right," Edith Knight said without interest. "She's been dead seventeen years next month." She continued knitting in silence.

"It's Francie again," she added at last, abandoning the hope of being prodded. "Helen Randall went up there one afternoon—Francie had invited her up, specifically in*vit*ed her for that afternoon—and Francie didn't even come downstairs. Joe made excuses for her. She starts in the morning with vermouth."

"Vermouth, is it." Lily laughed. So often had she heard her mother say of someone who drank that he or she started in the morning with vermouth that she could not drink vermouth without a pleasant sense of discreet raciness; thanks to Edith Knight, vermouth was for Lily one of the small adventures that frequently made her day. Lily's day could also be made by ordering stockings by the dozen rather than by the pair; wearing expensive perfume around the ranch in the mornings; and, among other things, focusing for a fraction of a minute on some stranger's eyes and making him look back just until, say, the traffic light changed.

"I don't know what's going to become of those twins," Edith Knight said, ignoring Lily. "They will no doubt grow up to be zoot-suiters. Look and see if there's any sherry left."

Lily picked up the decanter and filled her mother's glass.

"On the other hand," Edith Knight added, "there's no need to pity Joe. He's been quick enough to find comfort in the past."

Lily sat down again without saying anything.

"If you understand what I mean. About Joe."

"Yes." Lily picked up her knitting again. "I understand you all right."

"Not that she hasn't been a cross. Lord no. But Joe doesn't exactly wear himself out carrying it, either. If you see."

"I understand," Lily repeated.

She had understood well enough. As had Joe. That had required no *roman de la rose.* Once the speculative glances and the accidental meetings were out of the way (the procedure, she saw, was a *way* of doing rather than anything done; first the miraculous awareness of the possibility, then the almost inaudible overture, the response so subtle as to be uncertain), they met in the late afternoons of that winter and in the long spring twilights, met in cars parked off the levee, bars frequented by Mexicans, and in an empty shack on the piece downriver which belonged to Francie Templeton's mother. They did not talk much, and she was never certain that either derived from the other much pleasure, as that word is commonly defined. She knew only that they continued to interest each other. A tacit complicity between them cut that interest away from everything going on in other places and at other times; Lily discovered that she could see Joe later any evening, or perhaps the next day in town, and not only behave as she would have behaved before but think of him as she had thought of him before. She had always thought him rather a likable fool; she still did. She did not for the time being find it necessary to make frequent connections between Joe and Everett, whose letters came from Georgia now, and Francie lived in Everett's country. It concerned, she thought, neither Everett nor Francie; it did not even seem, in any real way, to concern her.

When the nights grew warm, come May of that year, they occasionally met late at night. The wind blew off the river through the shack, its windows broken long ago by children or transients, and they lay on a torn mattress and listened to the current. Once in a while she asked him something about the war, and he explained to her about Tunisia; once in a while she told him about something which had happened a long time before, a dance she had gone to or a slight she had imagined, but mostly they simply lay there in the dark in the bare room littered with dead wisteria, blown through the windows during a wind in April, and listened to the water. *I love you*, Joe said once, *Lily Knight*, and she turned away from him.

"I mean now," he said. "I meant I love you now."

"I know." She twisted her shoulder free from his hand. "I knew what you meant. That's all right."

"Lily Knight," he repeated, drawing the sheet she had brought up over her shoulders.

She sat up, pulling the sheet around her. "My name's not Lily Knight. If you recall. I'm married to Everett McClellan and he loves me *very very much* and nothing I do can change it."

Joe did not answer, and when he pulled her down again she said *I'm sorry, baby it's all right*, and it was all right, possibly sharper and better and more interesting than it had ever been before.

12

IN THE beginning the afternoon was no more than a question of sugar, or the lack of it. China Mary had baked four cakes and given them as prizes in a parish raffle; when Lily asked her what they were going to use for sugar during the rest of October—during the entire rest of 1944, for that matter, since China Mary had traded some of their November stamps to her sister for extra sugar—China Mary shrugged and continued whistling "Coming in on a Wing and a Prayer." Good works, Lily wanted her to know, would cut no ice down at the OPA. It was one thing for China Mary to go around ingratiating herself with Father Ford; it was quite another to do it with the whole family's sugar stamps.

There were some women in this world, announced China Mary, untying her apron and throwing it at Lily's feet, a great many women in this world—for example that saint (God rest her) who had been Everett's and Martha's and Sarah's mother—who would count God more important than a little bitty sugar. Thirty years she had worked on this ranch and no McClellan, not one, had ever tried to tell her how to run her kitchen, and there were some spoiled young ladies who were going to be punished by God if they didn't start thinking about their Church once in a while. "It's not my Church," Lily had snapped, aware that she was beaten: her error, as Martha observed immediately, had been the mention of Father Ford, who had personally brought about China Mary's conversion and secured a place high on her personal hagiology by assuring her that Dennis Kearney, who with several hundred exclusionist followers had set fire to a San Francisco laundry operated by China Mary's grandfather in 1877, had probably been a bad Catholic if indeed he had been a Catholic at all. As Martha pointed out, Lily would never learn how to get around China Mary if she couldn't get it through her head not to mention Father Ford.

That was at two o'clock. At three Joe Templeton called, and at five-thirty he arrived with twenty pounds of sugar. Although Martha had been sick for two days, she came downstairs in a new pale pink robe for which she had paid sixty dollars a few weeks after she had met Ryder Channing at the Mather Field Officers' Club that summer; she had torn the white silk roses from the sash, and Lily knew, from that, from the grateful satisfaction Martha was taking in a low-grade fever, and from the way she talked to Joe about Channing ("*Cap*tain Channing," she kept saying, and referring to his slight limp as "something he allegedly got over Normandy"), that the affair must be running cool. Martha talked animatedly, laughed extravagantly at Joe's mild jokes ("Joe, you're too *funny*, you ought to be on radio, don't you think Joe should be on radio, Lily? Giving imitations of canaries and people? I mean he couldn't have sounded *more* like Harry Hopkins"), and urged him to stay for dinner. It would be, she explained, a kind of cook-it-yourself operation, catch-as-catch-can, because China Mary was off brooding, but it would be scads of fun, she promised, and one thing they would have plenty of was sugar, one thing they definitely would not run short on, thanks to Lily's foresight and Joe's mysterious resources, was sugar. As a matter of fact it was providential that China Mary had used up all their sugar and inspired Lily to call upon Joe, because they had nowhere *near* twenty pounds to begin with. That was the old silver lining for you, all right. With interest. Joe must stay.

Joe could not. Joe was taking Francie and her mother out to dinner.

Which was, Martha said, very shrewd of Joe. Taking Francie's mother out to dinner. Making sure the bread stayed buttered, and all that.

Anyway, she added, picking up a bowl of camellias and starting for the kitchen, it was no wonder Joe didn't want to stay for dinner, the way this house was kept. Nothing but dead flowers in tasteless bowls, anywhere.

"It was a bowl of my mother's," Lily explained as she walked Joe out to his car, but the incident seemed to have eluded him. "What was?" he asked without interest, and then added immediately: "I met this Channing character." "He's quite a good friend of Martha's," Lily interrupted, annoyed at Joe's denseness about the bowl of camellias.

When she came back to the house Martha was lying on the couch, her face buried in a pillow. Lily pulled a comforter over

Martha's back, and sat down to finish the letter to Everett she had begun before Joe came.

"You writing Everett?" Martha sat up, throwing the comforter off.

Lily nodded without looking up. "I want to see if he can't come home for a few days. You keep warm." She had asked Everett, in almost every letter since his transfer to Fort Bliss in July, if he could not come home for a few days. In the back of her mind she was uneasily convinced that he could have gotten home, had he wanted to, between the time he had left Georgia and the time he had been due in Texas.

Martha lay down again. "Some days I certainly can't abide Joe Templeton."

"Some days you certainly are rude."

"I mean sometimes I wonder where old Joe would be today if Francie didn't drink. I mean he absolutely *trades* on it, he's made an absolute *career* of it."

She paused, watching Lily's reflection in the mirror above the couch. "When really it's just the other way around," she added finally. "I mean I guess everybody on the river knows who puts up with who in that house. Who needs who. And it's more than just her money. Her money's only the half of it. Don't you think."

"I don't know," Lily said.

"Well think about it a minute."

"All right."

"Now. Think about it right now."

"I want to finish this letter before dinner."

Martha pulled the comforter back up to her neck and resettled the pillow. "Tell Everett we're eating Joe Templeton's sugar, why don't you. Tell him you're sleeping around to keep us in black-market sugar. That should bring him. Write Everett-baby that."

Lily put the letter down. China Mary had been impossible about the sugar coupons. Knight had been running a fever; Julie cutting a tooth. Martha and her father had fought at dinner every night for a week, and Joe had been worried about Francie, who had sprained her wrist in a fall from a horse while she was drunk. Even that sure and quiet comfort had evolved into the garrulous ambiguity of friendship, a change that was probably irreversible; when Joe had tried, a few minutes ago, to draw her into a prolonged and clumsy kiss in the darkness by the car, she had turned her face away in irritation that he should try to so deceive both her and himself. Once they had admitted sugar coupons and sprained wrists, it no longer worked. She was too tired even to be shocked by Martha, let alone angry at her.

"Martha," she said. "Please."

Martha had begun to cry, tears welling in her fevered eyes and splashing down her flushed cheeks.

"Martha, baby."

"You've got no right to my brother," Martha whispered, standing up unsteadily. "No right."

Lily was, then, less angry than frightened: harsh words between women seemed to her unthinkable, an irreparable rent in the social fabric. On those few occasions when she had quarreled with her mother, they had ended, both terrified of the consequences, weeping together. She thought now of the picture of Everett above Martha's bed, the roses torn from the sash of the new robe, of Martha's delight when she graduated *summa cum laude* in June ("Wait until Everett hears," she had said. "He'll be appalled"); thought of Martha at Julie's christening, Sunday before last, whispering out loud *please help her to choose right every day she lives.* Martha had held Julie, and none of the omens were good: the sky was overcast with the peculiar yellow haze Edith Knight called earthquake weather, Everett's father jammed on his Stetson and walked out of the church before the christening because the minister had a favorable word for Harold Ickes, and Martha cried. (She cried because Ryder Channing had not come to the christening; she would have cried had he come. "That girl will have shed enough tears by the end of the year 1944," Mr. McClellan said before he left the church, "to drown the entire Jap army. She is what you call an untapped resource.") Lily had worn the silly John Frederics hat with the black veiling that had cost her mother seventy-five dollars, and had known even as she smiled at Martha that Julie was already beyond choice. The tellers of fairy tales knew about choosing what Martha did not know. An uninvited guest brings a gold ring or a spray of rue to the christening party.

"Martha," she called now, wanting to make it all right, but Martha had run upstairs.

*

Later, she arranged a tray for Martha with a roast-beef sandwich and an artichoke, soaked in olive oil as Martha liked artichokes best. ("Why can't she come down?" Mr. McClellan demanded, ripping the leaves from his own artichoke and clearly regretting the lost opportunity for another few rounds at dinner. "Why doesn't she just check into a hospital and stay there?")

She found Martha lying in bed in the dark, the blanket littered with damp shreds of Kleenex.

"I didn't mean what I said." Martha's eyes were closed. "I didn't mean anything like that. You're fine for Everett. Everett loves you."

"Don't talk about it now." Lily sat on the edge of the bed and turned on the light. The reconciliation made her quite as uncomfortable as the scene downstairs had; things said out loud had for her an aura of danger so volatile that it could be controlled only in that dark province inhabited by those who share beds. Although she could sometimes say things out loud to Everett, she did not know how to talk to Martha.

"My eyes are red." Martha turned off the light again. "Everett thinks the sun rises and sets with you. You should realize that."

"I realize it."

"I mean you should realize how really simple Everett is."

Martha sat up in bed and fumbled on the table for a package of cigarettes.

"You better eat," Lily said. "Everything's getting cold."

"You mean that cold artichoke and that cold roast-beef sandwich and that cold glass of milk." Martha lit a cigarette. "Just a minute. How really straight he is. I mean maybe Everett gets scared and has bad dreams like anybody else, I don't know, but the difference is Everett wouldn't ever explore it. All Everett wants is a little *or*der."

"I guess that's what everybody wants."

Martha lay down again. "Maybe everybody wants it. But most people don't want it more than anything else in the world. The way Everett does. You might want it, I might want it. But when the opportunity to *have* it practically hits us over the head, we just about knock ourselves out getting out of the way." She paused. "Take you for example."

Lily said nothing.

"All right, don't. Take me. What do I want. A nice ordered life right here on the river just like we've always had."

"Joe says the war is going to change everything." Snatching at what had seemed for a moment a chance to steer the conversation away from the particular and into the realm of topics so impersonal and so unweighted that they could be safely talked about, Lily had forgotten that Joe was for the time being a name loaded with peril.

"Never *mind* about Joe. He read it in *U.S. News & World Report.* Anyway. That's what I want. But what do I do about getting it. I get messed up with Ryder, who not only doesn't want to marry me, doesn't understand any of the things I need, but is so unfitted to everything I want that I get so nervous I practically break into tears every time he's in the same room with Daddy. That's what I do about it."

Lily looked away. "I don't know," she said. She did not want Martha to tell her anything more about Ryder Channing. She had written Everett about how impossible Martha had been since she met him, had told him he had better come talk to Martha, and she did not know what else she could do.

"I don't even *like* Ryder," Martha added, wadding up her baby pillow and holding it against her face with one hand, groping with the other for the shreds of Kleenex on the blanket.

Lily took a tissue from her pocket and handed it to Martha. "I'll get you some Luminal," she said with relief. She did not like to see Martha cry but the conversation was at any rate closed.

At twenty minutes to eleven, after Mr. McClellan had gone upstairs and left Lily to finish her letter to Everett (*I wish you would please reconsider about coming for a few days because neither your father nor I can talk to her and I don't believe she has passed one day without crying since she came home in June, and this man, although he is quite nice, does not seem good for her, Everett, baby, please*), Ryder Channing arrived to see Martha.

"Actually she's asleep," Lily said, straightening her skirt as she took his raincoat. "I guess you know she's been sick."

"I thought she might feel better."

He did not sit down, and she noticed for the first time that he was about Everett's height, about six feet. He would not have looked unlike Everett had there not been about his face both a hardness and a softness absent in Everett's, the look of someone who has been in some sense spoiled. She supposed he must be older than Everett by four or five years, must be twenty-nine or thirty.

"I thought she might feel up to driving into town for a drink. I'm sorry." He picked up a book from the hall table and opened it, pausing to read the inscription. "Maybe you'd like to go."

"I shouldn't go out. Won't you have a drink here."

"Sure. Sure I will." He smiled. She had thought before that he must calculate the effect of his smile; its peculiar intimacy was a study in timing. It was something like the way John Wayne said "Hell-o there" when he first met the girl, on a train or in a construction camp or riding past on a horse. There was no mistaking John Wayne and there was, in a limited way, no mistaking Ryder Channing.

"That's real nice of you," he added, smiling again, sitting down, and examining the envelope she had just addressed to Everett. Seeing that it was empty, he yawned, closed his eyes, and asked: "Where's that drink?"

It occurred to her, as she got the ice, that John Wayne had the jump on Ryder when it came to follow-through.

They had, in all, three drinks. At first Lily sat very straight on the wooden rocker by the desk; after he had made a second drink she sat across from the couch, where he lay sprawled with one leg propped on the arm. He told her about Memphis, where his mother and sisters lived, and about Charlottesville, where he had gone to school. ("You'd like that, Lily. You'd really like that, Charlottesville, springtime, you'd eat it up," he assured her in the Tennessee drawl that made everything he said seem a mild flirtation, made her feel that he had, in uncovering her previously unsuspected and more or less unprovable predilection for Charlottesville in the springtime, penetrated the very essence of her.) He praised Martha extravagantly (she had, he declared, one of the quickest minds he had ever encountered in a woman); asked to see a crayon drawing Knight had done; and announced that the three of them—he, Martha, and Lily—must have dinner at the Officers' Club at Mather Field the following Sunday. Or some Sunday. They would keep it loose. Under his gentle prodding, Lily found herself telling him about the parties her mother used to give, about the time her grandfather had challenged a neighbor to a gunfight over a right of way which (it turned out) belonged to neither of them; even about her father. It was the first time she had spoken about her father except in passing since his death. Ryder seemed fascinated by the most minute details of life on the river: he wanted to know why she had been sent to Dominican rather than to the union high school as Martha had been; why they did not belong to the country club and whether anyone else on the river did; why Walter Knight would not have been likely to belong to a San Francisco club, say the Pacific Union or the Bohemian. "He just wouldn't, that's all," Lily said, and it seemed to satisfy Ryder; he appeared to index it under *Growers, Social Eccentricities of*, and went on to explore whether Walter Knight had known anyone who voted for Culbert Olson for Governor in 1938.

As they were finishing their third drink and Lily was trying to explain why she had not liked going to the San Francisco dances when she was at Dominican, Martha appeared on the stair landing, tying the roseless sash and smiling wanly.

"I heard you all." Whatever Martha's malaise, it seemed to have so developed within the past few hours that she could not negotiate four steps without clutching the railing. "I'm sorry I didn't wake up before."

Channing swung his long legs off the couch and stood up, holding out his arms to Martha.

"You poor sick baby." He bent to kiss her neck. "You shouldn't be out of bed."

"I only wanted to say hello."

She stood there, neither sitting down nor taking Ryder's hand.

"Lily was telling me about the San Francisco Assembly," Ryder said. "Did you go to those dances?"

"No. I didn't go to those dances."

"Martha went to school up here," Lily said. "As you know."

"Listen," Martha said. "I meant to tell you. Daddy said something real funny the other night at dinner."

"What?"

"Well, see, he wanted to ask me something about you. But naturally he pretended not to remember your name. 'That fellow from Mississippi,' he said. 'Ryder's not from Mississippi,' I said. 'He's from Tennessee.' 'Mississippi, Tennessee, what's the difference,' Daddy said. 'It's all Del Paso Heights to me.'"

Lily laughed. Del Paso Heights was a district north of Sacramento noted for its large Negro population and its high incidence of minor social disorders.

"That's very funny," Channing said. He seemed obscurely pleased by the story, another entry under *Growers, Eccentricities of.*

"He really said it, didn't he, Lily."

"He really did. I have to go up," she added, kissing Martha on the cheek and taking Ryder's hand. He smiled at her.

As she walked upstairs she felt that Ryder was watching her, and kept her back straight. When she turned at the landing she saw that he was not watching her at all, but kissing Martha, pulling her very close, his hand at the small of her back. She wondered how Martha felt when Ryder smiled, and how much of the smile was calculated. Not that it mattered. Everyone had his own shell game, and if Ryder Channing had known tonight how to make her feel open and happy for an hour or so, they had, in the end, conned each other. He would probably understand that.

It occurred to her later, after she had undressed and turned down the sheets on Everett's and her bed, that Ryder Channing might have been someone to whom, under different circumstances, she could have said things out loud.

13

EVERETT WAS playing poker in the Officers' Club at Fort Bliss when they telephoned him on that Saturday after Thanksgiving, 1944. Lily had already called twice that week, asking if he could please come home for Christmas because everything was falling apart without him. First the baby had been down with measles, then Knight had caught whooping cough; there had been nothing but sickness since summer. *I need you*, she said. He could simply *not understand* unless he came; he must come. In the first place there was Martha. If he wanted to help Martha he had better come. She was still intimating that she was about to run off with that Air Corps captain from Tennessee; the week before Thanksgiving she did not come home for two days. She told her father she was in San Francisco. Which for all Lily knew she might have been but there was *one vital detail* missing in the version she told her father. (Not that it wasn't Martha's own business, but she managed to make it everyone's by making issues of everyone else's faults. If she heard once more from Martha that Ryder Channing said she had "no conversation" she was going to start screaming, and if any of them heard once more from Martha that Ryder Channing thought the house looked like something out of Charles Addams, Lily simply could not be responsible for what Everett's father might do. He objected to the way Ryder Channing wore his hat, without any stiffening, and referred to him always as "the fly-boy" or "the ninety-day wonder," phrases he had picked up Lily didn't know where since everything else about the war was more or less escaping him.) Anyway. Martha and her father fought every night at dinner until no one could eat, and then Martha would push her chair back and run upstairs. They could hear her crying at night and it upset everyone. She had in fact been behaving that way ever since she came home from school, so it did not in all fairness seem to have been brought on by Channing, but he was around all the time and when he was not around Martha was crying and it upset Everett's father especially. Not that it took much to upset him these days. Everett could not realize. Someone had approached him about subdividing the ranch after the war, and the man may have been rather unattractive and may even have been as Everett's father said an operator and a draft-dodger, but Everett's father still had no call to say the things he said to that man. There you had it. The children were sick and Martha was crying and Everett's father was losing his mind. If only Everett could come. *You don't know how I need you.*

Lily's letters and telephone calls had been the only disturbance in Everett's life that summer and fall; she seemed to have read none of the inspirational literature about building service morale, keeping the home fires burning, I'll be home for Christmas but only in my dreams. He missed her and the babies, but not as much as he told her he did, and then only in an abstract way. They were safe, and his absence from them was more than blameless; it was blessed by all the Allied Powers. More than he could remember being since his first few weeks at Stanford, he was peculiarly contented within the ordered limitations of his life at Bliss. Desultorily, he played poker and struck up guarded friendships at the bar; later, every night, he lay in bed and made new plans for the ranch: exquisitely rational arrangements, unmarred by the sloppy actualities of plans in operation. Once, when he had a pass, he went up to Dallas with another lieutenant, one of the group with whom he sometimes played poker; the lieutenant called some girls he had known in college at Austin, and they all went dancing at the Adolphus Hotel. Although he could not later remember how, Everett ended up alone with a girl who had pale strawberry-blond hair and access to her father's Cadillac. In the Cadillac they had driven out by a creek where they sat on the running board and drank bourbon out of paper cups and watched the sun come up, and the girl had made Everett feel her necklace (it liked to be touched, she told him, because it was made of real pearls from Neiman-Marcus) and had held his hand against her throat, but he had only kissed her gravely and driven her home. Later that morning, waiting for a transport he could hop back to El Paso, he tried to believe that it had been because she was a nice girl or at any rate because he was faithful to Lily, but he knew that he had left the girl alone for neither reason. He had left her alone because it was too much trouble; on a small scale she might have disturbed the even flow of his days at Bliss even as Lily did.

It was not that he did not like the idea of having Lily on the ranch, waiting: he did. Lily completed the picture, gave him the sense of having settled things, the sense he had missed before they were married. It was necessary, however, that things stay settled. During the past few weeks he had begun to regard Lily's messages as definite intrusions, to look upon life on the ranch as a bacchanalia of disorganization, peculiarly female disorder. No one, so far as Everett knew, cried all night in the Officers' Club at Bliss.

He had explained repeatedly that Christmas was out of the question; he had only a seventy-two-hour pass and transportation was at best uncertain. He would go instead to Mexico, although he did not tell her that. *You don't know how I need you*, she had repeated over the telephone two nights ago, and he had answered in a blaze of righteousness: *You don't seem to realize there's a war going on.* Immediately he had laughed, trying to cover not only his pomposity but his deception. It must be clear even to Lily that El Paso was not exactly Leyte Gulf, and that getting to the ranch for Christmas would not be impossible.

Now when the orderly told him that he had a call from California he felt the resentment return: they were forcing the issue, making him feel guilty. Annoyed with them all and with himself, he picked up the telephone ready to tell Lily once again that there was a war going on.

"Is that Everett?"

He was abruptly charmed by her small voice. For a moment it was as if he had never gone away from her, never discovered the siren lure of celibacy.

"Who does it sound like?"

There was a silence. "This is Lily."

"Not Lily McClellan, surely."

"Yes," she said, and paused again. "Now listen to me."

"What is it?"

She did not answer. He had stiffened, preparing himself for the last-ditch appeal, and now she did not make it, did not answer, said nothing.

"What is it?" he repeated, remembering suddenly what she had said about Martha.

She said nothing.

"*Operator*," he said. Then, with some relief, he heard Martha's voice, controlled and distant.

"We're at the hospital," she said rapidly. "Sutter Hospital. Daddy had a stroke and you'd better come home."

"Is he all right?" He realized the idiocy of the question as he asked it.

"Of course he isn't all right. He's dead. Or we wouldn't have bothered you."

All that night he sat in the washroom of a Pullman car, smoking cigarettes and watching the green-shaded lights flicker on and off as the train crawled across the desert to Los Angeles. He probably could have gotten a seat on a plane, but had not, even though Martha's sharp, precarious voice had finally broken: *I said he's dead, Everett, come home now oh Christ Daddy's dead and let's not have any more of that crap about how the lights are going out all over the world, Everett, please, come home fast.* The train would be at least two days, longer should he miss the Los Angeles connection. He had wired his father's lawyer to make arrangements for the funeral. He knew with certainty that although he might see Bliss again, he was as good as discharged now; although he had in 1942 given up his farm deferment in order to enlist, there was no one now to run the ranch. He would ask for and certainly get a hardship discharge.

That he would not see his father again did not really occur to him until he reached the ranch, six hours too late for the funeral (he had missed the connection in Los Angeles, and by then could not get a flight at all), and found that Sarah had flown home from Philadelphia. "It was sudden," she kept repeating to Everett, "it was terribly sudden." "Yes," he agreed each time, dimly reassuring her as he reassured himself; they seemed to share some burden, the guilt of the children out playing when the trouble happened.

It was all they shared. He had not seen Sarah since the day of her wedding, in August of 1936. She had been married in the garden, in their mother's wedding dress, to a boy named Peter. Although she had met Peter at Stanford he turned out to be from Philadelphia, a circumstance which seemed insurmountable to all the McClellans except Sarah. Seventeen years old, Everett had been an usher. He had gotten a little drunk on champagne (Peter had not approved of the champagne, which was California; it had been Peter's conviction, expressed in company which included two Napa Valley grape growers, that if you could not afford a decent French champagne you did better by sticking to Scotch) and toward the end of the afternoon, when Sarah was cutting the bride's cake, he had told her and Peter a not very funny but very dirty joke. Peter had looked faintly annoyed. He never looked more than faintly anything. "I guess we've had enough of the local *vino*," he said, slapping Everett's shoulder in what he seemed to consider an appropriately fraternal manner. "You ass," Everett had said, and Sarah had thrown her arms around Everett, laughing and kissing him with white frosting on her mouth. She had been home twice since then, once before and once after the six weeks on the Nevada side of Lake Tahoe which legalized the end of Peter, but Everett had been away that summer, working in a lumber camp out of Tacoma.

Her presence now, even the trace of her perfume that was all through the house (the same perfume: it smelled again like the summer she was married, when the house was full of silver and tissue paper and girls), indicated that this was indeed an event, a crisis, a death in the family. Sad and nervous, she walked aimlessly through the house straightening pictures, picking up plates and putting them back, opening and closing the shutters; through her alien's eyes Everett saw that what Lily had said was true: everything was falling apart.

It would be a difficult spring. Lily had not exaggerated; he had simply not wanted to believe her. Apparently his father had not been well for months before his stroke, and had lost interest in growing anything on the land he held so tenaciously. Everett could understand that; he never blamed his father. When it came down to it, beyond making enough to live on, he had little interest himself in using the land. Like his father, he wanted only to have it. The Braden place was a case in point. It was two hundred acres, near Auburn, virtually untillable, deserted for years. It had been in Everett's mother's estate. Although Joe Templeton had wanted to buy it, Everett had refused to sell, ostensibly because he planned to develop it himself. He knew now why he had not sold the Braden place.

He had thought about it in that Pullman washroom crossing the desert. He wanted, all of his life, to be able to go up to the Braden place and stand on the hill and look up the Valley to the Marysville buttes, and he wanted to be standing on his own land. It had nothing to do with crops, development, profit. He understood, all right, how his father, sick, could have let the river ranch run down. He had just dropped his guard temporarily, and there it went.

Moved by this example, Everett was on guard, now, armed with the brisk decision, the semblance of efficient appraisal. Their Japanese foreman had been evacuated in 1942, and his replacement, to whom Everett's father had increasingly left the day-to-day operation, had proved incompetent. Everett had said, when they hired him, that the man was not responsible; "never mind," his father had muttered, disturbed more than he saw fit to admit by the relocation of the Japanese. "Those bastards asked for it." It was typical of him to have thought that the loss incurred by an irresponsible foreman would be the government's; he had apparently never at any point seen that it was his own. On acre after acre, the redwood poles and wire trellises had been knocked down and left to rot with dead vines, unpicked the summer before. Part of last summer's crop, the foreman told Everett, had mildewed; in the shed Everett found, unopened, the copper sulfate which would have prevented it. Machinery, unreplaceable until after the war, had been left out to rust in the autumn rains; the kiln was in no condition to use, the main road rutted. Even the levee was eroded, neglected all one year. The Army Engineers, as far as that went, were supposed to watch the levees, but Everett did not suppose that the Engineers had been deeply concerned during 1943 and 1944 with the levee at McClellan's Landing.

"I kept writing you," Lily reminded him, never looking up from her knitting. It seemed to him that she had been knitting steadily since his arrival. Whenever she caught him looking at her she would bite her lip, ostentatiously readjust her needles, and knit faster.

He turned, wordless, to Martha.

"I never noticed anybody letting me run this ranch," she said. "I can't even write a check around here."

"We did everything we could," Lily said. "Your father wasn't asking for any advice from us."

"If only someone had let Everett know." Sarah closed the box of old dance programs and pressed orchids which had claimed her attention since dinner. "If only someone had let *me* know."

"If only someone had *thought*." Martha leaned to touch Lily's arm. "Sarah could have forwarded us some pamphlets from the United States Department of Agriculture. Or maybe she could have talked it over with *Peter*."

"I haven't seen Peter since 1939."

"This new one then," Martha said. "I can't ever think of his name."

"It's on all my note paper," Sarah said with an attempt at serenity. "Robert Carr Warfield, Jr." She paused. "Bud," she added doubtfully.

"Bud. That's it. Maybe you and Bud could have put your heads together and gotten this place in shape by air mail."

Lily put down her knitting and looked up at Everett.

He understood: he had never meant to cast doubts upon their intentions. Nonetheless, he would be away another few months until his discharge was processed, and someone would have to take hold. Could they do that, could they get the poles up and the fields cleared and above all could they get the Engineers to do something about the levee before they found themselves floating around the Delta?

"You tell the men I'm running it and I will," Martha said.

"Joe Templeton will help us," Lily said.

"Joe Templeton will help us," Martha repeated. "Oh my yes. Old Joe Templeton will absolutely leap at the opportunity to help us. Yes indeed. Joe Templeton can be depended upon, Everett, count on that." She had been playing nervously with one of Lily's knitting needles; now she jammed it into a ball of yarn and walked to the window.

Three days after the funeral Everett put Sarah on a plane back to Philadelphia ("back home," she said, apparently oblivious to the pain she could cause her brother simply by shifting the locus of her belonging), carrying a paper bag full of dried hops to show to her children and to the stranger who was now her husband. The hops had been Martha's idea. "They'll think I'm bringing candy," Sarah laughed, nervous as they stood in the rain at the gate. "I should have bought something, they won't realize I came for a funeral." Her voice trailed off as she watched the propellers catching. Tentatively, Everett put his arm around her shoulders, thick in her black fleece coat, too heavy for California. She turned, smiling brilliantly and blowing him a kiss. "You come visit us," she called as she ran to the plane, "come visit whenever you can."

After the plane had left the runway Everett sat in the empty parking lot, bent over the steering wheel of the station wagon with the rain blowing in through the open window and the strings of Christmas tinsel stars clinking in the wind between the low buildings, and cried for the first time that he could remember, not so much for his father as for Sarah's defection, because she had lost all memory of the family they had been on that day when he got a little drunk on champagne.

14

"EVERETT," she said. "Everett."

He turned toward her, fumbling blindly through the wrinkled sheets for her body, meaning to draw her to him in the hot bed and drop back into sleep, wanting only to quiet her.

"Everett. Please. Everett."

He opened his eyes. Lily lay on her back smoking a cigarette. He had been home from Bliss six months now, ever since his discharge in February, and through those two seasons of 1945 he had not slept one night without the dim troubled sense that Lily was awake, shifting in bed, walking around the room or sitting by the window in the dark. (She could not remember, she told him, a summer so hot: she had not been able to breathe for months.) Not until he woke in the morning would she be asleep, sometimes in the chair by the window, her legs stretched out across the low sill and her nightgown fallen from her shoulders; sometimes on the far edge of the bed, one hand flat on the floor, the other flung toward him but not touching him. She would lie for hours then without waking; one morning he had sat on the bed and held her hand for twenty minutes while she lay as if drugged, neither clenching nor withdrawing her fingers.

"Go to sleep," he said now. "Go to sleep, baby."

"I have to talk to you."

He ran his fingers over the moist ends of her hair and across her face. Her eyes were wet. *Jesus Christ.* How many nights had he heard Lily crying. As some parents sleep through fire, thunderstorms, and voices at the back door only to wake at a child's whisper, so Everett heard Lily crying at night. Her muffled sobs seemed to have broken his dreams for years. He had heard her even at Fort Lewis, even in Georgia, finally at Bliss. That was Lily crying in the wings whenever the priests came to tear up his mother's grave. Lily cried in the twilight field where he picked wild poppies with Martha; Lily's was the cry he heard those nights the kiln burned, the levee broke, the ranch went to nothing.

"What is it, Lily."

She crushed out her cigarette. "I have to tell you."

He brushed the damp hair back from her forehead and kissed her closed eyelids, tasting the salt on his tongue.

"I didn't want to tell you but I have to."

"What is it," he said. "What do you have to tell me, baby."

He did not want her to say it. He had known for maybe three weeks, since that morning (it was the morning the pump broke, the Monday after they had gone to Lake Tahoe with Marth and Channing) when he had gotten up and found Lily sitting on the edge of the bathtub, her head down, her arms crossed as if she were having a chill. Her nightgown was down around her waist and a glass of orange juice was spilled on the pink tile floor. Her hands were shaking, her eyes glazed; he knew she had been sick. As he helped her back to bed it occurred to him that she was overdue that month. He was not sure. She had not taken her eyes from his face as he pulled the sheet over her, and while he tried to clean up the orange juice with toilet paper (for some reason he had not wanted to leave it for China Mary to see) he recalled that she had been sick on orange juice the first few months both times before. He had hoped (so fiercely that it was a constant prayer, now after three weeks as automatic as breathing) that he was mistaken, about the one thing if not the other, hoped that she would not say the words. But he had known she would. He had known all along she would wake him some night. *I didn't want to tell you but I have to.*

He moved his arm beneath her shoulders. Her body was rigid. He would have to let her say it. He was the goddamn priest who would have to hear it.

"I'm pregnant." Her eyes were shut tight, as if she expected him to hit her. "I'm pregnant and I don't think by you."

Her voice was as smooth and anonymous as a recording. She must have rehearsed the words so often that all inflection had been erased. He threw off the sheet and sat up on the edge of the bed, reaching toward the table for a cigarette, stalling less from shock than from a sense of anticlimax. Spoken, the words had lost their power.

Lily had not moved. *Well let her sweat it out.*

"You don't think by me," he repeated finally.

She was sobbing convulsively now.

"Any Mexican would know better." He could hear the flatness in his voice. "Any West End whore."

"Leave me alone." She was choking. "Just leave me be."

"Crystal on your mother's place would know better. Crystal Gomez. Or whatever her name is."

He persisted only because he did not know what else to do, and thought she expected it of him.

"What do you want," she whispered, her head turned away from him. "What do you want me to say."

"Nothing." His voice was gentler now. "I don't want you to say anything at all."

She sat up suddenly, as if anticipating a trick, suspecting some incipient violence.

"You want to know who it *was*," she sobbed, almost screaming.

You want to know who it was. He did not know whether she meant it as question or accusation. Without looking at her, he reached for the shirt and the pair of khaki pants thrown on the chair the night before. He supposed he knew who it was, if it mattered. He would rather it had been a stranger, someone who came and left. For it to have been someone he knew made the fault more subtly Lily's: she had at once violated several contracts. That kind of thinking, however, did not apply. No kind of thinking that led to the word "contract" could possibly apply to whatever it was between him and Lily. He would prefer that it had been a stranger but it did not matter that it had not been. It might as well have been.

"No," he said. "I don't want to hear it. I don't want to hear anything more about it."

He pulled on the khaki pants and left the room, carrying the shirt and a pair of sneakers. When he dropped one of the sneakers on the stairs he did not bother to pick it up.

Mostly because a light had been left burning on the sun porch, he sat down there on the edge of the rattan couch, one sneaker still in his hand, and wondered how long he had been asleep and how long it would be until dawn.

He sat there the rest of the night, occasionally taking a swallow of bourbon from a bottle left on the table, staring blankly at an album of snapshots Martha had left out. She had been showing their pictures to Channing the night before. (Channing, of course, had missed the point about Martha's showing him the pictures, had studied a snapshot of Martha on a horse at eleven years old and remarked only upon the resemblance in pose to Elizabeth Taylor in *National Velvet*; had examined the pictures of Martha on the beach at Carmel and been struck not by Martha but by the cypress formations. "They just blow that way, Ryder," Martha explained again and again with more patience than Everett thought either characteristic or necessary. "They just get blown that way and stick." It had so irritated and saddened Everett to see Martha spreading out their vacations at Carmel before Channing's disregard that he had gone upstairs at ten o'clock. "Now, Everett, baby," Lily had said, that deceptive mildness in her voice, "Martha's baby pictures do not exactly constitute Mount Rushmore.")

He saw a snapshot taken on the verandah of the Knight place when they were all children: Lily, he and Marth, and Sarah holding Marth by the hand. It looked like a birthday party but he could not think whose. He remembered one party, perhaps this one, when Martha had become sick from excitement. They had found her huddled in the corner of Edith Knight's bathtub, the daisy wreath Sarah had made for her wilted and down over one eye. Everett smiled now, seeing that on that day they had all worn navy-blue reefer coats in different sizes. Knight had an identical reefer now; Lily's mother had bought it.

He wished that he could go upstairs to Lily, tell her it would be all right, brush away the physical fact by making her laugh over the snapshot with the reefer coats. *Red Rover, Red Rover, let Lily Knight come over.* He could remember how Martha had sometimes kept herself hidden for hours when they played hide-and-go-seek; how Lily, who had never liked being It, had never even liked games much, had sat down under the lilac once and cried because no one would come from hiding and it was getting dark. "I thought you'd all gone and drowned," she sobbed, hiccuping, when they finally ran in from the dry place under the dock where Martha had insisted on hiding. "I thought you'd fallen in and been caught in a whirlpool." (The prospect of falling in and being caught in a whirlpool had always loomed impressively in Lily's imagination; he knew that she believed remotely to this day that whirlpools the size and power of the Maelstrom were commonplace in the Sacramento River.) Somehow that day, he could not recall how, he had made Lily stop crying and laugh. He had intended always to take care of her, to make her laugh. But somewhere they had stopped listening to each other, and so he remained downstairs in a paralysis not of anger but of lassitude and pride.

He had stopped being angry months before, if he had ever been angry at all: had passed through shock, hurt, and compromise already, and alone. Even then he had been hurt not so much by Lily as by his own failure to see. *Have a drink with me, Everett,* Francie Templeton had said the night he finally saw; he had gone up to see Joe about buying a used Ford pickup, but Joe was in town.

"We'll have a drink together this fine June evening because Everett darling," Francie said firmly, "it's about to be one dry summer."

She emptied an ice tray into a pitcher and picked up a bottle of bourbon. Reluctantly, he followed her upstairs to the terrace of the second-floor landing; women who drank made him uncomfortable under any circumstances, and Francie fell besides into the category of women old enough to know better.

"I so enjoyed *talk*ing to you the other night," Francie said, dropping ice into two glasses. With an accuracy which surprised him, she threw one cube into the branches of an orange tree which brushed the terrace wall, tearing apart a spider's web.

"I enjoyed it too, Francie."

Everett was acutely uncomfortable; in the moonlight flooding the terrace Francie looked even more haggard than she had looked downstairs in the lamplight, and the other night had not been the other night at all, but a month before, on V-E Day, when he had drunk too much at a party down the river. "Walk me down to the water, Everett darling," Francie had said about midnight that evening, and he had walked with Francie across the lawn and over the levee to the dock, had half-carried her down under the cottonwoods and big oaks and had sat with her there maybe half an hour, singing. Perhaps because he had been drinking as much as she had, Francie's clear, slight voice did not seem in the least blurred to Everett, and she remembered all the lyrics to "The Battle Hymn of the Republic" and "The Yellow Rose of Texas" and even "There'll Always Be an England," a song which had always infuriated his father. On that warm May night with the lights on down the river and occasional strains of the *Oklahoma!* score drifting down from the house and Francie's head on his shoulder, Francie whom he had known all his life, the world had seemed to Everett fine and noble and sweet and brave, a place of infinite possibilities for faith and honor and the grace of commonplace pleasures, and he was moved beyond any expressing of it by the worn words *Oh beautiful for spacious skies, for amber waves of grain.* Her shoes off, one foot trailing in the water, Francie had gradually dropped her head into his lap and stopped singing, fading out halfway through "There'll Be Bluebirds over the White Cliffs of Dover." Thinking her asleep, Everett sat stroking her hair for a few minutes before she sat up abruptly and began to untie the knotted silk halter strap of her dress. "Let's go in swimming, Everett darling."

"It's too early, Francie," he kept repeating softly, sober enough to see that neither of them was in condition to swim in the river, "it's still running cold." As he extricated the halter strap from her fingers and began to tie it again at the back of her neck, she at first dropped her head docilely, then, without saying anything, reached between his legs. "Don't, Francie," he said, getting to his feet and lifting her up; she had begun crying then, her hands over her face and the big diamond she had inherited from her grandmother blazing suddenly in the spotlight from a passing cruiser. When he tried to take her hands and hold her she wrenched away. "Go screw yourself," she had whispered, "that's probably the only way you like it anyway." He had hoped she would not remember it later, and had not really thought she would. (The next morning he told Lily that while she was inside dancing he had been singing songs with Francie Templeton, and she had laughed: "Everett baby. That's not much your style.")

"We had quite a sing for ourselves, didn't we," Francie said now, handing him a glass and touching it with her own. "To the old songs."

"That's right, Francie. The old songs."

"Quite a sing," she repeated reflectively. "On the Occasion of the Victory in Europe. A regular narrative by Norman Corwin." She paused. "You think Francie's changed since you went away."

"You always look the same, Francie," he said quickly, embarrassed that she had caught him out. She was wearing an old denim skirt and a wrinkled shirt which probably belonged to Joe; he knew that she must have been drinking most of the day.

"Well, yes and no." She poured more bourbon into her glass and waved him toward a wicker bench. "Yes and no. I'm thirty-seven years old today."

"Happy birthday." He wondered if she had a celebration in mind.

"Ha. It's not my birthday at all. I've been thirty-seven years old for months. Now old *Joe*," she added thoughtfully, "is forty."

Everett smiled gamely. He knew that Joe was thirty-six. Joe was ten years older than he was almost to the day. He happened to know that much with certainty because once Joe had come down drunk for a game at Stanford and collared Everett after lunch at the Deke house and explained all through the first quarter how much they had in common, give or take ten years. One of the things they still had in common, Everett recalled, was fifty dollars Joe had borrowed that day because Francie had temporarily left him and transferred all the money in their joint checking account into her private account, where she said it belonged in the first place.

"Forty—years—old," Francie said. "Or anyway he is almost. *Sic transit* old Joe, and all that."

"That's right, Francie." She was sitting on the low brick wall that edged the terrace, her body in profile to him, and he was nervous that she would fall from the wall and down one story onto the lawn.

"Tell me about the war," she said, swaying gently, almost crooning. "Tell me about how you were out defending democracy in El Paso and other foreign fields while old Joe here kept the home fires burning."

"I appreciate Joe's helping out after my father died." He was uncomfortably aware that Francie had at some point passed beyond neighborly conversation.

"Oh yes," she said. "Oh my yes. Joe was helping out down there right along."

"Martha and Lily appreciated it."

Francie sat holding her knees with her arms, her eyes closed.

"I'll bet Lily did," she said pleasantly. "He's pretty good."

Everett said nothing. It did not seem possible that he had heard Francie correctly, but the words seemed to hang on in the warm air, as continually and unmistakably audible as a prolonged high note on a piano. Although he had never been good at extracting subtleties from conversations, he tried, now, to imagine something else Francie could mean, to remember a word he had missed that would, once inserted into its proper place in the conversation, clear the entire thing up. But all he could remember was Lily, how she had been this spring (had sat reading night after night until he had asked her to come to bed, had turned away afterwards every time all spring—*what do you care*, she had whispered once, *what did you care when you were in Texas*—had gotten up and brushed her hair and returned to one or another of a series of books on sacred architecture she brought home from the county library); he remembered Lily and he considered Francie.

"Or anyway he used to be," Francie said in the same pleasant voice, unmarred by any trace of alcohol. "I wouldn't know any more. These days I'm just old Joe's cross, or you might say I'm the curse that Joe was born to, his albatross, his middle of the night. His checkbook. You might put it that way."

Francie paused, chewing a piece of ice. "Because frankly, Everett," she added finally, "I like to drink."

Everett said nothing. Beginning immediately to preserve what could be preserved, extending his carefulness of heart, he remembered stories he had heard about wives in wartime, and how it meant nothing. It would mean nothing to him if he could stop thinking about Lily, and think instead of a generalized Wife.

"You might even say I'd *rather* drink. So you *see*."

Everett stood up.

"I have to go, Francie," he said gently.

He had not seen, but he could not much blame Joe.

He had not seen: there was the crux of it. He sat on the sun porch holding the picture of Lily and Martha and Sarah and himself in the reefer coats until the first light came through the east windows, as if by tracing his finger down the crack in that yellowed snapshot he could recoup all their mortal losses, as if by merely looking long enough and hard enough he could walk back into that afternoon, walk back into Lily Knight's house, holding Martha by the hand, and begin again; could run with Martha up from the dock to where Lily cried beneath the lilac in the twilight and be home free.

15

HE DID not want to see Lily that morning, did not want to face her reddened eyes, her exhausted voice. *You want to know who it was.* She had placed the burden on him; all that had happened was in some way his responsibility. When China Mary came to the house he asked her to take Lily a tray, no orange juice, and to see that she stayed in bed awhile. "She's tired," he said. "The heat gets her. Try to keep Knight and Julie out."

He left the house then for the south fields to watch the last hops come down. Although he normally came to the house for lunch, at noon he instead drove one of the trucks down to a bar on the highway and had two bottles of Lucky Lager and a bologna sandwich wrapped in cellophane. While he drank the second bottle of beer he listened on the bartender's radio to the Yankees beating the Red Sox in the seventh at Fenway Park and did not think about Lily. By seven o'clock, when he started back to the house, the entire ranch was stripped bare of the vines. They had been picking all week, and this was the day he had liked least all of his life: the day the last hops came down, the day summer ended. All he could see as he walked back to the house were the bare poles, the broken strings hanging motionless in the heat, the dust stirred up by the picking machines. Tomorrow they would start the kiln, and during the next four or five days while the hops dried the whole year could go to waste. The kiln and the crop with it could go up in a flash of dry flame, and beyond taking the most elementary precautions there was nothing he could do about it. During the next week the agents from the insurance companies would be dropping by the ranches where the hops were drying, watching their risks; almost every August a kiln burned somewhere in the Valley. Last year it had been on the Messner place, up the Cosumnes River, the night they were to have finished.

Everett walked up to the house alone. Although it had been a custom of his father's to invite the foreman and his wife to the house the night they finished picking, the new foreman

(Henry Sears was his name, he had come from down the San Joaquin, near Bakersfield, had arrived on the ranch a few days after Everett came home from Bliss) had driven a truck full of Mexicans into town, leaving before Everett could have spoken to him, even if Everett had intended speaking to him. At any rate Henry Sears would not know the custom since he had not known Everett's father, and anyway he had no wife. Everett did not know what he could have said to him if he had invited him. Everyone had always responded to his father: had liked him, disliked him, talked to him, talked about him; had become in one way or another involved with him. Five hundred and forty-seven people had sent flowers when he died, and every one of them had thought himself involved with John McClellan. He would have known, as Everett did not know, how to talk to Henry Sears. Even Martha would probably know, but Everett did not.

Everett did not even know how to talk to Lily. Although he had no idea now what he could say to her when he got to the house, he would have to make it all right, at least for this week. At some point during the afternoon he had worked out an inarticulate pact, and had invested in it all his unthinkable prayers: should the hops come through the drying, the child she was carrying was his. It differed from the game Lily had taught Knight to play with the evening star only that in Everett's game the odds were pretty much with him. *Make sure it's the first star you see at night, baby, and don't stop looking until you've finished the wish.* ("That's Venus," he had explained to Knight. "That's a planet, not a star at all. A planet named Venus." "I don't think so," Knight said politely, not looking away from the window; one twilight he waited at his bedroom window fifteen minutes so as not to risk seeing another star first.)

Even before Everett reached the steps to the verandah he heard Martha's laughter through the screened door and windows, and he heard in the particular pitch of that laughter the fact that Ryder Channing was with her. It was not that he disliked Channing. Channing in fact reminded him of Clark McCormack, his roommate at Stanford, and he admired their apparent easiness in the world even as he was vaguely troubled by it. Clark McCormack had seemed to Everett the center of a vast social network, the pivot for dozens of acquaintances, all of whom were constantly calling or dropping by the Deke house: one to bring Clark the stolen stencil for a mimeographed midterm; another to drop off a box of Glenn Miller records in anticipation of a party; others, usually extraordinarily pretty girls, to leave their convertibles for Clark to use. Like Clark McCormack, Channing conveyed the distinct impression that he could live by his wits alone. They were both free agents, adventurers who turned whatever came their way to some advantage; both pleasant, knowledgeable, and in some final way incomprehensible to Everett. Channing had once told Everett that wherever he was he made a point of getting a guest card to the best country club. It was that kind of thing, something Everett could not put his finger on. Channing had no business around Marth. He might even be married: you never knew about people like Channing. He would have to talk to Martha; he had meant to talk to her ever since he came home in February.

"Everett?" Martha called now from the living room.

He had wanted to see Lily before facing Marth and Channing, and he hesitated, playing for time by looking through the mail on the hall table. There were two pediatricians' bills, a notice of a sale on Germaine Monteil Superglow Solid Powder at the Bon Marché in Sacramento, and a report from the Pi Beta Phi Arrow Shop in Gatlinburg, Tennessee: all addressed to Lily.

"Everett," Martha called again. "Come here."

He walked into the living room, oddly conscious of the muscles moving in his legs. He was struck by the thought, although it did not sound scientific, that if he forgot where the muscles were he would be unable to walk.

"Ryder brought us some good gin for a change and I'm making martinis."

Everett did not look at Channing. "Where's Lily?" he asked with an effort.

Martha was sitting with her back to him, her rather too long hair hanging forward over her bare shoulders. She had on some kind of sun dress which made her look pale and thin, and the hair did not help. Although he had always liked it long she looked healthier when she kept it cut.

"She's in San Francisco," Martha said finally, measuring gin into a pitcher. "I drove her in this morning to get the train. *The City of San Francisco* was two hours late coming in over the mountains and that's why I wasn't here for lunch. I told China Mary to slice the ham," she added. "Was it all right?"

"I wasn't up for lunch." He paused. "You say Lily's gone to the City?"

"She just decided to go as long as it was so hot—you wouldn't be*lieve* how hot it was in town today, we saw Francie cashing a check in the Wells Fargo and she looked like *wrath*—and you're so busy. Anyway she had to shop. She claimed she didn't have anything to wear to the Horse Show in case you took her to the Fair."

"The Fair," Everett repeated.

Martha looked up. "The Fair starts Thursday. Anyway. She said to tell you she was going to spend all your money at Magnin's."

Sweet Christ. He could hear her saying it. *Tell your brother I'm going to spend all his money at Magnin's.*

"She staying at the St. Francis?"

"I wouldn't think so." Martha handed Channing a glass. "I don't know that she's ever stayed at the St. Francis in her life. I mean has she?"

He did not know. He had thought of the St. Francis only because it was her favorite hotel in San Francisco: *It makes me feel like violets, baby, violets and silver dollars from the Comstock Lode. All that tacky marble.*

"I mean I assumed she was staying with Mrs. Ives," Martha added. "I didn't really think. She said she might call tonight or tomorrow."

Charlotte Ives was Lily's great-aunt, a widow who lived out in the Marina. Lily might be at the St. Francis and she might not, but she would almost certainly not be with Mrs. Ives. *She said she might call tonight or tomorrow.* Wherever she was, he would not be able to reach her. That was all that meant. He knew now that he should have expected her to do this, knew that he would pay all of his life for letting her spend this one hour in some nameless doctor's office. If that was what she was doing, and he did not know what else she could be doing. She must have been ready to do it before she told him. She had

tried him at last and found no help. It occurred to him suddenly that something could go wrong, that everything could go all wrong and they would never let him know.

"What's going to happen to Knight and Julie?" He heard too late the uneven rise in his voice.

Martha looked at Channing, who shrugged, stood up, and walked over to the window.

"Now, Everett," Martha said finally. "Knight and Julie are at this moment asleep. China Mary has fed them and I have twice recounted for them the story of the little engine that could. Ryder has obtained at Knight's request three glasses of water, and perhaps you might—when you feel up to it—make certain that Julie has not misplaced her stuffed raccoon, which seems to do for Julie what Luminal does for Julie's Mommy. Now I would assume that we could carry on in this vein until Mommy's re*turn*."

Everett saw that Channing was watching him, and forced himself to smile. He was irritated, as he frequently was now, by Martha's tone: he was sure that if she could hear herself she would stop it, but did not know how to tell her that.

"We got the last of the hops down today," he said finally.

"Ah," Martha said to Channing. "We celebrate the harvest, chez McClellan."

"Some harvest festival." Channing smiled. "When the harvester won't have a drink."

"We call him the grim reaper." Martha blew Everett a kiss.

"You're wearing too much lipstick." He could at least tell her that. But as he watched her turn away, trying to bite the color off her lips, he was sorry that he had said anything.

He picked up his drink. There was nothing to do now but wait for Lily to call or come home, get through the next day or so without letting Martha see that something was wrong, that everything had gone all wrong. She should have waited. He would have helped her. He swore to himself that he would have helped her had she waited. It might even have been his, and it would not have mattered much finally if it had not been. What real difference would it have made: it would have been Lily's, and Lily was his, and as far as that went Joe Templeton was a distant cousin of his, distant enough for Everett to

seldom remember it but close enough to think about now. They went to the same weddings and funerals, which was what mattered.

"You should have gone down with Lily," Channing said now to Marth, filling his glass from the pitcher. "You look like hell."

"The heat bothers Martha." Everett wondered how much longer Channing would be at Mather Field now that the war was over.

"It sure doesn't bother that Lily-maid," Channing said. "She hasn't looked so good all year."

"She's tired," Everett said. "I don't care how she looks to you, she's tired and she needs a rest."

"She's your bride, Coop."

It was a great little thing with Channing, the Gary Cooper routine with Everett and especially the "that Lily-maid" business with Lily. When they had gone, the four of them, to Lake Tahoe three weeks before, he had kept it up all weekend, needling Lily unobtrusively at first but at last so constantly that it had begun not only to set Everett on edge but to humiliate Martha: Everett had watched her trying to divert Channing's attention from Lily, the strain on her face more and more visible as she began talking, too loudly, about things neither Channing nor Lily could know about, deliberately excluding them from recollections of how Sarah had behaved before her first dance, how China Mary had feared a Great Dane they had kept for three weeks a long time ago. But *aren't we happy*, Lily had said, and despite Channing and despite Martha they had been: he had not been away with Lily since before he left for Fort Lewis, and they drove to all the places they had gone so often during the first year of their marriage: Reno, Carson, down into Glenwood. In the shining clarity of that afternoon in the mountains, the air so clear and sharp and the horizons clean and distant, it had seemed to Everett for a while that they could have again what he had wanted them to have, could lie in bed and laugh, neither accusing the other of anything. Their betrayal of each other (for had he not betrayed her in his mind, wished to stay away, wanted no trouble, *you don't seem to realize there's a war going on*) seemed for a few hours that Saturday afternoon and evening a simple dislocation of war, a disturbance no more lasting than the wash from a stone thrown in the river. They had stayed Saturday night in a house which belonged to one of Lily's cousins, a brown-shingled place on the north shore of the lake, and they had gambled on the Nevada line until about two o'clock in the morning. Although Lily would not play ("Women don't ever win, Everett, can't you see. Because winners have to believe they can affect the dice"), she stayed close to the table, watching over his shoulder, reaching now and then into his pocket for a cigarette or change for a drink, playing idly with a stack of silver dollars he had given her but never taking her eyes from the play on the table. He had tried once again to explain the odds to her, but she claimed to understand nothing at all about the game: she liked only to watch the movement on the table, the chips and the silver and the dice and the rakes the dealers used. *Let the little lady roll*, the dealer said gallantly (it was a slow table), and Everett remembered now how she had leaned over the table and closed her eyes and thrown with one hand, *come seven baby*, while she clutched his arm with the other, delighted to be playing with the grownups; she put two dollars on the line and her yellow sweater fell to the floor and she had been his child bride all over again. All that evening he had pretended with her, had played her game because that was the way he wanted it too, and later they swam in the lake, the water so clear that with only the moonlight and the handful of lights strung out on the dock he could make out rocks thirty feet below the surface, so cold that swimming was like grappling with dry ice. Lily had turned white with cold, her pale tan fading at the first burning touch of water; long after they came up from the lake she sat shivering on the stone hearth, wrapped in a towel. He had found it absurdly endearing that she should warm her nightgown in front of the fire before she put it on. *Keep me warm, baby*, she had cried out later in bed, and he had forced her head sideways and her mouth into the pillow as she moved in his arms because he did not want Channing, in the next room, to hear her. *Keep me baby please keep me.* Well, he had not. He had lost her, and now she was in some San Francisco hotel room by herself and maybe it had happened already and maybe it had gone all wrong and she was dying there by herself (women died from abortions, you saw it in the paper every so often, you heard about it, and whether the odds were with her or not she would be afraid of it) and he was here drinking with Martha and Ryder Channing as if it did not matter what happened to Lily. It was all right for Martha to sit here. Martha could not know; had she known, she would have kept Lily from going. But he had known all along, and he sat here now with Ryder Channing, and it was all mixed up in some way with the war, and Sarah's not being home, and people like Ryder Channing. Not that it was Channing's fault.

The future was being made, he heard Channing say at some point that evening, right here in California. Starting now. Channing had the hunch they were in on the ground floor of the biggest boom this country had ever seen. Talk about your gold rush. And he wasn't the only one who believed in Northern California. Just one example, the Keller Brothers believed in Northern California to the tune of five million berries.

"The Keller Brothers," Everett said. "I don't believe I know them."

The Keller Brothers, Channing explained patiently, were developers. Los Angeles developers who believed in Northern California, in the Valley specifically, to the tune of five million smackeroos. Which they were putting into the Natomas District.

"I never heard of any Kellers in the Natomas," Everett said.

With what appeared to be infinite restraint, Channing inspected and crumpled three empty cigarette packages before answering. "They aren't *in* the Natomas right now. They want to de*vel*op the Natomas."

"Who's putting up the money? How can they raise five million dollars on land they haven't got?"

"Those sweethearts could raise five million dollars with a plot plan on the back of a goddamn napkin. Anyway," Channing added, apparently abandoning his effort to justify the Kellers' ways to Everett, "that's just one example. The point is we're sitting right here on the ground floor with the button pushed go."

"Cut yourself in, Channing, it's a free country, plenty of room for everybody."

Everett realized that he must be drunk; he did not know what Channing had on his mind, but resented the "we." Martha was asleep on the couch, her head on Channing's lap. Lily had not called; he had known she would not. A few hours ago he had tried seven San Francisco hotels, the only seven he could think of, as well as the Claremont and the Durant in Berkeley. No one was registered as McClellan at any one of the nine. There had been a Miss Knight at the Mark Hopkins but when Everett got her on the line it had not been Lily at all. It had been some woman who wanted to know if she had met him with the National Cash Register boys and hung up immediately when he said she had not.

Channing seemed not to have heard him. "The point is we need everything out here. Absolutely *tabula rasa*. Christ, within the next ten, fifteen years somebody could make a fortune in the *agency* business."

"You mean real estate? Insurance?" Everett made a determined effort to follow Channing. "Or automobiles?"

"I mean *ad*vertising. Advertising agencies. You think branch offices are going to be enough for long, you don't realize what we're sitting on out here."

Everett had never known anyone who worked for an advertising agency, and although he had from time to time read articles in *Fortune* about Bruce Barton and Albert Lasker, he had no clear idea of what people who worked for advertising agencies actually did. When he thought of an advertising agency at all, which was not very often, he thought about Albert Lasker sitting around an office looking out into the falling snow and thinking about toothpaste, maybe even squeezing toothpaste onto a toothbrush. The next panel in his mind showed an electric light bulb over Albert Lasker's head and the single word "Irium." The falling snow was for some reason an integral part of the picture, and Everett had never considered it happening in California. Albert Lasker and Irium belonged to another world, a world teeming with immigrants and women who spent the day in art galleries and elevator operators who called you by name if you were a crack *Life* photographer. There was a kind of movie that always began that way, an elevator operator saying good morning to a crack *Life* photographer. They never called it *Life* but it was all part of the same goddamn world and it was always the same goddamn elevator operator.

The elevator operator brought him back to Channing, who had claimed to be sitting on the ground floor with the button pushed go. Speaking of go, he began to wonder why Channing did not go home to Mather Field or wherever it was he slept and he began to wonder why Martha was asleep with her head in Channing's lap. Picking up her sweater from the floor, he moved to spread it across her bare legs.

She shifted in her sleep, flinging one arm back across Channing's knee. "Ry-der?" she whispered.

"Go back to sleep," Channing ordered.

Apparently reassured, she withdrew her arm. Everett dropped her sweater and poured what was left of a bottle of bourbon into his glass. They did not seem to be drinking martinis any more and there was only a puddle of warm water in the ice bucket.

"You're like a goddamn radio announcer," he said suddenly to Channing. "You'd make one hell of a radio announcer."

"Maybe so," Channing said amiably. "Maybe I'll look into it."

"Charm. That's what you got, Channing, is charm. C-H-A-R-M."

He could not now think why he had turned on Channing, but because he was now, whatever the reason, more or less committed to it, he stood up, rocking a little on the balls of his feet while he watched Channing.

Channing stood up, waking Martha, who lay rubbing her eyes with one hand and trying to smooth her hair with the other.

"What is it," she said, her eyes still closed.

"Your brother," Channing said, "could use a sandwich."

"Screw a sandwich. I've just been telling your gentleman friend, in words of one syllable, that he's not in your class."

"*Everett.*" Martha stood up, tucking her dress into her belt without taking her eyes from his face. "You shut your mouth, you hear me?"

"All right," he said. "I'm sorry."

She meant it, all right: he recognized that the tremor in her voice was not for Channing's ears alone. *She's in thrall*, Lily had laughed at the beginning of the summer. "Haven't you ever read in books about women in thrall? Martha's in thrall." "What does that mean out of books?" he had asked. "It means he's the first man she ever slept with," Lily said, not laughing then, and he had slapped her, had hit her across the face with all the revulsion he had felt that night on the terrace toward Francie Templeton. *He's pretty good. Or anyway he used to be, I wouldn't know.*

When he started upstairs Martha was still standing there with Channing. She did not move her eyes from Everett, and she shook her head, almost imperceptibly, as if she wanted Channing to stop stroking her hair but was not really aware he was doing it. For an instant Everett wanted to go back down and get her, tell her to pick up her sweater and a fresh bottle of bourbon and get in the car, tell her that they were going to San Francisco to bring Lily home. But he did not know where to find Lily, and he was afraid that Martha would begin screaming if he even paused on the stairs. He had not heard her scream since they were children, but it was a scream he had never forgotten, all panic and blind hatred, so piercing it was almost sweet, and as he looked down at Martha standing rigid in Channing's casual embrace it seemed to him that he could almost see the scream beginning in her eyes.

The bed was littered with things Lily had dropped when she was packing: her hairbrush, a satin case with stockings spilling from it, her book of telephone numbers, an alligator handbag he had given her on her last birthday. He looked in the bag and found nothing but pennies, tobacco crumbs, a couple of the silver dollars she always carried ("for luck, Everett baby"), and an old shopping list: *Arden hand lotion, white socks for Knight, birthday for E., two curtain rods for back bedroom, call Mother about platter.*

He brushed it all to the floor and pulled back the sheet. There was a note scribbled on a page from a calendar: *Everett darling I'll try to make everything all right. Please. L.* Well, no one could say Lily had not hit her stride with this one. Notes under the sheet.

He crumpled the note and dropped it, then bent to retrieve it because he did not want China Mary to find it when she came to clean in the morning. He sat then on the edge of the unmade bed and absently rubbed the satin tie of Lily's nightgown across his face and listened to the faint sound of the phonograph from downstairs.

Give me land, lots of land
Under starry skies a-bove
Don't fence me in . . .

Well to hell with Martha. Let her make her own bed. With a goddamn radio announcer.

16

Keep me baby please keep me, she had said that night with the fire down low and her hair still wet with the lake water: touched, Everett had accepted it as a trust. Or anyway he had wanted to, had longed to believe that she meant it, even as he knew that it was something women said; even as he remembered others who had said that or almost that.

Not that there had ever been, for Everett, that many others: the first had been Doris Jeanne Coe, Doris Jeanne of the glass-blue eyes, the lank blond hair, the bad teeth, and the smile that seemed to Everett at sixteen infinitely perverse. Two years older than Everett, Doris Jeanne was behind in school not from native inability, which had never held anyone back in the county consolidated school system, but simply because she had stayed out of school two years when her family moved out from Oklahoma in 1933. Her mother was tubercular and Doris Jeanne, the oldest child, stayed home to help with her brother and four sisters; their father used to be a farmer but now, according to Doris Jeanne, he fixed things, and Doris Jeanne thought California was strictly a drag.

Everett met her the week she enrolled, when they were assigned to debate the topic "John C. Frémont: Opportunist or Patriot?" She was wearing, he would remember always, a fuchsia-pink sweater with a harp embroidered in gilt threads over her left breast, a tight black gabardine skirt, and a coat which made Everett forever uneasy about Doris Jeanne, the coat about which Lily later said, when he told her about it one night in bed, "Didn't it make you cry? Didn't it make you want to cry for the world every time you looked at it?" Although he had laughed at Lily, there was little doubt in his mind that the coat had indeed lent his entire relationship with Doris Jeanne Coe certain aspects of a social passion play. A hand-me-down from someone for whom her father worked, it was a camel's-hair polo coat with an I. Magnin label, and she let it out of her sight so rarely that two of the buttons were missing and the pocket bore a year-old Coca-Cola stain.

After class, Everett had stopped Doris Jeanne and asked her which position she preferred, a phrasing which afforded her a great deal of unconcealed delight. When Everett explained, blushing, that he meant did she want to argue John C. Frémont was a Patriot or did she want to argue John C. Frémont was an Opportunist, Doris Jeanne looked at him a long time, slipped the polo coat off her shoulders, removed from her large red shoulder bag a blue vial of *Evening in Paris Eau de Cologne*, and dabbed the stopper behind her ears and in the crooks of her elbows. Then she replaced the vial, snapped the bag closed, and asked Everett who John C. Frémont was. After he had told her, she smiled crookedly, arranged the bag on her shoulder, and said, "It don't make me no never-mind, honey."

Mostly because he would have preferred it himself, Everett offered Doris Jeanne the "Patriot" position, and she eventually stood up before the class with her polo coat on, daintily applied *Evening in Paris* to her wrists in full view of twenty-four entranced students and Mrs. Nalley, the English teacher, and presented an original defense in which Jessie Benton and John C. Frémont emerged curiously as refugees from some early-day phenomenon not unlike the Dust Bowl. Although she had taken a clear fancy to the Frémonts, she could not escape the impression that they had first entered California in a second-hand Ford, and the entire exercise left Mrs. Nalley so unnerved that she excused her classes for the rest of the day.

The debate was otherwise without incident, and Everett did not speak to Doris Jeanne again until the class picnic, when her brother, who played baseball with Everett, urged him to sneak off to the river and share a half-gallon of valley red with him and Doris Jeanne, who was included in the first place only because she had negotiated the purchase. After a while Alfred Coe went to sleep over beyond an Indian mound, and Doris Jeanne, with lifeless dispatch, took care of Everett. A few days later she cornered him in the hall at school, pressed up against him as he stood backed against his open locker, and began playing lovingly with his collar; she wanted to do it again out behind the backstop during seventh period, when there were no teams on the field, but Everett hesitated, and Doris Jeanne said he was strictly a drag and could stew in his own juice.

Later that semester, after the intercession of her brother, Everett wrote a term paper for Doris Jeanne on the subject "Will Semple Green: Father of Irrigation in the Northern Valley." Unhappily neither Mrs. Nalley nor the vice-principal who was called in as arbitrator could be persuaded that "Will Semple Green: Father of Irrigation in the Northern Valley" was entirely Doris Jeanne's work, and in the pressure of this controversy Doris Jeanne quit school. That she never named Everett made him admire her, and feel obscurely guilty that he had failed to do a more convincing job for her. Several years later he saw a picture of her in the *San Francisco Examiner*; described as a "curvaceous model and sometime waitress at an El Camino Real supper club," she had instituted a paternity suit against a football player with a Polish name. Although she had changed her name to Dori Lee, Everett recognized the picture, and wondered if she would remember him. He thought not.

After Doris Jeanne it had been nobody: necking in cars on hot summer nights with the back doors open so you could lie with your legs out and sometimes even lying almost naked and covered with sweat, but never doing it; once or twice or three times even lying in somebody's bed at parties given by boys whose parents were away, lying naked under the sheet with girls who had been drinking bourbon and Seven-Up and wanted to go to sleep, lying there for hours and kissing girls who probably would have done it had anyone insisted, but Everett never insisted; it was not, as Lily would have said, much his style.

Then there had been, at Stanford, a couple of girls who required less insistence: Annis McMahon, whom everyone else called alternately "Annie" and "Pooh" but whom Everett always called Annis, wishing upon her the dignity implied by her tall, cold, blond good looks. He liked to watch her play tennis, and long before he knew her he developed the habit of walking back to the Deke house from his eleven o'clock class by way of the courts where she played every noon. When it reached a point where he thought he wanted to watch her play tennis for the rest of his life, he asked Clark McCormack to introduce him to her. Once introduced, he called her three times a day, played tennis with her every afternoon, took her to the movies every Sunday night, and in May of his sophomore year, still determined that she should be the girl he had hoped she would be in the face of mounting evidence to the contrary, he drove Annis McMahon down to Santa Cruz on two successive weekends. (On the third, he found out later, Clark McCormack drove her down to Santa Cruz.) They lay in a motel room with a mission tile table and a framed color photograph of Bridal Veil Falls at Yosemite, and she told him in the high nasal voice which had been his first disappointment about the difficulty she was having arranging her courses to obtain her teaching credential at the same time she received her degree in physical education and therapy. She got up from the bed every time as if she were getting out of a shower, ready, in a companionable way he found dispiriting in the extreme, to discuss it; stretched her incredible golden arms, lit a cigarette, opened all the blinds, and wrapped herself in his shirt, a gambit which might have seemed more winning had his shirt not fit her almost perfectly.

The next year there was Naomi Kahn, a Jewish girl from Beverly Hills whose grades were good, whose clothes smelled always as if they had just come from Bullock's-Wilshire boxes (as a matter of fact they had not: Naomi ordered all her clothes from Bergdorf Goodman in New York), and whose mother and father were both, as she put it, in the Industry. She told Everett that her deepest wishes for her mother and father involved their abandoning screenwriting in favor of writing something like *Winterset*, and when that day came she would be more than happy, in answer to Everett's query, to stop ordering her clothes from Bergdorf Goodman in New York, although for Everett's information, Maxwell Anderson was not exactly on the relief rolls. Everett ought to get around more. Once the Kahns came up to Stanford to visit Naomi, and Mrs. Kahn later wrote that she considered Everett divine, an honest-to-Christ set piece, whereupon Naomi's ardor for Everett began to cool. One night toward the end of their junior year she announced that she was driving to Reno the next day to marry a Berkeley graduate student who was active in the Young Communist League; the Kahns, after getting the marriage annulled, transferred Naomi to Sarah Lawrence. Although Everett never knew what happened to Naomi after that, he noticed the Kahns' names from time to time among the credits on B comedies, and years later he read in *Time* that they were up before the Tenney Committee for having participated in the October 1943 Writers' Congress at UCLA. They were listed as members of several oddly named organizations the function of which Everett did not entirely understand, were later indicted in Washington for contempt of Congress, and Everett reflected that Naomi, wherever she was, must have approved at last.

Actually Everett had liked Naomi Kahn: he had liked the way her clothes smelled and liked the slightly derisive way she went to bed; she did it exactly the way she wrote out a midterm or drove a car, with a style and efficiency he had never observed in any of the girls with whom he had grown up, and he loved it. He sometimes thought he even loved her, usually when she had gone to spend the weekend with her parents in Palm Springs and he was left with the alternatives of sitting around the house drinking beer or calling up somebody like Annis McMahon. Palo Alto the winter of 1939 seemed full of girls like Annis McMahon, and Everett's appreciation of Naomi's singular virtues grew until he actually regretted, for something like four days after she eloped with the Young Communist from Berkeley, that he had not asked her to marry him.

Nonetheless, Naomi Kahn had not been, any more than Annis McMahon or for that matter Doris Jeanne Coe had been, someone with whom he could have lived on the ranch. During those four days when he wished he had married Naomi he never once thought of living anywhere with her: they were always driving someplace together, or he was putting her on an airplane, or they were registering at the Fairmont in San Francisco and she had on a black hat with a veil.

In the end Naomi had been just like Annis McMahon and a dozen or so girls he had known not as well: something he had tried and abandoned, before the effort became too strenuous, and none of it had to do with Lily. Even as he imagined himself registering at the Fairmont with Naomi Kahn, Everett knew without thinking that what he would do was live on the ranch with Lily Knight, knew it so remotely that if he had heard, during the years he rarely saw her, that she had married someone else he would have wished her well and gone on thinking about Naomi Kahn at the Fairmont, and only somewhere in the unused part of his mind would he have begun wondering, with an urgency he would not have understood, what he was going to do with the rest of his life. Lily required no commitment: Lily was already there.

It had not occurred to him that he could lose her (had not occurred to him even that he wanted her) until the week he came home from Stanford and saw her sitting on her father's terrace in a faded pink dress, the late afternoon sun on her dusty bare feet and a large safety pin in place of a missing screw on her sunglass frames. It had seemed to him then that to risk losing her would be to risk losing Martha and Sarah and himself as well, that she alone could retrieve and keep for him the twenty-one years he had already spent. Convinced that he could ill afford to leave her untended for even that one night, he fell asleep finally with his clothes on, a cigarette still burning in the ashtray on his bedroom window sill, and when he woke in the morning he set out immediately to secure for himself the haven of her faded pink dress, her bare feet, the safety pin in her sunglasses.

As far as the safety pin went, it remained in her sunglasses until the summer she was pregnant with Julie, when he told her one night, irritated partly because she had just uncovered a grocery bill she had lost three months before and partly because she had dragged a sheet down to the sun porch the night before and slept there until ten o'clock but irritated mostly because it had been 105° for three days and she had accused him of not loving her as her father had loved her, that the safety pin in her sunglasses summed up all her unattractive habits, her sloppiness of mind, her inability to accomplish the routine tasks that could be done with one hand by any of the girls he had known at Stanford. She had gone upstairs without speaking. When he came to bed she had pretended to be asleep, and she had gotten up at seven the next morning to drive into Sacramento. She returned at noon with a new screw in her sunglasses and with, as well, a book called *The Managerial Revolution* in which she later read the first and last chapters (she pretended to have read it all but he read it himself and saw that she had not), an album of French language records which as far as he knew she never played, eight dollars' worth of closet bags and boxes, and a large account book in which she wrote down, for two weeks, the exact amounts both she and China Mary spent on food and household supplies. The book was in fact labeled "Food and Household Supplies," and she had shown it proudly to Martha. The first day's entry, Martha reported with a degree of admiration, began with an itemized list showing the unit prices, the amount saved by buying in quantity, and a tax breakdown wherever a tax was involved, on twenty-four bottles of beer, twelve cans of mixed carrots and peas, twelve cans of puréed liver, four quarts of milk, two cartons of Lucky Strikes, six tins of smoked oysters, and fifteen cans of Campbell's Soup; five consommé, five vegetable-beef, five cream of chicken. Totaled, these items came to $18.53, and were followed by an entry which read "Etc.—$27 (about)." When Martha asked what the $27 represented, Lily, absorbed in contemplating the neatness of her figuring, had shrugged. "You know. A mop handle. Things." After Lily had abandoned "Food and Household Supplies," Everett tore the entry from the book, carried it around with him for a couple of weeks and finally put it in a drawer where he kept his Stanford diploma, a clipping about a no-hit game he had pitched in high school, and a letter from Martha describing the only 4-H meeting she ever attended.

The truth was simply that he would not have known what to do with a wife who knew what to do with a book labeled "Food and Household Supplies": it was not Everett's idea of a wife's function. Although he was not sure what his idea of a wife's function was, he knew that Lily had been closest to fulfilling it when she had been trying least. She simply did not know how. She would concentrate upon the details while the essence eluded her, unable to see that one entry in the Pillsbury Bake-Off did not make a Mrs. America.

There as everywhere, Lily failed, even as she tried with pathetic concentration, to apprehend what was expected of her. The most insignificant social encounter was for Lily, as Martha had pointed out at dinner one night this spring, fraught with the apprehension of possible peril.

"I mean Lily can't say simple things like 'thank you' or 'I'd rather not' or 'please may I have more coffee,'" Martha had added, turning then to Lily. "I don't know what's wrong with you but you can't."

"Nothing's wrong with her," Everett said, although he saw Martha's point. He had only a week before learned that Lily was allergic to strawberries, which he had seen her eating with apparent delight innumerable times. "I thought your father liked them," she said, in explanation.

"Everett, it's *true*. I'm not being mean to Lily, I'm only observing something interesting. Somebody holds the door open for Lily in a hardware store, and she thinks she has a very complex situation on her hands."

Martha poured the rest of a bottle of wine into Lily's glass and sat back, watching Lily. "First Lily says thank you. Then she wonders: did he hear her? If he didn't, was he thinking how rude she was? Assuming that he heard her, was just 'thank you' enough? If not, what more? On the other hand maybe 'thank you' was too much. Maybe she should have just smiled. Maybe he thought she'd been forward. In fact maybe she'd been mistaken in thinking he was holding the door for her *at all*. Possibly he'd been holding it for someone behind her, his wife, or an old lady. If that was the case, thanking him made her look *a perfect fool*, and now she can't remember why she came to the hardware store in the first place, and every now and then all day she thinks about how she might have handled it. I mean the *crises* Lily faces from day to day."

Lily had blown out the candles on the table and transparently misunderstood Martha: "I don't think good manners are ever amiss," she said. But later, when she was brushing her hair and he was working at the card table he had covered with tax records, he looked up and saw that she was crying, crying and brushing her hair as if she wanted to brush it out. He had put aside the depreciation schedule and picked her up in his arms, the hairbrush still in her hand. Her voice muffled against his shoulder, she explained that she wanted to be like other people, wanted to be able to talk to people. "You're shy," he said. "There's nothing wrong with being shy." There was, Lily sobbed, something wrong with being shy when you were going on twenty-four years old, and anyway she was not shy, she was simply no good around people and that was that. He had lain on the bed with her and the hairbrush and told her that she was not to talk that way, that she was not other people. She was, he added, turning out the light, his baby. It occurred to Everett later that he had in that commonplace endearment put his finger on some of Lily's virtues and certain of her failings.

17

LILY CAME home from San Francisco on a Greyhound bus crowded with Mexican pickers and sailors. From San Francisco to Vallejo she sat next to a sailor who was going to meet his girl in Salt Lake City. She lived with her folks in Salt Lake but Frisco, he explained, was their lucky town. They had met there, in a gin mill on Market Street, four days before he shipped out in 1943. When she promised to wait had been the A-1 moment in his life, and the second A-1 moment had been a week before on the U.S.S. *Chester* when he got his first sight in two years of the Golden Gate Bridge. There had been fog in the morning and when the fog broke he saw it there, shining way off in the distance like it wasn't attached to anything. The band on the well deck had started in on "California Here I Come" and everybody had belted it out along with the band and it might sound cornball to her but it made him want to sit down and bawl like a baby. Lily began to cry, struck by the superiority of his appreciations to her own, and the sailor said wait a minute, hold your horses, it wasn't sad, honey, it was like women crying at weddings. She looked to him like the kind who cried at weddings. It was like that. When the sailor got off at Vallejo to wait for the Salt Lake express Lily wished him good luck and watched him covertly through the window. He was sitting on his duffel bag reading a comic book and eating a Milky Way, and she wanted to get off the bus and give him her garnet ring for his girl, but did not know how to go about it. It was not until the bus had rolled out of the station that Lily remembered that at any rate the garnet ring had been Everett's grandmother's and was therefore not in the strictest sense hers to give.

From Vallejo to Sacramento she sat next to a woman who was a part-time cashier at a drive-in across the highway from Hotel El Rancho, west of Sacramento. The woman had been in Vallejo visiting her daughter, who had a nice place, not large but fixed up cute, above a florist's shop on Tennessee Street. No doubt Lily knew the florist's shop. No? The woman had thought surely she would because they did all the society weddings in Vallejo, it was very well-known.

Regretful that she had not pretended to recognize the florist's name and anxious that the woman not think she had been trying to snub her, Lily hurried to surmount what seemed to her an impasse by asking if the daughter were married. Well, not exactly. It seemed that Sue Ann's husband, a seaman first class but a bastard from the word go, had got his at Okinawa —Sue Ann had been just about set to blow the whistle anyway, as far as that went—and Sue Ann was now supporting their six-year-old son, Billy Jack, by car-hopping at Stan's off U.S. 40.

The woman paused, and Lily quickly assured her that she knew Stan's. (As it happened, she did, because when Everett first went away she had listened nights on the radio to *Stan's Private Line*, and had even wondered academically from time to time whether or not she could have made the grade among the leather-jacketed *jeunesse dorée* who gathered nightly at Stan's to eat Double-Burgers and dedicate songs to one another.) The woman ignored her. Naturally Sue Ann got asked on a lot of dates—she was about Lily's age but a real doll, built like Rita Hayworth. You could hardly tell them apart except for the hair, and nobody would ever convince her that Rita's was natural anyway. But don't get her started on that. So Sue Ann had been playing the field, but now she had a once-in-a-lifetime opportunity to marry a young fellow who in turn had a once-in-a-lifetime opportunity to wrap up the Kirby Party franchise for the entire Greater Vallejo area. You know, Kirby Parties. You invite a congenial group to your home and serve a little something, doughnuts and soft drinks, and then the Kirby representative comes and demonstrates the vacuum cleaners and all. You get a bonus gift for getting a certain number to come and you get in a little girl-talk besides. If Lily wasn't on to Kirby Parties she ought to take Fred's number and call him the next time she was in the area, providing his deal went through. Anyway. The only catch was that Fred didn't know about Billy Jack. Or rather he knew about Billy Jack but believed him to be Sue Ann's little brother. She had warned Sue Ann it was a crazy mad thing to do, trying to pass off Billy Jack as her own mother's change-of-life baby, but what could you do. Sue Ann had her right to happiness as much as the next one. What did Lily think.

As the bus rolled out of the Coast Range and into the heat of the Valley, Lily stopped thinking altogether, lulled by the even rhythm of the telephone poles against field after dry yellow field, by the regular rise and fall of the woman's voice, by the grinding and shifting of gears as the bus swung off the highway and down the streets of towns in which she seemed to have spent her life: Fairfield-Suisun, Vacaville, Dixon. Although she did not suppose that she had driven through any one of the towns more than on the outside twenty times, they had about them an imprint which to perceive once, especially if that once was on an August afternoon when the streets looked abandoned and the frame buildings as fragile as tinder, was to possess forever. She could close her eyes and tick it off: the Bank of America building, the W.T. Grant store, the Lincoln-Mercury agency; the lone woman in a shapeless dress and flowered straw hat, sitting on the porch of the hotel until her husband was through in town. Off the main street there would be a few blocks of houses, three-storey houses in need of paint, each fronted by a patch of dry grass, maybe a tricycle overturned on the cracked concrete walk. The blinds would be drawn and there would not be any people, anywhere. The afternoon heat could bleach those towns so clean that the houses and the buildings seemed always on the verge of dematerializing; there was the sense that to close one's eyes on a Valley town was to risk opening them a moment later on dry fields, the sun bleaching out the last traces of habitation, a flowered straw hat, a neon advertisement which had blinked a moment before from a wall no longer visible: *More Yield from Every Acre with Seeds from Northrup-King.*

It was a great comfort, watching the towns come and go through the tinted window of the Greyhound bus. The heat drained the distinctions from things—marriage and divorce and new curtains and overdrafts at the bank, all the same—and Lily could not at the moment imagine any preoccupation strong enough to withstand the summer. At least any preoccupation of hers; Sue Ann, now, was another case. There would be nothing ambiguous about Sue Ann's responses, nothing ambivalent about her wants: Sue Ann would have kissed Joe Templeton goodbye with no second thoughts. Sue Ann's problems, unlike her own, offered the compression, the foreshortening of art; her own were inadvertent, makeshift affairs at best, and there with her head resting against the bus window she could not think why she had gone to San Francisco or why she had caused a scene with Everett or how she had gotten pregnant in the first place by somebody she did not much like or why, the heart of the matter, she had thought it made any difference.

When the bus arrived in Sacramento at six o'clock, however, she emerged as if from a darkened theater into the sudden glare, the sudden presence of people, and the sudden recollection of why it made any difference. Standing on the loading platform, holding her raincoat and her overnight bag, she could remember just about everything except why she had chosen a four-hour bus ride over two air-conditioned hours in a Southern Pacific club car. For reasons now lost to her, it had seemed in San Francisco the thing to do; had seemed the way of the Cross.

I've been worried, Joe said when she called him from the bus station. There seemed to her reproof in every syllable.

"I'm sorry. I just got into town." She did not want to talk to Joe and did not know why she had called him, except that she had promised to.

"I worried," he repeated. "I couldn't sleep. I yelled at Francie."

"You yelled at Francie." She leaned against the wall of the telephone booth and tried to open the glass door with her foot, succeeding only in catching her heel between the door and the jamb.

"How are you?"

"I'm all right." Working her foot free, she let the shoe drop. "I'm fine."

"You sound pretty good."

"How did you expect me to sound?"

In the prolonged silence which followed she reached to retrieve her shoe and saw that she had snagged her stocking on the lock of her overnight case.

"*Damn it*." She jammed her foot into her shoe and brushed her damp hair from her face.

"What's the matter?"

"Nothing's the matter. I was just putting my shoe on."

"Putting your shoe on? Why did you have your shoes off?"

"No reason, Joe, no reason. I'm just down here in the Greyhound bus station barefoot, see."

"Cut it out."

"I'm sorry."

After a silence Joe said tentatively: "You saw the doctor?"

"Yes."

"How did it go?"

"It was fine. Everything was just fine."

"I told you it would be."

She did not say anything.

"He didn't charge you any more, did he?"

"No. It went all right."

"I told you it would. He didn't want any more money?"

"*No*, I said." She was irritated by his preoccupation with the money; it had been her five hundred dollars in the first place. To get the cash she had sold ten shares of an oil stock her father had given her as a wedding present, and she did not like to be reminded of it. Although she had not thought of it before, there was something about Joe's inability to put his hands on five hundred dollars without Francie's knowing about it which summed up all his rather aggressive weaknesses.

"I would have cut off my right arm if I could have gone down there for you."

"Now you cut it out," she said, and was immediately touched with remorse: if he was dishonest so was she. If she were honest she would not even be talking to him on the telephone.

"There was nothing you could do," she added, ashamed.

"It's been pretty bad. You know how bad I felt about it." He paused. "Maybe I could see you tomorrow."

"No," she said rapidly. "I mean I can't. I have to rest."

"I guess you better." He sounded relieved. "I just thought you'd want to talk to someone."

"Oh Christ. No. I don't want to talk to someone. I don't want to talk to anyone."

She clicked off the connection with her finger and dropped the receiver in her lap. Her silk suit was damp with perspiration and stained not only with dust but tea, spilled at the counter in the San Francisco bus station. She should have let the waitress sponge it off but her bus had already been called and she had not wanted to run; she had been afraid that if she moved too quickly the bleeding would begin again.

If she had not wanted to talk to Joe, she certainly did not want to talk to Everett. Nonetheless, she had to get home and felt incapable of explaining to anyone else what she was doing with her suitcase in the Greyhound bus station. She had meant to take the river bus out to the ranch, but the drivers had gone on strike. If it was not one thing it was another. Fumbling in her bag for a cigarette, she dropped two coins in the telephone and dialed her mother's number. When her mother answered she felt tears rising, hung up without saying anything, and smoked the cigarette down to her fingers. *I would have cut off my right arm*, she thought viciously. He knew what he could cut off. She blew her nose, snapped her bag shut, and called the ranch.

Everett answered on the first ring. "Sweet Jesus, Lily. You all right?"

"I'm fine."

"Where the hell are you?"

She hesitated. Where was she. It was the giveaway, the proof of how she felt, the evidence that she would never be the kind who could carry things off.

"At the Greyhound bus station," she said at last.

"You fool," he said softly. "You goddamn little ass."

She drank some warm Coca-Cola in a sticky paper cup and went outside the station to wait for Everett. At six-thirty everything seemed still: the traffic had already thinned out and the thick branches of the plane trees hung heavy and motionless over the street. In front of the loading platform a sailor was trying to pick up two girls; both the girls wore white peasant blouses, pulled down off their shoulders, and one had her hair tied up in a magenta scarf. When the sailor, teasing, pulled off the scarf, Lily saw that the girl's head was covered with pin curls. Snatching the scarf back, the girl struck an exaggerated pose with it, and they all laughed. They seemed to be having a very good time and it tired Lily to think that she was probably no older than they were.

Depressed, she turned her attention across the street to a parking lot where a few men, apparently late from their offices and obviously all acquainted, were picking up their cars. She reflected sadly that they would no doubt arrive home to find their well-behaved sun-tanned wives getting out of their swimming suits and dressed for dinner. It was too hot a night to cook; all over town those loving summer wives were brushing the chlorine out of their hair and putting on dresses to go out to dinner. They would be at the country club tonight, wearing their bright clean linen dresses loosely, as if they were unaccustomed to wearing clothes at all. They would talk about their diets and their children and their golf scores, display their even dispositions and their gold charm bracelets, and presently they would go home to take off the bright clean linen dresses, to lie on hot sheets and wait patiently for the day to begin again. You would never catch one of them standing around the Greyhound bus station in a tea-stained wrinkled silk suit not wanting to see her husband. You would never even catch one of them standing around anywhere in a tea-stained wrinkled silk suit. There was the kind of wife Everett should have, and look what he had instead. Martha had said it all: Lily had no right to her brother. Everett, like Sue Ann, had his right to happiness as much as the next one.

It was almost seven-thirty before Everett arrived. Unshaven and wearing a dirty khaki shirt, he double-parked the station wagon, swung himself over the rear bumper of a parked Chevrolet, and took Lily's arm. She had not at first seen him, and smiled tentatively when he touched her. He picked up her suitcase, helped her around the Chevrolet, and opened the station-wagon door without speaking. Before they were home she had fallen asleep, dry-eyed for a change, her head in the way of the gear shift.

Later he put her to bed, opened the shutters which had been closed all day against the heat, and wiped her face with a washcloth soaked in witch hazel.

"Did you get the hops finished?" she whispered, opening her eyes.

"Yes," he said. "Everything's fine. Go to sleep."

"Listen." She took the washcloth from him and laid it across her eyes. "I love you."

He looked at her for a long time.

"Stop feeling sorry for yourself," he said finally.

She took the washcloth from her eyes and threw her arms around his neck. "Everett, baby. I do. I love you. I know you and you know me and nobody else does. Everett please baby *love* me."

She clung to him while he kissed her hair, and when he moved to take her arms from his neck she tighened her hold. "Lie here with me," she whispered. "Lie here with me until it's all dark."

"Later." He stood up. "Go to sleep now, baby."

He sat with Knight for half an hour on the third floor, from where they could see the fireworks in town, for that day happened also to be the opening of the State Fair. There would be fireworks every night for twelve days, great slow bursts of white and pink and green, barely visible from the ranch. Long before the last distant sparks had showered out and drifted down, Knight fell asleep in Everett's arms, and he carried him downstairs without waking him and put him to bed in his playsuit.

He went downstairs then, wandering absently from room to room. The house was quiet: Julie was at her grandmother's; Martha had gone to the Fair with Ryder Channing. Insisting that Lily and Everett must come with them, they had waited an hour to see if Lily might arrive; Everett had gotten rid of them only by saying that the four of them would go to the Fair over the weekend. After they had gone Everett had sat in the kitchen with a bottle of beer and an article Channing had brought him about what was described as a pioneer shopping center in Kansas City. The kitchen chairs were uncomfortable and Everett had found it increasingly difficult to concentrate on why some developers preferred shopping centers with mall layouts to shopping centers with cluster layouts, whatever a cluster layout was; the kitchen, however, was the only place in the house where he did not feel oppressed by the presence of telephones. Although he knew that there were only two telephones in the house and five on the entire ranch, the house had seemed, while he waited for Lily to call, equipped with enough telephones to service a handbook operation.

Now he sat down again in the kitchen and tried to finish the article Channing had given him, but after three or four more paragraphs abandoned it. For fifteen minutes he sat reading the labels on the beer bottle he had left on the table when Lily called, and finally he went outside and set sprinklers to run all night on the south lawn, an extravagance justified only by the possibility that it would cool Lily's and the children's room some. He thought automatically now of *Lily's room*, and when he went to sleep at eleven o'clock it was, for the first time of many, in his father's bed. Although during the night he thought he woke and heard voices in the driveway, first Channing's, *shut up you're almost shouting*, and then Martha's, *you think she's so interesting-looking maybe you could knock her up yourself the next time*, by morning it seemed easier to believe that he had only dreamed it.

18

THERE WAS nothing wrong with Ryder Channing, Martha observed, that could not be inferred from his habit, when he was at any house within fifty miles of San Francisco, of asking his hostess if she had at hand a copy of the 1948 San Francisco *Social Register* because he wanted to look up a new telephone number.

Actually, Martha amended, Ryder took her calling in San Francisco so infrequently that she had only once witnessed him asking for the 1948 *Social Register* to look up a telephone number, but she was certain that it had been no improvisation of the moment. It was of a piece with his routinely asking people from Cleveland where they lived in Shaker Heights.

"That's not fair of me," Martha added then with the instant contrition which tended, for a while quite successfully, to obscure the hostile edge on her voice; her standard conversational technique was that of a trial lawyer who pursues a tendentious line of questioning and then allows it stricken from the record.

"I mean that's perfectly true about Ryder and the *Social Register* but it's not fair. It's not the *whole* Ryder. I mean Ryder goes around talking about big deals that never go through and all but that doesn't mean Ryder's a phony. Ryder just wants things. That's not so bad, to want things. Is it."

"Not at all," Lily said, virtuously knotting a thread in a dress she was making by hand for Julie's first day at school. The dress was an economy measure: Everett had said that their 1949 taxes would be double this year's—both the riverfront and the Cosumnes ranches had been reassessed for the first time since the war—and Lily had resolved, without mentioning it to Everett, to save money. She had begun by saving the six or seven dollars she would normally have paid for Julie's dress, instead buying four dollars' worth of imported lawn and a sixty-cent pattern. After three weeks of intermittent work, the lawn was not only grimy from her fingers but spotted here and there with blood from her pricked fingers; it should, however, wash up very nicely. Good fabrics, good soap, and good hats, her mother often told her, were no extravagance.

Impressed with the fruit of her own economy, Lily added: "Wanting things and working to get them. It's the basis of the American way."

"*Balls.* You aren't even listening to me."

"Really, Martha." Although Lily had never known exactly what the word meant, it did not sound conversational to her. She had for that matter first heard it from Martha, the afternoon Mr. McClellan died in Sutter Hospital. Because Martha was having a cigarette with one of the doctors, Lily had been alone in the room, holding Mr. McClellan's hand, when he woke from the coma. "You're a good girl, Miss Lily Knight," he said, opening his eyes and squeezing her hand weakly. "You're sickly-looking but you're a good girl." "*Balls,*" Martha said from the doorway, seeing that her father's eyes were again closed and his hand fallen free of Lily's. Involuntarily, Lily had put her hand out to shield Mr. McClellan from Martha's voice, but ten minutes later he was dead and possibly he had heard neither Martha's invective nor, a minute later, her sobbing.

"I'm sorry," Martha said now. "It's only that you were at it again."

"At what again?"

"You know." Martha paused. "Your dress is coming along nicely. That blue should be very good on Julie."

Lily smiled, and held the dress up for Martha's further approval.

"If only there weren't that gap between her teeth."

Lily laid the dress aside and began threading a needle. Martha had told Julie that unless her teeth were straightened immediately she would grow up to be a very unattractive little girl. For several days Julie had been inconsolable, repeatedly climbing up on the washbasin to inspect her teeth in the bathroom mirror.

"I told you before, her second teeth aren't even in." Lily finished threading the needle and inadvertently jammed it into her index finger.

Martha shrugged, her interest in orthodontia apparently ebbing.

"Ryder just wants things," she repeated reflectively. "That's exactly the thing about Ryder."

"What does Ryder want now."

Martha looked at her a long while. "This is what they call a *mo-bile situation*, see, Lily. Ryder is what they call *up-ward mo-bile*. Or *on-the-make*. Didn't you ever take any courses? Didn't you ever read any books by Lloyd Warner?"

"There's—" Lily stopped. She had been about to say that there was nothing wrong in wanting to get ahead. She did not know what it was about Martha that inflexibly brought out in her diction the best of both Mr. McClellan and her mother.

"There's *what*?" Martha demanded.

"Nothing."

"'*There's nothing wrong in wanting to get ahead*,'" Martha mimicked. "I know you. Well there's not. But you don't understand about Ryder. He wants to *use* people."

"Martha. Don't get all upset."

"Well he can't use me." Martha paused. "I don't want anything from him. That's the reason he can't use me."

"Martha," Lily repeated.

"I don't want his *jobs*, I don't want his *favors*, I don't want anything *about* him."

What Martha did not want from Ryder Channing that morning was the job he had gotten her three weeks before on a Sacramento television station. It was the fourth or fifth such job for which he had arranged an interview; it was not only the first one Martha had taken but the first one, as far as Lily knew, for which she had even shown up for the initial appointment. The idea behind this particular job had been that Martha, after a month of answering letters from viewers and doing other small jobs around the station, would eventually work into doing both the morning interview program and the commercials during the afternoon movie, a job handled during the first year of the channel's operation by the manager's wife, now pregnant. It was, Ryder had declared, an unbeatable opportunity to get in on the ground floor of an industry with nowhere to go but up, and he had installed a borrowed television set on the sun porch so that Martha could observe the interview and commercial techniques developed by the manager's wife, Maribeth Sidell. Martha had only to consider that Maribeth Sidell was a household word the length and breadth of the Sacramento Valley to realize, he pointed out, the future in the job.

Together, Lily and Martha had watched several of Maribeth Sidell's programs, including one on which she interviewed, simultaneously, a retired disk jockey, Miss Sacramento, and two Japanese businessmen in the United States to arrange a trade fair. When the conversation turned to how Sacramento compared to Yokohama, Martha switched off the set and declared that she was a natural for the job. After avidly testing some of the products Maribeth advertised, in order to get what she called "fresh insights," Martha drove into town, met Mr. Sidell, and reported at dinner that he had asked her to call him "Buzz," had taken her to the Sacramento Hotel bar, and after two Manhattans (for him) and two sherries (for her) had announced that although she was no Jinx Falkenburg she had a lot of class and for his money ($75 a week) the ball was hers to run with. "I knew the sherry would get him," Martha added enthusiastically. "The cornball."

Although Lily never learned exactly where the ball had been dropped, Martha had worked only one full week and three days of last week. On the fourth day she had left the house as usual at seven-thirty, but by eleven, when Sidell called the ranch, she had not yet arrived at work.

Toward five o'clock she walked into the kitchen through the back door, runs in both her stockings and thistles caught along the hem of her white linen dress. "I was sick," she explained shortly. "I drove to Yuba City and climbed on some rocks and watched a stretch of rapids in the Feather for a while."

"Sidell called," Lily said. "So did Ryder."

"Did he." Martha turned on the faucet in the sink and splashed water on her face and arms. "There was a dead rattlesnake caught in a backwater," she said finally, reaching for a paper towel. "Bloated."

When Ryder Channing called again at seven o'clock Martha at first said to tell him she was out, then, as Lily hesitated, put down her drink, reached across the table for a cigarette from Lily's bag, and took the telephone from her.

"That's right, I didn't," she said. "I didn't feel good."

Holding the receiver with her shoulder she lit the cigarette and made a face at Julie, who was illuminating with red and blue crayons a Standard Oil brochure addressed to Everett. "I just didn't call, that's all."

"I'm not trying to do anything to you, Ryder," she added after a pause. "It's part of your *egocentricity* that you think everything I do is for the express purpose of getting on your nerves. I didn't go in and I didn't call and that's all there is to it. It hasn't got anything to do with you." She paused, turning her face to the wall. "Ryder, I was scared. I don't *know* why, I was just scared."

"All right," she said finally. "I never asked you to get me any jobs. I never asked you for anything but a little understanding and it's perfectly apparent to me that you aren't capable of giving anybody anything. All you want to do is *use* people." She put out her cigarette, and took Julie's hand, holding it very tightly. Julie looked at Lily and Lily shook her head. "I'm sure I don't *know* what advantage there could possibly be for you in my having a job. I don't know what goes through your mind. I only know there *was* an advantage or you wouldn't have pushed me into it. You are forever pushing me and using me and I'm through."

"Through," she repeated.

"Don't you get that way with me, Ryder Channing. I've heard that one before. I won't miss anything about you and most of all, first on the list of things I will not miss, most of all I will not miss that."

She hung up, picked up her drink, and walked outside.

Although no one mentioned it at dinner, Martha explained later to Everett that the job had been all right the first week but had become too difficult. The telephones distracted her and there was an enormous clock with a second hand that never stopped. Sidell insisted that letters from viewers be answered the day they came in, and frequently she did not know the answers to the questions raised. The week before she had stopped Sidell in the hall and asked him, in order to answer a letter, why the channel did not carry the program with Kukla, Fran, and Ollie. Sidell had looked at her for a long time and asked her if she had ever heard of networks and network affiliates. She had tried to tell him that of course she had—she had simply not thought of an answer so obvious—but he walked away and naturally she had not wanted to ask him any more questions. Instead she had begun putting difficult queries aside in a drawer of her desk, meaning to find out later how to answer them, but the days had gone by and the letters had not been answered and now Sidell would discover them and she simply could not go back. It would be all right if she could take the letters off somewhere and answer them by herself but there was no place in the office where you could get away from those clocks. She *knew* clocks weren't supposed to stop, don't be silly. She knew they needed a clock. But she could not work with it going every second. When it was going every second that way she could not seem to take her eyes off it, and because it made no noise she found herself making the noise for it in her mind.

Everett, who had thought the job a good idea because Martha's days did not seem to him generally constructive, suggested that possibly Martha would like to take a trip. Martha thought not.

For the rest of that week Martha had refused to answer the telephone, to look at her mail, or to leave the ranch, even for a wedding down the river in which she was to have been a bridesmaid. She was quite certain, she explained to Everett and Lily, that the four hundred guests, two flower girls, and seven remaining bridesmaids could sufficiently nerve Molly Bee to lose her cherry without any additional help from her. Everett walked out of the house then, neither speaking to Martha nor getting dressed for the wedding, and finally Lily had gone alone, late, to Molly Bee's reception, where she tried to apologize for Martha and Everett, drank nine glasses of champagne in an hour and fifteen minutes, was warned by her mother that she would end up with a well-deserved headache, and kissed two of the ushers, one of whom, Molly Bee's cousin from Tulare, insisted that she was in no condition to drive and that he would drive her home himself, later. That he would be returning the next day to Tulare lent him, when she was kissing him in the car, an air of infinite promise: she could make him want her and then never see him again, all of the possibilities still intact, neither his deficiencies nor her own ever revealed. *You make me feel good*, she whispered, and meant it.

When she arrived at the ranch not long after two A.M. Everett was sitting in the chair by their bedroom window, drinking a beer and looking at an old copy of *Life*. Although she tried to tell him who had been at Molly Bee's wedding he did not seem interested, and after he had picked up the pink silk dress she had dropped on the bed and looked first at the indelible wrinkles in the skirt and then at her and had dropped the dress on the floor and gone downstairs, she lay on the bedspread in her slip and turned out the lights: she had gone and lost him again and not for any reason, not for any good reason at all. After a while, because she had a headache from the champagne and from the gin she had been drinking in the car with Molly Bee's cousin and because she thought Everett would have to come if she told him she was sick, she went to the landing and called him. "Go back to sleep," he said without moving.

On the following Monday a letter had arrived for Martha from the television station, but Martha shoved it unopened into the back of a drawer where Lily found it after her death. It contained only a note from Sidell expressing concern for her illness and a check for the eight days she had worked.

19

AT TEN-THIRTY on the morning of December 18, 1948, while she was having a fourth cup of coffee and wishing that she had not already worked the crossword puzzle, Martha saw in the social pages of the *San Francisco Chronicle* the announcement of Ryder Channing's engagement to a Miss Nancy Dupree of Piedmont. After tearing the notice out of the *Chronicle* and securing it in the pocket of her jumper, Martha wrapped with her calling card—*Miss Martha Currier McClellan, McClellan's Landing*, let Miss Nancy Dupree figure out who it was—a silver dish which Channing had once admired. It was a small dish which had been her mother's, made to Mildred McClellan's order at Shreve's in San Francisco and marked *M.C.McC.* In a smaller box she placed another calling card, with her key to Channing's apartment in Sacramento Scotch-taped over her name.

She had both packages ready to mail by early afternoon, driving in to the main post office in Sacramento and stopping first at the library to look up the Piedmont address in an Oakland telephone book. In the library she located as well several photographs of Nancy Dupree in a University of California yearbook, Class of 1947. A member of Kappa Kappa Gamma and Senior Class Council, she had one year been chosen not only Soph Doll but Sweetheart of Sigma Chi Attendant. Her major was listed as General Curriculum. She appeared to be somewhat less blond than Martha, with prettier features, and as Martha studied first one and then another picture she remembered that she had met the girl at a party in Piedmont to which Ryder had taken her. She had simply not remembered her name. It had been one of those parties at which she drank too much and became depressed, a party at which she had known none of the people Channing seemed to know; as she once explained to Everett, Ryder's only real vocation was for remembering and being remembered by all the people he went out of his way to meet. At some point during the evening she had locked herself in the bathroom and stared at her reflection in the mirror for a long time and not looked like herself (*Your name is Martha McClellan*, she said again and again to the mirror, and then cried because it did not seem to be the Martha McClellan she had wanted to be), and when she came downstairs again she had told two strangers, a pretty girl and her husband who had made a perfunctory attempt to include her in a controversy over whether or not Ernie Heckscher had played for the hostess's debut, that she was sick. "Come sit down a minute," the pretty girl said, looking at Martha and then at her husband, but then Martha saw Ryder, standing by the piano singing "As Time Goes By" with his arm around a girl in Bermuda shorts and a Liberty lawn blouse, and she ran into the bedroom, pulled her sweater from beneath a pile of navy-blue and red and forest-green blazers, and walked out of the house. *Go ahead*, she screamed at Ryder when he followed her out to the car. *You go on back in there and play whatever games you want to play. Just don't think I don't see.* She could not now remember what she thought she saw, except that she had accidentally for once been right, because the girl at the piano singing "As Time Goes By," the girl in the Liberty lawn blouse who had earlier asked Ryder if she could count on him for a Scotch foursome Sunday at Claremont Country Club, had been Nancy Dupree. *Don't think I don't know*, Martha had screamed there in the driveway as Ryder tried to take the car keys from her. Although she had not screamed loudly, he shoved her into the car and slapped her. Her first thought had been that it was Everett's car and Ryder had no right to slap her in Everett's car, but then she had remembered that Everett surely cared as little for her as Ryder did, and all during the two-hour drive to Sacramento she sat rigid against the door, trying to think how to hurt them both. What she had done finally was spend the night in Ryder's apartment, an injury to Everett which, because he had assumed she was staying all night in Piedmont anyway, escaped him.

The more she remembered of the evening ("You're Ryder's best girl in the Valley," the girl had said, taking Martha's hand and smiling up at Ryder, "I've heard so much about you"), the more she resented Ryder now, and it was with a palpable knot of hatred in her stomach that she returned the yearbook to the librarian, crossed the street to the post office, and waited in line ten minutes to see that the clerk gave immediate attention to the key for Ryder, the silver dish for Nancy Dupree.

Rid of the boxes, she started back across the Plaza to the car, but because she felt both dizzy and a little silly, she stopped and sat on the edge of the fountain long enough to smoke two cigarettes and to chew, since an old man lay passed out at the foot of the water fountain, one of the phenobarbital tablets the doctor had told her to take three times a day. There were lighted Christmas wreaths strung across J Street and as the phenobarbital began to work she forgot about Ryder and began to wish, suddenly, that her father were alive, that Sarah could come home for Christmas. There was something about Christmas as managed by Lily that was not quite Christmas, although everyone tried very hard to pretend it was and although Edith Knight always came to stay on the ranch for a few days, decorating everything in sight, hanging stockings for Knight and Julie, and helping China Mary make quantities of eggnog which no one ever dropped by to drink.

A few minutes after she got back to the ranch, Ryder called her from a bar. She knew he was in a bar because she could hear the juke box.

Well, what a surprise. She wanted to offer him all her congratulations.

Oh, he said. He had called to see if she was home. He had planned to drive out and tell her himself. He had not thought of her seeing the San Francisco papers.

No, of course he would not have thought of her seeing the San Francisco papers. He had been on the ranch not more than a thousand, fourteen hundred times during the past four and a half years, and no one could have expected him to notice that they got the San Francisco papers. It wasn't a bit nice to think about how life went on—papers got delivered, papers got read, that kind of thing—when one wasn't counting on it, was it. But never mind. It was all very, very nice and she had only an hour before sent off her blessings to that most fortunate girl, Miss Nancy Dupree. Who was, she believed, the same Miss Nancy Dupree known to her friends in the East Bay Junior Assistance League as "Bugsy"? Just so. Nicknames. Cute as a bug's ear. You knew that any girl who'd call herself Bugsy had a sense of fun. There was one *little* thing. She did think, couldn't help thinking, that since his plans must have been more or *less* settled last night, he might have told her his surprise then. Of course they had been pretty busy last night, sorting his laundry, wondering where she had put the razor blades she had brought the day before, typing out his application for an extension on his personal loan at the Wells Fargo. There had been scarcely a minute for surprises, had there. Or possibly he had not known then. Possibly he and Bugsy had just decided late last night on the long-distance telephone and Bugsy had thrown on her forest-green blazer and rushed the news right over to the *Chronicle*. What a stroke of luck, deciding in time for the Valley Edition.

He did not know why he had called her at all. He should have known that she would only behave as stupidly as she was behaving now. Count on her to act like a gauche, bitchy little girl.

Oh. So he was drinking. She supposed he must be fairly proud of himself. She knew he was drinking or he would not have had the courage to call her in the first place. Drinking or not, his character was nothing to write home about. Even to his home, wherever and whatever that was. And as for that talent of which he was so proud, she could walk out the door and get it better from the first picker she came across. Without any of the games.

She could go to hell.

But Jesus Christ, baby. Anybody who'd call herself Bugsy.

Although she had torn the announcement from the paper expressly so that Everett and Lily would not see it, they would know by sundown anyway. Everyone on the river got the San Francisco papers. She had wanted them not to know because she did not want Ryder's name taken in vain. In the strictest sense, which was the sense Martha prided herself upon, Ryder was not in the least in the wrong. Ryder was simply the way he was, and she had known all along how he was. To have persisted, knowing that, was to have taken the responsibility upon herself. *I'm quite old enough and more than smart enough to know what I'm doing*, she had told Everett three years ago, had told Lily before that, had told even her father although not in so many words. She had known it so thoroughly that for the past two years she had not even thought of marrying Ryder, except as a dark contract they could undertake if all else failed, an unattended ritual during which both would avert their eyes, a civil ceremony incorporating the more lurid aspects of a black mass. But despite what she knew, she had, every time he smiled and put his hand on her neck and said *whose girl*, smiled back. *Your girl.*

To avoid Lily and Everett, she sat in her room for the rest of the afternoon, knitting and trying to call up a catalogue of Ryder's virtues against the probability that someone would question his possession of any. Ryder loved small children, at least if they were clean and attractive. He delighted in giving people presents. He had once driven straight through from Los Angeles in order to be at the ranch in time for her birthday. Occasionally when he thought she was asleep he would kiss her ear and whisper that he loved her, although he rarely did either when he thought she was awake. (That, however, was not a widely employable defense, and neither was the fact that he had once at a party knocked out a drunk, someone they did not know, for pointing at Lily and saying *There goes the easiest lay in the room, I can always spot them, something scared in their eyes.* As she had explained to Ryder, she had appreciated it for Everett's sake.) He always asked her if his tie looked all right with his jacket, expressed concern about the correct length for her skirts, and had once gotten up at four o'clock in the morning and met every plane into Sacramento until noon on the off chance that she might be flying home from Carmel that morning.

Again in the strictest sense, she had thought of nothing which could be accurately described as a virtue, but by six o'clock she had thought of so many things that had at one time or another pleased or amused her that she put her head between her knees and, although she had regularly screamed at him to get away from her and stay away from her, cried for the loss of Ryder Channing.

When she saw the candles lighted in the dining room, she knew that Lily had heard. Lily would have heard and lighted the candles and brought up a bottle of wine and told China Mary to find some artichokes because Martha liked them. Lily and her mother were both great little candle lighters. The river could be in flood, the barn could be on fire, an escaped convict could be holding them hostage: you'd find Lily and Edith Knight in the dining room, lighting the candles and chatting about silver patterns, asking the convict if he would mind a dry white instead of a red with the roast. It was so pronounced an act that Lily's every gesture toward domestic gaiety or grace aroused the suspicion that disaster was at hand.

Avoiding Lily's eyes, she let Lily and Everett know, before the artichokes were on the table, that she had known for months. She had not only known for months, but she could not be more pleased. Really. It was exactly what Ryder needed. Of course she had met her. She had met her a year ago, and had hoped then that Ryder would marry her. Lily would have to meet her. They would ask Ryder to bring her out.

Lily thought, although she was not certain, that she had known the girl's older sister the year she was at Berkeley. Sally Dupree. A Kappa, lived in Piedmont off Mountain, near that circle. Would that be the family, she wondered.

That would be the family.

Money, then.

Con*struct*ion money, Everett believed. Wartime. It was all mixed up in his mind with Henry Kaiser.

It had, Lily corrected him, nothing to do with Henry Kaiser. It was perhaps the same kind of thing, but not connected in any way. No *ships*. And although she was perfectly aware that Dupree Development Inc. had gotten big during and since the war, the Duprees had not exactly been on the street when she knew Sally in 1940.

Ships or no, Martha supposed that Nancy Dupree had probably come out at the Fairmont in a white dress ordered from Elizabeth Arden.

Lily was not sure. Those construction people were a little different, particularly if they lived in the East Bay. It was not as if her name were Crocker or Spreckels or something like that.

No, Martha agreed, it was not. It certainly was not as if her name were Crocker or Spreckels or something like that. What a revelation, Lily's sudden grasp on the San Francisco social scene. Was it possible that Lily had at hand a copy of the 1948 San Francisco *Social Register*?

Never mind about that, Lily said. Just never mind. Anyway. Sally Dupree, the sister, had been much the same type as that girl of Everett's who played tennis. Alice whatever her name was.

Annis, Everett said. Annis McMahon.

She had known it was something like Alice.

Perhaps, Everett suggested, Martha would like to take a trip.

A trip. Whenever Everett could think of nothing else to do with her, he urged her to take a trip. There was nothing like a trip.

She could, Everett pressed, visit Sarah in Philadelphia. Sarah could take her to New York and she could buy some new clothes, see some plays.

Philadelphia was not universally considered, or so Martha had heard, the ideal winter vacation spot. She had not heard of the smart San Francisco set—Crocker, Spreckels, names like that—wintering there in years.

Perhaps the Islands, Lily improvised. There were all kinds of people Martha knew in Honolulu right now and she could have a marvelous time. As a matter of fact she might plan to take the *Lurline* over with Francie Templeton in January.

It was all, Martha said, Del Paso Heights to her.

It was a joke, Lily explained to Everett. It was something funny his father had once said.

Speaking of funny things people said, Martha wanted to tell them something funny Nancy Dupree said the first night she met her. At a party in Piedmont. Nancy (who was, Lily and Everett should know, called "Bugsy," that's right, Bugsy Dupree) had told her that the only ships to take in the Pacific were the American President ships, because they were jammed with fascinating people—Japanese engineers, people like that.

There you were, Lily declared. She was exactly like her sister and they were both exactly like that Alice McMahon.

Annis. Annis McMahon.

Well, whatever. She would have said something like that. She would have told you about the fascinating Japanese engineers you met on the American President ships.

What was wrong with Japanese engineers, Everett wanted to know. If you were on a ship going to Japan you presumably liked Japanese people in the first place.

Everett was, Lily said, missing the point altogether. There was nothing wrong with Japanese engineers. It was simply that a certain kind of girl would say that. Sally Dupree. That tennis player.

Everett did not recall that Lily had even met Annis McMahon.

Well, she had. And if she was not mistaken Martha had too. Hadn't Martha met Annis McMahon?

Martha did not know. Possibly she had.

She did not raise her eyes from her own hand on the table, as if she could scarcely summon up enough interest to answer at all.

After Lily had left the table to put Knight and Julie to bed, Martha lit a cigarette from the candles and then blew them out one by one.

"I wish we had some brandy."

"We drank two bottles of wine between us."

"That's not the same thing, Everett. Get with it."

"You drink too much."

"Now Everett. Sometimes I drink too much. Sometimes you drink too much. But neither of us quote unquote drinks too much. Francie Templeton is practically the only person you know who categorically drinks too much."

"You are tight right now."

"All right," Martha said without interest, scraping candle wax off the tablecloth with her fingernail.

"I never did like Channing," Everett said suddenly. "I never did think you should be messing around with him."

"Everett. Ryder Channing has been and is now my best friend."

She pushed back her chair and stood up. "Now you sing some Christmas carols with me."

Everett stood behind her at the piano, singing an occasional phrase of "O Little Town of Bethlehem" as she picked out the notes with her right hand.

Still playing, she said abruptly: "Remember before Sarah got married when we used to go to Carmel at Christmas time?"

"Yes," he said. "I remember."

"You remember we'd go to the graveyard first and put a holly wreath on Mother's grave, then drive on down to Carmel?"

"I remember," he repeated. "Why?"

"It was nice then, that's all."

Over and over Martha played the same phrase: *Above thy deep and dreamless sleep the silent stars go by.* Because she had not turned on the lights, the blaze from the fireplace and the colored lights on the Christmas tree flickered all around the room.

"I always think about how nice it was at Christmas, that's all." She stopped playing. "I always thought it was you and me together, against Sarah and Daddy. Because they remembered Mother and you really didn't. I always figured they thought she wouldn't have died if it hadn't been for me."

"You shouldn't have thought that," Everett said absently, letting his hand drop to her hair.

"But anyway I did. And we always took that same house out on the point?"

"It was Aunt Grace's house."

"I thought it was ours. I looked for it when I was down last year but I couldn't find it. And you always carried me upstairs to bed?"

"I'd forgotten."

"But you did." As she turned to face him his hand dropped from her hair to her shoulder. "You *did.*"

"I remember now, baby." She turned back to the keyboard and began again to pick out notes. *How still we see thee lie.*

"What about it?" he said.

"Nothing about it." She twisted her shoulder away from his hand. "This piano needs *tun*ing."

Because Everett told her that she should see some people and buy some new clothes, she did. She went to parties every night between Christmas and New Year's, and on the first business day of 1949 she went to San Francisco and charged $758.90 to her and Lily's account at Magnin's. Because she could not see that dressing like what the elevator advertisements called a Marima Shop Young Fashionable had gotten her very far in the past, she went not to the sixth floor, where she and Lily normally shopped, but to the third, where nothing was on racks and all the labels were oversized, heavy enough to stand alone, and embroidered with such intrinsically expensive words as *Traina-Norell for I. Magnin.* "Something way out," she told the saleswoman, and she came home that night with a red coat, a white chiffon dinner dress, two black lace slips, and a white silk dress appliquéd with silk butterflies the exact pale color of her hair. The dress with the butterflies cost $250 and was expressly to wear on the twenty-second of January at Nancy Dupree's wedding. Although Everett thought $250 a great deal to pay for a little dress with some butterflies thrown on it, it was all, he agreed, way out, and on the day of the wedding, when she put on the dress for the first time, he assured her that she had never looked prettier. Because Lily and the children had a virus and Everett did not want to leave them, Martha drove down alone to the wedding, rehearsing out loud, in the car, things she could say. *Ryder's so lucky. She looks beautiful. I've never been busier.* By the time she reached Piedmont, however, she could remember none of them; her hands were shaking on the steering wheel and as she drove past the church she did not see how she could possibly go in. Anyway she would be late by the time she found a parking place, and anyway no one ever noticed who was at the church. She would drive around and pull herself together and by the time she got to the reception it would be all right. Although she began to feel better immediately, her hands began shaking again as she drove to the reception, and she sat in the Claremont Country Club parking lot for ten minutes, putting on lipstick and then blotting it off, trying to brush back a strand of hair which fell forward over her face, and smoking one cigarette after another. It was all right, however, once she went inside. Everyone said how marvelous she looked, and she kissed Ryder on the cheek and told him she already loved both his bride and his sister (whom she had just met and been delighted to find rather tackily dressed); she drank a great deal of champagne and danced with everyone—it was a good dress to dance in because the butterflies appeared to move—and when she left it was with a man who seemed to be about forty and who had a suite at the Claremont Hotel. She stayed there until 4 A.M., when she woke up and told him that the way he looked disgusted her, the way he talked disgusted her, and she disgusted herself, she was no better than Lily. Who was Lily, he wanted to know; *she's my sister*, Martha said, *and you aren't good enough to say her name.*

I've never been busier, she told them at the wedding, and in fact she had not been. Although neither she nor Lily had ever joined the Junior League, Martha now became a provisional member, spent every evening and most afternoons in town, and at the end of February calculated that she had received proposals of marriage from two of the boys with whom she had grown up and had gone to bed with three, counting one who was married and not counting the man she had met at Nancy Dupree's wedding reception whose last name she did not remember. (She believed he had something to do with shopping centers, but it was all mixed up in her mind, as in Everett's, with Henry Kaiser.) Since everyone else was at the moment married that just about cleaned the situation up, and when she tallied up their assets and their liabilities, the balance was, as she had hoped it would be, *nada*.

All the connections had been broken, all the bridges burned miles back in the country she had crossed to achieve this insular victory. Even Ryder was included in her pervasive contempt: he could no longer touch her. There, the battle had turned. All the others had been civilian casualties, lost somewhere beyond the front lines: Channing was her dam on the Ruhr, her Guadalcanal, her Stalingrad. Thinking herself victorious, she despised all the vulnerable: all those who liked or disliked, wanted or did not want, damaged themselves with loving and hating and migraine headaches. She imagined that she had emerged triumphant, and that the banner she planted read *Noli Me Tangere*.

20

IT WAS a season of promise for anyone with a little land or a little money or even nothing more than an eye on the main chance; it was a season of promise for Ryder Channing, back in town with his bride after a three-week honeymoon in Acapulco; and it should be, Martha thought some nights as she was going to sleep, a season of promise for her. The mornings were more difficult: some mornings she did not want to get up at all. Some mornings she could get up only if she had already scheduled every minute of the day, which she learned immediately to do. She went everywhere, met everyone. She met builders, promoters, people looking for factory sites and talking about a deep-water channel and lobbying for federal dams; people neither Everett nor Lily would have known existed had she not told them. She went to large parties at new country clubs, went to small parties at new apartment houses, and went, almost every afternoon, to inspect subdivisions opened by one or another of the boys she knew who were going into the real-estate business. Although Lily and Everett claimed to see no distinctions among the miles of pastel stucco houses, Martha knew better. It was, she explained, a matter of detail. Some builders used panels of redwood siding; others, an imitation fieldstone veneer around each door. In one tract ("Executive Living on Low F.H.A.") each back yard included a small kidney-shaped swimming pool, a cabaña, and a neatly framed placard listing "Pool Rules"; most subdivisions, however, had only Community Pools, sometimes known as Swimming Clubs, and in any case surrounded by Cyclone fencing. Robles de la Sierra, a tract north of town, afforded prospective buyers "a setting with the romance of An Old Spanish Land Grant plus No Sewer Bonds, 40-Gallon Fast-Recovery Water Heaters, and Sidewalks In"; at Rancho Valley, selling points included a leaded-glass window on the exterior of each three-car attached garage, for "the same gracious finish throughout, VETS NO DOWN." And if Lily and Everett wanted distinctions, they had only to consider Riverside City, the most distinctive feature of which was that it was "dedicated to the concept of Retirement." Another distinctive feature of Riverside City was that it was a project initiated by Dupree Development Inc., and another was that Ryder Channing had in February been placed in nominal charge of development, but never mind that. It was a far, far grander scheme than might be indicated by the fact that Ryder was in charge of it. Although none of Riverside City's projected 37,000 houses had yet been built, quarter-acre lots had been sold by agents all over the country, an artificial lake was under construction, and *esprit* among future citizens was renewed weekly by the four-page *Riverside City Sun*, mailed from the Dupree Building in Oakland. "QUESTION: Although we live at present in Chicago, we enjoy our subscription to the *Sun* because we intend to build a home on our lot in the near future. My question is, about the plastic lining now being installed in the bottom of Riverside Lake, won't it make our lake look peculiar? ANSWER: *You can relax. The lining will be covered with six inches of earth, so unless you come out to inspect it now, you'll never even see it.* QUESTION: What kind of plants grow best in Riverside City? ANSWER: *We suggest you correspond with two of our pioneer citizens-to-be, the Mesdames Ada Travers and Bertha Kling, founders of the Riverside City Garden Club. They have already collected an impressive file of government pamphlets on the horticulture of the area. There are no weeds growing under these ladies.*"

Some nights at dinner Martha would announce that she planned to take some land and develop it herself and make them all rich; some nights she would sit at the table, not eating, and make Everett promise, again and again, that he and Sarah would never try to sell the ranch without her. Other nights she would not come to dinner at all, but would go instead to her room and lie in the dark with the sheet over her head, pretending, when Everett or Lily opened the door, to be asleep.

At six o'clock on the sixteenth of March, Martha was sitting in the bar at Del Paso Country Club wondering how it would feel to get laid in the rain on the golf course and listening to Sam Bradley, one of the river boys who had gone into real estate, explain how he had happened to join Del Paso: it was deductible and it was good business. Although they had been sitting in the bar an hour, Martha had seen no one she had ever seen before with two exceptions, the bartender and a gynecologist's wife whose picture was frequently in the paper in connection with the Opera Guild. "Meet a President," the pictures were always captioned. "No Stranger to the Gavel." No matter how hard you tried it was difficult to keep up with who was who now, and on the whole Martha would rather be on the golf course, but there were always too many people, everywhere.

Did Sam know any of these people, she wanted to know.

What the hell difference did it make if he knew any of these people. All he wanted to do, as he had been telling her off and on for twenty minutes, was get the hell out of here and drive up to that Mexican place in Jackson for dinner.

She *loved* that Mexican place. She had told him three times she loved that Mexican place. But Jackson was fifty miles away and it had been raining for three days and she really did not feel like driving fifty miles and back in the rain in his Austin-Healey.

They could get another car. They could get his brother's car. They could get her car. He hadn't planned to take the goddamn Austin-Healey.

Since both his brother's car and her car were approximately thirty-five miles from Del Paso and in the opposite direction from Jackson, that made it a drive of eighty-five miles each way. Besides, she did not even think the Mexican place was open week nights. Anyway there was illegal gambling there and he did not want, did he, to get caught in a raid. That wouldn't be very good business, would it.

Go to hell, he said. He would telephone ahead.

All right, she said, go find out, and as Sam got up from the table she saw Ryder Channing walk in from the golf course with a balding fat man. It was the first time she had seen Ryder without Nancy Dupree since December and she was faintly depressed to find that she still could not look at him as she looked at other people. She had seen him walking through the door and had thought *Ryder*, just as she always had, without any of the instant judgments she normally made about people she saw. She had been making judgments upon Sam Bradley from the moment he picked her up; she had already made maybe twenty small judgments upon the man with Ryder. But when she looked at Ryder all she thought was *Ryder*.

The other man was, she learned when Ryder brought him to the table, a Cadillac dealer from down the Valley who played, although Ryder had beaten him 79–88, a great game of golf.

"The rain put you off your game," Martha suggested to the Cadillac dealer.

He shrugged.

"You must have known Martha's father," Ryder said, not looking at Martha.

"Who's your dad, Marty?"

"John McClellan."

The Cadillac dealer looked blankly at Ryder. "Sure. Sure I know him. I probably run into him at Sacramento Rotary."

"I don't think so," Martha said. "Actually he's been dead since 1944."

"Well," said the dealer, "I wasn't here in 1944."

"How you been?" Martha asked Ryder.

"I'm fine. You look real good."

"I've been sleeping and eating a lot. I hear you're living in the old Carmelo place."

"A friend of Bugsy's family bought it and lent it to us until he decides what to do with it. We're going to build as soon as Bugsy finds some plans she likes."

"Great little girl," the dealer said. "The finest."

"I always liked the Carmelo place." Martha smoothed her gloves in her lap. "They gave a dance once on the third floor and lined both the stairways with azalea. It was about the first dance I ever went to."

"Termites," the dealer said. "Rotten with termites."

"Bugsy wants one storey," Ryder said.

"Where is she?" the Cadillac dealer demanded querulously. "Why aren't they here?" He turned to Martha. "She's shopping with my wife. Mitzi said they'd meet us here at six-thirty."

"It's not quite six-thirty," Ryder said. "I saw you last week at Nancy Slaughter's. You were just leaving."

"That's right," she said. "We were there a few minutes."

"Listen, Marth." He absently transferred some change from one pocket to another. "I'm glad I ran into you. I'm going to be out the river road tomorrow. Maybe I'll stop by."

"I won't be home. But I'm sure Lily and Everett would like seeing you."

"Some other time." He stood up as Sam came back.

"Remember me to your dad, Marty," the Cadillac dealer said. "*Hasta luego* for now."

When Ryder arrived the next afternoon at two o'clock Martha was alone in the house: Lily had taken China Mary and the children to have their chest X-rays; Everett was out working on the levees. The rain had gone to the mountains and was melting the snow too fast. Although Lily had wanted Martha to come have her chest X-rayed with them ("Talk about sickly, you look tubercular right now"), Martha had refused: she wanted to lie down. She had not gotten home from Jackson until three A.M., and Sam Bradley, although she had told him it was not good business, had stayed until nearly five. *I can't abide your kind*, she had ended up screaming at him; she did not know what had happened but it was the same thing that always happened. She would have a couple of drinks or simply get very tired or sometimes just wake up in the morning despising someone, everyone. If it happened in the morning she could lie there, hating, until it wore itself out, but if it happened around people she always ended up screaming. The very presence of Sam Bradley had seemed a personal affront to her: his bow tie a monument to both his vacuity and her lack of taste; his enthusiasm for the Mexican place in Jackson an affectation so transparent that she was mortified to have abetted it (he had greeted the cook warmly as "Mamacita," and Martha had looked on with approval); his brand of cigarettes (not her own) the crushing evidence of his mediocrity, his blatancy, his subtle lack of the male principle. It had begun when Sam said that no matter what Everett said, Earl Warren was an intelligent and reasonable man; it could have begun as well had he merely said he liked her dress, or did not like a book he was reading. She had once turned viciously on Ryder for changing his shirt before dinner. His vanity. His shallowness. His carelessness. His thoughtlessness, his selfishness. Did he think the whole world existed simply to provide him with clean shirts. Even remembering it, she felt quite dizzy with loathing for Ryder.

*

"I thought you might be here," Ryder said when she opened the door.

"I'm trying to sleep." She did not ask him to take off his raincoat but simply stood there, trying for once to examine him closely, to make some final damning judgment. She remembered once seeing in his apartment a postcard from a girl, possibly even Nancy Dupree—it had been signed "XXXX and you know what, from B"—which read "Loved seeing you Saturday nite you looked so sexy in your white pants." Although "sexy" was not a word she had ever applied to anyone, she had tried to see Ryder that way for several days. But all she had seen, then as now, was *Ryder*, and when she said, the next time he wore white pants, "You look fat-assed in those pants, Ryder, they don't flatter you," it was no judgment, only response.

"What are you looking at," he said.

"I've been trying to sleep," she repeated, defeated. "I'm not looking at anything."

Fifteen minutes later he had her down on the floor; she had refused to go near the couch.

"You want it," he said. She had her legs crossed and her face turned away from him.

"I do not."

"What difference do you think it makes now." He pushed her skirt up around her waist. "After I've screwed you maybe four, five times a week every week for the past five years."

"Four and a half years," she said faintly; his logic remained intact.

"Four and a half years."

"I never wanted it." Recognizing immediately that this clear untruth tended only to weaken her position, she amended it: "A lot of times I only pretended to want it."

"You want it now, all right. You don't have to start acting half-assed with me."

After he had gone (*Whose girl? Your girl*) Martha went upstairs and lay on her bed until she heard, just as it was getting dark, the children's voices downstairs.

She found Lily in the kitchen, pulling off Julie's galoshes. "Where's Everett?" she asked.

"Still working on the levees. I don't know."

"I'm going to see if I can find him." Martha pulled on a raincoat, buttoned it briskly, and then, as if she had forgotten why she wanted the raincoat in the first place, sat down and slowly began to unbutton it again.

"You're undoing your coat," Julie said, laying her head in Martha's lap. "Where you going?"

Martha smoothed Julie's hair. "I guess nowhere. I guess I couldn't find him."

"I guess not," Julie agreed. She was the kind of child who agreed with anything said by an adult. "You coming to the parade?"

"What parade is that?"

"The Saint Patrick's Day Parade. It's Saint Patrick's Day in town."

"Who all's going?"

"Me and Mommy and Knight. Only Knight can't go if he doesn't apologize for breaking my pedometer."

"Knight broke your pedometer? However will you figure mileage?"

"That's the thing. Anyway, two of our cousins are in it."

"In what?"

"In the par*ade*," Lily said. "You aren't following this very closely. Sally Randall's children are marching and I thought we should go wave at them. We're going to have hamburgers first. Why don't you get dressed and come."

"I guess I'm *dressed* all right. I don't guess I have to get all done up for the Saint Patrick's Day Parade, do I. You know what it'll be. There'll be a bagpipe band playing 'The Campbells Are Coming.' The Air Force Band playing 'Loch Lomond.' And a battalion of small girls in spangled two-piece bathing suits and white plastic Stetsons doing close-order drill to 'Temptation.' *You-came-Ah was a-lone-Ah should-a-known —You were Taymp-tay-shun*."

"*Mar*tha," Julie screamed, throwing herself at Martha's knees. "Stop making fun."

"I'm not making fun." Martha picked Julie up and swung her around. "I am telling you gospel. Because baby, I have seen Saint Patrick's Day before, *seen it all*. 'Temptation' will be *sung*—through a public-address system on a truck behind the small girls—by a mother wearing a rose crêpe dress with bugle beads, a short red car coat, and harlequin-framed glasses. So much for that. There will also be the Sheriff's Posse: fifteen dentists on fifteen palominos. And Julie baby, we're so wide open out here there'll probably even be the Masons."

"The Masons are not our cousins."

"That's right, baby. The Randalls are our cousins."

Lily stood up and picked up a lipstick from the shelf beside the sink. "You coming or not?"

Suddenly listless, Martha did not answer.

"If you're coming you better put on some shoes."

"What time is it?"

"Six. A little before."

"I was supposed to go somewhere. Sam Bradley and his brother were supposed to pick me up at six-thirty."

Lily blotted her lipstick on a piece of paper toweling and looked at Martha. "Then you can't come."

"Yes I can. I can come all right." Martha stood up and took from the pocket of her raincoat the dark glasses she wore almost constantly now.

"You want to call Sam before we go?"

"If I wanted to call Sam I'd *call* him, I mean wouldn't I?"

By the time they had driven into town ("Knight can look for Nevada plates and Julie for Arizona. That's right, there *are* more people in Arizona but you forget Nevada is closer. All right, *both* of you look for Arizona plates") and stopped at a drive-in for hamburgers ("I said hamburgers, Knight, I did not say steak sandwich and I did not say chicken-in-a-basket. All right, chiliburgers. You don't even *like* chili"), the parade was already underway: they had missed, a policeman told them as Lily was locking the station wagon, the Mayor's Cavalcade and the Knights of Columbus. "Cheer up, sweetie," he said to Julie. "There'll be more."

"You bet there will, sweetie," Martha whispered, giggling with Julie as fifteen palominos pranced into view, and then Knight was yelling *Hey Horse! Why did the chicken cross the road?* and Horse turned out to be not a horse at all but the name by which Sally Randall's son was known to his intimates; not long after Horse Randall and the Elk Grove Firehouse Five passed by, followed by a shivering blond drum majorette and a ragged line of high-school boys whistling and hooting, the rain began again, and when they looked for Martha she was gone. By the time they saw her, standing in front of the Rexall drugstore on the corner, the crowd was breaking up, going for cover, scattering into doorways and automobiles.

"Meet us at the car," Lily shouted over the idling of motors, the shifting of gears.

Instead Martha ran back down the block to where Lily stood with the children. Rain streamed down her face, across her sunglasses, down the neck of her unbuttoned raincoat.

"I was trying to call Sarah. Nobody answered."

"Sarah? In Philadelphia?"

Martha took Julie's hand and followed Lily and Knight to the station wagon. "I wanted to tell her about the parade," she said, lifting Julie into the middle seat.

"The parade," Lily repeated after her, fumbling beneath the brake pedal for the keys she had just found and dropped.

"Honestly," Martha said. "You'd think there might have been *some*body there."

"You can try her again when we get home." Lily fitted the key into the ignition with meticulous care while she tried to work the parade, the rain, and Sarah into some reasonable sequence. "By then it'll be after midnight in Philadelphia. Maybe they'll be home then."

"Oh no," Martha said. "It's only five-thirty there now. The man in the Rexall told me."

"It's almost eight-thirty here. You *know* it's later there."

"I'm sure I don't know why the man in the Rexall would have told me a deliberate *lie*."

"If he told you that he just didn't *know*. We *know*."

Martha shrugged. "I don't know. I don't know what to believe."

Lily switched on the windshield wipers but did not start the engine.

"Anyway it's too late," Martha said. "If it's midnight there, as you insist it is, it's too late."

"Too late for what?"

Martha leaned against the window and took off her sunglasses. Her eyes were closed. "I don't know," she said. "I didn't want to go home and I thought I might go there, but it's too late."

"I don't know what you're *talk*ing about."

"Sarah. I'm talking about my sister. I wanted to talk to Sarah. If you don't mind."

21

THEY BURIED Martha's body beneath the cherry tree near the levee on the morning of the twenty-second of March. Everett and Henry Sears (who had been sleeping off the flu and a four-day drunk when Everett had the night before begun shouting and pounding at the door of the foreman's cottage *Sears you bastard Sears get out here*) carried the coffin: a long rope-handled sea chest, packed for the past thirty years with Mildred McClellan's linens, ends of lace, a box of jet beading from a dress, and the ivory fan carried by Martha's great-great-grandmother Currier at Governor Leland Stanford's Inaugural Ball in 1862; unpacked the night before when Everett said *I'm telling you for the last time, Lily, get McGrath out of here, get his deputy out of here, and get that son of a bitch quack doctor out of here, she's my sister, I'm going to bury her, and I'm going to bury her on the ranch.*

Lily walked behind them, her arms full of flowers. Everett had been out before dawn, pulling up every daffodil left after the rain, tearing down whole branches of camellias. When they reached the place Everett had chosen they laid the sea chest on the wet ground, and Everett spelled Sears digging the grave. Numb with the morning cold, Lily stood holding the flowers and listening to the water. Every hour now, the river ran faster and higher with the melting mountain snow: tearing at the banks, jamming together logs and debris and then smashing through the jams.

As she watched Sears dig it occurred to her that Martha's body could well be washed out by evening, the unnailed lid of the sea chest ripped open and Martha free again in the water in the white silk dress with the butterflies. (*$250, I should wear it every day, every evening, and every night to bed*, she had said last night when she was dressing for the party and Lily had warned the rain might spot the silk, *Just ask Everett if I shouldn't.*) It was not right to bury her this way: McGrath had said it (*I'm telling you, Everett, it's against the law of the State of California*); Edith Knight had said it this morning when she came in her robe to pick up the children (*I'm not talking* *about the law. I'm not talking about any law run through by the undertakers' lobby. I'm talking about what's right and what's wrong*); the doctor had said it; she had said it herself. *Everett baby you don't know what you're doing*. They had each said it for different reasons and Everett had listened to none of them.

"You hear it rising?" Everett said, looking up at the levee.

Sears stopped digging to fasten his jacket against the wind. "Going to crest at thirty-eight."

"When's that?"

"Near to noon. Thiel's Landing." Sears was coughing now. He wiped the back of his hand across his mouth and picked up the shovel again.

Everett put his hand on Lily's shoulder.

"You want to move into town?"

She shook her head. "I don't see any need."

Sears looked up. "There ain't no problem this far up. Downriver maybe."

"The Engineers might blast it tonight. Upstream. We'd get some water."

"They wouldn't blast a levee until they'd evacuated," Lily said. "We'd know."

Everett shrugged and took the shovel from Sears.

Because she did not want Everett to see that she was crying Lily shifted the flowers close to her face. It would be all right, these next few hours, if she could keep her mind on the water. Where and when would the levee go, were the levee to go at all: there was the question to consider. Somewhere in her mind was a file of information, gathered and classified every year there was high water, and it was upon those facts that she must now focus her attention. At what point had they opened the Colusa Weir. How many gates were open at the Sacramento Weir. When would the Bypass reach capacity. What was the flood stage at Wilkins Slough. At Rough and Ready Bend. Fremont Weir. Rio Vista.

Obscurely comforted by her ability to remember, however uselessly, flood stages which bore no relation to this year's flood, she stood with her eyes closed and did not think of Martha for half an hour.

"All right," Everett said then, propping the shovel against the tree. "That's enough."

He took one end of the chest by its rope handle and Sears took the other; together they lowered it into the grave, already filling with seepage. Lily kneeled in the mud to drop the flowers on the chest, but Everett pulled her up.

"Not yet." He motioned Sears to stand back from the grave.

Oh Christ, Lily thought. He'll say that prayer and they'll cover her with dirt and that's all there is. *Christ in heaven.* How many people did you bury before you stopped screaming inside at the thought of that first night in the dark.

"*Gentle Jesus, meek and mild*," Everett repeated without inflection. It was the prayer he and Martha had learned as children. "*Look upon a little child. Pity her simplicity and suffer her to come to thee.*"

"God bless Martha, amen," Lily whispered.

Everett did not look at her. "Now," he said.

She dropped the camellias into the grave and stood back.

"Henry's going back to the house with you." Everett picked up the shovel. "Get him some breakfast."

China Mary was not in the kitchen: she had gone, late the afternoon before, to visit her sister in Courtland. They should have called her after it happened. They should have called and brought her home before they buried Martha; she had raised Martha. But there had been so many people last night: the sheriff, the deputy, the respirator squad, the doctor, Sears, even the children, wakened by the sirens; and by the time they were alone there was no use calling anyone because Everett wanted no one there. They should have called Sarah. They should have called maybe fifty people but above all they should have called China Mary and they should have called Sarah. *Sarah can't come, there's no reason to call her*, Everett had said. *It's too late. She left here of her own will and anyway it's too late now.* She had said *You're getting worse than your father was*, knowing that Sarah would hear about it from her, would read that her sister had drowned when the mail arrived one morning next week at her ivied brick house in Bryn Mawr, Pennsylvania, for Lily could never call her alone. She had tried to call Everett when his father died but had been unable to say it. Martha had finally taken the telephone and said it.

Lily dropped her raincoat on the table and held out her hand for Sears's jacket.

"Sit down. I'll fix bacon and eggs and biscuits. I had the biscuit batter made for Everett but he didn't eat."

"No bacon." Sears paused. "He don't seem so good."

"He's upset. That's all. All his family's gone now." She forgot for the moment Sarah, and when she did remember Sarah it did not much change the sense of what she had said to Sears.

"Got you and two kids. That's family."

Lily did not say anything.

"I didn't figure her that way," Sears said after a while.

"What way."

"I didn't figure her to do something like that. She grew up on the river, she should have known enough not to take a boat like that out when it's in flood."

"I don't know."

"Where'd she think she was going to get to?"

"I don't know," Lily repeated.

She knew, she knew better than that: Everett had said it, almost shouted it, after he carried Martha's drenched body up from the dock. Down there on the dock he had not said anything much to anyone. He said nothing to Lily from the time he first shouted from the driveway *Get McGrath the hell over here with a respirator* until the time, almost an hour and a half later, he laid Martha's body on her bed upstairs. By the time she had called McGrath at home and run down to the dock, Everett was already in the water, on the end of the rope Sears was still knotting around a piling. *What happened*, she kept saying, and finally Sears said *Martha. She was holding onto the boat but I don't know how long.* In the dark (they did not have the flares until McGrath arrived a few minutes later) she could see nothing, neither Everett nor Martha, not even the boat, overturned and caught on a trunk off the far bank. If Sears had not told her about the boat she would not have known that much, because Everett, after he brought Martha in with him on the rope, said nothing. In the brilliant cold light of the flares they had watched then for an hour while the boys with the respirator knelt over Martha on the wet dock, but it was nowhere near an hour before they all knew, all but Everett and maybe Everett knew too. "Thank Christ he didn't lose his head and go out there without the rope," McGrath said to Lily after the first fifteen minutes. "You'd have lost them both." "We haven't lost anybody," Everett said flatly, looking up from where he crouched at Martha's head, staring at McGrath with confused malice; McGrath looked at his deputy and they both looked away from Lily. It had been five or six minutes later when the doctor arrived and two or three minutes after that when he pronounced Martha dead. "She's alive," Everett said. "You don't know anything about her." Thirty minutes later he admitted what they all knew: "All right," he said. "All right."

She knew better than that: Edith Knight had said it, when Lily called her to come for the children. "That little girl, that little fool," she repeated again and again. "She knew better." It was for Edith Knight that rare event, a happening in which she could not immediately perceive the providential pattern, the point, the unmistakable, however elusive, benefit. Usually she was able to make death seem the most fortunate of circumstances, an unlooked-for circumvention of further bother for the deceased; sudden death was, logically, the supreme economy. "What a blessing he went without a long illness," she said regularly of Walter Knight; "One thing, she had certainly gotten the good of her furs," she reflected with sincere satisfaction when informed that a cousin had met death in the crash of a Piper Apache over Pyramid Lake. Of Martha's and Everett's mother, she frequently observed to Lily: "Mildred went the best way to go, everything in order, and I only hope I can do as well." This observation usually accompanied the cleaning of a closet or the discarding of a memento, because what she meant by "order" was that Mildred McClellan, shortly before her death in childbirth, had cleaned two back bedrooms of the McClellan house, disposing of several cartons of snapshots, dance programs, newspaper clippings, unmatched gloves too good to throw away, sketches of the Yosemite Valley made on her wedding trip, and the souvenirs of a trip to Chicago taken before her marriage. Having one's things in order was a persistent note in Edith Knight's reflections upon death: the ideal life, as she saw it, was characterized by the continual jettisoning of accumulated debris. One could leave this world, with planning, exactly as one came into it. Possibly because Martha had accomplished so little in the direction of having her things in order, Edith Knight was pressed to find a rationale for her death, although after a few minutes she had managed to glimpse, in the fact that Martha had not left behind a husband and small babies, an interim silver lining. "A blessing," Lily had agreed wearily on the telephone, and then: "I don't know. I don't know."

She knew better than that: Everett said it, Henry Sears said it, her mother said it, and all she could say was *I don't know*. It did not seem possible that they could not see what had been happening, but then she had not seen it herself until she had looked last night at the notebook. It was not that there was anything in the pages she read that she had not known about Martha. It was only that she had not seen the pattern, and maybe she would not have seen the pattern even last night had Martha not been lying there dead. She had found the notebook in Martha's dressing table when she looked for a brush to untangle her wet hair. It went back three years, with only occasional entries, some in pencil and some in ballpoint pen, hard to read because Martha's handwriting had grown increasingly illegible. The last entry, dated *March 20 1949* and scribbled over seven pages, could not be read at all. In addition to the entries from day to day, there had been separate pages headed "REASONS NOT TO LOVE RYDER," "REASONS NOT TO LOVE EVERETT," "REASONS NOT TO REMEMBER DADDY WITH LOVE." When she heard Everett in the hall Lily had dropped the book into the pocket of her apron, and early this morning she had burned it. She had wanted Everett never to see it, even if he went on thinking the things he thought now. (He had, he told her last night, killed Martha himself. She had been in his care and he had killed her. He had let her go, had not kept her safe. Martha had been, Lily reminded him, twenty-six-years old. He could not have kept her in a glass box. He could have kept care of her, he insisted. He could have done that much. Martha had not been well, Lily said, as close to saying it as she ever came; Martha had not been well a long while. She knew better, he said again. *Christ almighty she looked like a kitten that's been dropped in water and all you see are the little bones. You saw her, Lily. You saw how she looked.*)

The notebook would have changed nothing. Everett would only have blamed himself more for not having seen before what she now saw with ineluctible clarity: the pattern there all along, worked through it all as subtly and delicately as, in a drawing she had loved as a child, the tiger's face had been worked into the treetops. Once you had seen the tiger's face, you could never again see the treetops.

At ten minutes past one Ryder Channing called and asked for Martha.

"She's not here. She died last night."

Channing did not say anything.

"She drowned in the river," Lily added in an expressionless voice, the only one she could master. "She took the boat out and drowned."

"I saw her last night. I saw her at Cassie Waugh's."

"It was later. It was after the party. I didn't see her but it was after that. She drove up in front of the house and Everett went out and she was down at the boat. I don't know what happened."

"I *saw* her. I didn't talk to her but I saw her."

"Well," Lily said, "I didn't see her but she's dead."

"Where is she."

"She's *dead*."

"I mean her body."

She had known what he meant. "We buried her this morning," she said finally.

"Where?"

"Here on the ranch."

Channing said nothing.

"I'm sorry," Lily said before she hung up. "I'm sorry we didn't let you know."

I'm sorry. She was. No matter what she or Everett or even Martha had thought about Ryder Channing, none of it had been his doing. *November 18 1947: In bed all day, told E and L with flu. Ryder sent lilies of the valley, meant no doubt for L. Found field mouse in bathroom closet. Do not tell E because L will make him kill it. April 27 1948: Dinner at R's, things to remember about: (1) making me bring gin (2) sleeping while I fixed dinner (3) asking if I intended to eat dinner in my slip (4) calling me slatternly (5) asking if I had forgotten how to cook spare ribs along with everything else (6) pretending to read while I finished my dinner and his too (7) difficulty of eating spare ribs and artichokes with someone watching (8) getting sick and telling him he was impotent and knowing it reached him because he hit me. July 4 1948: Told R at picnic he was a redneck, white trash, not fit to eat off E's plates. I am reaching him all the time at last. The ways to do it were always transparently clear but I was too much on the defensive to see them. Now he is on the defensive and thrashing blindly: called me "you Okie bitch." February 20 1949: E could fall down dead in front of me and I would think it was nice he didn't live to be old. I am so far away from them all it is incredible when you consider.*

At three o'clock the doorbell rang. It was Joe Templeton, the rain running off his bare head and down his rubber poncho. He had been working on the levees with Ed McGrath. He wanted to say he was sorry about Martha. He had seen Everett about noon but Everett had said nothing.

"Come in for a minute." She did not want to talk to him but could think of nothing else to say. "I'm upstairs sewing."

He followed her upstairs to the sitting room and stood by the window behind her chair. She had not seen him in three weeks and had been trying all winter to avoid seeing him alone.

"Put another stick on the fire," she said. "Everything's too wet to burn."

"I thought you'd have your mother here."

"She took the children this morning. Everett told me to send them to school but they were too upset. I tried to keep them away but Julie saw them carrying her in and started screaming and screaming and finally I gave her some warm milk with bourbon in it and she quieted down."

"I remember I saw them downtown a couple of weeks ago, Julie hanging onto Martha's hand, they looked like mother and daughter. They looked a lot alike."

"Not so much, actually." Lily knew that she was talking too much and too fast but could not seem to stop: she had been unable to talk to Everett. "Martha took her places, played games with her. Anyway Julie kept screaming 'my Martha, my Martha' and Knight was trying not to let his father see him cry but anyway." She trailed off and finished lamely: "They both loved her."

"We saw her last night."

Lily looked at her hands for a long while. "How did she seem," she said finally.

"She looked pretty. She had on a pretty dress."

"Yes."

"We asked her to come to dinner with us. She said she would and then we all had another drink and she turned on Francie. She said Francie was drunk and I was getting drunk and she didn't want to sit around at dinner with a pair of lushes."

He paused, as if demanding an explanation.

"Well," Lily said. "I guess she didn't."

"She was very rude."

"Well, then. It served her right, didn't it. *Sweet Christ.*"

Joe said nothing. Instead he walked across the room and began examining the framed photographs above the fireplace: Martha the night she took all the jumping firsts at the State Fair horse show; Everett at sixteen in an American Legion baseball uniform; Walter Knight, Lily in his lap, in the driver's seat of the Hispano-Suiza he had bought when she was very small.

She got up to close the door to the bedroom. She did not want Joe looking at her unmade bed, the sheets and blankets and her nightgown and Everett's sneakers tumbled together at its foot.

"How are Francie and the twins." She sat down again.

"Francie still wants the divorce," he said after a while. "She was talking about it again last night."

"She was drunk. You said she was drunk."

"I said Martha said she was drunk. What about it. She brings it up cold sober."

"I told you. I don't want to talk about it."

It had been a month since Joe first told her that Francie had again decided to divorce him. Unless he filed a cross-complaint for custody of the twins she would not name Lily. She would simply say mental cruelty if he would keep his hands off the twins. Although she had made this latest decision in the Islands and in order to tell Joe immediately had flown home instead of waiting for the *Lurline*, she still had taken no action. She never did. Francie had been divorcing Joe off and on for fifteen years that Lily knew of; it was their way, although neither seemed to realize it, of periodically reviving interest in each other.

"I told you," Lily added. "If Francie files for divorce you file for custody if you want it. It wouldn't bother me."

"It wouldn't?"

"I said it wouldn't." It was a question so academic as to be absurd.

Joe poked at the fire. "Would you leave him and marry me if Francie goes through with it?"

Lily stood up without saying anything.

"I don't believe you'll ever leave him," Joe said.

"What would you give if I would? I mean *if Francie goes through with it.*"

"What do you mean, what would I give?"

"Would you cut off your right arm?"

"Yes. I'd cut off my right arm. What's the matter with you."

"That's right. You'd cut off your right arm." Lily paused. "You all would. Listen. You get out now but listen to me first: you think you've got some claim on me? You think it was some special thing that made any difference to me? Listen to me. Nothing we did matters to me. Nothing touched Everett and nothing touched me."

She followed Joe downstairs and closed the door behind him, and by the time Everett came home she had straightened the bedrooms, talked twice to Ed McGrath (*Well, it's done. All I can tell you is it's done. We'll try to make it all right later*), and made soup from potatoes and onions and cream, a kind that had comforted her as a child, but before she gave it to Everett she took him to bed and held him against the night and the rain and Martha lying outside the house. When she finally went downstairs in the dark, barefooted, to get the soup, the telephone was ringing.

"You're lying to me," Ryder Channing said.

"Ryder. Stop shouting."

"You lied to me. Get her on the telephone."

"You've been drinking. Go to sleep."

"I said get me Marth."

"Ryder. Please."

"You're lying to me. Get her to the phone."

"I told you. She's dead."

"Screw you," he said. "Screw you all."

*

Everett sat by the bedroom window, the rain splashing from the peeling window sill onto his knees.

"Who called?" he asked without looking up.

She put the tray on the table in front of him and closed the window. "My mother," she said.

22

THE THIRD spring after Martha died (it was 1952, but that was not the way time was reckoned on the ranch) Lily asked Everett if he wanted to divorce her.

He did not. Of course he did not.

What, then, did he want.

He did not, he said, want anything.

It was the year they seldom talked. When they did talk, they talked always about the same thing, although they never called it by name, never even referred to it out loud except very late at night or when they were very tired: *You made me get it*, she would say. Over seven years, the August day she went to San Francisco by herself had become, in its manifold evidence of mutual error, the heaviest weapon in both their arsenals, the massive retaliation each withheld until all else had been exhausted. She was convinced that year not only that she had gone to San Francisco *for Everett* (in a sense she had, and he knew it, and there was the lever) but that Everett had in fact robbed her of her womanhood: she had heard stories of women who after abortions could not become pregnant again, and although she did not want another child, Everett did. *You made me get it.* At such times she would pack a bag for Knight and Julie and take them to stay at her mother's. There in her own room, with the ebony chest brought from the Orient, the stacks of unread Dominican alumnae magazines, and the flowered lawn curtains she had made on her mother's treadle sewing machine the summer she was thirteen, the corrosiveness within her would subside, and she would begin to see Everett not as the blight of her womanhood but, on the contrary, as her only hold on sanity. *He had not held on to Martha but he would hold on to her.* She would imagine Everett dead then, and cry inconsolably for half an hour or forty-five minutes. *None of the others could help her. Joe could not help her and none of the others could help her, none of the one-night, two-night stands, none of the times when she had simply not known what else to do, how else to talk to someone, none of it could help her but Everett, and she would make Everett love her.* After she had stopped crying she would resolutely put on her dark glasses, kiss her mother goodbye in front of the television set (if it was an afternoon when the Dodger games were being televised, her mother sometimes seemed not to have known she was even in the house), and drive back to the ranch. Occasionally she would be gone only a few hours, and she would not then tell Everett that she had left him again.

The fourth spring after Martha died, Lily decided that it would be all right if they could go away together occasionally, leave the ranch. Again and again she asked Everett to take her somewhere, and at last they went, one weekend in June, to a party in San Francisco with some people Everett had known at Stanford. There were two views of the Bay Bridge, one of California Street, and four potted avocado trees (all the girls with whom he had gone to Stanford were now, Everett explained, mysteriously bent upon breaking the Calavo trust); there were repeated assurances that (alternately) Herb Caen or Barnaby Conrad or Dolly Fritz would be dropping by later; and there was Ryder Channing.

She had not seen Ryder since before Martha's death; she had not even talked to him on the telephone since those first few months, when he would sometimes call the house, drunk, and talk, about nothing in particular, for thirty or forty minutes. When he called during the day she had talked to him, but when he began calling late at night she had finally, without telling Everett, made a point before she went to bed of muffling the telephone so that they could not hear it ringing. After that she had only heard about him, here and there, from one or another of the few people they saw: none of the reports quite tallied but none of them were good. She would hear first that he was seen with a succession of unidentified girls in bars frequented by the very young; then that he was never seen, had become a virtual recluse. He was asking for sympathy all over town; he was rude, abusive, burning all his bridges. Nancy was leaving him; he had left Nancy. He had been taken off the Riverside City project because he was pulling some fast ones on Larry Dupree; he had been removed because he never appeared, showed no interest.

Finally: he had moved to San Francisco to follow Nancy; they had moved together to San Francisco because her father ordered them to.

When she first saw him, standing by the bar and laughing, none of it seemed possible: Ryder had never looked better. Deeply tanned and wearing a blue blazer, he had about him the air of the men one saw in liquor advertisements, an air which suggested untroubled afternoons spent sailing off Belvedere, expensive steaks in good restaurants, and the smooth absence of eccentricity achieved only by the recently rich. It was not until she had talked to him for a few minutes that she saw that there was something about his face which belied the sun tan, made the blue blazer seem a kind of fancy dress. His gaze flickered around her without ever quite settling upon her; his smile was less a smile than a tic.

He had, he assured her, the world by the tail. Or just about.

"I'm glad, Ryder."

He just about had it licked, he insisted. He guessed she had heard things were rough for a while, but she could rest assured that it would be smooth sailing from here on in.

"I'm glad," she said again. She had heard that he sometimes hinted, drunk, that Martha's death had caused the disorder in his life, and wondered if he had so deceived himself. The disorder had been there always. Even Martha had seen it: *He's the kind of man*, she had once said, *who when your father's dying or you're having a miscarriage or a note's due at the bank, depend on him, he won't be around.*

"How's Nancy," she added.

Nancy, he declared, could not be better. Nor could he. And they had been meaning to get in touch with her because—what a coincidence running into her tonight!—they were moving back to the Valley. He was going into an operation of his own, had some deals going, nothing he was free to talk about but very big irons in the fire. He'd be working his ass off but it was going to be worth it.

"That's fine, Ryder," she said; she wondered where Nancy was.

Although she heard, in July, that Ryder and Nancy Channing were in Sacramento again, she did not talk to him until one afternoon in September when he called and asked her to meet him in town. She couldn't possibly, she told him; *please*, he said, all pretense gone from his voice. *I need you. You're the only friend I've got.*

When she arrived at the address he had given her, a one-storey house in a new subdivision south of town, she saw that he had been alone for days, perhaps weeks: there were books thrown on the floor (he had always been sloppy and she recalled Martha saying that he did not sleep well), dirty shorts and socks and shirts strewn on the chairs, and every flat surface was littered with the remnants of whatever he had been eating —celery stalks, stale ends of bread, the torn plastic wrappings from processed cheese. In the bathroom there were dark hairpins on the floor, distinctly not Nancy's, and the sheets on the bed where she sat with him and finally lay with him had not been changed when Nancy would have changed them. He looked as disheveled as the house did, and talked incoherently: he had clearly been drinking. Nancy was in Piedmont, he did not know for how long. The deal on which he had been working had not quite gone through, but never mind that. It would. You had to wait these things out, they didn't build Stonestown in a day.

Before she left she gave him what cash she had, about $20, and straightened the bedroom so that he could sleep.

"Don't worry," she said.

He sat slumped in a chair.

"I said don't worry," she repeated, holding his head against her.

It was apparent that he needed someone, and as she drove out to the ranch she imagined that he needed not someone but her. Whether it was true or not did not much matter: she was already committed.

23

"YOU CAN'T dance at all," Everett said to her. "You never could dance worth a damn."

He said it in a motel room outside Salinas on a spring evening in 1957; they had driven down to look at a stock ranch, 840 acres for $225,000, which was, Everett thought, on the high side for a stock ranch but was $85,000 less than the eventual buyer, a Stockton syndicate, asked one year later for the eight acres of it with cloverleaf access to a proposed freeway south. (In the end, however, the joke was not upon Everett after all, since the route of the freeway was shifted five miles east.) In the motel there had been glass doors to the lighted swimming pool, Muzak piped in through the walls, and wall-to-wall tweed carpeting on which they had tried, after three drinks before dinner, to dance.

"Nobody can dance on a rug," she said.

"You couldn't dance at the Palladium."

Although she had never considered herself even a mediocre dancer, she was hurt; in the haze of three drinks she embroidered bitterly upon past hurts. A month before she had bought a red chiffon dress which he claimed not to like on her, although he knew (in fact *because* he knew, he said it because he knew) that she had wanted a red chiffon dinner dress from the time she was in school and had seen one on a girl at a dance; before Christmas, the day she came home from two weeks in Carmel, he had not been at home but (by a deliberate effort, she was certain now) in Reno.

"I'm not that bad a dancer," she said, wondering what had happened to the girl in the red chiffon dress, what brilliant marriage she had made, what adoring husband was even then leading her (*leading*: there was the key to good dancing) across the polished floor of what fashionable hotel.

"I told you, you can't dance at all. You don't listen to the beat. I don't know what you're listening to but it isn't the beat."

"Then let's not dance." She sat down on the bed and began brushing her hair.

He sat down, without speaking, and pretended interest in an advertising leaflet bearing a photograph of a man identified as "The Salinas Valley's Number One Restaurateur, a Ph.D. of Beef." There was also a drawing of a steer wearing a crown, with the legend "Where Premium Beef Is King."

"You're deliberately starting it again," she said. "You're deliberately doing it again."

Everett said nothing.

"You do it," she added, "because you're insecure."

"Cut it out, Lily." He stood up and straightened his tie in the mirror. "You ready to go?"

She picked up her sweater, and they did not speak again (if you did not count queries for the benefit of the waiter, and she did not) until halfway through dinner, after Everett had left the table to say hello to a cattleman he had seen in the bar.

"Eat your dinner," he said when he sat down again. "Or is there something the matter with it."

"I was waiting for you."

"You were."

She did not say anything.

"That'd be the first time." He picked up his drink. "That'd be the goddamn first time."

"When did you ever care."

"That's right. When did I ever care. When did you."

"I care right now."

"That'd be the goddamn first time," he repeated.

She saw the vein tightened on his forehead and tried to eat a bite of abalone. Everett had not touched his dinner and was on his sixth or seventh martini, she did not know which. *That'd be the goddamn first time.* What it was not the first time for, at any rate, was this scene: she supposed they said different words each time but it was always the same scene, and although she could not remember when or how it had begun, it seemed now that they were condemned to play it out together all the days of their lives, raking their memories for fresh grievances, cherishing familiar ones, nourishing the already indestructible shoots of their resentment with alcohol and with the inexhaustible adrenalin generated by what she supposed was (at least she did not know any other name for it) love. It did not seem to matter any more who had first resented whom, or for what. It did not seem to matter what either of them did any more: it could begin out of nothing. It could begin when they were trying hardest to keep it away, could tear apart all their tacit promises, could invade even the cunningly achieved anonymity of motel rooms with wall-to-wall tweed carpeting, rooms in which they had thought they might begin again; rooms in which she could feel, in the first glow of the first drink, that Everett was someone she did not know at all, someone to whom she might seem the gifted, graced, charmed woman she had wanted to be.

"Stop it," she said, putting down her fork.

He beckoned to the waiter. "Stop what."

By midnight Everett had fallen asleep in his clothes on one of the two double beds. Lily sat rigid in a straight chair on the far side of the room; to have lain on even the other bed would have implied domesticity, a truce. When he woke and told her to go to bed she turned away, turned her face toward the window which looked out on nothing but the Lincoln. She could not sleep, she said, in the same room with him. She had managed to sleep, he said, in the same room with plenty of other people, hadn't she. No, she had not. And what did it matter if she had. When had he ever cared. He had slapped her then and she twisted away, and he took her in his arms and it was all right again for a while. *It's going to be all right baby*, he said, *it's going to be fine now*, and she said over and over *Please Christ Everett keep us*, and he said *Lily, baby, we'll get through the next few months all right and then you take a trip, you take the kids on a trip, go somewhere you want to go and baby when you come home it'll be all right, you'll see.*

Later she had begged Everett to go with them on the trip that summer but he would not. Knight liked everything, liked Paris and London and Rome and New York, but Julie was homesick and wanted her father, and Lily was homesick too. Although she sent postcards almost every day to Everett and to her mother, neither wrote frequently: her mother twice, once to observe that Duke Snider had been off his game for a week, once to complain that the Wells Fargo Bank would allow her to subordinate not three hundred but only one hundred acres to the Paradise Valley All-Electric Homes people; Everett three times, each letter an exercise in the stiff, impenetrable optimism he reserved for all mailed communications. In Paris she received a cable from Ryder, asking if she could lend him five thousand dollars; she cabled that she could not, and then wondered guiltily where he would get the money.

After she was home, all she could remember of the trip at all was the fat Italian on the flight from New York to San Francisco, the Italian not from Italy but from New Jersey; she remembered him with a clarity she would have preferred to forego. He lived in New Jersey, was married to a woman who weighed 234 pounds, and had business in San Francisco: those were the only three facts she ever knew about him.

Idlewild that night had been hot and swept by fitful warm rains, everything smelling of the same sweet mildew that had always meant New York to her. The plane was delayed, and Lily sat (alone, because Knight and Julie were staying over a week to visit Sarah in Bryn Mawr) in the surgically lighted litter of the waiting room reading the real-estate advertisements in a *Town and Country* someone had left behind. She had on a white silk suit she had bought on sale the day before at Hattie Carnegie, and thought she presented rather a pleasant contrast to the other passengers, one of whom, an aging blonde, had on Capri pants; another of whom, an extraordinarily seedy minister, had stripped down to his pants, an undershirt, and a clerical bib. He was fanning himself with the *New York Daily Mirror*, and Lily hoped that he would not sit next to her on the plane, because she was quite certain that before they reached San Francisco she would be telling him, in a helpless drive to win his approval, what faith and works meant to her.

She smiled distantly at a man who had smiled at her. Apparently Italian, about her age, the man wore a suit of such deliberately obscure cut and color that it appeared to be a parody on a Brooks Brothers suit. The suit was complemented by—and such would be the phrase—a narrow black string tie with a heavy gold tie clasp, an absurdly small hat, and a candy-striped shirt with French cuffs, which he shot several times as he repeatedly opened and closed the attaché case in which he had for some reason secured his ticket. It was not until after he had settled himself next to her on the plane that she noticed the cuff links, which were representations of two of the

Caesars, and it was not until he accidently brushed his hand against her knee and then drew it away that she noticed the ring, which was large, diamond, and on his little finger.

It was about then that she noticed, as well, that he had been and was still drinking. *You're skinny but you're good-looking*, he announced thickly, his first words to her. Although she was taken back she smiled, lowered her head and looked up at him and smiled. She always smiled that way at men she did not know, unable to think of anything else to do and wanting them to want her, recognize her as the princess in the tower. In this particular case, however, she smiled also because the stewardess had looked with disapproval upon the man, who was making little effort to conceal his intention to stay drunk for the next three thousand miles. The disapproval of the stewardess suggested a kind of pact between Lily and her seat mate, and she sealed it by accepting a swallow of what seemed to be very good Scotch, although she did not like Scotch, from his flask.

Perhaps ten minutes after they had left Idlewild, when the lights had been turned off and the engines had settled to a low roar, the incredible thing happened, only it did not seem incredible until later, on the ground, in the light: the man began a low, loving, brutally obscene monologue. Did she know what he wanted to do to her. Did she know what he was going to do to her as soon as they reached San Francisco. How would she like that. He guessed she'd like that all right. *Be quiet*, she whispered from time to time, lulled almost unconscious by the dark, the moan of the engines, the slight vibration of the cold window next to her cheek, the void beyond the window; *don't talk that way*. There was, however, something about being at 25,000 feet in the dark that drained her voice of urgency. Occasionally she would even drop into sleep, waking each time to the quiet, unthinkable monotone; he never touched her and stopped talking only once, for about an hour, between the lights of Denver and the lights of Salt Lake, when he fell into deep sleep. She rather missed the sound of his voice. He woke not only with his imaginative powers still intact but with, for the first time, a definite program: *You're going to love it, baby, you're just going to give me three hours and you're going to love it and then you'll walk out that door and never see me again*. He saw this tryst as taking place in the airport hotel in San Francisco. It seemed he did not have to be into town until two o'clock in the afternoon. *Just three hours, baby. I can't,* she heard herself saying again and again, and when he demanded to know why not she heard herself, absurdly, making up reasons: she had to be here, there, her time was committed. Three hours wouldn't matter, he declared, if she wanted it: *Do you want it or don't you. I don't want it,* she said finally, almost inaudibly, trying to cover herself entirely with the blanket the stewardess had given her.

You want it all right baby, you want it. Three hours of it.

She said nothing. What held her in trance was his total lack of interest in anything else about her, his promise of being what she had looked for over and over: the point beyond which she could not go, the unambiguous undiluted article, the place where the battle would be on her terms. There could be no question of whether he liked her or disliked her, no question of approval or disapproval, no rôles at all: three hours he said and three hours he meant.

And if he had not passed out shortly before the plane landed in San Francisco, and if Everett had not driven down unexpectedly to meet her (given the second, she could thank God for the first), three hours it would probably, she knew with a blend of distaste and interest, have been. A few days later the incident had seemed so improbable as to be of obsessive interest, and she mentioned, tentatively, that she had sat next to a drunk on the plane. She had, Everett supposed, moved. Yes, she said. Of course I moved. She could not see then why she had not, and was moved, a few weeks later, to describe the flight in relentless detail to Ryder. Clearly impatient with her unresponsiveness to the details of a venture he had recently conceived (*a chain of espresso shops, see Lily, it's a natural*), Ryder said only that it could have happened to anyone. ("I'm not sure a chain of espresso shops would go, Ryder": that was all she said, but it occurred to her that Ryder found her as tiresome as she sometimes found him, and she reflected admiringly upon people in movies—and it was not only people in movies—who when they could not talk to each other said goodbye, had renunciations, made decisions: started fresh, apparently lobotomized. If there was one thing that she and Everett and Ryder all had in common, it was that none of their decisions ever came to much; they seemed afflicted with memory.)

24

LILY KNEW that she should not have been in town at all. Let alone sitting in the bar at the Capitol Tamale for two hours. Sarah and her new husband had arrived the day before on their way to the Islands; Knight had called up a San Francisco boy who would be in his class at Princeton and invited him up for dinner; China Mary had declared it unseasonably hot for June and gone to bed. Lily should be home. She had told Ryder half an hour ago that she was leaving; now she repeated it.

"Just finish your drink," Ryder said. "I want to talk to you."

"What about."

"For Christ's sake I haven't *seen* you in six weeks."

"That's not my fault," Lily said automatically. She had not particularly wanted to see Ryder anyway, but it had not in fact been her doing: he had spent all of May and part of June in Phoenix, trying to raise money for a project she did not entirely understand. After a while all of Ryder's projects tended to look alike, and whenever she had not seen him for a period of weeks or months she was struck, when she did see him, not only by that but by his appearance: his features seemed constantly heavier, his eyes less focused. Looking directly into his eyes this afternoon, she had felt that she was looking right through them: *You depress me, Ryder*, she had said, *you're acting like everything you do is reflex.* But then he had ordered another drink and she had taken a Miltown and they had both laughed. *So you think I'm a shadow of my former self*, he had said, making fun of her, and she had kissed her finger and pressed it against his cheek.

"Anyway," she said now, looking at her watch and trying to finish a story she had begun before. "There Knight was, shouting that his grandmother reminded him more every day of something out of *The Cherry Orchard*. 'By Anton Chekhov,' he said. 'If anybody on this ranch has even *heard* of Anton Chekhov.' Which he supposed was asking *too much*. And there I was, trying to point out that Mother's passion for turning her particular orchard into Paradise Valley All-Electric Homes was not exactly what I would call Chekhovian. And so Knight said, straight-faced—I swear, Ryder, he meant it—why didn't she tear down the big house and move into one? It would save on electricity."

Although Ryder laughed she could see that he was not much interested by the story.

Dampened, she added: "And that's pretty much all we've been doing."

"Except for Everett's sister," Ryder corrected her.

"That's right." Lily had only had three drinks but felt a little reckless. "Ex*cept* for the arrival of the prodigal sister."

"I saw them at the airport. Everett introduced me." He paused. "I would have recognized her anyway."

"Everett thinks she looks tired."

"She looks like Martha." Ryder paused. "She looks the way Martha might have looked at that age if she hadn't been Martha."

Lily said nothing.

"Listen," Ryder said at last, taking her hand. "You look good. You look a hell of a lot better than you did when I went away."

"I'm tired." Lily stood up and reached for the packages she had bought before she met Ryder. "I'm tired and I look terrible."

When she walked into the house, obscurely pleased that she had diverted Ryder from asking her to meet him somewhere more private than the Capitol Tamale, it occurred to her that no one had moved since noon, with the single exception of Sarah's husband, who appeared to have gone upstairs. Knight still lay on the verandah reading, Julie was still out by the pool, completely in shadow now; Everett and Sarah still sat in the living room. Not even the level of their drinks appeared to have changed appreciably in seven hours.

Sarah smiled uncertainly at Lily. "I was just telling Everett that I *rec*ognize how you both feel about it."

"About what," Lily said, taking off her gloves; she knew perfectly well about what. Sarah had been talking about selling since breakfast.

Ignoring Lily, Sarah turned back to Everett. "Surely we've had offers."

"We've had offers, all right. You know we've had offers."

"How would I know what we've had. Lily never writes about anything but the weather. How would I know about anything." Sarah paused. "I *do* know that what's-his-name, that man we ran into at the baggage counter last night, mentioned some Honolulu interest."

"Honolulu *interests*," Everett said. "That means Chinese investors. That's what they call Chinese money now. Honolulu interests. That guy's always got a deal going. I wouldn't bank on the money." Everett turned to Lily. "Channing," he added. "We saw Channing at the airport."

"Channing," Sarah repeated. "That's his name. Wasn't he a beau of Martha's?"

"No," Everett said.

"Ryder Channing was married for a while to one of Larry Dupree's daughters," Lily added hurriedly. She did not want Sarah moved to dwell again upon either Ryder or Martha; last night, going on about Martha, she had so upset Everett that he had not slept at all.

"Dupree Development," she added.

"As a matter of fact," Everett said, "Dupree has expressed some interest in the Cosumnes ranch."

"I don't *care* so much about the Cosumnes," Sarah said. "The Cosumnes at least brings in a little cash."

"I've been telling you for fifteen years, Sarah, a lot of the Cosumnes expenses come out of the riverfront's operating budget." Everett paused. "You thinking I'm bleeding the riverfront?"

"Everett, sweet," Sarah laughed. She stood up and walked over to the window. "The pool kills me. It looks like Pickfair."

Everett said nothing.

Sarah wandered around the room, picking up a silver platter and reading the inscription on the bottom, studying the photograph of her mother on the piano, returning to the window and looking out into the sunset, picking out, in the silence, a few notes on the piano.

When she sat down again her vivacity seemed suddenly exhausted. "Nothing's very different, is it," she said to no one in particular.

She smiled then at Everett but Everett did not smile back.

"'And it will not be a very *jolly* corner,'" she quoted. "T.S. Eliot. *The Family Reunion.*"

On the fourth Wednesday in June, exactly one week after they had put Sarah and her husband on the plane for the Islands, Knight had the accident with the Ford. Although the accident was neither serious nor entirely Knight's fault, he would almost certainly have his driver's license suspended for six weeks; he had admitted two beers to the Highway Patrol. "You're too honest for your own good," Julie observed with disgust. "They never could've proved two beers." "That's no way to talk," Lily said, but by lunch on Thursday she had begun to wish, if only for Everett's sake, that Knight had been less straightforward with the Highway Patrol.

It was 102° outside and Knight was not speaking to her. He talked only to Everett; except for yes and no and please, he had not spoken to her since Sunday, when he had seen her in Harrah's Club at the lake with Ryder. She had gone up alone to her cousin's house on Saturday morning (*I can't stand it*, she had told Everett, *I can't stand one more minute of your taking it out on me about Sarah, I can't stand your brooding, I can't stand any more scenes, and I can't stand the heat*, and she had walked out of the house—resolutely not thinking about the three hours she had spent with somebody's houseguest in a room at the Senator Hotel the night before—and driven straight to the lake); she had not even known Ryder was there until she ran into him outside Harrah's Club on Sunday. For once she had been totally blameless, but she could scarcely explain this small irony to Knight. She did not know what Knight had been doing in Harrah's Club in the first place. When she saw him she had called out and made her way past two crap tables to talk to him, but he had walked away.

"Just this one thing," Knight pleaded now. He wanted Everett to talk to someone at the Department of Motor Vehicles. "It'd be so *easy.* All you've got to say is you need me to drive the trucks. Can't you just do this one thing for me."

"It won't hurt you," Everett said.

"You might just talk to them," Lily said, mostly, she realized with shame, to ingratiate herself with Knight.

Knight looked at her coldly.

"It won't hurt him," Everett repeated.

She tried again. "Nobody said it would *hurt* him, Everett. But it might be nice if he could drive this summer."

"This is between my father and me," Knight said distantly.

"Apologize to your mother."

"I'm sorry." Knight turned back to Everett. "Just *one little phone call*."

Everett said nothing.

"All right. Don't do it. I didn't expect you to do it. Nobody expects you to do anything."

Knight pushed back his chair and watched Everett expectantly, but Everett did not respond.

"You just sit here," Knight added, his voice rising. "Just sit here like you've always done and don't pay any attention to what's going on. Just pretend we don't exist. Just sit here while your son gets his license lifted and your daughter lets anybody on the river get her drunk and goes swimming nude—"

"Shut up," Everett said.

Knight stood up. "*Last Saturday night* with both the Templeton twins. That's *last Saturday night* while your wife was shacked up at Lake Tahoe."

Lily looked first at Everett, then at Knight; neither looked at her.

"Get out," Everett said. "You want to say every trashy thing you hear, you get off this place to say it."

"You think I want to stay on this place? You think I want one lousy acre of it?"

"Get off now."

"It's not what I hear, it's what I know. Nobody says it out loud, not around here. But you know what they call her? You know how they think of her still? They call her Lily Knight, not McClellan, *Knight*. Like she was never married at all. *So I guess you didn't count for much*."

When Julie asked that night where her brother was, Lily said that he had gone out. "He's not coming back," Everett said. "He's disloyal." Julie looked at her father and then at her mother and her large eyes filled with tears: "I don't believe that," she said in her steady voice. "I wouldn't believe Knight could be disloyal." "I wouldn't believe you could go swimming without any clothes on, either," Everett said flatly.

After Julie had gone to sleep Lily sat down in the dark by her bed. She wanted to hold Julie's hand, flung out from the striped lavender and white sheets, but was afraid that she would wake her. Instead she sat with her hands in her lap listening to Julie's even breathing, and when Julie woke and looked at her with the tears beginning in her eyes again, Lily only smoothed her hair. "Go to sleep, baby," she said, unable to explain to Julie, any more than she could explain to herself, just where the trouble had begun. "It's all right."

When Knight came home two days later ("That was absurd," Lily heard Julie telling him, "running away in your mother's car. That's childish"), Lily prevailed upon Everett to accept, as she had done, his inarticulate, embarrassed apology. He brought Lily a dozen white roses, but was ashamed to tell her that he had bought them ("This guy gave them to me," he explained. "This guy I know in a florist's shop had them left over"); he asked Everett, carefully casual, if Everett minded if he stuck around and listened when the hop broker came at four o'clock. That was the day they began to be very polite to one another, dimly aware that they had been, more than they had ever been before, vis-à-vis the complexities, the downright complicity, of family love. (*It had nothing to do with you*, she tried to explain to Ryder, talking to him about it night after night. He did not understand what she was talking about, but it was better than talking to herself.)

August 1959

25

EVERETT LOOSENED his tie and unfastened the top button of his shirt. Exhausted, he remembered for the first time that the gun still lay on the dock.

"Sit down," Lily said. "Sit down, baby."

He let her lead him to a chair. The house looked no different than it had earlier in the evening; he could not think why he had expected it to.

"Wait here," she said. "I'll get you a drink."

"What time is it?"

Lily looked at her wrist. She was wearing the watch he had given her the September of 1957, when she and the children came home from abroad. He had bought it the week she left and saved it until she came home in September, telling her then, embarrassed, that she could count it an anniversary present. Once he had seen it on her thin wrist, he had seen how wrong the heavy diamonds were for Lily, but in the jeweler's that afternoon he had so wanted something which would make irrevocable his love and determination that if the jeweler could have worked the Cullinan Diamond into a wrist watch (the point of a wrist watch being that she could wear it every day) he would have borrowed on the ranches and bought it. Although he was quite sure that Lily did not like the watch, she wore it not only every day but so frequently in the shower and in the swimming pool that the parts were rusted and it seldom ran.

"One-thirty," she said. "One-twenty-five."

He looked at her. "The children," he said finally.

"They'll be a while. We have time."

She poured some bourbon into two glasses and handed him one.

"I meant to," he said. "I came here and got the gun. If I hadn't meant to I wouldn't have come here and gotten the gun. Would I."

"I don't know. That's not the point."

He said nothing.

"Listen," she said. "We're going to make it all right. I'm going to tell McGrath what happened."

"That didn't happen."

"It could have happened."

"It didn't."

"Don't you want it to be all right?"

He did not say anything.

She swallowed half the bourbon in her glass. "Everett. Listen to me. If you don't listen to me you're going to go to prison. You're going to go to Alcatraz and maybe *die* if you don't start listening to me."

"San Quentin. Not Alcatraz. San Quentin."

"Everett."

He looked at her. He had been wrong about her down on the dock: she was no older, she was still the thin little girl with the safety pin in her sunglasses, and whatever had happened in the years between did not signify much. Channing did not signify much: he thought of Channing sitting there on the log smoking a cigarette, switching his flashlight toward the levee and calling *Lily*? then springing up and flipping his cigarette into the water when he saw that it was not Lily. (*You better get off, Channing, you better get off this property*, he had said, and Channing had laughed: *O.K., Coop, O.K.* He had imagined Channing maybe telling Lily, later, what had happened, imagined Lily laughing with him. *O.K., Coop*, Channing had said, *you're going to hurt somebody with that, and she's no good to you dead.*) None of it signified: whether Channing had tried to grab the gun to protect himself or because he thought Everett intended to shoot Lily; whether he had shot Channing because he had intended to all along or because he was angered by Channing's thinking he could hurt Lily; none of it mattered. Channing pitching forward over the log, his flashlight rolling into the water: they were events of equal importance. After a while it had all been quiet again and he had wondered how the shot could have been so accurate when he could not remember aiming.

He smoothed the hair back from Lily's face.

"Anyway," he said, trying to make her smile. "We call it Quentin. Or just plain 'Q.'"

"*Everett.*" She buried her face in his sleeve.

"Never mind. Don't worry."

"Listen." She looked up at him. "You wouldn't do it now."

"No," he said. "I wouldn't."

"Then it doesn't matter."

"I think it does." He got up and walked over to the window.

"The swimming-pool lights are on again," he said. It suddenly irritated him: the pool lights left on when they were all at a party, the dock light burned out and not replaced, the waste everywhere, waste and erosion. "There's no reason to have the lights on when nobody's home."

"Julie thinks they're beautiful," Lily said faintly. "I left them on for Julie."

"Julie's not home," he said reasonably. "We can burn them all day and all night if Julie thinks they're beautiful, but Julie has not been home all evening."

"Everett. *Please.*"

"Don't worry," he said. "Just a minute."

"Sit down and listen to me."

He opened and closed the screen door, examined the hinges absently, picked up his drink and finished it.

"It's all right," he said. "I'm going to call McGrath now."

She sat forward on the edge of the couch. "You're going to tell him what we planned? Everett?"

"Sure. Sure, baby."

"Let me call."

He closed the telephone book and dialed.

"Ed? Everett McClellan."

Lily crossed the room and sat down by the telephone looking up at him.

"That's right," he said. "*Once* before. I called you in the middle of the night once before. Ten years ago."

"You know Ryder Channing? That's right. No, they're divorced." He paused. "Listen. I shot him."

"*Tell him why,*" Lily whispered.

"I just shot him. We had a fight over a gun and I shot him. My gun. You get on over here and I'll tell you about it."

Everett hung up.

"You didn't tell him why."

"No," Everett said. "It doesn't matter."

He took Lily's hand.

"Lily. Lily baby."

She did not take her eyes from him.

"I'm going down to get the gun," he said.

"Leave the gun. Wait until McGrath comes."

He shook his head.

"Leave me be," he said gently. "You sit here."

Holding her, her head pressed against his chest, he felt the sobs beginning in her frame and knew that she realized it was not going to be the way she had wanted it.

"Wait for the children," she said. "Julie will be here."

"I don't want to see her."

"Everett—"

"It was all right," he whispered. "It's been all right."

"I love you."

"I know that. Don't you think I know that."

"Nobody would have known it," she said. "Nobody. The way it's been."

"Known what."

"That I loved you."

"I knew it. You knew it."

She clung to him. He could feel her ribs beneath her dress.

"Listen," he said. "You have to put on some weight. You have to start eating more and getting some rest. You promise."

"I promise."

"All right then." He kissed her closed eyes.

26

SITTING ON the needlepoint chair where Everett had told her to sit she felt her hands wet, her head hurting (hurting, not aching; it had stopped aching upstairs, an hour ago, when she had first heard the shot), nothing very real. The only real thing had been the shot and she could hear it still, cracking reflexively through all the years before, spinning through the darkness between the games they had all played as children and the games they played now, between the child she had been and whoever she was now, sitting on the needlepoint chair and knowing that he was not going to let her make it all right.

Leave me be. What had it all been about: all the manqué promises, the failures of love and faith and honor; Martha buried out there by the levee in a $250 dress from Magnin's with river silt in the seams; Sarah in Bryn Mawr, Pennsylvania; her father, who had not much cared, the easy loser (*He never could have been*, her mother had said and still loved him); her mother sitting alone this afternoon in the big house upriver writing out invitations for the Admission Day Fiesta and watching *Dick Clark's American Bandstand* because the Dodgers were rained out; Everett down there on the dock with his father's .38. She, her mother, Everett, Martha, the whole family gallery: they carried the same blood, come down through twelve generations of circuit riders, county sheriffs, Indian fighters, country lawyers, Bible readers, one obscure United States Senator from a frontier state a long time ago; two hundred years of clearings in Virginia and Kentucky and Tennessee and then the break, the void into which they gave their rosewood chests, their silver brushes; the cutting clean which was to have redeemed them all. They had been a particular kind of people, their particular virtues called up by a particular situation, their particular flaws waiting there through all those years, unperceived, unsuspected, glimpsed only cloudily by one or two in each generation, by a wife whose bewildered eyes wanted to look not upon Eldorado but upon her mother's dogwood, by a blue-eyed boy who was at sixteen the best shot in the county and who when there was nothing left to shoot rode out one day and shot his brother, an accident. It had been above all a history of accidents: of moving on and of accidents. What is it you want, she had asked Everett tonight. It was a question she might have asked them all.

Leave him be. It was all she could do now, the only present she could make him. *Drive far away our ghostly foe and thine abiding peace bestow.* Christ on the cross couldn't drive away that ghostly foe. And maybe once you realized you had to do it alone, you were on your way home. Maybe the most difficult, most important thing anyone could do for anyone else was to leave him alone; it was perhaps the only gratuitous act, the act of love.

She sat on the needlepoint chair until she heard it, the second shot. When she found him, face down with his arm flung out and his head hanging over the edge of the dock, she lay down beside him on the wet boards and talked to him, telling him things for which there had never been any other words: *Remember, Everett baby once at the Fair, you lifted me onto the golden bear in front of the Counties Building and kissed me and we laughed. And remember we used to lie in bed mornings, sometimes with Knight in bed between us and I would say don't go to sleep, he'll smother, remember how it was and remember the day we took the children to the Cosumnes and it rained and we all sat drinking Cokes under the cottonwood and the rain coming through remember Everett baby remember.* She hoped that although he could not hear her she could somehow imprint her ordinary love upon his memory through all eternity, hoped he would rise thinking of her, *we were each other, we were each other, not that it mattered much in the long run but what else mattered as much.*

As she lay holding him against the dark she heard the sirens on the highway, but did not move until the two cars, one McGrath's and one the Highway Patrol, swung off the levee and down the drive to the house. She stood up then, left Everett and climbed the wooden stairs to the road. In the light down on the verandah McGrath, his pants pulled on with a pajama top, stood with two other men; another man, in a Highway Patrol uniform, waited on the lawn, looking not at the house but at the lighted pool. Watching them as she brushed the leaves from her skirt and licked the blood from the arm she had held around Everett, she began to wonder what she would say, not to them but to Knight and to Julie. She did not know what she could tell anyone except that he had been a good man. She was not certain that he had been but it was what she would have wished for him, if they gave her one wish.

SLOUCHING TOWARDS BETHLEHEM

For Quintana

Turning and turning in the widening gyre
The falcon cannot hear the falconer;
Things fall apart; the center cannot hold;
Mere anarchy is loosed upon the world,
The blood-dimmed tide is loosed, and everywhere
The ceremony of innocence is drowned;
The best lack all conviction, while the worst
Are full of passionate intensity.

Surely some revelation is at hand;
Surely the Second Coming is at hand.
The Second Coming! Hardly are those words out
When a vast image out of Spiritus Mundi
Troubles my sight: somewhere in the sands of the desert
A shape with lion body and the head of a man,
A gaze blank and pitiless as the sun,
Is moving its slow thighs, while all about it
Reel shadows of the indignant desert birds.
The darkness drops again; but now I know
That twenty centuries of stony sleep
Were vexed to nightmare by a rocking cradle,
And what rough beast, its hour come round at last,
Slouches towards Bethlehem to be born?

W. B. YEATS

I learned courage from Buddha, Jesus, Lincoln, Einstein, and Cary Grant.

MISS PEGGY LEE

A Preface

THIS BOOK IS CALLED *Slouching Towards Bethlehem* because for several years now certain lines from the Yeats poem which appears two pages back have reverberated in my inner ear as if they were surgically implanted there. The widening gyre, the falcon which does not hear the falconer, the gaze blank and pitiless as the sun; those have been my points of reference, the only images against which much of what I was seeing and hearing and thinking seemed to make any pattern. "Slouching Towards Bethlehem" is also the title of one piece in the book, and that piece, which derived from some time spent in the Haight-Ashbury district of San Francisco, was for me both the most imperative of all these pieces to write and the only one that made me despondent after it was printed. It was the first time I had dealt directly and flatly with the evidence of atomization, the proof that things fall apart: I went to San Francisco because I had not been able to work in some months, had been paralyzed by the conviction that writing was an irrelevant act, that the world as I had understood it no longer existed. If I was to work again at all, it would be necessary for me to come to terms with disorder. That was why the piece was important to me. And after it was printed I saw that, however directly and flatly I thought I had said it, I had failed to get through to many of the people who read and even liked the piece, failed to suggest that I was talking about something more general than a handful of children wearing mandalas on their foreheads. Disc jockeys telephoned my house and wanted to discuss (on the air) the incidence of "filth" in the Haight-Ashbury, and acquaintances congratulated me on having finished the piece "just in time," because "the whole fad's dead now, *fini*, *kaput*." I suppose almost everyone who writes is afflicted some of the time by the suspicion that nobody out there is listening, but it seemed to me then (perhaps because the piece was important to me) that I had never gotten a feedback so universally beside the point.

Almost all of the pieces here were written for magazines during 1965, 1966, and 1967, and most of them, to get that question out of the way at the outset, were "my idea." I was asked to go up to the Carmel Valley and report on Joan Baez's school there; I was asked to go to Hawaii; I think I was asked to write about John Wayne; and I was asked for the short essays on "morality," by *The American Scholar*, and on "self-respect," by *Vogue*. Thirteen of the twenty pieces were published in *The Saturday Evening Post*. Quite often people write me from places like Toronto and want to know (demand to know) how I can reconcile my conscience with writing for *The Saturday Evening Post*; the answer is quite simple. The *Post* is extremely receptive to what the writer wants to do, pays enough for him to be able to do it right, and is meticulous about not changing copy. I lose a nicety of inflection now and then to the *Post*, but do not count myself compromised. Of course not all of the pieces in this book have to do, in a "subject" sense, with the general breakup, with things falling apart; that is a large and rather presumptuous notion, and many of these pieces are small and personal. But since I am neither a camera eye nor much given to writing pieces which do not interest me, whatever I do write reflects, sometimes gratuitously, how I feel.

I am not sure what more I could tell you about these pieces. I could tell you that I liked doing some of them more than others, but that all of them were hard for me to do, and took more time than perhaps they were worth; that there is always a point in the writing of a piece when I sit in a room literally papered with false starts and cannot put one word after another and imagine that I have suffered a small stroke, leaving me apparently undamaged but actually aphasic. I was in fact as sick as I have ever been when I was writing "Slouching Towards Bethlehem"; the pain kept me awake at night and so for twenty and twenty-one hours a day I drank gin-and-hot-water to blunt the pain and took Dexedrine to blunt the gin and wrote the piece. (I would like you to believe that I kept working out of some real professionalism, to meet the deadline, but that would not be entirely true; I did have a deadline, but it was also a troubled time, and working did to the trouble what gin did to the pain.) What else is there to tell? I am bad at interviewing people. I avoid situations in which I have to talk to anyone's press agent. (This precludes doing pieces on most actors, a bonus in itself.)

I do not like to make telephone calls, and would not like to count the mornings I have sat on some Best Western motel bed somewhere and tried to force myself to put through the call to the assistant district attorney. My only advantage as a reporter is that I am so physically small, so temperamentally unobtrusive, and so neurotically inarticulate that people tend to forget that my presence runs counter to their best interests. And it always does. That is one last thing to remember: *writers are always selling somebody out.*

I

LIFE STYLES IN THE GOLDEN LAND

Some Dreamers of the Golden Dream

THIS IS A STORY about love and death in the golden land, and begins with the country. The San Bernardino Valley lies only an hour east of Los Angeles by the San Bernardino Freeway but is in certain ways an alien place: not the coastal California of the subtropical twilights and the soft westerlies off the Pacific but a harsher California, haunted by the Mojave just beyond the mountains, devastated by the hot dry Santa Ana wind that comes down through the passes at 100 miles an hour and whines through the eucalyptus windbreaks and works on the nerves. October is the bad month for the wind, the month when breathing is difficult and the hills blaze up spontaneously. There has been no rain since April. Every voice seems a scream. It is the season of suicide and divorce and prickly dread, wherever the wind blows.

The Mormons settled this ominous country, and then they abandoned it, but by the time they left the first orange tree had been planted and for the next hundred years the San Bernardino Valley would draw a kind of people who imagined they might live among the talismanic fruit and prosper in the dry air, people who brought with them Midwestern ways of building and cooking and praying and who tried to graft those ways upon the land. The graft took in curious ways. This is the California where it is possible to live and die without ever eating an artichoke, without ever meeting a Catholic or a Jew. This is the California where it is easy to Dial-A-Devotion, but hard to buy a book. This is the country in which a belief in the literal interpretation of Genesis has slipped imperceptibly into a belief in the literal interpretation of *Double Indemnity*, the country of the teased hair and the Capris and the girls for whom all life's promise comes down to a waltz-length white wedding dress and the birth of a Kimberly or a Sherry or a Debbi and a Tijuana divorce and a return to hairdressers' school. "We were just crazy kids," they say without regret, and look to the future. The future always looks good in the golden land, because no one remembers the past. Here is where the hot wind blows and the old ways do not seem relevant, where the divorce rate is double the national average and where one person in every thirty-eight lives in a trailer. Here is the last stop for all those who come from somewhere else, for all those who drifted away from the cold and the past and the old ways. Here is where they are trying to find a new life style, trying to find it in the only places they know to look: the movies and the newspapers. The case of Lucille Marie Maxwell Miller is a tabloid monument to that new life style.

Imagine Banyan Street first, because Banyan is where it happened. The way to Banyan is to drive west from San Bernardino out Foothill Boulevard, Route 66: past the Santa Fe switching yards, the Forty Winks Motel. Past the motel that is nineteen stucco tepees: "SLEEP IN A WIGWAM—GET MORE FOR YOUR WAMPUM." Past Fontana Drag City and the Fontana Church of the Nazarene and the Pit Stop A Go-Go; past Kaiser Steel, through Cucamonga, out to the Kapu Kai Restaurant-Bar and Coffee Shop, at the corner of Route 66 and Carnelian Avenue. Up Carnelian Avenue from the Kapu Kai, which means "Forbidden Seas," the subdivision flags whip in the harsh wind. "HALF-ACRE RANCHES! SNACK BARS! TRAVERTINE ENTRIES! $95 DOWN." It is the trail of an intention gone haywire, the flotsam of the New California. But after a while the signs thin out on Carnelian Avenue, and the houses are no longer the bright pastels of the Springtime Home owners but the faded bungalows of the people who grow a few grapes and keep a few chickens out here, and then the hill gets steeper and the road climbs and even the bungalows are few, and here —desolate, roughly surfaced, lined with eucalyptus and lemon groves—is Banyan Street.

Like so much of this country, Banyan suggests something curious and unnatural. The lemon groves are sunken, down a three- or four-foot retaining wall, so that one looks directly into their dense foliage, too lush, unsettlingly glossy, the greenery of nightmare; the fallen eucalyptus bark is too dusty, a place for snakes to breed. The stones look not like natural stones but like the rubble of some unmentioned upheaval. There are smudge pots, and a closed cistern. To one side of Banyan there is the flat valley, and to the other the San Bernardino Mountains, a dark mass looming too high, too fast, nine, ten, eleven thousand feet, right there above the lemon groves. At midnight on

Banyan Street there is no light at all, and no sound except the wind in the eucalyptus and a muffled barking of dogs. There may be a kennel somewhere, or the dogs may be coyotes.

Banyan Street was the route Lucille Miller took home from the twenty-four-hour Mayfair Market on the night of October 7, 1964, a night when the moon was dark and the wind was blowing and she was out of milk, and Banyan Street was where, at about 12:30 A.M., her 1964 Volkswagen came to a sudden stop, caught fire, and began to burn. For an hour and fifteen minutes Lucille Miller ran up and down Banyan calling for help, but no cars passed and no help came. At three o'clock that morning, when the fire had been put out and the California Highway Patrol officers were completing their report, Lucille Miller was still sobbing and incoherent, for her husband had been asleep in the Volkswagen. "What will I tell the children, when there's nothing left, nothing left in the casket," she cried to the friend called to comfort her. "How can I tell them there's nothing left?"

In fact there was something left, and a week later it lay in the Draper Mortuary Chapel in a closed bronze coffin blanketed with pink carnations. Some 200 mourners heard Elder Robert E. Denton of the Seventh-Day Adventist Church of Ontario speak of "the temper of fury that has broken out among us." For Gordon Miller, he said, there would be "no more death, no more heartaches, no more misunderstandings." Elder Ansel Bristol mentioned the "peculiar" grief of the hour. Elder Fred Jensen asked "what shall it profit a man, if he shall gain the whole world, and lose his own soul?" A light rain fell, a blessing in a dry season, and a female vocalist sang "Safe in the Arms of Jesus." A tape recording of the service was made for the widow, who was being held without bail in the San Bernardino County Jail on a charge of first-degree murder.

Of course she came from somewhere else, came off the prairie in search of something she had seen in a movie or heard on the radio, for this is a Southern California story. She was born on January 17, 1930, in Winnipeg, Manitoba, the only child of Gordon and Lily Maxwell, both schoolteachers and both dedicated to the Seventh-Day Adventist Church, whose members observe the Sabbath on Saturday, believe in an apocalyptic

Second Coming, have a strong missionary tendency, and, if they are strict, do not smoke, drink, eat meat, use makeup, or wear jewelry, including wedding rings. By the time Lucille Maxwell enrolled at Walla Walla College in College Place, Washington, the Adventist school where her parents then taught, she was an eighteen-year-old possessed of unremarkable good looks and remarkable high spirits. "Lucille wanted to see the world," her father would say in retrospect, "and I guess she found out."

The high spirits did not seem to lend themselves to an extended course of study at Walla Walla College, and in the spring of 1949 Lucille Maxwell met and married Gordon ("Cork") Miller, a twenty-four-year-old graduate of Walla Walla and of the University of Oregon dental school, then stationed at Fort Lewis as a medical officer. "Maybe you could say it was love at first sight," Mr. Maxwell recalls. "Before they were ever formally introduced, he sent Lucille a dozen and a half roses with a card that said even if she didn't come out on a date with him, he hoped she'd find the roses pretty anyway." The Maxwells remember their daughter as a "radiant" bride.

Unhappy marriages so resemble one another that we do not need to know too much about the course of this one. There may or may not have been trouble on Guam, where Cork and Lucille Miller lived while he finished his Army duty. There may or may not have been problems in the small Oregon town where he first set up private practice. There appears to have been some disappointment about their move to California: Cork Miller had told friends that he wanted to become a doctor, that he was unhappy as a dentist and planned to enter the Seventh-Day Adventist College of Medical Evangelists at Loma Linda, a few miles south of San Bernardino. Instead he bought a dental practice in the west end of San Bernardino County, and the family settled there, in a modest house on the kind of street where there are always tricycles and revolving credit and dreams about bigger houses, better streets. That was 1957. By the summer of 1964 they had achieved the bigger house on the better street and the familiar accouterments of a family on its way up: the $30,000 a year, the three children for the Christmas card, the picture window, the family room, the newspaper photographs that showed "Mrs. Gordon Miller, Ontario Heart Fund Chairman. . . ." They were paying the familiar price for it. And they had reached the familiar season of divorce.

It might have been anyone's bad summer, anyone's siege of heat and nerves and migraine and money worries, but this one began particularly early and particularly badly. On April 24 an old friend, Elaine Hayton, died suddenly; Lucille Miller had seen her only the night before. During the month of May, Cork Miller was hospitalized briefly with a bleeding ulcer, and his usual reserve deepened into depression. He told his accountant that he was "sick of looking at open mouths," and threatened suicide. By July 8, the conventional tensions of love and money had reached the conventional impasse in the new house on the acre lot at 8488 Bella Vista, and Lucille Miller filed for divorce. Within a month, however, the Millers seemed reconciled. They saw a marriage counselor. They talked about a fourth child. It seemed that the marriage had reached the traditional truce, the point at which so many resign themselves to cutting both their losses and their hopes.

But the Millers' season of trouble was not to end that easily. October 7 began as a commonplace enough day, one of those days that sets the teeth on edge with its tedium, its small frustrations. The temperature reached 102° in San Bernardino that afternoon, and the Miller children were home from school because of Teachers' Institute. There was ironing to be dropped off. There was a trip to pick up a prescription for Nembutal, a trip to a self-service dry cleaner. In the early evening, an unpleasant accident with the Volkswagen: Cork Miller hit and killed a German shepherd, and afterward said that his head felt "like it had a Mack truck on it." It was something he often said. As of that evening Cork Miller was $63,479 in debt, including the $29,637 mortgage on the new house, a debt load which seemed oppressive to him. He was a man who wore his responsibilities uneasily, and complained of migraine headaches almost constantly.

He ate alone that night, from a TV tray in the living room. Later the Millers watched John Forsythe and Senta Berger in *See How They Run*, and when the movie ended, about eleven, Cork Miller suggested that they go out for milk. He wanted some hot chocolate. He took a blanket and pillow from the couch and climbed into the passenger seat of the Volkswagen.

Lucille Miller remembers reaching over to lock his door as she backed down the driveway. By the time she left the Mayfair Market, and long before they reached Banyan Street, Cork Miller appeared to be asleep.

There is some confusion in Lucille Miller's mind about what happened between 12:30 A.M., when the fire broke out, and 1:50 A.M., when it was reported. She says that she was driving east on Banyan Street at about 35 m.p.h. when she felt the Volkswagen pull sharply to the right. The next thing she knew the car was on the embankment, quite near the edge of the retaining wall, and flames were shooting up behind her. She does not remember jumping out. She does remember prying up a stone with which she broke the window next to her husband, and then scrambling down the retaining wall to try to find a stick. "I don't know how I was going to push him out," she says. "I just thought if I had a stick, I'd push him out." She could not, and after a while she ran to the intersection of Banyan and Carnelian Avenue. There are no houses at that corner, and almost no traffic. After one car had passed without stopping, Lucille Miller ran back down Banyan toward the burning Volkswagen. She did not stop, but she slowed down, and in the flames she could see her husband. He was, she said, "just black."

At the first house up Sapphire Avenue, half a mile from the Volkswagen, Lucille Miller finally found help. There Mrs. Robert Swenson called the sheriff, and then, at Lucille Miller's request, she called Harold Lance, the Millers' lawyer and their close friend. When Harold Lance arrived he took Lucille Miller home to his wife, Joan. Twice Harold Lance and Lucille Miller returned to Banyan Street and talked to the Highway Patrol officers. A third time Harold Lance returned alone, and when he came back he said to Lucille Miller, "O.K. . . . you don't talk any more."

When Lucille Miller was arrested the next afternoon, Sandy Slagle was with her. Sandy Slagle was the intense, relentlessly loyal medical student who used to baby-sit for the Millers, and had been living as a member of the family since she graduated from high school in 1959. The Millers took her away from a difficult home situation, and she thinks of Lucille Miller not only as "more or less a mother or a sister" but as "the most wonderful character" she has ever known. On the night of the accident, Sandy Slagle was in her dormitory at Loma Linda University, but Lucille Miller called her early in the morning and asked her to come home. The doctor was there when Sandy Slagle arrived, giving Lucille Miller an injection of Nembutal. "She was crying as she was going under," Sandy Slagle recalls. "Over and over she'd say, 'Sandy, all the hours I spent trying to save him and now what are they trying to *do* to me?'"

At 1:30 that afternoon, Sergeant William Paterson and Detectives Charles Callahan and Joseph Karr of the Central Homicide Division arrived at 8488 Bella Vista. "One of them appeared at the bedroom door," Sandy Slagle remembers, "and said to Lucille, 'You've got ten minutes to get dressed or we'll take you as you are.' She was in her nightgown, you know, so I tried to get her dressed."

Sandy Slagle tells the story now as if by rote, and her eyes do not waver. "So I had her panties and bra on her and they opened the door again, so I got some Capris on her, you know, and a scarf." Her voice drops. "And then they just took her."

The arrest took place just twelve hours after the first report that there had been an accident on Banyan Street, a rapidity which would later prompt Lucille Miller's attorney to say that the entire case was an instance of trying to justify a reckless arrest. Actually what first caused the detectives who arrived on Banyan Street toward dawn that morning to give the accident more than routine attention were certain apparent physical inconsistencies. While Lucille Miller had said that she was driving about 35 m.p.h. when the car swerved to a stop, an examination of the cooling Volkswagen showed that it was in low gear, and that the parking rather than the driving lights were on. The front wheels, moreover, did not seem to be in exactly the position that Lucille Miller's description of the accident would suggest, and the right rear wheel was dug in deep, as if it had been spun in place. It seemed curious to the detectives, too, that a sudden stop from 35 m.p.h.—the same jolt which was presumed to have knocked over a gasoline can in the back seat and somehow started the fire—should have left two milk cartons upright on the back floorboard, and the remains of a Polaroid camera box lying apparently undisturbed on the back seat.

No one, however, could be expected to give a precise account of what did and did not happen in a moment of terror, and none of these inconsistencies seemed in themselves incontrovertible evidence of criminal intent. But they did interest the Sheriff's Office, as did Gordon Miller's apparent unconsciousness at the time of the accident, and the length of time it had taken Lucille Miller to get help. Something, moreover, struck the investigators as wrong about Harold Lance's attitude when he came back to Banyan Street the third time and found the investigation by no means over. "The way Lance was acting," the prosecuting attorney said later, "they thought maybe they'd hit a nerve."

And so it was that on the morning of October 8, even before the doctor had come to give Lucille Miller an injection to calm her, the San Bernardino County Sheriff's Office was trying to construct another version of what might have happened between 12:30 and 1:50 A.M. The hypothesis they would eventually present was based on the somewhat tortuous premise that Lucille Miller had undertaken a plan which failed: a plan to stop the car on the lonely road, spread gasoline over her presumably drugged husband, and, with a stick on the accelerator, gently "walk" the Volkswagen over the embankment, where it would tumble four feet down the retaining wall into the lemon grove and almost certainly explode. If this happened, Lucille Miller might then have somehow negotiated the two miles up Carnelian to Bella Vista in time to be home when the accident was discovered. This plan went awry, according to the Sheriff's Office hypothesis, when the car would not go over the rise of the embankment. Lucille Miller might have panicked then—after she had killed the engine the third or fourth time, say, out there on the dark road with the gasoline already spread and the dogs baying and the wind blowing and the unspeakable apprehension that a pair of headlights would suddenly light up Banyan Street and expose her there—and set the fire herself.

Although this version accounted for some of the physical evidence—the car in low because it had been started from a dead stop, the parking lights on because she could not do what needed doing without some light, a rear wheel spun in repeated attempts to get the car over the embankment, the milk cartons upright because there had been no sudden stop

—it did not seem on its own any more or less credible than Lucille Miller's own story. Moreover, some of the physical evidence did seem to support her story: a nail in a front tire, a nine-pound rock found in the car, presumably the one with which she had broken the window in an attempt to save her husband. Within a few days an autopsy had established that Gordon Miller was alive when he burned, which did not particularly help the State's case, and that he had enough Nembutal and Sandoptal in his blood to put the average person to sleep, which did: on the other hand Gordon Miller habitually took both Nembutal and Fiorinal (a common headache prescription which contains Sandoptal), and had been ill besides.

It was a spotty case, and to make it work at all the State was going to have to find a motive. There was talk of unhappiness, talk of another man. That kind of motive, during the next few weeks, was what they set out to establish. They set out to find it in accountants' ledgers and double-indemnity clauses and motel registers, set out to determine what might move a woman who believed in all the promises of the middle class—a woman who had been chairman of the Heart Fund and who always knew a reasonable little dressmaker and who had come out of the bleak wild of prairie fundamentalism to find what she imagined to be the good life—what should drive such a woman to sit on a street called Bella Vista and look out her new picture window into the empty California sun and calculate how to burn her husband alive in a Volkswagen. They found the wedge they wanted closer at hand than they might have at first expected, for, as testimony would reveal later at the trial, it seemed that in December of 1963 Lucille Miller had begun an affair with the husband of one of her friends, a man whose daughter called her "Auntie Lucille," a man who might have seemed to have the gift for people and money and the good life that Cork Miller so noticeably lacked. The man was Arthwell Hayton, a well-known San Bernardino attorney and at one time a member of the district attorney's staff.

In some ways it was the conventional clandestine affair in a place like San Bernardino, a place where little is bright or graceful, where it is routine to misplace the future and easy to start looking for it in bed. Over the seven weeks that it would take to try

Lucille Miller for murder, Assistant District Attorney Don A. Turner and defense attorney Edward P. Foley would between them unfold a curiously predictable story. There were the falsified motel registrations. There were the lunch dates, the afternoon drives in Arthwell Hayton's red Cadillac convertible. There were the interminable discussions of the wronged partners. There were the confidantes ("I knew everything," Sandy Slagle would insist fiercely later. "I knew every time, places, everything") and there were the words remembered from bad magazine stories ("Don't kiss me, it will trigger things," Lucille Miller remembered telling Arthwell Hayton in the parking lot of Harold's Club in Fontana after lunch one day) and there were the notes, the sweet exchanges: "Hi Sweetie Pie! You are my cup of tea!! Happy Birthday—you don't look a day over 29!! Your baby, Arthwell."

And, toward the end, there was the acrimony. It was April 24, 1964, when Arthwell Hayton's wife, Elaine, died suddenly, and nothing good happened after that. Arthwell Hayton had taken his cruiser, *Captain's Lady*, over to Catalina that weekend; he called home at nine o'clock Friday night, but did not talk to his wife because Lucille Miller answered the telephone and said that Elaine was showering. The next morning the Haytons' daughter found her mother in bed, dead. The newspapers reported the death as accidental, perhaps the result of an allergy to hair spray. When Arthwell Hayton flew home from Catalina that weekend, Lucille Miller met him at the airport, but the finish had already been written.

It was in the breakup that the affair ceased to be in the conventional mode and began to resemble instead the novels of James M. Cain, the movies of the late 1930's, all the dreams in which violence and threats and blackmail are made to seem commonplaces of middle-class life. What was most startling about the case that the State of California was preparing against Lucille Miller was something that had nothing to do with law at all, something that never appeared in the eight-column afternoon headlines but was always there between them: the revelation that the dream was teaching the dreamers how to live. Here is Lucille Miller talking to her lover sometime in the early summer of 1964, after he had indicated that, on the advice of his minister, he did not intend to see her any more:

"First, I'm going to go to that dear pastor of yours and tell him a few things. . . . When I do tell him that, you won't be in the Redlands Church any more. . . . Look, Sonny Boy, if you think your reputation is going to be ruined, your life won't be worth two cents." Here is Arthwell Hayton, to Lucille Miller: "I'll go to Sheriff Frank Bland and tell him some things that I know about you until you'll wish you'd never heard of Arthwell Hayton." For an affair between a Seventh-Day Adventist dentist's wife and a Seventh-Day Adventist personal-injury lawyer, it seems a curious kind of dialogue.

"Boy, I could get that little boy coming and going," Lucille Miller later confided to Erwin Sprengle, a Riverside contractor who was a business partner of Arthwell Hayton's and a friend to both the lovers. (Friend or no, on this occasion he happened to have an induction coil attached to his telephone in order to tape Lucille Miller's call.) "And he hasn't got one thing on me that he can prove. I mean, I've got concrete—he has nothing concrete." In the same taped conversation with Erwin Sprengle, Lucille Miller mentioned a tape that she herself had surreptitiously made, months before, in Arthwell Hayton's car.

"I said to him, I said 'Arthwell, I just feel like I'm being used.' . . . He started sucking his thumb and he said 'I love you. . . . This isn't something that happened yesterday. I'd marry you tomorrow if I could. I don't love Elaine.' He'd love to hear that played back, wouldn't he?"

"Yeah," drawled Sprengle's voice on the tape. "That would be just a little incriminating, wouldn't it?"

"Just a *little* incriminating," Lucille Miller agreed. "It really *is*."

Later on the tape, Sprengle asked where Cork Miller was.

"He took the children down to the church."

"You didn't go?"

"No."

"You're naughty."

It was all, moreover, in the name of "love"; everyone involved placed a magical faith in the efficacy of the very word. There was the significance that Lucille Miller saw in Arthwell's saying that he "loved" her, that he did not "love" Elaine. There was Arthwell insisting, later, at the trial, that he had never said it, that he may have "whispered sweet nothings in her ear" (as her defense hinted that he had whispered in many ears), but he did not remember bestowing upon her the special seal, saying the word, declaring "love." There was the summer evening when Lucille Miller and Sandy Slagle followed Arthwell Hayton down to his new boat in its mooring at Newport Beach and untied the lines with Arthwell aboard, Arthwell and a girl with whom he later testified he was drinking hot chocolate and watching television. "I did that on purpose," Lucille Miller told Erwin Sprengle later, "to save myself from letting my heart do something crazy."

January 11, 1965, was a bright warm day in Southern California, the kind of day when Catalina floats on the Pacific horizon and the air smells of orange blossoms and it is a long way from the bleak and difficult East, a long way from the cold, a long way from the past. A woman in Hollywood staged an all-night sit-in on the hood of her car to prevent repossession by a finance company. A seventy-year-old pensioner drove his station wagon at five miles an hour past three Gardena poker parlors and emptied three pistols and a twelve-gauge shotgun through their windows, wounding twenty-nine people. "Many young women become prostitutes just to have enough money to play cards," he explained in a note. Mrs. Nick Adams said that she was "not surprised" to hear her husband announce his divorce plans on the Les Crane Show, and, farther north, a sixteen-year-old jumped off the Golden Gate Bridge and lived.

And, in the San Bernardino County Courthouse, the Miller trial opened. The crowds were so bad that the glass courtroom doors were shattered in the crush, and from then on identification disks were issued to the first forty-three spectators in line. The line began forming at 6 A.M., and college girls camped at the courthouse all night, with stores of graham crackers and No-Cal.

All they were doing was picking a jury, those first few days, but the sensational nature of the case had already suggested itself. Early in December there had been an abortive first trial, a trial at which no evidence was ever presented because on the day the jury was seated the San Bernardino *Sun-Telegram* ran an "inside" story quoting Assistant District Attorney Don Turner, the prosecutor, as saying, "We are looking into the circumstances of Mrs. Hayton's death. In view of the current trial concerning the death of Dr. Miller, I do not feel I should comment on Mrs. Hayton's death." It seemed that there had been barbiturates in Elaine Hayton's blood, and there had seemed some irregularity about the way she was dressed on that morning when she was found under the covers, dead. Any doubts about the death at the time, however, had never gotten as far as the Sheriff's Office. "I guess somebody didn't want to rock the boat," Turner said later. "These were prominent people."

Although all of that had not been in the *Sun-Telegram*'s story, an immediate mistrial had been declared. Almost as immediately, there had been another development: Arthwell Hayton had asked newspapermen to an 11 A.M. Sunday morning press conference in his office. There had been television cameras, and flash bulbs popping. "As you gentlemen may know," Hayton had said, striking a note of stiff bonhomie, "there are very often women who become amorous toward their doctor or lawyer. This does not mean on the physician's or lawyer's part that there is any romance toward the patient or client."

"Would you deny that you were having an affair with Mrs. Miller?" a reporter had asked.

"I would deny that there was any romance on my part whatsoever."

It was a distinction he would maintain through all the wearing weeks to come.

So they had come to see Arthwell, these crowds who now milled beneath the dusty palms outside the courthouse, and they had also come to see Lucille, who appeared as a slight, intermittently pretty woman, already pale from lack of sun, a woman who would turn thirty-five before the trial was over and whose tendency toward haggardness was beginning to show, a meticulous woman who insisted, against her lawyer's advice, on coming to court with her hair piled high and lacquered. "I would've been happy if she'd come in with it hanging loose, but Lucille wouldn't do that," her lawyer said. He was Edward P. Foley, a small, emotional Irish Catholic who several times wept in the courtroom. "She has a great honesty, this woman," he added, "but this honesty about her appearance always worked against her."

By the time the trial opened, Lucille Miller's appearance included maternity clothes, for an official examination on December 18 had revealed that she was then three and a half months pregnant, a fact which made picking a jury even more difficult than usual, for Turner was asking the death penalty. "It's unfortunate but there it is," he would say of the pregnancy to each juror in turn, and finally twelve were seated, seven of them women, the youngest forty-one, an assembly of the very peers—housewives, a machinist, a truck driver, a grocery-store manager, a filing clerk—above whom Lucille Miller had wanted so badly to rise.

That was the sin, more than the adultery, which tended to reinforce the one for which she was being tried. It was implicit in both the defense and the prosecution that Lucille Miller was an erring woman, a woman who perhaps wanted too much. But to the prosecution she was not merely a woman who would want a new house and want to go to parties and run up high telephone bills ($1,152 in ten months), but a woman who would go so far as to murder her husband for his $80,000 in insurance, making it appear an accident in order to collect another $40,000 in double indemnity and straight accident policies. To Turner she was a woman who did not want simply her freedom and a reasonable alimony (she could have had that, the defense contended, by going through with her divorce suit), but wanted everything, a woman motivated by "love and greed." She was a "manipulator." She was a "user of people."

To Edward Foley, on the other hand, she was an impulsive woman who "couldn't control her foolish little heart." Where Turner skirted the pregnancy, Foley dwelt upon it, even calling the dead man's mother down from Washington to testify that her son had told her they were going to have another baby because Lucille felt that it would "do much to weld our home again in the pleasant relations that we used to have." Where the prosecution saw a "calculator," the defense saw a "blabbermouth," and in fact Lucille Miller did emerge as an ingenuous conversationalist. Just as, before her husband's death, she had confided in her friends about her love affair, so she chatted about it after his death, with the arresting sergeant. "Of course Cork lived with it for years, you know," her voice was heard to tell Sergeant Paterson on a tape made the morning after her arrest. "After Elaine died, he pushed the panic button one night and just asked me right out, and that, I think, was when he really—the first time he really faced it." When the sergeant asked why she had agreed to talk to him, against the specific instructions of her lawyers, Lucille Miller said airily, "Oh, I've always been basically quite an honest person. . . . I mean I can put a hat in the cupboard and say it cost ten dollars less, but basically I've always kind of just lived my life the way I wanted to, and if you don't like it you can take off."

The prosecution hinted at men other than Arthwell, and even, over Foley's objections, managed to name one. The defense called Miller suicidal. The prosecution produced experts who said that the Volkswagen fire could not have been accidental. Foley produced witnesses who said that it could have been. Lucille's father, now a junior-high-school teacher in Oregon, quoted Isaiah to reporters: "*Every tongue that shall rise against thee in judgment thou shalt condemn.*" "Lucille did wrong, her affair," her mother said judiciously. "With her it was love. But with some I guess it's just passion." There was Debbie, the Millers' fourteen-year-old, testifying in a steady voice about how she and her mother had gone to a supermarket to buy the gasoline can the week before the accident. There was Sandy Slagle, in the courtroom every day, declaring that on at least one occasion Lucille Miller had prevented her husband not only from committing suicide but from committing suicide in such a way that it would appear an accident and ensure the double-indemnity payment. There was Wenche Berg, the pretty twenty-seven-year-old Norwegian governess to Arthwell Hayton's children, testifying that Arthwell had instructed her not to allow Lucille Miller to see or talk to the children.

Two months dragged by, and the headlines never stopped. Southern California's crime reporters were headquartered in San Bernardino for the duration: Howard Hertel from the *Times*, Jim Bennett and Eddy Jo Bernal from the *Herald-Examiner*. Two months in which the Miller trial was pushed off the *Examiner*'s front page only by the Academy Award nominations and Stan Laurel's death. And finally, on March 2, after Turner had reiterated that it was a case of "love and greed," and Foley had protested that his client was being tried for adultery, the case went to the jury.

They brought in the verdict, guilty of murder in the first degree, at 4:50 P.M. on March 5. "She didn't do it," Debbie Miller cried, jumping up from the spectators' section. "She didn't *do* it." Sandy Slagle collapsed in her seat and began to scream. "Sandy, for God's sake please *don't*," Lucille Miller said in a voice that carried across the courtroom, and Sandy Slagle was momentarily subdued. But as the jurors left the courtroom she screamed again: "You're murderers. . . . Every last one of you is a *murderer*." Sheriff's deputies moved in then, each wearing a string tie that read "1965 SHERIFF'S RODEO," and Lucille Miller's father, that sad-faced junior-high-school teacher who believed in the word of Christ and the dangers of wanting to see the world, blew her a kiss off his fingertips.

The California Institution for Women at Frontera, where Lucille Miller is now, lies down where Euclid Avenue turns into country road, not too many miles from where she once lived and shopped and organized the Heart Fund Ball. Cattle graze across the road, and Rainbirds sprinkle the alfalfa. Frontera has a softball field and tennis courts, and looks as if it might be a California junior college, except that the trees are not yet high enough to conceal the concertina wire around the top of the Cyclone fence. On visitors' day there are big cars in the parking area, big Buicks and Pontiacs that belong to grandparents and sisters and fathers (not many of them belong to husbands), and some of them have bumper stickers that say "SUPPORT YOUR LOCAL POLICE."

A lot of California murderesses live here, a lot of girls who somehow misunderstood the promise. Don Turner put Sandra Garner here (and her husband in the gas chamber at San Quentin) after the 1959 desert killings known to crime reporters as "the soda-pop murders." Carole Tregoff is here, and has been ever since she was convicted of conspiring to murder Dr. Finch's wife in West Covina, which is not too far from San Bernardino. Carole Tregoff is in fact a nurse's aide in the prison hospital, and might have attended Lucille Miller had her baby been born at Frontera; Lucille Miller chose instead to have it outside, and paid for the guard who stood outside the delivery room in St. Bernardine's Hospital. Debbie Miller came to take the baby home from the hospital, in a white dress with pink ribbons, and Debbie was allowed to choose a name. She named the baby Kimi Kai. The children live with Harold and Joan Lance now, because Lucille Miller will probably spend ten years at Frontera. Don Turner waived his original request for the death penalty (it was generally agreed that he had demanded it only, in Edward Foley's words, "to get anybody with the slightest trace of human kindness in their veins off the jury"), and settled for life imprisonment with the possibility of parole. Lucille Miller does not like it at Frontera, and has had trouble adjusting. "She's going to have to learn humility," Turner says. "She's going to have to use her ability to charm, to manipulate."

The new house is empty now, the house on the street with the sign that says

PRIVATE ROAD
BELLA VISTA
DEAD END

The Millers never did get it landscaped, and weeds grow up around the fieldstone siding. The television aerial has toppled on the roof, and a trash can is stuffed with the debris of family life: a cheap suitcase, a child's game called "Lie Detector." There is a sign on what would have been the lawn, and the sign reads "ESTATE SALE." Edward Foley is trying to get Lucille Miller's case appealed, but there have been delays. "A trial always comes down to a matter of sympathy," Foley says wearily now. "I couldn't create sympathy for her." Everyone is a little weary now, weary and resigned, everyone except Sandy Slagle, whose bitterness is still raw. She lives in an apartment near the medical school in Loma Linda, and studies reports of the case in *True Police Cases* and *Official Detective Stories.* "I'd much rather we not talk about the Hayton business too much," she tells visitors, and she keeps a tape recorder running. "I'd rather talk about Lucille and what a wonderful person she is and how her rights were violated." Harold Lance does not talk to visitors at all. "We don't want to give away what we can sell," he explains pleasantly; an attempt was made to sell Lucille Miller's personal story to *Life*, but *Life* did not want to buy it. In the district attorney's offices they are prosecuting other murders now, and do not see why the Miller trial attracted so much attention. "It wasn't a very interesting murder as murders go," Don Turner says laconically. Elaine Hayton's death is no longer under investigation. "We know everything we want to know," Turner says.

Arthwell Hayton's office is directly below Edward Foley's. Some people around San Bernardino say that Arthwell Hayton suffered; others say that he did not suffer at all. Perhaps he did not, for time past is not believed to have any bearing upon time present or future, out in the golden land where every day the world is born anew. In any case, on October 17, 1965, Arthwell Hayton married again, married his children's pretty governess, Wenche Berg, at a service in the Chapel of the Roses at a retirement village near Riverside. Later the newlyweds were feted at a reception for seventy-five in the dining room of Rose Garden Village. The bridegroom was in black tie, with a white carnation in his buttonhole. The bride wore a long white *peau de soie* dress and carried a shower bouquet of sweetheart roses with stephanotis streamers. A coronet of seed pearls held her illusion veil.

1966

John Wayne: A Love Song

IN THE SUMMER OF 1943 I was eight, and my father and mother and small brother and I were at Peterson Field in Colorado Springs. A hot wind blew through that summer, blew until it seemed that before August broke, all the dust in Kansas would be in Colorado, would have drifted over the tar-paper barracks and the temporary strip and stopped only when it hit Pikes Peak. There was not much to do, a summer like that: there was the day they brought in the first B-29, an event to remember but scarcely a vacation program. There was an Officers' Club, but no swimming pool; all the Officers' Club had of interest was artificial blue rain behind the bar. The rain interested me a good deal, but I could not spend the summer watching it, and so we went, my brother and I, to the movies.

We went three and four afternoons a week, sat on folding chairs in the darkened Quonset hut which served as a theater, and it was there, that summer of 1943 while the hot wind blew outside, that I first saw John Wayne. Saw the walk, heard the voice. Heard him tell the girl in a picture called *War of the Wildcats* that he would build her a house, "at the bend in the river where the cottonwoods grow." As it happened I did not grow up to be the kind of woman who is the heroine in a Western, and although the men I have known have had many virtues and have taken me to live in many places I have come to love, they have never been John Wayne, and they have never taken me to that bend in the river where the cottonwoods grow. Deep in that part of my heart where the artificial rain forever falls, that is still the line I wait to hear.

I tell you this neither in a spirit of self-revelation nor as an exercise in total recall, but simply to demonstrate that when John Wayne rode through my childhood, and perhaps through yours, he determined forever the shape of certain of our dreams. It did not seem possible that such a man could fall ill, could carry within him that most inexplicable and ungovernable of diseases. The rumor struck some obscure anxiety, threw our very childhoods into question. In John Wayne's world, John Wayne was supposed to give the orders.

"Let's ride," he said, and "Saddle up." "Forward *ho*," and "A man's gotta do what he's got to do." "Hello, there," he said when he first saw the girl, in a construction camp or on a train or just standing around on the front porch waiting for somebody to ride up through the tall grass. When John Wayne spoke, there was no mistaking his intentions; he had a sexual authority so strong that even a child could perceive it. And in a world we understood early to be characterized by venality and doubt and paralyzing ambiguities, he suggested another world, one which may or may not have existed ever but in any case existed no more: a place where a man could move free, could make his own code and live by it; a world in which, if a man did what he had to do, he could one day take the girl and go riding through the draw and find himself home free, not in a hospital with something going wrong inside, not in a high bed with the flowers and the drugs and the forced smiles, but there at the bend in the bright river, the cottonwoods shimmering in the early morning sun.

"Hello, there." Where did he come from, before the tall grass? Even his history seemed right, for it was no history at all, nothing to intrude upon the dream. Born Marion Morrison in Winterset, Iowa, the son of a druggist. Moved as a child to Lancaster, California, part of the migration to that promised land sometimes called "the west coast of Iowa." Not that Lancaster was the promise fulfilled; Lancaster was a town on the Mojave where the dust blew through. But Lancaster was still California, and it was only a year from there to Glendale, where desolation had a different flavor: antimacassars among the orange groves, a middle-class prelude to Forest Lawn. Imagine Marion Morrison in Glendale. A Boy Scout, then a student at Glendale High. A tackle for U.S.C., a Sigma Chi. Summer vacations, a job moving props on the old Fox lot. There, a meeting with John Ford, one of the several directors who were to sense that into this perfect mold might be poured the inarticulate longings of a nation wondering at just what pass the trail had been lost. "Dammit," said Raoul Walsh later, "the son of a bitch looked like a man." And so after a while the boy from Glendale became a star. He did not become an actor, as he has always been careful to point out to interviewers ("How many times do I gotta tell you, I don't act at all, I *re*-act"), but a star, and the star called John Wayne would spend most of the rest of his life with one or another of those directors, out on some forsaken location, in search of the dream.

Out where the skies are a trifle bluer
Out where friendship's a little truer
That's where the West begins.

Nothing very bad could happen in the dream, nothing a man could not face down. But something did. There it was, the rumor, and after a while the headlines. "I licked the Big C," John Wayne announced, as John Wayne would, reducing those outlaw cells to the level of any other outlaws, but even so we all sensed that this would be the one unpredictable confrontation, the one shoot-out Wayne could lose. I have as much trouble as the next person with illusion and reality, and I did not much want to see John Wayne when he must be (or so I thought) having some trouble with it himself, but I did, and it was down in Mexico when he was making the picture his illness had so long delayed, down in the very country of the dream.

It was John Wayne's 165th picture. It was Henry Hathaway's 84th. It was number 34 for Dean Martin, who was working off an old contract to Hal Wallis, for whom it was independent production number 65. It was called *The Sons of Katie Elder*, and it was a Western, and after the three-month delay they had finally shot the exteriors up in Durango, and now they were in the waning days of interior shooting at Estudio Churubusco outside Mexico City, and the sun was hot and the air was clear and it was lunchtime. Out under the pepper trees the boys from the Mexican crew sat around sucking caramels, and down the road some of the technical men sat around a place which served a stuffed lobster and a glass of tequila for one dollar American, but it was inside the cavernous empty commissary where the talent sat around, the reasons for the exercise, all sitting around the big table picking at *huevos con queso* and Carta Blanca beer. Dean Martin, unshaven. Mack Gray, who goes where Martin goes. Bob Goodfried, who was in charge of Paramount publicity and who had flown down to arrange for a trailer and who had a delicate stomach. "Tea and toast," he warned repeatedly. "That's the ticket. You can't trust the lettuce." And Henry Hathaway, the director, who did not seem to be listening to Goodfried. And John Wayne, who did not seem to be listening to anyone.

"This week's gone slow," Dean Martin said, for the third time.

"How can you say that?" Mack Gray demanded.

"*This . . . week's . . . gone . . . slow*, that's how I can say it."

"You don't mean you want it to end."

"I'll say it right out, Mack, I want it to *end*. Tomorrow night I shave this beard, I head for the airport, I say *adiós amigos*! Bye-bye *muchachos*!"

Henry Hathaway lit a cigar and patted Martin's arm fondly. "Not tomorrow, Dino."

"Henry, what are you planning to add? A World War?"

Hathaway patted Martin's arm again and gazed into the middle distance. At the end of the table someone mentioned a man who, some years before, had tried unsuccessfully to blow up an airplane.

"He's still in jail," Hathaway said suddenly.

"In jail?" Martin was momentarily distracted from the question whether to send his golf clubs back with Bob Goodfried or consign them to Mack Gray. "What's he in jail for if nobody got killed?"

"Attempted murder, Dino," Hathaway said gently. "A felony."

"You mean some guy just *tried* to kill me he'd end up in jail?"

Hathaway removed the cigar from his mouth and looked across the table. "Some guy just tried to kill *me* he wouldn't end up in jail. How about you, Duke?"

Very slowly, the object of Hathaway's query wiped his mouth, pushed back his chair, and stood up. It was the real thing, the authentic article, the move which had climaxed a thousand scenes on 165 flickering frontiers and phantasmagoric battlefields before, and it was about to climax this one, in the commissary at Estudio Churubusco outside Mexico City. "Right," John Wayne drawled. "I'd kill him."

*

Almost all the cast of *Katie Elder* had gone home, that last week; only the principals were left, Wayne, and Martin, and Earl Holliman, and Michael Anderson, Jr., and Martha Hyer. Martha Hyer was not around much, but every now and then someone referred to her, usually as "the girl." They had all been together nine weeks, six of them in Durango. Mexico City was not quite Durango; wives like to come along to places like Mexico City, like to shop for handbags, go to parties at Merle Oberon Pagliai's, like to look at her paintings. But Durango. The very name hallucinates. Man's country. Out where the West begins. There had been ahuehuete trees in Durango; a waterfall, rattlesnakes. There had been weather, nights so cold that they had postponed one or two exteriors until they could shoot inside at Churubusco. "It was the girl," they explained. "You couldn't keep the girl out in cold like that." Henry Hathaway had cooked in Durango, *gazpacho* and ribs and the steaks that Dean Martin had ordered flown down from the Sands; he had wanted to cook in Mexico City, but the management of the Hotel Bamer refused to let him set up a brick barbecue in his room. "You really missed something, *Durango*," they would say, sometimes joking and sometimes not, until it became a refrain, Eden lost.

But if Mexico City was not Durango, neither was it Beverly Hills. No one else was using Churubusco that week, and there inside the big sound stage that said LOS HIJOS DE KATIE ELDER on the door, there with the pepper trees and the bright sun outside, they could still, for just so long as the picture lasted, maintain a world peculiar to men who like to make Westerns, a world of loyalties and fond raillery, of sentiment and shared cigars, of interminable desultory recollections; campfire talk, its only point to keep a human voice raised against the night, the wind, the rustlings in the brush.

"Stuntman got hit accidentally on a picture of mine once," Hathaway would say between takes of an elaborately choreographed fight scene. "What was his name, married Estelle Taylor, met her down in Arizona."

The circle would close around him, the cigars would be fingered. The delicate art of the staged fight was to be contemplated.

"I only hit one guy in my life," Wayne would say. "Accidentally, I mean. That was Mike Mazurki."

"Some guy. Hey, Duke says he only hit one guy in his life, Mike Mazurki."

"Some choice." Murmurings, assent.

"It wasn't a choice, it was an accident."

"I can believe it."

"You bet."

"Oh boy. Mike Mazurki."

And so it would go. There was Web Overlander, Wayne's makeup man for twenty years, hunched in a blue Windbreaker, passing out sticks of Juicy Fruit. "*Insect* spray," he would say. "Don't tell us about insect spray. We saw insect spray in Africa, all right. Remember Africa?" Or, "*Steamer* clams. Don't tell us about steamer clams. We got our fill of steamer clams all right, on the *Hatari!* appearance tour. Remember Bookbinder's?" There was Ralph Volkie, Wayne's trainer for eleven years, wearing a red baseball cap and carrying around a clipping from Hedda Hopper, a tribute to Wayne. "This Hopper's some lady," he would say again and again. "Not like some of these guys, all they write is sick, sick, sick, how can you call that guy *sick*, when he's got pains, coughs, works all day, *never complains*. That guy's got the best hook since Dempsey, not *sick*."

And there was Wayne himself, fighting through number 165. There was Wayne, in his thirty-three-year-old spurs, his dusty neckerchief, his blue shirt. "You don't have too many worries about what to wear in these things," he said. "You can wear a blue shirt, or, if you're down in Monument Valley, you can wear a yellow shirt." There was Wayne, in a relatively new hat, a hat which made him look curiously like William S. Hart. "I had this old cavalry hat I loved, but I lent it to Sammy Davis. I got it back, it was unwearable. I think they all pushed it down on his head and said *O.K., John Wayne*—you know, a joke."

There was Wayne, working too soon, finishing the picture with a bad cold and a racking cough, so tired by late afternoon that he kept an oxygen inhalator on the set. And still nothing mattered but the Code. "That guy," he muttered of a reporter who had incurred his displeasure. "I admit I'm balding. I admit I got a tire around my middle. What man fifty-seven doesn't? Big news. Anyway, that guy."

He paused, about to expose the heart of the matter, the root of the distaste, the fracture of the rules that bothered him more than the alleged misquotations, more than the intimation that he was no longer the Ringo Kid. "He comes down, uninvited, but I ask him over anyway. So we're sitting around drinking mescal out of a water jug."

He paused again and looked meaningfully at Hathaway, readying him for the unthinkable denouement. "He had to be *assisted* to his room."

They argued about the virtues of various prizefighters, they argued about the price of J & B in pesos. They argued about dialogue.

"As rough a guy as he is, Henry, I still don't think he'd raffle off his mother's *Bible*."

"I like a shocker, Duke."

They exchanged endless training-table jokes. "You know why they call this memory sauce?" Martin asked, holding up a bowl of chili.

"Why?"

"Because you *remember it in the morning*."

"Hear that, Duke? Hear why they call this memory sauce?"

They delighted one another by blocking out minute variations in the free-for-all fight which is a set piece in Wayne pictures; motivated or totally gratuitous, the fight sequence has to be in the picture, because they so enjoy making it. "Listen—this'll really be funny. Duke picks up the kid, see, and then it takes both Dino and Earl to throw him out the door—*how's that?*"

They communicated by sharing old jokes; they sealed their camaraderie by making gentle, old-fashioned fun of wives, those civilizers, those tamers. "So Señora Wayne takes it into her head to stay up and have one brandy. So for the rest of the night it's 'Yes, Pilar, you're right, dear. I'm a bully, Pilar, you're right, I'm impossible.'"

"You hear that? Duke says Pilar threw a table at him."

"Hey, Duke, here's something funny. That finger you hurt today, get the Doc to bandage it up, go home tonight, show it to Pilar, tell her she did it when she threw the table. You know, make her think she was really cutting up."

They treated the oldest among them respectfully; they treated the youngest fondly. "You see that kid?" they said of Michael Anderson, Jr. "What a kid."

"He don't act, it's right from the heart," said Hathaway, patting his heart.

"Hey kid," Martin said. "You're gonna be in my next picture. We'll have the whole thing, no beards. The striped shirts, the girls, the hi-fi, the eye lights."

They ordered Michael Anderson his own chair, with "BIG MIKE" tooled on the back. When it arrived on the set, Hathaway hugged him: "You see that?" Anderson asked Wayne, suddenly too shy to look him in the eye. Wayne gave him the smile, the nod, the final accolade. "I saw it, kid."

On the morning of the day they were to finish *Katie Elder*, Web Overlander showed up not in his Windbreaker but in a blue blazer. "Home, Mama," he said, passing out the last of his Juicy Fruit. "I got on my getaway clothes." But he was subdued. At noon, Henry Hathaway's wife dropped by the commissary to tell him that she might fly over to Acapulco. "Go ahead," he told her. "I get through here, all I'm gonna do is take Seconal to a point just this side of suicide." They were all subdued. After Mrs. Hathaway left, there were desultory attempts at reminiscing, but man's country was receding fast; they were already halfway home, and all they could call up was the 1961 Bel Air fire, during which Henry Hathaway had ordered the Los Angeles Fire Department off his property and saved the place himself by, among other measures, throwing everything flammable into the swimming pool. "Those fire guys might've just given it up," Wayne said. "Just let it burn." In fact this was a good story, and one incorporating several of their favorite themes, but a Bel Air story was still not a Durango story.

In the early afternoon they began the last scene, and although they spent as much time as possible setting it up, the moment finally came when there was nothing to do but shoot it. "Second team out, first team in, *doors closed*," the assistant director shouted one last time. The stand-ins walked off the set, John Wayne and Martha Hyer walked on. "All right, boys, *silencio*, this is a picture." They took it twice. Twice the girl offered John Wayne the tattered Bible. Twice John Wayne told her that "there's a lot of places I go where that wouldn't fit in." Everyone was very still. And at 2:30 that Friday afternoon Henry Hathaway turned away from the camera, and in the hush that followed he ground out his cigar in a sand bucket. "O.K.," he said. "That's it."

Since that summer of 1943 I had thought of John Wayne in a number of ways. I had thought of him driving cattle up from Texas, and bringing airplanes in on a single engine, thought of him telling the girl at the Alamo that "Republic is a beautiful word." I had never thought of him having dinner with his family and with me and my husband in an expensive restaurant in Chapultepec Park, but time brings odd mutations, and there we were, one night that last week in Mexico. For a while it was only a nice evening, an evening anywhere. We had a lot of drinks and I lost the sense that the face across the table was in certain ways more familiar than my husband's.

And then something happened. Suddenly the room seemed suffused with the dream, and I could not think why. Three men appeared out of nowhere, playing guitars. Pilar Wayne leaned slightly forward, and John Wayne lifted his glass almost imperceptibly toward her. "We'll need some Pouilly-Fuissé for the rest of the table," he said, "and some red Bordeaux for the Duke." We all smiled, and drank the Pouilly-Fuissé for the rest of the table and the red Bordeaux for the Duke, and all the while the men with the guitars kept playing, until finally I realized what they were playing, what they had been playing all along: "The Red River Valley" and the theme from *The High and the Mighty*. They did not quite get the beat right, but even now I can hear them, in another country and a long time later, even as I tell you this.

1965

Where the Kissing Never Stops

OUTSIDE THE MONTEREY COUNTY COURTHOUSE in Salinas, California, the Downtown Merchants' Christmas decorations glittered in the thin sunlight that makes the winter lettuce grow. Inside, the crowd blinked uneasily in the blinding television lights. The occasion was a meeting of the Monterey County Board of Supervisors, and the issue, on this warm afternoon before Christmas 1965, was whether or not a small school in the Carmel Valley, the Institute for the Study of Nonviolence, owned by Miss Joan Baez, was in violation of Section 32-C of the Monterey County Zoning Code, which prohibits land use "detrimental to the peace, morals, or general welfare of Monterey County." Mrs. Gerald Petkuss, who lived across the road from the school, had put the problem another way. "We wonder what kind of people would go to a school like this," she asked quite early in the controversy. "Why they aren't out working and making money."

Mrs. Petkuss was a plump young matron with an air of bewildered determination, and she came to the rostrum in a strawberry-pink knit dress to say that she had been plagued "by people associated with Miss Baez's school coming up to ask where it was although they knew perfectly *well* where it was—one gentleman I remember had a beard."

"Well I don't *care*," Mrs. Petkuss cried when someone in the front row giggled. "I have three small children, that's a big responsibility, and I don't like to have to worry about . . ." Mrs. Petkuss paused delicately. "About who's around."

The hearing lasted from two until 7:15 P.M., five hours and fifteen minutes of participatory democracy during which it was suggested, on the one hand, that the Monterey County Board of Supervisors was turning our country into Nazi Germany, and, on the other, that the presence of Miss Baez and her fifteen students in the Carmel Valley would lead to "Berkeley-type" demonstrations, demoralize trainees at Fort Ord, paralyze Army convoys using the Carmel Valley road, and send property values plummeting throughout the county. "Frankly, I can't conceive of anyone buying property near such an operation," declared Mrs. Petkuss's husband, who is a veterinarian. Both Dr. and Mrs. Petkuss, the latter near tears, said that they were particularly offended by Miss Baez's presence on her property during weekends. It seemed that she did not always stay inside. She sat out under trees, and walked around the property.

"We don't start until one," someone from the school objected. "Even if we did make noise, which we don't, the Petkusses could sleep until one, I don't see what the problem is."

The Petkusses' lawyer jumped up. "The *prob*lem is that the Petkusses happen to have a very beautiful swimming pool, they'd like to have guests out on weekends, like to use the pool."

"They'd have to stand up on a table to see the school."

"They will, too," shouted a young woman who had already indicated her approval of Miss Baez by reading aloud to the supervisors a passage from John Stuart Mill's *On Liberty*. "They'll be out with spyglasses."

"That is *not* true," Mrs. Petkuss keened. "We see the school out of three bedroom windows, out of one living-room window, it's the only direction we can *look*."

Miss Baez sat very still in the front row. She was wearing a long-sleeved navy-blue dress with an Irish lace collar and cuffs, and she kept her hands folded in her lap. She is extraordinary looking, far more so than her photographs suggest, since the camera seems to emphasize an Indian cast to her features and fails to record either the startling fineness and clarity of her bones and eyes or, her most striking characteristic, her absolute directness, her absence of guile. She has a great natural style, and she is what used to be called a lady. "Scum," hissed an old man with a snap-on bow tie who had identified himself as "a veteran of two wars" and who is a regular at such meetings. "*Spaniel.*" He seemed to be referring to the length of Miss Baez's hair, and was trying to get her attention by tapping with his walking stick, but her eyes did not flicker from the rostrum. After a while she got up, and stood until the room was completely quiet. Her opponents sat tensed, ready to spring up and counter whatever defense she was planning to make of her politics, of her school, of beards, of "Berkeley-type" demonstrations and disorder in general.

"Everybody's talking about their forty- and fifty-thousand-dollar houses and their property values going down," she drawled finally, keeping her clear voice low and gazing levelly at the supervisors. "I'd just like to say one thing. I have more than one *hundred* thousand dollars invested in the Carmel Valley, and I'm interested in protecting my property too." The property owner smiled disingenuously at Dr. and Mrs. Petkuss then, and took her seat amid complete silence.

She is an interesting girl, a girl who might have interested Henry James, at about the time he did Verena Tarrant, in *The Bostonians.* Joan Baez grew up in the more evangelistic thickets of the middle class, the daughter of a Quaker physics teacher, the granddaughter of two Protestant ministers, an English-Scottish Episcopalian on her mother's side, a Mexican Methodist on her father's. She was born on Staten Island, but raised on the edges of the academic community all over the country; until she found Carmel, she did not really come from anywhere. When it was time to go to high school, her father was teaching at Stanford, and so she went to Palo Alto High School, where she taught herself "House of the Rising Sun" on a Sears, Roebuck guitar, tried to achieve a vibrato by tapping her throat with her finger, and made headlines by refusing to leave the school during a bomb drill. When it was time to go to college, her father was at M.I.T. and Harvard, and so she went a month to Boston University, dropped out, and for a long while sang in coffee bars around Harvard Square. She did not much like the Harvard Square life ("They just lie in their pads, smoke pot, and do stupid things like that," said the ministers' granddaughter of her acquaintances there), but she did not yet know another.

In the summer of 1959, a friend took her to the first Newport Folk Festival. She arrived in Newport in a Cadillac hearse with "JOAN BAEZ" painted on the side, sang a few songs to 13,000 people, and there it was, the new life. Her first album sold more copies than the work of any other female folksinger in record history. By the end of 1961 Vanguard had released her second album, and her total sales were behind those of only Harry Belafonte, the Kingston Trio, and the Weavers. She had finished her first long tour, had given a concert at

Carnegie Hall which was sold out two months in advance, and had turned down $100,000 worth of concert dates because she would work only a few months a year.

She was the right girl at the right time. She had only a small repertory of Child ballads ("What's Joanie still doing with this Mary Hamilton?" Bob Dylan would fret later), never trained her pure soprano and annoyed some purists because she was indifferent to the origins of her material and sang everything "sad." But she rode in with the folk wave just as it was cresting. She could reach an audience in a way that neither the purists nor the more commercial folksingers seemed to be able to do. If her interest was never in the money, neither was it really in the music: she was interested instead in something that went on between her and the audience. "The easiest kind of relationship for me is with ten thousand people," she said. "The hardest is with one."

She did not want, then or ever, to entertain; she wanted to move people, to establish with them some communion of emotion. By the end of 1963 she had found, in the protest movement, something upon which she could focus the emotion. She went into the South. She sang at Negro colleges, and she was always there where the barricade was, Selma, Montgomery, Birmingham. She sang at the Lincoln Memorial after the March on Washington. She told the Internal Revenue Service that she did not intend to pay the sixty percent of her income tax that she calculated went to the defense establishment. She became the voice that meant protest, although she would always maintain a curious distance from the movement's more ambiguous moments. ("I got pretty sick of those Southern marches after a while," she could say later. "All these big entertainers renting little planes and flying down, always about 35,000 people in town.") She had recorded only a handful of albums, but she had seen her face on the cover of *Time*. She was just twenty-two.

Joan Baez was a personality before she was entirely a person, and, like anyone to whom that happens, she is in a sense the hapless victim of what others have seen in her, written about her, wanted her to be and not to be. The roles assigned to her are various, but variations on a single theme. She is the Madonna of the disaffected. She is the pawn of the protest movement. She is the unhappy analysand. She is the singer who would not train her voice, the rebel who drives the Jaguar too fast, the Rima who hides with the birds and the deer. Above all, she is the girl who "feels" things, who has hung on to the freshness and pain of adolescence, the girl ever wounded, ever young. Now, at an age when the wounds begin to heal whether one wants them to or not, Joan Baez rarely leaves the Carmel Valley.

Although all Baez activities tend to take on certain ominous overtones in the collective consciousness of Monterey County, what actually goes on at Miss Baez's Institute for the Study of Nonviolence, which was allowed to continue operating in the Carmel Valley by a three-two vote of the supervisors, is so apparently ingenuous as to disarm even veterans of two wars who wear snap-on bow ties. Four days a week, Miss Baez and her fifteen students meet at the school for lunch: potato salad, Kool-Aid, and hot dogs broiled on a portable barbecue. After lunch they do ballet exercises to Beatles records, and after that they sit around on the bare floor beneath a photomural of Cypress Point and discuss their reading: *Gandhi on Nonviolence*, Louis Fischer's *Life of Mahatma Gandhi*, Jerome Frank's *Breaking the Thought Barrier*, Thoreau's *On Civil Disobedience*, Krishnamurti's *The First and Last Freedom* and *Think on These Things*, C. Wright Mills's *The Power Elite*, Huxley's *Ends and Means*, and Marshall McLuhan's *Understanding Media*. On the fifth day, they meet as usual but spend the afternoon in total silence, which involves not only not talking but also not reading, not writing, and not smoking. Even on discussion days, this silence is invoked for regular twenty-minute or hour intervals, a regimen described by one student as "invaluable for clearing your mind of personal hangups" and by Miss Baez as "just about the most important thing about the school."

There are no admission requirements, other than that applicants must be at least eighteen years old; admission to each session is granted to the first fifteen who write and ask to come. They come from all over, and they are on the average very young, very earnest, and not very much in touch with the larger scene, less refugees from it than children who do not quite apprehend it. They worry a great deal about "responding to one another with beauty and tenderness," and their response to one another is in fact so tender that an afternoon at the school tends to drift perilously into the never-never. They debate whether or not it was a wise tactic for the Vietnam Day Committee at Berkeley to try to reason with Hell's Angels "on the hip level."

"O.K.," someone argues. "So the Angels just shrug and say 'our thing's violence.' How can the V.D.C. guy answer that?"

They discuss a proposal from Berkeley for an International Nonviolent Army: "The idea is, we go to Vietnam and we go into these villages, and then if they burn them, we burn too."

"It has a beautiful simplicity," someone says.

Most of them are too young to have been around for the memorable events of protest, and the few who have been active tell stories to those who have not, stories which begin "One night at the Scranton Y . . ." or "Recently when we were sitting in at the A.E.C. . . ." and "We had this eleven-year-old on the Canada-to-Cuba march who was at the time corresponding with a Gandhian, and he. . . ." They talk about Allen Ginsberg, "the only one, the only beautiful voice, the only one talking." Ginsberg had suggested that the V.D.C. send women carrying babies and flowers to the Oakland Army Terminal.

"Babies and flowers," a pretty little girl breathes. "But that's so *beautiful*, that's the whole *point*."

"Ginsberg was down here one weekend," recalls a dreamy boy with curly golden hair. "He brought a copy of the *Fuck Songbag*, but we burned it." He giggles. He is holding a clear violet marble up to the window, turning it in the sunlight. "Joan gave it to me," he says. "One night at her house, when we all had a party and gave each other presents. It was like Christmas but it wasn't."

The school itself is an old whitewashed adobe house quite far out among the yellow hills and dusty scrub oaks of the Upper Carmel Valley. Oleanders support a torn wire fence around the school, and there is no sign, no identification at all. The adobe was a one-room county school until 1950; after that it was occupied in turn by the So Help Me Hannah Poison Oak Remedy Laboratory and by a small shotgun-shell manufacturing business, two enterprises which apparently did not present the threat to property values that Miss Baez does. She bought the place in the fall of 1965, after the County Planning Commission told her that zoning prohibited her from running the school in her house, which is on a ten-acre piece a few miles away. Miss Baez is the vice president of the Institute, and its sponsor; the $120 fee paid by each student for each six-week session includes lodging, at an apartment house in Pacific Grove, and does not meet the school's expenses. Miss Baez not only has a $40,000 investment in the school property but is responsible as well for the salary of Ira Sandperl, who is the president of the Institute, the leader of the discussions, and in fact the *eminence gris* of the entire project. "You might think we're starting in a very small way," Ira Sandperl says. "Sometimes the smallest things can change the course of history. Look at the Benedictine order."

In a way it is impossible to talk about Joan Baez without talking about Ira Sandperl. "One of the men on the Planning Commission said I was being led down the primrose path by the lunatic fringe," Miss Baez giggles. "Ira said maybe he's the lunatic and his beard's the fringe." Ira Sandperl is a forty-two-year-old native of St. Louis who has, besides the beard, a shaved head, a large nuclear-disarmament emblem on his corduroy jacket, glittering and slightly messianic eyes, a high cracked laugh and the general look of a man who has, all his life, followed some imperceptibly but fatally askew rainbow. He has spent a good deal of time in pacifist movements around San Francisco, Berkeley, and Palo Alto, and was, at the time he and Miss Baez hit upon the idea of the Institute, working in a Palo Alto bookstore.

Ira Sandperl first met Joan Baez when she was sixteen and was brought by her father to a Quaker meeting in Palo Alto. "There was something magic, something different about her even then," he recalls. "I remember once she was singing at a meeting where I was speaking. The audience was so responsive that night that I said 'Honey, when you grow up we'll have to be an evangelical team.'" He smiles, and spreads his hands.

The two became close, according to Ira Sandperl, after Miss Baez's father went to live in Paris as a UNESCO advisor. "I was the oldest friend around, so naturally she turned to me."

He was with her at the time of the Berkeley demonstrations in the fall of 1964. "We were actually the outside agitators you heard so much about," he says. "Basically we wanted to turn an *un*violent movement into a *non*violent one. Joan was e*nor*mously instrumental in pulling the movement out of its slump, although the boys may not admit it now."

A month or so after her appearance at Berkeley, Joan Baez talked to Ira Sandperl about the possibility of tutoring her for a year. "She found herself among politically knowledgeable people," he says, "and while she had strong *feel*ings, she didn't know any of the socio-economic-political-historical terms of nonviolence."

"It was all vague," she interrupts, nervously brushing her hair back. "I want it to be less vague."

They decided to make it not a year's private tutorial but a school to go on indefinitely, and enrolled the first students late in the summer of 1965. The Institute aligns itself with no movements ("Some of the kids are just leading us into another long, big, violent mess," Miss Baez says), and there is in fact a marked distrust of most activist organizations. Ira Sandperl, for example, had little use for the V.D.C., because the V.D.C. believed in nonviolence only as a limited tactic, accepted conventional power blocs, and even ran one of its leaders for Congress, which is anathema to Sandperl. "Darling, let me put it this way. In civil rights, now, the President signs a bill, who does he call to witness it? Adam Powell? No. He calls Rustin, Farmer, King, *none* of them in the conventional power structure." He pauses, as if envisioning a day when he and Miss Baez will be called upon to witness the signing of a bill outlawing violence. "I'm not optimistic, darling, but I'm hopeful. There's a difference. I'm hopeful."

The gas heater sputters on and off and Miss Baez watches it, her duffel coat drawn up around her shoulders. "Everybody says I'm politically naïve, and I am," she says after a while. It is something she says frequently to people she does not know. "So are the people running politics, or we wouldn't be in wars, would we."

The door opens and a short middle-aged man wearing handmade sandals walks in. He is Manuel Greenhill, Miss Baez's manager, and although he has been her manager for five years, he has never before visited the Institute, and he has never before met Ira Sandperl.

"At last!" Ira Sandperl cries, jumping up. "The disembodied voice on the telephone is here at last! There *is* a Manny Greenhill! There *is* an Ira Sandperl! Here I am! Here's the villain!"

It is difficult to arrange to see Joan Baez, at least for anyone not tuned to the underground circuits of the protest movement. The New York company for which she records, Vanguard, will give only Manny Greenhill's number, in Boston. "Try Area Code 415, prefix DA 4, number 4321," Manny Greenhill will rasp. Area Code 415, DA 4-4321 will connect the caller with Kepler's Bookstore in Palo Alto, which is where Ira Sandperl used to work. Someone at the bookstore will take a number, and, after checking with Carmel to see if anyone there cares to hear from the caller, will call back, disclosing a Carmel number. The Carmel number is not, as one might think by now, for Miss Baez, but for an answering service. The service will take a number, and, after some days or weeks, a call may or may not be received from Judy Flynn, Miss Baez's secretary. Miss Flynn says that she will "try to contact" Miss Baez. "I don't see people," says the heart of this curiously improvised web of wrong numbers, disconnected telephones, and unreturned calls. "I lock the gate and hope nobody comes, but they come anyway. Somebody's been telling them where I live."

She lives quietly. She reads, and she talks to the people who have been told where she lives, and occasionally she and Ira Sandperl go to San Francisco, to see friends, to talk about the peace movement. She sees her two sisters and she sees Ira Sandperl. She believes that her days at the Institute talking and listening to Ira Sandperl are bringing her closer to contentment than anything she has done so far. "Certainly than the singing. I used to stand up there and think I'm getting so many thousand dollars, and for what?" She is defensive about her income ("Oh, I have some money from somewhere"), vague about her plans. "There are some things I want to do. I want to try some rock 'n' roll and some classical music. But I'm not going to start worrying about the charts and the sales because then where are you?"

Exactly where it is she wants to be seems an open question,

bewildering to her and even more so to her manager. If he is asked what his most celebrated client is doing now and plans to do in the future, Manny Greenhill talks about "lots of plans," "other areas," and "her own choice." Finally he hits upon something: "Listen, she just did a documentary for Canadian television, *Variety* gave it a great review, let me read you."

Manny Greenhill reads. "Let's see. Here *Variety* says '*planned only a twenty-minute interview but when CBC officials in Toronto saw the film they decided to go with a special—*'" He interrupts himself. "That's pretty newsworthy right there. Let's see now. Here they quote her ideas on peace . . . you know those . . . here she says '*every time I go to Hollywood I want to throw up*' . . . let's not get into that . . . here now, '*her impersonations of Ringo Starr and George Harrison were dead-on*,' get that, that's good."

Manny Greenhill is hoping to get Miss Baez to write a book, to be in a movie, and to get around to recording the rock 'n' roll songs. He will not discuss her income, although he will say, at once jaunty and bleak, "but it won't be much *this* year." Miss Baez let him schedule only one concert for 1966 (down from an average of thirty a year), has accepted only one regular club booking in her entire career, and is virtually never on television. "What's she going to do on Andy Williams?" Manny Greenhill shrugs. "One time she sang one of Pat Boone's songs with him," he adds, "which proves she can get along, but still. We don't want her up there with some dance routine behind her." Greenhill keeps an eye on her political appearances, and tries to prevent the use of her name. "We say, if they use her name it's a concert. The point is, if they haven't used her name, then if she doesn't like the looks of it she can get out." He is resigned to the school's cutting into her schedule. "Listen," he says. "I've always encouraged her to be political. I may not be active, but let's say I'm concerned." He squints into the sun. "Let's say maybe I'm just too old."

To encourage Joan Baez to be "political" is really only to encourage Joan Baez to continue "feeling" things, for her politics are still, as she herself said, "all vague." Her approach is instinctive, pragmatic, not too far from that of any League of Women Voters member. "Frankly, I'm down on Communism," is her latest word on that subject. On recent events in the pacifist movement, she has this to say: "Burning draft cards doesn't make sense, and burning themselves makes even less." When she was at Palo Alto High School and refused to leave the building during a bomb drill, she was not motivated by theory; she did it because "it was the practical thing to do, I mean it seemed to me this drill was impractical, all these people thinking they could get into some kind of little shelter and be saved with canned water." She has made appearances for Democratic administrations, and is frequently quoted as saying: "There's never been a good Republican folksinger"; it is scarcely the diction of the new radicalism. Her concert program includes some of her thoughts about "waiting on the eve of destruction," and her thoughts are these:

> *My life is a crystal teardrop. There are snowflakes falling in the teardrop and little figures trudging around in slow motion. If I were to look into the teardrop for the next million years, I might never find out who the people are, and what they are doing.*
>
> *Sometimes I get lonesome for a storm. A full-blown storm where everything changes. The sky goes through four days in an hour, the trees wail, little animals skitter in the mud and everything gets dark and goes completely wild. But it's really God—playing music in his favorite cathedral in heaven—shattering stained glass—playing a gigantic organ—thundering on the keys—perfect harmony—perfect joy.*

Although Miss Baez does not actually talk this way when she is kept from the typewriter, she does try, perhaps unconsciously, to hang on to the innocence and turbulence and capacity for wonder, however ersatz or shallow, of her own or of anyone's adolescence. This openness, this vulnerability, is of course precisely the reason why she is so able to "come through" to all the young and lonely and inarticulate, to all those who suspect that no one else in the world understands about beauty and hurt and love and brotherhood. Perhaps because she is older now, Miss Baez is sometimes troubled that she means, to a great many of her admirers, everything that is beautiful and true.

"I'm not very happy with my thinking about it," she says. "Sometimes I tell myself, 'Come on, Baez, you're just like everybody else,' but then I'm not happy with that either."

"Not everybody else has the voice," Ira Sandperl interrupts dotingly.

"Oh, it's all right to have the *voice*, the *voice* is all right . . ."

She breaks off and concentrates for a long while on the buckle of her shoe.

So now the girl whose life is a crystal teardrop has her own place, a place where the sun shines and the ambiguities can be set aside a little while longer, a place where everyone can be warm and loving and share confidences. "One day we went around the room and told a little about ourselves," she confides, "and I discovered that *boy*, I'd had it pretty easy." The late afternoon sun streaks the clean wooden floor and the birds sing in the scrub oaks and the beautiful children sit in their coats on the floor and listen to Ira Sandperl.

"Are you a vegetarian, Ira?" someone asks idly.

"Yes. Yes, I am."

"Tell them, Ira," Joan Baez says. "It's nice."

He leans back and looks toward the ceiling. "I was in the Sierra once." He pauses, and Joan Baez smiles approvingly. "I saw this magnificent tree *grow*ing out of bare rock, *thrust*ing itself . . . and I thought *all right, tree*, if you want to live that much, *all right*! All *right*! O.K.! I won't chop you! I won't eat you! The one thing we all have in common is that we all want to *live*!"

"But what about vegetables," a girl murmurs.

"Well, I realized, of course, that as long as I was in *this flesh* and *this blood* I couldn't be *per*fectly nonviolent."

It is getting late. Fifty cents apiece is collected for the next day's lunch, and someone reads a request from the Monterey County Board of Supervisors that citizens fly American flags to show that "Kooks, Commies, and Cowards do not represent our County," and someone else brings up the Vietnam Day Committee, and a dissident member who had visited Carmel.

"Marv's an honest-to-God nonviolenter," Ira Sandperl declares. "A man of honesty and love."

"He said he's an anarchist," someone interjects doubtfully.

"Right," Ira Sandperl agrees. "Absolutely."

"Would the V.D.C. call Gandhi bourgeois?"

"Oh, they must know better, but they lead such bourgeois lives themselves . . ."

"That's so true," says the dreamy blond boy with the violet marble. "You walk into their office, they're so unfriendly, so unfriendly and cold . . ."

Everyone smiles lovingly at him. By now the sky outside is the color of his marble, but they are all reluctant about gathering up their books and magazines and records, about finding their car keys and ending the day, and by the time they are ready to leave Joan Baez is eating potato salad with her fingers from a bowl in the refrigerator, and everyone stays to share it, just a little while longer where it is warm.

1966

Comrade Laski, C.P.U.S.A. (M.-L.)

MICHAEL LASKI, also known as M. I. Laski, is a relatively obscure young man with deep fervent eyes, a short beard, and a pallor which seems particularly remarkable in Southern California. With his striking appearance and his relentlessly ideological diction, he looks and talks precisely like the popular image of a professional revolutionary, which in fact he is. He was born twenty-six years ago in Brooklyn, moved as a child to Los Angeles, dropped out of U.C.L.A. his sophomore year to organize for the Retail Clerks, and now, as General Secretary of the Central Committee of the Communist Party U.S.A. (Marxist-Leninist), a splinter group of Stalinist-Maoists who divide their energies between Watts and Harlem, he is rigidly committed to an immutable complex of doctrine, including the notions that the traditional American Communist Party is a "revisionist bourgeois clique," that the Progressive Labor Party, the Trotskyites, and "the revisionist clique headed by Gus Hall" prove themselves opportunistic bourgeois lackeys by making their peace appeal not to the "workers" but to the liberal imperialists; and that H. Rap Brown is the tool, if not the conscious agent, of the ruling imperialist class.

Not long ago I spent some time with Michael Laski, down at the Workers' International Bookstore in Watts, the West Coast headquarters of the C.P.U.S.A. (M.-L.). We sat at a kitchen table beneath the hammer-and-sickle flag and the portraits of Marx, Engels, Mao Tse-tung, Lenin, and Stalin (Mao in the favored center position), and we discussed the revolution necessary to bring about the dictatorship of the proletariat. Actually I was interested not in the revolution but in the revolutionary. He had with him a small red book of Mao's poems, and as he talked he squared it on the table, aligned it with the table edge first vertically and then horizontally. To understand who Michael Laski is you must have a feeling for that kind of compulsion. One does not think of him eating, or in bed. He has nothing in common with the passionate personalities who tend to turn up on the New Left. Michael Laski scorns deviationist reformers. He believes with Mao that political power grows out of the barrel of a gun, a point he insists upon with blazing and self-defeating candor. His place in the geography of the American Left is, in short, an almost impossibly lonely and quixotic one, unpopular, unpragmatic. He believes that there are "workers" in the United States, and that, when the time comes, they will "arise," not in anarchy but in conscious concert, and he also believes that "the ruling class" is self-conscious, and possessed of demonic powers. He is in all ways an idealist.

As it happens I am comfortable with the Michael Laskis of this world, with those who live outside rather than in, those in whom the sense of dread is so acute that they turn to extreme and doomed commitments; I know something about dread myself, and appreciate the elaborate systems with which some people manage to fill the void, appreciate all the opiates of the people, whether they are as accessible as alcohol and heroin and promiscuity or as hard to come by as faith in God or History.

But of course I did not mention dread to Michael Laski, whose particular opiate is History. I did suggest "depression," did venture that it might have been "depressing" for him to see only a dozen or so faces at his last May Day demonstration, but he told me that depression was an impediment to the revolutionary process, a disease afflicting only those who do not have ideology to sustain them. Michael Laski, you see, did not feel as close to me as I did to him. "I talk to you at all," he said, "only as a calculated risk. Of course your function is to gather information for the intelligence services. Basically you want to conduct the same probe the F.B.I. would carry out if they could put us in a chair." He paused and tapped the small red book with his fingernails. "And yet," he said finally, "there's a definite advantage to me in talking to you. Because of one fact: these interviews provide a public record of my existence."

Still, he was not going to discuss with me what he called "the underground apparatus" of the C.P.U.S.A. (M.-L.), any more than he would tell me how many members constituted the cadre. "Obviously I'm not going to give you that kind of information," he said. "We know as a matter of course that we'll be outlawed." The Workers' International Bookstore, however, was "an open facility," and I was free to look around. I leafed through some of the literature out of Peking (*Vice-Premier*

Chen Yi Answers Questions Put by Correspondents), Hanoi (*President Ho Chi Minh Answers President L. B. Johnson*), and Tirana, Albania (*The Hue and Cry About a Change in Tito's Policy and the Undeniable Truth*), and I tried to hum, from a North Vietnamese song book, "When the Party Needs Us Our Hearts Are Filled with Hatred." The literature was in the front of the store, along with a cash register and the kitchen table; in back, behind a plywood partition, were a few cots and the press and mimeograph machine on which the Central Committee prints its "political organ," *People's Voice*, and its "theoretical organ," *Red Flag*. "There's a cadre assigned to this facility in order to guarantee the security," Michael Laski said when I mentioned the cots. "They have a small arsenal in back, a couple of shotguns and a number of other items."

So much security may seem curious when one considers what the members of the cadre actually do, which is, aside from selling the *People's Voice* and trying to set up People's Armed Defense Groups, largely a matter of perfecting their own ideology, searching out "errors" and "mistakes" in one another's attitudes. "What we do may seem a waste of time to some people," Michael Laski said suddenly. "Not having any ideology yourself, you might wonder what the Party offers. It offers nothing. It offers thirty or forty years of putting the Party above everything. It offers beatings. Jail. On the high levels, assassination."

But of course that was offering a great deal. The world Michael Laski had constructed for himself was one of labyrinthine intricacy and immaculate clarity, a world made meaningful not only by high purpose but by external and internal threats, intrigues and apparatus, an immutably ordered world in which things mattered. Let me tell you about another day at the Workers' International Bookstore. The Marxist-Leninists had been out selling the *People's Voice*, and now Michael Laski and three other members of the cadre were going over the proceeds, a ceremony as formal as a gathering of the Morgan partners.

"Mr.—*Comrade*—Simmons—what was the total income?" Michael Laski asked.

"Nine dollars and ninety-one cents."

"Over what period of time?"

"Four hours."

"What was the total number of papers sold?"

"Seventy-five."

"And the average per hour?"

"Nineteen."

"The average contribution?"

"Thirteen and a half cents."

"The largest contribution?"

"Sixty cents."

"The smallest?"

"Four cents."

"It was not a very good day, Comrade Simmons. Can you explain?"

"It's always bad the day before welfare and unemployment checks arrive."

"Very good, Comrade Simmons."

You see what the world of Michael Laski is: a minor but perilous triumph of being over nothingness.

1967

7000 Romaine, Los Angeles 38

SEVEN THOUSAND Romaine Street is in that part of Los Angeles familiar to admirers of Raymond Chandler and Dashiell Hammett: the underside of Hollywood, south of Sunset Boulevard, a middle-class slum of "model studios" and warehouses and two-family bungalows. Because Paramount and Columbia and Desilu and the Samuel Goldwyn studios are nearby, many of the people who live around here have some tenuous connection with the motion-picture industry. They once processed fan photographs, say, or knew Jean Harlow's manicurist. 7000 Romaine looks itself like a faded movie exterior, a pastel building with chipped *art moderne* detailing, the windows now either boarded or paned with chicken-wire glass and, at the entrance, among the dusty oleander, a rubber mat that reads WELCOME.

Actually no one is welcome, for 7000 Romaine belongs to Howard Hughes, and the door is locked. That the Hughes "communications center" should lie here in the dull sunlight of Hammett-Chandler country is one of those circumstances that satisfy one's suspicion that life is indeed a scenario, for the Hughes empire has been in our time the only industrial complex in the world—involving, over the years, machinery manufacture, foreign oil-tool subsidiaries, a brewery, two airlines, immense real-estate holdings, a major motion-picture studio, and an electronics and missile operation—run by a man whose *modus operandi* most closely resembles that of a character in *The Big Sleep*.

As it happens, I live not far from 7000 Romaine, and I make a point of driving past it every now and then, I suppose in the same spirit that Arthurian scholars visit the Cornish coast. I am interested in the folklore of Howard Hughes, in the way people react to him, in the terms they use when they talk about him. Let me give you an example. A few weeks ago I lunched with an old friend at the Beverly Hills Hotel. One of the other guests was a well-married woman in her thirties who had once been a Hughes contract starlet, and another was a costume designer who had worked on a lot of Hughes pictures and who still receives a weekly salary from 7000 Romaine, on the understanding that he work for no one else. He has done nothing but cash that weekly check for some years now. They sat there in the sun, the one-time starlet and the sometime costume designer for a man whose public appearances are now somewhat less frequent than those of The Shadow, and they talked about him. They wondered how he was and why he was devoting 1967 to buying up Las Vegas.

"You can't tell me it's like they say, that he bought the Desert Inn just because the high rollers were coming in and they wouldn't let him keep the penthouse," the ex-starlet mused, fingering a diamond as big as the Ritz. "It must be part of some larger mission."

The phrase was exactly right. Anyone who skims the financial press knows that Hughes never has business "transactions," or "negotiations"; he has "missions." His central mission, as *Fortune* once put it in a series of love letters, has always been "to preserve his power as the proprietor of the largest pool of industrial wealth still under the absolute control of a single individual." Nor does Hughes have business "associates"; he has only "adversaries." When the adversaries "appear to be" threatening his absolute control, Hughes "might or might not" take action. It is such phrases as "appear to be" and "might or might not," peculiar to business reportage involving Hughes, that suggested the special mood of a Hughes mission. And here is what the action might or might not be: Hughes might warn, at the critical moment, "You're holding a gun to my head." If there is one thing Hughes dislikes, it is a gun to his head (generally this means a request for an appearance, or a discussion of policy), and at least one president of T.W.A., a company which, as Hughes ran it, bore an operational similarity only to the government of Honduras, departed on this note.

The stories are endless, infinitely familiar, traded by the faithful like baseball cards, fondled until they fray around the edges and blur into the apocryphal. There is the one about the barber, Eddie Alexander, who was paid handsomely to remain on "day and night standby" in case Hughes wanted a haircut. "Just checking, Eddie," Hughes once said when he called Alexander at two in the morning. "Just wanted to see if you were standing by." There was the time Convair wanted to sell Hughes 340 transports and Hughes insisted that, to insure "secrecy," the mission be discussed only between midnight and dawn, by flashlight, in the Palm Springs Municipal Dump. There was the evening when both Hughes and Greg Bautzer, then his lawyer, went incommunicado while, in the conference room of the Chemical Bank in New York, the money men waited to lend T.W.A. $165 million. There they were, $165 million in hand, the men from two of the country's biggest insurance companies and nine of its most powerful banks, all waiting, and it was 7 P.M. of the last day the deal could be made and the bankers found themselves talking by phone not to Hughes, not even to Bautzer, but to Bautzer's wife, the movie star Dana Wynter. "I hope he takes it in pennies," a Wall Street broker said when Hughes, six years later, sold T.W.A. for $546 million, "and drops it on his toes."

Then there are the more recent stories. Howard Hughes is en route to Boston aboard the Super Chief with the Bel Air Patrol riding shotgun. Howard Hughes is in Peter Bent Brigham Hospital. Howard Hughes commandeers the fifth floor of the Boston Ritz. Howard Hughes is or is not buying 37½ percent of Columbia Pictures through the Swiss Banque de Paris. Howard Hughes is ill. Howard Hughes is dead. No, Howard Hughes is in Las Vegas. Howard Hughes pays $13 million for the Desert Inn. $15 million for the Sands. Gives the State of Nevada $6 million for a medical school. Negotiates for ranches, Alamo Airways, the North Las Vegas Air Terminal, more ranches, the rest of the Strip. By July of 1967 Howard Hughes is the largest single landholder in Clark County, Nevada. "Howard likes Las Vegas," an acquaintance of Hughes's once explained, "because he likes to be able to find a restaurant open in case he wants a sandwich."

Why do we like those stories so? Why do we tell them over and over? Why have we made a folk hero of a man who is the antithesis of all our official heroes, a haunted millionaire out of the West, trailing a legend of desperation and power and white sneakers? But then we have always done that. Our favorite people and our favorite stories become so not by any inherent virtue, but because they illustrate something deep in the grain, something unadmitted. Shoeless Joe Jackson, Warren Gamaliel Harding, the *Titanic: how the mighty are fallen.* Charles Lindbergh, Scott and Zelda Fitzgerald, Marilyn Monroe: *the beautiful and damned.* And Howard Hughes. That we have made a hero of Howard Hughes tells us something interesting about ourselves, something only dimly remembered, tells us that the secret point of money and power in America is neither the things that money can buy nor power for power's sake (Americans are uneasy with their possessions, guilty about power, all of which is difficult for Europeans to perceive because they are themselves so truly materialistic, so versed in the uses of power), but absolute personal freedom, mobility, privacy. It is the instinct which drove America to the Pacific, all through the nineteenth century, the desire to be able to find a restaurant open in case you want a sandwich, to be a free agent, live by one's own rules.

Of course we do not admit that. The instinct is socially suicidal, and because we recognize that this is so we have developed workable ways of saying one thing and believing quite another. A long time ago, Lionel Trilling pointed out what he called "the fatal separation" between "the ideas of our educated liberal class and the deep places of the imagination." "I mean only," he wrote, "that our educated class has a ready if mild suspiciousness of the profit motive, a belief in progress, science, social legislation, planning and international cooperation. . . . Those beliefs do great credit to those who hold them. Yet it is a comment, if not on our beliefs then on our way of holding them, that not a single first-rate writer has emerged to deal with these ideas, and the emotions that are consonant with them, in a great literary way." Officially we admire men who exemplify those ideas. We admire the Adlai Stevenson character, the rational man, the enlightened man, the man not dependent upon the potentially psychopathic mode of action. Among rich men, we officially admire Paul Mellon, a socially responsible inheritor in the European mold. There has always been that divergence between our official and our unofficial heroes. It is impossible to think of Howard Hughes without seeing the apparently bottomless gulf between what we say we want and what we do want, between what we officially admire and secretly desire, between, in the largest sense, the people we marry and the people we love. In a nation which increasingly appears to prize social virtues, Howard Hughes remains not merely antisocial but grandly, brilliantly, surpassingly, asocial. He is the last private man, the dream we no longer admit.

1967

California Dreaming

EVERY WEEKDAY MORNING at eleven o'clock, just about the time the sun burns the last haze off the Santa Barbara hills, fifteen or twenty men gather in what was once the dining room of a shirt manufacturer's mansion overlooking the Pacific Ocean and begin another session of what they like to call "clarifying the basic issues." The place is the Center for the Study of Democratic Institutions, the current mutation of the Fund for the Republic, and since 1959, when the Fund paid $250,000 for the marble villa and forty-one acres of eucalyptus, a favored retreat for people whom the Center's president, Robert M. Hutchins, deems controversial, stimulating, and, perhaps above all, cooperative, or *our kind.* "If they just want to work on their own stuff," Hutchins has said, "then they ought not to come here. Unless they're willing to come in and work with the group as a group, then this place is not for them."

Those invited to spend time at the Center get an office (there are no living quarters at the Center) and a salary, the size of which is reportedly based on the University of California pay scale. The selection process is usually described as "mysterious," but it always involves "people we know." Paul Hoffman, who was at one time president of the Ford Foundation and then director of the Fund for the Republic, is now the Center's honorary chairman, and his son is there quite a bit, and Robert Hutchins's son-in-law. Rexford Tugwell, one of the New Deal "brain trust," is there ("Why not?" he asked me. "If I weren't here I'd be in a rest home"), and Harvey Wheeler, the co-author of *Fail-Safe.* Occasionally someone might be asked to the Center because he has built-in celebrity value, *e.g.*, Bishop James Pike. "What we are is a group of highly skilled public-relations experts," Harry Ashmore says. Harry Ashmore is a fixture at the Center, and he regards Hutchins—or, as the president of the Center is inflexibly referred to in the presence of outsiders, Dr. Hutchins—as "a natural intellectual resource." What these highly skilled public-relations experts do, besides clarifying the basic issues and giving a lift to Bennett

Cerf ("My talk with Paul Hoffman on the Coast gave me a lift I won't forget," Bennett Cerf observed some time ago), is to gather every weekday for a few hours of discussion, usually about one of several broad areas that the Center is concentrating upon at any given time—The City, say, or The Emerging Constitution. Papers are prepared, read, revised, reread, and sometimes finally published. This process is variously described by those who participate in it as "pointing the direction for all of us toward a greater understanding" and "applying human reason to the complex problems of our brand-new world."

I have long been interested in the Center's rhetoric, which has about it the kind of ectoplasmic generality that always makes me sense I am on the track of the real soufflé, the genuine American *kitsch*, and so not long ago I arranged to attend a few sessions in Santa Barbara. It was in no sense time wasted. The Center is the most perfectly indigenous cultural phenomenon since the Encyclopaedia Britannica's *Syntopicon*, which sets forth "The 102 Great Ideas of Western Man" and which we also owe to Robert, or Dr., Hutchins. "Don't make the mistake of taking a chair at the big table," I was warned *sotto voce* on my first visit to the Center. "The talk there is pretty high-powered."

"Is there any evidence that living in a violent age encourages violence?" someone was asking at the big table.

"That's hard to measure."

"I think it's the Westerns on television."

"I tend [*pause*] to agree."

Every word uttered at the Center is preserved on tape, and not only colleges and libraries but thousands of individuals receive Center tapes and pamphlets. Among the best-selling pamphlets have been A. A. Berle, Jr.'s *Economic Power and the Free Society*, Clark Kerr's *Unions and Union Leaders of Their Own Choosing*, Donald Michael's *Cybernation: The Silent Conquest*, and Harrison Brown's *Community of Fear*. Seventy-five thousand people a year then write fan letters to the Center, confirming the staff in its conviction that everything said around the place mystically improves the national, and in fact the international, weal. From a Colorado country-day-school teacher: "I use the Center's various papers in my U.S. history–current events course. It seems to me that there is no institution in the

U.S. today engaged in more valuable and first-rate work than the Center." From a California mother: "Now my fifteen-year-old daughter has discovered your publications. This delights me as she is one of those regular teenagers. But when she curls up to read, it is with your booklets."

The notion that providing useful papers for eighth-grade current-events classes and reading for regular teenagers might not be at all times compatible with establishing "a true intellectual community" (another Hutchins aim) would be considered, at the Center, a downbeat and undemocratic cavil. "People are entitled to learn what we're thinking," someone there told me. The place is in fact avidly anti-intellectual, the deprecatory use of words like "egghead" and "ivory tower" reaching heights matched only in a country-club locker room. Hutchins takes pains to explain that by "an intellectual community" he does not mean a community "whose members regard themselves as 'intellectuals.'" Harry Ashmore frets particularly that "men of affairs" may fail to perceive the Center's "practical utility." Hutchins likes to quote Adlai Stevenson on this point: "The Center can be thought of as a kind of national insurance plan, a way of making certain that we will deserve better and better."

Although one suspects that this pragmatic Couéism as a mode of thought comes pretty naturally to most of the staff at the Center, it is also vital to the place's survival. In 1959 the Fund for the Republic bequeathed to the Center the $4 million left of its original $15 million Ford Foundation grant, but that is long gone, and because there was never any question of more Ford money, the Center must pay its own way. Its own way costs about a million dollars a year. Some twelve thousand contributors provide the million a year, and it helps if they can think of a gift to the Center not as a gift to support some visionaries who never met a payroll but "as an investment [tax-exempt] in the preservation of our free way of life." It helps, too, to present the donor with a fairly broad-stroke picture of how the Center is besieged by the forces of darkness, and in this effort the Center has had an invaluable, if unintentional, ally in the Santa Barbara John Birch Society. "You can't let the fascists drive them out of town," I was advised by an admirer of the Center.

Actually, even without the Birch Society as a foil, Hutchins has evolved the $E{=}mc^2$ of all fund-raising formulae. The Center is supported on the same principle as a vanity press. People who are in a position to contribute large sums of money are encouraged to participate in clarifying the basic issues. Dinah Shore, a founding member, is invited up to discuss civil rights with Bayard Rustin. Steve Allen talks over "Ideology and Intervention" with Senator Fulbright and Arnold Toynbee, and Kirk Douglas, a founding member, speaks his piece on "The Arts in a Democratic Society." Paul Newman, in the role of "concerned citizen," is on hand to discuss "The University in America" with Dr. Hutchins, Supreme Court Justice William O. Douglas, Arnold Grant, Rosemary Park, and another concerned citizen, Jack Lemmon. "Apropos of absolutely nothing," Mr. Lemmon says, pulling on a pipe, "just for my own amazement—I don't *know*, but I *want* to know—" At this juncture he wants to know about student unrest, and, at another, he worries that government contracts will corrupt "pure research."

"You mean maybe they get a grant to develop some new kind of *plastic*," Mr. Newman muses, and Mr. Lemmon picks up the cue: "What happens then to the humanities?"

Everyone goes home flattered, and the Center prevails. Well, why not? One morning I was talking with the wife of a big contributor as we waited on the terrace for one of the Center's ready-mixed martinis and a few moments' chat with Dr. Hutchins. "These sessions are way over my head," she confided, "but I go out floating on air."

1967

Marrying Absurd

TO BE MARRIED in Las Vegas, Clark County, Nevada, a bride must swear that she is eighteen or has parental permission and a bridegroom that he is twenty-one or has parental permission. Someone must put up five dollars for the license. (On Sundays and holidays, fifteen dollars. The Clark County Courthouse issues marriage licenses at any time of the day or night except between noon and one in the afternoon, between eight and nine in the evening, and between four and five in the morning.) Nothing else is required. The State of Nevada, alone among these United States, demands neither a premarital blood test nor a waiting period before or after the issuance of a marriage license. Driving in across the Mojave from Los Angeles, one sees the signs way out on the desert, looming up from that moonscape of rattlesnakes and mesquite, even before the Las Vegas lights appear like a mirage on the horizon: "GETTING MARRIED? Free License Information First Strip Exit." Perhaps the Las Vegas wedding industry achieved its peak operational efficiency between 9:00 P.M. and midnight of August 26, 1965, an otherwise unremarkable Thursday which happened to be, by Presidential order, the last day on which anyone could improve his draft status merely by getting married. One hundred and seventy-one couples were pronounced man and wife in the name of Clark County and the State of Nevada that night, sixty-seven of them by a single justice of the peace, Mr. James A. Brennan. Mr. Brennan did one wedding at the Dunes and the other sixty-six in his office, and charged each couple eight dollars. One bride lent her veil to six others. "I got it down from five to three minutes," Mr. Brennan said later of his feat. "I could've married them *en masse*, but they're people, not cattle. People expect more when they get married."

What people who get married in Las Vegas actually do expect—what, in the largest sense, their "expectations" are—strikes one as a curious and self-contradictory business. Las Vegas is the most extreme and allegorical of American settlements, bizarre and beautiful in its venality and in its devotion to immediate gratification, a place the tone of which is set by mobsters and call girls and ladies' room attendants with amyl nitrite poppers in their uniform pockets. Almost everyone notes that there is no "time" in Las Vegas, no night and no day and no past and no future (no Las Vegas casino, however, has taken the obliteration of the ordinary time sense quite so far as Harold's Club in Reno, which for a while issued, at odd intervals in the day and night, mimeographed "bulletins" carrying news from the world outside); neither is there any logical sense of where one is. One is standing on a highway in the middle of a vast hostile desert looking at an eighty-foot sign which blinks "STARDUST" or "CAESAR'S PALACE." Yes, but what does that explain? This geographical implausibility reinforces the sense that what happens there has no connection with "real" life; Nevada cities like Reno and Carson are ranch towns, Western towns, places behind which there is some historical imperative. But Las Vegas seems to exist only in the eye of the beholder. All of which makes it an extraordinarily stimulating and interesting place, but an odd one in which to want to wear a candlelight satin Priscilla of Boston wedding dress with Chantilly lace insets, tapered sleeves and a detachable modified train.

And yet the Las Vegas wedding business seems to appeal to precisely that impulse. "Sincere and Dignified Since 1954," one wedding chapel advertises. There are nineteen such wedding chapels in Las Vegas, intensely competitive, each offering better, faster, and, by implication, more sincere services than the next: Our Photos Best Anywhere, Your Wedding on A Phonograph Record, Candlelight with Your Ceremony, Honeymoon Accommodations, Free Transportation from Your Motel to Courthouse to Chapel and Return to Motel, Religious or Civil Ceremonies, Dressing Rooms, Flowers, Rings, Announcements, Witnesses Available, and Ample Parking. All of these services, like most others in Las Vegas (sauna baths, payroll-check cashing, chinchilla coats for sale or rent) are offered twenty-four hours a day, seven days a week, presumably on the premise that marriage, like craps, is a game to be played when the table seems hot.

But what strikes one most about the Strip chapels, with their wishing wells and stained-glass paper windows and their artificial bouvardia, is that so much of their business is by no means a matter of simple convenience, of late-night liaisons between show girls and baby Crosbys. Of course there is some of that. (One night about eleven o'clock in Las Vegas I watched a bride in an orange minidress and masses of flame-colored hair stumble from a Strip chapel on the arm of her bridegroom, who looked the part of the expendable nephew in movies like *Miami Syndicate*. "I gotta get the kids," the bride whimpered. "I gotta pick up the sitter, I gotta get to the midnight show." "What you gotta get," the bridegroom said, opening the door of a Cadillac Coupe de Ville and watching her crumple on the seat, "is sober.") But Las Vegas seems to offer something other than "convenience"; it is merchandising "niceness," the facsimile of proper ritual, to children who do not know how else to find it, how to make the arrangements, how to do it "right." All day and evening long on the Strip, one sees actual wedding parties, waiting under the harsh lights at a crosswalk, standing uneasily in the parking lot of the Frontier while the photographer hired by The Little Church of the West ("Wedding Place of the Stars") certifies the occasion, takes the picture: the bride in a veil and white satin pumps, the bridegroom usually in a white dinner jacket, and even an attendant or two, a sister or a best friend in hot-pink *peau de soie*, a flirtation veil, a carnation nosegay. "When I Fall in Love It Will Be Forever," the organist plays, and then a few bars of Lohengrin. The mother cries; the stepfather, awkward in his role, invites the chapel hostess to join them for a drink at the Sands. The hostess declines with a professional smile; she has already transferred her interest to the group waiting outside. One bride out, another in, and again the sign goes up on the chapel door: "One moment please—Wedding."

I sat next to one such wedding party in a Strip restaurant the last time I was in Las Vegas. The marriage had just taken place; the bride still wore her dress, the mother her corsage. A bored waiter poured out a few swallows of pink champagne ("on the house") for everyone but the bride, who was too young to be served. "You'll need something with more kick than that," the bride's father said with heavy jocularity to his new son-in-law;

the ritual jokes about the wedding night had a certain Panglossian character, since the bride was clearly several months pregnant. Another round of pink champagne, this time not on the house, and the bride began to cry. “It was just as nice,” she sobbed, “as I hoped and dreamed it would be.”

1967

Slouching Towards Bethlehem

THE CENTER WAS not holding. It was a country of bankruptcy notices and public-auction announcements and commonplace reports of casual killings and misplaced children and abandoned homes and vandals who misspelled even the four-letter words they scrawled. It was a country in which families routinely disappeared, trailing bad checks and repossession papers. Adolescents drifted from city to torn city, sloughing off both the past and the future as snakes shed their skins, children who were never taught and would never now learn the games that had held the society together. People were missing. Children were missing. Parents were missing. Those left behind filed desultory missing-persons reports, then moved on themselves.

It was not a country in open revolution. It was not a country under enemy siege. It was the United States of America in the cold late spring of 1967, and the market was steady and the G.N.P. high and a great many articulate people seemed to have a sense of high social purpose and it might have been a spring of brave hopes and national promise, but it was not, and more and more people had the uneasy apprehension that it was not. All that seemed clear was that at some point we had aborted ourselves and butchered the job, and because nothing else seemed so relevant I decided to go to San Francisco. San Francisco was where the social hemorrhaging was showing up. San Francisco was where the missing children were gathering and calling themselves "hippies." When I first went to San Francisco in that cold late spring of 1967 I did not even know what I wanted to find out, and so I just stayed around awhile, and made a few friends.

A sign on Haight Street, San Francisco:

> *Last Easter Day*
> *My Christopher Robin wandered away.*
> *He called April 10th*
> *But he hasn't called since*

He said he was coming home
But he hasn't shown.

If you see him on Haight
Please tell him not to wait
I need him now
I don't care how
If he needs the bread
I'll send it ahead.

If there's hope
Please write me a note
If he's still there
Tell him how much I care
Where he's at I need to know
For I really love him so!

Deeply,
Marla

Marla Pence
12702 NE. Multnomah
Portland, Ore. 97230
503/252-2720.

I am looking for somebody called Deadeye and I hear he is on the Street this afternoon doing a little business, so I keep an eye out for him and pretend to read the signs in the Psychedelic Shop on Haight Street when a kid, sixteen, seventeen, comes in and sits on the floor beside me.

"What are you looking for," he says.

I say nothing much.

"I been out of my mind for three days," he says. He tells me he's been shooting crystal, which I already pretty much know because he does not bother to keep his sleeves rolled down over the needle tracks. He came up from Los Angeles some number of weeks ago, he doesn't remember what number, and now he'll take off for New York, if he can find a ride. I show him a sign offering a ride to Chicago. He wonders where Chicago is. I ask where he comes from. "Here," he says. I mean before here. "San Jose, Chula Vista, I dunno. My mother's in Chula Vista."

A few days later I run into him in Golden Gate Park when the Grateful Dead are playing. I ask if he found a ride to New York. "I hear New York's a bummer," he says.

Deadeye never showed up that day on the Street, and somebody says maybe I can find him at his place. It is three o'clock and Deadeye is in bed. Somebody else is asleep on the living-room couch, and a girl is sleeping on the floor beneath a poster of Allen Ginsberg, and there are a couple of girls in pajamas making instant coffee. One of the girls introduces me to the friend on the couch, who extends one arm but does not get up because he is naked. Deadeye and I have a mutual acquaintance, but he does not mention his name in front of the others. "The man you talked to," he says, or "that man I was referring to earlier." The man is a cop.

The room is overheated and the girl on the floor is sick. Deadeye says she has been sleeping for twenty-four hours now. "Lemme ask you something," he says. "You want some grass?" I say I have to be moving on. "You want it," Deadeye says, "it's yours." Deadeye used to be an Angel around Los Angeles but that was a few years ago. "Right now," he says, "I'm trying to set up this groovy religious group—'Teenage Evangelism.'"

Don and Max want to go out to dinner but Don is only eating macrobiotic so we end up in Japantown again. Max is telling me how he lives free of all the old middle-class Freudian hang-ups. "I've had this old lady for a couple of months now, maybe she makes something special for my dinner and I come in three days late and tell her I've been balling some other chick, well, maybe she shouts a little but then I say 'That's me, baby,' and she laughs and says 'That's you, Max.'" Max says it works both ways. "I mean if she comes in and tells me she wants to ball Don, maybe, I say 'O.K., baby, it's your trip.'"

Max sees his life as a triumph over "don'ts." Among the don'ts he had done before he was twenty-one were peyote, alcohol, mescaline, and Methedrine. He was on a Meth trip for three years in New York and Tangier before he found acid. He first tried peyote when he was in an Arkansas boys' school and got down to the Gulf and met "an Indian kid who was doing a don't. Then every weekend I could get loose I'd hitchhike seven hundred miles to Brownsville, Texas, so I could cop peyote. Peyote went for thirty cents a button down in Brownsville on the street." Max dropped in and out of most of the schools and fashionable clinics in the eastern half of America, his standard technique for dealing with boredom being to leave. Example: Max was in a hospital in New York and "the night nurse was a groovy spade, and in the afternoon for therapy there was a chick from Israel who was interesting, but there was nothing much to do in the morning, so I left."

We drink some more green tea and talk about going up to Malakoff Diggings in Nevada County because some people are starting a commune there and Max thinks it would be a groove to take acid in the diggings. He says maybe we could go next week, or the week after, or anyway sometime before his case comes up. Almost everybody I meet in San Francisco has to go to court at some point in the middle future. I never ask why.

I am still interested in how Max got rid of his middle-class Freudian hang-ups and I ask if he is now completely free.

"Nah," he says. "I got acid."

Max drops a 250- or 350-microgram tab every six or seven days.

Max and Don share a joint in the car and we go over to North Beach to find out if Otto, who has a temporary job there, wants to go to Malakoff Diggings. Otto is pitching some electronics engineers. The engineers view our arrival with some interest, maybe, I think, because Max is wearing bells and an Indian headband. Max has a low tolerance for straight engineers and their Freudian hang-ups. "Look at 'em," he says. "They're always yelling 'queer' and then they come sneaking down to the Haight-Ashbury trying to get the hippie chick because she fucks."

We do not get around to asking Otto about Malakoff Diggings because he wants to tell me about a fourteen-year-old he knows who got busted in the Park the other day. She was just walking through the Park, he says, minding her own, carrying her schoolbooks, when the cops took her in and booked her and gave her a pelvic. "*Fourteen years old*," Otto says. "A *pelvic*."

"Coming down from acid," he adds, "that could be a real bad trip."

*

I call Otto the next afternoon to see if he can reach the fourteen-year-old. It turns out she is tied up with rehearsals for her junior-high-school play, *The Wizard of Oz*. "Yellow-brick-road time," Otto says. Otto was sick all day. He thinks it was some cocaine-and-wheat somebody gave him.

There are always little girls around rock groups—the same little girls who used to hang around saxophone players, girls who live on the celebrity and power and sex a band projects when it plays—and there are three of them out here this afternoon in Sausalito where the Grateful Dead rehearse. They are all pretty and two of them still have baby fat and one of them dances by herself with her eyes closed.

I ask a couple of the girls what they do.

"I just kind of come out here a lot," one of them says.

"I just sort of know the Dead," the other says.

The one who just sort of knows the Dead starts cutting up a loaf of French bread on the piano bench. The boys take a break and one of them talks about playing the Los Angeles Cheetah, which is in the old Aragon Ballroom. "We were up there drinking beer where Lawrence Welk used to sit," Jerry Garcia says.

The little girl who was dancing by herself giggles. "Too much," she says softly. Her eyes are still closed.

Somebody said that if I was going to meet some runaways I better pick up a few hamburgers and Cokes on the way, so I did, and we are eating them in the Park together, me, Debbie who is fifteen, and Jeff who is sixteen. Debbie and Jeff ran away twelve days ago, walked out of school one morning with $100 between them. Because a missing-juvenile is out on Debbie—she was already on probation because her mother had once taken her down to the police station and declared her incorrigible—this is only the second time they have been out of a friend's apartment since they got to San Francisco. The first time they went over to the Fairmont Hotel and rode the outside elevator, three times up and three times down. "Wow," Jeff says, and that is all he can think to say, about that.

I ask why they ran away.

"My parents said I had to go to church," Debbie says. "And they wouldn't let me dress the way I wanted. In the seventh grade my skirts were longer than anybody's—it got better in the eighth grade, but still."

"Your mother was kind of a bummer," Jeff agrees.

"They didn't like Jeff. They didn't like my girlfriends. My father thought I was cheap and he told me so. I had a C average and he told me I couldn't date until I raised it, and that bugged me too."

"My mother was just a genuine all-American bitch," Jeff says. "She was really troublesome about hair. Also she didn't like boots. It was really weird."

"Tell about the chores," Debbie says.

"For example I had chores. If I didn't finish ironing my shirts for the week I couldn't go out for the weekend. It was weird. Wow."

Debbie giggles and shakes her head. "This year's gonna be wild."

"We're just gonna let it all happen," Jeff says. "Everything's in the future, you can't pre-plan it. First we get jobs, then a place to live. Then, I dunno."

Jeff finishes off the French fries and gives some thought to what kind of job he could get. "I always kinda dug metal shop, welding, stuff like that." Maybe he could work on cars, I say. "I'm not too mechanically minded," he says. "Anyway you can't pre-plan."

"I could get a job baby-sitting," Debbie says. "Or in a dime store."

"You're always talking about getting a job in a dime store," Jeff says.

"That's because I worked in a dime store already."

Debbie is buffing her fingernails with the belt to her suède jacket. She is annoyed because she chipped a nail and because I do not have any polish remover in the car. I promise to get her to a friend's apartment so that she can redo her manicure, but something has been bothering me and as I fiddle with the ignition I finally ask it. I ask them to think back to when they were children, to tell me what they had wanted to be when they were grown up, how they had seen the future then.

Jeff throws a Coca-Cola bottle out the car window. "I can't remember I ever thought about it," he says.

"I remember I wanted to be a veterinarian once," Debbie says. "But now I'm more or less working in the vein of being an artist or a model or a cosmetologist. Or something."

I hear quite a bit about one cop, Officer Arthur Gerrans, whose name has become a synonym for zealotry on the Street. "He's our Officer Krupke," Max once told me. Max is not personally wild about Officer Gerrans because Officer Gerrans took Max in after the Human Be-In last winter, that's the big Human Be-In in Golden Gate Park where 20,000 people got turned on free, or 10,000 did, or some number did, but then Officer Gerrans has busted almost everyone in the District at one time or another. Presumably to forestall a cult of personality, Officer Gerrans was transferred out of the District not long ago, and when I see him it is not at the Park Station but at the Central Station on Greenwich Avenue.

We are in an interrogation room, and I am interrogating Officer Gerrans. He is young and blond and wary and I go in slow. I wonder what he thinks "the major problems" in the Haight are.

Officer Gerrans thinks it over. "I would say the major problems there," he says finally, "the major problems are narcotics and juveniles. Juveniles and narcotics, those are your major problems."

I write that down.

"Just one moment," Officer Gerrans says, and leaves the room. When he comes back he tells me that I cannot talk to him without permission from Chief Thomas Cahill.

"In the meantime," Officer Gerrans adds, pointing at the notebook in which I have written *major problems: juveniles, narcotics*, "I'll take those notes."

The next day I apply for permission to talk to Officer Gerrans and also to Chief Cahill. A few days later a sergeant returns my call.

"We have finally received clearance from the Chief per your request," the sergeant says, "and that is taboo."

I wonder why it is taboo to talk to Officer Gerrans.

Officer Gerrans is involved in court cases coming to trial.

I wonder why it is taboo to talk to Chief Cahill.

The Chief has pressing police business.

I wonder if I can talk to anyone at all in the Police Department.

"No," the sergeant says, "not at the particular moment."

Which was my last official contact with the San Francisco Police Department.

Norris and I are standing around the Panhandle and Norris is telling me how it is all set up for a friend to take me to Big Sur. I say what I really want to do is spend a few days with Norris and his wife and the rest of the people in their house. Norris says it would be a lot easier if I'd take some acid. I say I'm unstable. Norris says all right, anyway, *grass*, and he squeezes my hand.

One day Norris asks how old I am. I tell him I am thirty-two. It takes a few minutes, but Norris rises to it. "Don't worry," he says at last. "There's old hippies too."

It is a pretty nice evening and nothing much happening and Max brings his old lady, Sharon, over to the Warehouse. The Warehouse, which is where Don and a floating number of other people live, is not actually a warehouse but the garage of a condemned hotel. The Warehouse was conceived as total theater, a continual happening, and I always feel good there. What happened ten minutes ago or what is going to happen a half hour from now tends to fade from mind in the Warehouse. Somebody is usually doing something interesting, like working on a light show, and there are a lot of interesting things around, like an old Chevrolet touring car which is used as a bed and a vast American flag fluttering up in the shadows and an overstuffed chair suspended like a swing from the rafters, the point of that being that it gives you a sensory-deprivation high.

One reason I particularly like the Warehouse is that a child named Michael is staying there now. Michael's mother, Sue Ann, is a sweet wan girl who is always in the kitchen cooking seaweed or baking macrobiotic bread while Michael amuses himself with joss sticks or an old tambourine or a rocking horse with the paint worn off. The first time I ever saw Michael was on that rocking horse, a very blond and pale and dirty child on a rocking horse with no paint. A blue theatrical spotlight was the only light in the Warehouse that afternoon, and there was Michael in it, crooning softly to the wooden horse. Michael is three years old. He is a bright child but does not yet talk.

This particular night Michael is trying to light his joss sticks and there are the usual number of people floating through and they all drift into Don's room and sit on the bed and pass joints. Sharon is very excited when she arrives. "*Don*," she cries, breathless. "We got some STP today." At this time STP is a pretty big deal, remember; nobody yet knew what it was and it was relatively, although just relatively, hard to come by. Sharon is blond and scrubbed and probably seventeen, but Max is a little vague about that since his court case comes up in a month or so and he doesn't need statutory rape on top of it. Sharon's parents were living apart when last she saw them. She does not miss school or anything much about her past, except her younger brother. "I want to turn him on," she confided one day. "He's fourteen now, that's the perfect age. I know where he goes to high school and someday I'll just go get him."

Time passes and I lose the thread and when I pick it up again Max seems to be talking about what a beautiful thing it is the way Sharon washes dishes.

"Well it *is* beautiful," Sharon says. "*Every*thing is. I mean you watch that blue detergent blob run on the plate, watch the grease cut—well, it can be a real trip."

Pretty soon now, maybe next month, maybe later, Max and Sharon plan to leave for Africa and India, where they can live off the land. "I got this little trust fund, see," Max says, "which is useful in that it tells cops and border patrols I'm O.K., but living off the land is the thing. You can get your high and get your dope in the city, O.K., but we gotta get out somewhere and live organically."

"Roots and things," Sharon says, lighting another joss stick for Michael. Michael's mother is still in the kitchen cooking seaweed. "You can eat them."

Maybe eleven o'clock, we move from the Warehouse to the place where Max and Sharon live with a couple named Tom and Barbara. Sharon is pleased to get home ("I hope you got some hash joints fixed in the kitchen," she says to Barbara by way of greeting) and everybody is pleased to show off the apartment, which has a lot of flowers and candles and paisleys. Max and Sharon and Tom and Barbara get pretty high on hash, and everyone dances a little and we do some liquid projections and set up a strobe and take turns getting a high on that. Quite late, somebody called Steve comes in with a pretty, dark girl. They have been to a meeting of people who practice a Western yoga, but they do not seem to want to talk about that. They lie on the floor awhile, and then Steve stands up.

"Max," he says, "I want to say one thing."

"It's your trip." Max is edgy.

"I found love on acid. But I lost it. And now I'm finding it again. With nothing but grass."

Max mutters that heaven and hell are both in one's karma.

"That's what bugs me about psychedelic art," Steve says.

"What about psychedelic art," Max says. "I haven't seen much psychedelic art."

Max is lying on a bed with Sharon, and Steve leans down to him. "Groove, baby," he says. "You're a groove."

Steve sits down then and tells me about one summer when he was at a school of design in Rhode Island and took thirty trips, the last ones all bad. I ask why they were bad. "I could tell you it was my neuroses," he says, "but fuck that."

A few days later I drop by to see Steve in his apartment. He paces nervously around the room he uses as a studio and shows me some paintings. We do not seem to be getting to the point.

"Maybe you noticed something going on at Max's," he says abruptly.

It seems that the girl he brought, the dark pretty one, had once been Max's girl. She had followed him to Tangier and now to San Francisco. But Max has Sharon. "So she's kind of staying around here," Steve says.

Steve is troubled by a lot of things. He is twenty-three, was raised in Virginia, and has the idea that California is the beginning of the end. "I feel it's insane," he says, and his voice drops. "This chick tells me there's no meaning to life but it doesn't matter, we'll just flow right out. There've been times I felt like packing up and taking off for the East Coast again, at least there I had a *target*. At least there you expect that it's going to *happen.*" He lights a cigarette for me and his hands shake. "Here you know it's not going to."

I ask what it is that is supposed to happen.

"I don't know," he says. "Something. Anything."

Arthur Lisch is on the telephone in his kitchen, trying to sell VISTA a program for the District. "We already *got* an emergency," he says into the telephone, meanwhile trying to disentangle his daughter, age one and a half, from the cord. "We don't get help here, nobody can guarantee what's going to happen. We've got people sleeping in the streets here. We've got people starving to death." He pauses. "All right," he says then, and his voice rises. "So they're doing it by choice. So what."

By the time he hangs up he has limned what strikes me as a pretty Dickensian picture of life on the edge of Golden Gate Park, but then this is my first exposure to Arthur Lisch's "riot-on-the-Street-unless" pitch. Arthur Lisch is a kind of leader of the Diggers, who, in the official District mythology, are supposed to be a group of anonymous good guys with no thought in their collective head but to lend a helping hand. The official District mythology also has it that the Diggers have no "leaders," but nonetheless Arthur Lisch is one. Arthur Lisch is also a paid worker for the American Friends' Service Committee and he lives with his wife, Jane, and their two small children in a railroad flat, which on this particular day lacks organization. For one thing the telephone keeps ringing. Arthur promises to attend a hearing at city hall. Arthur promises to "send Edward, he's O.K." Arthur promises to get a good group, maybe the Loading Zone, to play free for a Jewish benefit. For a second thing the baby is crying, and she does not stop until Jane Lisch appears with a jar of Gerber's Junior Chicken Noodle Dinner. Another confusing element is somebody named Bob, who just sits in the living room and looks at his toes. First he looks at the toes on one foot, then at the toes on the other. I make several attempts to include Bob in the conversation before I realize he is on a bad trip. Moreover, there are two people hacking up what looks like a side of beef on the kitchen floor, the idea being that when it gets hacked up, Jane Lisch can cook it for the daily Digger feed in the Park.

Arthur Lisch does not seem to notice any of this. He just keeps talking about cybernated societies and the guaranteed annual wage and riot on the Street, unless.

I call the Lisches a day or so later and ask for Arthur. Jane Lisch says he's next door taking a shower because somebody is coming down from a bad trip in their bathroom. Besides the freak-out in the bathroom they are expecting a psychiatrist in to look at Bob. Also a doctor for Edward, who is not O.K. at all but has the flu. Jane says maybe I should talk to Chester Anderson. She will not give me his number.

Chester Anderson is a legacy of the Beat Generation, a man in his middle thirties whose peculiar hold on the District derives from his possession of a mimeograph machine, on which he prints communiqués signed "the communication company." It is another tenet of the official District mythology that the communication company will print anything anybody has to say, but in fact Chester Anderson prints only what he writes himself, agrees with, or considers harmless or dead matter. His statements, which are left in piles and pasted on windows around Haight Street, are regarded with some apprehension in the District and with considerable interest by outsiders, who study them, like China watchers, for subtle shifts in obscure ideologies. An Anderson communiqué might be doing something as specific as fingering someone who is said to have set up a marijuana bust, or it might be working in a more general vein:

> Pretty little 16-year-old middle-class chick comes to the Haight to see what it's all about & gets picked up by a 17-year-old street dealer who spends all day shooting her full of speed again & again, then feeds her 3,000 mikes & raffles off her temporarily unemployed body for the biggest Haight Street gangbang since the night before last. The politics and ethics of ecstasy. Rape is as common as bullshit on Haight Street. Kids are starving on the Street. Minds and bodies are being maimed as we watch, a scale model of Vietnam.

Somebody other than Jane Lisch gave me an address for Chester Anderson, 443 Arguello, but 443 Arguello does not exist. I telephone the wife of the man who gave me 443 Arguello and she says it's 742 Arguello.

"But don't go up there," she says.

I say I'll telephone.

"There's no number," she says. "I can't give it to you."

"742 Arguello," I say.

"No," she says. "I don't know. And don't go there. And don't use either my name or my husband's name if you do."

She is the wife of a full professor of English at San Francisco State College. I decide to lie low on the question of Chester Anderson for awhile.

Paranoia strikes deep—
Into your life it will creep—
is a song the Buffalo
Springfield sings.

The appeal of Malakoff Diggings has kind of faded out but Max says why don't I come to his place, just be there, the next time he takes acid. Tom will take it too, probably Sharon, maybe Barbara. We can't do it for six or seven days because Max and Tom are in STP space now. They are not crazy about STP but it has advantages. "You've still got your forebrain," Tom says. "I could write behind STP, but not behind acid." This is the first time I have heard of anything you can't do behind acid, also the first time I have heard that Tom writes.

Otto is feeling better because he discovered it wasn't the cocaine-and-wheat that made him sick. It was the chicken pox, which he caught baby-sitting for Big Brother and the Holding Company one night when they were playing. I go over to see him and meet Vicki, who sings now and then with a group called the Jook Savages and lives at Otto's place. Vicki dropped out of Laguna High "because I had mono," followed the Grateful Dead up to San Francisco one time and has been here "for a while." Her mother and father are divorced, and she does not see her father, who works for a network in New York. A few months ago he came out to do a documentary on the District and tried to find her, but couldn't. Later he wrote her a letter in care of her mother urging her to go back to school. Vicki guesses maybe she will sometime but she doesn't see much point in it right now.

*

We are eating a little tempura in Japantown, Chet Helms and I, and he is sharing some of his insights with me. Until a couple of years ago Chet Helms never did much besides hitchhiking, but now he runs the Avalon Ballroom and flies over the Pole to check out the London scene and says things like "Just for the sake of clarity I'd like to categorize the aspects of primitive religion as I see it." Right now he is talking about Marshall McLuhan and how the printed word is finished, out, over. "The *East Village Other* is one of the few papers in America whose books are in the black," he says. "I know that from reading *Barron's*."

A new group is supposed to play in the Panhandle today but they are having trouble with the amplifier and I sit in the sun listening to a couple of little girls, maybe seventeen years old. One of them has a lot of makeup and the other wears Levi's and cowboy boots. The boots do not look like an affectation, they look like she came up off a ranch about two weeks ago. I wonder what she is doing here in the Panhandle trying to make friends with a city girl who is snubbing her but I do not wonder long, because she is homely and awkward and I think of her going all the way through the consolidated union high school out there where she comes from and nobody ever asking her to go into Reno on Saturday night for a drive-in movie and a beer on the riverbank, so she runs. "I know a thing about dollar bills," she is saying now. "You get one that says '1111' in one corner and '1111' in another, you take it down to Dallas, Texas, they'll give you $15 for it."

"Who will?" the city girl asks.

"I don't know."

"There are only three significant pieces of data in the world today," is another thing Chet Helms told me one night. We were at the Avalon and the big strobe was going and the colored lights and the Day-Glo painting and the place was full of high-school kids trying to look turned on. The Avalon sound system projects 126 decibels at 100 feet but to Chet Helms the sound is just there, like the air, and he talks through it. "The first is," he said, "God died last year and was obited by the press. The second is, fifty percent of the population is or will be under twenty-five." A boy shook a tambourine toward us and Chet smiled benevolently at him. "The third," he said, "is that they got twenty billion irresponsible dollars to spend."

Thursday comes, some Thursday, and Max and Tom and Sharon and maybe Barbara are going to take some acid. They want to drop it about three o'clock. Barbara has baked fresh bread, Max has gone to the Park for fresh flowers, and Sharon is making a sign for the door which reads "DO NOT DISTURB, RING, KNOCK, OR IN ANY OTHER WAY DISTURB. LOVE." This is not how I would put it to either the health inspector, who is due this week, or any of the several score narcotics agents in the neighborhood, but I figure the sign is Sharon's trip.

Once the sign is finished Sharon gets restless. "Can I at least play the new record?" she asks Max.

"Tom and Barbara want to save it for when we're high."

"I'm getting bored, just sitting around here."

Max watches her jump up and walk out. "That's what you call pre-acid uptight jitters," he says.

Barbara is not in evidence. Tom keeps walking in and out. "All these innumerable last-minute things you have to do," he mutters.

"It's a tricky thing, acid," Max says after a while. He is turning the stereo on and off. "When a chick takes acid, it's all right if she's alone, but when she's living with somebody this edginess comes out. And if the hour-and-a-half process before you take the acid doesn't go smooth . . ." He picks up a roach and studies it, then adds, "They're having a little thing back there with Barbara."

Sharon and Tom walk in.

"You pissed off too?" Max asks Sharon.

Sharon does not answer.

Max turns to Tom. "Is she all right?"

"Yeh."

"Can we take acid?" Max is on edge.

"I don't know what she's going to do."

"What do you want to do?"

"What I want to do depends on what she wants to do." Tom is rolling some joints, first rubbing the papers with a marijuana resin he makes himself. He takes the joints back to the bedroom, and Sharon goes with him.

"Something like this happens every time people take acid," Max says. After a while he brightens and develops a theory around it. "Some people don't like to go out of themselves, that's the trouble. You probably wouldn't. You'd probably like only a quarter of a tab. There's still an ego on a quarter tab, and it wants things. Now if that thing is balling—and your old lady or your old man is off somewhere flashing and doesn't want to be touched—well, you get put down on acid, you can be on a bummer for months."

Sharon drifts in, smiling. "Barbara might take some acid, we're all feeling better, we smoked a joint."

At three-thirty that afternoon Max, Tom, and Sharon placed tabs under their tongues and sat down together in the living room to wait for the flash. Barbara stayed in the bedroom, smoking hash. During the next four hours a window banged once in Barbara's room, and about five-thirty some children had a fight on the street. A curtain billowed in the afternoon wind. A cat scratched a beagle in Sharon's lap. Except for the sitar music on the stereo there was no other sound or movement until seven-thirty, when Max said "Wow."

I spot Deadeye on Haight Street, and he gets in the car. Until we get off the Street he sits very low and inconspicuous. Deadeye wants me to meet his old lady, but first he wants to talk to me about how he got hip to helping people.

"Here I was, just a tough kid on a motorcycle," he says, "and suddenly I see that young people don't have to walk alone." Deadeye has a clear evangelistic gaze and the reasonable rhetoric of a car salesman. He is society's model product. I try to meet his gaze directly because he once told me he could read character in people's eyes, particularly if he has just dropped acid, which he did, about nine o'clock this morning. "They just have to remember one thing," he says. "The Lord's Prayer. And that can help them in more ways than one."

He takes a much-folded letter from his wallet. The letter is from a little girl he helped. "My loving brother," it begins. "I thought I'd write you a letter since I'm a part of you. Remember that: When you feel happiness, I do, when you feel . . ."

"What I want to do now," Deadeye says, "is set up a house where a person of any age can come, spend a few days, talk over his problems. *Any age.* People your age, they've got problems too."

I say a house will take money.

"I've found a way to make money," Deadeye says. He hesitates only a few seconds. "I could've made eighty-five dollars on the Street just then. See, in my pocket I had a hundred tabs of acid. I had to come up with twenty dollars by tonight or we're out of the house we're in, so I knew somebody who had acid, and I knew somebody who wanted it, so I made the connection."

> *Since the Mafia moved into the LSD racket, the quantity is up and the quality is down . . . Historian Arnold Toynbee celebrated his 78th birthday Friday night by snapping his fingers and tapping his toes to the Quicksilver Messenger Service* . . . are a couple of items from Herb Caen's column one morning as the West declined in the spring of 1967.

When I was in San Francisco a tab, or a cap, of LSD-25 sold for three to five dollars, depending upon the seller and the district. LSD was slightly cheaper in the Haight-Ashbury than in the Fillmore, where it was used rarely, mainly as a sexual ploy, and sold by pushers of hard drugs, *e.g.*, heroin, or "smack." A great deal of acid was being cut with Methedrine, which is the trade name for an amphetamine, because Methedrine can simulate the flash that low-quality acid lacks. Nobody knows how much LSD is actually in a tab, but the standard trip is supposed to be 250 micrograms. Grass was running ten dollars a lid, five dollars a matchbox. Hash was considered "a luxury item." All the amphetamines, or "speed"—Benzedrine, Dexedrine, and particularly Methedrine—were in far more common use in the late spring than they had been in the early spring. Some attributed this to the presence of the Syndicate; others to a general deterioration of the scene, to the incursions of gangs and younger part-time, or "plastic," hippies, who like the amphetamines and the illusions of action and power they give. Where Methedrine is in wide use, heroin tends to be available, because, I was told, "You can get awful damn high shooting crystal, and smack can be used to bring you down."

*

Deadeye's old lady, Gerry, meets us at the door of their place. She is a big, hearty girl who has always counseled at Girl Scout camps during summer vacations and was "in social welfare" at the University of Washington when she decided that she "just hadn't done enough living" and came to San Francisco. "Actually the heat was bad in Seattle," she adds.

"The first night I got down here," she says, "I stayed with a gal I met over at the Blue Unicorn. I looked like I'd just arrived, had a knapsack and stuff." After that, Gerry stayed at a house the Diggers were running, where she met Deadeye. "Then it took time to get my bearings, so I haven't done much work yet."

I ask Gerry what work she does. "Basically I'm a poet," she says, "but I had my guitar stolen right after I arrived, and that kind of hung up my thing."

"Get your books," Deadeye orders. "Show her your books."

Gerry demurs, then goes into the bedroom and comes back with several theme books full of verse. I leaf through them but Deadeye is still talking about helping people. "Any kid that's on speed," he says, "I'll try to get him off it. The only advantage to it from the kids' point of view is that you don't have to worry about sleeping or eating."

"Or sex," Gerry adds.

"That's right. When you're strung out on crystal you don't need *nothing*."

"It can lead to the hard stuff," Gerry says. "Take your average Meth freak, once he's started putting the needle in his arm, it's not too hard to say, well, let's shoot a little smack."

All the while I am looking at Gerry's poems. They are a very young girl's poems, each written out in a neat hand and finished off with a curlicue. Dawns are roseate, skies silver-tinted. When Gerry writes "crystal" in her books, she does not mean Meth.

"You gotta get back to your writing," Deadeye says fondly, but Gerry ignores this. She is telling about somebody who propositioned her yesterday. "He just walked up to me on the Street, offered me six hundred dollars to go to Reno and do the thing."

"You're not the only one he approached," Deadeye says.

"If some chick wants to go with him, fine," Gerry says.

"Just don't bum my trip." She empties the tuna-fish can we are using for an ashtray and goes over to look at a girl who is asleep on the floor. It is the same girl who was sleeping on the floor the first day I came to Deadeye's place. She has been sick a week now, ten days. "Usually when somebody comes up to me on the Street like that," Gerry adds, "I hit him for some change."

When I saw Gerry in the Park the next day I asked her about the sick girl, and Gerry said cheerfully that she was in the hospital, with pneumonia.

Max tells me about how he and Sharon got together. "When I saw her the first time on Haight Street, I flashed. I mean flashed. So I started some conversation with her about her beads, see, but I didn't care about her beads." Sharon lived in a house where a friend of Max's lived, and the next time he saw her was when he took the friend some bananas. "It was during the great banana bubble. You had to kind of force your personality and the banana peels down their throats. Sharon and I were like kids—we just smoked bananas and looked at each other and smoked more bananas and looked at each other."

But Max hesitated. For one thing he thought Sharon was his friend's girl. "For another I didn't know if I wanted to get hung up with an old lady." But the next time he visited the house, Sharon was on acid.

"So everybody yelled 'Here comes the banana man,'" Sharon interrupts, "and I got all excited."

"She was living in this crazy house," Max continues. "There was this one kid, all he did was scream. His whole trip was to practice screams. It was too much." Max still hung back from Sharon. "But then she offered me a tab, and I knew."

Max walked to the kitchen and back with the tab, wondering whether to take it. "And then I decided to flow with it, and that was that. Because once you drop acid with somebody you flash on, you see the whole world melt in her eyes."

"It's stronger than anything in the world," Sharon says.

"Nothing can break it up," Max says. "As long as it lasts."

*

No milk today—
My love has gone away . . .
The end of my hopes—
The end of all my dreams—
is a song I heard every morning in the
cold late spring of 1967 on KFRC, the
Flower Power Station, San Francisco.

Deadeye and Gerry tell me they plan to be married. An Episcopal priest in the District has promised to perform the wedding in Golden Gate Park, and they will have a few rock groups there, "a real community thing." Gerry's brother is also getting married, in Seattle. "Kind of interesting," Gerry muses, "because, you know, his is the traditional straight wedding, and then you have the contrast with ours."

"I'll have to wear a tie to his," Deadeye says.

"Right," Gerry says.

"Her parents came down to meet me, but they weren't ready for me," Deadeye notes philosophically.

"They finally gave it their blessing," Gerry says. "In a way."

"They came to me and her father said, 'Take care of her,'" Deadeye reminisces. "And her mother said, 'Don't let her go to jail.'"

Barbara baked a macrobiotic apple pie and she and Tom and Max and Sharon and I are eating it. Barbara tells me how she learned to find happiness in "the woman's thing." She and Tom had gone somewhere to live with the Indians, and although she first found it hard to be shunted off with the women and never to enter into any of the men's talk, she soon got the point. "That was where the *trip* was," she says.

Barbara is on what is called the woman's trip to the exclusion of almost everything else. When she and Tom and Max and Sharon need money, Barbara will take a part-time job, modeling or teaching kindergarten, but she dislikes earning more than ten or twenty dollars a week. Most of the time she keeps house and bakes. "Doing something that shows your love that way," she says, "is just about the most beautiful thing I know." Whenever I hear about the woman's trip, which is often, I think a lot about nothin'-says-lovin'-like-something-from-the-oven and the Feminine Mystique and how it is possible for people to be the unconscious instruments of values they would strenuously reject on a conscious level, but I do not mention this to Barbara.

It is a pretty nice day and I am just driving down the Street and I see Barbara at a light.

What am I doing, she wants to know.

I am just driving around.

"Groovy," she says.

It's a beautiful day, I say.

"Groovy," she agrees.

She wants to know if I will come over. Sometime soon, I say.

"Groovy," she says.

I ask if she wants to drive in the Park but she is too busy. She is out to buy wool for her loom.

Arthur Lisch gets pretty nervous whenever he sees me now because the Digger line this week is that they aren't talking to "media poisoners," which is me. So I still don't have a tap on Chester Anderson, but one day in the Panhandle I run into a kid who says he is Chester's "associate." He has on a black cape, black slouch hat, mauve Job's Daughters sweatshirt and dark glasses, and he says his name is Claude Hayward, but never mind that because I think of him just as The Connection. The Connection offers to "check me out."

I take off my dark glasses so he can see my eyes. He leaves his on.

"How much you get paid for doing this kind of media poisoning?" he says for openers.

I put my dark glasses back on.

"There's only one way to find out where it's at," The Connection says, and jerks his thumb at the photographer I'm with. "Dump him and get out on the Street. Don't take money. You won't need money." He reaches into his cape and pulls out a Mimeographed sheet announcing a series of classes at the Digger Free Store on How to Avoid Getting Busted, Gangbangs, VD, Rape, Pregnancy, Beatings, and Starvation. "You oughta come," The Connection says. "You'll need it."

I say maybe, but meanwhile I would like to talk to Chester Anderson.

"If we decide to get in touch with you at all," The Connection says, "we'll get in touch with you real quick." He kept an eye on me in the Park after that but never called the number I gave him.

It is twilight and cold and too early to find Deadeye at the Blue Unicorn so I ring Max's bell. Barbara comes to the door.

"Max and Tom are seeing somebody on a kind of business thing," she says. "Can you come back a little later?"

I am hard put to think what Max and Tom might be seeing somebody about in the way of business, but a few days later in the Park I find out.

"Hey," Max calls. "Sorry you couldn't come up the other day, but *business* was being done." This time I get the point. "We got some great stuff," he says, and begins to elaborate. Every third person in the Park this afternoon looks like a narcotics agent and I try to change the subject. Later I suggest to Max that he be more wary in public. "Listen, I'm very cautious," he says. "You can't be too careful."

By now I have an unofficial taboo contact with the San Francisco Police Department. What happens is that this cop and I meet in various late-movie ways, like I happen to be sitting in the bleachers at a baseball game and he happens to sit down next to me, and we exchange guarded generalities. No information actually passes between us, but after a while we get to kind of like each other.

"The kids aren't too bright," he is telling me on this particular day. "They'll tell you they can always spot an undercover, they'll tell you about 'the kind of car he drives.' They aren't talking about undercovers, they're talking about plainclothesmen who just happen to drive unmarked cars, like I do. They can't tell an undercover. An undercover doesn't drive some black Ford with a two-way radio."

He tells me about an undercover who was taken out of the District because he was believed to be overexposed, too familiar. He was transferred to the narcotics squad, and by error was sent immediately back into the District as a narcotics undercover.

The cop plays with his keys. "You want to know how smart these kids are?" he says finally. "The first week, this guy makes forty-three cases."

*

The Jook Savages are supposed to be having a May Day party in Larkspur and I go by the Warehouse and Don and Sue Ann think it would be nice to drive over there because Sue Ann's three-year-old, Michael, hasn't been out lately. The air is soft and there is a sunset haze around the Golden Gate and Don asks Sue Ann how many flavors she can detect in a single grain of rice and Sue Ann tells Don maybe she better learn to cook *yang*, maybe they are all too *yin* at the Warehouse, and I try to teach Michael "Frère Jacques." We each have our own trip and it is a nice drive. Which is just as well because there is nobody at all at the Jook Savages' place, not even the Jook Savages. When we get back Sue Ann decides to cook up a lot of apples they have around the Warehouse and Don starts working with his light show and I go down to see Max for a minute. "Out of sight," Max says about the Larkspur caper. "Somebody thinks it would be groovy to turn on five hundred people the first day in May, and it would be, but then they turn on the last day in April instead, so it doesn't happen. If it happens, it happens. If it doesn't, it doesn't. Who cares. Nobody cares."

Some kid with braces on his teeth is playing his guitar and boasting that he got the last of the STP from Mr. O. himself and somebody else is talking about how five grams of acid will be liberated within the next month and you can see that nothing much is happening this afternoon around the *San Francisco Oracle* office. A boy sits at a drawing board drawing the infinitesimal figures that people do on speed, and the kid with the braces watches him. "*I'm gonna shoot my wo–man*," he sings softly. "*She been with a–noth–er man*." Someone works out the numerology of my name and the name of the photographer I'm with. The photographer's is all white and the sea ("If I were to make you some beads, see, I'd do it mainly in white," he is told), but mine has a double death symbol. The afternoon does not seem to be getting anywhere, so it is suggested that we go over to Japantown and find somebody named Sandy who will take us to the Zen temple.

Four boys and one middle-aged man are sitting on a grass mat at Sandy's place, sipping anise tea and watching Sandy read Laura Huxley's *You Are Not the Target*.

We sit down and have some anise tea. "Meditation turns us on," Sandy says. He has a shaved head and the kind of cherubic face usually seen in newspaper photographs of mass murderers. The middle-aged man, whose name is George, is making me uneasy because he is in a trance next to me and stares at me without seeing me.

I feel that my mind is going—George is *dead*, or we *all* are —when the telephone rings.

"It's for George," Sandy says.

"George, *tele*phone."

"George."

Somebody waves his hand in front of George and George finally gets up, bows, and moves toward the door on the balls of his feet.

"I think I'll take George's tea," somebody says. "George— are you coming back?"

George stops at the door and stares at each of us in turn. "In a *mo*ment," he snaps.

Do you know who is the first eternal spaceman
of this universe?
The first to send his wild wild vibrations
To all those cosmic superstations?
For the song he always shouts
Sends the planets flipping out . . .
But I'll tell you before you think me loony
That I'm talking about Narada Muni . . .
Singing
HARE KRISHNA HARE KRISHNA
KRISHNA KRISHNA HARE HARE
HARE RAMA HARE RAMA
RAMA RAMA HARE HARE
is a Krishna song. Words by
Howard Wheeler and music by
Michael Grant.

Maybe the trip is not in Zen but in Krishna, so I pay a visit to Michael Grant, the Swami A.C. Bhaktivedanta's leading disciple in San Francisco. Michael Grant is at home with his brother-in-law and his wife, a pretty girl wearing a cashmere pullover, a jumper, and a red caste mark on her forehead.

"I've been associated with the Swami since about last July," Michael says. "See, the Swami came here from India and he was at this ashram in upstate New York and he just kept to himself and chanted a lot. For a couple of months. Pretty soon I helped him get his storefront in New York. Now it's an international movement, which we spread by teaching this chant." Michael is fingering his red wooden beads and I notice that I am the only person in the room with shoes on. "It's catching on like wildfire."

"If everybody chanted," the brother-in-law says, "there wouldn't be any problem with the police or anybody."

"Ginsberg calls the chant ecstasy, but the Swami says that's not exactly it." Michael walks across the room and straightens a picture of Krishna as a baby. "Too bad you can't meet the Swami," he adds. "The Swami's in New York now."

"Ecstasy's not the right word at all," says the brother-in-law, who has been thinking about it. "It makes you think of some . . . mun*dane* ecstasy."

The next day I drop by Max and Sharon's, and find them in bed smoking a little morning hash. Sharon once advised me that half a joint even of grass would make getting up in the morning a beautiful thing. I ask Max how Krishna strikes him.

"You can get a high on a mantra," he says. "But I'm holy on acid."

Max passes the joint to Sharon and leans back. "Too bad you couldn't meet the Swami," he says. "The Swami was the turn-on."

Anybody who thinks this is all about drugs has his head in a bag. It's a social movement, quintessentially romantic, the kind that recurs in times of real social crisis. The themes are always the same. A return to innocence. The invocation of an earlier authority and control. The mysteries of the blood. An itch for the transcendental, for purification. Right there you've got the ways that romanticism historically ends up in trouble, lends itself to authoritarianism. When the direction appears. How long do you think it'll take for that to happen? is a question a San Francisco psychiatrist asked me.

*

At the time I was in San Francisco the political potential of what was then called the movement was just becoming clear. It had always been clear to the revolutionary core of the Diggers, whose every guerrilla talent was now bent toward open confrontations and the creation of a summer emergency, and it was clear to many of the straight doctors and priests and sociologists who had occasion to work in the District, and it could rapidly become clear to any outsider who bothered to decode Chester Anderson's call-to-action communiqués or to watch who was there first at the street skirmishes which now set the tone for life in the District. One did not have to be a political analyst to see it; the boys in the rock groups saw it, because they were often where it was happening. "In the Park there are always twenty or thirty people below the stand," one of the Dead complained to me. "Ready to take the crowd on some militant trip."

But the peculiar beauty of this political potential, as far as the activists were concerned, was that it remained not clear at all to most of the inhabitants of the District, perhaps because the few seventeen-year-olds who are political realists tend not to adopt romantic idealism as a life style. Nor was it clear to the press, which at varying levels of competence continued to report "the hippie phenomenon" as an extended panty raid; an artistic avant-garde led by such comfortable YMHA regulars as Allen Ginsberg; or a thoughtful protest, not unlike joining the Peace Corps, against the culture which had produced Saran-Wrap and the Vietnam War. This last, or they're-trying-to-tell-us-something approach, reached its apogee in a *Time* cover story which revealed that hippies "scorn money—they call it 'bread'" and remains the most remarkable, if unwitting, extant evidence that the signals between the generations are irrevocably jammed.

Because the signals the press was getting were immaculate of political possibilities, the tensions of the District went unremarked upon, even during the period when there were so many observers on Haight Street from *Life* and *Look* and CBS that they were largely observing one another. The observers believed roughly what the children told them: that they were a generation dropped out of political action, beyond power games, that the New Left was just another ego trip.

Ergo, there really were no activists in the Haight-Ashbury, and those things which happened every Sunday were spontaneous demonstrations because, just as the Diggers say, the police are brutal and juveniles have no rights and runaways are deprived of their right to self-determination and people are starving to death on Haight Street, a scale model of Vietnam.

Of course the activists—not those whose thinking had become rigid, but those whose approach to revolution was imaginatively anarchic—had long ago grasped the reality which still eluded the press: we were seeing something important. We were seeing the desperate attempt of a handful of pathetically unequipped children to create a community in a social vacuum. Once we had seen these children, we could no longer overlook the vacuum, no longer pretend that the society's atomization could be reversed. This was not a traditional generational rebellion. At some point between 1945 and 1967 we had somehow neglected to tell these children the rules of the game we happened to be playing. Maybe we had stopped believing in the rules ourselves, maybe we were having a failure of nerve about the game. Maybe there were just too few people around to do the telling. These were children who grew up cut loose from the web of cousins and great-aunts and family doctors and lifelong neighbors who had traditionally suggested and enforced the society's values. They are children who have moved around a lot, *San Jose, Chula Vista, here.* They are less in rebellion against the society than ignorant of it, able only to feed back certain of its most publicized self-doubts, *Vietnam, Saran-Wrap, diet pills, the Bomb.*

They feed back exactly what is given them. Because they do not believe in words—words are for "typeheads," Chester Anderson tells them, and a thought which needs words is just one more of those ego trips—their only proficient vocabulary is in the society's platitudes. As it happens I am still committed to the idea that the ability to think for one's self depends upon one's mastery of the language, and I am not optimistic about children who will settle for saying, to indicate that their mother and father do not live together, that they come from "a broken home." They are sixteen, fifteen, fourteen years old, younger all the time, an army of children waiting to be given the words.

*

Peter Berg knows a lot of words.

"Is Peter Berg around?" I ask.

"Maybe."

"Are you Peter Berg?"

"Yeh."

The reason Peter Berg does not bother sharing too many words with me is because two of the words he knows are "media poisoning." Peter Berg wears a gold earring and is perhaps the only person in the District on whom a gold earring looks obscurely ominous. He belongs to the San Francisco Mime Troupe, some of whose members started the Artist's Liberation Front for "those who seek to combine their creative urge with socio-political involvement." It was out of the Mime Troupe that the Diggers grew, during the 1966 Hunter's Point riots, when it seemed a good idea to give away food and do puppet shows in the streets making fun of the National Guard. Along with Arthur Lisch, Peter Berg is part of the shadow leadership of the Diggers, and it was he who more or less invented and first introduced to the press the notion that there would be an influx into San Francisco during the summer of 1967 of 200,000 indigent adolescents. The only conversation I ever have with Peter Berg is about how he holds me personally responsible for the way *Life* captioned Henri Cartier-Bresson's pictures out of Cuba, but I like to watch him at work in the Park.

Janis Joplin is singing with Big Brother in the Panhandle and almost everybody is high and it is a pretty nice Sunday afternoon between three and six o'clock, which the activists say are the three hours of the week when something is most likely to happen in the Haight-Ashbury, and who turns up but Peter Berg. He is with his wife and six or seven other people, along with Chester Anderson's associate The Connection, and the first peculiar thing is, they're in blackface.

I mention to Max and Sharon that some members of the Mime Troupe seem to be in blackface.

"It's street theater," Sharon assures me. "It's supposed to be really groovy."

The Mime Troupers get a little closer, and there are some other peculiar things about them. For one thing they are tapping people on the head with dime-store plastic nightsticks, and for another they are wearing signs on their backs. "HOW MANY TIMES YOU BEEN RAPED, YOU LOVE FREAKS?" and "WHO STOLE CHUCK BERRY'S MUSIC?", things like that. Then they are distributing communication company fliers which say:

> & this summer thousands of un-white un-suburban boppers are going to want to know why you've given up what they can't get & how you get away with it & how come you not a faggot with hair so long & they want haight street one way or the other. IF YOU DON'T KNOW, BY AUGUST HAIGHT STREET WILL BE A CEMETERY.

Max reads the flier and stands up. "I'm getting bad vibes," he says, and he and Sharon leave.

I have to stay around because I'm looking for Otto so I walk over to where the Mime Troupers have formed a circle around a Negro. Peter Berg is saying if anybody asks that this is street theater, and I figure the curtain is up because what they are doing right now is jabbing the Negro with the nightsticks. They jab, and they bare their teeth, and they rock on the balls of their feet and they wait.

"I'm beginning to get annoyed here," the Negro says. "I'm gonna get mad."

By now there are several Negroes around, reading the signs and watching.

"Just beginning to get annoyed, are you?" one of the Mime Troupers says. "Don't you think it's about time?"

"Nobody *stole* Chuck Berry's music, man," says another Negro who has been studying the signs. "Chuck Berry's music belongs to *every*body."

"Yeh?" a girl in blackface says. "Everybody *who*?"

"Why," he says, confused. "Everybody. In America."

"In *America*," the blackface girl shrieks. "Listen to him talk about *America*."

"Listen," he says helplessly. "Listen here."

"What'd *America* ever do for you?" the girl in blackface jeers. "White kids here, they can sit in the Park all summer long, listening to the music they stole, because their bigshot parents keep sending them money. Who ever sends you money?"

"Listen," the Negro says, his voice rising. "You're gonna start something here, this isn't right—"

"You tell us what's right, black boy," the girl says.

The youngest member of the blackface group, an earnest tall kid about nineteen, twenty, is hanging back at the edge of the scene. I offer him an apple and ask what is going on. "Well," he says, "I'm new at this, I'm just beginning to study it, but you see the capitalists are taking over the District, and that's what Peter—well, ask Peter."

I did not ask Peter. It went on for a while. But on that particular Sunday between three and six o'clock everyone was too high and the weather was too good and the Hunter's Point gangs who usually come in between three and six on Sunday afternoon had come in on Saturday instead, and nothing started. While I waited for Otto I asked a little girl I knew slightly what she had thought of it. "It's something groovy they call street theater," she said. I said I had wondered if it might not have political overtones. She was seventeen years old and she worked it around in her mind awhile and finally she remembered a couple of words from somewhere. "Maybe it's some John Birch thing," she said.

When I finally find Otto he says "I got something at my place that'll blow your mind," and when we get there I see a child on the living-room floor, wearing a reefer coat, reading a comic book. She keeps licking her lips in concentration and the only off thing about her is that she's wearing white lipstick.

"Five years old," Otto says. "On acid."

The five-year-old's name is Susan, and she tells me she is in High Kindergarten. She lives with her mother and some other people, just got over the measles, wants a bicycle for Christmas, and particularly likes Coca-Cola, ice cream, Marty in the Jefferson Airplane, Bob in the Grateful Dead, and the beach. She remembers going to the beach once a long time ago, and wishes she had taken a bucket. For a year now her mother has given her both acid and peyote. Susan describes it as getting stoned.

I start to ask if any of the other children in High Kindergarten get stoned, but I falter at the key words.

"She means do the other kids in your class turn on, *get stoned*," says the friend of her mother's who brought her to Otto's.

"Only Sally and Anne," Susan says.

"What about Lia?" her mother's friend prompts.

"Lia," Susan says, "is not in High Kindergarten."

Sue Ann's three-year-old Michael started a fire this morning before anyone was up, but Don got it out before much damage was done. Michael burned his arm though, which is probably why Sue Ann was so jumpy when she happened to see him chewing on an electric cord. "You'll fry like rice," she screamed. The only people around were Don and one of Sue Ann's macrobiotic friends and somebody who was on his way to a commune in the Santa Lucias, and they didn't notice Sue Ann screaming at Michael because they were in the kitchen trying to retrieve some very good Moroccan hash which had dropped down through a floorboard damaged in the fire.

1967

II

PERSONALS

On Keeping a Notebook

"'THAT WOMAN ESTELLE,'" the note reads, "'is partly the reason why George Sharp and I are separated today.' *Dirty crepe-de-Chine wrapper, hotel bar, Wilmington RR, 9:45* A.M. *August Monday morning.*"

Since the note is in my notebook, it presumably has some meaning to me. I study it for a long while. At first I have only the most general notion of what I was doing on an August Monday morning in the bar of the hotel across from the Pennsylvania Railroad station in Wilmington, Delaware (waiting for a train? missing one? 1960? 1961? why Wilmington?), but I do remember being there. The woman in the dirty crepe-de-Chine wrapper had come down from her room for a beer, and the bartender had heard before the reason why George Sharp and she were separated today. "Sure," he said, and went on mopping the floor. "You told me." At the other end of the bar is a girl. She is talking, pointedly, not to the man beside her but to a cat lying in the triangle of sunlight cast through the open door. She is wearing a plaid silk dress from Peck & Peck, and the hem is coming down.

Here is what it is: the girl has been on the Eastern Shore, and now she is going back to the city, leaving the man beside her, and all she can see ahead are the viscous summer sidewalks and the 3 A.M. long-distance calls that will make her lie awake and then sleep drugged through all the steaming mornings left in August (1960? 1961?). Because she must go directly from the train to lunch in New York, she wishes that she had a safety pin for the hem of the plaid silk dress, and she also wishes that she could forget about the hem and the lunch and stay in the cool bar that smells of disinfectant and malt and make friends with the woman in the crepe-de-Chine wrapper. She is afflicted by a little self-pity, and she wants to compare Estelles. That is what that was all about.

Why did I write it down? In order to remember, of course, but exactly what was it I wanted to remember? How much of it actually happened? Did any of it? Why do I keep a notebook at all? It is easy to deceive oneself on all those scores. The impulse to write things down is a peculiarly compulsive one, inexplicable to those who do not share it, useful only accidentally, only secondarily, in the way that any compulsion tries to justify itself. I suppose that it begins or does not begin in the cradle. Although I have felt compelled to write things down since I was five years old, I doubt that my daughter ever will, for she is a singularly blessed and accepting child, delighted with life exactly as life presents itself to her, unafraid to go to sleep and unafraid to wake up. Keepers of private notebooks are a different breed altogether, lonely and resistant rearrangers of things, anxious malcontents, children afflicted apparently at birth with some presentiment of loss.

My first notebook was a Big Five tablet, given to me by my mother with the sensible suggestion that I stop whining and learn to amuse myself by writing down my thoughts. She returned the tablet to me a few years ago; the first entry is an account of a woman who believed herself to be freezing to death in the Arctic night, only to find, when day broke, that she had stumbled onto the Sahara Desert, where she would die of the heat before lunch. I have no idea what turn of a five-year-old's mind could have prompted so insistently "ironic" and exotic a story, but it does reveal a certain predilection for the extreme which has dogged me into adult life; perhaps if I were analytically inclined I would find it a truer story than any I might have told about Donald Johnson's birthday party or the day my cousin Brenda put Kitty Litter in the aquarium.

So the point of my keeping a notebook has never been, nor is it now, to have an accurate factual record of what I have been doing or thinking. That would be a different impulse entirely, an instinct for reality which I sometimes envy but do not possess. At no point have I ever been able successfully to keep a diary; my approach to daily life ranges from the grossly negligent to the merely absent, and on those few occasions when I have tried dutifully to record a day's events, boredom has so overcome me that the results are mysterious at best. What is this business about "shopping, typing piece, dinner with E, depressed"? Shopping for what? Typing what piece? Who is E? Was this "E" depressed, or was I depressed? Who cares?

In fact I have abandoned altogether that kind of pointless

entry; instead I tell what some would call lies. "That's simply not true," the members of my family frequently tell me when they come up against my memory of a shared event. "The party was *not* for you, the spider was *not* a black widow, *it wasn't that way at all*." Very likely they are right, for not only have I always had trouble distinguishing between what happened and what merely might have happened, but I remain unconvinced that the distinction, for my purposes, matters. The cracked crab that I recall having for lunch the day my father came home from Detroit in 1945 must certainly be embroidery, worked into the day's pattern to lend verisimilitude; I was ten years old and would not now remember the cracked crab. The day's events did not turn on cracked crab. And yet it is precisely that fictitious crab that makes me see the afternoon all over again, a home movie run all too often, the father bearing gifts, the child weeping, an exercise in family love and guilt. Or that is what it was to me. Similarly, perhaps it never did snow that August in Vermont; perhaps there never were flurries in the night wind, and maybe no one else felt the ground hardening and summer already dead even as we pretended to bask in it, but that was how it felt to me, and it might as well have snowed, could have snowed, did snow.

How it felt to me: that is getting closer to the truth about a notebook. I sometimes delude myself about why I keep a notebook, imagine that some thrifty virtue derives from preserving everything observed. See enough and write it down, I tell myself, and then some morning when the world seems drained of wonder, some day when I am only going through the motions of doing what I am supposed to do, which is write—on that bankrupt morning I will simply open my notebook and there it will all be, a forgotten account with accumulated interest, paid passage back to the world out there: dialogue overheard in hotels and elevators and at the hat-check counter in Pavillon (one middle-aged man shows his hat check to another and says, "That's my old football number"); impressions of Bettina Aptheker and Benjamin Sonnenberg and Teddy ("Mr. Acapulco") Stauffer; careful *aperçus* about tennis bums and failed fashion models and Greek shipping heiresses, one of whom taught me a significant lesson (a lesson I could have learned from F. Scott Fitzgerald, but perhaps we all must meet the very rich for ourselves) by asking, when I arrived to interview her in her orchid-filled sitting room on the second day of a paralyzing New York blizzard, whether it was snowing outside.

I imagine, in other words, that the notebook is about other people. But of course it is not. I have no real business with what one stranger said to another at the hat-check counter in Pavillon; in fact I suspect that the line "That's my old football number" touched not my own imagination at all, but merely some memory of something once read, probably "The Eighty-Yard Run." Nor is my concern with a woman in a dirty crepe-de-Chine wrapper in a Wilmington bar. My stake is always, of course, in the unmentioned girl in the plaid silk dress. *Remember what it was to be me*: that is always the point.

It is a difficult point to admit. We are brought up in the ethic that others, any others, all others, are by definition more interesting than ourselves; taught to be diffident, just this side of self-effacing. ("You're the least important person in the room and don't forget it," Jessica Mitford's governess would hiss in her ear on the advent of any social occasion; I copied that into my notebook because it is only recently that I have been able to enter a room without hearing some such phrase in my inner ear.) Only the very young and the very old may recount their dreams at breakfast, dwell upon self, interrupt with memories of beach picnics and favorite Liberty lawn dresses and the rainbow trout in a creek near Colorado Springs. The rest of us are expected, rightly, to affect absorption in other people's favorite dresses, other people's trout.

And so we do. But our notebooks give us away, for however dutifully we record what we see around us, the common denominator of all we see is always, transparently, shamelessly, the implacable "I." We are not talking here about the kind of notebook that is patently for public consumption, a structural conceit for binding together a series of graceful *pensées*; we are talking about something private, about bits of the mind's string too short to use, an indiscriminate and erratic assemblage with meaning only for its maker.

And sometimes even the maker has difficulty with the meaning. There does not seem to be, for example, any point in my knowing for the rest of my life that, during 1964, 720 tons of soot fell on every square mile of New York City, yet there it is in my notebook, labeled "FACT." Nor do I really need to remember that Ambrose Bierce liked to spell Leland Stanford's name "£eland $tanford" or that "smart women almost always wear black in Cuba," a fashion hint without much potential for practical application. And does not the relevance of these notes seem marginal at best?:

> In the basement museum of the Inyo County Courthouse in Independence, California, sign pinned to a mandarin coat: "This MANDARIN COAT was often worn by Mrs. Minnie S. Brooks when giving lectures on her TEAPOT COLLECTION."
>
> Redhead getting out of car in front of Beverly Wilshire Hotel, chinchilla stole, Vuitton bags with tags reading:
>
> MRS LOU FOX
> HOTEL SAHARA
> VEGAS

Well, perhaps not entirely marginal. As a matter of fact, Mrs. Minnie S. Brooks and her MANDARIN COAT pull me back into my own childhood, for although I never knew Mrs. Brooks and did not visit Inyo County until I was thirty, I grew up in just such a world, in houses cluttered with Indian relics and bits of gold ore and ambergris and the souvenirs my Aunt Mercy Farnsworth brought back from the Orient. It is a long way from that world to Mrs. Lou Fox's world, where we all live now, and is it not just as well to remember that? Might not Mrs. Minnie S. Brooks help me to remember what I am? Might not Mrs. Lou Fox help me to remember what I am not?

But sometimes the point is harder to discern. What exactly did I have in mind when I noted down that it cost the father of someone I know $650 a month to light the place on the Hudson in which he lived before the Crash? What use was I planning to make of this line by Jimmy Hoffa: "I may have my faults, but being wrong ain't one of them"? And although I think it interesting to know where the girls who travel with the Syndicate have their hair done when they find themselves on the West Coast, will I ever make suitable use of it? Might I not be better off just passing it on to John O'Hara? What is a recipe for sauerkraut doing in my notebook? What kind of magpie keeps this notebook? *"He was born the night the Titanic went down."* That seems a nice enough line, and I even recall who said it, but is it not really a better line in life than it could ever be in fiction?

But of course that is exactly it: not that I should ever use the line, but that I should remember the woman who said it and the afternoon I heard it. We were on her terrace by the sea, and we were finishing the wine left from lunch, trying to get what sun there was, a California winter sun. The woman whose husband was born the night the *Titanic* went down wanted to rent her house, wanted to go back to her children in Paris. I remember wishing that I could afford the house, which cost $1,000 a month. "Someday you will," she said lazily. "Someday it all comes." There in the sun on her terrace it seemed easy to believe in someday, but later I had a low-grade afternoon hangover and ran over a black snake on the way to the supermarket and was flooded with inexplicable fear when I heard the checkout clerk explaining to the man ahead of me why she was finally divorcing her husband. "He left me no choice," she said over and over as she punched the register. "He has a little seven-month-old baby by her, he left me no choice." I would like to believe that my dread then was for the human condition, but of course it was for me, because I wanted a baby and did not then have one and because I wanted to own the house that cost $1,000 a month to rent and because I had a hangover.

It all comes back. Perhaps it is difficult to see the value in having one's self back in that kind of mood, but I do see it; I think we are well advised to keep on nodding terms with the people we used to be, whether we find them attractive company or not. Otherwise they turn up unannounced and surprise us, come hammering on the mind's door at 4 A.M. of a bad night and demand to know who deserted them, who betrayed them, who is going to make amends. We forget all too soon the things we thought we could never forget. We forget the loves and the betrayals alike, forget what we whispered and what we screamed, forget who we were. I have already lost touch with a couple of people I used to be; one of them, a seventeen-year-old, presents little threat, although it would be of some interest to me to know again what it feels like to sit on a river levee drinking vodka-and-orange-juice and listening to Les Paul and Mary Ford and their echoes sing "How High the Moon" on the car radio. (You see I still have the scenes, but I no longer perceive myself among those present, no longer could even improvise the dialogue.) The other one, a twenty-three-year-old, bothers me more. She was always a good deal of trouble, and I suspect she will reappear when I least want to see her, skirts too long, shy to the point of aggravation, always the injured party, full of recriminations and little hurts and stories I do not want to hear again, at once saddening me and angering me with her vulnerability and ignorance, an apparition all the more insistent for being so long banished.

It is a good idea, then, to keep in touch, and I suppose that keeping in touch is what notebooks are all about. And we are all on our own when it comes to keeping those lines open to ourselves: your notebook will never help me, nor mine you. *"So what's new in the whiskey business?"* What could that possibly mean to you? To me it means a blonde in a Pucci bathing suit sitting with a couple of fat men by the pool at the Beverly Hills Hotel. Another man approaches, and they all regard one another in silence for a while. "So what's new in the whiskey business?" one of the fat men finally says by way of welcome, and the blonde stands up, arches one foot and dips it in the pool, looking all the while at the cabaña where Baby Pignatari is talking on the telephone. That is all there is to that, except that several years later I saw the blonde coming out of Saks Fifth Avenue in New York with her California complexion and a voluminous mink coat. In the harsh wind that day she looked old and irrevocably tired to me, and even the skins in the mink coat were not worked the way they were doing them that year, not the way she would have wanted them done, and there is the point of the story. For a while after that I did not like to look in the mirror, and my eyes would skim the newspapers and pick out only the deaths, the cancer victims, the premature coronaries, the suicides, and I stopped riding the Lexington Avenue IRT because I noticed for the first time that all the strangers I had seen for years—the man with the seeing-eye dog, the spinster who read the classified pages every day, the fat girl who always got off with me at Grand Central—looked older than they once had.

It all comes back. Even that recipe for sauerkraut: even that brings it back. I was on Fire Island when I first made that sauerkraut, and it was raining, and we drank a lot of bourbon and ate the sauerkraut and went to bed at ten, and I listened to the rain and the Atlantic and felt safe. I made the sauerkraut again last night and it did not make me feel any safer, but that is, as they say, another story.

1966

On Self-Respect

ONCE, IN A DRY SEASON, I wrote in large letters across two pages of a notebook that innocence ends when one is stripped of the delusion that one likes oneself. Although now, some years later, I marvel that a mind on the outs with itself should have nonetheless made painstaking record of its every tremor, I recall with embarrassing clarity the flavor of those particular ashes. It was a matter of misplaced self-respect.

I had not been elected to Phi Beta Kappa. This failure could scarcely have been more predictable or less ambiguous (I simply did not have the grades), but I was unnerved by it; I had somehow thought myself a kind of academic Raskolnikov, curiously exempt from the cause-effect relationships which hampered others. Although even the humorless nineteen-year-old that I was must have recognized that the situation lacked real tragic stature, the day that I did not make Phi Beta Kappa nonetheless marked the end of something, and innocence may well be the word for it. I lost the conviction that lights would always turn green for me, the pleasant certainty that those rather passive virtues which had won me approval as a child automatically guaranteed me not only Phi Beta Kappa keys but happiness, honor, and the love of a good man; lost a certain touching faith in the totem power of good manners, clean hair, and proven competence on the Stanford-Binet scale. To such doubtful amulets had my self-respect been pinned, and I faced myself that day with the nonplused apprehension of someone who has come across a vampire and has no crucifix at hand.

Although to be driven back upon oneself is an uneasy affair at best, rather like trying to cross a border with borrowed credentials, it seems to me now the one condition necessary to the beginnings of real self-respect. Most of our platitudes notwithstanding, self-deception remains the most difficult deception. The tricks that work on others count for nothing in that very well-lit back alley where one keeps assignations with oneself: no winning smiles will do here, no prettily drawn lists of good intentions. One shuffles flashily but in vain through one's marked cards—the kindness done for the wrong reason, the apparent triumph which involved no real effort, the seemingly heroic act into which one had been shamed. The dismal fact is that self-respect has nothing to do with the approval of others —who are, after all, deceived easily enough; has nothing to do with reputation, which, as Rhett Butler told Scarlett O'Hara, is something people with courage can do without.

To do without self-respect, on the other hand, is to be an unwilling audience of one to an interminable documentary that details one's failings, both real and imagined, with fresh footage spliced in for every screening. *There's the glass you broke in anger, there's the hurt on X's face; watch now, this next scene, the night Y came back from Houston, see how you muff this one.* To live without self-respect is to lie awake some night, beyond the reach of warm milk, phenobarbital, and the sleeping hand on the coverlet, counting up the sins of commission and omission, the trusts betrayed, the promises subtly broken, the gifts irrevocably wasted through sloth or cowardice or carelessness. However long we postpone it, we eventually lie down alone in that notoriously uncomfortable bed, the one we make ourselves. Whether or not we sleep in it depends, of course, on whether or not we respect ourselves.

To protest that some fairly improbable people, some people who *could not possibly respect themselves*, seem to sleep easily enough is to miss the point entirely, as surely as those people miss it who think that self-respect has necessarily to do with not having safety pins in one's underwear. There is a common superstition that "self-respect" is a kind of charm against snakes, something that keeps those who have it locked in some unblighted Eden, out of strange beds, ambivalent conversations, and trouble in general. It does not at all. It has nothing to do with the face of things, but concerns instead a separate peace, a private reconciliation. Although the careless, suicidal Julian English in *Appointment in Samarra* and the careless, incurably dishonest Jordan Baker in *The Great Gatsby* seem equally improbable candidates for self-respect, Jordan Baker had it, Julian English did not. With that genius for accommodation more often seen in women than in men, Jordan took her own measure, made her own peace, avoided threats to that peace: "I hate careless people," she told Nick Carraway. "It takes two to make an accident."

Like Jordan Baker, people with self-respect have the courage of their mistakes. They know the price of things. If they choose to commit adultery, they do not then go running, in an access of bad conscience, to receive absolution from the wronged parties; nor do they complain unduly of the unfairness, the undeserved embarrassment, of being named co-respondent. In brief, people with self-respect exhibit a certain toughness, a kind of moral nerve; they display what was once called *character*, a quality which, although approved in the abstract, sometimes loses ground to other, more instantly negotiable virtues. The measure of its slipping prestige is that one tends to think of it only in connection with homely children and United States senators who have been defeated, preferably in the primary, for reelection. Nonetheless, character—the willingness to accept responsibility for one's own life—is the source from which self-respect springs.

Self-respect is something that our grandparents, whether or not they had it, knew all about. They had instilled in them, young, a certain discipline, the sense that one lives by doing things one does not particularly want to do, by putting fears and doubts to one side, by weighing immediate comforts against the possibility of larger, even intangible, comforts. It seemed to the nineteenth century admirable, but not remarkable, that Chinese Gordon put on a clean white suit and held Khartoum against the Mahdi; it did not seem unjust that the way to free land in California involved death and difficulty and dirt. In a diary kept during the winter of 1846, an emigrating twelve-year-old named Narcissa Cornwall noted coolly: "Father was busy reading and did not notice that the house was being filled with strange Indians until Mother spoke about it." Even lacking any clue as to what Mother said, one can scarcely fail to be impressed by the entire incident: the father reading, the Indians filing in, the mother choosing the words that would not alarm, the child duly recording the event and noting further that those particular Indians were not, "fortunately for us," hostile. Indians were simply part of the *donnée*.

In one guise or another, Indians always are. Again, it is a question of recognizing that anything worth having has its price. People who respect themselves are willing to accept the risk that the Indians will be hostile, that the venture will go bankrupt, that the liaison may not turn out to be one in which *every day is a holiday because you're married to me.* They are willing to invest something of themselves; they may not play at all, but when they do play, they know the odds.

That kind of self-respect is a discipline, a habit of mind that can never be faked but can be developed, trained, coaxed forth. It was once suggested to me that, as an antidote to crying, I put my head in a paper bag. As it happens, there is a sound physiological reason, something to do with oxygen, for doing exactly that, but the psychological effect alone is incalculable: it is difficult in the extreme to continue fancying oneself Cathy in *Wuthering Heights* with one's head in a Food Fair bag. There is a similar case for all the small disciplines, unimportant in themselves; imagine maintaining any kind of swoon, commiserative or carnal, in a cold shower.

But those small disciplines are valuable only insofar as they represent larger ones. To say that Waterloo was won on the playing fields of Eton is not to say that Napoleon might have been saved by a crash program in cricket; to give formal dinners in the rain forest would be pointless did not the candlelight flickering on the liana call forth deeper, stronger disciplines, values instilled long before. It is a kind of ritual, helping us to remember who and what we are. In order to remember it, one must have known it.

To have that sense of one's intrinsic worth which constitutes self-respect is potentially to have everything: the ability to discriminate, to love and to remain indifferent. To lack it is to be locked, within oneself, paradoxically incapable of either love or indifference. If we do not respect ourselves, we are on the one hand forced to despise those who have so few resources as to consort with us, so little perception as to remain blind to our fatal weaknesses. On the other, we are peculiarly in thrall to everyone we see, curiously determined to live out—since our self-image is untenable—their false notions of us. We flatter ourselves by thinking this compulsion to please others an attractive trait: a gist for imaginative empathy, evidence of our willingness to give. *Of course* I will play Francesca to your Paolo, Helen Keller to anyone's Annie Sullivan: no expectation is too misplaced, no role too ludicrous. At the mercy of those we cannot but hold in contempt, we play roles doomed to failure before they are begun, each defeat generating fresh despair at the urgency of divining and meeting the next demand made upon us.

It is the phenomenon sometimes called "alienation from self." In its advanced stages, we no longer answer the telephone, because someone might want something; that we could say *no* without drowning in self-reproach is an idea alien to this game. Every encounter demands too much, tears the nerves, drains the will, and the specter of something as small as an unanswered letter arouses such disproportionate guilt that answering it becomes out of the question. To assign unanswered letters their proper weight, to free us from the expectations of others, to give us back to ourselves—there lies the great, the singular power of self-respect. Without it, one eventually discovers the final turn of the screw: one runs away to find oneself, and finds no one at home.

1961

I Can't Get That Monster out of My Mind

QUITE EARLY in the action of an otherwise unmemorable monster movie (I do not even remember its name), having to do with a mechanical man who walks underwater down the East River as far as Forty-ninth Street and then surfaces to destroy the United Nations, the heroine is surveying the grounds of her country place when the mechanical monster bobs up from a lake and attempts to carry off her child. (Actually we are aware that the monster wants only to make friends with the little girl, but the young mother, who has presumably seen fewer monster movies than we have, is not. This provides pathos, and dramatic tension.) Later that evening, as the heroine sits on the veranda reflecting upon the day's events, her brother strolls out, tamps his pipe, and asks: "Why the brown study, Deborah?" Deborah smiles, ruefully. "It's nothing, Jim, really," she says. "I just can't get that monster out of my mind."

I just can't get that monster out of my mind. It is a useful line, and one that frequently occurs to me when I catch the tone in which a great many people write or talk about Hollywood. In the popular imagination, the American motion-picture industry still represents a kind of mechanical monster, programmed to stifle and destroy all that is interesting and worthwhile and "creative" in the human spirit. As an adjective, the very word "Hollywood" has long been pejorative and suggestive of something referred to as "the System," a phrase delivered with the same sinister emphasis that James Cagney once lent to "the Syndicate." The System not only strangles talent but poisons the soul, a fact supported by rich webs of lore. Mention Hollywood, and we are keyed to remember Scott Fitzgerald, dying at Malibu, attended only by Sheilah Graham while he ground out college-weekend movies (he was also writing *The Last Tycoon*, but that is not part of the story); we are conditioned to recall the brightest minds of a generation, deteriorating around the swimming pool at the Garden of Allah while they waited for calls from the Thalberg Building. (Actually it takes a fairly romantic sensibility to discern why the Garden of Allah should have been a more insidious ambiance than the Algonquin, or why the Thalberg Building, and Metro-Goldwyn-Mayer, should have been more morally debilitating than the Graybar Building, and *Vanity Fair*. Edmund Wilson, who has this kind of sensibility, once suggested that it has something to do with the weather. Perhaps it does.)

Hollywood the Destroyer. It was essentially a romantic vision, and before long Hollywood was helping actively to perpetuate it: think of Jack Palance, as a movie star finally murdered by the System in *The Big Knife*; think of Judy Garland and James Mason (and of Janet Gaynor and Fredric March before them), their lives blighted by the System, or by the Studio—the two phrases were, when the old major studios still ran Hollywood, more or less interchangeable—in *A Star Is Born*. By now, the corruption and venality and restrictiveness of Hollywood have become such firm tenets of American social faith—and of Hollywood's own image of itself—that I was only mildly surprised, not long ago, to hear a young screenwriter announce that Hollywood was "ruining" him. "As a writer," he added. "As a writer," he had previously written, over a span of ten years in New York, one comedy (as opposed to "comic") novel, several newspaper reviews of other people's comedy novels, and a few years' worth of captions for a picture magazine.

Now. It is not surprising that the specter of Hollywood the Destroyer still haunts the rote middle intelligentsia (the monster lurks, I understand, in the wilds between the Thalia and the Museum of Modern Art), or at least those members of it who have not yet perceived the *chic* conferred upon Hollywood by the *Cahiers du Cinéma* set. (Those who have perceived it adopt an equally extreme position, speculating endlessly about what Vincente Minnelli was up to in *Meet Me in St. Louis*, attending seminars on Nicholas Ray, that kind of thing.) What is surprising is that the monster still haunts Hollywood itself—and Hollywood knows better, knows that the monster was laid to rest, dead of natural causes, some years ago. The Fox back lot is now a complex of office buildings called Century City; Paramount makes not forty movies a year but "Bonanza." What was once The Studio is now a releasing operation, and even the Garden of Allah is no more. Virtually every movie made is an independent production—and is that not what we once wanted? Is that not what we once said could revolutionize American movies? The millennium is here, the era of "fewer and better" motion pictures, and what have we? We have fewer pictures, but not necessarily better pictures. Ask Hollywood why, and Hollywood resorts to murmuring about the monster. It has been, they say, impossible to work "honestly" in Hollywood. Certain things have prevented it. The studios, or what is left of the studios, thwart their every dream. The moneymen conspire against them. New York spirits away their prints before they have finished cutting. They are bound by clichés. There is something wrong with "the intellectual climate." If only they were allowed some freedom, if only they could exercise an individual voice. . . .

If only. These protests have about them an engaging period optimism, depending as they do upon the Rousseauean premise that most people, left to their own devices, think not in clichés but with originality and brilliance; that most individual voices, once heard, turn out to be voices of beauty and wisdom. I think we would all agree that a novel is nothing if it is not the expression of an individual voice, of a single view of experience—and how many good or even interesting novels, of the thousands published, appear each year? I doubt that more can be expected of the motion-picture industry. Men who do have interesting individual voices have for some time now been making movies in which those voices are heard; I think of Elia Kazan's *America America*, and, with a good deal less enthusiasm for the voice, of Stanley Kubrick's *Dr. Strangelove*.

But it is not only the "interesting" voices who now have the opportunity to be heard. John Frankenheimer was quoted in *Life* as admitting: "You can't call Hollywood 'The Industry' any more. Today we have a chance to put our personal fantasies on film." Frankenheimer's own personal fantasies have included *All Fall Down*, in which we learned that Warren Beatty and Eva Marie Saint were in love when Frankenheimer dissolved to some swans shimmering on a lake, and *Seven Days in May*, which, in its misapprehension of the way the American power elite thinks and talks and operates (the movie's United States Senator from California, as I recall, drove a Rolls-Royce), appeared to be fantasy in the most clinical sense of that word. Carl Foreman, who, before he was given a chance to put his personal fantasies on film, worked on some very good (of their type) movies—*High Noon* and *The Guns of Navarone*, for two—

later released what he called his "personal statement": *The Victors*, a phenomenon which suggests only that two heads are perhaps better than one, if that one is Foreman's.

One problem is that American directors, with a handful of exceptions, are not much interested in style; they are at heart didactic. Ask what they plan to do with their absolute freedom, with their chance to make a personal statement, and they will pick an "issue," a "problem." The "issues" they pick are generally no longer real issues, if indeed they ever were —but I think it a mistake to attribute this to any calculated venality, to any conscious playing it safe. (I am reminded of a screenwriter who just recently discovered dwarfs—although he, like the rest of us, must have lived through that period when dwarfs turned up on the fiction pages of the glossier magazines with the approximate frequency that Suzy Parker turned up on the advertising pages. This screenwriter sees dwarfs as symbols of modern man's crippling anomie. There is a certain cultural lag.) Call it instead—this apparent calculation about what "issues" are now safe—an absence of imagination, a sloppiness of mind in some ways encouraged by a comfortable feedback from the audience, from the bulk of the reviewers, and from some people who ought to know better. Stanley Kramer's *Judgment at Nuremberg*, made in 1961, was an intrepid indictment not of authoritarianism in the abstract, not of the trials themselves, not of the various moral and legal issues involved, but of Nazi war atrocities, about which there would have seemed already to be some consensus. (You may remember that *Judgment at Nuremberg* received an Academy Award, which the screenwriter Abby Mann accepted on the behalf of "all intellectuals.") Later, Kramer and Abby Mann collaborated on *Ship of Fools*, into which they injected "a little more compassion and humor" and in which they advanced the action from 1931 to 1933—the better to register another defiant protest against the National Socialist Party. Foreman's *The Victors* set forth, interminably, the proposition that war defeats the victors equally with the vanquished, a notion not exactly radical. (Foreman is a director who at first gives the impression of having a little style, but the impression is entirely spurious, and prompted mostly by his total recall for old Eisenstein effects.) Stanley Kubrick's *Dr. Strangelove*, which did have a little style, was scarcely a picture of relentless originality; rarely have we seen so much made over so little. John Simon, in the *New Leader*, declared that the "altogether admirable thing" about *Dr. Strangelove* was that it managed to be "thoroughly irreverent about everything the Establishment takes seriously: atomic war, government, the army, international relations, heroism, sex, and what not." I don't know who John Simon thinks makes up the Establishment, but skimming back at random from "what not," sex is our most durable communal joke; Billy Wilder's *One, Two, Three* was a boffo (*cf. Variety*) spoof of international relations; the army as a laugh line has filtered right down to Phil Silvers and "Sergeant Bilko"; and, if "government" is something about which the American Establishment is inflexibly reverent, I seem to have been catching some pretty underground material on prime time television. And what not. *Dr. Strangelove* was essentially a one-line gag, having to do with the difference between all other wars and nuclear war. By the time George Scott had said "I think I'll mosey on over to the War Room" and Sterling Hayden had said "Looks like we got ourselves a shootin' war" and the SAC bomber had begun heading for its Soviet targets to the tune of "When Johnny Comes Marching Home Again," Kubrick had already developed a full fugue upon the theme, and should have started counting the minutes until it would begin to pall.

What we have, then, are a few interesting minds at work; and a great many less interesting ones. The European situation is not all that different. Antonioni, among the Italians, makes beautiful, intelligent, intricately and subtly built pictures, the power of which lies entirely in their structure; Visconti, on the other hand, has less sense of form than anyone now directing. One might as well have viewed a series of stills, in no perceptible order, as his *The Leopard*. Federico Fellini and Ingmar Bergman share a stunning visual intelligence and a numbingly banal view of human experience; Alain Resnais, in *Last Year at Marienbad* and *Muriel*, demonstrated a style so intrusive that one suspected it to be a smoke screen, suspected that it was intruding upon a vacuum. As for the notion that European movies tend to be more original than American movies, no one who saw *Boccaccio '70* could ever again automatically modify the word "formula" with "Hollywood."

*

So. With perhaps a little prodding from abroad, we are all grown up now in Hollywood, and left to set out in the world on our own. We are no longer in the grip of a monster; Harry Cohn no longer runs Columbia like, as the saying went, a concentration camp. Whether or not a picture receives a Code seal no longer matters much at the box office. No more curfew, no more Daddy, *anything goes.* Some of us do not quite like this permissiveness; some of us would like to find "reasons" why our pictures are not as good as we know in our hearts they might be. Not long ago I met a producer who complained to me of the difficulties he had working within what I recognized as the System, although he did not call it that. He longed, he said, to do an adaptation of a certain Charles Jackson short story. "Some really terrific stuff," he said. "Can't touch it, I'm afraid. About masturbation."

1964

On Morality

AS IT HAPPENS I am in Death Valley, in a room at the Enterprise Motel and Trailer Park, and it is July, and it is hot. In fact it is 119°. I cannot seem to make the air conditioner work, but there is a small refrigerator, and I can wrap ice cubes in a towel and hold them against the small of my back. With the help of the ice cubes I have been trying to think, because *The American Scholar* asked me to, in some abstract way about "morality," a word I distrust more every day, but my mind veers inflexibly toward the particular.

Here are some particulars. At midnight last night, on the road in from Las Vegas to Death Valley Junction, a car hit a shoulder and turned over. The driver, very young and apparently drunk, was killed instantly. His girl was found alive but bleeding internally, deep in shock. I talked this afternoon to the nurse who had driven the girl to the nearest doctor, 185 miles across the floor of the Valley and three ranges of lethal mountain road. The nurse explained that her husband, a talc miner, had stayed on the highway with the boy's body until the coroner could get over the mountains from Bishop, at dawn today. "You can't just leave a body on the highway," she said. "It's immoral."

It was one instance in which I did not distrust the word, because she meant something quite specific. She meant that if a body is left alone for even a few minutes on the desert, the coyotes close in and eat the flesh. Whether or not a corpse is torn apart by coyotes may seem only a sentimental consideration, but of course it is more: one of the promises we make to one another is that we will try to retrieve our casualties, try not to abandon our dead to the coyotes. If we have been taught to keep our promises—if, in the simplest terms, our upbringing is good enough—we stay with the body, or have bad dreams.

I am talking, of course, about the kind of social code that is sometimes called, usually pejoratively, "wagon-train morality." In fact that is precisely what it is. For better or worse, we are what we learned as children: my own childhood was illuminated by graphic litanies of the grief awaiting those who failed in their loyalties to each other. The Donner-Reed Party, starving in the Sierra snows, all the ephemera of civilization gone save that one vestigial taboo, the provision that no one should eat his own blood kin. The Jayhawkers, who quarreled and separated not far from where I am tonight. Some of them died in the Funerals and some of them died down near Badwater and most of the rest of them died in the Panamints. A woman who got through gave the Valley its name. Some might say that the Jayhawkers were killed by the desert summer, and the Donner Party by the mountain winter, by circumstances beyond control; we were taught instead that they had somewhere abdicated their responsibilities, somehow breached their primary loyalties, or they would not have found themselves helpless in the mountain winter or the desert summer, would not have given way to acrimony, would not have deserted one another, would not have *failed*. In brief, we heard such stories as cautionary tales, and they still suggest the only kind of "morality" that seems to me to have any but the most potentially mendacious meaning.

You are quite possibly impatient with me by now; I am talking, you want to say, about a "morality" so primitive that it scarcely deserves the name, a code that has as its point only survival, not the attainment of the ideal good. Exactly. Particularly out here tonight, in this country so ominous and terrible that to live in it is to live with antimatter, it is difficult to believe that "the good" is a knowable quantity. Let me tell you what it is like out here tonight. Stories travel at night on the desert. Someone gets in his pickup and drives a couple of hundred miles for a beer, and he carries news of what is happening, back wherever he came from. Then he drives another hundred miles for another beer, and passes along stories from the last place as well as from the one before; it is a network kept alive by people whose instincts tell them that if they do not keep moving at night on the desert they will lose all reason. Here is a story that is going around the desert tonight: over across the Nevada line, sheriff's deputies are diving in some underground pools, trying to retrieve a couple of bodies known to be in the hole. The widow of one of the drowned boys is over there; she is eighteen, and pregnant, and is said not to leave the hole. The divers go down and come up, and she just stands there and stares into the water. They have been diving for ten days but have found no bottom to the caves, no bodies and no trace of them, only the black 90° water going down and down and down, and a single translucent fish, not classified. The story tonight is that one of the divers has been hauled up incoherent, out of his head, shouting—until they got him out of there so that the widow could not hear—about water that got hotter instead of cooler as he went down, about light flickering through the water, about magma, about underground nuclear testing.

That is the tone stories take out here, and there are quite a few of them tonight. And it is more than the stories alone. Across the road at the Faith Community Church a couple of dozen old people, come here to live in trailers and die in the sun, are holding a prayer sing. I cannot hear them and do not want to. What I can hear are occasional coyotes and a constant chorus of "Baby the Rain Must Fall" from the jukebox in the Snake Room next door, and if I were also to hear those dying voices, those Midwestern voices drawn to this lunar country for some unimaginable atavistic rites, *rock of ages cleft for me*, I think I would lose my own reason. Every now and then I imagine I hear a rattlesnake, but my husband says that it is a faucet, a paper rustling, the wind. Then he stands by a window, and plays a flashlight over the dry wash outside.

What does it mean? It means nothing manageable. There is some sinister hysteria in the air out here tonight, some hint of the monstrous perversion to which any human idea can come. "I followed my own conscience." "I did what I thought was right." How many madmen have said it and meant it? How many murderers? Klaus Fuchs said it, and the men who committed the Mountain Meadows Massacre said it, and Alfred Rosenberg said it. And, as we are rotely and rather presumptuously reminded by those who would say it now, Jesus said it. Maybe we have all said it, and maybe we have been wrong. Except on that most primitive level—our loyalties to those we love—what could be more arrogant than to claim the primacy of personal conscience? ("Tell me," a rabbi asked Daniel Bell when he said, as a child, that he did not believe in God. "Do you think God cares?") At least some of the time, the world appears to me as a painting by Hieronymous Bosch; were I to follow my conscience then, it would lead me out onto the desert with Marion Faye, out to where he stood in *The Deer Park* looking east to Los Alamos and praying, as if for rain, that it would happen: "*. . . let it come and clear the rot and the stench and the stink, let it come for all of everywhere, just so it comes and the world stands clear in the white dead dawn.*"

Of course you will say that I do not have the right, even if I had the power, to inflict that unreasonable conscience upon you; nor do I want you to inflict your conscience, however reasonable, however enlightened, upon me. ("We must be aware of the dangers which lie in our most generous wishes," Lionel Trilling once wrote. "Some paradox of our nature leads us, when once we have made our fellow men the objects of our enlightened interest, to go on to make them the objects of our pity, then of our wisdom, ultimately of our coercion.") That the ethic of conscience is intrinsically insidious seems scarcely a revelatory point, but it is one raised with increasing infrequency; even those who do raise it tend to *segue* with troubling readiness into the quite contradictory position that the ethic of conscience is dangerous when it is "wrong," and admirable when it is "right."

You see I want to be quite obstinate about insisting that we have no way of knowing—beyond that fundamental loyalty to the social code—what is "right" and what is "wrong," what is "good" and what "evil." I dwell so upon this because the most disturbing aspect of "morality" seems to me to be the frequency with which the word now appears; in the press, on television, in the most perfunctory kinds of conversation. Questions of straightforward power (or survival) politics, questions of quite indifferent public policy, questions of almost anything: they are all assigned these factitious moral burdens. There is something facile going on, some self-indulgence at work. Of course we would all like to "believe" in something, like to assuage our private guilts in public causes, like to lose our tiresome selves; like, perhaps, to transform the white flag of defeat at home into the brave white banner of battle away from home. And of course it is all right to do that; that is how, immemorially, things have gotten done. But I think it is all right only so long as we do not delude ourselves about what we are doing, and why. It is all right only so long as we remember that all the *ad hoc* committees, all the picket lines, all the brave signatures in *The New York Times*, all the tools of agitprop straight across the spectrum, do not confer upon anyone any *ipso facto* virtue. It is all right only so long as we recognize that the end may or may not be expedient, may or may not be a good idea, but in any case has nothing to do with "morality." Because when we start deceiving ourselves into thinking not that we want something or need something, not that it is a pragmatic necessity for us to have it, but that it is a *moral imperative* that we have it, then is when we join the fashionable madmen, and then is when the thin whine of hysteria is heard in the land, and then is when we are in bad trouble. And I suspect we are already there.

1965

On Going Home

I AM HOME for my daughter's first birthday. By "home" I do not mean the house in Los Angeles where my husband and I and the baby live, but the place where my family is, in the Central Valley of California. It is a vital although troublesome distinction. My husband likes my family but is uneasy in their house, because once there I fall into their ways, which are difficult, oblique, deliberately inarticulate, not my husband's ways. We live in dusty houses ("D-U-S-T," he once wrote with his finger on surfaces all over the house, but no one noticed it) filled with mementos quite without value to him (what could the Canton dessert plates mean to him? how could he have known about the assay scales, why should he care if he did know?), and we appear to talk exclusively about people we know who have been committed to mental hospitals, about people we know who have been booked on drunk-driving charges, and about property, particularly about property, land, price per acre and C-2 zoning and assessments and freeway access. My brother does not understand my husband's inability to perceive the advantage in the rather common real-estate transaction known as "sale-leaseback," and my husband in turn does not understand why so many of the people he hears about in my father's house have recently been committed to mental hospitals or booked on drunk-driving charges. Nor does he understand that when we talk about sale-leasebacks and right-of-way condemnations we are talking in code about the things we like best, the yellow fields and the cottonwoods and the rivers rising and falling and the mountain roads closing when the heavy snow comes in. We miss each other's points, have another drink and regard the fire. My brother refers to my husband, in his presence, as "Joan's husband." Marriage is the classic betrayal.

Or perhaps it is not any more. Sometimes I think that those of us who are now in our thirties were born into the last generation to carry the burden of "home," to find in family life the source of all tension and drama. I had by all objective accounts a "normal" and a "happy" family situation, and yet I was almost thirty years old before I could talk to my family on the telephone without crying after I had hung up. We did not fight. Nothing was wrong. And yet some nameless anxiety colored the emotional charges between me and the place that I came from. The question of whether or not you could go home again was a very real part of the sentimental and largely literary baggage with which we left home in the fifties; I suspect that it is irrelevant to the children born of the fragmentation after World War II. A few weeks ago in a San Francisco bar I saw a pretty young girl on crystal take off her clothes and dance for the cash prize in an "amateur-topless" contest. There was no particular sense of moment about this, none of the effect of romantic degradation, of "dark journey," for which my generation strived so assiduously. What sense could that girl possibly make of, say, *Long Day's Journey into Night*? Who is beside the point?

That I am trapped in this particular irrelevancy is never more apparent to me than when I am home. Paralyzed by the neurotic lassitude engendered by meeting one's past at every turn, around every corner, inside every cupboard, I go aimlessly from room to room. I decide to meet it head-on and clean out a drawer, and I spread the contents on the bed. A bathing suit I wore the summer I was seventeen. A letter of rejection from *The Nation*, an aerial photograph of the site for a shopping center my father did not build in 1954. Three teacups hand-painted with cabbage roses and signed "E.M.," my grandmother's initials. There is no final solution for letters of rejection from *The Nation* and teacups hand-painted in 1900. Nor is there any answer to snapshots of one's grandfather as a young man on skis, surveying around Donner Pass in the year 1910. I smooth out the snapshot and look into his face, and do and do not see my own. I close the drawer, and have another cup of coffee with my mother. We get along very well, veterans of a guerrilla war we never understood.

Days pass. I see no one. I come to dread my husband's evening call, not only because he is full of news of what by now seems to me our remote life in Los Angeles, people he has seen, letters which require attention, but because he asks what I have been doing, suggests uneasily that I get out, drive to San Francisco or Berkeley. Instead I drive across the river to a family graveyard. It has been vandalized since my last visit and the monuments are broken, overturned in the dry grass. Because I once saw a rattlesnake in the grass I stay in the car and listen to a country-and-western station. Later I drive with my father to a ranch he has in the foothills. The man who runs his cattle on it asks us to the roundup, a week from Sunday, and although I know that I will be in Los Angeles I say, in the oblique way my family talks, that I will come. Once home I mention the broken monuments in the graveyard. My mother shrugs.

I go to visit my great-aunts. A few of them think now that I am my cousin, or their daughter who died young. We recall an anecdote about a relative last seen in 1948, and they ask if I still like living in New York City. I have lived in Los Angeles for three years, but I say that I do. The baby is offered a horehound drop, and I am slipped a dollar bill "to buy a treat." Questions trail off, answers are abandoned, the baby plays with the dust motes in a shaft of afternoon sun.

It is time for the baby's birthday party: a white cake, strawberry-marshmallow ice cream, a bottle of champagne saved from another party. In the evening, after she has gone to sleep, I kneel beside the crib and touch her face, where it is pressed against the slats, with mine. She is an open and trusting child, unprepared for and unaccustomed to the ambushes of family life, and perhaps it is just as well that I can offer her little of that life. I would like to give her more. I would like to promise her that she will grow up with a sense of her cousins and of rivers and of her great-grandmother's teacups, would like to pledge her a picnic on a river with fried chicken and her hair uncombed, would like to give her *home* for her birthday, but we live differently now and I can promise her nothing like that. I give her a xylophone and a sundress from Madeira, and promise to tell her a funny story.

1967

III

SEVEN PLACES OF THE MIND

Notes from a Native Daughter

It is very easy to sit at the bar in, say, La Scala in Beverly Hills, or Ernie's in San Francisco, and to share in the pervasive delusion that California is only five hours from New York by air. The truth is that La Scala and Ernie's are only five hours from New York by air. California is somewhere else.

Many people in the East (or "back East," as they say in California, although not in La Scala or Ernie's) do not believe this. They have been to Los Angeles or to San Francisco, have driven through a giant redwood and have seen the Pacific glazed by the afternoon sun off Big Sur, and they naturally tend to believe that they have in fact been to California. They have not been, and they probably never will be, for it is a longer and in many ways a more difficult trip than they might want to undertake, one of those trips on which the destination flickers chimerically on the horizon, ever receding, ever diminishing. I happen to know about that trip because I come from California, come from a family, or a congeries of families, that has always been in the Sacramento Valley.

You might protest that no family has been in the Sacramento Valley for anything approaching "always." But it is characteristic of Californians to speak grandly of the past as if it had simultaneously begun, *tabula rasa*, and reached a happy ending on the day the wagons started west. *Eureka*—"I Have Found It"—as the state motto has it. Such a view of history casts a certain melancholia over those who participate in it; my own childhood was suffused with the conviction that we had long outlived our finest hour. In fact that is what I want to tell you about: what it is like to come from a place like Sacramento. If I could make you understand that, I could make you understand California and perhaps something else besides, for Sacramento *is* California, and California is a place in which a boom mentality and a sense of Chekhovian loss meet in uneasy suspension; in which the mind is troubled by some buried but ineradicable suspicion that things had better work here, because here, beneath that immense bleached sky, is where we run out of continent.

In 1847 Sacramento was no more than an adobe enclosure, Sutter's Fort, standing alone on the prairie; cut off from San Francisco and the sea by the Coast Range and from the rest of the continent by the Sierra Nevada, the Sacramento Valley was then a true sea of grass, grass so high a man riding into it could tie it across his saddle. A year later gold was discovered in the Sierra foothills, and abruptly Sacramento was a town, a town any moviegoer could map tonight in his dreams—a dusty collage of assay offices and wagonmakers and saloons. Call that Phase Two. Then the settlers came—the farmers, the people who for two hundred years had been moving west on the frontier, the peculiar flawed strain who had cleared Virginia, Kentucky, Missouri; they made Sacramento a farm town. Because the land was rich, Sacramento became eventually a rich farm town, which meant houses in town, Cadillac dealers, a country club. In that gentle sleep Sacramento dreamed until perhaps 1950, when something happened. What happened was that Sacramento woke to the fact that the outside world was moving in, fast and hard. At the moment of its waking Sacramento lost, for better or for worse, its character, and that is part of what I want to tell you about.

But the change is not what I remember first. First I remember running a boxer dog of my brother's over the same flat fields that our great-great-grandfather had found virgin and had planted; I remember swimming (albeit nervously, for I was a nervous child, afraid of sinkholes and afraid of snakes, and perhaps that was the beginning of my error) the same rivers we had swum for a century: the Sacramento, so rich with silt that we could barely see our hands a few inches beneath the surface; the American, running clean and fast with melted Sierra snow until July, when it would slow down, and rattlesnakes would sun themselves on its newly exposed rocks. The Sacramento, the American, sometimes the Cosumnes, occasionally the Feather. Incautious children died every day in those rivers; we read about it in the paper, how they had miscalculated a current or stepped into a hole down where the American runs into the Sacramento, how the Berry Brothers had been called in from Yolo County to drag the river but how the bodies remained unrecovered. "They were from away," my grandmother would extrapolate from the newspaper stories. “Their parents had no *business* letting them in the river. They were visitors from Omaha.” It was not a bad lesson, although a less than reliable one; children we knew died in the rivers too.

When summer ended—when the State Fair closed and the heat broke, when the last green hop vines had been torn down along the H Street road and the tule fog began rising off the low ground at night—we would go back to memorizing the Products of Our Latin American Neighbors and to visiting the great-aunts on Sunday, dozens of great-aunts, year after year of Sundays. When I think now of those winters I think of yellow elm leaves wadded in the gutters outside the Trinity Episcopal Pro-Cathedral on M Street. There are actually people in Sacramento now who call M Street Capitol Avenue, and Trinity has one of those featureless new buildings, but perhaps children still learn the same things there on Sunday mornings:

Q. In what way does the Holy Land resemble the Sacramento Valley?
A. In the type and diversity of its agricultural products.

And I think of the rivers rising, of listening to the radio to hear at what height they would crest and wondering if and when and where the levees would go. We did not have as many dams in those years. The bypasses would be full, and men would sandbag all night. Sometimes a levee would go in the night, somewhere upriver; in the morning the rumor would spread that the Army Engineers had dynamited it to relieve the pressure on the city.

After the rains came spring, for ten days or so; the drenched fields would dissolve into a brilliant ephemeral green (it would be yellow and dry as fire in two or three weeks) and the real-estate business would pick up. It was the time of year when people’s grandmothers went to Carmel; it was the time of year when girls who could not even get into Stephens or Arizona or Oregon, let alone Stanford or Berkeley, would be sent to Honolulu, on the *Lurline*. I have no recollection of anyone going to New York, with the exception of a cousin who visited there (I cannot imagine why) and reported that the shoe salesmen at Lord & Taylor were “intolerably rude.” What happened in New York and Washington and abroad seemed to impinge not at all upon the Sacramento mind. I remember being taken to call upon a very old woman, a rancher's widow, who was reminiscing (the favored conversational mode in Sacramento) about the son of some contemporaries of hers. "That Johnston boy never did amount to much," she said. Desultorily, my mother protested: Alva Johnston, she said, had won the Pulitzer Prize, when he was working for *The New York Times.* Our hostess looked at us impassively. "He never amounted to anything in Sacramento," she said.

Hers was the true Sacramento voice, and, although I did not realize it then, one not long to be heard, for the war was over and the boom was on and the voice of the aerospace engineer would be heard in the land. VETS NO DOWN! EXECUTIVE LIVING ON LOW FHA!

Later, when I was living in New York, I would make the trip back to Sacramento four and five times a year (the more comfortable the flight, the more obscurely miserable I would be, for it weighs heavily upon my kind that we could perhaps not make it by wagon), trying to prove that I had not meant to leave at all, because in at least one respect California—the California we are talking about—resembles Eden: it is assumed that those who absent themselves from its blessings have been banished, exiled by some perversity of heart. Did not the Donner-Reed Party, after all, eat its own dead to reach Sacramento?

I have said that the trip back is difficult, and it is—difficult in a way that magnifies the ordinary ambiguities of sentimental journeys. Going back to California is not like going back to Vermont, or Chicago; Vermont and Chicago are relative constants, against which one measures one's own change. All that is constant about the California of my childhood is the rate at which it disappears. An instance: on Saint Patrick's Day of 1948 I was taken to see the legislature "in action," a dismal experience; a handful of florid assemblymen, wearing green hats, were reading Pat-and-Mike jokes into the record. I still think of the legislators that way—wearing green hats, or sitting around on the veranda of the Senator Hotel fanning themselves and being entertained by Artie Samish's emissaries. (Samish was the lobbyist who said, "Earl Warren may be the governor of the state, but I'm the governor of the legislature.") In fact there is no longer a veranda at the Senator Hotel—it was turned into an airline ticket office, if you want to embroider the point—and in any case the legislature has largely deserted the Senator for the flashy motels north of town, where the tiki torches flame and the steam rises off the heated swimming pools in the cold Valley night.

It is hard to *find* California now, unsettling to wonder how much of it was merely imagined or improvised; melancholy to realize how much of anyone's memory is no true memory at all but only the traces of someone else's memory, stories handed down on the family network. I have an indelibly vivid "memory," for example, of how Prohibition affected the hop growers around Sacramento: the sister of a grower my family knew brought home a mink coat from San Francisco, and was told to take it back, and sat on the floor of the parlor cradling that coat and crying. Although I was not born until a year after Repeal, that scene is more "real" to me than many I have played myself.

I remember one trip home, when I sat alone on a night jet from New York and read over and over some lines from a W. S. Merwin poem I had come across in a magazine, a poem about a man who had been a long time in another country and knew that he must go home:

> *. . . But it should be*
> *Soon. Already I defend hotly*
> *Certain of our indefensible faults,*
> *Resent being reminded; already in my mind*
> *Our language becomes freighted with a richness*
> *No common tongue could offer, while the mountains*
> *Are like nowhere on earth, and the wide rivers.*

You see the point. I want to tell you the truth, and already I have told you about the wide rivers.

It should be clear by now that the truth about the place is elusive, and must be tracked with caution. You might go to Sacramento tomorrow and someone (although no one I know) might take you out to Aerojet-General, which has, in the Sacramento phrase, "something to do with rockets." Fifteen thousand people work for Aerojet, almost all of them imported; a Sacramento lawyer's wife told me, as evidence of how Sacramento was opening up, that she believed she had met one of them, at an open house two Decembers ago. ("Couldn't have been nicer, actually," she added enthusiastically. "I think he and his wife bought the house next *door* to Mary and Al, something like that, which of course was how *they* met him.") So you might go to Aerojet and stand in the big vendors' lobby where a couple of thousand components salesmen try every week to sell their wares and you might look up at the electrical wallboard that lists Aerojet personnel, their projects and their location at any given time, and you might wonder if I have been in Sacramento lately. MINUTEMAN, POLARIS, TITAN, the lights flash, and all the coffee tables are littered with airline schedules, very now, very much in touch.

But I could take you a few miles from there into towns where the banks still bear names like The Bank of Alex Brown, into towns where the one hotel still has an octagonal-tile floor in the dining room and dusty potted palms and big ceiling fans; into towns where everything—the seed business, the Harvester franchise, the hotel, the department store and the main street —carries a single name, the name of the man who built the town. A few Sundays ago I was in a town like that, a town smaller than that, really, no hotel, no Harvester franchise, the bank burned out, a river town. It was the golden anniversary of some of my relatives and it was 110° and the guests of honor sat on straight-backed chairs in front of a sheaf of gladioluses in the Rebekah Hall. I mentioned visiting Aerojet-General to a cousin I saw there, who listened to me with interested disbelief. Which is the true California? That is what we all wonder.

Let us try out a few irrefutable statements, on subjects not open to interpretation. Although Sacramento is in many ways the least typical of the Valley towns, it *is* a Valley town, and must be viewed in that context. When you say "the Valley" in Los Angeles, most people assume that you mean the San Fernando Valley (some people in fact assume that you mean Warner Brothers), but make no mistake: we are talking not about the valley of the sound stages and the ranchettes but about the real Valley, the Central Valley, the fifty thousand square miles drained by the Sacramento and the San Joaquin Rivers and further irrigated by a complex network of sloughs, cutoffs, ditches, and the Delta-Mendota and Friant-Kern Canals.

A hundred miles north of Los Angeles, at the moment when you drop from the Tehachapi Mountains into the outskirts of Bakersfield, you leave Southern California and enter the Valley. "You look up the highway and it is straight for miles, coming at you, with the black line down the center coming at you and at you . . . and the heat dazzles up from the white slab so that only the black line is clear, coming at you with the whine of the tires, and if you don't quit staring at that line and don't take a few deep breaths and slap yourself hard on the back of the neck you'll hypnotize yourself."

Robert Penn Warren wrote that about another road, but he might have been writing about the Valley road, U.S. 99, three hundred miles from Bakersfield to Sacramento, a highway so straight that when one flies on the most direct pattern from Los Angeles to Sacramento one never loses sight of U.S. 99. The landscape it runs through never, to the untrained eye, varies. The Valley eye can discern the point where miles of cotton seedlings fade into miles of tomato seedlings, or where the great corporation ranches—Kern County Land, what is left of DiGiorgio—give way to private operations (somewhere on the horizon, if the place is private, one sees a house and a stand of scrub oaks), but such distinctions are in the long view irrelevant. All day long, all that moves is the sun, and the big Rainbird sprinklers.

Every so often along 99 between Bakersfield and Sacramento there is a town: Delano, Tulare, Fresno, Madera, Merced, Modesto, Stockton. Some of these towns are pretty big now, but they are all the same at heart, one- and two- and three-story buildings artlessly arranged, so that what appears to be the good dress shop stands beside a W. T. Grant store, so that the big Bank of America faces a Mexican movie house. *Dos Peliculas, Bingo Bingo Bingo.* Beyond the downtown (pronounced *down*town, with the Okie accent that now pervades Valley speech patterns) lie blocks of old frame houses—paint peeling, sidewalks cracking, their occasional leaded amber windows overlooking a Foster's Freeze or a five-minute car wash or a State Farm Insurance office; beyond those spread the shopping centers and the miles of tract houses, pastel with redwood siding, the unmistakable signs of cheap building already blossoming on those houses which have survived the first rain. To a stranger driving 99 in an air-conditioned car (he would be on business, I suppose, any stranger driving 99, for 99 would never get a tourist to Big Sur or San Simeon, never get him to the California he came to see), these towns must seem so flat, so impoverished, as to drain the imagination. They hint at evenings spent hanging around gas stations, and suicide pacts sealed in drive-ins.

But remember:

Q. In what way does the Holy Land resemble the Sacramento Valley?

A. In the type and diversity of its agricultural products.

U.S. 99 in fact passes through the richest and most intensely cultivated agricultural region in the world, a giant outdoor hothouse with a billion-dollar crop. It is when you remember the Valley's wealth that the monochromatic flatness of its towns takes on a curious meaning, suggests a habit of mind some would consider perverse. There is something in the Valley mind that reflects a real indifference to the stranger in his air-conditioned car, a failure to perceive even his presence, let alone his thoughts or wants. An implacable insularity is the seal of these towns. I once met a woman in Dallas, a most charming and attractive woman accustomed to the hospitality and social hypersensitivity of Texas, who told me that during the four war years her husband had been stationed in Modesto, she had never once been invited inside anyone's house. No one in Sacramento would find this story remarkable ("She probably had no *rel*atives there," said someone to whom I told it), for the Valley towns understand one another, share a peculiar spirit. They think alike and they look alike. *I* can tell Modesto from Merced, but I have visited there, gone to dances there; besides, there is over the main street of Modesto an arched sign which reads:

WATER — WEALTH
CONTENTMENT — HEALTH

There is no such sign in Merced.

*

I said that Sacramento was the least typical of the Valley towns, and it is—but only because it is bigger and more diverse, only because it has had the rivers and the legislature; its true character remains the Valley character, its virtues the Valley virtues, its sadness the Valley sadness. It is just as hot in the summertime, so hot that the air shimmers and the grass bleaches white and the blinds stay drawn all day, so hot that August comes on not like a month but like an affliction; it is just as flat, so flat that a ranch of my family's with a slight rise on it, perhaps a foot, was known for the hundred-some years which preceded this year as "the hill ranch." (It is known this year as a subdivision in the making, but that is another part of the story.) Above all, in spite of its infusions from outside, Sacramento retains the Valley insularity.

To sense that insularity a visitor need do no more than pick up a copy of either of the two newspapers, the morning *Union* or the afternoon *Bee*. The *Union* happens to be Republican and impoverished and the *Bee* Democratic and powerful ("THE VALLEY OF THE BEES!" as the McClatchys, who own the Fresno, Modesto, and Sacramento *Bees*, used to headline their advertisements in the trade press. "ISOLATED FROM ALL OTHER MEDIA INFLUENCE!"), but they read a good deal alike, and the tone of their chief editorial concerns is strange and wonderful and instructive. The *Union*, in a county heavily and reliably Democratic, frets mainly about the possibility of a local takeover by the John Birch Society; the *Bee*, faithful to the letter of its founder's will, carries on overwrought crusades against phantoms it still calls "the power trusts." Shades of Hiram Johnson, whom the *Bee* helped elect governor in 1910. Shades of Robert La Follette, to whom the *Bee* delivered the Valley in 1924. There is something about the Sacramento papers that does not quite connect with the way Sacramento lives now, something pronouncedly beside the point. The aerospace engineers, one learns, read the San Francisco *Chronicle*.

The Sacramento papers, however, simply mirror the Sacramento peculiarity, the Valley fate, which is to be paralyzed by a past no longer relevant. Sacramento is a town which grew up on farming and discovered to its shock that land has more profitable uses. (The chamber of commerce will give you crop figures, but pay them no mind—what matters is the feeling, the knowledge that where the green hops once grew is now Larchmont Riviera, that what used to be the Whitney ranch is now Sunset City, thirty-three thousand houses and a country-club complex.) It is a town in which defense industry and its absentee owners are suddenly the most important facts; a town which has never had more people or more money, but has lost its *raison d'être*. It is a town many of whose most solid citizens sense about themselves a kind of functional obsolescence. The old families still see only one another, but they do not see even one another as much as they once did; they are closing ranks, preparing for the long night, selling their rights-of-way and living on the proceeds. Their children still marry one another, still play bridge and go into the real-estate business together. (There is no other business in Sacramento, no reality other than land—even I, when I was living and working in New York, felt impelled to take a University of California correspondence course in Urban Land Economics.) But late at night when the ice has melted there is always somebody now, some Julian English, whose heart is not quite in it. For out there on the outskirts of town are marshaled the legions of aerospace engineers, who talk their peculiar condescending language and tend their dichondra and plan to stay in the promised land; who are raising a new generation of native Sacramentans and who do not care, really do not care, that they are not asked to join the Sutter Club. It makes one wonder, late at night when the ice is gone; introduces some air into the womb, suggests that the Sutter Club is perhaps not, after all, the Pacific Union or the Bohemian; that Sacramento is not *the city*. In just such self-doubts do small towns lose their character.

I want to tell you a Sacramento story. A few miles out of town is a place, six or seven thousand acres, which belonged in the beginning to a rancher with one daughter. That daughter went abroad and married a title, and when she brought the title home to live on the ranch, her father built them a vast house—music rooms, conservatories, a ballroom. They needed a ballroom because they entertained: people from abroad, people from San Francisco, house parties that lasted weeks and involved special trains. They are long dead, of course, but their only son, aging and unmarried, still lives on the place. He does not live in the house, for the house is no longer there. Over the years it burned, room by room, wing by wing. Only the chimneys of the great house are still standing, and its heir lives in their shadow, lives by himself on the charred site, in a house trailer.

That is a story my generation knows; I doubt that the next will know it, the children of the aerospace engineers. Who would tell it to them? Their grandmothers live in Scarsdale, and they have never met a great-aunt. "Old" Sacramento to them will be something colorful, something they read about in *Sunset.* They will probably think that the Redevelopment has always been there, that the Embarcadero, down along the river, with its amusing places to shop and its picturesque fire houses turned into bars, has about it the true flavor of the way it was. There will be no reason for them to know that in homelier days it was called Front Street (the town was not, after all, settled by the Spanish) and was a place of derelicts and missions and itinerant pickers in town for a Saturday-night drunk: VICTORIOUS LIFE MISSION, JESUS SAVES, BEDS 25¢ A NIGHT, CROP INFORMATION HERE. They will have lost the real past and gained a manufactured one, and there will be no way for them to know, no way at all, why a house trailer should stand alone on seven thousand acres outside town.

But perhaps it is presumptuous of me to assume that they will be missing something. Perhaps in retrospect this has been a story not about Sacramento at all, but about the things we lose and the promises we break as we grow older; perhaps I have been playing out unawares the Margaret in the poem:

Margaret, are you grieving
Over Goldengrove unleaving? . . .
It is the blight man was born for,
It is Margaret you mourn for.

1965

Letter from Paradise, 21° 19′ N., 157° 52′ W.

BECAUSE I HAD BEEN TIRED too long and quarrelsome too much and too often frightened of migraine and failure and the days getting shorter, I was sent, a recalcitrant thirty-one-year-old child, to Hawaii, where winter does not come and no one fails and the median age is twenty-three. There I could become a new woman, there with the life-insurance salesmen on million-dollar-a-year incentive trips, there with the Shriners and the San Francisco divorcées and the splurging secretaries and the girls in the string bikinis and the boys in search of the perfect wave, children who understood the insouciant economy of buying a Honda or a surfboard for one dollar down and $2.50 a week and then abandoning it, children who have never been told, as I was told, that golden lads and girls all must as chimney sweepers come to dust. I was to lie beneath the same sun that had kept Doris Duke and Henry Kaiser forever hopeful. I was to play at sipping frozen daiquiris and wear flowers in my hair as if ten years had never happened. I was to see for myself that just beyond the end of the line lay not Despond but Diamond Head.

I went, a wary visitor. I do not believe that the stories told by lovely hula hands merit extensive study. I have never heard a Hawaiian word, including and perhaps most particularly *aloha*, which accurately expressed anything I had to say. I have neither enough capacity for surprise nor enough heart for twice-told tales to make you listen again to tedious vignettes about Midwesterners in souvenir shirts and touring widows in muumuus and simulated pearls, about the Kodak Hula Show or the Sunday Night Luau or the Schoolteacher and the Beach Boy. And so, now that it is on the line between us that I lack all temperament for paradise, real or facsimile, I am going to find it difficult to tell you precisely how and why Hawaii moves me, touches me, saddens and troubles and engages my imagination, what it is in the air that will linger long after I have forgotten the smell of pikake and pineapple and the way the palms sound in the trade winds.

Perhaps because I grew up in California, Hawaii figured

large in my fantasies. I sat as a child on California beaches and imagined that I saw Hawaii, a certain shimmer in the sunset, a barely perceptible irregularity glimpsed intermittently through squinted eyes. The curious void in this fantasy was that I had not the slightest idea what Hawaii would look like if I did see it, for in my child's mind there were three distant Hawaiis, and I could perceive no connections among the three.

There was, to begin with, the Hawaii first shown to me in an atlas on December 7, 1941, the pastel pinpoints that meant war and my father going away and makeshift Christmases in rented rooms near Air Corps bases and nothing the same ever again. Later, when the war was over, there was another Hawaii, a big rock candy mountain in the Pacific which presented itself to me in newspaper photographs of well-fed Lincoln-Mercury dealers relaxing beside an outrigger at the Royal Hawaiian Hotel or disembarking *en famille* from the *Lurline*, a Hawaii where older cousins might spend winter vacations learning to surfboard (for that is what it was called in those simpler days, surfboarding, and it was peculiar to Hawaii) and where godmothers might repair to rest and to learn all the lyrics to "My Little Grass Shack in Kealakekua Hawaii." I do not remember how many nights I lay awake in bed and listened to someone downstairs singing "My Little Grass Shack in Kealakekua Hawaii," but I do remember that I made no connection between that Hawaii and the Hawaii of December 7, 1941.

And then, always, there was a third Hawaii, a place which seemed to have to do neither with war nor with vacationing godmothers but only with the past, and with loss. The last member of my direct family ever to live in Hawaii was a great-great-grandfather who taught there as a young missionary in 1842, and I was given to understand that life in the Islands, as we called Hawaii on the West Coast, had been declining steadily since. My aunt married into a family which had lived for generations in the Islands, but they did not even visit there any more; "Not since Mr. *Kais*er," they would say, as if the construction of the Hawaiian Village Hotel on a few acres of reclaimed tidal flat near Fort De Russy had in one swing of the builder's crane wiped out their childhoods and their parents' childhoods, blighted forever some subtropical cherry orchard where every night in the soft blur of memory the table was set for forty-eight in case someone dropped by; as if Henry Kaiser had personally condemned them to live out their lives in California exile among only their token mementos, the calabashes and the carved palace chairs and the flat silver for forty-eight and the diamond that had been Queen Liliuokalani's and the heavy linens embroidered on all the long golden afternoons that were no more.

Of course as I grew older I recognized that the name "Henry Kaiser" carried more symbolic than literal freight, but even then I missed the point, imagined that it was merely the proliferation of hotels and hundred-dollar thrift flights that had disturbed the old order, managed to dismiss the Hawaii of my first memory, the Hawaii which meant war, as an accident of history, a freak relevant neither to the gentle idyll that must have been the past nor to the frenetic paean to middle-income leisure that must be the present. In so doing I misapprehended Hawaii completely, for if there is a single aura which pervades Honolulu, one mood which lends the lights a feverish luster and the pink catamarans a heartbreaking absurdity and which engages the imagination as mere paradise never could, that mood is, inescapably, one of war.

It begins, of course, in what we remember.

> *Hawaii is our Gibraltar, and almost our Channel Coast. Planes, their eyes sharpened by the year-round clearness of blue Pacific days, can keep easy watch over an immense sea-circle, of which Hawaii is the centre. With Hawaii on guard, a surprise attack on us from Asia, the experts believe, would be quite impossible. So long as the great Pearl Harbor Naval Base, just down the road from Honolulu, is ours, American warships and submarines can run their un-Pacific errands with a maximum of ease. Pearl Harbor is one of the greatest, if not the very greatest, maritime fortresses in the world. Pearl Harbor has immense reserves of fuel and food, and huge and clanging hospitals for the healing of any wounds which steel can suffer. It is the one sure sanctuary in the whole of the vast Pacific both for ships and men.*
>
> John W. Vandercook, in
> *Vogue*, January 1, 1941

Every afternoon now, twenty-five years after the fact, the bright pink tour boats leave Kewalo Basin for Pearl Harbor. It has a kind of sleazy festivity at first, the prospect of an outing on a fine day, the passengers comparing complaints about their tour directors and their accommodations and the food at Canlis' Charcoal Broiler, the boys diving for coins around the boats; "Hey Mister Big," they scream. "How's about a coin." Sometimes a woman will throw a bill, and then be outraged when the insolent brown bodies pluck it from the air and jeer at her expectations. As the boat leaves the basin the boys swim back, their cheeks stuffed with money, and the children pout that they would rather be at the beach, and the women in their new Liberty House shifts and leftover leis sip papaya juice and study a booklet billed as *An Ideal Gift—Picture Story of December 7.*

It is, after all, a familiar story that we have come to hear—familiar even to the children, for of course they have seen John Wayne and John Garfield at Pearl Harbor, have spent countless rainy afternoons watching Kirk Douglas and Spencer Tracy and Van Johnson wonder out loud why Hickam does not answer this morning—and no one listens very closely to the guide. Sugar cane now blows where the *Nevada* went aground. An idle figure practices putting on Ford Island. The concessionaire breaks out more papaya juice. It is hard to remember what we came to remember.

And then something happens. I took that bright pink boat to Pearl Harbor on two afternoons, but I still do not know what I went to find out, which is how other people respond a quarter of a century later. I do not know because there is a point at which I began to cry, and to notice no one else. I began to cry at the place where the *Utah* lies in fifty feet of water, water neither turquoise nor bright blue here but the gray of harbor waters everywhere, and I did not stop until after the pink boat had left the *Arizona*, or what is visible of the *Arizona*: the rusted after-gun turret breaking the gray water, the flag at full mast because the Navy considers the *Arizona* still in commission, a full crew aboard, 1,102 men from forty-nine states. All I know about how other people respond is what I am told: that everyone is quiet at the *Arizona*.

*

A few days ago someone just four years younger than I am told me that he did not see why a sunken ship should affect me so, that John Kennedy's assassination, not Pearl Harbor, was the single most indelible event of what he kept calling "our generation." I could tell him only that we belonged to different generations, and I did not tell him what I want to tell you, about a place in Honolulu that is quieter still than the *Arizona*: the National Memorial Cemetery of the Pacific. They all seem to be twenty years old, the boys buried up there in the crater of an extinct volcano named Punchbowl, twenty and nineteen and eighteen and sometimes not that old. "SAMUEL FOSTER HARMON," one stone reads. "PENNSYLVANIA. PVT 27 REPL DRAFT 5 MARINE DIV. WORLD WAR II. APRIL 10 1928—MARCH 25 1945." Samuel Foster Harmon died, at Iwo Jima, fifteen days short of his seventeenth birthday. Some of them died on December 7 and some of them died after the *Enola Gay* had already bombed Hiroshima and some of them died on the dates of the landings at Okinawa and Iwo Jima and Guadalcanal and one whole long row of them, I am told, died on the beach of an island we no longer remember. There are 19,000 graves in the vast sunken crater above Honolulu.

I would go up there quite a bit. If I walked to the rim of the crater I could see the city, look down over Waikiki and the harbor and the jammed arterials, but up there it was quiet, and high enough into the rain forest so that a soft mist falls most of the day. One afternoon a couple came and left three plumeria leis on the grave of a California boy who had been killed, at nineteen, in 1945. The leis were already wilting by the time the woman finally placed them on the grave, because for a long time she only stood there and twisted them in her hands. On the whole I am able to take a very long view of death, but I think a great deal about what there is to remember, twenty-one years later, of a boy who died at nineteen. I saw no one else there but the men who cut the grass and the men who dig new graves, for they are bringing in bodies now from Vietnam. The graves filled last week and the week before that and even last month do not yet have stones, only plastic identification cards, streaked by the mist and splattered with mud. The earth is raw and trampled in that part of the crater, but the grass grows fast, up there in the rain cloud.

It is not very far from the crater down to Hotel Street, which is to Honolulu what Market Street is to San Francisco, the bright night street in a port city. The carrier *Coral Sea* was in Honolulu that week, and 165 men in from Vietnam on rest-and-recuperation leave, and 3,500 Marines on their way to Okinawa and then to Vietnam (they were part of the reactivated 5th Marine Division, and it was the 5th, if you will remember, to which the sixteen-year-old Samuel Foster Harmon belonged), and besides that there was the regular complement of personnel for Pearl and Hickam and Camp H. M. Smith and Fort Shafter and Fort De Russy and Bellows A.F.B. and the Kaneohe Marine Air Station and Schofield Barracks, and sooner or later they all got downtown to Hotel Street. They always have. The Navy cleaned out the red-light houses at the end of World War II, but the Hotel Streets of this world do not change perceptibly from war to war. The girls with hibiscus in their hair stroll idly in front of the penny arcades and the Japanese pool halls and the massage studios. "GIRLS WANTED FOR MASSAGE WORK," the signs say. "WHAT A REFRESHING NEW TINGLE." The fortunetellers sit and file their nails behind flowered paper curtains. The boys from the cast of the Boys Will Be Girls Revue stand out on the sidewalk in lamé evening dresses, smoking cigarettes and looking the sailors over.

And the sailors get drunk. They all seem to be twenty years old on Hotel Street, too, twenty and nineteen and eighteen and drunk because they are no longer in Des Moines and not yet in Danang. They look in at the taxi-dance places and they look in at the strip places with the pictures of Lili St. Cyr and Tempest Storm outside (Lili St. Cyr was in California and Tempest Storm in Baltimore, but never mind, they all look alike on Saturday night in Honolulu) and they fish in their pockets for quarters to see the Art Movie in the back of the place that sells *Sunshine* and *Nude* and all the paperbacks with chained girls on the cover. They have snapshots laminated. They record their own voices (*Hi, Sweetheart, I'm in Honolulu tonight*) and they talk to the girls with hibiscus in their hair.

But mostly they just get a little drunker, and jostle around on the sidewalk avoiding the Hawaii Armed Forces Patrol and daring one another to get tattooed. In a show of bravado they rip off their shirts a half block before they reach Lou Normand's

Tattoo Parlor and then they sit with glazed impassivity while the needle brands them with a heart or an anchor or, if they are particularly flush or particularly drunk, a replica of Christ on the cross with the stigmata in red. Their friends cluster outside the glass cubicle watching the skin redden and all the while, from a country-and-western bar on the corner, "King of the Road" reverberates down Hotel Street. The songs change and the boys come and go but Lou Normand has been Thirty Years in the Same Location.

Perhaps it seems not surprising that there should be a mood of war at the scenes of famous defeats and at the graves of seventeen-year-olds and downtown in a port city. But the mood is not only there. War is in the very fabric of Hawaii's life, ineradicably fixed in both its emotions and its economy, dominating not only its memory but its vision of the future. There is a point at which every Honolulu conversation refers back to war. People sit in their gardens up on Makiki Heights among their copa de oro and their star jasmine and they look down toward Pearl Harbor and get another drink and tell you about the morning it happened. Webley Edwards was on the radio, they remember that, and what he said that morning again and again was "This is an air raid, take cover, *this is the real McCoy*." That is not a remarkable thing to say, but it is a remarkable thing to have in one's memory. And they remember how people drove up into the hills and parked to watch the fires, just as they do now when a tsunami wave is due. They remember emergency wards in school auditoriums and how the older children were dispatched to guard reservoirs with unloaded guns. They laugh about trying to drive over the Pali in the fog after the 9 P.M. blackout, and about how their wives took thick books and large handkerchiefs down to the Y.W.C.A. and used them to show girls from the outer islands how to make a hospital bed, and they remember how it was when there were only three hotels on all two miles of Waikiki, the Royal for the Navy, the Halekulani for the press, and the Moana. In fact they contrive to leave an indistinct impression that it was in 1945, or perhaps '46, that they last got down to Waikiki. "I suppose the Royal hasn't changed," one Honolulan who lives within eight minutes of the Royal remarked to me. "The Halekulani," another said, as if it had just flickered into memory and she was uncertain it still existed. "*That* used to be kind of fun for drinks." Everyone was younger then, and in the telling a certain glow suffuses those years.

And then, if they have a stake in selling Hawaii, and there are very few people left in Hawaii who refuse to perceive that they do have a stake in selling it, they explain why Hawaii's future is so bright. In spite of what might be considered a classic false economy, based first upon the military, next upon the tourist, and third upon subsidized sugar, Hawaii's future is bright because Hawaii is the hub of the Pacific, a phrase employed in Honolulu only slightly less frequently than "our wonderful *aloha* spirit." They point out that Hawaii is the hub of the Pacific as far as the travel industry goes, and that Hawaii is also the hub of the Pacific as far as—they pause, and perhaps pick up a glass and study it before continuing. "And, well, frankly, if it goes the other way, what I mean by that is if the *situation* goes the other way, we're in the right spot for that, too." Perhaps nowhere else in the United States is the prospect of war regarded with so much equanimity.

Of course it is easy to suggest reasons, to say that after all Hawaii has already lived through one war, or to point out that Honolulu is even now in a war zone, steeped in the vocabulary of the military, deeply committed to the business of war. But it runs deeper than that. War is viewed with a curious ambivalence in Hawaii because the largest part of its population interprets war, however unconsciously, as a force for good, an instrument of social progress. And of course it was precisely World War II which cracked the spine of sugar feudalism, opened up a contracting economy and an immobile society, shattered forever the pleasant but formidable colonial world in which a handful of families controlled everything Hawaii did, where it shopped, how it shipped its goods, who could come in and how far they could go and at what point they would be closed out.

We have, most of us, some image of prewar Hawaii. We have heard the phrase "Big Five," and we have a general notion that certain families acquired a great deal of money and power in Hawaii and kept that money and that power for a very long while. The reality of Hawaiian power was at once more obvious and more subtle than one might imagine it to have been. The Big Five companies—C. Brewer, Theo. H. Davies, American Factors, Castle & Cooke, and Alexander & Baldwin—began as "factors" for the sugar planters; in effect they were plantation management. Over the years, the Big Five families and a few others—the Dillinghams, say, who were descended from a stranded sailor who built Hawaii's first railroad—intermarried, sat on one another's boards, got into shipping and insurance and money, and came to comprise a benevolent oligarchy unlike any on the mainland.

For almost half a century this interlocking directorate extended into every area of Hawaiian life, and its power could be exercised immediately and personally. American Factors, for example, owned (and still owns) the major Hawaiian department store, Liberty House. In 1941, Sears, Roebuck, working secretly through intermediaries, bought land for a store in suburban Honolulu. Sears finally opened its store, but not until the Sears president, Robert E. Wood, had threatened to buy his own ship; there had been some question as to whether Matson Navigation, controlled by Castle & Cooke and Alexander & Baldwin, would ship merchandise for anyone so baldly attempting to compete with a Big Five enterprise.

That was Hawaii. And then World War II came. Island boys went to war, and came home with new ideas. Mainland money came in, against all Island opposition. After World War II, the late Walter Dillingham could come down to a public hearing from his house on Diamond Head and cast at Henry Kaiser the most meaningful epithet of ante-bellum Hawaii—"*visitor*"—and have its significance lost on perhaps half his audience. In spirit if never quite in fact, World War II made everyone a Dillingham, and anyone in Hawaii too slow to perceive this for himself was constantly told it, by politicians and by labor leaders and by mainland observers.

The extent of the change, of course, has often been overstated, for reasons sometimes sentimental and sometimes strategic, but it is true that Hawaii is no more what it once was. There is still only one "Lowell" in Honolulu, and that is Lowell Dillingham, still only one "Ben," and that is his brother—but Ben Dillingham was overwhelmingly defeated in his 1962 campaign for the United States Senate by Daniel Inouye, a Nisei. (In the 1920's, when a congressional committee asked Ben Dillingham's father and Henry Baldwin why so few Japanese voted in Hawaii, they could suggest only that perhaps the Japanese were under instructions from Tokyo not to register.) There is still a strong feeling in old-line Honolulu that the Big Five "caved in" to labor—but Jack Hall, the tough I.L.W.U. leader who was once convicted under the Smith Act for conspiring to teach the overthrow of the United States Government by force and violence, now sits on the board of the Hawaii Visitors' Bureau and commends the ladies of the Outdoor Circle for their efforts in "preserving the loveliness that is Hawaii." And Chinn Ho, who as a schoolboy used to chalk up quotations for a downtown broker, now owns not only a few score million dollars' worth of real estate but also that broker's own house, out on Diamond Head, hard by Ben Dillingham's. "The thing is," the broker's niece told me, "I suppose he wanted it when he was fourteen."

But perhaps there is no clearer way to understand the change than to visit Punahou School, the school the missionaries founded "for their children and their children's children," a statement of purpose interpreted rather literally until quite recently. To leaf through Punahou's old class books is a briefing in Hawaiian oligarchy, for the same names turn up year after year, and the names are the same as those which appear in cut stone or discreet brass letters down around what Honolulu calls The Street, Merchant Street, down on those corners where the Big Five have their offices and most Island business is done. In 1881 an Alexander delivered the commencement address and a Dillingham the commencement poem; at the 1882 graduation a Baldwin spoke on "Chinese Immigration," an Alexander on "Labor Ipse Voluptas," and a Bishop on "Sunshine." And although high-caste Hawaiians have always coexisted with and in fact intermarried with the white oligarchy, their Punahou classmates usually visualized them, when it came time for class prophecies, "playing in a band."

It is not that Punahou is not still the school of the Island power elite; it is. "There will always be room at Punahou for those children who belong here," Dr. John Fox, headmaster since 1944, assured alumni in a recent bulletin. But where in 1944 there were 1,100 students and they had a median IQ of 108, now there are 3,400 with a median IQ of 125. Where once the enrollment was ten percent Oriental, now it is a fraction under thirty percent. And so it is that outside Punahou's new Cooke Library, where the archives are kept by a great-great-granddaughter of the Reverend Hiram Bingham, there sit, among the plumeria blossoms drifted on the steps, small Chinese boys with their books in Pan American flight bags.

"John Fox is rather controversial, I guess you know," old-family alumni will sometimes say now, but they do not say exactly wherein the controversy lies. Perhaps because Hawaii sells itself so assiduously as the very model of a modern melting pot, the entire area of race relations is conversationally delicate. "I wouldn't exactly say we had discrimination here," one Honolulu woman explained tactfully. "I'd say we had a wonderful, wonderful competitive feeling." Another simply shrugs. "It's just something that's never pressed. The Orientals are—well, discreet's not really the word, but they aren't like the Negroes and the Jews, they don't push in where they're not wanted."

Even among those who are considered Island liberals, the question of race has about it, to anyone who has lived through these hypersensitive past years on the mainland, a curious and rather engaging ingenuousness. "There are very definitely people here who know the Chinese socially," one woman told me. "They have them to their houses. The uncle of a friend of mine, for example, has Chinn Ho to his house all the time." Although this seemed a statement along the lines of "Some of my best friends are Rothschilds," I accepted it in the spirit in which it was offered—just as I did the primitive progressivism of an Island teacher who was explaining, as we walked down a corridor of her school, about the miracles of educational integration the war had wrought. "Look," she said suddenly, grabbing a pretty Chinese girl by the arm and wheeling her around to face me. "You wouldn't have seen this here before the war. Look at those eyes."

And so, in the peculiar and still insular mythology of Hawaii, the dislocations of war became the promises of progress. Whether or not the promises have been fulfilled depends of course upon who is talking, as does whether or not progress is a virtue, but in any case it is war that is pivotal to the Hawaiian imagination, war that fills the mind, war that seems to hover over Honolulu like the rain clouds on Tantalus. Not very many people talk about that. They talk about freeways on Oahu and condominiums on Maui and beer cans at the Sacred Falls and how much wiser it is to bypass Honolulu altogether in favor of going directly to Laurance Rockefeller's Mauna Kea, on Hawaii. (In fact the notion that the only place to go in the Hawaiian Islands is somewhere on Maui or Kauai or Hawaii has by now filtered down to such wide acceptance that one can only suspect Honolulu to be due for a revival.) Or, if they are of a more visionary turn, they talk, in a kind of James Michener rhetoric, about how Hawaii is a multiracial paradise and a labor-management paradise and a progressive paradise in which the past is now reconciled with the future, where the I.L.W.U.'s Jack Hall lunches at the Pacific Club and where that repository of everything old-line in Hawaii, the Bishop Estate, works hand in hand with Henry Kaiser to transform Koko Head into a $350 million development named Hawaii Kai. If they are in the travel business they talk about The Million Visitor Year (1970) and The Two Million Visitor Year (1980) and twenty thousand Rotarians convening in Honolulu in 1969 and they talk about The Product. "The reports show what we need," one travel man told me. "We need more attention to shaping and molding the product." The product is the place they live.

If they are from Honolulu but a little *arriviste*—say if they have been here only thirty years—they drop the name "Lowell" and talk about their charity work. If they are from Honolulu but not at all *arriviste* they talk about opening boutiques and going into the real-estate business and whether or not it was rude for Jacqueline Kennedy to appear for dinner at Henry Kaiser's in a muumuu and bare feet. ("I mean I *know* people come here to relax and not get dressed up, but still. . . .") They get to the mainland quite often but not often enough to be well-informed about what is going on there. They like to entertain and to be entertained and to have people coming through. ("What would it be like without them?" one woman asked me rhetorically. "It'd be Saturday night at the club in Racine, Wisconsin.") They are very gracious and very enthusiastic, and give such an appearance of health and happiness and hope that I sometimes find it difficult to talk to them. I think that they would not understand why I came to Hawaii, and I think that they will perhaps not understand what I am going to remember.

1966

Rock of Ages

ALCATRAZ ISLAND is covered with flowers now: orange and yellow nasturtiums, geraniums, sweet grass, blue iris, black-eyed Susans. Candytuft springs up through the cracked concrete in the exercise yard. Ice plant carpets the rusting catwalks. "WARNING! KEEP OFF! U.S. PROPERTY," the sign still reads, big and yellow and visible for perhaps a quarter of a mile, but since March 21, 1963, the day they took the last thirty or so men off the island and sent them to prisons less expensive to maintain, the warning has been only *pro forma*, the gun turrets empty, the cell blocks abandoned. It is not an unpleasant place to be, out there on Alcatraz with only the flowers and the wind and a bell buoy moaning and the tide surging through the Golden Gate, but to like a place like that you have to want a moat.

I sometimes do, which is what I am talking about here. Three people live on Alcatraz Island now. John and Marie Hart live in the same apartment they had for the sixteen years that he was a prison guard; they raised five children on the island, back when their neighbors were the Birdman and Mickey Cohen, but the Birdman and Mickey Cohen are gone now and so are the Harts' children, moved away, the last married in a ceremony on the island in June 1966. One other person lives on Alcatraz, a retired merchant seaman named Bill Doherty, and, between them, John Hart and Bill Doherty are responsible to the General Services Administration for maintaining a twenty-four-hour watch over the twenty-two-acre island. John Hart has a dog named Duffy, and Bill Doherty has a dog named Duke, and although the dogs are primarily good company they are also the first line of defense on Alcatraz Island. Marie Hart has a corner window which looks out to the San Francisco skyline, across a mile and a half of bay, and she sits there and paints "views" or plays her organ, songs like "Old Black Joe" and "Please Go 'Way and Let Me Sleep." Once a week the Harts take their boat to San Francisco to pick up their mail and shop at the big Safeway in the Marina, and occasionally Marie Hart gets off the island to visit her children. She likes to keep in touch with them by telephone, but for ten months recently, after a Japanese freighter cut the cable, there was no telephone service to or from Alcatraz. Every morning the KGO traffic reporter drops the San Francisco *Chronicle* from his helicopter, and when he has time he stops for coffee. No one else comes out there except a man from the General Services Administration named Thomas Scott, who brings out an occasional congressman or somebody who wants to buy the island or, once in a while, his wife and small son, for a picnic. Quite a few people would like to buy the island, and Mr. Scott reckons that it would bring about five million dollars in a sealed-bid auction, but the General Services Administration is powerless to sell it until Congress acts on a standing proposal to turn the island into a "peace park." Mr. Scott says that he will be glad to get Alcatraz off his hands, but the charge of a fortress island could not be something a man gives up without ambivalent thoughts.

I went out there with him a while ago. Any child could imagine a prison more like a prison than Alcatraz looks, for what bars and wires there are seem perfunctory, beside the point; the island itself was the prison, and the cold tide its wall. It is precisely what they called it: the Rock. Bill Doherty and Duke lowered the dock for us, and in the station wagon on the way up the cliff Bill Doherty told Mr. Scott about small repairs he had made or planned to make. Whatever repairs get made on Alcatraz are made to pass the time, a kind of caretaker's scrimshaw, because the government pays for no upkeep at all on the prison; in 1963 it would have cost five million dollars to repair, which is why it was abandoned, and the $24,000 a year that it costs to maintain Alcatraz now is mostly for surveillance, partly to barge in the 400,000 gallons of water that Bill Doherty and the Harts use every year (there is no water at all on Alcatraz, one impediment to development), and the rest to heat two apartments and keep some lights burning. The buildings seem quite literally abandoned. The key locks have been ripped from the cell doors and the big electrical locking mechanisms disconnected. The tear-gas vents in the cafeteria are empty and the paint is buckling everywhere, corroded by the sea air, peeling off in great scales of pale green and ocher. I stood for a while in Al Capone's cell, five by nine feet, number 200 on the second tier of B Block, not one of the view cells, which were awarded on seniority, and I walked through the solitary block, totally black when the doors were closed. "Snail Mitchel," read a pencil scrawl on the wall of Solitary 14. "The only man that ever got shot for walking too slow." Beside it was a calendar, the months penciled on the wall with the days scratched off, May, June, July, August of some unnumbered year.

Mr. Scott, whose interest in penology dates from the day his office acquired Alcatraz as a potential property, talked about escapes and security routines and pointed out the beach where Ma Barker's son Doc was killed trying to escape. (They told him to come back up, and he said he would rather be shot, and he was.) I saw the shower room with the soap still in the dishes. I picked up a yellowed program from an Easter service (*Why seek ye the living among the dead? He is not here, but is risen*) and I struck a few notes on an upright piano with the ivory all rotted from the keys and I tried to imagine the prison as it had been, with the big lights playing over the windows all night long and the guards patrolling the gun galleries and the silverware clattering into a bag as it was checked in after meals, tried dutifully to summon up some distaste, some night terror of the doors locking and the boat pulling away. But the fact of it was that I liked it out there, a ruin devoid of human vanities, clean of human illusions, an empty place reclaimed by the weather where a woman plays an organ to stop the wind's whining and an old man plays ball with a dog named Duke. I could tell you that I came back because I had promises to keep, but maybe it was because nobody asked me to stay.

1967

The Seacoast of Despair

I WENT TO NEWPORT not long ago, to see the great stone *fin-de-siècle* "cottages" in which certain rich Americans once summered. The places loom still along Bellevue Avenue and Cliff Walk, one after another, silk curtains frayed but gargoyles intact, monuments to something beyond themselves; houses built, clearly, to some transcendental point. No one had made clear to me exactly what that point was. I had been promised that the great summer houses were museums and warned that they were monstrosities, had been assured that the way of life they suggested was graceful beyond belief and that it was gross beyond description, that the very rich were different from you and me and yes, they had lower taxes, and if "The Breakers" was perhaps not entirely tasteful, still, *où sont les croquet wickets d'antan.* I had read Edith Wharton and I had read Henry James, who thought that the houses should stand there always, reminders "of the peculiarly awkward vengeances of affronted proportion and discretion."

But all that turns out to be beside the point, all talk of taxes and taste and affronted proportion. If, for example, one pursues the course, as Mrs. Richard Gambrill did in 1900, of engaging the architect who did the New York Public Library, approving plans for an eighteenth-century French château on a Rhode Island beach, ordering the garden copied after one Henry VIII gave to Anne Boleyn, and naming the result "Vernon Court," one moves somehow beyond the charge of breached "discretion." Something else is at work here. No aesthetic judgment could conceivably apply to the Newport of Bellevue Avenue, to those vast follies behind their hand-wrought gates; they are products of the metastasis of capital, the Industrial Revolution carried to its logical extreme, and what they suggest is how recent are the notions that life should be "comfortable," that those who live it should be "happy."

"Happiness" is, after all, a consumption ethic, and Newport is the monument of a society in which production was seen as the moral point, the reward if not exactly the end, of the economic process. The place is devoid of the pleasure principle.

To have had the money to build "The Breakers" or "Marble House" or "Ochre Court" and to choose to build at Newport is in itself a denial of possibilities; the island is physically ugly, mean without the saving grace of extreme severity, a landscape less to be enjoyed than dominated. The prevalence of topiary gardening in Newport suggests the spirit of the place. And it was not as if there were no other options for these people: William Randolph Hearst built not at Newport but out on the edge of the Pacific. San Simeon, whatever its peculiarities, is in fact *la cuesta encantada*, swimming in golden light, sybaritic air, a deeply romantic place. But in Newport the air proclaims only the sources of money. Even as the sun dapples the great lawns and the fountains plash all around, there is something in the air that has nothing to do with pleasure and nothing to do with graceful tradition, a sense not of how prettily money can be spent but of how harshly money is made, an immediate presence of the pits and the rails and the foundries, of turbines and pork-belly futures. So insistent is the presence of money in Newport that the mind springs ineluctably to the raw beginnings of it. A contemplation of "Rosecliff" dissolves into the image of Big Jim Fair, digging the silver out of a mountain in Nevada so that his daughter might live in Newport. "Old Man Berwind, he'd turn in his grave to see that oil truck parked in the driveway," a guard at "The Elms" said to me as we surveyed the sunken garden there. "He made it in coal, soft coal." It had been on my mind as well as on the guard's, even as we stood in the sunlight outside the marble summer house, coal, soft coal, words like *bituminous* and *anthracite*, not the words of summer fancy.

In that way Newport is curiously Western, closer in spirit to Virginia City than to New York, to Denver than to Boston. It has the stridency usually credited to the frontier. And, like the frontier, it was not much of a game for women. Men paid for Newport, and granted to women the privilege of living in it. Just as gilt vitrines could be purchased for the correct display of biscuit Sèvres, so marble stairways could be bought for the advantageous display of women. In the filigreed gazebos they could be exhibited in a different light; in the French sitting rooms, in still another setting. They could be cajoled, flattered, indulged, given pretty rooms and Worth dresses, allowed to imagine that they ran their own houses and their own lives, but when it came time to negotiate, their freedom proved *trompe l'oeil.* It was the world of Bailey's Beach which made a neurasthenic of Edith Wharton, and, against her will, the Duchess of Marlborough of Consuelo Vanderbilt. The very houses are men's houses, factories, undermined by tunnels and service railways, shot through with plumbing to collect salt water, tanks to store it, devices to collect rain water, vaults for table silver, equipment inventories of china and crystal and "Tray cloths—fine" and "Tray cloths—ordinary." Somewhere in the bowels of "The Elms" is a coal bin twice the size of Julia Berwind's bedroom. The mechanics of such houses take precedence over all desires or inclinations; neither for great passions nor for morning whims can the factory be shut down, can production—of luncheons, of masked balls, of *marrons glacés*—be slowed. To stand in the dining room of "The Breakers" is to imagine fleeing from it, pleading migraine.

What Newport turns out to be, then, is homiletic, a fantastically elaborate stage setting for an American morality play in which money and happiness are presented as antithetical. It is a curious theatrical for these particular men to have conceived, but then we all judge ourselves sometime; it is hard for me to believe that Cornelius Vanderbilt did not sense, at some point in time, in some dim billiard room of his unconscious, that when he built "The Breakers" he damned himself. The world must have seemed greener to all of them, out there when they were young and began laying the rails or digging for high-grade ore in the Comstock or daring to think that they might corner copper. More than anyone else in the society, these men had apparently dreamed the dream and made it work. And what they did then was to build a place which seems to illustrate, as in a child's primer, that the production ethic led step by step to unhappiness, to restrictiveness, to entrapment in the mechanics of living. In that way the lesson of Bellevue Avenue is more seriously radical than the idea of Brook Farm. Who could fail to read the sermon in the stones of Newport? Who could think that the building of a railroad could guarantee salvation, when there on the lawns of the men who built the railroad nothing is left but the shadows of migrainous women, and the pony carts waiting for the long-dead children?

1967

Guaymas, Sonora

IT HAD RAINED in Los Angeles until the cliff was crumbling into the surf and I did not feel like getting dressed in the morning, so we decided to go to Mexico, to Guaymas, where it was hot. We did not go for marlin. We did not go to skin-dive. We went to get away from ourselves, and the way to do that is to drive, down through Nogales some day when the pretty green places pall and all that will move the imagination is some place difficult, some desert. The desert, any desert, is indeed the valley of the shadow of death; come back from the desert and you feel like Alcestis, reborn. After Nogales on Route 15 there is nothing but the Sonoran desert, nothing but mesquite and rattlesnakes and the Sierra Madre floating to the east, no trace of human endeavor but an occasional Pemex truck hurtling north and once in a while in the distance the dusty Pullman cars of the Ferrocarril del Pacífico. Magdalena is on Route 15, and then Hermosillo, where the American ore and cattle buyers gather in the bar at the Hotel San Alberto. There is an airport in Hermosillo, and Hermosillo is only eighty-five miles above Guaymas, but to fly is to miss the point. The point is to become disoriented, shriven, by the heat and the deceptive perspectives and the oppressive sense of carrion. The road shimmers. The eyes want to close.

And then, just past that moment when the desert has become the only reality, Route 15 hits the coast and there is Guaymas, a lunar thrust of volcanic hills and islands with the warm Gulf of California lapping idly all around, lapping even at the cactus, the water glassy as a mirage, the ships in the harbor whistling unsettlingly, moaning, ghost schooners, landlocked, lost. That is Guaymas. As far as the town goes, Graham Greene might have written it: a shadowy square with a filigree pergola for the Sunday band, a racket of birds, a cathedral in bad repair with a robin's-egg-blue tile dome, a turkey buzzard on the cross. The wharves are piled with bales of Sonoran cotton and mounds of dark copper concentrates; out on the freighters with the Panamanian and Liberian flags the Greek and German boys stand in the hot twilight and stare sullenly at the grotesque and claustrophobic hills, at the still town, a curious limbo at which to call.

Had we really been intent upon losing ourselves we might have stayed in town, at a hotel where faded and broken turquoise-blue shutters open onto the courtyard, where old men sit in the doorways and nothing moves, but instead we stayed outside town, at the Playa de Cortés, the big old hotel built by the Southern Pacific before the railways were nationalized. That place was a mirage, too, lovely and cool with thick whitewashed walls and dark shutters and bright tiles, tables made from ebony railroad ties, pale appliqued muslin curtains, shocks of corn wrapped around the heavy beams. Pepper trees grew around the swimming pool, and lemons and bananas in the courtyard. The food was unremarkable, but after dinner one could lie in a hammock on the terrace and listen to the fountains and the sea. For a week we lay in hammocks and fished desultorily and went to bed early and got very brown and lazy. My husband caught eight sharks, and I read an oceanography textbook, and we did not talk much. At the end of the week we wanted to do something, but all there was to do was visit the tracking station for an old space program or go see John Wayne and Claudia Cardinale in *Circus World*, and we knew it was time to go home.

1965

Los Angeles Notebook

There is something uneasy in the Los Angeles air this afternoon, some unnatural stillness, some tension. What it means is that tonight a Santa Ana will begin to blow, a hot wind from the northeast whining down through the Cajon and San Gorgonio Passes, blowing up sandstorms out along Route 66, drying the hills and the nerves to the flash point. For a few days now we will see smoke back in the canyons, and hear sirens in the night. I have neither heard nor read that a Santa Ana is due, but I know it, and almost everyone I have seen today knows it too. We know it because we feel it. The baby frets. The maid sulks. I rekindle a waning argument with the telephone company, then cut my losses and lie down, given over to whatever it is in the air. To live with the Santa Ana is to accept, consciously or unconsciously, a deeply mechanistic view of human behavior.

I recall being told, when I first moved to Los Angeles and was living on an isolated beach, that the Indians would throw themselves into the sea when the bad wind blew. I could see why. The Pacific turned ominously glossy during a Santa Ana period, and one woke in the night troubled not only by the peacocks screaming in the olive trees but by the eerie absence of surf. The heat was surreal. The sky had a yellow cast, the kind of light sometimes called "earthquake weather." My only neighbor would not come out of her house for days, and there were no lights at night, and her husband roamed the place with a machete. One day he would tell me that he had heard a trespasser, the next a rattlesnake.

"On nights like that," Raymond Chandler once wrote about the Santa Ana, "every booze party ends in a fight. Meek little wives feel the edge of the carving knife and study their husbands' necks. Anything can happen." That was the kind of wind it was. I did not know then that there was any basis for the effect it had on all of us, but it turns out to be another of those cases in which science bears out folk wisdom. The Santa Ana, which is named for one of the canyons it rushes through, is a *foehn* wind, like the *foehn* of Austria and Switzerland and the *hamsin* of Israel. There are a number of persistent malevolent winds, perhaps the best known of which are the mistral of France and the Mediterranean sirocco, but a *foehn* wind has distinct characteristics: it occurs on the leeward slope of a mountain range and, although the air begins as a cold mass, it is warmed as it comes down the mountain and appears finally as a hot dry wind. Whenever and wherever a *foehn* blows, doctors hear about headaches and nausea and allergies, about "nervousness," about "depression." In Los Angeles some teachers do not attempt to conduct formal classes during a Santa Ana, because the children become unmanageable. In Switzerland the suicide rate goes up during the *foehn*, and in the courts of some Swiss cantons the wind is considered a mitigating circumstance for crime. Surgeons are said to watch the wind, because blood does not clot normally during a *foehn*. A few years ago an Israeli physicist discovered that not only during such winds, but for the ten or twelve hours which precede them, the air carries an unusually high ratio of positive to negative ions. No one seems to know exactly why that should be; some talk about friction and others suggest solar disturbances. In any case the positive ions are there, and what an excess of positive ions does, in the simplest terms, is make people unhappy. One cannot get much more mechanistic than that.

Easterners commonly complain that there is no "weather" at all in Southern California, that the days and the seasons slip by relentlessly, numbingly bland. That is quite misleading. In fact the climate is characterized by infrequent but violent extremes: two periods of torrential subtropical rains which continue for weeks and wash out the hills and send subdivisions sliding toward the sea; about twenty scattered days a year of the Santa Ana, which, with its incendiary dryness, invariably means fire. At the first prediction of a Santa Ana, the Forest Service flies men and equipment from northern California into the southern forests, and the Los Angeles Fire Department cancels its ordinary non-firefighting routines. The Santa Ana caused Malibu to burn the way it did in 1956, and Bel Air in 1961, and Santa Barbara in 1964. In the winter of 1966–67 eleven men were killed fighting a Santa Ana fire that spread through the San Gabriel Mountains.

Just to watch the front-page news out of Los Angeles during

a Santa Ana is to get very close to what it is about the place. The longest single Santa Ana period in recent years was in 1957, and it lasted not the usual three or four days but fourteen days, from November 21 until December 4. On the first day 25,000 acres of the San Gabriel Mountains were burning, with gusts reaching 100 miles an hour. In town, the wind reached Force 12, or hurricane force, on the Beaufort Scale; oil derricks were toppled and people ordered off the downtown streets to avoid injury from flying objects. On November 22 the fire in the San Gabriels was out of control. On November 24 six people were killed in automobile accidents, and by the end of the week the Los Angeles *Times* was keeping a box score of traffic deaths. On November 26 a prominent Pasadena attorney, depressed about money, shot and killed his wife, their two sons, and himself. On November 27 a South Gate divorcée, twenty-two, was murdered and thrown from a moving car. On November 30 the San Gabriel fire was still out of control, and the wind in town was blowing eighty miles an hour. On the first day of December four people died violently, and on the third the wind began to break.

It is hard for people who have not lived in Los Angeles to realize how radically the Santa Ana figures in the local imagination. The city burning is Los Angeles's deepest image of itself: Nathanael West perceived that, in *The Day of the Locust*; and at the time of the 1965 Watts riots what struck the imagination most indelibly were the fires. For days one could drive the Harbor Freeway and see the city on fire, just as we had always known it would be in the end. Los Angeles weather is the weather of catastrophe, of apocalypse, and, just as the reliably long and bitter winters of New England determine the way life is lived there, so the violence and the unpredictability of the Santa Ana affect the entire quality of life in Los Angeles, accentuate its impermanence, its unreliability. The wind shows us how close to the edge we are.

2

"Here's why I'm on the beeper, Ron," said the telephone voice on the all-night radio show. "I just want to say that this *Sex for the Secretary* creature—whatever her name is—certainly isn't contributing anything to the morals in this country. It's pathetic. Statistics *show*."

"It's *Sex and the Office*, honey," the disc jockey said. "That's the title. By Helen Gurley Brown. Statistics show what?"

"I haven't got them right here at my fingertips, naturally. But they *show*."

"I'd be interested in hearing them. Be constructive, you Night Owls."

"All right, let's take *one* statistic," the voice said, truculent now. "Maybe I haven't read the book, but what's this business she recommends about *going out with married men for lunch*?"

So it went, from midnight until 5 A.M., interrupted by records and by occasional calls debating whether or not a rattlesnake can swim. Misinformation about rattlesnakes is a leitmotiv of the insomniac imagination in Los Angeles. Toward 2 A.M. a man from "out Tarzana way" called to protest. "The Night Owls who called earlier must have been thinking about, uh, *The Man in the Gray Flannel Suit* or some other book," he said, "because Helen's one of the few authors trying to tell us what's really going *on*. Hefner's another, and he's also controversial, working in, uh, another area."

An old man, after testifying that he "personally" had seen a swimming rattlesnake, in the Delta-Mendota Canal, urged "moderation" on the Helen Gurley Brown question. "We shouldn't get on the beeper to call things pornographic before we've read them," he complained, pronouncing it porn-ee-oh-graphic. "I say, get the book. Give it a chance." The original *provocateur* called back to agree that she would get the book. "And then I'll burn it," she added.

"Book burner, eh?" laughed the disc jockey good-naturedly.

"I wish they still burned witches," she hissed.

3

It is three o'clock on a Sunday afternoon and 105° and the air so thick with smog that the dusty palm trees loom up with a sudden and rather attractive mystery. I have been playing in the sprinklers with the baby and I get in the car and go to Ralph's Market on the corner of Sunset and Fuller wearing an old bikini bathing suit. That is not a very good thing to wear to the market but neither is it, at Ralph's on the corner of Sunset and Fuller, an unusual costume. Nonetheless a large woman in a cotton muumuu jams her cart into mine at the butcher counter. "*What a thing to wear to the market*," she says in a loud but strangled voice. Everyone looks the other way and I study a plastic package of rib lamb chops and she repeats it. She follows me all over the store, to the Junior Foods, to the Dairy Products, to the Mexican Delicacies, jamming my cart whenever she can. Her husband plucks at her sleeve. As I leave the check-out counter she raises her voice one last time: "*What a thing to wear to Ralph's*," she says.

4

A party at someone's house in Beverly Hills: a pink tent, two orchestras, a couple of French Communist directors in Cardin evening jackets, chili and hamburgers from Chasen's. The wife of an English actor sits at a table alone; she visits California rarely although her husband works here a good deal. An American who knows her slightly comes over to the table.

"Marvelous to see you here," he says.

"Is it," she says.

"How long have you been here?"

"Too long."

She takes a fresh drink from a passing waiter and smiles at her husband, who is dancing.

The American tries again. He mentions her husband.

"I hear he's marvelous in this picture."

She looks at the American for the first time. When she finally speaks she enunciates every word very clearly. "He . . . is . . . also . . . a . . . fag," she says pleasantly.

5

The oral history of Los Angeles is written in piano bars. "Moon River," the piano player always plays, and "Mountain Greenery." "There's a Small Hotel" and "This Is Not the First Time." People talk to each other, tell each other about their first wives and last husbands. "Stay funny," they tell each other, and "This is to die over." A construction man talks to an unemployed screenwriter who is celebrating, alone, his tenth wedding anniversary. The construction man is on a job in Montecito: "Up in Montecito," he says, "they got one square mile with 135 millionaires."

"Putrescence," the writer says.

"That's all you got to say about it?"

"Don't read me wrong, I think Santa Barbara's one of the most—Christ, *the* most—beautiful places in the world, but it's a beautiful place that contains a . . . *putrescence.* They just live on their putrescent millions."

"So give me putrescent."

"No, no," the writer says. "I just happen to think millionaires have some sort of lacking in their . . . in their elasticity."

A drunk requests "The Sweetheart of Sigma Chi." The piano player says he doesn't know it. "Where'd you learn to play the piano?" the drunk asks. "I got two degrees," the piano player says. "One in musical education." I go to a coin telephone and call a friend in New York. "Where are you?" he says. "In a piano bar in Encino," I say. "Why?" he says. "Why not," I say.

1965–67

Goodbye to All That

How many miles to Babylon?
Three score miles and ten—
Can I get there by candlelight?
Yes, and back again—
If your feet are nimble and light
You can get there by candlelight.

IT IS EASY to see the beginnings of things, and harder to see the ends. I can remember now, with a clarity that makes the nerves in the back of my neck constrict, when New York began for me, but I cannot lay my finger upon the moment it ended, can never cut through the ambiguities and second starts and broken resolves to the exact place on the page where the heroine is no longer as optimistic as she once was. When I first saw New York I was twenty, and it was summertime, and I got off a DC-7 at the old Idlewild temporary terminal in a new dress which had seemed very smart in Sacramento but seemed less smart already, even in the old Idlewild temporary terminal, and the warm air smelled of mildew and some instinct, programmed by all the movies I had ever seen and all the songs I had ever heard sung and all the stories I had ever read about New York, informed me that it would never be quite the same again. In fact it never was. Some time later there was a song on all the jukeboxes on the upper East Side that went "but where is the schoolgirl who used to be me," and if it was late enough at night I used to wonder that. I know now that almost everyone wonders something like that, sooner or later and no matter what he or she is doing, but one of the mixed blessings of being twenty and twenty-one and even twenty-three is the conviction that nothing like this, all evidence to the contrary notwithstanding, has ever happened to anyone before.

Of course it might have been some other city, had circumstances been different and the time been different and had I been different, might have been Paris or Chicago or even San Francisco, but because I am talking about myself I am talking here about New York. That first night I opened my window on the bus into town and watched for the skyline, but all I could see were the wastes of Queens and the big signs that said MIDTOWN TUNNEL THIS LANE and then a flood of summer rain (even that seemed remarkable and exotic, for I had come out of the West where there was no summer rain), and for the next three days I sat wrapped in blankets in a hotel room air-conditioned to 35° and tried to get over a bad cold and a high fever. It did not occur to me to call a doctor, because I knew none, and although it did occur to me to call the desk and ask that the air conditioner be turned off, I never called, because I did not know how much to tip whoever might come—was anyone ever so young? I am here to tell you that someone was. All I could do during those three days was talk long-distance to the boy I already knew I would never marry in the spring. I would stay in New York, I told him, just six months, and I could see the Brooklyn Bridge from my window. As it turned out the bridge was the Triborough, and I stayed eight years.

In retrospect it seems to me that those days before I knew the names of all the bridges were happier than the ones that came later, but perhaps you will see that as we go along. Part of what I want to tell you is what it is like to be young in New York, how six months can become eight years with the deceptive ease of a film dissolve, for that is how those years appear to me now, in a long sequence of sentimental dissolves and old-fashioned trick shots—the Seagram Building fountains dissolve into snowflakes, I enter a revolving door at twenty and come out a good deal older, and on a different street. But most particularly I want to explain to you, and in the process perhaps to myself, why I no longer live in New York. It is often said that New York is a city for only the very rich and the very poor. It is less often said that New York is also, at least for those of us who came there from somewhere else, a city for only the very young.

I remember once, one cold bright December evening in New York, suggesting to a friend who complained of having been around too long that he come with me to a party where there would be, I assured him with the bright resourcefulness of twenty-three, "new faces." He laughed literally until he choked, and I had to roll down the taxi window and hit him on the back. "New faces," he said finally, "don't tell me about *new faces.*" It seemed that the last time he had gone to a party where he had been promised "new faces," there had been fifteen people in the room, and he had already slept with five of the women and owed money to all but two of the men. I laughed with him, but the first snow had just begun to fall and the big Christmas trees glittered yellow and white as far as I could see up Park Avenue and I had a new dress and it would be a long while before I would come to understand the particular moral of the story.

It would be a long while because, quite simply, I was in love with New York. I do not mean "love" in any colloquial way, I mean that I was in love with the city, the way you love the first person who ever touches you and never love anyone quite that way again. I remember walking across Sixty-second Street one twilight that first spring, or the second spring, they were all alike for a while. I was late to meet someone but I stopped at Lexington Avenue and bought a peach and stood on the corner eating it and knew that I had come out of the West and reached the mirage. I could taste the peach and feel the soft air blowing from a subway grating on my legs and I could smell lilac and garbage and expensive perfume and I knew that it would cost something sooner or later—because I did not belong there, did not come from there—but when you are twenty-two or twenty-three, you figure that later you will have a high emotional balance, and be able to pay whatever it costs. I still believed in possibilities then, still had the sense, so peculiar to New York, that something extraordinary would happen any minute, any day, any month. I was making only $65 or $70 a week then ("Put yourself in Hattie Carnegie's hands," I was advised without the slightest trace of irony by an editor of the magazine for which I worked), so little money that some weeks I had to charge food at Bloomingdale's gourmet shop in order to eat, a fact which went unmentioned in the letters I wrote to California. I never told my father that I needed money because then he would have sent it, and I would never know if I could do it by myself. At that time making a living seemed a game to me, with arbitrary but quite inflexible rules. And except on a certain kind of winter evening—six-thirty in the Seventies, say, already dark and bitter with a wind off the river, when

I would be walking very fast toward a bus and would look in the bright windows of brownstones and see cooks working in clean kitchens and imagine women lighting candles on the floor above and beautiful children being bathed on the floor above that—except on nights like those, I never felt poor; I had the feeling that if I needed money I could always get it. I could write a syndicated column for teenagers under the name "Debbi Lynn" or I could smuggle gold into India or I could become a $100 call girl, and none of it would matter.

Nothing was irrevocable; everything was within reach. Just around every corner lay something curious and interesting, something I had never before seen or done or known about. I could go to a party and meet someone who called himself Mr. Emotional Appeal and ran The Emotional Appeal Institute or Tina Onassis Blandford or a Florida cracker who was then a regular on what he called "the Big C," the Southampton–El Morocco circuit ("I'm well-connected on the Big C, honey," he would tell me over collard greens on his vast borrowed terrace), or the widow of the celery king of the Harlem market or a piano salesman from Bonne Terre, Missouri, or someone who had already made and lost two fortunes in Midland, Texas. I could make promises to myself and to other people and there would be all the time in the world to keep them. I could stay up all night and make mistakes, and none of it would count.

You see I was in a curious position in New York: it never occurred to me that I was living a real life there. In my imagination I was always there for just another few months, just until Christmas or Easter or the first warm day in May. For that reason I was most comfortable in the company of Southerners. They seemed to be in New York as I was, on some indefinitely extended leave from wherever they belonged, disinclined to consider the future, temporary exiles who always knew when the flights left for New Orleans or Memphis or Richmond or, in my case, California. Someone who lives always with a plane schedule in the drawer lives on a slightly different calendar. Christmas, for example, was a difficult season. Other people could take it in stride, going to Stowe or going abroad or going for the day to their mothers' places in Connecticut; those of us who believed that we lived somewhere else would spend it making and canceling airline reservations, waiting for weatherbound flights as if for the last plane out of Lisbon in 1940, and finally comforting one another, those of us who were left, with the oranges and mementos and smoked-oyster stuffings of childhood, gathering close, colonials in a far country.

Which is precisely what we were. I am not sure that it is possible for anyone brought up in the East to appreciate entirely what New York, the idea of New York, means to those of us who came out of the West and the South. To an Eastern child, particularly a child who has always had an uncle on Wall Street and who has spent several hundred Saturdays first at F. A. O. Schwarz and being fitted for shoes at Best's and then waiting under the Biltmore clock and dancing to Lester Lanin, New York is just a city, albeit *the* city, a plausible place for people to live. But to those of us who came from places where no one had heard of Lester Lanin and Grand Central Station was a Saturday radio program, where Wall Street and Fifth Avenue and Madison Avenue were not places at all but abstractions ("Money," and "High Fashion," and "The Hucksters"), New York was no mere city. It was instead an infinitely romantic notion, the mysterious nexus of all love and money and power, the shining and perishable dream itself. To think of "living" there was to reduce the miraculous to the mundane; one does not "live" at Xanadu.

In fact it was difficult in the extreme for me to understand those young women for whom New York was not simply an ephemeral Estoril but a real place, girls who bought toasters and installed new cabinets in their apartments and committed themselves to some reasonable future. I never bought any furniture in New York. For a year or so I lived in other people's apartments; after that I lived in the Nineties in an apartment furnished entirely with things taken from storage by a friend whose wife had moved away. And when I left the apartment in the Nineties (that was when I was leaving everything, when it was all breaking up) I left everything in it, even my winter clothes and the map of Sacramento County I had hung on the bedroom wall to remind me who I was, and I moved into a monastic four-room floor-through on Seventy-fifth Street. "Monastic" is perhaps misleading here, implying some chic severity; until after I was married and my husband moved some furniture in, there was nothing at all in those four rooms except a cheap double mattress and box springs, ordered by telephone the day I decided to move, and two French garden chairs lent me by a friend who imported them. (It strikes me now that the people I knew in New York all had curious and self-defeating sidelines. They imported garden chairs which did not sell very well at Hammacher Schlemmer or they tried to market hair straighteners in Harlem or they ghosted exposés of Murder Incorporated for Sunday supplements. I think that perhaps none of us was very serious, *engagé* only about our most private lives.)

All I ever did to that apartment was hang fifty yards of yellow theatrical silk across the bedroom windows, because I had some idea that the gold light would make me feel better, but I did not bother to weight the curtains correctly and all that summer the long panels of transparent golden silk would blow out the windows and get tangled and drenched in the afternoon thunderstorms. That was the year, my twenty-eighth, when I was discovering that not all of the promises would be kept, that some things are in fact irrevocable and that it had counted after all, every evasion and every procrastination, every mistake, every word, all of it.

That is what it was all about, wasn't it? Promises? Now when New York comes back to me it comes in hallucinatory flashes, so clinically detailed that I sometimes wish that memory would effect the distortion with which it is commonly credited. For a lot of the time I was in New York I used a perfume called *Fleurs de Rocaille*, and then *L'Air du Temps*, and now the slightest trace of either can short-circuit my connections for the rest of the day. Nor can I smell Henri Bendel jasmine soap without falling back into the past, or the particular mixture of spices used for boiling crabs. There were barrels of crab boil in a Czech place in the Eighties where I once shopped. Smells, of course, are notorious memory stimuli, but there are other things which affect me the same way. Blue-and-white striped sheets. Vermouth cassis. Some faded nightgowns which were new in 1959 or 1960, and some chiffon scarves I bought about the same time.

I suppose that a lot of us who have been young in New York have the same scenes on our home screens. I remember sitting in a lot of apartments with a slight headache about five o'clock in the morning. I had a friend who could not sleep, and he knew a few other people who had the same trouble, and we would watch the sky lighten and have a last drink with no ice and then go home in the early morning light, when the streets were clean and wet (had it rained in the night? we never knew) and the few cruising taxis still had their headlights on and the only color was the red and green of traffic signals. The White Rose bars opened very early in the morning; I recall waiting in one of them to watch an astronaut go into space, waiting so long that at the moment it actually happened I had my eyes not on the television screen but on a cockroach on the tile floor. I liked the bleak branches above Washington Square at dawn, and the monochromatic flatness of Second Avenue, the fire escapes and the grilled storefronts peculiar and empty in their perspective.

It is relatively hard to fight at six-thirty or seven in the morning without any sleep, which was perhaps one reason we stayed up all night, and it seemed to me a pleasant time of day. The windows were shuttered in that apartment in the Nineties and I could sleep a few hours and then go to work. I could work then on two or three hours' sleep and a container of coffee from Chock Full O' Nuts. I liked going to work, liked the soothing and satisfactory rhythm of getting out a magazine, liked the orderly progression of four-color closings and two-color closings and black-and-white closings and then The Product, no abstraction but something which looked effortlessly glossy and could be picked up on a newsstand and weighed in the hand. I liked all the minutiae of proofs and layouts, liked working late on the nights the magazine went to press, sitting and reading *Variety* and waiting for the copy desk to call. From my office I could look across town to the weather signal on the Mutual of New York Building and the lights that alternately spelled out TIME and LIFE above Rockefeller Plaza; that pleased me obscurely, and so did walking uptown in the mauve eight o'clocks of early summer evenings and looking at things, Lowestoft tureens in Fifty-seventh Street windows, people in evening clothes trying to get taxis, the trees just coming into full leaf, the lambent air, all the sweet promises of money and summer.

Some years passed, but I still did not lose that sense of wonder about New York. I began to cherish the loneliness of it, the sense that at any given time no one need know where I was or what I was doing. I liked walking, from the East River over to the Hudson and back on brisk days, down around the Village on warm days. A friend would leave me the key to her apartment in the West Village when she was out of town, and sometimes I would just move down there, because by that time the telephone was beginning to bother me (the canker, you see, was already in the rose) and not many people had that number. I remember one day when someone who did have the West Village number came to pick me up for lunch there, and we both had hangovers, and I cut my finger opening him a beer and burst into tears, and we walked to a Spanish restaurant and drank Bloody Marys and *gazpacho* until we felt better. I was not then guilt-ridden about spending afternoons that way, because I still had all the afternoons in the world.

And even that late in the game I still liked going to parties, all parties, bad parties, Saturday-afternoon parties given by recently married couples who lived in Stuyvesant Town, West Side parties given by unpublished or failed writers who served cheap red wine and talked about going to Guadalajara, Village parties where all the guests worked for advertising agencies and voted for Reform Democrats, press parties at Sardi's, the worst kinds of parties. You will have perceived by now that I was not one to profit by the experience of others, that it was a very long time indeed before I stopped believing in new faces and began to understand the lesson in that story, which was that it is distinctly possible to stay too long at the Fair.

I could not tell you when I began to understand that. All I know is that it was very bad when I was twenty-eight. Everything that was said to me I seemed to have heard before, and I could no longer listen. I could no longer sit in little bars near Grand Central and listen to someone complaining of his wife's inability to cope with the help while he missed another train to Connecticut. I no longer had any interest in hearing about the advances other people had received from their publishers, about plays which were having second-act trouble in Philadelphia, or about people I would like very much if only I would come out and meet them. I had already met them, always. There were certain parts of the city which I had to avoid. I could not bear upper Madison Avenue on weekday mornings (this was a particularly inconvenient aversion, since I then lived just fifty or sixty feet east of Madison), because I would see women walking Yorkshire terriers and shopping at Gristede's, and some Veblenesque gorge would rise in my throat. I could not go to Times Square in the afternoon, or to the New York Public Library for any reason whatsoever. One day I could not go into a Schrafft's; the next day it would be Bonwit Teller.

I hurt the people I cared about, and insulted those I did not. I cut myself off from the one person who was closer to me than any other. I cried until I was not even aware when I was crying and when I was not, cried in elevators and in taxis and in Chinese laundries, and when I went to the doctor he said only that I seemed to be depressed, and should see a "specialist." He wrote down a psychiatrist's name and address for me, but I did not go.

Instead I got married, which as it turned out was a very good thing to do but badly timed, since I still could not walk on upper Madison Avenue in the mornings and still could not talk to people and still cried in Chinese laundries. I had never before understood what "despair" meant, and I am not sure that I understand now, but I understood that year. Of course I could not work. I could not even get dinner with any degree of certainty, and I would sit in the apartment on Seventy-fifth Street paralyzed until my husband would call from his office and say gently that I did not have to get dinner, that I could meet him at Michael's Pub or at Toots Shor's or at Sardi's East. And then one morning in April (we had been married in January) he called and told me that he wanted to get out of New York for a while, that he would take a six-month leave of absence, that we would go somewhere.

It was three years ago that he told me that, and we have lived in Los Angeles since. Many of the people we knew in New York think this a curious aberration, and in fact tell us so. There is no possible, no adequate answer to that, and so we give certain stock answers, the answers everyone gives. I talk about how difficult it would be for us to "afford" to live in New York right now, about how much "space" we need. All I mean is that I was very young in New York, and that at some point the golden rhythm was broken, and I am not that young any more. The last time I was in New York was in a cold January, and everyone was ill and tired. Many of the people I used to know there had moved to Dallas or had gone on Antabuse or had bought a farm in New Hampshire. We stayed ten days, and then we took an afternoon flight back to Los Angeles, and on the way home from the airport that night I could see the moon on the Pacific and smell jasmine all around and we both knew that there was no longer any point in keeping the apartment we still kept in New York. There were years when I called Los Angeles "the Coast," but they seem a long time ago.

1967

PLAY IT AS IT LAYS

For John

Maria

WHAT MAKES IAGO EVIL? some people ask. I never ask. Another example, one which springs to mind because Mrs. Burstein saw a pygmy rattler in the artichoke garden this morning and has been intractable since: I never ask about snakes. Why should Shalimar attract kraits. Why should a coral snake need two glands of neurotoxic poison to survive while a king snake, *so similarly marked*, needs none. Where is the Darwinian logic there. You might ask that. I never would, not any more. I recall an incident reported not long ago in the Los Angeles *Herald-Examiner*: two honeymooners, natives of Detroit, found dead in their Scout camper near Boca Raton, a coral snake still coiled in the thermal blanket. Why? Unless you are prepared to take the long view, there is no satisfactory "answer" to such questions.

Just so. I am what I am. To look for "reasons" is beside the point. But because the pursuit of reasons is their business here, they ask me questions. Maria, yes or no: I see a cock in this inkblot. Maria, yes or no: A large number of people are guilty of bad sexual conduct, I believe my sins are unpardonable, I have been disappointed in love. How could I answer? How could it apply? NOTHING APPLIES, I print with the magnetized IBM pencil. What does apply, they ask later, as if the word "nothing" were ambiguous, open to interpretation, a questionable fragment of an Icelandic rune. There are only certain facts, I say, trying again to be an agreeable player of the game. Certain facts, certain things that happened. (Why bother, you might ask. I bother for Kate. What I play for here is Kate. Carter put Kate in there and I am going to get her out.) They will misread the facts, invent connections, will extrapolate reasons where none exist, but I told you, that is their business here.

So they suggested that I set down the facts, and the facts are these: My name is Maria Wyeth. That is pronounced Mar-*eye*-ah, to get it straight at the outset. Some people here call me "Mrs. Lang," but I never did. Age, thirty-one. Married. Divorced. One daughter, age four. (I talk about Kate to no one here. In the place where Kate is they put electrodes on her head and needles in her spine and try to figure what went wrong. It is one more version of why does a coral snake have two glands of neurotoxic poison. Kate has soft down on her spine and an aberrant chemical in her brain. Kate is Kate. Carter could not remember the soft down on her spine or he would not let them put needles there.) From my mother I inherited my looks and a tendency to migraine. From my father I inherited an optimism which did not leave me until recently.

Details: I was born in Reno, Nev., and moved nine years later to Silver Wells, Nev., pop. then 28, now 0. We moved down to Silver Wells because my father lost the Reno house in a private game and happened to remember that he owned this town, Silver Wells. He had bought it or won it or maybe his father left it to him, I'm not sure which and it doesn't matter to you. We had a lot of things and places that came and went, a cattle ranch with no cattle and a ski resort picked up on somebody's second mortgage and a motel that would have been advantageously situated at a freeway exit had the freeway been built; I was raised to believe that what came in on the next roll would always be better than what went out on the last. I no longer believe that, but I am telling you how it was. What we had in Silver Wells was three hundred acres of mesquite and some houses and a Flying A and a zinc mine and a Tonopah & Tidewater RR siding and a trinket shop and later, after my father and his partner Benny Austin hit on the idea that Silver Wells was a natural tourist attraction, a midget golf course and a reptile museum and a restaurant with some slots and two craps tables. The slots were not exactly moneymakers because the only person who played them was Paulette, with nickels from the cashbox. Paulette ran the restaurant and (I see now) balled my father and sometimes let me pretend to cashier after school. I say "pretend" because there were no customers. As it happened the highway my father counted on came nowhere near and the money ran out and my mother got sick and Benny Austin went back to Vegas, I ran into him in the Flamingo a few years ago. "Your father's only Waterloo was he was a man always twenty years before his time," Benny advised me that night in the Flamingo. "The ghost-town scheme, the midget golf, the automatic blackjack concept, what do you see today? Harry Wyeth could be a *Rock*efeller in Silver Wells today."

"There isn't any Silver Wells today," I said. "It's in the middle of a missile range."

"I'm speaking about *then*, Maria. *As it was.*"

Benny called for a round of Cuba Libres, a drink I have never known anyone but my mother and father and Benny Austin to order, and I gave him some chips to play for me and went to the ladies' room and never came back. I told myself it was because I didn't want Benny to see the kind of man I was with, I was with a man who was playing baccarat with hundred-dollar bills behind the rope, but that wasn't all of it. I might as well lay it on the line, I have trouble with *as it was.*

I mean it leads nowhere. Benny Austin, my mother sitting in Paulette's empty restaurant when it was 120° outside looking through her magazines for contests we could enter (Waikiki, Paris France, Roman Holiday, my mother's yearnings suffused our life like nerve gas, *cross the ocean in a silver plane*, she would croon to herself and mean it, *see the jungle when it's wet with rain*), the three of us driving down to Vegas in the pickup and then driving home again in the clear night, a hundred miles down and a hundred back and nobody on the highway either way, just the snakes stretched on the warm asphalt and my mother with a wilted gardenia in her dark hair and my father keeping a fifth of Jim Beam on the floorboard and talking about his plans, he always had a lot of plans, I never in my life had any plans, none of it makes any sense, none of it adds up.

New York: what sense did that make? An eighteen-year-old girl from Silver Wells, Nevada, graduates from the Consolidated Union High School in Tonopah and goes to New York to take acting lessons, how do you figure it? My mother thought being an actress was a nice idea, she used to cut my hair in bangs to look like Margaret Sullavan, and my father said not to be afraid to go because if certain deals worked out as anticipated he and my mother would be regular airline passengers between Las Vegas and New York City, so I went. As it turned out, the last time but once I ever saw my mother was sitting in the Vegas airport drinking a Cuba Libre, but there you are. Everything goes. I am working very hard at not thinking about how everything goes. I watch a hummingbird, throw the I Ching but never read the coins, keep my mind in the now. New York. Let me stick to certain facts. What happened was this: I looked all right (I'm not telling you I was blessed or cursed, I'm telling a fact, I know it from all the pictures) and somebody photographed me and before long I was getting $100 an hour from the agencies and $50 from the magazines which in those days was not bad and I knew a lot of Southerners and faggots and rich boys and that was how I spent my days and nights. The night my mother ran the car off the highway outside Tonopah I was with a drunk rich boy at the old Morocco, as close as I could figure later: I didn't know about it for a couple of weeks because the coyotes tore her up before anybody found her and my father couldn't tell me. ("Jesus but we had a good thing going in Silver Wells," Benny Austin said that night in the Flamingo, and maybe they did, maybe I did, maybe I never should have left, but that line of thinking leads nowhere because as I told Benny *there is no Silver Wells.* The last I heard of Paulette she was living in a Sun City. Think that one over.) My father's letter was mailed to an old address and forwarded, I read it in a taxi one morning when I was late for a sitting and when I hit the fact in the middle of the second paragraph I began to scream and did not work for a month after. The letter is still in my makeup box but I am careful not to read it unless I am drunk, which in my current situation is never. "This is a bad hand but God if there is one, and Honey I sincerely believe there must be 'Something', never meant it to set you back in your Plans," is how it ends. "Don't let them bluff you back there because you're holding all the aces."

Easy aces. I am not sure what year it was because I have this problem with *as it was*, but after a while I had a bad time. (There, you will say now, she believed her sins were unpardonable, but I told you, nothing applies.) The tulips on Park Avenue looked dirty and I was sent twice to Montego Bay to get some color back in my face but I could not sleep alone and stayed up late and it was falling apart with Ivan Costello and everything showed in the camera by then. Of course I did not get back to Nevada that year because that was the year I screamed at Ivan and married Carter, and the next was the year we came here and Carter put me in a couple of little pictures (one you may have seen, a doctor here claims to have seen it but he will say anything to make me talk, the other never distributed) and I don't know what happened the year after that and then I started getting to Nevada quite a bit, but by then my father was dead and I was not married any more.

Those are the facts. Now I lie in the sun and play solitaire and listen to the sea (the sea is down the cliff but I am not allowed to swim, only on Sundays when we are accompanied) and watch a hummingbird. I try not to think of dead things and plumbing. I try not to hear the air conditioner in that bedroom in Encino. I try not to live in Silver Wells or in New York or with Carter. I try to live in the now and keep my eye on the hummingbird. I see no one I used to know, but then I'm not just crazy about a lot of people. I mean maybe I was holding all the aces, but what was the game?

Helene

I SAW MARIA TODAY. Or at least I tried to see Maria today: I made the effort. I didn't make it for Maria I don't mind saying, I made it for Carter, or for BZ, or for old times or for something, not for Maria. "I don't much want to talk to you, Helene," was what she said the last time. "It's not personal, Helene, I just don't talk any more." Not for Maria.

Anyway I didn't. See her. I drove all the way out there, took the entire morning and packed a box for her, all the new books and a chiffon scarf she left at the beach once (she was careless, it must have cost thirty dollars, she was always careless) and a pound of caviar, maybe not Beluga but Maria shouldn't bitch now, plus a letter from Ivan Costello and a long profile somebody did in *The New York Times* about Carter, you'd think that would at least interest her except Maria has never been able to bear Carter's success, all that, and Maria wouldn't see me. "Mrs. Lang is resting," the nurse said. I could see her resting, I could see her down by the pool in the same bikini she was wearing the summer she killed BZ, lying by that swimming pool with a shade over her eyes as if she hadn't a care or a responsibility in the world. She never puts on any weight, you'll notice that's often true of selfish women. Not that I blame Maria for anything that happened to me, although I'm the one who suffered, I'm the one who should be "resting," I'm the one who lost BZ through her carelessness, her selfishness, but I blame her only *on Carter's behalf.* Half a chance and she would have killed Carter too. She was always a very selfish girl, it was first last and always Maria.

Carter

HERE ARE SOME SCENES I have very clear in my mind.

"I always get breakfast out," I say to someone. This is at a dinner party, a group of friends. Maria would say that they were not her friends, but Maria has never understood friendship, conversation, the normal amenities of social exchange. Maria has difficulty talking to people with whom she is not sleeping.

"I go to the Wilshire or the Beverly Hills," I say. "I read the trades, I like to be alone at breakfast."

"In fact he doesn't always get breakfast out," Maria says, very low, to no one in particular. "In fact the last time he got breakfast out was on April 17."

The others at the table look first at her and then away, astonished, uneasy: something in the way her hands are tensed on the edge of the table prevents passing this off. Only BZ continues to look directly at her.

"Oh fuck it," she says then, and tears run down her cheeks. She still looks very straight ahead at no one in particular.

Another scene: she is playing on the lawn with the baby, tossing up drops of water from a clear plastic hose. "Watch out she doesn't get chilled," I say from the terrace; Maria looks up, drops the hose, and walks away from the baby toward the poolhouse. She turns, and looks back at the baby. "Your father wants to talk to you," she says. Her voice is neutral.

After BZ's death there was a time when I played and replayed these scenes and others like them, composed them as if for the camera, trying to find some order, a pattern. I found none. All I can say is this: it was after a succession of such small scenes that I began to see the improbability of a rapprochement with Maria.

I

IN THE FIRST HOT MONTH of the fall after the summer she left Carter (the summer Carter left her, the summer Carter stopped living in the house in Beverly Hills), Maria drove the freeway. She dressed every morning with a greater sense of purpose than she had felt in some time, a cotton skirt, a jersey, sandals she could kick off when she wanted the touch of the accelerator, and she dressed very fast, running a brush through her hair once or twice and tying it back with a ribbon, for it was essential (to pause was to throw herself into unspeakable peril) that she be on the freeway by ten o'clock. Not somewhere on Hollywood Boulevard, not on her way to the freeway, but actually on the freeway. If she was not she lost the day's rhythm, its precariously imposed momentum. Once she was on the freeway and had maneuvered her way to a fast lane she turned on the radio at high volume and she drove. She drove the San Diego to the Harbor, the Harbor up to the Hollywood, the Hollywood to the Golden State, the Santa Monica, the Santa Ana, the Pasadena, the Ventura. She drove it as a riverman runs a river, every day more attuned to its currents, its deceptions, and just as a riverman feels the pull of the rapids in the lull between sleeping and waking, so Maria lay at night in the still of Beverly Hills and saw the great signs soar overhead at seventy miles an hour, *Normandie ¼ Vermont ¾ Harbor Fwy 1.* Again and again she returned to an intricate stretch just south of the interchange where successful passage from the Hollywood onto the Harbor required a diagonal move across four lanes of traffic. On the afternoon she finally did it without once braking or once losing the beat on the radio she was exhilarated, and that night slept dreamlessly. By then she was sleeping not in the house but out by the pool, on a faded rattan chaise left by a former tenant. There was a jack for a telephone there, and she used beach towels for blankets. The beach towels had a special point. Because she had an uneasy sense that sleeping outside on a rattan chaise could be construed as the first step toward something unnameable (she did not know what it was she feared, but it had to do with empty sardine cans in the sink, vermouth bottles in the wastebaskets, slovenliness past the point of return) she told herself that she was sleeping outside just until it was too cold to sleep beneath beach towels, just until the heat broke, just until the fires stopped burning in the mountains, sleeping outside only because the bedrooms in the house were hot, airless, only because the palms scraped against the screens and there was no one to wake her in the mornings. The beach towels signified how temporary the arrangement was. Outside she did not have to be afraid that she would not wake up, outside she could sleep. Sleep was essential if she was to be on the freeway by ten o'clock. Sometimes the freeway ran out, in a scrap metal yard in San Pedro or on the main street of Palmdale or out somewhere no place at all where the flawless burning concrete just stopped, turned into common road, abandoned construction sheds rusting beside it. When that happened she would keep in careful control, portage skillfully back, feel for the first time the heavy weight of the becalmed car beneath her and try to keep her eyes on the mainstream, the great pilings, the Cyclone fencing, the deadly oleander, the luminous signs, the organism which absorbed all her reflexes, all her attention.

So that she would not have to stop for food she kept a hard-boiled egg on the passenger seat of the Corvette. She could shell and eat a hard-boiled egg at seventy miles an hour (crack it on the steering wheel, never mind salt, salt bloats, no matter what happened she remembered her body) and she drank Coca-Cola in Union 76 stations, Standard stations, Flying A's. She would stand on the hot pavement and drink the Coke from the bottle and put the bottle back in the rack (she tried always to let the attendant notice her putting the bottle in the rack, a show of thoughtful responsibility, no sardine cans in her sink) and then she would walk to the edge of the concrete and stand, letting the sun dry her damp back. To hear her own voice she would sometimes talk to the attendant, ask advice on oil filters, how much air the tires should carry, the most efficient route to Foothill Boulevard in West Covina. Then she would retie the ribbon in her hair and rinse her dark glasses in the drinking fountain and be ready to drive again. In the first hot month of the fall after the summer she left Carter, the summer Carter left her, the summer Carter stopped living in the house in Beverly

Hills, a bad season in the city, Maria put seven thousand miles on the Corvette. Sometimes at night the dread would overtake her, bathe her in sweat, flood her mind with sharp flash images of Les Goodwin in New York and Carter out there on the desert with BZ and Helene and the irrevocability of what seemed already to have happened, but she never thought about that on the freeway.

2

THE SECOND PICTURE she had made with Carter was called *Angel Beach*, and in it she played a girl who was raped by the members of a motorcycle gang. Carter had brought the picture in for $340,000 and the studio had saturation-booked it and by the end of the first year the domestic and foreign gross was just under eight million dollars. Maria had seen it twice, once at a studio preview and a second time by herself, at a drive-in in Culver City, and neither time did she have any sense that the girl on the screen was herself. "I look at you and I know that . . . *what happened* just didn't mean anything," the girl on the screen would say, and "There's a lot more to living than just kicks, I see that now, kicks are nowhere." Carter's original cut ended with a shot of the motorcycle gang, as if they represented some reality not fully apprehended by the girl Maria played, but the cut released by the studio ended with a long dolly shot of Maria strolling across a campus. Maria preferred the studio's cut. In fact, she liked watching the picture: the girl on the screen seemed to have a definite knack for controlling her own destiny.

The other picture, the first picture, the picture never distributed, was called *Maria*. Carter had simply followed Maria around New York and shot film. It was not until they moved to California and Carter began cutting the film together that she entirely realized what he was doing. The picture showed Maria doing a fashion sitting, Maria asleep on a couch at a party, Maria on the telephone arguing with the billing department at Bloomingdale's, Maria cleaning some marijuana with a kitchen strainer, Maria crying on the IRT. At the end she was thrown into negative and looked dead. The picture lasted seventy-four minutes and had won a prize at a festival in Eastern Europe and Maria did not like to look at it. She had once heard that students at UCLA and USC talked about using her the way commercial directors talked about using actresses who got a million dollars a picture, but she had never talked to any of them (sometimes they walked up to Carter in front of a theater or a bookstore and introduced themselves, and Carter would introduce Maria, and they would look sidelong at Maria while they talked to Carter about coming to see their film programs, but Maria had nothing to say to them, avoided their eyes) and she disliked their having seen her in that first picture. She never thought of it as *Maria*. She thought of it always as that first picture. Carter took her to BZ and Helene's one night when BZ was running the picture and she had to leave the house after the titles, had to sit outside on the beach smoking cigarettes and fighting nausea for seventy-two of the seventy-four minutes.

"Why does he run it so often," she had said to Carter later. "Why do you let him keep a print out there, he *keeps a print in the house*."

"He owns it, Maria. He owns all the prints."

"That's not what I mean. I said why does he run it so often."

"He wants Helene to see it."

"Helene's seen it a dozen times. Helene doesn't even *like* it, she told me so."

"You don't understand anything," Carter had said finally, and they had gone to bed that night without speaking. Maria did not want to understand why BZ ran that first picture so often or what it had to do with Helene. The girl on the screen in that first picture had no knack for anything.

3

"MARIA WYETH," she repeated to Freddy Chaikin's receptionist. The reception room was full of glossy plants in chinoiserie pots and Maria had an abrupt conviction that the plants were consuming the oxygen she needed to breathe. She should not have come here without calling. Only people in trouble came unannounced to see their agents. If Freddy Chaikin thought she carried trouble with her he would avoid her, because trouble was something no one in the city liked to be near. Failure, illness, fear, they were seen as infectious, contagious blights on glossy plants. It seemed to Maria that even the receptionist was avoiding her eyes, fearing contamination. "He's kind of expecting me," Maria added in a near whisper.

"Maria Wyeth," the receptionist said. "Mr. Chaikin is in the projection room, do you want to wait? Or could he call you."

"No. I mean yes. But tell him it has to be today or—"

The receptionist waited.

"Or I'll talk to him tomorrow," Maria said finally.

In the elevator was an actor she recognized but had never met, the star of a canceled television Western. He was with a short agent in a narrow dark suit, and the agent smiled at Maria as the elevator door closed.

"The word on Carter's dailies is sensational," the agent said.

Maria smiled and nodded. It did not require an answer: it was a cue for the actor, who waited a suitable instant and then picked it up. "Your pocketbook's open," he drawled, and the look he gave Maria was dutifully charged with sexual appreciation, meant not for Maria herself but for Carter Lang's wife. She leaned against the padded elevator wall and closed her eyes. If she could tell Les Goodwin about the actor in the elevator he would laugh. When she got home she thought about calling him, but instead she went upstairs and lay face down on Kate's empty bed, cradled Kate's blanket, clutched Kate's baby pillow to her stomach and fought off a wave of the dread. The time seemed to have passed for telling Les Goodwin funny stories.

4

SHE SAT ON THE RATTAN CHAISE in the hot October twilight and watched BZ throw the ice cubes from his drink one by one into the swimming pool. They had already talked about Helene's week at La Costa and they had already talked about an actress who had been admitted to UCLA Neuropsychiatric with her wrists cut (the papers said exhaustion, but BZ knew things like that, knew about people, that was why she had called him) and now it was the hour when in all the houses all around the pretty women were putting on perfume and enameled bracelets and kissing the pretty children goodnight, the hour of apparent grace and promised music, and even here in Maria's own garden the air smelled of jasmine and the water in the pool was 85°. The water in the pool was always 85° and it was always clean. It came with the rent. Whether or not Carter could afford the rent, whether it was a month like this one when he was making a lot of money or a month when the lawyers were talking about bankruptcy, the boy came twice a week to vacuum the pool and the man came four days a week to work on the roses and the water in the pool was 85°. Sometimes it occurred to Maria that maybe the pretty children and the enameled bracelets came the same way, but she did not like to think about that.

"Tell me who you've seen," she said. She did not much want to hear who BZ had seen but neither did she want BZ to leave. BZ had not yet mentioned Carter. BZ was the producer on the picture, BZ had come in from the location two days before and he was going back to the location tomorrow and he had not once mentioned Carter. "Tell me about the Willards' dance."

"Strobe lights in Pasadena." BZ stood up. "On nights like that you could kill yourself for being a Gentile."

"Don't leave."

"I'm late now. I'm supposed to be somewhere."

"Who is it," she said, not looking at him.

"Nobody special, I'm meeting Tommy Loew, you know Tommy, he's in from New York."

"I don't mean you." She wondered without interest if Tommy Loew was a faggot. "You know I don't mean you."

"I don't know what you're talking about." BZ put his glass on a table, and looked at Maria for a long while. "Just let him finish."

"Who is it." She did not know why she persisted.

"Listen, Maria. I don't know if you know this, but he wanted you in this picture very badly. At one point he was ready to scrap the deal, jeopardize the entire project, just because he wanted to use you."

"I know that."

"Then why not stop thinking Carter designs his every move expressly to thwart you. Why not stop thinking like Carlotta."

"You don't have any idea in your mind how I think." Carlotta was BZ's mother. Carlotta had $35 million and was engaged in constant litigation with her estranged second husband. Maria sat down on the edge of the pool and splashed the clear water over her bare feet. "Listen to the music from the Kuliks'. They're having a party."

"You going?"

"Of course I'm not going. He's a gangster."

"I just asked if you were going to a party, Maria, I didn't ask for a grand-jury indictment." BZ paused. "In the second place he's not a gangster. He's a lawyer."

"For gangsters."

BZ shrugged. "I think of him more as a philosopher king. He told me once he understood the whole meaning of life, it came to him in a blinding flash one time when he almost died on the table at Cedars."

"Larry Kulik's not going to die at Cedars. Larry Kulik's going to die in a barber chair."

"It's uphill work making you laugh, Maria. Anyway, Larry Kulik's a great admirer of yours. You know what he said to Carter? He said, 'What I like about your wife, Carter, is she's not a cunt.'"

Maria said nothing.

"That's very funny, Maria, Kulik saying that to Carter, you lost your sense of humor?"

"I've already heard it. Give me your glass."

"I told you, Tommy Loew. I'm already late."

"Who is it," she repeated.

"He's two weeks behind schedule now, Maria. Just let him finish the picture." BZ stood up, and ran the tips of his fingers very lightly across Maria's bare back. "Seen anything of Les Goodwin?" he said finally.

Maria watched a leaf in the water and tried not to recoil from BZ's fingers. "Les and Felicia are in New York," she said carefully, and then reached for a towel. "You're already late for Tommy Loew, I mean aren't you?"

Later in the week she saw in one of the columns that BZ had been at the Kuliks' party with Tommy Loew and a starlet whose name she did not recognize. She did not know why it annoyed her but it did. She wondered if Tommy Loew and the starlet had gone back to BZ's later, and who had watched whom, and if Helene had been back from La Costa.

5

"JUST WANTED YOU TO KNOW I'm thinking of you," Freddy Chaikin said on the telephone. "I'll be frank, I was surprised to hear you wanted to work again. After that debacle with Mark Ross, I just naturally thought—"

"I've always wanted to work." Maria tried to keep her voice even. Freddy would be sitting in his office with the Barcelona chairs and the Giacometti sculpture and anything he wanted to say Maria would have to hear.

"—an actress walks off a set, people tend to think she doesn't want to work."

"That was almost a year ago. I was sick. I was upset about Kate. I haven't walked off any more sets, you *know* that, Freddy."

"You haven't had any sets *to* walk off."

Maria closed her eyes. "What are you doing right now, Freddy," she said finally. "You sitting there playing with a Fabergé Easter egg? Or what?"

"Calm down. Actually I talked to Morty Landau about you today at lunch. I said, Morty, you know Maria Wyeth, and he did—"

"I should think so. I had the lead in two features."

"Right, Maria, of course you did. You know that. I know that. And they were very interesting little pictures. Carter parlayed those two little pictures, one of them never distributed, into a very nice thing. Carter's in the enviable position now where he wants to do something, it's just a question of working out the numbers. I'm proud to represent him. I'm proud to represent both of you, Maria. Maybe I could arrange for Morty Landau to see some film, you give me your word that you really want to work."

"See some *film*."

"Where's the problem, Maria? There's something so unusual about wanting to see some film? I show film on talent getting two, two-fifty a picture."

"Morty Landau makes television."

"Let's get to the bottom line, Maria, if Carter were around he'd say the same thing. You want to work, I'll arrange for Morty Landau to see film."

"Carter is around."

There was a silence, and when Freddy Chaikin spoke again his voice was gentle. "All I meant, Maria, was that Carter's on location. All I meant."

6

ON THE TENTH DAY OF OCTOBER at quarter past four in the afternoon with a dry hot wind blowing through the passes Maria found herself in Baker. She had never meant to go as far as Baker, had started out that day as every day, her only destination the freeway. But she had driven out the San Bernardino and up the Barstow and instead of turning back at Barstow (she had been out that far before but never that late in the day, it was past time to navigate back, she was out too far too late, the rhythm was lost) she kept driving. When she turned off at Baker it was 115° and she was picking up Vegas on the radio and she was within sixty miles of where Carter was making the picture. He could be in the motel right now. They could be through shooting for the day and he could be having a drink with BZ and Helene, thinking about going into Vegas for dinner or just resting, resting on the unmade bed with his shirt off. The woman who ran the motel only made the beds once a week, Carter had made a joke about it in an interview, Maria had read it in the trades. She could call. "Listen," she could say. "I'm in Baker. I just happen to be in Baker."

"So you just happen to be in Baker," he could say. "Get on up here."

Or he could even say: "Listen. Get up here quick."

Those were things he could say but because she did not know if he would say them or even if she wanted to hear them she just sat in the car behind the 76 station in Baker and studied the pay phone by the Coke machine. Whatever he began by saying he would end by saying nothing. He would say something and she would say something and before either of them knew it they would be playing out a dialogue so familiar that it drained the imagination, blocked the will, allowed them to drop words and whole sentences and still arrive at the cold conclusion. "Oh Christ," he would say. "I felt good today, really good for a change, you fixed that, you really pricked the balloon."

"How did I fix that."

"You know how."

"I don't know how."

She would wait for him to answer but he would say nothing then, would just sit with his head in his hands. She would feel first guilty, resigned to misery, then furious, trapped, white with anger. "*Listen* to me," she would say then, almost shouting, trying to take him by the shoulders and shake him out of what she could not see as other than an elaborate pose; he would knock her away, and the look on his face, contorted, teeth bared, would render her paralyzed. "Why don't you just get it over with," he would say then, leaning close, his face still contorted. "Why don't you just go in that bathroom and take every pill in it. Why don't you die."

After that he would leave for a while, breaking things as he went, slamming doors to kick them open, picking up decanters to hurl at mirrors, detouring by way of chairs to smash them against the floor. Always when he came back he would sleep in their room, shutting the door against her. Rigid with self-pity she would lie in another room, wishing for the will to leave. Each believed the other a murderer of time, a destroyer of life itself. She did not know what she was doing in Baker. However it began it ended like that.

"Listen," she would say.

"Don't touch me," he would say.

Maria looked at the pay phone for a long while, and then she got out of the car and drank a warm Coke. With the last of the Coke she swallowed two Fiorinal tablets, then closed her eyes against the sun and waited for the Fiorinal to clear her head of Carter and what Carter would say. On the way back into the city the traffic was heavy and the hot wind blew sand through the windows and the radio got on her nerves and after that Maria did not go back to the freeway except as a way of getting somewhere.

7

"C'EST MOI, MARIA," the voice said on the telephone. "BZ."

Maria tried to untangle the cord from the receiver and fight her way out of sleep. Sleeping in the afternoon was a bad sign. She had been trying not to notice the signs but she could not avoid this one, and a sharp fear contracted her stomach muscles. "Where are you," she said finally.

"At the beach."

Maria groped on the edge of the pool for her dark glasses.

"Did I catch you in the middle of an overdose, Maria? Or what?"

"I thought you were on the desert."

"We're shutting down for a week, don't you read the trades? Because of the fire."

"What fire."

"On top of the news as ever," BZ said. "The fire, we had a fire, we have to rebuild the set. Carter's coming in tomorrow. I'll take you to Anita Garson's tonight if you're not doing anything, all right?"

"Where's Helene?"

"Helene's in bed, Helene's depressed. Helene has these very *cop*ious menstruations." There was a pause. "Seven-thirty all right?"

"I don't know about Anita Garson's, I don't—"

"I meant of course unless you've got *plans*." His voice rose almost imperceptibly. "Unless you've got an *à deux* going at the Marmont. Or wherever it is he stays."

Maria said nothing.

"You're a lot of laughs this afternoon, Maria, I'm glad I called. I just meant that you and Les Goodwin were friends. As in just-good. No innuendo. No offense." He paused. "You still sulking in there?"

"I'll see you at seven-thirty," she said finally.

Later she could not think how she had been coerced by BZ into going to Anita Garson's party, which was large and noisy and crowded with people she did not much like. There was a rock group and a pink tent and everywhere Maria looked she saw someone who registered on her only as a foreigner or a faggot or a gangster. She tried to keep her eyes bright and her lips slightly parted and she stayed close to BZ. "How's Carter," someone said behind her, and when she turned she saw that it was Larry Kulik.

"Carter's on location," she said, but Larry Kulik was not listening. He was watching a very young girl in a white halter dress dancing on the terrace.

"I'd like to get into that," he said contemplatively to BZ.

"I wouldn't call it the impossible dream," BZ said.

Maria twisted the napkin around her glass. She had already smiled too long and she did not want to look any more at Larry Kulik's careful manicure and expensively tailored suit and she did not want to consider why Larry Kulik was talking to BZ about the girl in the white dress.

"Not that many guys," Larry Kulik was saying. "Not just anybody."

"Shit no. You have to be able to get her into the Whisky."

Larry Kulik was still watching the girl. "Only six guys."

"How do you know, six?"

Larry Kulik shrugged. "I had her researched. Six." He patted Maria's arm absently. "How's it going, baby? How's Carter?"

At the table on the terrace where Maria and BZ sat for dinner there were a French director, his cinematographer, and two English Lesbians who lived in Santa Monica Canyon. Maria sat next to the cinematographer, who spoke no English, and during dinner BZ and the French director disappeared into the house. Maria could smell marijuana, but it was not mentioned on the terrace. The cinematographer and the two Lesbians discussed the dehumanizing aspect of American technology, in French.

"You have to come over sometime and use the sauna," Larry Kulik said when he brushed by the table on his way inside. "Stereo piped in, beaucoup fantastic."

At midnight one of the amplifiers broke down, and the band packed up to leave. BZ was getting together a group to go back to his house: the French director, Larry Kulik, the girl in the white halter dress. "Simplicity itself," he said to Maria. "The chickie wants the frog."

"I have to go home."

"You're not exactly a shot of meth tonight anyway."

"I feel beaucoup fantastic," Maria said, and turned her face away so that he would not see her tears. When Les Goodwin called from New York the next morning at seven o'clock she began to cry again. Why was she crying, he wanted to know. Because he made her so happy, she said, and for that moment believed it.

8

"YOU HAVEN'T ASKED ME how it went after we left Anita's," BZ said.

"How did it go," Maria said without interest.

"Everybody got what he came for."

"Don't you ever get tired of doing favors for people?"

There was a long silence. "You don't know how tired," BZ said.

9

SHE LOOKED AT CARTER sitting in the living room and all she could think was that he had put on weight. The blue work shirt he was wearing pulled at the buttons. She supposed that he had weighed that much when he left, she noticed it now only because she had not seen him.

"You going to stay here?" she said.

He rubbed his knuckles across the stubble on his chin. "All my things are here, aren't they?"

Maria sat down across from him. She wished she had a cigarette but there were none on the table and it seemed frivolous to go get one. Carter's saying that all his things were in the house did not seem entirely conclusive, did not address itself to the question. Quite often with Carter she felt like Ingrid Bergman in *Gaslight*, another frivolous thought.

"I mean I thought we were kind of separated." That did not sound exactly right either.

"If that's the way you want it."

"It wasn't me. I mean was it me?"

"Never, Maria. Never you."

There was a silence. Something real was happening: this was, as it were, her life. If she could keep that in mind she would be able to play it through, do the right thing, whatever that meant.

"I guess we could try," she said uncertainly.

"Only if you want to."

"Of course I do." She did not know what else to say. "Of course I want to."

"Why don't you sound like it."

"Carter, I *do*." She paused, abruptly exhausted. "Maybe it's not such a good idea."

"Do what you want," he said, and went upstairs.

Maria sat with her eyes closed until the vein in her temple stopped pulsing, then followed him upstairs. He lay on the bed in their room, staring at the ceiling. Only by an increased immobility did he acknowledge her presence.

"I was going out to see Kate," she said finally.

"How many times you been out there lately?" He still did not look at her.

"Hardly at all," she said, and then: "In the past few weeks, maybe a couple of times."

"You've been there four times since Sunday."

Resolutely Maria walked into the dressing room and began pinning her hair back.

"They called me," Carter said from the bedroom, speaking as if by rote. "They called me to point out that unscheduled parental appearances tend to disturb the child's adjustment."

"Adjustment to what." Maria jabbed a pin into her hair.

"We've been through this, Maria. We've done this number about fifty times."

Maria put her head in her arms on the dressing table. When she looked into the mirror again she saw Carter's reflection. There had come a time when she felt anesthetized in the presence of Ivan Costello and now that time had come with Carter.

"Don't cry," Carter said. "I know it upsets you, we're doing all we can, I said don't cry."

"I'm not crying," she said, and she was not.

10

"I'M ADAMANT about the mixes, I'm sorry, I just won't use them," the masseur who wanted to be a writer called from the kitchen. Maria lay face down on the sand beyond the sun deck and tried to neutralize, by concentrating on images of Kate (Kate's hair, brushing Kate's hair, the last time she went to the hospital Kate's hair was tangled and she had sat on the lawn and brushed it, worked out the tangles into fine golden strands, they told her not to come so often but how could she help it, they never brushed Kate's hair), the particular rise and inflection of the masseur's voice. There was always someone Maria tried not to hear at BZ and Helene's. Either there were the sulky young men BZ met in places like Acapulco and Kitzbühel and Tangier or there were Helene's friends, the women with whom she shopped and planned restorative weeks at Palm Springs and La Costa, the women with the silk Pucci shirts and the periodically tightened eye lines and the husbands on perpetual location. They were always in their middle forties, those friends of Helene's, always about ten years older than Helene herself. "Heaven pajamas," Helene's friends would say to one another, and they would exchange the addresses of new astrologers and the tag lines of old jokes. One of Helene's friends had been at the house when Maria and Carter arrived. "I'll tell you one thing, he's a great *phone*," she said several times, and she and Helene would laugh. It seemed to be a joke but Maria had failed to hear the beginning of it. Usually Maria could avoid hearing Helene's friends but BZ's friends were more difficult, and this one was particularly difficult. Part of it was his voice and part of it was that Maria had met him before, she was certain she had. He did not seem to recognize her but she was sure that she had met him three years before, at someone's house in Santa Barbara. He had come in after a polo game with some people who spoke only to the host and to one another, never to Carter and Maria—there had been an actor whose last several pictures had failed, the actor's mother, and a nervous steel heiress with whom the others seemed to have spent a week in Palm Beach—and then he had been not a masseur but the actor's secretary. Even lying in the noon sun on this blazing dry October day Maria felt a physical chill when she thought about that afternoon in Santa Barbara. The way he looked was the problem. He looked exactly the same. He looked untouched, and she did not.

"BZ, you've planned this to torment me," he was saying now. He stood on the deck, holding a plastic lemon at elaborate arm's-length. "You couldn't possibly buy artificial lemon juice, someone left it here, it's a bad joke."

"All BZ's friends are purists," Helene murmured without opening her eyes.

"You're a nasty," BZ said, and laughed. He twisted a silver medallion on his chest so that it flashed in the sun. BZ was perpetually tanned, oiled, gleaming, not the negotiable health-club tan of people like Freddy Chaikin but tanned as evidence of a lifetime spent in season. "Isn't Helene a nasty, Carter? Haven't I got a bitch for a wife? And question number three, *who am I impersonating*?"

"Yourself," Helene suggested.

"Carter's not listening," the masseur said. "Don't be draggy, Helene, run down the beach and ask Audrey Wise for a couple of lemons. Ask Audrey and Jerry for Bloodys even. I mean we could definitely stand a few giggles."

Helene opened her eyes. "You know what Jerry gave Audrey for her birthday?"

"Let me guess." BZ touched a finger to his tongue and held it to the wind. "One perfect white rose."

"One perfect thousand-dollar bill," Helene said. "Smartass."

"Maybe she can buy herself a good fuck," BZ said.

Helene giggled. "Jerry's a good phone."

"The *lemons*," the masseur said.

Carter threw down the script he was reading and stood up. "I'll get the goddamn lemons," he said. Maria lay perfectly still until she knew that he was beyond the dunes and then she sat up, everything swimming in her vision. Beneath the faded American flag hanging over the sun deck they were arranged in tableau: BZ and the masseur, their bodies gleaming, unlined, as if they had an arrangement with mortality. Helene stood on the edge of the deck, looking down the beach toward Audrey and Jerry Wise's house. Helene was not quite so immune to time, there was a certain texture to Helene's thighs, a certain lack of resilience where fabric cut into Helene's flesh. It occurred to Maria that whatever arrangements were made, they worked less well for women. That nervous steel heiress with whom Maria had last met the masseur, something bad had happened to her. She had been shot in the face by her fourteen-year-old son. It had been in the newspapers a few years ago. After the boy killed his mother he shot himself, and was later described by his father as a victim of divorce and drugs. Maria imagined that she had sunstroke. She closed her eyes and concentrated on a prayer she had learned as a child.

"That's one less for lunch," Helene said.

"I seem to have come in after the main titles," the masseur said petulantly. "Is he going to get the lemons or isn't he?"

"Faggots make Carter nervous," Helene said pleasantly.

BZ laughed and blew Helene a kiss off his fingertips. "Actually, Nelson," he said then, "that lemon is not artificial. That lemon is re*con*stituted."

Maria stood up and grabbed a beach towel from the deck and ran into the house with the towel clutched to her mouth and a few minutes later when, pale under her sunburn and covered with cold sweat, she stopped the dry heaves and pulled off her bathing suit she saw that for the fifty-first day she was not bleeding.

II

"I WASN'T JUST CRAZY about your asking Helene how much money BZ's mother gives them to stay married," Carter said on the way back in from the beach. The top was down and Carter was driving too fast because he had to meet Freddy Chaikin and a writer from New York at Chasen's at seven o'clock. "I wasn't just crazy about that at all."

"Well, she does."

"Does what."

"Carlotta gives them money to stay married."

"So what."

"I'm sick of everybody's sick arrangements."

"You've got a fantastic vocabulary."

She looked at him and she spoke very fast and low. "I've got a fantastic vocabulary and I'm having a baby."

Carter slowed the car down. "I missed a transition," he said finally.

Maria did not look at him.

"It's not mine," he said, his voice raised. "I suppose you're going to tell me it's not mine."

"I don't know."

She did not know why she had said it but she had to. She had to get it straight. For a moment Carter said nothing.

"You don't fucking know," he said then.

She put her bare feet on the dashboard and pressed her face against her knees. Now it was a fact. He could stay or he could leave, she had set forth the fact.

"Who was it," he said.

"You know."

He kept his eyes on the highway and his foot hard on the accelerator. She wanted to tell him she was sorry, but saying she was sorry did not seem entirely adequate, and in any case what she was sorry about seemed at once too deep and too evanescent for any words she knew, seemed so vastly more complicated than the immediate fact that it was perhaps better left unraveled. The late sun glazed the Pacific. The wind burned on her face. Once they were off the Coast Highway he pulled over to the curb and stopped the car.

"I know," he said. "But Felicia doesn't."

She said nothing. It was going to be bad.

"What makes you so sure," he said then.

"I didn't say I was sure." The air seemed suddenly still and close and she pulled off her scarf. "I said I didn't know."

"I mean what makes you so sure it's happening."

"Because I went to this doctor." She spoke very fast and kept her mind on something else. It seemed to her that they had once been to dinner at somebody's house who lived off San Vicente around here, she could not remember whose house it had been but there had been Japanese food and women with long handcrafted earrings and it had been summer. "Because I went to this doctor and the test he did in his office was positive but that's not an absolutely certain test so he had me bring in some urine for a rabbit test. And he gave me this shot. And if I really wasn't the shot would make me bleed in three to five days." She paused. It came to her that in the scenario of her life this would be what was called an obligatory scene, and she wondered with distant interest just how long the scene would play. "And it was six days ago I had the shot."

"What about the test."

"What test?"

"The test you were talking about. The second test."

"The rabbit test." She was suddenly almost too exhausted to speak. "I just never called back about it."

"You were afraid to call back about it." He was speaking in a careful monotone, a prosecutor with an open-and-shut case. "You thought if you didn't call back it would just go away."

She closed her eyes. "I guess so. I guess that's right."

"But now it's certain anyway. Otherwise the shot would have made you bleed."

She nodded mutely.

"What doctor. Who was the doctor."

"Just a doctor. On Wilshire."

"A doctor you didn't know. You thought that was smart."

She said nothing.

"I'm interested in the mechanics of this, Maria. I'm interested in how your mind works. How exactly you picked this doctor out, why this particular doctor."

Maria folded her scarf and smoothed it carefully over her bare knees. "He was near Saks," she whispered finally. "I was having my hair done at Saks."

12

LATE THAT NIGHT sitting alone in the dark by the pool she remembered whose house it had been out off San Vicente with the Japanese food, it had been the house of a couple named Sidney and Ruth Loomis. Sidney Loomis was a television writer and Ruth Loomis was very active in the civil-rights movement and group therapy. Maria had never been able to think of anything to say to Ruth Loomis, but in retrospect that was not why Carter had stopped seeing Sidney and Ruth Loomis. He had stopped seeing them because the show Sidney Loomis was writing had been canceled in midseason and he did not pick up another. Maria tried very hard to keep thinking of Carter in this light, Carter as a dropper of friends and names and obligations, because if she thought of Carter as he was tonight she would begin to cry again. He had left the house. He had neither met Freddy Chaikin at Chasen's nor called to say that he was not coming. She knew that because Freddy Chaikin had called for him. She had at last done something that reached him, but now it was too late. "What am I supposed to do," he had said before he left the house. "What in fuck am I supposed to do?"

13

WHEN CARTER CALLED the next morning it was from the motel on the desert. His voice was measured, uninflected, as if he had been saying the words to himself all night. "I love you," she whispered, but it was more a plea than a declaration and in any case he made no response. "Get a pencil," he ordered. He was going to give her a telephone number. He was going to give her the telephone number of the only man in Los Angeles County who did clean work.

"Then we'll see."

"I'm not sure I want to do that," she said carefully.

"All right, don't do it. Go ahead and have this kid." He paused, confident in his hand. She waited for him to play it through. "And I'll take Kate."

After he hung up she sat very still. She had a remote sense that everything was happening exactly the way it was supposed to happen. By the time she called him back she was calm, neutral, an intermediary calling to clarify the terms. "Listen," she said. "If I do this, then you promise I can have Kate? You promise there won't be trouble later?"

"I'm not promising anything," he said. "I said we'll see."

14

AT FOUR THAT AFTERNOON, after a day spent looking at the telephone and lighting cigarettes and putting the cigarettes out and getting glasses of water and looking at the telephone again, Maria dialed the number. A man answered, and said that he would call back. When he did he asked who had referred her.

"You want an appointment with the doctor," he said.

"When could he see me."

"The doctor will want to know how many weeks."

"How many weeks what?"

There was a silence. "How advanced is the *problem*, Maria," the voice said finally.

15

"THE FOOD WAS UNSPEAKABLE, my clothes mildewed in the closet, you can *have* Cozumel," BZ's mother said. She was playing solitaire and Maria sat transfixed by the light striking off the diamond bracelets on her thin tanned wrists. "Also Machu Picchu," she added, slapping down another card.

"I can't even dream why you stopped at Cozumel," Helene said. "I mean since you can't bear Mexicans."

"BZ said it was marvelous, that's why."

"BZ likes Mexicans."

"I know why BZ likes Mexicans." Carlotta Mendenhall Fisher shuffled the cards once and pointed at Maria. "Did you ask this child for dinner?" she demanded. "Or didn't you?"

"It's just seven, Carlotta. I thought we'd have another drink."

"I always serve at seven."

"The last time I was in Pebble Beach," Helene said, "you served at quarter to eleven."

Helene and her mother-in-law looked at each other for an instant and then Carlotta began to laugh. "This girl is my own natural child," she said finally to Maria, gasping through her laughter. "The daughter I didn't have."

"Speaking of the one you did have," Helene said, "does Nikki know you're back in the country?"

"*Nikki.* Nikki's like this child, I bore her." She looked at Maria. "Don't I bore you. Admit it."

Maria looked up uncertainly. The voice on the telephone had known what she wanted without either of them saying it. The voice on the telephone had said that this would be expensive. The voice on the telephone had told her that on the day set she was to bring a pad and a belt and $1,000 in cash. In confusion Maria looked away from Carlotta's bright blue eyes, glittering like her bracelets.

"Isn't it kind of . . ." Maria trailed off.

"Isn't *what*?"

"I mean Cozumel," Maria said finally. "Isn't it the off season."

"Of *course* the off season," Carlotta said triumphantly.

The voice had called her Maria.

The voice had said that he would be in touch.

"Carlotta's a demon for thrift," Helene said.

"Now what about my boring you," Carlotta said.

16

THE NEXT MORNING in the dry still heat she woke crying for her mother. She had not cried for her mother since the bad season in New York, the season when she had done nothing but walk and cry and lose so much weight that the agency refused to book her. She had not been able to eat that year because every time she looked at food the food would seem to arrange itself into ominous coils. She had known that there was no rattlesnake on her plate but once the image had seized her there was no eating the food. She was consumed that year by questions. Exactly what time had it happened, precisely what had she been doing in New York at the instant her mother lost control of the car outside Tonopah. What was her mother wearing, thinking. What was she doing in Tonopah anyway. She imagined her mother having a doctor's appointment in Tonopah, and the doctor saying cancer, and her mother cracking up the car on purpose. She imagined her mother trying to call her from a pay phone in Tonopah, standing in a booth with all her quarters and dimes and nickels spread on the shelf and getting the operator and getting New York and then the answering service picking up the call. Maria did not know whether any of that had actually happened but she used to think it, used to think it particularly around the time the sun set in New York, think about the mother dying in the desert light, the daughter unavailable in the Eastern dark. She would imagine the quarters and dimes and nickels spread out on the shelf and the light in the cottonwoods and she would wonder what she was doing in the dark. What time is it there, her mother would have asked had she gotten Maria. What's the weather. She might never have said what was on her mind but she would have left a coded message, said goodbye. One time Maria had saved enough money to give her mother a trip around the world, but instead she had lent the money to Ivan Costello, and then her mother was dead.

"I'm not crying," Maria said when Carter called from the desert at 8 A.M. "I'm perfectly all right."

"You don't sound perfectly all right."

"I had a bad dream."

There was a silence. "You called the doctor?"

"Yes. I called the doctor." She spoke very rapidly and distantly. "Everything's arranged. Everything's perfectly taken care of."

"What did—"

"I have to go now. I have to hang up. I have to see somebody about a job."

"Just hold on a minute, Maria, I want to know what the doctor said."

She was staring into a hand mirror, picking out her mother's features. Sometime in the night she had moved into a realm of miseries peculiar to women, and she had nothing to say to Carter.

"I said what did they *say*, Maria."

"They said they'd call me up some day and on the day they called me up I'd meet them some place with a pad and a belt and $1,000 in cash. All right, Carter? All right?"

17

ALTHOUGH THE HEAT had not yet broken she began that week to sleep inside, between white sheets, hoping dimly that the white sheets would effect some charm, that she would wake in the morning and find them stained with blood. She did this in the same spirit that she had, a month before, thrown a full box of Tampax into the garbage: to be without Tampax was to insure bleeding, to sleep naked between white sheets was to guarantee staining. To give the charm every opportunity she changed the immaculate sheets every morning. She wore white crêpe pajamas and no underwear to a party. She pretended to herself that she was keeping the baby, the better to invite disappointment, court miscarriage. "I'm having a baby," she heard herself telling the parking-lot attendant at Saks as they tried vainly to get a wicker bassinette into the Corvette. When it became clear that she would have to leave the bassinette for delivery she sat in the driver's seat of the Corvette and cried. She was crying too much. All the time now, when she was driving and when she was trying to clean a bathroom and when she was pretending to herself that she could have the baby, she was wondering where and when it was going to happen.

"Any calls," she asked the service.

"Mr. Goodwin, New York, three times, you're to call immediately."

She looked again into the hand mirror and again saw her mother. "Tell him I haven't picked up my messages." She had nothing to say to any of them.

18

"MONDAY," the voice on the telephone said. "Monday at five o'clock. We'll be in touch again on Monday."

"Where," she said. "Where do I go."

"I said we'll be in touch, Maria. We will."

She drove to the beach, but there was oil scum on the sand and a red tide in the flaccid surf and mounds of kelp at the waterline. The kelp hummed with flies. The water lapped warm, forceless. When she got back into town she drove aimlessly down Sunset, pulled into a drive-in at the corner of La Brea, and, briefly flushed into purposefulness by a Coca-Cola, walked barefoot across the hot asphalt to a telephone booth.

"This is Maria," she said helplessly when Felicia Goodwin picked up the telephone in New York. She did not know why but she had not counted on talking to Felicia. "I just wondered when you were coming back."

"We've been trying to get you for *days*." Felicia always spoke on the telephone as if a spurious urgency could mask her radical lack of interest in talking to anyone. Sometimes Maria was depressed by how much she and Felicia had in common. "Les was worried something had happened to you, I said no, she's on the desert with Carter—didn't you call the service?"

"Not exactly."

"Anyway we'll be out in a few days, this time to stay, we're going to buy a house—" Felicia's voice faded, as if she had stretched her capacity for communication to its limit.

"Les finished the script?"

"I'll get him," Felicia said with relief.

"Never mind," Maria said, but it was too late.

"Where've you been," he said.

"Nowhere." When she heard his voice she felt a rush of well-being. "I didn't want to call because—"

"I can't hear you, Maria, where are you?"

"In a phone booth. I just wanted—"

"You all right?"

"No. I mean yes." A bus was shifting gears on Sunset and she raised her voice. "Listen. Call me."

She walked back to the car and sat for a long while in the parking lot, idling the engine and watching a woman in a muumuu walk out of the Carolina Pines Motel and cross the street to a supermarket. The woman walked in small mincing steps and kept raising her hand to shield her eyes from the vacant sunlight. As if in trance Maria watched the woman, for it seemed to her then that she was watching the dead still center of the world, the quintessential intersection of nothing. She did not know why she had told Les Goodwin to call her.

19

"YOU WANT IT IN CASH," the teller said doubtfully.

"I'm taking a trip." She did not know why she was saying this but she kept on. "Mexico City, Guadalajara."

"You don't want traveler's checks?"

"*Cash*," she said, and when the teller handed her the bills she ran from the bank with them still in her hand.

In the car she counted the stiff bills. They stuck together and she missed one and she counted them four more times before she was certain she had them all. Since early morning she had been trying to remember something Les Goodwin had said to her, anything Les Goodwin had said to her. When she was not actually talking to him now she found it hard to keep him distinct from everyone else, everyone with whom she had ever slept or almost slept or refused to sleep or wanted to sleep. It had seemed this past month as if they were all one, that her life had been a single sexual encounter, one dreamed fuck, no beginnings or endings, no point beyond itself. She tried to remember how it had been to drag Fremont Street in Vegas with Earl Lee Atkins when she was sixteen years old, how it had been to go out on the desert between Vegas and Boulder and drink beer from half-quart cans and feel her sunburn when he touched her and smell the chlorine from her own hair and the Lava soap from his and the sweet sharp smell of starched cotton soaked with sweat. *How High the Moon*, the radio would play, Les Paul and Mary Ford. She tried to remember Ivan Costello, tried to fix in her mind the exact way the light came through the shutters in his bedroom in New York, the exact colors of the striped sheets she had put on his bed and the way those sheets looked in the morning and the look of a motel room in which they had once spent a week in Maryland. She tried to remember Carter. She tried to remember Les Goodwin. She could remember it all but none of it seemed to come to anything. She had a sense the dream had ended and she had slept on.

20

"NOTHING'S WRONG," she repeated to Les Goodwin on the telephone.

"I know something's wrong."

"Nothing."

"O.K.," he said finally. "All right. I'm coming out alone on Monday, meet my plane at four."

"I can't."

"I want to *talk* to you, Maria. I want to see you."

"Monday night," she said. "Listen. You make me happy."

She hung up very fast then because she did not want to find herself telling him why she could not meet his flight.

21

IN THE DREAM from which she woke when the telephone rang again that night she had the baby, and she and the baby and Kate were living on West Twelfth Street with Ivan Costello. In the dream she did not yet know Carter, but somehow had Carter's daughter and Carter's blessing. In the dream it was all right. She supposed that she had dreamed of Ivan Costello because the telephone was ringing, and he used to call her in the middle of the night. "How much do you want it," he used to say. "Tell me what you'd do to get it from me." The telephone was still ringing and she pulled the cord loose from the jack. She could not remember what she would have done to get it from any of them.

22

"YOU SHOULD ALWAYS CALL before you come," the nurse in charge of Kate's cottage said on Sunday. The nurse had short hair and a faint moustache and Kate clung to her knees and Maria did not like her. "The new medication, new treatment, naturally she's not—"

"What new medication," Maria heard herself saying. "You keep talking about the new medication, I mean *what is it*."

Kate screamed. The nurse looked reproachfully at Maria. "Methylphenidate hydrochloride."

Maria closed her eyes. "All right. Your point."

"We definitely would have suggested you wait until next week."

"I won't be here next week."

"You're going away?"

"Cozumel," Maria said. "Mexico."

On the way to the parking lot she twice invented pretexts to run back, kiss Kate's small fat hands, tell her to be good. The third time she ran back it was to find the nurse.

"One thing. You know when she wakes up at night and says '*oise, oise*,' it means she's . . ." Maria faltered. She realized that she expected to die. All along she had expected to die, as surely as she expected that planes would crash if she boarded them in bad spirit, as unquestionably as she believed that loveless marriage ended in cancer of the cervix and equivocal adultery in fatal accidents to children. Maria did not particularly believe in rewards, only in punishments, swift and personal. "It means she's having a nightmare," she said finally.

The nurse looked at her impassively.

"I mean I don't know if I ever told you that."

"I'm sure you did," the nurse said.

That night the house crackled with malign electricity. A hot wind came up at midnight and the leaves scraped the screens, a loose storm drain slapped against the roof. Sometime in the night Maria wrote three letters which, before dawn, she tore up and flushed down the toilet. The bits of paper kept floating back into the toilet bowl and by the time she finally got rid of them it was light, and all the daisies in the garden had been snapped by the wind, and the concrete around the swimming pool was littered with fallen palm fronds. At six-thirty that morning she placed a call to Carter at the motel on the desert but Carter had already left for the location. She interpreted that as a sign and did not try to call the location. She would do what he wanted. She would do this one last thing and then they would never be able to touch her again.

23

SHE TRIED TO STRAIGHTEN a drawer, and abandoned it. She heard fire reports on the radio, and turned the sprinklers on the ivy. For almost two hours she studied an old issue of *Vogue* she picked up in the poolhouse, her attention fixed particularly on the details of the life led in New York and Rome by the wife of an Italian industrialist. The Italian seemed to find a great deal of purpose in her life, seemed to make decisions and stick by them, and Maria studied the photographs as if a key might be found among them. When she had exhausted the copy of *Vogue* she got out her checkbook and a stack of bills and spread them on the kitchen table. Paying bills sometimes lent her the illusion of order but now each bill she opened seemed fresh testimony to her life's disorder, its waste and diffusion: flowers sent to people whom she had failed to thank for parties, sheets bought for beds in which no one now slept, an old bill from F.A.O. Schwarz for a tricycle Kate had never ridden. When she wrote out the check to Schwarz her hand trembled so hard that she had to void the first check, and smoke a cigarette before she could write another.

"Get it right, Maria," the voice on the telephone said. "You got a pencil there? You writing this down?"

"Yes," Maria said.

"Ventura Freeway north, you got that all right? You know what exit?"

"I wrote it down."

"All set, then. I'll meet you in the parking lot of the Thriftimart."

"What Thriftimart," Maria whispered.

"Maria, I told you, you can't miss it. Under the big red T."

In the aftermath of the wind the air was dry, burning, so clear that she could see the ploughed furrows of firebreaks on distant mountains. Not even the highest palms moved. The stillness and clarity of the air seemed to rob everything of its perspective, seemed to alter all perception of depth, and Maria drove as carefully as if she were reconnoitering an atmosphere without gravity. Taco Bells jumped out at her. Oil rockers creaked ominously. For miles before she reached the Thriftimart she could see the big red T, a forty-foot cutout letter which seemed peculiarly illuminated against the harsh unclouded light of the afternoon sky.

24

"YOU DRIVE," the man had said. "We'll pick up my car after."

He was wearing white duck pants and a white sport shirt and he had a moon face and a eunuch's soft body. The hand resting on his knee was pale and freckled and boneless and ever since he got in the car he had been humming *I Get a Kick Out of You*.

"You familiar with this area, Maria?"

The question seemed obscurely freighted. "No," Maria said finally.

"Nice homes here. Nice for kids." The voice was bland, ingratiating, the voice on the telephone. "Let me ask you one question, all right?"

Maria nodded, and tightened her grip on the steering wheel.

"Get pretty good mileage on this? Or no?"

"Pretty good," she heard herself saying after only the slightest pause. "Not too bad."

"You may have noticed, I drive a Cadillac. Eldorado. Eats gas but I like it, like the feel of it."

Maria said nothing. That, then, had actually been the question. She had not misunderstood.

"If I decided to get rid of the Cad," he said, "I might pick myself up a little Camaro. Maybe that sounds like a step down, a Cad to a Camaro, but I've got my eye on this par*tic*ular Camaro, exact model of the pace car in the Indianapolis 500."

"You think you'll buy a Camaro," Maria said in the neutral tone of a therapist.

"Get the right price, I just might. I got a friend, he can write me a sweet deal if it's on the floor much longer. They almost had a buyer last week but lucky for me—here, Maria, right here, pull into this driveway."

Maria turned off the ignition and looked at the man in the white duck pants with an intense and grateful interest. In the past few minutes he had significantly altered her perception of reality: she saw now that she was not a woman on her way to have an abortion. She was a woman parking a Corvette outside a tract house while a man in white pants talked about buying a Camaro. There was no more to it than that. "Lucky for you what?"

"Lucky for me, the guy's credit didn't hold up."

25

THE FLOOR OF THE BEDROOM where it happened was covered with newspapers. She remembered reading somewhere that newspapers were antiseptic, it had to do with the chemicals in the ink, to deliver a baby in a farmhouse you covered the floor with newspapers. There was something else to be done with newspapers, something unexpected, some emergency trick: quilts could be made with newspapers. In time of disaster you could baste newspapers to both sides of a cotton blanket and end up with a warm quilt. She knew a lot of things about disaster. She could manage. Carter could never manage but she could. She could not think where she had learned all these tricks. Probably in her mother's *American Red Cross Handbook*, gray with a red cross on the cover. There, that was a good thing to think about, at any rate not a bad thing if she kept her father out of it. If she could concentrate for even one minute on a picture of herself as a ten-year-old sitting on the front steps of the house in Silver Wells reading the gray book with the red cross on the cover (splints, shock, rattlesnake bite, rattlesnake bite was why her mother made her read it) with the heat shimmering off the corrugated tin roof of the shed across the road (her father was not in this picture, keep him out of it, say he had gone into Vegas with Benny Austin), if she could concentrate for one more minute on that shed, on whether this minute twenty years later the heat still shimmered off its roof, those were two minutes during which she was not entirely party to what was happening in this bedroom in Encino.

Two minutes in Silver Wells, two minutes here, two minutes there, it was going to be over in this bedroom in Encino, it could not last forever. The walls of the bedroom were cream-colored, yellow, a wallpaper with a modest pattern. Whoever had chosen that wallpaper would have liked maple furniture, a maple bedroom set, a white chenille bedspread and a white Princess telephone, all gone now but she could see it as it must have been, could see even the woman who had picked the wallpaper, she would be a purchaser of Audubon prints and scented douches, a hoarder of secret sexual grievances, a wife.

Two minutes in Silver Wells, two minutes on the wallpaper, it could not last forever. The table was a doctor's table but not fitted with stirrups: instead there were two hardbacked chairs with pillows tied over the backs. "Tell me if it's too cold," the doctor said. The doctor was tall and haggard and wore a rubber apron. "Tell me now because I won't be able to touch the air conditioner once I start."

She said that it was not too cold.

"No, it's too cold. You don't weigh enough, it's too cold."

He adjusted the dial but the sound remained level. She closed her eyes and tried to concentrate on the sound. Carter did not like air conditioners but there had been one somewhere. She had slept in a room with an air conditioner, the question was where, never mind the question, that question led nowhere. "This is just induced menstruation," she could hear the doctor saying. "Nothing to have any emotional difficulties about, better not to think about it at all, quite often the pain is worse when we think about it, don't like anesthetics, anesthetics are where we run into trouble, just a little local on the cervix, there, relax, Maria, I said *relax*."

No moment more or less important than any other moment, all the same: the pain as the doctor scraped signified nothing beyond itself, no more constituted the pattern of her life than did the movie on television in the living room of this house in Encino. The man in the white duck pants was sitting out there watching the movie and she was lying in here not watching the movie, and that was all there was to that. Why the volume on the set was turned up so high seemed another question better left unasked. "Hear that scraping, Maria?" the doctor said. "That should be the sound of music to you . . . don't scream, Maria, there are people next door, almost done, almost over, better to get it all now than do it again a month from now . . . I said don't make any noise, Maria, now I'll tell you what's going to happen, you'll bleed a day or so, not heavily, just spotting, and then a month, six weeks from now you'll have a normal period, not this month, this month you just had it, it's in that pail."

He went into the bathroom then (later she would try to fix in her mind the exact circumstances of his leaving the bedroom, would try to remember if he took the pail with him, later that would seem important to her) and by the time he came back the contractions had stopped. He gave her one envelope of tetracycline capsules and another of ergot tablets and by six o'clock of that hot October afternoon she was out of the bedroom in Encino and back in the car with the man in the white duck pants. The late sun seemed warm and benevolent on her skin and everything she saw looked beautiful, the summer pulse of life itself made manifest. As she backed out of the driveway she smiled radiantly at her companion.

"You missed a pretty fair movie," he said. "Paula Raymond." He reached into his pocket for what seemed to be a cigarette holder. "Ever since I gave up smoking I carry these by the dozen, they look like regular holders but all you get is air."

Maria stared at his outstretched hand.

"*Take* it. I noticed you're still smoking. You'll thank me some day."

"Thank you."

"I'm a regular missionary." The man in the white duck pants resettled his soft bulk and gazed out the car window. "Gee, Paula Raymond was a pretty girl," he said then. "Funny she never became a star."

26

"I WANT A VERY LARGE STEAK," she said to Les Goodwin in a restaurant on Melrose at eight o'clock that night. "And before the very large steak I want three drinks. And after the steak I want to go somewhere with very loud music."

"Like where."

"I don't know where. You ought to know *where.* You know a lot of places with loud music."

"What's the matter with you."

"I am just very very very tired of listening to you all."

27

SILVER WELLS was with her again. She wanted to see her mother. She wanted to go back to the last day she had spent with her mother: a Sunday. She had flown out from New York on Friday and then it was Sunday and Benny Austin was there for Sunday dinner and after dinner they would all drive down to Vegas to put Maria back on the airplane.

"Your mom's O.K., don't worry about your mom," Benny muttered when he and Maria were alone for a moment at the table. "Believe me it's nothing."

"What's nothing? What's the matter with her?"

"Nothing on God's earth, Maria, that's what I'm telling you. You might say she's a little depressed, naturally your father doesn't want to talk about it."

"Depressed," Maria repeated.

"Nothing, Maria, believe me. Here they come, we're talking about the zinc boom." Benny cleared his throat. "I've been telling Maria about the zinc boom, Harry."

"You into zinc?" Maria said finally. She was watching her mother but her mother looked just as she always had.

"We've been buying a few rights." Harry Wyeth began whistling through his teeth.

"Meal fit for the Queen of Spain," Benny said. "Francine, you could make a fortune in the take-out spare-rib business."

Francine Wyeth laughed. "Maria and I can always open a hash house. When we get sick of you all."

"Hash house on 95," Harry Wyeth said. "Pretty picture."

"*Not* on 95," Francine Wyeth said. "*Somewhere else.*"

Maria closed her eyes.

"I'm talking about a quantity operation. Franchises, you rent out your name and your receipt." Benny Austin talked as if nothing had happened at the table. "Franchised services, that's where the future lies."

"I don't want to go back," Maria said.

"That's natural." Harry Wyeth did not look at his wife or daughter. "That's only natural. Don't think about it, you'll be out again in a month or two, plan on it now."

"She's too thin," Francine Wyeth said. "Look at her, see for yourself."

"She can't win if she's not at the table, Francine." Harry Wyeth threw down his napkin and stood up. "You wouldn't understand that."

That night as the plane taxied out onto the runway at McCarran Maria had kept her face pressed against the window for as long as she could see them, her mother and father and Benny Austin, waving at the wrong window.

28

"HELENE'S GOING UP to Pebble Beach to spend the weekend with BZ's mother," Carter said when he called from the desert. "Why don't you fly up and meet her there."

"I can't."

"Too busy, I suppose."

Maria said nothing.

"Or maybe you're afraid you might have a good time."

"I said I *can't*."

"Why can't you, just for the record."

"She's not my mother," Maria said.

29

THE BLEEDING BEGAN a few weeks later. "It's nothing," the doctor on Wilshire said when she finally went. "Who-ever did it did all right. It's clean, no infection, count your blessings."

"The pain."

"You're just menstruating early, I'll give you some Edrisal."

The Edrisal did not work and neither did some Darvon she found in the bathroom and she slept that night with a gin bottle by her bed. She did not think she was menstruating. She wanted to talk to her mother.

30

"I'VE GOT NEWS," Freddy Chaikin said after the waiter had brought her Bloody Mary and his Perrier water. "I didn't want to break it until it was set. Morty Landau, I predicted it, he's in love with you. You've got a guest-star on a two-part *Interstate 80*."

"That's fine, Freddy." She tried for more conviction. "That's really fine."

He watched her drain her glass. "It'll get you seen."

"Actually I'm not feeling too well."

"You mean you don't want to work."

"I didn't say that. I just said I wasn't feeling too well."

"Maria, I empathize. What you and Carter are going through, it tears my heart out. Believe me, I've been through it. Which is why I know that *work is the best medicine for things wrong in the private-life department.* And I don't want to sound like an agent, but ten percent of nothing doesn't pay the bar bill." He laughed, and then looked at her. "A joke, Maria. Just a joke."

31

THE BLEEDING CAME AND WENT and came again. By late afternoon of her third day's work on *Interstate 80* there were involuntary pain lines on her forehead and she could not stand entirely upright for more than a few seconds. She sat back in the shadows on the edge of the set and prayed that the cameramen would be so slow with the set-ups that the day's last shot would be delayed until morning. At five-thirty they got the shot in three takes and later in the parking lot she could not remember doing it.

By midnight the blood was coming so fast that she soaked three pads in fifteen minutes. There was blood on the bed, blood on the floor, blood on the bathroom tiles. She thought about calling Les Goodwin—it would be all right to call him, she knew that Felicia was in San Francisco—but she did not. She called Carter.

"Get the doctor," Carter said.

"I don't exactly want to do that."

"For Christ's sake then get to an emergency hospital."

"I can't," she said finally. "The thing is, I'm working tomorrow."

"What do you mean, *work*ing. What in fuck does *work*ing mean. You just told me you were *dying*."

"I never said that."

"You said you were afraid."

Maria said nothing.

"Jesus Christ, Maria, I'm out here on the desert, I can't do anything, will you please get to a hospital or do you want me to call the police to come *get* you."

"You just want me in a hospital so that nothing'll happen to make you feel guilty," she said then, said it before she meant to speak, and when she heard the words she broke out in a sweat. "*Listen*," she said. "I didn't mean that. I'm just tired. Listen. I'll call the doctor right now."

"You have to swear to me." Carter's voice was drained, exhausted. "You have to swear you'll call the doctor. And call me back if something's wrong."

"I promise."

Instead she took a Dexedrine to stay awake. Awake she could always call an ambulance. Awake she could save herself if it came to that. In the morning, from the studio, she called the doctor.

"I'll meet you at St. John's," he said.

"I can't go to the hospital. I told you before, I'm working."

"You're hemorrhaging, you can't work."

"Oh yes I can work," she said, and hung up. She had wanted to ask him for more Dexedrine, but instead she got some from a hairdresser on the set. While she was changing she found a large piece of bloodied tissue on the pad she had been wearing, and she put it in an envelope and dropped it by the doctor's office on her way home from the studio. When she called the next day the doctor said that the tissue was part of the placenta, and that was the end of that. For the first time in two weeks she slept through the night, and was an hour late for her morning call.

32

"YOU WERE GOING to come over and use the sauna," Larry Kulik said.

"I've been—"

"So I hear."

"Hear what."

"Hear you're ready for a nuthouse, you want to know."

"You think I need a sauna."

"I think you need something."

Maria said nothing.

"I'm a good friend to people I like," Larry Kulik said. "Think it over."

33

A FEW DAYS LATER the dreams began. She was in touch with a member of a shadowy Syndicate. Sometimes the contact was Freddy Chaikin, sometimes an F.B.I. man she had met once in New York and not thought of since. Certain phrases remained constant. Always he explained that he was "part of that operation." Always he wanted to discuss "a business proposition." Always he mentioned a plan to use the house in Beverly Hills for "purposes which would in no way concern" her. She need only supply certain information: the condition of the plumbing, the precise width of the pipes, the location and size of all the clean-outs. Workmen appeared, rooms were prepared. The man in the white duck pants materialized and then the doctor, in his rubber apron. At that point she would fight for consciousness but she was never able to wake herself before the dream revealed its inexorable intention, before the plumbing stopped up, before they all fled and left her there, gray water bubbling up in every sink. Of course she could not call a plumber, because she had known all along what would be found in the pipes, what hacked pieces of human flesh.

34

IN NOVEMBER THE HEAT BROKE, and Carter went to New York to cut the picture, and Maria still had the dream. On the morning a sink backed up in the house in Beverly Hills she looked in the classified for another place to sleep.

"You'd be surprised the history this place has," the man said as he showed her the apartment. He was wearing a pumpkin velour beach robe and wraparound glasses and she had found him not in the apartment marked "Mgr." but out on Fountain Avenue, hosing down the sidewalk. "As a writer, it might interest you to know that Philip Dunne once had 2-D."

"I'm not a writer," Maria said.

"Excuse me, it was Sidney Howard." He took off his glasses and wiped them on a sleeve of the beach robe. "Or so the legend goes."

In December the Christmas tree on top of the Capitol Records Tower came and went, and Maria had Kate for three days. They drove up and down La Brea looking for a Christmas tree and had Christmas dinner at Les and Felicia Goodwin's new house and Kate smashed the Victorian doll Felicia had given her against a large mirror.

"She misses Carter," Felicia murmured, distraught beyond the immediate breakage.

"You don't know what the fuck you're talking about," Les Goodwin said.

Kate's eyes darted from Maria to Les to Felicia and back to Maria and then, preternaturally attuned to the threat of voices not even raised, she began to scream. The mother apologizing, the child screaming, the polished floor covered with shards of broken mirror and flesh-colored ceramic, they left the Christmas dinner. All that night the two of them held each other with a dumb protective ferocity but the next day at the hospital, parting, only Maria cried.

In January there were poinsettias in front of all the bungalows between Melrose and Sunset, and the rain set in, and Maria wore not sandals but real shoes and a Shetland sweater she had bought in New York the year she was nineteen. For days during the rain she did not speak out loud or read a newspaper. She could not read newspapers because certain stories leapt at her from the page: the four-year-olds in the abandoned refrigerator, the tea party with Purex, the infant in the driveway, rattlesnake in the playpen, the peril, unspeakable peril, in the everyday. She grew faint as the processions swept before her, the children alive when last scolded, dead when next seen, the children in the locked car burning, the little faces, helpless screams. The mothers were always reported to be under sedation. In the whole world there was not as much sedation as there was instantaneous peril. Maria ate frozen enchiladas, looked at television for word of the world, thought of herself as under sedation and did not leave the apartment on Fountain Avenue.

35

"I DON'T KNOW if you noticed, I'm mentally ill," the woman said. The woman was sitting next to Maria at the snack counter in Ralph's Market. "I'm *talking* to you."

Maria turned around. "I'm sorry."

"I've been mentally ill for seven years. You don't know what a struggle it is to get through a day like this."

"This is a bad day for you," Maria said in a neutral voice.

"What's so different about this day."

Maria looked covertly at the pay phones but there was still a line. The telephone in the apartment was out of order and she had to report it. The line at the pay phones in Ralph's Market suddenly suggested to Maria a disorganization so general that the norm was to have either a disconnected telephone or some clandestine business to conduct, some extramarital error. She had to have a telephone. There was no one to whom she wanted to talk but she had to have a telephone. If she could not be reached it would happen, the peril would find Kate. Beside her the woman's voice rose and fell monotonously.

"I mean you can't fathom the despair. Believe me I've thought of ending it. Kaput. Over. Head in the oven."

"A doctor," Maria said.

"*Doctor.* I've talked to doctors."

"You'll feel better. Try to feel better." The girl now using the nearest telephone seemed to be calling a taxi to take her home from Ralph's. The girl had rollers in her hair and a small child in her basket and Maria wondered whether her car had been repossessed or her husband had left her or just what had happened, why was she calling a taxi from Ralph's. "I mean you have to try, you can't feel this way forever."

"I'll say I can't." Tears began to roll down the woman's face. "You don't even want to talk to me."

"But I do." Maria touched her arm. "I do."

"*Get your whore's hands off me,*" the woman screamed.

36

"THERE'S SOME PRINCIPLE I'm not grasping, Maria," Carter said on the telephone from New York. "You've got a $1,500-a-month house sitting empty in Beverly Hills, and you're living in a furnished apartment on Fountain Avenue. You want to be closer to Schwab's? Is that it?"

Maria lay on the bed watching a television news film of a house about to slide into the Tujunga Wash. "I'm not living here, I'm just staying here."

"I still don't get the joke."

She kept her eyes on the screen. "Then don't get it," she said at the exact instant the house splintered and fell.

After Carter had hung up Maria wrapped her robe close and smoked part of a joint and watched an interview with the woman whose house it had been. "You boys did a really outstanding camera job," the woman said. Maria finished the cigarette and repeated the compliment out loud. The day's slide and flood news was followed by a report of a small earth tremor centered near Joshua Tree, 4.2 on the Richter Scale, and, of corollary interest, an interview with a Pentecostal minister who had received prophecy that eight million people would perish by earthquake on a Friday afternoon in March. The notion of general devastation had for Maria a certain sedative effect (the rattlesnake in the playpen, that was different, that was particular, that was punitive), suggested an instant in which all anxieties would be abruptly gratified, and between the earthquake prophecy and the marijuana and the cheerful detachment of the woman whose house was in the Tujunga Wash, she felt a kind of resigned tranquillity. Within these four rented walls she was safe. She was more than safe, she was all right: she had seen herself on *Interstate 80* just before the news and she looked all right. Warm, content, suffused with tentative small resolves, Maria fell asleep before the news was over.

But the next morning when the shower seemed slow to drain she threw up in the toilet, and after she had stopped trembling packed the few things she had brought to Fountain Avenue and, in the driving rain, drove back to the house in Beverly Hills. There would be plumbing anywhere she went.

37

"I'M GOING TO DO IT," she would say on the telephone.

"Then do it," Carter would say. "It's better."

"You think it's better."

"If it's what you want."

"What do *you* want."

"It's never been right," he would say. "It's been shit."

"I'm sorry."

"I know you're sorry. I'm sorry."

"We could try," one or the other would say after a while.

"We've already tried," the other would say.

By the time Carter came back to town in February the dialogue was drained of energy, the marriage lanced.

"I've got a new lawyer," she told him. "You can use Steiner."

"I'll call him today."

"I'll need a witness."

"Helene," he said. "Helene can do it." He seemed relieved that the dialogue had worn itself down to legal details, satisfied that he could offer Helene. He would be staying in BZ and Helene's guest house while they were looping and scoring the picture. He would speak to Helene immediately. Maria felt herself a sleepwalker to the courthouse.

"Let's see . . . an afternoon hearing." Helene spaced the words as if she were consulting an engagement book. "That means lunch before instead of after."

"We don't have to have lunch."

"Day of days, Maria. Of course lunch."

On the day of the hearing Maria overslept, thick with Seconal. When she walked into the Bistro half an hour late for lunch she could only think dimly how healthy Helene looked, how suntanned and somehow invincible with her silk shirt and tinted glasses and long streaked hair and a new square emerald that covered one of her fingers to the knuckle.

"Straighten your shoulders," Helene said, lifting her drink

slightly as Maria sat down. "You look spectral. We should go to the Springs together." Helene's eyes were not on Maria but on two women who sat across the room. "Allene Walsh has a new *friend*," she murmured to Maria as she smiled at the older of the two women. "They've been spooning food into each other's mouths for the past half hour."

"She's an actress named Sharon Carroll, I worked with her once." Maria tried to summon up some other detail to assuage Helene's avid interest in other people. "She kept a dildo in her dressing room."

"Allene Walsh has more dildoes around her house than anybody I ever knew. Look at my new ring."

"I saw it."

"From Carlotta." Helene studied the emerald. "For staying on the desert. Speaking of *new friends.* I mean he was shuttling them in and out of that motel like the dailies, I couldn't even get up for a Nembutal without knocking over somebody's bottle of *Monsieur Y.*" For an instant Helene's face seemed to lose its animation, and when she spoke again her voice was flat and preoccupied. "You look like hell, Maria, this isn't any excuse for you to fall apart, I mean a *divorce.* I've done it twice."

"I thought only once."

"Twice," Helene said without interest. "BZ says once because that's what he told his mother." She was intent upon her reflection in the mirror behind the table, tracing a line with one finger from her chin to her temple. "You can really tell," she said finally.

"Tell what?"

"Tell I haven't done my Laszlo in three days." Helene's voice was still flat but her interest seemed revived.

At two o'clock they met Carter and the lawyers outside the courtroom in Santa Monica, and at two-thirty Maria swore and Helene confirmed that the defendant, Carter Lang, had repeatedly struck and in other ways humiliated the plaintiff, Mrs. Maria Lang. The charge was mental cruelty, uncontested. This Mrs. Maria Lang to whom the lawyers referred seemed to Maria someone other than herself, an aggrieved wife she might see interviewed on television. As they waited for the details to be cleared up, the papers to be signed, Maria sat very still with her hands in her lap. Helene stirred restlessly beside her, her eyes across the aisle, on Carter and his lawyer. "*Carter,*" Helene whispered finally, leaning across Maria to attract his attention. "*Puzzle of the week. Guess which two dykes were seen feeding each other cheese soufflé in the Bistro today.*"

38

"WHAT HAVE YOU BEEN DOING," Carter said the next time she saw him.

"Working. I'm going to be working very soon."

"I mean who've you been seeing."

"Nobody. Helene. BZ. BZ comes by sometimes."

"Don't get into that," Carter said.

"He's your friend," Maria said.

39

THE FIRST TIME Maria ever met BZ it had been at the beach house and it had been two o'clock on a weekday afternoon and it was the summer Carter was cutting *Angel Beach.*

"I've got a meeting at the beach with this guy from San Francisco I told you about," Carter had said. "You come along and swim."

"I don't feel like swimming."

"Maria," Carter had said finally, "he's going to maybe put up some money. Maybe. All right?"

When they walked into the beach house she thought there must have been some misunderstanding, some mixup of time or day, because the man to whom Carter spoke was sitting alone with a projector in the darkened living room running a blue movie of extraordinary technical quality.

"Stroke of two, very prompt," the man had said, and looked at Maria for a long while before he turned off the projector.

"Did you get by the studio yesterday?" Carter seemed oblivious to the meeting's peculiar circumstance. "They show you the rough cut?"

"Fantastic."

"Did Helene see it?" Carter persisted. "Where's Helene?"

"On the beach."

"I'll get my suit on," Maria said, uneasy in the darkened room, and BZ had looked at her again, then flicked the projector back on.

"It's too cold to swim," he said, and then to Carter: "The rough cut looked fantastic, except you're missing the story."

"Meaning what."

"Meaning," BZ said, "how did Maria feel about the gang-bang, the twelve cocks, did she get the sense they're doing it not to her but to each *other*, does that *interest* her, you don't get that, you're missing the story."

The reel had run out and the only sound was the film slapping against the projector. "It's a commercial piece, BZ," Carter said finally.

BZ only shrugged, and changed the reel. Again the figures flooded the screen. Wordlessly, BZ sat on a pillow and began watching Maria. He rolled a cigarette and passed it to her, and when she passed it on to Carter he took it without looking away from the screen. Between the marijuana and the figures on the screen Maria felt flushed and not entirely in control.

"Look at the film, BZ," Carter had said suddenly. "Incredible, they've got opticals."

"I've seen the *film*, Carter," BZ had said, and never took his eyes from Maria.

40

"LET'S GO TO MEXICO CITY tonight," BZ said.

"Who?"

"You, me, Helene, I don't know, maybe Larry Kulik, just fly down for a couple of days, Susannah Wood's there now doing some interiors at Churubusco."

"I don't want to do that," Maria said.

"Yes you do," BZ said.

41

EVERY NIGHT she named to herself what she must do: she must ask Les Goodwin to come keep her from peril. Calmed, she would fall asleep pretending that even then she lay with him in a house by the sea. The house was like none she had ever seen but she thought of it so often that she knew even where the linens were kept, the plates, knew how the wild grass ran down to the beach and where the rocks made tidal pools. Every morning in that house she would make the bed with fresh sheets. Every day in that house she would cook while Kate did her lessons. Kate would sit in a shaft of sunlight, her head bent over a pine table, and later when the tide ran out they would gather mussels together, Kate and Maria, and still later all three of them would sit down together at the big pine table and Maria would light a kerosene lamp and they would eat the mussels and drink a bottle of cold white wine and after a while it would be time to lie down again, on the clean white sheets. In the story Maria told herself at three or four in the morning there were only three people and none of them had histories, only the man and the woman and the child and, in the lamplight, the opalescent mussel shells.

But by dawn she was always back in the house in Beverly Hills, uneasy in the queer early light, plagued by her own and his own and Kate's own manifold histories, certain that BZ and Larry Kulik and all their kind recognized her in a way that Les Goodwin might not want to, recognized her, knew her, had her number, understood as she did that the still center of the daylight world was never a house by the sea but the corner of Sunset and La Brea. In that empty sunlight Kate could do no lessons, and the mussels on any shore Maria knew were toxic. Instead of calling Les Goodwin she bought a silver vinyl dress, and tried to stop thinking about *what had he done with the baby. The tissue. The living dead thing, whatever you called it.*

42

"I'M GOING TO NEW YORK for a few days," she said to Carter. Going to New York had not before occurred to her but in the instant's confusion of running into Carter on the street in Beverly Hills the idea simultaneously materialized and assumed a real plausibility. It was something people did when they did not know what else to do, they went to New York for a few days. "Tomorrow morning," she added.

"What are you going to do in New York?"

"What do people usually do in New York."

He looked at her for a long time. She was aware that her hair was unkempt, her face puffy. She did not meet his eyes.

"They see a few plays," he said finally. "Maybe you can see a few plays."

"Maybe I can," she said, and walked away.

All that day Maria thought of fetuses in the East River, translucent as jellyfish, floating past the big sewage outfalls with the orange peels. She did not go to New York.

43

ONCE A LONG TIME BEFORE Maria had worked a week in Ocho Rios with a girl who had just had an abortion. She could remember the girl telling her about it while they sat huddled next to a waterfall waiting for the photographer to decide the sun was high enough to shoot. It seemed that it was a hard time for abortions in New York, there had been arrests, no one wanted to do it. Finally the girl, her name was Ceci Delano, had asked a friend in the District Attorney's office if he knew of anyone. "Quid pro quo," he had said, and, late the same day that Ceci Delano testified to a blue-ribbon jury that she had been approached by a party-girl operation, she was admitted to Doctors' Hospital for a legal D & C, arranged and paid for by the District Attorney's office.

It had seemed a funny story as she told it, both that morning by the waterfall and later at dinner, when she repeated it to the photographer and the agency man and the fashion coordinator for the client. Maria tried now to put what had happened in Encino into the same spirited perspective, but Ceci Delano's situation seemed not to apply. In the end it was just a New York story.

44

THE LETTER from the hypnotist was mimeographed, and came to Maria in care of the studio that had released *Angel Beach*. "YOUR WORRIES MAY DATE FROM WHEN YOU WERE A BABY," the letter began, and then, after a space, were the words "IN YOUR MOTHER'S WOMB." Maria read the letter very carefully. The hypnotist had found that many people could be regressed not only to infancy but to the very instant of their conception. The hypnotist would receive a few interested clients in the privacy of his Silverlake home. With a sense that she was about to confirm a nightmare, Maria telephoned the number he gave.

45

"YOU'VE BEEN BRUSHING IT wet," the hairdresser said, lifting a strand of Maria's hair and letting it drop with distaste.

"I guess so." Maria could never keep up her end of the dialogue with hairdressers.

"I told you before, you split the ends," he said with no real interest, and then transferred his attention to a thin girl who had just come up and kissed the back of his neck. "How are you, babe."

"I had an operation."

"No kidding."

"Pelvic abscess." The girl loosened her wrapper and absently stroked her collarbone. "All through my tubes."

"Listen, I hear his new act is just lying there," the hairdresser said. "Bibi Markel was just over there and she heard they were trying to transfer his contract to the lounge."

"*Macht nicht* to me," the girl said. "Except maybe I'll have to go to court for the separate maintenance." She slipped one big roller away from her scalp and touched the hair to see if it was dry. "Listen," she said suddenly. "Finish her and then comb me out and come up for a drink on your way home."

"Where you living now."

"Off Coldwater, same place. O.K.? Promise?"

"I'll think about it."

"Please. Promise."

He ignored her, and handed Maria a mirror. "You want to use a drier, Maria honey?"

But Maria only shook her head and took the fifteen dollars from her bag and walked very fast toward the dressing room.

"Maybe I can get Sandy to come up." Even from the dressing room Maria could hear the girl wheedling, the thin beautiful girl with the pelvic abscess and the separate maintenance and her hair all done and nobody to drink with. She fixed her attention on the mounds of used wrappers and damp towels and tried not to hear whatever it was the girl would say next. The girl was a presentiment of something. "*Listen*," the girl said then. *"Maybe I can get Bibi Markel."*

46

SHE HAD WATCHED THEM in supermarkets and she knew the signs. At seven o'clock on a Saturday evening they would be standing in the checkout line reading the horoscope in *Harper's Bazaar* and in their carts would be a single lamb chop and maybe two cans of cat food and the Sunday morning paper, the early edition with the comics wrapped outside. They would be very pretty some of the time, their skirts the right length and their sunglasses the right tint and maybe only a little vulnerable tightness around the mouth, but there they were, one lamb chop and some cat food and the morning paper. To avoid giving off the signs, Maria shopped always for a household, gallons of grapefruit juice, quarts of green chile salsa, dried lentils and alphabet noodles, rigatoni and canned yams, twenty-pound boxes of laundry detergent. She knew all the indices to the idle lonely, never bought a small tube of toothpaste, never dropped a magazine in her shopping cart. The house in Beverly Hills overflowed with sugar, corn-muffin mix, frozen roasts and Spanish onions. Maria ate cottage cheese.

47

"YOU'RE LYING IN WATER," the hypnotist said. "You're lying in water and it's warm and you hear your mother's voice."

"No," Maria said. "I don't."

The hypnotist stood up. He always seemed cold and he was always sipping Pernod and water and his house was dusty and cluttered with torn newspaper clippings and stained file folders. "What do you hear," he said finally. "What do you hear and see in your mind right now. What are you doing."

"I'm driving over here," Maria said. "I'm driving Sunset and I'm staying in the left lane because I can see the New Havana Ballroom and I'm going to turn left at the New Havana Ballroom. That's what I'm doing."

48

THERE WAS AT FIRST that spring an occasional faggot who would take her to parties. Never a famous faggot, never one of those committed months in advance to escorting the estranged wives of important directors, but a third-string faggot. At first she was even considered a modest asset by several of them: they liked her not only because she would listen to late-night monologues about how suicidal they felt but because the years she spent modeling had versed her in precisely the marginal distinctions which preoccupied them. She understood, for example, about shoes, and could always distinguish among the right bracelet and the amusing impersonation of the right bracelet and the bracelet that was merely a witless copy. Still, there remained some fatal lack of conviction in her performance, some instant of flushed inattention that would provoke them finally to a defensive condescension. Eventually they would raise their eyebrows helplessly at one another when they were with her, and be oversolicitous. "Darling," they would say, "have another drink." And she would. She was drinking a good deal in the evenings now because when she drank she did not dream. "This way to the gas, ladies and gentlemen," a loudspeaker kept repeating in her dreams now, and she would be checking off names as the children filed past her, the little children in the green antechamber, she would be collecting their lockets and baby rings in a fine mesh basket. Her instructions were to whisper a few comforting words to those children who cried or held back, because this was a humane operation.

49

"LEONARD'S IN NEW YORK for ten days," Helene said as soon as Maria had hung up the telephone. "Did I tell you?"

"Three times," Maria said. Leonard was Helene's hairdresser.

"I don't mind if I'm out of town, but if I'm *in* town and Leonard's *not*—who was that on the telephone?"

"Somebody's leg man."

"What do you mean, somebody's? Whose?"

"Some columnist in the trades. I don't know."

"What did he want?"

"He wanted to know if I was dating anyone in particular. He also wanted to know what I thought of Carter's dating Susannah Wood."

Helene shrugged. "You knew that."

"I mean the word dating? Doesn't it strike you funny?"

"Not particularly." Helene was studying her hair line in a small mirror. "If I'm *in* town, and Leonard's *not*, I feel almost . . . frightened."

Maria said nothing.

"I don't suppose you understand that."

Maria watched the tears welling in Helene's eyes. "Don't, Helene," she said finally. "Don't be depressed."

"It's shit," Helene said. "It's all shit."

50

Everything Maria could think to do in the town she had already done. She had checked into the motel, she had eaten a crab at the marina. At three in the afternoon she had been the only customer in the marina restaurant and it had been a dispiriting thirty or forty minutes, sliced beets staining the crab legs and a couple of waitresses arguing listlessly and a piped medley from *Showboat.* After that she had walked on the gravelly sand and she had driven aimlessly to Port Hueneme and back to Oxnard and now she sat on a bench in the downtown plaza, watching some boys in ragged Levi jackets and dark goggles who sat on the grass near her car. Their Harleys were pulled up to the curb and they seemed to be passing a joint with furtive daring and every now and then they would look over at her and laugh. Because there was an oil fire somewhere to the north a yellow haze hung over the town, a stillness over the plaza. On the next bench an old man coughed soundlessly, spit phlegm that seemed to hang in the heavy air. A woman in a nurse's uniform wheeled a bundled neuter figure silently past the hedges of dead camellias. Maria closed her eyes and imagined the woman coming toward her with a hypodermic needle. When she opened her eyes again the boys in the Levi jackets seemed to be rifling the glove compartments of parked cars. To hear the sound of her own footsteps Maria stood up and walked to the pay phone by the public toilet and asked the operator to try the number in Los Angeles again.

She would tell him she could not wait.

She would tell him she was sitting in a park watching some hoods rifling cars and she could not wait.

Maybe she would not feel this way if she talked to him, maybe he would make her laugh. Maybe she would hear his voice and the silence would break, the woman in the nurse's uniform would speak to her charge and the boys would get on their Harleys and roar off.

But when the operator got the studio a voice said only that Mr. Goodwin could not be reached.

When she hung up the phone the silence was absolute. The boys in the Levi jackets were all watching her now, because they were standing around her car, they knew it was her car, they had watched her lock it. They were trying various keys. They were watching to see what she would do. As if in slowed motion she began walking across the grass toward the car, and as she got closer they melted back, formed a semicircle. Abstractly she admired the way that she and they together were evolving a choreography, hearing the same silent beat. She kept her eyes steady, her pace even, and when she found herself unlocking the car under their blank gaze it was with extreme deliberation. As she slid into the driver's seat she stared directly at each of them, one by one, and in that instant of total complicity one of them leaned across the hood and raised a hand in recognition of what had passed between them, his palm out, inscribing an arc in the still air. Later those few minutes in the plaza in Oxnard would come back to Maria and she would replay them, change the scenario. It ended that way badly, or well, depending on what you wanted.

51

SHE SAT IN THE MOTEL ROOM near the Southern Pacific tracks in Oxnard and waited for Les Goodwin to call. He had said nine-thirty or ten but she had driven past the theater in the afternoon, the marquee read MAJOR STUDIO PREVIEW 8 P.M. An eight o'clock sneak meant eleven, by the time they counted the cards. When the telephone rang, it was quarter to eleven and he said it would be another half hour. Maria took two Librium, washed her face although she had showered an hour before, straightened the immaculate room as if to erase any sign of herself. When there was nothing left to straighten she walked across the parking lot to the ice machine by the swimming pool and filled a paper bucket with ice. After she had arranged the bucket on a tray with two water glasses and a bottle of whisky she sat on the bed and turned the pages of the Oxnard–Port Hueneme telephone book. There were fourteen Wyeths listed, twenty-three Langs and twenty Goodwins.

When she finally opened the door for him she avoided his eyes, buried her face against his shirt. They were both shaking. He poured Scotch into the two glasses without ice and they sat down on the bed and still they had not looked at each other.

"I almost didn't come," he said then. "I called the house this afternoon, I was going to tell you I wasn't coming up, they'd canceled the preview."

"I know."

"You know."

"I was going to tell you I was here and couldn't wait."

"You came up this afternoon?"

"I didn't have anything in particular to do in town," she said, and then she looked at him. "I came up this afternoon because I was afraid you'd call me up and tell me they'd canceled the preview."

"This is a lousy place," he said finally. "Let's get out of here."

They drove up the coast until they were exhausted enough to sleep, and then they did sleep, wrapped together like children in a room by the sea in Morro Bay.

"I've got until tomorrow, we can go on up the coast," he said the next morning.

"We could go up to Big Sur."

"We could have a picnic, we could stay at the Lodge."

"We could buy a sleeping bag and sleep on the beach."

"I've got to call Felicia," he said then.

"Wait until I'm dressed."

She dressed with her back to him, then left the motel room and walked down to the water. A culvert had washed out and the equipment brought in to lift it was mired in the sandy mud. Bare-legged and bare-armed, shivering in her cotton jersey dress, she stood for a long while watching them try to free the equipment. When she got back to the motel he was dressed, sitting on the unmade bed.

"Don't cry," he said.

"There's no point."

"No point in what."

"No point in our doing any of those things."

He looked at her for a long while. "Later," he said then.

"I'm sorry."

"It's all right."

On the drive back they told each other that it had been the wrong time, the wrong place, that it was bad because he had lied to arrange it, that it would be all right another time, idyllic later. He mentioned the strain he had been under, he mentioned that the preview had gone badly. She mentioned that she was getting the curse. They mentioned Kate, Carter, Felicia, the weather, Oxnard, his dislike of motel rooms, her fear of subterfuge. They mentioned everything but one thing: that she had left the point in a bedroom in Encino.

52

MARIA MADE A LIST of things she would never do. She would never: *walk through the Sands or Caesar's alone after midnight*. She would never: *ball at a party, do S-M unless she wanted to, borrow furs from Abe Lipsey, deal*. She would never: *carry a Yorkshire in Beverly Hills*.

53

"I'LL BE AWAY a few weeks," Carter said. "I came by because I'll be away, I wanted to tell you—you know the picture's entered at Cannes."

"I read that."

"You seen it yet?"

"How would I have seen it, it's not in release, I mean is it?"

"Maria, for Christ's fucking sake, they've been screening it every night for a month, you know that—oh shit."

"I didn't mean to be that way," she said after a while.

"You never mean to be any way."

It was always that way when he came by but sometimes later, after he had left, the spectre of his joyless face would reach her, talk about heart's needle, would flash across her hapless consciousness all the images of the family they might have been: Carter throwing a clear plastic ball filled with confetti, Kate missing the ball. Kate crying. Carter swinging Kate by her wrists. The spray from the sprinklers and the clear plastic ball with the confetti falling inside and Kate's fat arms stretched up again for the catch she would always miss. Freeze frame. Kate fevered, Carter sponging her back while Maria called the pediatrician. Kate's birthday, Kate laughing, Carter blowing out the candle. The images would flash at Maria like slides in a dark room. On film they might have seemed a family.

"Listen," Maria said to Carter the night before he left for Cannes. She had put off calling until almost midnight but had finally made herself do it. "The picture's fine. I went to a screening, it's a beautiful picture."

There was a silence. "If you need to reach me call BZ," he said then. "He'll know where I am."

"The picture. I really liked it."

"Fine. Thanks."

"What's the matter."

"Just forget it, Maria." His voice was tired. "There hasn't been a print in Los Angeles all week."

During the next few weeks Maria bought *Daily Variety* and *The Hollywood Reporter* and studied them dutifully for small mentions of Carter. After Cannes he seemed to be in London, and after that in Paris again, where he appeared on television discussing the *auteur* principle.

"Carter's staying another week in Paris, I guess you know," Helene said on the telephone.

"The touring *auteur*," Maria said.

Helene paused only slightly. "BZ called them last night, apparently she has to stay over to talk about a picture."

"I suppose he was pleased about Cannes."

"He didn't talk about it much but she said—"

"You think you're telling me something, Helene, you're missing the point."

Helene giggled. "Whose point."

That afternoon Maria had a small accident with the Corvette, received a call from the bank about her overdrawn account, and learned from the drugstore that the doctor would no longer renew her barbiturate prescriptions. In a way she was relieved.

54

MARIA STOOD IN THE SUN on the Western street and waited for the young agent from Freddy Chaikin's office to back his Volkswagen past the Writers' Building to where she was. It was hot and no one had left her name at the gate and there was a spot on her skirt and she was annoyed because of the trouble at the gate and because Freddy Chaikin had not come himself. He had arranged for her to see a director who wanted her for a bike picture and the least he could have done was show up himself. She did not even want to do another bike picture.

"Looks like we missed him," the young agent said. He did not turn the motor off.

"How do you mean, we missed him."

"I mean I guess he's already left for lunch." The agent looked uncomfortably past Maria. "Actually it wasn't two hundred percent confirmed, he told Freddy he might be tied up with the girl they're looking at for the lead."

Maria pushed her hair back and watched the agent avoid her eyes. "What exactly did they want me for," she said finally.

"The high-school teacher, Freddy must've told you that. You read the script, that's the *part*, the lead's just any teeny fluff. I mean the *teacher*, she . . . she carries the picture."

"The teacher," Maria said. "Who plays the Angel Mama?"

"His girlfriend."

"I have to go now," Maria said, and without waiting for him to speak she turned and began walking toward the gate. Once in her car she drove as far as Romaine and then pulled over, put her head on the steering wheel and cried as she had not cried since she was a child, cried out loud. She cried because she was humiliated and she cried for her mother and she cried for Kate and she cried because something had just come through to her, there in the sun on the Western street: she had deliberately not counted the months but she must have been counting them unawares, must have been keeping a relentless count somewhere, because this was the day, the day the baby would have been born.

55

"I WANT TO TELL YOU right now I'm never going to do anything again," Ivan Costello had said in the beginning. "If you want to live that way, O.K. There's not going to be any money and there's not going to be any eating breakfast together and there's not going to be any getting married and there's not going to be any baby makes three. And if you make any money, I'll spend it."

She had said she wanted to live that way.

"What if I did," she had said a long time later.

"Did what."

"Got pregnant. Then at least I'd have a baby."

"No you wouldn't," he had said.

56

"MAYBE NEXT TIME," the hypnotist said. "Next week."

"I'm not coming next week." Maria did not look at him. "I can't come any more."

The hypnotist watched her as she opened her bag, found her car keys, dropped them beneath a sofa cushion and groped for them. The room was overheated but he was wearing two faded cardigan sweaters and standing over a furnace vent.

"It doesn't prove anything, you know," he said.

"What doesn't."

"That you couldn't open enough doors to get back. Your failure. It doesn't prove anything at all."

"I have to leave."

He shrugged. As she stood up he was pouring water into a cheese glass coated with Pernod, swirling the mixture into a milky fluid.

"Some people resist," he said. "Some people don't want to know."

Maria drove down to the New Havana Ballroom on Sunset and, trembling, made a telephone call.

"I need help," she said. "Ivan, I need help bad."

57

"WHO'S YOUR FRIEND," Ivan Costello said. "Who loves you."

It was five o'clock in Los Angeles and eight in New York and he was drunk. She should have known better than to call him. She did not even like him. She could not bring herself to give the answer he expected, could not pick up the old litany, could not say *you do.*

"I don't know," she said.

"What's the matter with you."

"I just wanted to talk to you."

"You just wanted . . ." He paused, and she knew that he was turning on her. "To *talk* to me."

She said nothing. The bar in the New Havana was empty and smelled of disinfectant and the bartender was watching her distrustfully.

"You mean you want to talk to me direct, you don't want me to make an appointment? Go through your agent?"

"All right. I get it."

"You're *feel*ing good enough to talk to me? You aren't sick? You aren't asleep? You aren't out of town? You aren't just fucking una*vail*able?"

"Ivan—"

"'Ivan' *shit.*"

"All right," she said. "O.K."

"You want to know what I think of your life?"

"No," she said, but he was already spitting into the telephone.

In the morning he left four messages on the service and Maria returned none of them. She did call Larry Kulik.

58

MARIA SAT ON A COUCH in the ladies' room of the Flamingo with the attendant and a Cuban who was killing the hour between her ten o'clock and midnight dates and she knew that she could not go back out to the craps tables.

"Like a cemetery," the Cuban said.

The attendant shrugged. "Every place the same."

"Not the Sands, I could hardly get through the Sands tonight."

"So do business at the Sands."

"Fucking negrita," the Cuban said without rancor, and looked at Maria appraisingly. "You sick? You need something?"

"I'm all right," Maria said. "Thank you."

She could not go back to the tables because Benny Austin was out there. Somehow she had never expected to see Benny Austin again: in her mind he was always in her father's pickup, or standing with her mother and father on the tarmac at McCarran waving at the wrong window. There was something wrong with running into Benny Austin in the Flamingo. "Maria?" he had called when he saw her. "*Maria?* That you?" He was shorter than she remembered him, shorter and more frail, almost bald, a failed man wearing a lariat tie clasp. "Jesus if you aren't the picture of Francine," he kept saying. "Jesus but you're her daughter." He had asked her if she was married. He had shrugged and said that the course of true love never was a straight flush. He had ordered Cuba Libres for the two of them and he had talked about *as it was* and finally she had run. He would be waiting there still, trying to run up a stake for her with the chips she had left, that was like Benny, he would play her chips until they were gone and then he would play his own for her, waiting, holding the Cuba Libre until the ice was gone. Benny would wait there all night. Benny would lay anybody in the Flamingo five-to-one that Harry and Francine Wyeth's daughter would not run out on him, and five-to-one were the best odds Benny would lay on the sun rising.

When Maria heard herself being paged she asked the Cuban for a match and gave no sign that she was Maria Wyeth.

Maybe it was Benny paging her but having people paged was not much Benny's style, more likely it was Larry Kulik. She smoked a cigarette and tried not to think about Benny hearing her name and looking around, adjusting his tie clasp and holding his bets, wondering who was calling Harry and Francine's girl, waiting for her to reappear and introduce her friend, make it an evening. After Maria had finished the cigarette she took a back elevator up to Larry Kulik's suite.

59

"TELL HIM TO COME UP," Larry Kulik said, handing her a drink while she waited for the operator to page Benny Austin. In the other room there were some of Larry Kulik's well-manicured friends and a couple of girls, one of them the Cuban she had seen in the ladies' room. The Cuban had given her no sign of recognition. "Guys like that interest me, you'd be surprised."

"I wouldn't be surprised at all. Tell that spic to turn the music down."

She waited. "Benny?" She raised her voice over the clatter of the slot machines downstairs. "Benny, I got sick, I—"

"Christ, Maria, why didn't you say something, I got a good friend, house doctor at the Mint."

"I just need some rest. Benny? Can you hear me? You come see me the next time you're in Los Angeles, all right? Promise?"

"Sure, honey, swell. I'd like that."

Maria felt a rush of shame. Benny Austin never came to Los Angeles. "Listen," she said suddenly. "You remember the last time you saw me? Remember? You and Mother and Daddy put me on the plane at McCarran? And before that we ate spare ribs at the house? Remember?"

"Sure, honey, you bet. Next time I'm over we'll paint the town."

For a long while Maria lay on the bed and stared at a large oil painting of a harlequin. In a sense the day they ate spare ribs and drove to McCarran had ceased to exist, had never happened at all: she was the only one left who remembered it. Maria followed this thought for as far as it would go, which was not very far, and then she got up and opened the door. A second-string comedian had come in with some of his entourage, and a girl Maria had seen drinking in the lounge.

"New talent," the comedian said, looking at Maria.

"She's not talent," Larry Kulik said.

At dawn she woke Larry Kulik and told him she was taking the seven o'clock flight out.

"Stick around," he said. "What is it with you, you want to get paid for your time or something? So I crapped out on you last night. So what."

"That's not it."

"Suit yourself," Larry Kulik said.

60

AT A PARTY IN MAY she left not with the choreographer who had brought her but with an actor she had never before met. They had danced together and shared a joint in the garden and he told her that they would leave and go up to his house. He had some friends there. Maria was wearing the silver vinyl dress she had bought to make her feel better and her hair was loose and her feet were bare and driving up through the canyon in the actor's Ferrari she felt good for the first time in a long while. The actor had a tape in the car that played *Midnight Hour* over and over again and when they got to his house he introduced her to the eight or ten people in the living room as Myra. "This is Myra," he said. "I just found her some place." Four or five joints were being passed in the living room and she smoked one and then went to find a Coca-Cola. In the kitchen she danced by herself and felt a little dizzy but still good. She liked his not knowing her. She did not much like him but she liked his not knowing her.

"Let's fuck," the actor said from the doorway.

"You mean right here."

"Not here, in the bed." He seemed annoyed.

She shook her head.

"Then do it here," he said. "Do it with the Coke bottle."

When they finally did it they were on the bed and at the moment before he came he reached under the pillow and pulled out an amyl nitrite popper and broke it under his nose, breathed in rapidly, and closed his eyes.

"Don't move," he said. *"I said don't move."*

Maria did not move.

"Terrific," he said then. His eyes were still closed.

Maria said nothing.

"Wake me up in three hours," he said. "With your tongue."

After he had gone to sleep she got dressed very quietly and walked out of the house. She was in the driveway before she remembered that she had no car. The keys were in his Ferrari and she took it, hesitating when she came out to the main canyon road, turning then not toward Beverly Hills but toward the Valley, and the freeway. It was dawn before she reached Vegas and, because she stopped in Vegas to buy cigarettes, eight o'clock before she reached Tonopah. She was not sure what she had meant to do in Tonopah. There was something about seeing her mother's and father's graves, but her mother and father were not buried in Tonopah. They were buried in Silver Wells, or what had been Silver Wells. In any case she was stopped for speeding outside Tonopah and when the highway patrolman saw the silver dress and the bare feet and the Ferrari registered to someone else, he checked California to see if the car had been reported stolen, and it had.

61

THEY LET HER make one call, and she called Freddy Chaikin. It was not as easy for Freddy to fix as it might have been, because when they vacuumed the car they picked up marijuana, but still, by sundown, she was flying back across the desert with Freddy in a Lear he had borrowed from a client. Freddy had done everything. Freddy had driven out to the Malibu ranch where the actor was shooting a Western and had told the actor whom to call to retract the complaint. Freddy had waited there while the actor did it. Freddy had gotten in touch with one of the big savings-and-loan Democrats, who got in touch with someone in Nevada and the marijuana came off the report. And now as the jet gained altitude Freddy was handing Maria a drink. She was still wearing the silver dress and she was still barefoot and her face was streaked with dust and when she tasted the drink it all came up, all the pills and the not eating and the liquor and the fear and the way she had felt about the actor and the way she had felt when the matron had her finger up her looking for drugs, all that came up in a trail of mucous on the floor of the Lear that Freddy had borrowed in his day-long effort to protect Carter. Freddy watched her clean it up.

"I don't understand girls like you," he said finally.

She clutched a towel to her mouth but the convulsion passed.

"I mean there's something in your behavior, Maria, I would almost go so far as to call it . . ." Freddy paused, and lit a cigarillo with his gold Cartier lighter. When he spoke again he measured each word. "Almost go so far as to call it a very self-destructive personality structure."

Maria closed her eyes. "You know what, Freddy?"

"What."

"I'd almost go so far as to call you—"

Freddy Chaikin flicked the gold lighter closed and smiled at her.

Maria took his hand, and went to sleep.

62

TWO DOZEN ROSES ARRIVED from the actor, or rather from his business manager. Maria knew that the business manager had sent them because his name was on the delivery slip.

"Hey, babe," the actor said when he called. "You didn't have to call out the tactical nukes."

"I don't know what you're talking about."

"I'm talking about Freddy Chaikin, he shows up at ten o'clock in the morning and tries to lay it on me I'll never be in a package with any of his clients again. I mean I was *shoot*ing."

"I was in *jail*."

"Just hold on, cunt," the actor said, his voice rising. *"You never told me who you were."*

"I hear you had a rather baroque morning-after," Helene said.

Helene came to the house all the time now. Sometimes Maria would pretend no one was home but today Helene had walked in without ringing and come directly upstairs. She sat on the edge of the bed and took out a cigarette.

"How exactly did you hear that," Maria said finally. She had taken so many showers during the past several hours that her skin felt damp between the sheets, but the smell of Helene's cigarette and perfume was making her feel dirty again. "I mean what exactly did you hear."

"Just that. Carter called from New York and told BZ."

"I haven't even talked to Carter."

"Freddy did, naturally." Helene picked up Maria's lipstick and studied the effect of the color on the back of her wrist. "I mean Freddy is seriously worried about you, Carter is seriously worried about you, BZ and *I* are—"

"I'm *all right*."

"Of course. You're really on top of it. I mean for example there's nothing at all peculiar about hiding here under the covers shaking at three o'clock in the afternoon. Nothing at all off about leaving a party with Johnny Waters and ending up in jail in Nevada at eight o'clock the next morning. Nothing wrong there."

"I've got a headache. I'm in bed because my head aches."

"I'll get a Darvon."

Maria pulled the sheet up to her chin.

"I'm just trying to help you, Maria."

"I'll be all right." Maria sat up and touched Helene's arm. "Really, Helene. I promise."

"All right, never mind, I'm leaving." Helene stood up and smoothed the bed where she had been sitting and then stared at herself for a long while in the mirror on the dressing-room door. "What kind of fuck is Johnny Waters?" she asked finally.

During the next week Freddy Chaikin made a number of telephone calls to various television producers asking, "as a personal favor to Carter," that Maria be considered for parts, even day work. "Anything to take her mind off herself," Freddy said to each of them. "What we've got here is a slightly suicidal situation." Maria knew about these calls because Helene told her about them.

"I saw a picture of you today," Helene said.

"Where." Every time she went downstairs Helene seemed to be there.

"You know that employment agency on Beverly? The one where you got the Guatemalan who stole your diaphragm?"

"I don't know." Maria did not want to think about the Guatemalan who had taken her diaphragm.

"You do too know. They've got all those studio stills on the wall? Satisfied customers? Anyway, now they've got a picture of you, signed 'Good luck, Maria Wyeth.'"

"Well, fine," Maria said. "I didn't think you'd be in town again today."

Helene looked at her and giggled. "BZ sent me," she said finally. "BZ wants me to get you to spend a few weeks at the beach."

Maria said nothing.

"You looked years younger in this picture, I must say." Helene laughed again. "'Good luck, Maria Wyeth.'"

"Dear Maria," the note read. *"Well don't know when I'll get over to LA but wanted to give you a telephone where you can*

call if you are in Nevada again or need help. Have some things of your Dad's I want to give you, also because you are like my own daughter there will be a little windfall from this quarter some day, not too soon let's hope. Have all your Dad's papers plus mineral certificates, no action now but quien sabe, once knew a man who thought his rights were worthless and he was sitting on pitchblende so loaded with U. the counters went haywire. Call me at number below and ask for Benny, phone belongs to lady next door, also she cooks for me sometimes. Not like your Mom. Ha ha. Your Friend Benny C. Austin."

Maria was listening to someone talk and every now and then she would hear herself making what she thought was an appropriate response but mostly she was just swaying slightly with the music and wondering where her drink was when suddenly Felicia Goodwin took her arm.

"We're leaving now, Maria. We'll drop you."

"I have my car, thanks, I'm fine."

"Les?" Felicia was talking over her shoulder. "I need you."

Maria picked up someone else's drink and smiled past Felicia at Les. "Crowd scene," she said. "Principals emerge."

"You come with Felicia and me, Maria. I'll get your car tomorrow."

Maria put the glass down and looked at him for a long while.

"I didn't come with you," she said very clearly then. "Thank Christ."

After that she was crying, and Helene was holding her arm while BZ got her coat.

"I thought it merited a mention," Felicia Goodwin whispered.

"Let it *go*," Helene said. Grateful, Maria put her head on Helene's shoulder and let herself be led outside. In the car she was sick on Helene's lap, and told BZ he was a degenerate.

When she woke before dawn in Helene's bedroom she saw that someone had undressed and bathed and creamed her body. At first she thought she was alone in the room but then she saw BZ and Helene, sprawled together on a chaise. She had only the faintest ugly memory of what had brought BZ and Helene together, and to erase it from her mind she fixed her imagination on a needle dripping sodium pentathol into her

arm and began counting backward from one hundred. When that failed she imagined herself driving, conceived audacious lane changes, strategic shifts of gear, the Hollywood to the San Bernardino and straight on out, past Barstow, past Baker, driving straight on into the hard white empty core of the world. She slept and did not dream.

63

"I GUESS I DRANK too much last night," Maria said carefully.

"Don't talk about it." Helene was staring out the kitchen window, holding a cup of coffee in her two hands as if for warmth. Her eyes were puffy and there was a bruise on her left cheekbone and her voice was soft and vague. "I don't want to talk about it. The wind makes me feel bad."

"I just don't remember getting here." Maria had a flash image of BZ holding a belt and Helene laughing and she tried not to look at the bruise on Helene's face. "That's all I was saying."

Tears began falling down Helene's face. "Don't *talk* about it. And don't say you don't remember, either."

"I didn't—" Maria broke off. BZ was standing in the doorway.

"I picked up your car." BZ dropped the keys on the table and looked from Maria to Helene. "What have we here," he said softly. "A little hangover terror? A few second thoughts? Is that about the size of it?"

Helene said nothing.

"I can't take this, Helene." BZ was wearing tinted glasses and for the first time Maria noticed a sag beneath his eyes. "If you can't deal with the morning, get out of the game. You've been around a long time, you know what it is, it's play-or-pay."

"Why don't you go tell that to Carlotta," Helene whispered.

Maria closed her eyes at the instant BZ's hand hit Helene's face. "Stop it," she screamed.

BZ looked at Maria and laughed. "You weren't talking that way last night," he said.

64

FROM A PAY PHONE on the highway outside Las Vegas she called the number Benny Austin had given her. The number was no longer in service.

"You here all alone?" the bellboy in the Sands asked, lingering after she had tipped him.

"My husband's meeting me here."

"Is that right? Today? Tomorrow?"

She looked at him. "Go away," she said.

The room was painted purple, with purple Lurex threads in the curtains and bedspread. Because her mother had once told her that purple rooms could send people into irreversible insanity she thought about asking for a different room, but the boy had unnerved her. She did not want to court further appraisal by asking anyone for anything. To hear someone's voice she looked in the telephone book and dialed a few prayers, then took three aspirin and tried not to think about BZ and Helene.

In the morning she went to the post office. Because it was Saturday the long corridors were deserted, and all but one of the grilled windows shuttered. Her sandals clattered against the marble and echoed as she walked.

"Could you put this in Box 674," she said to the clerk at the one open window. 674 was the number on the envelope of Benny Austin's letter.

"Can't."

"Why not."

"It's got to have postage. It's got to go through the United States mail."

Sullenly he studied the nickel and penny she gave him, then pushed one stamp under the grill and watched her stamp the note.

"Now could you put it in 674?"

"No," he said, and threw the letter into a canvas bin.

She found a bench near Box 674 and sat down. At noon the last window slammed shut. Maria drank from the water cooler, smoked cigarettes, read the F.B.I. posters. Wandering the country somewhere were Negro Females Armed with Lye, Caucasian Males posing as Baby Furniture Representatives, Radio Station Employees traveling out of Texas with wives and children and embezzled cash and Schemes for Getting Money and Never Delivering on Piecework, an inchoate army on the move. Maria crossed the street to a diner with a view of the post office and tried to eat a grilled-cheese sandwich.

On the third day a woman unlocked Box 674. She was wearing a soiled white uniform and she had a hard sad face and Maria did not want to speak to her.

"Excuse me," she said finally. "I'm trying to reach Benny Austin—"

"What *is* this." The woman was holding Maria's letter and her eyes darted from the letter to Maria.

"Actually I sent that letter—"

"And now you want it back."

"No. Not at all. I want you to give it to Benny Austin and tell—"

"I don't know any Benny person. And I think it's pretty funny this letter addressed to some Benny person in my box and then right off you sashay up and start dropping the same name, either you've been tampering in my box, a federal offense, or you're trying some other mickey mouse and believe me you've got the wrong party."

Maria backed away. The woman's face was white and twisted and she was following Maria, her voice rising. "You're Luanne's foster mother, is exactly who you are, and you're nosing around Vegas because you heard about the injury settlement, well just you *forget* it. I said *forget it.*"

65

"WHAT DO YOU THINK," Maria could hear one of the men saying. She was trying to eat an egg roll in the Sands and the two men and the girl had been watching her ever since she sat down.

"About what," the girl said.

"That."

The girl shrugged. "Maybe."

The other man said something that Maria did not hear and when she looked up again the girl was still watching her.

"Thirty-six," the girl said. "But a good thirty-six."

For the rest of the time Maria was in Las Vegas she wore dark glasses. She did not decide to stay in Vegas: she only failed to leave. She spoke to no one. She did not gamble. She neither swam nor lay in the sun. She was there on some business but she could not seem to put her finger on what that business was. All day, most of every night, she walked and she drove. Two or three times a day she walked in and out of all the hotels on the Strip and several downtown. She began to crave the physical flash of walking in and out of places, the temperature shock, the hot wind blowing outside, the heavy frigid air inside. She thought about nothing. Her mind was a blank tape, imprinted daily with snatches of things overheard, fragments of dealers' patter, the beginnings of jokes and odd lines of song lyrics. When she finally lay down nights in the purple room she would play back the day's tape, a girl singing into a microphone and a fat man dropping a glass, cards fanned on a table and a dealer's rake in closeup and a woman in slacks crying and the opaque blue eyes of the guard at some baccarat table. A child in the harsh light of a crosswalk on the Strip. A sign on Fremont Street. A light blinking. In her half sleep the point was ten, the jackpot was on eighteen, *the only man that could ever reach her was the son of a preacher man*, someone was down sixty, someone was up, Daddy wants a popper and she *rode a painted pony let the spinning wheel spin*.

*

By the end of a week she was thinking constantly about where her body stopped and the air began, about the exact point in space and time that was the difference between *Maria* and *other*. She had the sense that if she could get that in her mind and hold it for even one micro-second she would have what she had come to get. As if she had fever, her skin burned and crackled with a pinpoint sensitivity. She could feel smoke against her skin. She could feel voice waves. She was beginning to feel color, light intensities, and she imagined that she could be put blindfolded in front of the signs at the Thunderbird and the Flamingo and know which was which. "Maria," she felt someone whisper one night, but when she turned there was nobody.

She began to feel the pressure of Hoover Dam, there on the desert, began to feel the pressure and pull of the water. When the pressure got great enough she drove out there. All that day she felt the power surging through her own body. All day she was faint with vertigo, sunk in a world where great power grids converged, throbbing lines plunged finally into the shallow canyon below the dam's face, elevators like coffins dropped into the bowels of the earth itself. With a guide and a handful of children Maria walked through the chambers, stared at the turbines in the vast glittering gallery, at the deep still water with the hidden intakes sucking all the while, even as she watched; clung to the railings, leaned out, stood finally on a platform over the pipe that carried the river beneath the dam. The platform quivered. Her ears roared. She wanted to stay in the dam, lie on the great pipe itself, but reticence saved her from asking.

"Just how long have you been here now," Freddy Chaikin asked when she ran into him in Caesar's. "You planning on making a year of it? Or what?"

"Two weeks, Freddy. I haven't been here *even* two weeks."

"Jesus Christ, two weeks in Vegas."

"I like the good talk."

"I'm over for Lenny's opening, you coming?"

She tried to think who Lenny was. "I'm not seeing too many people, actually."

"That's not healthy, you're morbid enough. Do me a favor, come on over after. Lenny's suite. A *lot* of people you know."

"I'll see."

"Maria. A personal favor. You owe me one, O.K.? 1202, that's in the *new* building."

"Could you tell me how to find 1202," she asked the man at the desk in the hotel. When she had called up from the lobby there was too much noise to understand Freddy's directions.

She waited. The desk clerk did not look up.

"I'm looking for 1202."

He lifted his eyes only slightly. "No," he said.

"You don't understand. I don't know how to get to the new building."

"I do understand, honey. I understand *very well.* No dice. If they want you up there they'd tell you how to get there. Freelance some place else."

When she got back to the Sands she looked at herself in the mirror for a long while, then called room service and asked for a double bourbon. When the boy came he looked at her.

"Pretty early still," he said.

She poured a few drops of bourbon over the ice and watched it coat the glass. It seemed to her now that she had been driving all week toward precisely this instant. "I don't know anyone," she heard herself saying.

"Lots of guys around."

"I don't know any."

"I could make an introduction."

She looked at him. "All right," she said. "In an hour."

After he left she waited five minutes and then walked into the corridor and out onto the burning floodlit parking lot and an hour later she was deep into the desert, driving west at eighty miles an hour. Early in the morning she called Freddy Chaikin from Los Angeles and asked him to pay her bill and bring back her clothes.

"What happened."

Maria did not answer.

"I don't even want to know," Freddy Chaikin said.

"Don't forget my dark glasses," Maria said.

66

"WHAT DO YOU WEIGH NOW? About eighty-two?"

Maria opened her eyes. The voice was Carter's but for an instant in the bright afternoon light on the sun deck she could not make out his features.

"I didn't know you'd be here today," she said finally.

"Helene told me you were coming out."

"Helene is a veritable Celebrity Register."

"Just calm down. I want to talk about something." He looked back toward the house. BZ was on the telephone in the living room. "Let's walk down the beach."

"We can talk here."

"Have it your way, we can talk here." He kicked aside her sandals and sat down. "I've been trying to get hold of you for two weeks."

"I know it."

"No games, Maria, O.K.? I came all the way out here, I walked out of a meeting, a meeting with Carl Kastner, just to—"

She reached for his hand and put it over his mouth. She was absurdly touched by the detail about Carl Kastner: Carter was still Carter. "I haven't wanted to see you because I didn't feel good. That's all. Talk to me."

Carter took out a cigarette, crumpled the package, then smoothed out the package and replaced the cigarette. "You know I'm starting the new picture on the desert in ten days," he said finally. "You knew about that." He was not looking at her. "Which means this: it means—"

"It means," she prompted after a pause.

He looked at her. "I want you out there."

Maria said nothing.

"We could do it."

"Why should we."

Carter looked uncomfortable. "It just might be better."

"You mean you don't think I can take care of myself."

"No." Carter stood up. "I do not. I do not think you can take care of yourself. Things I've been hearing, things I—"

"What things."

"You know goddamn fucking well what things."

He stood over Maria with his hand frozen in air. He had been about to hit her.

"Go ahead," she said. "You can't hurt me."

"Fantastic day," a clear voice said, and Carter dropped his arm. A girl with long tangled hair and a short chemise nightgown stood in the doorway, yawning and shaking out her hair. "You suppose there's any coffee?" The girl examined what seemed to be a bite on her arm and walked out into the sun. "I mean I could die for some."

"I don't know," Maria said.

"BZ honey?" the girl called. "Is there coffee made?"

"No," BZ said from the house. "There is no coffee. There is *not any coffee*."

"Honey, there must be instant," the girl drawled. From the doorway she smiled back at Carter. "I'm Jeanelle," she said.

"Who the fuck was that," Carter said after a moment.

Maria sat huddled in a towel. "I guess that's Jeanelle."

"Who's she for?"

"How should I know."

Carter looked at her. "Stop it," he said finally. "Stop crying. Baby, listen. Stop."

"I don't know what to do."

"You're going to come to the desert with me."

"Just as a point of interest, you going to be fucking Susannah Wood out there?"

Carter pulled her to her feet and kissed her. She stood without moving and after a while he let his arms drop.

"What's the matter now," he said.

"Nothing."

"It's all gone with you," he said. "It used to be there but it's gone."

"Listen," she said as if by rote. "I love you."

"You know what I wish it was tonight?" the girl in the nightgown was saying when Maria came inside at four o'clock. "I wish it was New Year's Eve. Most people think New Year's Eve is a bore but I love it."

Helene lay on a couch staring at the ceiling. "You do," she said.

"Helene," BZ said. "Maria's going to the desert with us, isn't that interesting?" BZ smiled at Maria. "I said Maria's going to the desert, Helene."

"I heard you."

"I also love Christmas," the girl said.

"Jeanelle," BZ said, "there's some coke in the bedroom if you want to go get it. Some Merck."

"You've been holding out," Jeanelle said.

BZ watched the girl leave and then turned to Helene. "Get her out of here," he said.

Helene stared at him. "You started it," she whispered.

67

"YOU TOLD ME YOU'D COME," Carter said.

"What for."

"I want you out there."

"It's all gone, you said so yourself."

"All right," Carter said. "Stay here and kill yourself. Something interesting like that."

Carter and BZ and Helene left for the desert. Maria found a doctor who would give her barbiturates again, and in the evenings she drove.

"Who is it," she whispered when she saw the lighted cigar in the dark living room. She had just let herself into the house and locked the door behind her and now she leaned against it. "I said who is it."

The cigar moved. She closed her eyes.

"Who do you think it is," Ivan Costello said. "Maybe if you'd call your answering service once in a while you'd know when I was in town."

"What are you doing in my house."

"Come here."

She turned on a light.

"I said come here."

"No." She could see that he was drunk. "I'm going out."

"You aren't going anywhere. Don't tell me no."

"No."

"All right," he said. "Fight me. You'll like it better that way anyway."

"What did you come here for," she said at three or four in the morning.

"What I got."

"What did you come here for," she repeated.

"I didn't come here to hurt you, if that's what you mean."

She said nothing.

"Oh Christ," he said. "Baby. I just came to make you remember."

"I can't remember."

"You remembered all right the last three hours."

She wrapped her arms around her bare shoulders. "That hasn't got anything to do with me."

"Baby, it used to."

"Get out of here," she said, and this time he did.

In the morning he came again. She answered the door and went back to the couch where she had spent the rest of the night.

"You don't have to crack up over this," he said. "You used to tell me you'd do it for me until you died. You used to tell me—"

"I used to tell you a lot of things." She could still smell cigar smoke on his coat. "Leave me alone."

"I'll leave you alone," he said finally. "See how you like it."

She lay on the couch, her eyes fixed on a bowl of dead roses, until four o'clock in the afternoon. At four she called Les Goodwin.

"Something bad is going to happen to me," she said.

"Something bad is going to happen to all of us."

She could hear a typewriter in the background. "I mean it. Take me somewhere."

"You got a map of Peru?"

She said nothing.

"That's funny, Maria. That's a line from *Dark Passage*."

"I know it."

"I had a fight with Felicia at lunch, I've got to have a rewrite by tomorrow morning, I tell you something funny and you don't laugh."

"When I want to hear something funny I'll call you up again."

After she hung up she packed one bag and drove to the desert.

68

When I first married Carter and my name began appearing in columns I received mail from mad people. I am not much engaged by the problems of what you might call our day but I am burdened by the particular, the mad person who writes me a letter. It is no longer necessary for them even to write me. I know when someone is thinking of me. I learn to deal with this.

69

THE FIRST NIGHT in the still heat of the motel on the desert Carter turned away from Maria without speaking. The second night he got up and lay down on the bed in the other room.

"What's the matter," Maria said, standing in the doorway in the dark.

"It isn't any better."

"How do you know."

He said nothing.

"I mean we didn't even try."

"You don't want it."

"I do too."

"No," he said. "You don't."

Maria turned away. After that either she or Carter slept most nights in the other room. Some nights he said that he was tired, and some nights she said that she wanted to read, and other nights no one said anything.

In the motel on the desert there were the two rooms, and a bathroom with a scaling metal shower stall, and a kitchenette with a few chipped dishes and an oilcloth-covered table. The air conditioner was broken, and through the open windows at night Maria could hear the jukebox from the bar across the road. On those nights when Carter could not sleep she lay perfectly still, her eyes closed, and waited for the moment when Carter would begin banging drawers, slamming doors, throwing a magazine across the bed where she lay.

"You aren't waking me up," she would say then. "I'm not asleep."

"Well *go* to sleep, cunt. Go to sleep. Die. Fucking vegetable."

After that point he would sleep. She would not.

By the time Maria woke at eight-thirty or nine in the morning it would already be 105°, 110°. Carter would be gone. For the first week Maria would wash in the trickle that came from the shower and drink a Coca-Cola in the bathroom and then drive out to the location, but on Monday of the second week Carter asked her to leave at lunchtime.

"You're making Susannah nervous," he said. "It's only her second picture, she's worried about working against Harrison, now you're here—the point is, when an actress is working, there's a certain—"

"I've worked once or twice. As an actress."

Carter avoided her eyes. "Maybe you and Helene could do something."

"Maybe we could see some plays."

70

THE TOWN WAS ON A DRY RIVER bed between Death Valley and the Nevada line. Carter and BZ and Helene and Susannah Wood and Harrison Porter and most of the crew did not think of it as a town at all, but Maria did: it was larger than Silver Wells. Besides the motel, which was built of cinder block and operated by the wife of the sheriff's deputy who patrolled the several hundred empty square miles around the town, there were two gas stations, a store which sold fresh meat and vegetables one day a week, a coffee shop, a Pentecostal church, and the bar, which served only beer. The bar was called The Rattler Room.

There was a bathhouse in the town, an aluminum lean-to with a hot spring piped into a shallow concrete pool, and because of the hot baths the town attracted old people, believers in cures and the restorative power of desolation, eighty- and ninety-year-old couples who moved around the desert in campers. There were a few dozen cinder-block houses in the town, two trailer courts, and, on the dirt road that was the main street, the office for an abandoned talc mine called the Queen of Sheba. The office was boarded up. Fifty miles north there was supposed to be a school, but Maria saw no children.

"You can't call this a bad place," the woman who ran the coffee shop told Maria. The fan was broken and the door open and the woman swatted listlessly at flies. "I've lived in worse."

"So have I," Maria said. The woman shrugged.

By late day the thermometer outside the motel office would register between 120° and 130°. The old people put aluminum foil in their trailer windows to reflect the heat. There were two trees in the town, two cottonwoods in the dry river bed, but one of them was dead.

71

"YOU'RE WITH THE MOVIE," the boy at the gate to the bathhouse said. He was about eighteen and he had fair pimpled skin and he wore a straw field hat to ward off the sun. "I guessed it yesterday."

"My husband is."

"You want to know how I guessed?"

"How," Maria said.

"Because I—" The boy studied his grimy fingernails, as if no longer confident that the story illustrated a special acumen. "Because I personally know everybody from around here," he said then, his eyes on his fingernails. "I mean I guessed right away you weren't somebody I already knew."

"Actually I come from around here." Maria had spoken to no one else all day and she did not want to go into the bathhouse. She did not even know why she had come to the bathhouse. The bathhouse was full of old people, their loose skin pink from the water, sitting immobile on the edge of the pool nursing terminal cancers and wens and fear. "Actually I grew up in Silver Wells."

The boy looked at her impassively.

"It's across the line. I mean it's on the test range."

"How about that," the boy said, and then he leaned forward. "Your husband couldn't be Harrison Porter, could he?"

"No," Maria said, and then there seemed nothing more to say.

"My room, my game." Susannah Wood was sitting on her bed rolling cigarettes. "So turn up the sound."

Carter walked over to the bank of amplifiers and speakers and tape reels that Susannah had brought with her to the desert.

"Somebody's going to complain," Maria repeated.

"So what," Susannah Wood said, and then she laughed. "Maria thinks we're going to get ar*rest*ed for pos*ses*sion. Maria thinks she's already *done* that number in Nevada."

BZ looked up. "Turn it down, Carter."

Susannah Wood looked first at BZ and then at Maria. "Turn it up, Carter."

Maria stood up. It was midnight and she was wearing only an old bikini bathing suit and her hair clung damply to the back of her neck. "I don't like any of you," she said. "You are all making me sick."

Susannah Wood laughed.

"That's not funny, Maria," Helene said.

"I mean sick. Physically sick."

Helene picked up a jar from the clutter on Susannah Wood's dressing table and began smoothing cream into Maria's shoulders. "If it's not funny don't say it, Maria."

"What about Susannah," Maria asked Carter. She was standing in the sun by the window brushing her hair.

"What about her."

Maria brushed her hair another twenty strokes and went into the bathroom. "I mean did you really like fucking her."

"Not particularly."

"I wonder why not," Maria said, and closed the bathroom door.

"Where's Carter," Maria said when she came into BZ's room.

"We had some trouble with Harrison, Carter stayed out there to block a scene with him. You want a drink?"

"I guess so. They coming back here?"

"I said we'd meet them in Vegas. Helene's there already."

"Let's not have dinner at the Riviera again."

"Harrison likes the Riviera."

Maria leaned back on Helene's bed. "I'm tired of Harrison." She licked the inside of her glass and let the bourbon coat her tongue. "Some ice might help."

"The refrigerator's broken. Roll a number."

Maria closed her eyes. "And I'm also tired of Susannah."

"What else are you tired of."

"I don't know."

"You're getting there," BZ said.

"Getting where."

"Where I am."

72

THEY HAD BEEN on the desert three weeks when Susannah Wood got beaten up in a hotel room in Las Vegas. The unit publicity man got over there right away and Harrison Porter did a surprise Telethon for Southern Nevada Cystic Fibrosis and there was no mention of the incident. When Maria asked Carter what had happened he shrugged.

"What difference does it make," he said.

Susannah Wood was not badly hurt but her face was bruised and she could not be photographed. Carter tried to shoot around her until the bruise was down enough to be masked by makeup but by the end of the fourth week they were running ten days over schedule.

"Was it Harrison?"

"It's over, she's O.K., drop it." Carter was standing by the window watching for BZ's car. BZ had been in town for meetings at the studio. "Susannah doesn't take things quite as hard as you do. So just forget it."

"Was it you?"

Carter looked at her. "You think that way, get your ass out of here."

In silence Maria pulled out a suitcase and began taking her clothes from hangers. In silence Carter watched her. By the time BZ walked in, neither of them had spoken for ten minutes.

"They're on your back," BZ said. He dropped his keys on the bed and took an ice tray from the refrigerator.

"I thought they liked the dailies."

"Ralph likes them. Kramer says they're very interesting."

"What does that mean."

"It means he wants to know why he's not seeing a master, two, closeup and reaction on every shot."

"If I started covering myself on every shot we'd bring it in at about two-five."

"All right, then, it doesn't mean that. It means he wants Ralph to hang himself with your rope." BZ looked at Maria. "What's she doing?"

"Ask her," Carter said, and walked out.

*

"Harrison did it," BZ said. "What's the problem."

"Carter was there. Wasn't Carter there."

"It was just something that got a little out of hand."

Maria sat down on the bed beside her suitcase. "Carter was there."

BZ looked at her for a long while and then laughed. "Of course Carter was there. He was there with Helene."

Maria said nothing.

"If you're pretending that it makes some difference to you, who anybody fucks and where and when and why, you're faking yourself."

"It does make a difference to me."

"No," BZ said. "It doesn't."

Maria stared out the window into the dry wash behind the motel.

"You know it doesn't. If you thought things like that mattered you'd be gone already. You're not going anywhere."

"Why don't you get me a drink," Maria said finally.

"What's the matter," Carter would ask when he saw her sitting in the dark at two or three in the morning staring out at the dry wash. "What do you want. I can't help you if you don't tell me what you want."

"I don't want anything."

"Tell me."

"I just told you."

"Fuck it then. Fuck it and fuck you. I'm up to here with you. I've had it. I've had it with the circles under your eyes and the veins showing on your arms and the lines starting on your face and your fucking menopausal depression—"

"Don't say that word to me."

"*Menopause. Old.* You're going to get *old*."

"You talk crazy any more and I'll leave."

"Leave. For Christ's sake *leave*."

She would not take her eyes from the dry wash. "All right."

"Don't," he would say then. "Don't."

"Why do you say those things. Why do you fight."

He would sit on the bed and put his head in his hands. "To find out if you're alive."

In the heat some mornings she would wake with her eyes swollen and heavy and she would wonder if she had been crying.

73

THEY HAD TEN DAYS LEFT on the desert.

"Come out and watch me shoot today," Carter said.

"Later," she said. "Maybe later."

Instead she sat in the motel office and studied the deputy sheriff's framed photographs of highway accidents, imagined the moment of impact, tasted blood in her own dry mouth and searched the grain of the photographs with a magnifying glass for details not immediately apparent, the false teeth she knew must be on the pavement, the rattlesnake she suspected on the embankment. The next day she borrowed a gun from a stunt man and drove out to the highway and shot at road signs.

"That was edifying," Carter said. "Why'd you do it."

"I just did it."

"I want you to give that gun back to Farris."

"I already did."

"I don't want any guns around here."

Maria looked at him. "Neither do I," she said.

"I can't take any more of that glazed expression," Carter said. "I want you to wake up. I want you to come out with us today."

"Later," Maria said.

Instead she sat in the coffee shop and talked to the woman who ran it.

"I close down now until four," the woman said at two o'clock. "You'll notice it says that on the door, hours 6 A.M. to 2 P.M., 4 P.M. to—"

"6:30 P.M.," Maria said.

"Well. You saw it."

"What do you do between two and four."

"I go home, I usually—" The woman looked at Maria. "Look. You want to come out and see my place?"

The house was on the edge of the town, a trailer set on a concrete foundation. In place of a lawn there was a neat expanse of concrete, bordered by a split-rail fence, and beyond the fence lay a hundred miles of drifting sand.

"I got the only fence around here. Lee built it before he took off."

"Lee." Maria tried to remember in which of the woman's stories Lee had figured. "Where'd he go."

"Found himself a girl down to Barstow. I told you. Doreen Baker."

The sand was blowing through the rail fence onto the concrete, drifting around the posts, coating a straight-backed chair with pale film. Maria began to cry.

"Honey," the woman said. "You pregnant or something?"

Maria shook her head and looked in her pocket for a Kleenex. The woman picked up a broom and began sweeping the sand into small piles, then edging the piles back to the fence. New sand blew in as she swept.

"You ever made a decision?" she said suddenly, letting the broom fall against the fence.

"About what."

"I made my decision in '61 at a meeting in Barstow and I never shed one tear since."

"No," Maria said. "I never did that."

74

When I was ten years old my father taught me to assess quite rapidly the shifting probabilities on a craps layout: I could trace a layout in my sleep, the field here and the pass line all around, even money on Big Six or Eight, five-for-one on Any Seven. Always when I play back my father's voice it is with a professional rasp, it goes as it lays, don't do it the hard way. My father advised me that life itself was a crap game: it was one of the two lessons I learned as a child. The other was that overturning a rock was apt to reveal a rattlesnake. As lessons go those two seem to hold up, but not to apply.

75

SHE SAT IN THE MOTEL in the late afternoon light looking out at the dry wash until its striations and shifting grains seemed to her a model of the earth and the moon. When BZ came in she did not look up.

"Let me entertain you," BZ said finally.

Maria said nothing.

"I could do my turn about Harrison calling one of the grips a vicious cunt."

"Please don't smoke in here, BZ."

"Why not."

She got up and filled a glass with the warm water from the tap. "Because it's a felony."

BZ laughed. Maria sat on the bed and drank the water and watched him roll a cigarette.

"I said don't, BZ."

"I get the feeling you want me to leave."

"I don't feel like talking to anybody."

"You don't have to talk to me." He lit the cigarette and handed it to her. "You want to know where Carter is?"

"Still shooting."

"Maria, it's seven-thirty."

"I give up."

"He's with Helene."

"I thought I didn't have to talk to you."

"You aren't paying attention, Maria. Carter is fucking Helene. I thought these things made a big difference to you."

Maria got up and walked back to the window. In the few minutes that BZ had been distracting her the light had changed on the dry wash. Tomorrow she would borrow a camera, and station it on the dry wash for twenty-four hours.

"Tell me what matters," BZ said.

"Nothing," Maria said.

76

If Carter and Helene want to think it happened because I was insane, I say let them. They have to lay it off on someone. Carter and Helene still believe in cause-effect. Carter and Helene also believe that people are either sane or insane. Just once, the week after the desert, when Helene came to see me in Neuropsychiatric, I tried to explain how wrong she had been when she screamed that last night about my carelessness, my selfishness, my insanity, as if it had somehow slipped my attention what BZ was doing. I told her: there was no carelessness involved. Helene, I said: I knew precisely what BZ was doing. But Helene only screamed again.

Fuck it, I said to Helene. Fuck it, I said to them all, a radical surgeon of my own life. Never discuss. Cut. In that way I resemble the only man in Los Angeles County who does clean work.

77

"WHAT DO YOU THINK about it," Maria asked Carter.

"About what."

"What I just told you. About the man at the trailer camp who told his wife he was going out for a walk in order to talk to God."

"I wasn't listening, Maria. Just give me the punch line."

"There isn't any punch line, the highway patrol just found him dead, bitten by a rattlesnake."

"I'll say there isn't any punch line."

"Do you think he talked to God?"

Carter looked at her.

"I mean do you think God answered? Or don't you?"

Carter walked out of the room.

The heat stuck. The air shimmered. An underground nuclear device was detonated where Silver Wells had once been, and Maria got up before dawn to feel the blast. She felt nothing.

"I'm giving this one more chance," Carter said when he saw her sitting by the window. "Tell me what you want."

"Nothing."

"I want to help you. Tell me what you feel."

She looked at the hand he held out to her. "Nothing," she said.

"You say that again and I swear to Christ—"

She shrugged. He left the motel.

They had three days left on the desert.

78

Except when they let Carter or Helene in, I never minded Neuropsychiatric and I don't mind here. Nobody bothers me. The only problem is Kate. I want Kate.

79

"WE SHOT THE LAST MASTER after you left this afternoon," Carter said when he came in with Helene. "Three setups in the morning and we're home. Fantastic."

"Susannah was fabulous," Helene said. "Super-good."

BZ said nothing. Maria stared out the window.

"You should have seen Carter working with her."

"I bet he was fabulous," BZ said. "Fab."

80

The one time Ivan Costello got through the switchboard to me here he told me that I had lost my sense of humor. In spite of what Carter and Helene think, maybe my sense of humor was all I did lose.

81

"YOU WERE FANTASTIC TODAY," Helene said when Susannah Wood came in.

"Super-good," BZ said. "Really key."

Susannah Wood lay down on Maria's bed. "Let's go into Vegas."

"It's all planned." Helene did not look at BZ. "Sylvie Roth's over, and Cassie and Leona and—"

BZ stood up. "You go into Vegas."

"Don't you want to see Sylvie?"

"No."

"Don't you want to see Leona's last show?"

"No."

The cords tightened on Helene's neck. "Exactly what do you want."

Susannah Wood giggled. "I saw the charts today, Leona's single stopped at 85."

BZ looked at Helene. "Exactly nothing," he said pleasantly.

Maria dropped a tray of ice on the floor.

82

Carter and Helene still ask questions. I used to ask questions, and I got the answer: nothing. The answer is "nothing." Now that I have the answer, my plans for the future are these: (1) get Kate, (2) live with Kate alone, (3) do some canning. Damson plums, apricot preserves. Sweet India relish and pickled peaches. Apple chutney. Summer squash succotash. There might even be a ready market for such canning: you will note that after everything I remain Harry and Francine Wyeth's daughter and Benny Austin's godchild. For all I know they knew the answer too, and pretended they didn't. You call it as you see it, and stay in the action. BZ thought otherwise. If Carter and Helene aren't careful they'll get the answer too.

83

"I THOUGHT YOU'D BE in Vegas," BZ said when Maria opened the door. He was holding a bottle of vodka and in spite of the heat he was wearing a blazer and a tie. "With Carter and Helene and Susannah and Harrison and Sylvia and Cassie and Leona and—"

"You knew I wasn't going." Maria lay down on the bed again.

"All right, I knew." He sat on the edge of the bed and loosened his tie. "Look at me all duded up. Why are you in bed at nine o'clock."

"Why not."

"Beautiful."

Maria looked at him. "Tell me why you're sad."

"You're a good girl." All the musculature seemed gone from BZ's face. He put down the bottle of vodka and reached into his pocket. "You know what these are?"

He poured twenty or thirty capsules onto the bed before she answered.

"Grain-and-a-half Seconal."

"You want some?"

She looked at him. "No."

"You're still playing." BZ did not take his eyes from hers. "Some day you'll wake up and you just won't feel like playing any more."

"That's a queen's way of doing it."

"I never expected you to fall back on style as an argument."

"I'm not arguing."

"I know that. You think I'd be here if I didn't know that?"

She took his hand and held it. "Why are you here."

"Because you and I, we *know* something. Because we've been out there where nothing is. Because I wanted—you know why."

"Lie down here," she said after a while. "Just go to sleep."

When he lay down beside her the Seconal capsules rolled on the sheet. In the bar across the road somebody punched *King of the Road* on the jukebox again, and there was an argument outside, and the sound of a bottle breaking. Maria held onto BZ's hand.

"Listen to that," he said. "Try to think about having enough left to break a bottle over it."

"It would be very pretty," Maria said. "Go to sleep."

She was almost asleep when she sensed that his weight had shifted.

"Don't." After she had said it she opened her eyes.

He was swallowing the capsules with a glass of water. There were not very many left on the bed.

"Don't start faking me now." BZ turned off the light and lay down again. "Take my hand. Go back to sleep."

"I'm sorry," she said after a while.

"Hold onto me," BZ said.

When Maria woke again the room was blazing with light and Carter was shaking her and Helene was screaming. Maria thought she had never heard anyone scream the way Helene screamed. She closed her eyes against the light and her ears against Helene and her mind against what was going to happen in the next few hours and tightened her hold on BZ's hand.

84

Carter called today, but I saw no point in talking to him. On the whole I talk to no one. I concentrate on the way light would strike filled Mason jars on a kitchen windowsill. I lie here in the sunlight, watch the hummingbird. This morning I threw the coins in the swimming pool, and they gleamed and turned in the water in such a way that I was almost moved to read them. I refrained.

One thing in my defense, not that it matters: I know something Carter never knew, or Helene, or maybe you. I know what "nothing" means, and keep on playing.

Why, BZ would say.

Why not, I say.

A BOOK OF COMMON PRAYER

This book is for Brenda Berger Garner,

for James Jerrett Didion,

and also for Allene Talmey and Henry Robbins.

ONE

I

I WILL BE HER WITNESS.

That would translate *seré su testigo*, and will not appear in your travelers' phrasebook because it is not a useful phrase for the prudent traveler.

Here is what happened: she left one man, she left a second man, she traveled again with the first; she let him die alone. She lost one child to "history" and another to "complications" (I offer in each instance the evaluation of others), she imagined herself capable of shedding that baggage and came to Boca Grande, a tourist. *Una turista*. So she said. In fact she came here less a tourist than a sojourner but she did not make that distinction.

She made not enough distinctions.

She dreamed her life.

She died, hopeful. In summary. So you know the story. Of course the story had extenuating circumstances, weather, cracked sidewalks and paregorina, but only for the living.

Charlotte would call her story one of passion. I believe I would call it one of delusion. My name is Grace Strasser-Mendana, *née* Tabor, and I have been for fifty of my sixty years a student of delusion, a prudent traveler from Denver, Colorado. My mother died of influenza one morning when I was eight. My father died of gunshot wounds, not self-inflicted, one afternoon when I was ten. From that afternoon until my sixteenth birthday I lived alone in our suite at the Brown Palace Hotel. I have lived in equatorial America since 1935 and only twice had fever. I am an anthropologist who lost faith in her own method, who stopped believing that observable activity defined anthropos. I studied under Kroeber at California and worked with Lévi-Strauss at São Paulo, classified several societies, catalogued their rites and attitudes on occasions of birth, copulation, initiation and death; did extensive and well-regarded studies on the rearing of female children in the Mato Grosso and along certain tributaries of the Rio Xingu, and still

I did not know why any one of these female children did or did not do anything at all.

Let me go further.

I did not know why I did or did not do anything at all.

As a result I "retired" from that field, married a planter of San Blas Green coconut palms here in Boca Grande and took up the amateur study of biochemistry, a discipline in which demonstrable answers are commonplace and "personality" absent. I am interested for example in learning that such a "personality" trait as fear of the dark exists irrelative to patterns of child-rearing in the Mato Grosso or in Denver, Colorado. Fear of the dark can be synthesized in the laboratory. Fear of the dark is an arrangement of fifteen amino acids. Fear of the dark is a protein. I once diagrammed this protein for Charlotte. "I don't quite see why calling it a protein makes it any different," Charlotte said, her eyes flickering covertly back to a battered Neiman-Marcus Christmas catalogue she had received in the mail that morning in May. She had reached that stage in her sojourn when she lived for mail, sent away for every catalogue, filled out every coupon, wrote many letters and received some answers. "I mean I don't quite see your point."

I explained my point.

"I've never been afraid of the dark," Charlotte said after a while, and then, tearing out a photograph of a small child in a crocheted dress: "This would be pretty on Marin."

Since Marin was the child Charlotte had lost to history and was at the time of her disappearance eighteen years old, I could conclude only that Charlotte did not care to pursue my point.

Also, for the record, Charlotte was afraid of the dark.

Give me the molecular structure of the protein which defined Charlotte Douglas.

In at least two of the several impenetrably euphemistic "Letters from Central America" which Charlotte wrote during her stay here and tried unsuccessfully to sell to *The New Yorker*, she characterized Boca Grande as a "land of contrasts." Boca Grande is not a land of contrasts. On the contrary Boca Grande is relentlessly "the same": the cathedral is not Spanish Colonial but corrugated aluminum. There is a local currency but the American dollar is legal tender. The politics of the country at first appear to offer contrast, involving as they do the "colorful" Latin juxtaposition of *guerrilleros* and colonels, but when the tanks are put away and the airport reopens nothing has actually changed in Boca Grande. There are no waterfalls of note, no ruins of interest, no chic boutiques (Charlotte went so far as to rent a storefront for one such boutique, but my son Gerardo turned the storefront to his own purposes and it has been since the October Violence a Pentecostal reading room) to provide dramatic cultural foil to voodoo in the hills.

In fact there is no voodoo in the hills.

In fact there are no hills, only the flat bush and the lifeless sea.

And the light. The opaque equatorial light. The bush and the sea do not reflect the light but absorb it, suck it in, then glow morbidly.

Boca Grande is the name of the country and Boca Grande is also the name of the city, as if the place defeated the imagination of even its first settler. At least once each year, usually on the afternoon of the Anniversary of Independence, the Boca Grande Intellectual Union sponsors a debate, followed by a no-host cocktail party, as to who that first settler might have been, but the arguments are desultory, arbitrary. Information is missing here. Evidence goes unrecorded. Every time the sun falls on a day in Boca Grande that day appears to vanish from local memory, to be reinvented if necessary but never recalled. I once asked the librarian at the Intellectual Union to recommend for Charlotte a history of Boca Grande. "Boca Grande has no history," the librarian said, and he seemed gratified that I had asked, as if we had together hit upon a catechistic point of national pride.

"Boca Grande has no history," I repeated to Charlotte, but again Charlotte did not quite see my point. Charlotte was at that time preparing a "Letter" describing Boca Grande as the "economic fulcrum of the Americas." It was true that planes between, say, Los Angeles and Bogotá, or New York and Quito, sometimes stopped in Boca Grande to refuel, and paid an inflated landing fee. It was also true that passengers on such flights often left a dollar or two in the airport slot machines during the time required for refueling, but revenue from an airport landing fee and eighteen slot machines did not seem to me to constitute, in the classical sense, an economic fulcrum.

I suggested this to Charlotte.

Boca Grande exported copra, Charlotte said. Principally your own.

Boca Grande did export copra, principally my own, and, in about the same dollar volume, Boca Grande also exported parrots, anaconda skins, and macramé shawls.

What I was overlooking entirely, Charlotte said, was what Boca Grande "could become."

A "Letter" from a city or country, I suggested, was conventionally understood to be a factual report on that city or country, not as it "could become" but as it "was."

Not necessarily, Charlotte said.

Another of Charlotte's Letters covered the "spirit of hope" she divined in the Boca Grande *favelas*. Boca Grande has no *favelas*, even the word is Portuguese. There is poverty here, but it is obdurately indistinguishable from comfort. We all live in cinderblock houses. Charlotte wanted color. By way of color I could tell her only that the Hotel del Caribe was said to have Central America's largest ballroom, but Charlotte was not satisfied with that. Nor with the light.

2

CALL THIS MY own letter from Boca Grande.

No. Call it what I said. Call it my witness to Charlotte Douglas.

One or two facts about the place where Charlotte died and I live. Boca Grande means "big mouth," or big bay, and describes the country's principal physical feature precisely as it appears. Almost everything in Boca Grande describes itself precisely as it appears, as if any ambiguity in the naming of things might cause the present to sink as tracelessly as the past. The Rio Blanco looks white. The Rio Colorado looks red. The Avenida del Mar runs by the sea, the Avenida de la Punta Verde runs by the green point. The green point is in fact green. On reflection I know only two place names in Boca Grande which evoke an idea or an event or a person, which suggest a past either Indian or colonial.

One of these two exceptions is "Millonario."

As in Millonario Province.

So named because our palms grow there and our copra is milled there, and my husband's father was the rich man, the *millonario*, a St. Louis confidence man named Victor Strasser who at age twenty-three floated some Missouri money to buy oil rights, at age twenty-four fled Mexico after an abortive attempt to invade Sonora, and at age twenty-five arrived in Boca Grande. Upon his recovery from cholera he married a Mendana and proceeded to divest her family of interior Boca Grande.

Victor Strasser died at ninety-five and for the last sixty years of his life preferred to be addressed as Don Victor.

I called him Mr. Strasser.

There is Millonario and there is also "Progreso." In fact there are two Progresos, El Progreso *primero* and El Progreso *otro*. The first Progreso was the grand design of my brother-in-law Luis, the toy of his fifteen-month presidency, his new city, his capital, twenty matched glass pyramids intersected by four eight-lane boulevards, all laid out on fill in the bay and connected to the mainland until recently by causeway. The matched glass pyramids were never finished but the eight-lane boulevards were. Until a few years ago, when the causeway collapsed, I would take lunch out to the first Progreso and eat there alone, sitting on the site of a projected monument where all four empty boulevards converged. On the fill between the boulevards bamboo grew up through the big Bechtel cranes, abandoned the day Luis was shot. Luis was the last of my brothers-in-law to place himself in so exposed a position as that of *El Presidente.* Since Luis they have tended to favor the Ministry of Defense for themselves, and the presidency for expendable cousins by marriage. In the years after Luis was shot water hyacinths clogged the culverts at Progreso and after rain the boulevards would remain all day in shallow flood, the film of water shimmering with mosquito larvae and with the rainbow slick from rusting oil tanks. Until the collapse I would go out there maybe once a week, and stay most of the afternoon. It occurs to me that I was perhaps the only person in Boca Grande inconvenienced by the collapse of the Progreso causeway.

At some point after the collapse Gerardo took Charlotte to Progreso by boat.

I recall asking Charlotte at dinner if she found Progreso *primero* as peaceful as I did.

Charlotte began to cry.

As for Progreso *otro*, which might have even more radically challenged Charlotte's rather teleological view of human settlement, I have not seen it in some years. Neither has anyone else. This second Progreso was another new city, in the interior, built on leased land (ours) by an American aluminum combine during the bauxite chimera here. (There was bauxite, yes, but not as much as the geologists had predicted, not enough to justify Progreso *otro.*) After the mines closed a handful of engineers stayed on, trying to find some economic use for the aluminous laterite which made up the bulk of the deposit, but one by one they got fever or quit or moved to the combine's operation in Venezuela. The last two left in 1965. The road in, which cost thirty-four-million American dollars to build, can still be discerned from the air, quite clearly, a straight line of paler vegetation. My husband wanted to maintain the road, said always that the interior had things we might want access to, but after Edgar died I let it grow over. What I wanted from the interior had nothing to do with access.

Edgar was the oldest of the four sons of Victor Strasser and Alicia Mendana.

It was the brother nearest Edgar's age, Luis, who was shot on the steps of the presidential palace in April 1959.

You will have gathered that I married into one of the three or four solvent families in Boca Grande. In fact Edgar's death left me in putative control of fifty-nine-point-eight percent of the arable land and about the same percentage of the decision-making process in La República (recently La República Libre) de Boca Grande. *El Presidente* this year wears a yachting cap. The two younger Strasser-Mendana brothers, Little Victor and Antonio, the two Edgar and Luis called *los mosquitos*, participate in the estate only via a trust administered by me. Victor and Antonio do not much like this arrangement, nor do their wives Bianca and Isabel, nor does Luis's widow Elena, but there it is. The joint decision of Edgar and his father. *Fait accompli* on the morning Edgar died. There it was and there it is. (A small example of why it is. The day Luis was shot Elena flew to exile in Geneva, a theatrical gesture but unnecessary, since even before her plane left the runway the coup was over and Little Victor had assumed temporary control of the government. The wife of any other Latin president would have known immediately that a coup in which the airport remained open was a coup doomed to fail, but Elena had no instinct for being the wife of a Latin president. Nor does she make a particularly appropriate presidential widow. In any case. A few weeks later Elena came back. Edgar and his father and I met her at the airport. She was wearing tinted glasses and a new Balenciaga coat, lettuce-green. She was carrying a matching parrot. She had not taken this parrot with her from Boca Grande. She had bought this parrot that morning in Geneva, for seven hundred dollars.) In any event there is not as much money in all of Boca Grande as Victor and Bianca and Antonio and Isabel and Elena accuse me of having secreted in Switzerland.

Strike Bianca.

Bianca does not accuse me of having secreted money in Switzerland because Bianca was taught at Sacre Coeur in New Orleans that discussions of money are not genteel. Also strike Isabel. Isabel does not accuse me of having secreted money in Switzerland because Isabel is so rarely here, and has been told by her doctor in Arizona that discussions of money disturb the flow of transcendental energy.

I continue to live here only because I like the light.

And because I am intermittently engaged by the efforts of my extant brothers-in-law to turn a profit on the Red Cross.

And because my days are too numbered to spend them in New York or Paris or Denver imagining the light in Boca Grande, how flat it is, how harsh and still. How dead white at noon.

One thing at least I share with Charlotte: I lost my child. Gerardo is lost to me. I hear from him regularly, see him all too often, talk to him about politics and new films and the bud rot we are experiencing in the interior groves, but I talk to him as an acquaintance. In Boca Grande he drives an Alfa Romeo 1750. In Paris, where he has lived off and on for fifteen years on a succession of student visas, he rides a Suzuki 500 motorcycle. I always think of Gerardo on wheels, or skis. I like him but not too much any more. Gerardo embodies many of the failings of this part of the world, the rather wishful machismo, the defeating touchiness, the conviction that his heritage must be aristocratic; a general attitude I do not admire. Gerardo is the grandson of two American wildcatters who got rich, my father in Colorado minerals and Edgar's father in Boca Grande politics, and of the Irish nursemaid and the *mestiza* from the interior they respectively married. Still he persists in tracing his line to the court of Castile. On the delusion front I would have to say that Gerardo and Charlotte were well met.

I tell you these things about myself only to legitimize my voice. We are uneasy about a story until we know who is telling it. In no other sense does it matter who "I" am: "the narrator" plays no motive role in this narrative, nor would I want to.

Gerardo of course does play a motive role. I do not delude myself there.

Unlike Charlotte I do not dream my life.

I try to make enough distinctions.

I will die (and rather soon, of pancreatic cancer) neither hopeful nor its opposite. I am interested in Charlotte Douglas only insofar as she passed through Boca Grande, only insofar as the meaning of that sojourn continues to elude me.

3

ACCORDING TO HER passport, entry visa, and International Certificate of Vaccination, Charlotte Amelia Douglas was born in Hollister, California, forty years before her entry into Boca Grande; was at the time of that entry a married resident of San Francisco, California; was five-feet-five inches tall, had red hair, brown eyes, and no visible distinguishing marks; and had been successfully inoculated against smallpox, cholera, yellow fever, typhus, typhoid, and paratyphoid A and B. The passport had been renewed four months before at New Orleans, Louisiana, and bore entry and departure stamps for Antigua and Guadeloupe, unused visas for Australia and the British Solomon Islands Protectorate, a Mexican tourist card stamped at Mérida, a visa and entry stamp for Boca Grande, and no indication that the bearer had reentered the United States during the four months since the renewal of the passport. Nationality NORTEAMERICANA. Type of Visa TURISTA. Occupation MADRE.

There seemed to me many elusive anomalies on these documents, not the least of them Charlotte Amelia Douglas's decision to enter Boca Grande, but none of these nuances suggested themselves to Victor, Little Victor, who had ordered the passport surreptitiously removed from the Hotel del Caribe safe because its number appeared on a United States Department of State list indicating travelers who were to receive certain special treatment.

4

WHEN CHARLOTTE FIRST came to Boca Grande she was referred to always as *la norteamericana. La norteamericana* had been heard typing in her room at the Caribe all night, *la norteamericana* had woken a doctor at two in the morning to ask the symptoms of infant framboesia. *La norteamericana* had advised the manager of the Caribe that he was derelict in allowing the maids to fill the water carafes from the tap. *La norteamericana* had asked a waiter at the Jockey Club if marijuana was in general use in the kitchen. *La norteamericana* had come downstairs in a thin cotton dressing gown one night when the Caribe generator failed and sat alone in the dark at the ballroom piano until three A.M., picking out with one hand, over and over again and in every possible tempo, the melodic line of a single song. This story was told to me by a bellman at the Caribe, the brother of a woman who cooked for Victor and Bianca, and he tried to hum the song that *la norteamericana* had played over and over again. The song was "Mountain Greenery."

In those first few weeks before any of us had met her she seemed to appear only in the evenings. An hour or so after the sunset one could see her walking through the empty casino at the Caribe, nodding pleasantly at the idle croupiers and the national police assigned to the casino, breathing deeply at the windows quite as if fresh air could possibly penetrate the dusty blue velvet curtains that lined the room. She would inspect the tables one by one but did not play. After this ritual turn through the casino she would walk on out through the lobby, her step buoyant, purposeful. Later one could see her eating alone on the porch at the Capilla del Mar or at the Jockey Club, always the same table at the Jockey Club, the table beneath the photograph of the Venezuelan polo team which visited Boca Grande in 1948. She would draw the legs of a spiny lobster between her remarkably white teeth and read the *Miami Herald*, reading the classified as attentively as she read the front page, reading both as avidly and as thoroughly as she ate the spiny lobster.

I saw her at the Jockey Club on a few evenings, and heard about her on others. Like so many works of man in Boca Grande the Jockey Club is less than it seems: an aluminum-sided bungalow with rattan card tables and a menu written in French but translated in the kitchen into ambiguous gumbos based mainly on plantains and rice. Although any traveler could obtain a guest card to the Jockey Club by asking for one at an airline ticket office, not many bothered. There was once a nine-hole golf course, but the greens first went spongy and then reverted to swamp. There was once an artificial lake for swimming, but the lake first became infested with freshwater snails and then with the *Schistosoma mansoni* worms that infest the snails. The lake was not drained until after one of Antonio and Isabel's children suffered gastrointestinal bleeding from what was diagnosed in New Orleans as schistosomiasis. The draining of the artificial lake did not go unremarked upon at the Jockey Club. Elena opposed it. Elena recently resigned from the Jockey Club after the membership, led by Victor, defeated her motion to rename the club Le Cercle Sportif. Elena was born and raised on the Guatemalan coast but favors all things French. Elena's resignation did not go unremarked upon at the Jockey Club.

In short.

The presence at the same table night after night of this conspicuous *norteamericana* was not likely to go unremarked upon at the Jockey Club. Actually it would have been hard to overlook Charlotte Douglas anywhere. There was the extreme and volatile thinness of the woman. There was the pale red hair which curled in the damp heat and stood out around her face and seemed almost more weight than she could bear. There was the large square emerald she wore in place of a wedding ring, there were the expensive clothes that seemed to betray in their just perceptible disrepair (the safety pin that puckered the hem of the Irish linen skirt, the clasp that did not quite close the six-hundred-dollar handbag) some equivalent disrepair of the morale, some vulnerability, or abandon.

And there was that strain of exhibitionism, perverse and sometimes witty until it bloomed too long, and tired the observer. If Charlotte Douglas heard someone speaking English at another table she would invade the conversation, offer suggestions for touring, sights not to be missed. As there were neither any conventional "sights" in Boca Grande nor any tourists, only the occasional mineral geologist or CIA man traveling on one or another incorporeal AID mission, these encounters tended to end in obscurely sexual misunderstandings and bewilderment. After dinner she would walk back to the hotel alone, walking very deliberately, tying and retying a scarf which whipped in the hot night wind, seeming to concentrate on the scarf as if oblivious to the potholes in the sidewalk and the places where waste ran into the gutters. At the Caribe desk she would ask for her messages in a halting but flawlessly memorized Castilian Spanish which the night clerk found difficult to understand. As reported to Victor there were never any messages in any case.

5

UNTIL I LOST a filling and had occasion to see a dentist in Miami I never knew what *la norteamericana* did during the day. At least one thing she did during the day those first few weeks was this: she went to the airport. She did not go to the airport to catch a plane, nor to meet one. She just went to the airport. She was at the counter of the airport coffee shop the morning I left for Miami, not sitting at the counter but standing behind it, holding a watch in her hand. "I certainly wouldn't think yet," she said to the sullen girl whose space she had arrogated, and she tapped the face of the watch with her fingernail. "Nine minutes more. See for yourself."

The girl stared at Charlotte Douglas a moment and then, without speaking, plunged her index finger into the sugar bowl on the counter. Still gazing at Charlotte she licked the sugar from her finger. In another country she might have gone the extra step, made her point explicit, jammed her grimy finger between *la norteamericana*'s teeth, but the expression of proletarian resentment in Boca Grande remains largely symbolic. The *guerrilleros* here would have nothing to say to this girl in the airport. The *guerrilleros* here spend their time theorizing in the interior, and are covertly encouraged to emerge from time to time as foils to the actual politics of the country. Our notoriously frequent revolutions are made not by the *guerrilleros* but entirely by people we know. This is a hard point for the outsider of romantic sensibility to grasp.

"Gastrointestinal infection is the leading natural cause of death in this country," Charlotte said after a while. She said it in English and did not look at the girl. "If you call it natural."

The girl sucked the last grains of sugar from under her scabbed fingernail and rolled it again in the bowl.

"Which I don't particularly."

When the water for Charlotte Douglas's tea had boiled the requisite twenty minutes she made the tea herself, took it to a table by the window and sat there reading an article on the cultivation of vanilla in *Revista Boca Grande*. She moved her lips slightly and seemed entirely absorbed in what she read. When the Miami plane was called she continued reading *Revista Boca Grande*. She never looked up, or out the window. The next afternoon when I came back from Miami Charlotte Douglas was sitting at the same table reading the same copy of *Revista Boca Grande*. It did not occur to me that day that I would ever have reason to consider Charlotte an outsider of romantic sensibility. In any case I am no longer sure that she was. Possibly this is the question I am trying to answer.

Once I knew Charlotte I realized that although she spoke Spanish she had trouble reading it, and tended to lose the sense of even the simplest newspaper story somewhere in the first paragraph, but it could not have mattered in this case since she had no interest in the cultivation of vanilla.

Or in the reform of the Boca Grande tax structure.

Or in the contradiction inherent in a Central American common market.

All of which topics, and others, Charlotte Douglas read about in the Boca Grande airport, her concentration apparently passionate, her expression miming comprehension, here a nod of approval, there a moue of disagreement; her eyes scanning the Spanish words as if she understood them.

When there was nothing else to read.

When, say, the *Miami Herald* did not come in and she had already committed to memory the revised schedules of all five airlines chartered to land at Boca Grande.

6

THE STATE DEPARTMENT list on which Charlotte Douglas's name and passport number appeared stated simply that the United States Embassy should be advised of the entry, the departure, the arrest, the hospitalization, or the participation in civil disorder of anyone listed. Various forms were provided for this purpose, but the immigration officer in charge of the list had mislaid them; as far as he could remember Charlotte Douglas was the only person on the list ever to enter Boca Grande. Victor himself had never before heard of the list, had seen it for the first time when the immigration officer's report on Charlotte Douglas arrived on his desk at the Ministry of Defense, and he regarded the thin leaflet with the eagle on the top page as a mesmeric challenge to his powers of deduction. The list animated a slow week for Victor. The list was a code Victor could not crack. The list so obsessed Victor that he had even solicited Antonio's opinion as to whether those listed were politically suspect, criminal, indigent, or very important.

"Scratch indigent," I suggested.

"The little brother suggested indigent."

Victor routinely referred to Antonio as "the little brother," I think in a stab at ironic distance. Antonio was at that time Minister of Public Works, whatever "Public Works" mean in Boca Grande.

"I don't think indigent," I said.

"Then what."

"Show me the list."

"The list is for official eyes only."

"You won't show me the list, how should I know 'what.' Ask Bradley."

"I'm asking you."

"I'm not the American ambassador, Victor, Bradley is."

Victor sucked at his teeth and drummed his glossy fingernails on a Steuben paperweight Bradley had given him as a gesture of ambassadorial good will. Victor believed the pale moons of his fingernails to be evidence of noble blood and had a manicurist meet him every day at noon to shape his cuticles and perform other services characterized by Elena as beyond Bianca's range. Elena's faith in the sexual virtuosity of working women was touching and childlike. If I did not completely misapprehend Victor the cuticles came first.

"Ask Bradley," I repeated. "Call the Embassy and ask Bradley."

"We don't run this country at Bradley's convenience."

Put a Strasser-Mendana behind a desk and you have a *tableau vivant* of the famous touchiness of command. Antonio once urinated on the foot of an Italian newspaperwoman who suggested that Boca Grande was perhaps not ready to join the nuclear club. Victor was displeased with Bradley because the week before Bradley had allowed his wife to leave one of Victor's official lunches in the courtyard at three-thirty, before the food was served, pleading faintness from the heat. Victor felt insulted by Americans who grew faint before lunch, even Americans who were, as Ardis Bradley was, forty-four years old and seven months pregnant.

"In any case." Victor studied his nails. "In fact. Bradley is in Caracas."

In any case in fact Bradley was not in Caracas, I had seen him the night before, but it was a theme of Victor's that Tuck Bradley neglected Boca Grande for livelier capitals.

"About those four o'clock lunches in the courtyard," I said.

"I wasn't aware we were talking about any four o'clock lunches in the courtyard."

"Just one detail. While I think of it. Pass it on to Bianca. I don't think the baba au rhum should be out in the sun from twelve-thirty on."

Victor said that he had not called me into his office for advice on serving baba au rhum.

I asked if he had called me into his office to admire the new 380 Mauser automatic pistol mounted on his desk.

Victor snapped his fingers. The aide at the door sprang to my chair and bowed.

"As another *norteamericana* you could meet her," Victor said as I got up. He did not look at me. That he continued this conversation at all confirmed his obsession with the list, because it was past noon. At noon exactly his car always took him to meet his manicurist at the apartment he kept in the

Residencia Vista del Palacio. The Residencia was only a block and a half from the Ministry but Victor fancied that his car, a black Mercedes limousine with the license BOCA GRANDE 2 (Victor always allowed *El Presidente* the BOCA GRANDE 1 plate), was the discreet way to go. "In the most natural way you could meet this woman. You could ask her for a coffee. Or a drink."

"Or a baba au rhum."

Victor swiveled his chair to face the window. Many of my visits to Victor's office at the Ministry ended this way, and still do, although the office is now Antonio's. I suppose Isabel is pleased that the office is finally Antonio's but Isabel is spending her usual season at the private hospital her doctor operates in Arizona.

When it was reported to Victor that Charlotte Douglas went to the airport every day he construed immediately that her presence on the list had to do with Kasindorf and Riley. Kasindorf was Bradley's cultural attaché at the Embassy and Riley was a young man who ran an OAS "educational" office called "Operación Simpático" downtown. The connection with Charlotte Douglas, transparent to Victor, was that Kasindorf and Riley also went to the airport every day, met there for coffee at precisely seven-thirty A.M., a time which coincided with the arrival of the night Braniff from Mexico.

In fact Kasindorf and Riley went to the airport not because of the night Braniff from Mexico but because they assumed correctly that Victor had microphones in their offices.

In fact Charlotte Douglas just went to the airport.

7

LA NORTEAMERICANA TOLD a story about playing hide-and-seek with Marin among the thousand trunks of the Great Banyan at the Calcutta Botanical Garden. It had been "the most lyrical" day. She and Marin had "devoured" coconut ice for lunch. She and Marin had wandered beneath the Great Banyan at noon and stayed until after dark.

She leaned toward Victor and me as if the end of the story were a secret never before revealed. "And when Leonard finished his meeting and couldn't find us at the Hilton he was wild, he had people combing Calcutta for us, it was hilarious."

The absence of banyan trees at the American Embassy reminded Charlotte Douglas of this story.

She told a story about sitting in the rain in a limousine at Lod Airport eating caviar with an Israeli general. They had "devoured" the caviar from the tin with their fingers and pieces of unsalted matzoh. The Israeli and Leonard could meet only between planes and the Israeli had brought the caviar.

Again she leaned toward us. "And when Leonard saw the Iranian seal on the tin he wouldn't eat the caviar, and the general said 'don't be a fool, don't make me go to war for it,' it was hilarious."

The absence of caviar at the American Embassy Christmas party reminded Charlotte Douglas of this story.

She talked constantly. She talked feverishly. She talked as if Victor had released her from vows of silence by walking up to where she stood with Ardis Bradley and offering her a crab puff. Every memory was "lyrical," every denouement "hilarious," and sometimes "ironic" as well. Her face was flushed but she was not drunk: she stood very straight and refused even the weak rum punches the Bradleys favored for general entertainments. She seemed to be receiving these pointless but bizarrely arresting stories out of some deep vacuum of nervous exhaustion, transmitting them dutifully in a voice soft and clear and oddly confidential. She used words as a seven-year-old might, as if she had heard them and liked their adult sound but had only the haziest idea of their meaning, and she also mentioned names as a seven-year-old might, with a bewildering disregard for who was listening. "Leonard," she would say, as if we would naturally know who Leonard was, as if the Minister of Defense of a Central American republic and his *norteamericana* sister-in-law, acquaintances of an hour in the crush of an official reception, were of course privy to all the people and places in her life.

There was "Leonard."

There was "Warren."

There was "Marin."

There was the house on California Street in San Francisco and there were the meetings in Calcutta and La Paz and in limousines at Lod Airport.

There were the hotel suites, always "flooded with flowers."

There was the missed plane and its happy ending: Air Force One.

"Imagine Leonard on Air Force One." She had one of those odd intimate laughs that seemed simultaneously to include everyone within hearing and to exclude all possibility of inquiry. "Ardis. Tell them. You know Leonard."

"Actually I don't quite," Ardis Bradley said.

"For that matter imagine Leonard on a camel," Charlotte Douglas said.

"Leonard," Victor said tentatively, looking at Ardis Bradley. "Leonard would be her—"

"Actually I think Tuck might know him," Ardis Bradley said. Ardis had spent twenty years in places like Sierra Leone and Boca Grande and Chevy Chase learning to go look for Tuck when she did not want to answer a question. "Actually I don't want Tuck to miss this."

"Leonard on that camel." Still laughing Charlotte Douglas touched Victor's arm. "After lunch one day in Kuwait."

Victor had the look of someone who had waded out too far. Ardis Bradley had vanished. I was myself unclear as to why this Leonard declined Iranian caviar in one story and lunched in Kuwait in another.

"The inevitable five-course lunch. In the inevitable Valerian Rybar dining room. Followed by the inevitable camel. I tried to postpone the camel part, I kept eating and eating, everything had this vile mint taste, I kept trying to distract the sheikh, I kept asking him what I could—"

She broke off abruptly and shrugged.

"What you could—?"

"It was hilarious." She was looking around the room as if unsure how she had gotten there. "I used to like mint but I don't any more, do you?"

"You kept asking the sheikh what you could—?"

"I suppose it's one of those abandoned tastes. As opposed to acquired. Mint." She focused on Victor with difficulty. "I kept asking the sheikh what I could send him from America. Of course."

"And then," Victor prompted.

"He wanted eight-track cassettes and flowered sheets." Her voice was absent. "They all do."

"But after lunch?"

"After lunch?"

"The camel?"

"The *camel*." She seemed relieved to be handed the thread to her story but had lost interest in telling it. "So Leonard rode the camel. Of course. Leonard had to ride the camel."

"Leonard would be—"

"You know how the Kuwaiti are."

"Your husband? Leonard would be your husband?"

"One of them." Her voice was still absent. "I mean they lay on a camel, you have to ride the camel."

"And he has occasion to travel a great deal." Victor was not to be deflected. "Your husband. Leonard. He travels. For business. For pleasure. For whatever."

"He runs guns," Charlotte Douglas said. "I wish they had caviar."

Victor stared at her.

She speared a shrimp, dipped it in mayonnaise and offered it to Victor. Victor made no response.

"I don't mean literally." She spoke with disinterested patience and still held out the shrimp to Victor. "I don't mean he literally buys and sells the hardware."

"The hardware," Victor said.

She ate the shrimp herself and seemed about to drop the toothpick into the six-hundred-dollar handbag with the broken clasp when Tuck Bradley appeared. To my astonishment she handed Tuck Bradley the toothpick. To my further astonishment he stood there holding it, between two fingers, looking prissy and foolish. Beyond handing him the toothpick Charlotte seemed entirely unaware of Tuck Bradley's presence. "He's kind of a lawyer," she said finally. "He's kind of a lawyer in San Francisco."

"If you're talking about Leonard he's a very well-known lawyer," Tuck Bradley said.

"In a way," Charlotte said.

"In San Francisco," Tuck Bradley said.

"And in some other places," Charlotte said.

And then, her animation returning, she again touched Victor's arm in that way she had of physically touching strangers, of reaching out unconsciously and then drawing back as if she had just realized the gesture's sexual freight; that mannerism, that tic, that way of barely suggesting impossible intimacy. She did this only to strangers but she did not do it to all strangers. I never saw her do it to a woman and I never saw her do it to Antonio. She never did it to Gerardo either but that was because Gerardo did it first, to her. Sexual freight was another area in which I would have to say that Gerardo and Charlotte were well met.

"You know what you need here," she said to Victor, lifting her fingers from his arm as if burned. "You know what Boca Grande needs."

"We're making great headway with the People-to-People program," Tuck Bradley said. "Leaps and bounds."

Neither Charlotte nor Victor looked at him.

"I know what you need here," Charlotte said.

"What do I need here," Victor said. His voice was almost hoarse. "Say it."

She studied the square emerald on the hand that had touched Victor and slid it up and down. She seemed aware of nothing she was doing. She was reflexively seductive. I did not want to watch this happening. I did not want to think of Victor and this woman in the apartment in the Residencia Vista del Palacio and I did not want to see the black Mercedes limousine with the BOCA GRANDE 2 plates parked outside the Caribe.

"Think of what made Acapulco," she said finally. "Think of what turned Acapulco around overnight."

Victor stared at the emerald as if transfixed.

Tuck Bradley snapped the toothpick in two.

I looked away.

"I'm not sure Mrs. Douglas realizes the problems," Tuck Bradley said.

"Think," Charlotte repeated.

"Say it," Victor repeated.

"A film festival," Charlotte Douglas said.

"You won't want the details but it's rather a tragic situation," Ardis Bradley said. "Tuck could tell you better than I."

"I won't bore you with the details but it's rather an interesting situation," Tuck Bradley said. "Don't ask her about her daughter."

I could not have asked Charlotte Douglas about her daughter in any case because Charlotte Douglas had already left, with Victor. I went as planned to Victor's and ate with Bianca, alone. The black Mercedes limousine with the BOCA GRANDE 2 plates was seen first at the Residencia Vista del Palacio and later at the Caribe. Bianca did not then and does not now go out, nor does she express interest in her husband's arrivals and departures. That is another example of the genteel behavior Bianca was taught at Sacre Coeur in New Orleans.

The next afternoon when I saw Charlotte Douglas arguing with the pharmacist in the big drugstore on the Avenida Centrale she did not look at me. She looked disheveled and unwell, her eyes puffy beneath dark glasses, her bright hair unkempt and only partly covered by a bandana.

"You tell me chloromycetin." The pharmacist slapped the counter with his palm. "I give you chloromycetin."

"This is tincture of opium."

"Different type chloromycetin."

"I can smell it, it's opium."

"Same thing. *Para la disentería.*"

"But they're not the same thing at all." Even in her distress she seemed determined to instruct him on this point. "They're both *para la disentería*, but they're quite different. Chloromycetin is a—"

"I give you chloromycetin."

"Forget the whole thing," she said, her voice low and her eyes averted from where I stood.

Later that afternoon I sent a maid to the Caribe with twenty chloromycetin and a note asking Charlotte Douglas to have dinner when she was recovered.

8

"CHARLOTTE DOUGLAS IS ILL," I said after Christmas lunch in the courtyard at Victor and Bianca's.

No one had spoken for twenty minutes. I had timed it. I had counted the minutes while I watched two mating flies try to extricate themselves from a melting chocolate shaving on the untouched Bûche de Noël. The children had already been trundled off quarreling to distribute nut cups to veterans, Gerardo had already made his filial call from St. Moritz, Elena had already been photographed in her Red Cross uniform and had changed back into magenta crepe de chine pajamas. Isabel had drunk enough champagne to begin crying softly. Antonio had grown irritable enough with Isabel's mournful hiccups to borrow a pistol from the guard at the gate and take aim at a lizard in the creche behind Bianca's fountain. Antonio was always handling guns, or smashing plates. As a gesture toward the spirit of Christmas he had refrained from smashing any plates at lunch, but the effort seemed to have exhausted his capacity for congeniality. Had Antonio been born in other circumstances he would have been put away early as a sociopath.

Bianca remained oblivious.

Bianca remained immersed in the floor plan for an apartment she wanted Victor to take for her in the Residencia Vista del Palacio. Bianca had never been apprised of the fact that Victor already had an apartment in the Residencia Vista del Palacio. For five of these twenty minutes it had seemed to me up in the air whether Antonio was about to shoot up Bianca's creche or tell Bianca about the Residencia Vista del Palacio.

"I said *la norteamericana* is sick."

"Send her to Dr. Schiff," Antonio muttered. Dr. Schiff was Isabel's doctor in Arizona. "Let the great healer tell *la norteamericana* who's making her sick."

Victor only gazed at the sky. I did not know whether Victor had seen Charlotte Douglas since the night he took her from the Embassy to the Residencia but I did know that a Ministry courier had delivered twenty-four white roses to the Caribe on Christmas Eve.

"So is Jackie Onassis sick," Elena said. Elena was leafing fretfully through a back issue of *Paris-Match*. "Or she was in September."

"So am I sick," Isabel said. "I need complete quiet."

"I should think that's what you have," Elena said.

"Not like Arizona," Isabel said. "I should have stayed through December, Dr. Schiff begged me. The air. The solitude. The long walks, the simple meals. Yoghurt at sunset. You can't imagine the sunsets."

"Sounds very lively," Elena said without looking up. "I wonder if Gerardo knows Jackie Onassis."

"If that's the *norteamericana* Grace is talking about I think she had every right to marry the Greek," Bianca said. "Not that I would ever care to live in Athens. I wonder about the view from the Residencia."

"Grace was talking about a different *norteamericana*, Bianca." Victor leaned back and clipped a cigar. "Of no interest to you. Or Grace."

"This *norteamericana* is of interest only to Victor." Antonio seemed to be having trouble drawing a bead on the lizard. "But she could tell you about the view from the Residencia. She's an expert on the view from the Residencia. Victor should introduce you to her."

"I don't meet strangers," Bianca said. "As you know. I take no interest. Look here, the plan for the eleventh floor. If we lived up that high we'd have clear air. No fevers."

"Almost like Arizona," Elena said. "I wonder if Gerardo knows Jacqueline de Ribes."

"Arizona," Isabel said. "I wonder what Dr. Schiff is doing today."

Antonio fired twice at the lizard.

The lizard darted away.

Two porcelain wise men shattered.

"Eating yoghurt in the sunset I presume," Elena said.

"Dr. Schiff doesn't believe in guns," Isabel said.

"What do you mean exactly, Isabel, '*Dr. Schiff doesn't believe in guns*'?" Antonio thrust the pistol into Isabel's line of sight. "Does Dr. Schiff not believe in the 'existence' of guns? *Look* at it. *Touch* it. It's *there. What does Dr. Schiff mean exactly?*"

Isabel closed her eyes.

Elena closed the copy of *Paris-Match*.

Bianca began to gather up the fragments of porcelain.

Victor looked at me and spoke very deliberately. "There's no longer any need for you to see the *norteamericana*, Grace. An extremely silly woman."

"But then so is your manicurist," Elena murmured.

"If I could live on the eleventh floor I think I'd take an interest again," Bianca said.

"Quite frankly it's better when you don't," Isabel said, abruptly and unsettlingly lucid, and in the silence that followed she stood up and put her arms around Bianca.

For a moment two of my three sisters-in-law stood there in the courtyard with the guard at the gate on Christmas afternoon and buried their faces in each other's shoulders and stroked each other's hair. Only their silence suggested their tears. They were little sisters crying.

Elena rubbed at a drop of champagne on her magenta crepe de chine pajamas.

Antonio drummed his nails on the table.

"It might be better if you left," Victor said to Antonio.

"Maybe I'll go get your *norteamericana* to sit on my face," Antonio said to Victor.

Victor smoked his cigar and looked at me. "Feliz Navidad," he said after a while.

Here is what Charlotte Douglas was said by Elena to have done with the twenty-four white roses Victor sent her on Christmas Eve: left them untouched in their box and laid the box in the hallway for the night maid.

9

"IT'S DEPRESSING TO BE sick in a hotel."

"I don't mind it." She said it as a child might, and she said nothing more.

"At Christmas."

"I didn't mind."

I tried again. "You're at the mercy of the maids."

"They're very nice here."

I watched Charlotte Douglas unwrap a cracker and fold the cellophane into a neat packet. She had insisted that we meet not at my house but at the Capilla del Mar, that I be her guest.

"Actually I'm never depressed." The act of saying this seemed to convince her that it was so, and she picked up the wine list in a show of resolute conviviality. "Actually I don't believe in being depressed. It's hard to keep wine in this climate, isn't it? Wine and crackers?"

Through two courses of that difficult dinner she never mentioned Victor.

She guided every topic to its most general application.

She talked as if she had no specific history of her own.

No Leonard.

No Warren.

As dessert was served she mentioned Marin for the first time: she said that she preferred the Capilla del Mar to the Jockey Club because the colored lights strung outside the Capilla del Mar reminded her of the Tivoli Gardens, where she had once flown with Marin for the weekend. Her face came alive with pleasure as she described this adult's dream of a weekend a child might like, described the puppet shows, the watermills, the picnics with the child. They had made dinners of salami and petits fours. They had scarcely slept. They had wandered beneath the colored lights until Marin's heels blistered, and then they had taken off their shoes and wandered barefoot.

"And when we got back to the hotel we ordered cocoa from room service." Charlotte Douglas leaned across the table. "And I let Marin place the order and tip the waiter and I taught her how to wash out her underwear at night."

I asked if her husband had gone to Copenhagen on business, but she said no. Her husband had not gone to Copenhagen at all. She had just woken up one morning in the house on California Street and decided to fly Marin to Copenhagen. "To see Tivoli. I mean before she was too old to like it."

Her eyes were fixed on the colored lights strung over our table on the porch at the Capilla del Mar. The lights at the Capilla del Mar were not Christmas lights but souvenirs of the season I married Edgar in São Paulo, the season a deranged Haitian dentist convinced the Minister of Health to string the entire city of Boca Grande with a web of colored lights as a specific against typhoid. The red and blue strings mostly shorted out in the first rain, leaving the city in the evening bathed in a necrotic yellow. So it was the night Edgar and I first arrived in Boca Grande from São Paulo. Edgar took me directly to Millonario and left me there until the epidemic waned. When I next saw the city many people had died and the rest seemed immune and the only lights left were at the Capilla del Mar.

I mentioned this to Charlotte.

"That's very interesting," Charlotte said politely, her eyes still on the lights. She had been smoking a cigarette as I talked and there was no ashtray and now, instead of just tossing the cigarette over the porch railing, she flicked off the lighted head with her fingernail, stripped the paper with the same fingernail and crumbled the tobacco neatly into the loam of a potted plant. I had seen men do this often and I had seen women do it in the field but I had never before seen a woman in a beige silk St. Laurent dress do it in a restaurant which passed for fashionable, and the casual dispatch with which Charlotte Douglas did it seemed at distinct odds with her rather demented account of the trip to Copenhagen. "By the way," she said then. "Marin and I are inseparable."

Some weeks later Charlotte again mentioned the weekend she had taken Marin to see Tivoli before she was too old to like it. She said that because Marin had run a fever all weekend, a reaction to her smallpox vaccination, they had never left the Hôtel Angleterre. She had obtained a doctor who was very understanding and nice. The manager at the Angleterre had been very understanding and nice and had sent Marin a marzipan carousel to make up for not seeing Tivoli. In any case it had rained all weekend.

One of two things was true: either Charlotte had gone with Marin to the Tivoli Gardens or Charlotte had wanted to go with Marin to the Tivoli Gardens.

Type of Visa TURISTA. Occupation MADRE.

10

THE NEXT TIME I saw Charlotte Douglas she grabbed up a chicken on the run and snapped the vertebrae in its neck. I had taken her to the annual picnic for the children of the workers in the Millonario groves and the men were killing chickens with machetes but Charlotte's kill was clean. There was no blood. She killed this chicken as efficiently and reflexively as she had field-stripped the cigarette at the Capilla del Mar.

"All the children have red shoes," she said to me and Elena as she handed the dead chicken to the man who had been trying to catch it. She had only smiled vaguely at the man's attempt to congratulate her. She seemed entirely unaware that for a guest of the *dueña* to kill a chicken with her hands was at Millonario an event worth remark. Even Elena had forgotten her sulky pique at being in Millonario and was staring at Charlotte, speechless.

"Red cardboard patent-leather shoes," Charlotte said. "All of them. Why do the children wear red shoes?"

"That chicken," Elena said.

"I mean you see them all over the tropics. Those red shoes."

"How exactly did you kill that chicken?" Elena said.

"Not the right way at all, actually." Charlotte's expression did not change. "Actually they're better if you bleed them live. Marin wanted a pair of red shoes once. When she was six. She cried, I wouldn't buy them."

Charlotte looked away and lifted the hair off her neck.

"I did have a baby who had red shoes," she said after a while. She stood up then and rinsed her hands in a ditch and when she straightened up she dried her hands on her skirt and gazed for a long time at the men still killing chickens with machetes. "You ought to tell them, chickens are better if you bleed them live. There was no reason not to buy Marin those shoes."

Nationality NORTEAMERICANA.

II

A GOLD CIGARETTE lighter engraved "D.N.C. ATLANTIC CITY '64."

A letter of introduction from the Wells-Fargo Bank in San Francisco to the Banco de la República, collapsed two regimes back.

A California drivers' license, recently expired, and credit cards from American Express, Gulf Oil, the Ochsner Clinic in New Orleans, I. Magnin and Saks Fifth Avenue.

$26 American and an equivalent amount in local currency.

An unsealed envelope addressed only to a post-office box in Buffalo, New York. An unfinished letter describing the resemblance of the Capilla del Mar to the Tivoli Gardens.

Two lipsticks, one broken pencil, a folded envelope containing four sulfathalidine and two salt tablets, a vial containing a scent predominantly gardenia, a fortune-cookie tape printed "A surprise is in store for someone you love," and a frayed clipping of one day's horoscope from *Prensa Latina*.

This is a list of the items said to be in Charlotte Douglas's possession (and later returned to the manager of the Hotel del Caribe) at the time of her death in the Estadio Nacional. The square emerald she wore in place of a wedding ring was neither listed nor returned. I took the gold cigarette lighter to Marin in Buffalo but Marin said she had no interest in the past. I do.

TWO

I

THE WIND IS UP TONIGHT.
Palm fronds clatter.

Shutters bang against the sills but I cannot close the windows because the house smells of cancer. Gerardo is somewhere over the sea, due home on the midnight Air France. When I think of the sea here tonight I imagine the water abruptly receding, then swelling back in the tidal surge, *la marejada*, drowning the sea wall, silencing the dogs, softening my burning skin and rinsing my brittle hair and floating the Liberian tanker in the harbor across the submerged boulevards of Progreso *primero.*

Sand-strewn caverns cool and deep
Where the winds are all asleep.

Wishful thinking.

La marejada will not come tonight, nor will I die tonight.

All that will happen tonight is that the generator will fail as usual and I will sit in the dark reciting Matthew Arnold as usual and when Gerardo arrives from the airport I will pretend to be asleep.

Again as usual.

Since Charlotte's death Gerardo and I have had to learn how to make conversation by day and avoid it in the dark, how to pretend together that my indifference to his presence derives from my being asleep, or in pain, or hallucinating. I am not in such pain that I hallucinate but other people prefer to think that I am. When I speak above a whisper Gerardo and Elena and Victor and Antonio avert their eyes. Even Isabel and Bianca avert their eyes. Even the dim Mendana cousin they brought in from Millonario to nurse me averts her eyes, and crosses herself every time I vomit or ask for a rum-and-quinine or suggest that she is repeating herself. This particularly tedious Mendana was trained as a Sister of Mercy, left the order in 1944 but continues to wear her full habit around Millonario and at family deathbeds, and fancies herself the dispatch-rider between the rest of us and heaven. When I interrupt her accounts of local miracles on the third telling she consoles herself by dismissing me as "*de afuera*," an outsider. I am *de afuera.*

I have been *de afuera* all my life. I was *de afuera* even at the Brown Palace Hotel. It is a little more than a year now since Charlotte Douglas's death and almost two years since her arrival in Boca Grande.

Charlotte Douglas's death.

Charlotte Douglas's murder.

Neither word works.

Charlotte Douglas's previous engagement.

Some of what I know about Marin Bogart's disappearance I know from Charlotte. Some of it I know from Leonard Douglas. Some of it I know from having once seen Warren Bogart and some of it I know from having once seen Marin but most of what I know, the most reliable part of what I know, derives from my training in human behavior.

I do not mean my training under Kroeber at California, nor with Lévi-Strauss at São Paulo.

I mean my training in being *de afuera*.

Nothing I know about Marin's disappearance comes from the "pages" Charlotte apparently wrote during her first weeks in Boca Grande, the pages she was heard typing at night in her room at the Caribe, the pages given to me with her other personal effects by the manager of the Caribe. On those pages she had tried only to rid herself of her dreams, and these dreams seemed to deal only with sexual surrender and infant death, commonplaces of the female obsessional life. We all have the same dreams.

2

THE MORNING THE FBI men first came to the house on California Street Charlotte did not understand why. She had read newspaper accounts of the events they recited, she listened attentively to everything they said, but she could make no connection between the pitiless revolutionist they described and Marin, who at seven had stood on a chair to make her own breakfast and wept helplessly when asked to clean her closet.

Sweet Marin.

Who at sixteen had been photographed with her two best friends wearing the pink-and-white candy-striped pinafores of Children's Hospital volunteers, and had later abandoned her Saturdays at the hospital as "too sad."

Soft Marin.

Who at eighteen had been observed with her four best friends detonating a crude pipe bomb in the lobby of the Transamerica Building at 6:30 A.M., hijacking a P.S.A. L–1011 at San Francisco Airport and landing it at Wendover, Utah, where they burned it in time for the story to interrupt the network news and disappeared.

Marin.

Or so the two FBI men tried to tell Charlotte.

Marin who had eaten coconut ice beneath the Great Banyan at Calcutta.

Marin who had been flown to Copenhagen to see the lights at Tivoli.

Marin who was at that moment, even as the two FBI men occupied Leonard's Barcelona chairs, even as the fat FBI man toyed with one of Leonard's porcelain roses and even as the thin FBI man gazed over Charlotte's head at the 10′ by 16′ silk screen of Mao Tse-tung given to Leonard by one of the Alameda Three, skiing at Squaw Valley.

Or so Charlotte tried to tell the fat FBI man.

The thin one did not seem to be listening.

I am talking here about a day in November one year before the day in November when Charlotte Douglas first appeared in Boca Grande.

One amplification. Some of what Charlotte said about the months which followed Marin's disappearance she did not even say to me. She said it to Gerardo.

I would call that the least reliable part of what I know.

Three or four things I do know about Charlotte.

As a child of comfortable family in the temperate zone she had been as a matter of course provided with clean sheets, orthodontia, lamb chops, living grandparents, attentive god-parents, one brother named Dickie, ballet lessons, and casual timely information about menstruation and the care of flat silver, as well as with a small wooden angel, carved in Austria, to sit on her bed table and listen to her prayers. In these prayers the child Charlotte routinely asked that "it" turn out all right, "it" being unspecified and all-inclusive, and she had been an adult for some years before the possibility occurred to her that "it" might not. She had put this doubt from her mind. As a child of the western United States she had been provided as well with faith in the value of certain frontiers on which her family had lived, in the virtues of cleared and irrigated land, of high-yield crops, of thrift, industry and the judicial system, of progress and education, and in the generally upward spiral of history. She was a *norteamericana*.

She was immaculate of history, innocent of politics. There were startling vacuums in her store of common knowledge. During the two years she spent at Berkeley before she ran away to New York with an untenured instructor named Warren Bogart, she had read mainly the Brontës and *Vogue*, bought a loom, gone home to Hollister on weekends and slept a great deal during the week. In those two years she had entered the main library once, during a traveling exhibition of the glass flowers from Harvard. She recalled having liked the glass flowers. From books Warren Bogart gave her to read when she was twenty Charlotte learned for the first time about the Spanish Civil War, memorized the ideological distinctions among the various PSUC brigades and POUM militia, but until she was twenty-two and Warren Bogart divined and corrected her misapprehension she believed that World War II had begun at Pearl Harbor. From Leonard Douglas she had absorbed a passing fluency in Third World power, had learned what the initials meant in Algeria and Indochina and the Caribbean, but on a blank map of the world she could not actually place the countries where the initials were in conflict. She considered the conflict dubious in any case. She understood that something was always going on in the world but believed that it would turn out all right. She believed the world to be peopled with others like herself. She associated the word "revolution" with the Boston Tea Party, one of the few events in the history of the United States prior to the westward expansion to have come to her attention. She also associated it with events in France and Russia that had probably turned out all right, otherwise why had they happened.

A not atypical *norteamericana.*

Of her time and place.

It occurs to me tonight that give or take twenty years and a thousand miles Charlotte Douglas's time and place and my time and place were not too different.

Some things about Charlotte I never understood. She was a woman who grew faint when she noticed the blue arterial veins in her wrists, could not swim in clouded water, and once suffered an attack of acute terror while wading in water where an artesian well churned up the sand. Yet during the time she was in Boca Grande I saw her perform a number of tasks with the same instinctive lack of squeamishness I had seen that day at Millonario. I once saw her skin an iguana for stew. I once saw her make the necessary incision in the trachea of an OAS field worker who was choking on a piece of steak at the Jockey Club. A doctor had been called but the OAS man was turning blue. Charlotte did it with a boning knife plunged first in a vat of boiling rice. A few nights later the OAS man caused a scene because Charlotte refused to fellate him on the Caribe terrace, but that, although suggestive of the ambiguous signals Charlotte tended to transmit, is neither here nor there. Similarly, during the cholera outbreak that year Charlotte volunteered to give inoculations, and she did, for thirty-four hours without sleeping, until the remaining Lederle vaccine was appropriated by one of Victor's colonels. When the colonel suggested that as a *norteamericana* she might be in a position to buy back some of the vaccine Charlotte only smiled, took off the white smock she had borrowed from the clinic, and dropped it at the colonel's feet. For the rest of that day Charlotte sat on the edge of the Caribe pool with her feet in the water and stared at the birds circling in the white sky. She did not wear dark glasses and by five o'clock the pale skin around her eyes was burned and puffy. For a few days Charlotte spoke to Gerardo about leaving Boca Grande, but within a week she had revised the incident to coincide with her own view of human behavior and assured me that the vaccine had been taken only so that the army could lend its resources to the inoculation program. I used to think that the only event in Charlotte Douglas's life to resist her revisions and erasures was Marin's disappearance.

"Interesting portrait there," the thin FBI man said, his eyes still on the 10′ by 16′ silk screen given to Leonard by one of the Alameda Three.

"Warhol," Charlotte said.

"I would have guessed Mao."

"Mao. Of course." Charlotte had no idea how one of the Alameda Three had happened to come by a Warhol silk screen. Or maybe it had not been one of the Alameda Three at all, maybe it had been one of the Tacoma Eleven or some Indian or Panther or heir to a motion-picture studio, Charlotte could never keep Leonard's clients straight. They came in packs and they ate and they asked for odd drinks and they went through her medicine cabinet and they borrowed and did not return her sweaters and they never addressed her directly and she could never remember their names. She wished that she could. She also wished that Marin would walk through the door of the house on California Street with a tow ticket tied to her windbreaker.

"You see you don't know Marin," she added finally. "I know her."

The fat FBI man coughed. The other examined a matchbook he had picked up from a table.

"I mean I'm her mother."

"Of course you are," the fat FBI man said.

"I don't quite follow what she's saying about this Chinese couple," one of the new FBI men said. It was almost time for lunch and Charlotte had not yet eaten breakfast and the house on California Street seemed to be filling with men who spoke to each other as if Charlotte were not there. "What Chinese couple."

"The Chinese couple who come to the house," Charlotte repeated. "And do the Peking duck."

"I don't quite follow what she's talking about."

"She's talking about caterers, Eddie, it's not a point."

"Maybe if she could run through it again. Marin arrives from Berkeley. Start there. Day before yesterday. Approximately twenty hours prior to the bombing. Marin arrives from Berkeley to—"

"To borrow a windbreaker." Charlotte spoke by rote. "To go skiing."

"To borrow a windbreaker. But she doesn't leave right away. She goes up to her room and she's up there alone maybe three, four hours, ballpark figure, you aren't sure which. Up in her room she—"

"You wanted her to tell it, Eddie, let her tell it."

Charlotte raised her voice. "She went through some things in her drawers."

"What things?"

"I don't know what things. She's eighteen years old, I don't go through her drawers."

"Mrs. Douglas mentioned a gold bracelet, Eddie, don't forget the gold bracelet."

"You mentioned a gold bracelet, Mrs. Douglas."

"I said she found a gold bracelet she thought she'd lost."

"In a drawer."

"In a drawer, behind a drawer." There was something about the gold bracelet Charlotte wanted not to think about. Marin had dropped the bracelet on the kitchen table and told Charlotte to keep it. Marin had called the bracelet "dead metal." Charlotte wished suddenly that she had not mentioned the bracelet and she also wished suddenly that Leonard were not in Nicosia. Or Damascus. Or wherever he was. He had written out the cities and the hotels and the telephone numbers on a legal pad upstairs but Charlotte had not looked at it since he left. Her left temple was beginning to hurt and she resented the FBI men for remembering the gold bracelet.

"Now we get to the part where I call the Chinese couple and ask them to do the Peking duck." She could hear the edge in her voice but could not control it. "All right?"

"We're back to the Chinese couple, Eddie."

"Caterers," the man the others called Eddie said.

"Not exactly," Charlotte said.

"They come to your house? They cook dinner?"

Charlotte nodded.

"Then they're caterers. Wasn't that kind of an exceptional thing to do, Mrs. Douglas, telephoning these caterers?"

"I don't quite see the exceptional part." Charlotte wished that the FBI man would not insist on calling the Chinese couple "caterers." They were not caterers, they were a couple. Under certain circumstances which had not yet arisen they might come to the house on California Street not as cooks but as guests. Charlotte knew a lot of couples like the Chinese couple who did the Peking duck. She knew the Algerian couple who did the couscous, she knew the Indonesian couple who did the rijsttafel, she knew the Mexican couple who were actually second-generation Chicano but who did the authentic Mexican dinner, not common enchiladas and refried beans but exquisite recipes they had learned while vacationing at the Hotel Inglaterra in Tampico. She knew the Filipino couple, she knew the Korean couple. She had recently uncovered the Vietnamese couple. In the kitchen of the house on California Street these and other couples regularly reproduced the menus of underdeveloped countries around the world, but usually for twelve or twenty-four people. Charlotte had never before called one of these couples to cook for fewer than twelve. This time she had. That might be the exceptional part. She began to see calling the Chinese couple to do Peking duck for herself and Marin in a different light, a light not necessarily more revealing but different.

In this light the gold bracelet she had made Marin take had been too loose on Marin's wrist.

In this light Marin had been too thin and pale for a child who skied and played tennis and was supposed to have spent the week before celebrating Thanksgiving off Cabo San Lucas.

In this light Charlotte had lit the fire and turned on the record-player and called the Chinese couple for the same reason she had insisted that Marin take the bracelet: to keep Marin from the harm outside.

"I mean a catered dinner for two must be quite an expensive proposition," the FBI man said.

"They're quite reasonable." Charlotte spoke automatically. "Considering."

"Catered dinner for *one*," the FBI man said. "Technically. Since Marin didn't stay."

"Marin had a paper to finish before she went skiing, I told you." Charlotte avoided the blank gaze of the FBI men. "She had a paper to finish for her seminar in I think *Moby Dick*."

The fat FBI man spoke for the first time since the arrival of the others. "She's not registered as a student, Mrs. Douglas, I suppose you know that."

"Actually you should try this couple." Charlotte spoke very clearly to shut out his voice. She did not know why she had said it was a seminar in *Moby Dick*. Marin had never mentioned any seminar in *Moby Dick*.

"She hasn't been registered for two quarters, and the quarter before that she took all incompletes, but I'm sure you know this."

"I mean if you like Cantonese food at all."

Moby Dick had something to do with Warren.

At nineteen Charlotte had written a paper on Melville and Warren had failed her. Warren had failed her and had rung her doorbell for the first time at midnight with the paper torn in half and a bag of cherries and a bottle of bourbon and they had not left the apartment for forty-eight hours. For the first three she called him Mr. Bogart and for the next forty-five she called him nothing at all and it was not until the third day, when he took her to his apartment and asked her to clean it up and she came across the letter from the department chairman advising him that his contract would not be renewed, that she ever called him Warren.

Still not looking at the FBI man Charlotte stood up and began placing their coffee cups on a tray.

"They also do a marvelous Szechuan beef thing."

The fat FBI man signaled the others to leave the room.

"Marin's father taught a seminar in *Moby Dick* once," Charlotte said before she broke.

After the FBI men left that morning Charlotte went upstairs to Marin's room. The Raggedy Ann Warren had sent for Marin's twelfth birthday was on its shelf. The teddy bear Warren had sent for Marin's fourteenth Easter was on its chair. The guitar once used by Joan Baez was on the windowseat, where it had been since the night Leonard bought it for Marin at an ACLU auction. The embroidered Swiss organdy curtains were as pristine as they had been the day Marin picked them out. The old valentines beneath the glass on the dressing table were unchanged, the tray of silver bangles and bath oil and eye shadow untouched. All that Marin had removed from the room was every picture, every snapshot, every clipping or class photograph, which contained her own image.

3

ONE IMAGINES A SWEET indolent girl, soft with baby fat, her attention span low and her range of interests limited. Marin approved of infants and puppies. Marin disapproved of "meanness" and "showing off." She appeared to approve equally of Leonard and Warren, and tailored her performance to please each of them. When Warren came to San Francisco she would appear instinctively in the navy-blue blazer no longer required by the progressive Episcopal day school she attended. For Leonard and his friends she would wear blue jeans, and a *dashiki* which scratched her skin. On principle she "adored madly" the presents Warren occasionally sent, although by her fifteenth birthday these presents still ran to the sporadic stuffed animal in a box bearing the charge-plate stamp of whatever woman he was living with at the time. In principle she was tolerant of Leonard's efforts on the behalf of social justice, although in practice she often found the beneficiaries of these efforts "weird" and their predicaments "unnecessary." That Episcopal day school Marin attended from the age of four until she entered Berkeley had as its aim "the development of a realistic but optimistic attitude," and it was characteristic of Charlotte that whenever the phrase "realistic but optimistic" appeared in a school communiqué she read it as "realistic and optimistic."

That was Charlotte.

Not Marin.

Marin would never bother changing a phrase to suit herself because she perceived the meanings of words only dimly, and without interest. Perhaps because of her realistic but optimistic attitude Marin was easily confused by such moral questions as were raised by the sight of someone disfigured (would a good God make ugly people?) or the problem of dividing her Halloween candy with the Episcopal orphans (do six licorice balls for the orphans equal one Almond Hershey for Marin, if Marin dislikes licorice?), and when confused could turn sulky, and withdrawn.

What else do I know about Marin.

I know that her posture toward all adult women was agreeably patronizing.

I know that her posture toward all adult men, toward Leonard and toward Warren and toward any man at all who was not disfigured, was uncomplicatedly seductive. Her mind was empty of grudges and hurts and family malice. Her energies were simple and physical and in the summertime her blond hair had the cast of pale verdigris from the chlorine in swimming pools. Charlotte adored her, brushed her pale hair and licked the tears from her cheeks, held her hand crossing streets and wanted never to let go, believed that when she walked through the valley of the shadow she would be sustained by the taste of Marin's salt tears, her body and blood. The night Charlotte was interrogated in the Estadio Nacional she cried not for God but for Marin. Gerardo told me that. I prefer not to know who told Gerardo.

4

"I SEE," Leonard kept saying from wherever he was on the day the FBI first came to the house on California Street. "I see."

"I don't see," Charlotte said. "Frankly I don't see at all."

There was a silence. "You're calling from the house."

"What difference does it make."

Charlotte could hear only the faint crackle on the cable. Actually she had forgotten that she was never supposed to call Leonard from the house if she had anything important to tell him. She was supposed to lose any possible surveillance and place the call on what Leonard called a neutral line. During the Mendoza trial in Cleveland she had called Leonard every day from a pay phone in Magnin's and once she had taken a room in a motel on Van Ness just to call London and tell Leonard that she missed him, but now that she had to tell him that Marin was said to have bombed the Transamerica Building she was calling from the white Princess phone in Marin's room.

"I mean what difference could it possibly make if they're listening, since I'm only telling you what they told me in the first place."

Still Leonard said nothing.

"I mean," Charlotte said, "I can't leave the house."

"I want you to leave the house. I want you to stay with Polly Orben in Sausalito. I want you to call Polly Orben right away—"

"I don't want to stay with Polly Orben." Polly Orben had been Leonard's analyst for eight years. Charlotte did not know what Polly Orben and Leonard had been talking about for eight years but Polly Orben frequently reported that they were within a year or so of "terminating," or "ending." She seemed to mean finishing the analysis. "I don't want to leave the house."

"It's Wednesday, Polly counsels at Glide on Wednesday, call her at Glide—"

"I have to be here when Marin calls."

"My point is this." Leonard spoke very carefully. "You don't know where Marin is."

"That's exactly why I have to be here."

"And if you don't know where Marin is, then you can't *tell* anyone where Marin is. Under oath. Can you."

Charlotte said nothing.

"If you see my point."

Still Charlotte said nothing.

"Get in touch with Warren. Tell him exactly what I just told you. Tell him he doesn't want to hear from her."

"I guess I'll just wait here and perjure myself," Charlotte said finally. "And then hire you."

Charlotte did not call Polly Orben at Glide. Charlotte did not get in touch with Warren. For the rest of that day Charlotte only lay on Marin's bed, staring at the black-button eyes of the Raggedy Ann Warren had sent for Marin's twelfth birthday. Charlotte did not see how Marin could have played any useful role in flying an L-1011 to Wendover, Utah. Marin could not even drive a car with a manual transmission.

Marin could not fly an L-1011 so Marin must be skiing at Squaw Valley.

Marin had called her great-grandmother's wedding bracelet dead metal.

Marin had been in bed with the flu on her twelfth birthday and as if she were four instead of twelve had slept all night with Warren's Raggedy Ann in her arms.

When it began to rain at six o'clock Charlotte wrapped herself in Marin's blanket but did not close the windows. She went downstairs only once, when two of the FBI men came back to ask if she had a recent photograph of Marin.

"I don't know." In a drawer upstairs she had three recent photographs that Marin had overlooked but there was some quite definite reason why she did not want the FBI men to have them. She could not put her finger on the reason but she knew that there was one. "I'd have to look."

She made no move to look.

She realized suddenly that she was still holding the Raggedy Ann, with its dress pulled up to show the red heart that said I LOVE YOU.

One of the FBI men cleared his throat.

"I don't suppose you've heard from her," he said finally.

"I'm sure you'd tell us if you had," the other said.

She wanted to slide the Raggedy Ann behind a pillow but she was sitting in one of Leonard's Barcelona chairs and there were no pillows.

"Actually I wouldn't," she said finally.

"Mrs. Douglas—"

"Actually I'd lie. I'd lie to you and I'd perjure myself in court. You know that. You heard me tell my husband that on the telephone."

The two FBI men looked away from each other.

"Or if you didn't hear me *someone* in your office certainly did, you should compare notes down there." She did not want to talk to the FBI this way but she could hear her own voice and it sounded bright and social and it did not stop. "Someone down there's been listening to me on the telephone for at least five years, you should know me by now. I'd lie."

"I'm sure you know that under the law a parent has no special—"

The other FBI man held up his hand as if to silence his partner.

"Maybe you'd like someone to stay with you tonight, Mrs. Douglas. Keep an eye on things."

"I *have* someone keeping an eye on things. I have all those people you moved into the apartment across the street. Haven't I. I mean I didn't see you move them in, but I know how you operate." She could not seem to stop herself. It was the Raggedy Ann. She resented their catching her with the Raggedy Ann. "One thing I *don't* know. I don't know if you kept tapes of all those telephone calls."

Neither man spoke.

"I mean it could be very useful if you did. If you could sit down now and listen to those telephone calls you'd probably know more about Marin and me and Leonard and Warren than I even remember. You could probably figure the whole thing out."

One of the men closed his briefcase. The other reached for his raincoat.

"You must have six or seven hundred hours on Marin and Lisa Harper alone. Doing their algebra." Charlotte smoothed the Raggedy Ann's dress over its red heart and did not look at the FBI men. "Lisa's at Stanford this year. In case you missed the installment when Lisa got into Stanford and Marin didn't."

"We're not on opposing sides, Mrs. Douglas."

"Marin cried when the letter came from Stanford. You probably remember that. Marin crying."

The next morning when Charlotte woke in Marin's bed the rain was streaming down Marin's organdy curtains and puddling on the parquet floor. Charlotte knew as she woke why she could not give the FBI a recent photograph of Marin. She could not give the FBI a recent photograph of Marin because any photograph useful to them would show Marin's eyes, and then Marin's eyes would stare back at her from newspapers and television screens, and she was not yet ready to deliver her child to history.

Another day passed and still Charlotte did not place a call to Warren. It was not possible to actually "call" Warren: it was necessary instead to "place a call" to Warren, to leave messages at various offices and apartments he frequented around New York and wait for him to call back. Usually he called back between one and three A.M. San Francisco time, or four and six A.M. New York time.

"Where's your interesting Jew husband," Warren would say if Charlotte did place the call and he did call back. He would say this if Charlotte had placed the call to say that Marin had a cold and he would say this if Charlotte had placed the call to say that Marin was going to tennis camp and he would also say this if Charlotte were to place a call to say that Marin was wanted by the FBI.

"I'm calling about something important," she would say.

She knew what she would say because she knew what he would say.

"I said where's your interesting Jew husband," he would say.

"Leonard is not Jewish. As you know. I'm calling—"

"There's nothing wrong with being 'Jewish.' As you say. Has he made an anti-Semite out of you along with everything else?"

"I have to tell you—"

"All you 'have to tell' me is where the well-known radical lawyer is. Come on. Admit it. He's at Bohemian Grove, isn't he. He's . . . let me get it right, he's *making the revolution at Bohemian Grove*."

She would not place a call to Warren just yet.

In any case Warren could not learn about Marin from the FBI because the FBI would not know how to place a call to Warren.

In any case there was no need to place a call to Warren because Marin was skiing at Squaw Valley.

In any case Leonard would place the call to Warren.

Charlotte settled many problems this way.

Leonard flew home immediately but because of an airport strike at Beirut and a demonstration at Orly it took him thirty-six hours to arrive in San Francisco, and by then they had sifted the debris and identified Marin's gold bracelet attached like a charm to the firing pin of the bomb. They had also received the tape, and released Marin's name to the press. Charlotte learned about the tape when she opened the door of the house on California Street and found a television crew already filming. On the six o'clock news there was film that showed Charlotte opening the door, turning from the camera and running upstairs as a young Negro pursued her with a microphone. When this film was repeated at eleven it was followed for the first time by the picture of Marin, the famous picture of Marin Bogart, the two-year-old newspaper picture of Marin in her pink-and-white candy-striped Children's Hospital volunteer's pinafore. The newspaper had apparently lost the negative and simply cropped and enlarged a newsprint reproduction in which Marin was almost indistinguishable, clearly a complaisant young girl in a pinafore but enigmatically expressionless, her eyes only smudges on the gravure screen. In the weeks that followed the appearance of the picture those two photogravure smudges would eradicate every other image Charlotte had of Marin's eyes. The day I finally saw Marin I was surprised by her eyes. She has Charlotte's eyes. She has nothing else of Charlotte's but she has Charlotte's eyes.

5

YOU NO DOUBT heard the tape.

"This is not an isolated action. We ask no one's permission to make the revolution."

I heard only part of it, on a Radio Jamaica relay, but I read excerpts from it in *Time* and in *Prensa Latina* and in the *Caracas Daily Journal*, excerpts always illustrated by the impenetrable picture of the child in the candy-striped pinafore. I heard only part of the Radio Jamaica relay because Gerardo was at the house the night it was played, and he had arranged the evening as usual to annoy and discomfit everyone involved. I used to think the design of such evenings Gerardo's only true amusement.

Or more accurately his only true vocation.

Since he was only fitfully amused by anything at all.

In the first place Gerardo had asked Elena to come for dinner that night. That Elena came was a tribute to Gerardo's sexual power over her, because Elena was not speaking to me. Elena was not speaking to me because I had that morning advised her that she and Gerardo would be better off exhibiting their tedious interest in each other's bodies in the Caribe ballroom than at political meetings under surveillance by both Victor and the Americans. I did not like hearing about Elena and Gerardo from Tuck Bradley. I did not like Tuck Bradley hearing about Elena and Gerardo from Kasindorf and Riley. As a matter of fact I had already heard about Elena and Gerardo, from Victor, and I did not like that either.

Elena said that Gerardo was the only person in the entire family who understood dancing or "fun."

I said that this might be true but in this case Gerardo's "fun" lay not in dancing but in embarrassing the family by parading the widow of a family *presidente* at meetings of people opposed to the family. It made no difference if Gerardo went to these meetings, because Gerardo's image in the community, deserved or not, was that of someone "worthless," and "young." It did make a difference if she, Elena, went to these meetings, because her image in the community, again deserved or not, was that of someone "virtuous," and "older."

A national treasure as it were.

But Elena had stopped speaking. Elena did not even know that these events to which Gerardo took her were "meetings." She believed them to be "parties." I think she still does.

In any case.

In the second place.

Just asking Elena to dinner had not quite sated Gerardo's craving for social piquancy. He had asked Elena and then he had proceeded to ask an extremely sullen girl he had been seeing off and on for years, an ambitious *mestiza* who had once gone to Paris with him and left him first for a minor Thyssen and then for an English rock-and-roll singer and had recently returned to Boca Grande to redeploy her resources. The girl was the daughter of the cashier at the Jockey Club and her name was Carmen Arrellano but she called herself Camilla de Arrellano y Bolívar and did not visit the Jockey Club. On this particular evening she was sulking because Gerardo was listening to the radio, and possibly also because I had told the cook to ignore her demand to be served a separate dinner of three boiled shrimp on a white plate with half a lemon wrapped in gauze. The cook had found this demand particularly offensive because her son was married to Carmen Arrellano's cousin.

"All class enemies must suffer exemplary punishment."

The voice on Radio Jamaica was sweetly instructive.

"When the fascist police think we are near we will be far away. When the fascist police think we are far away we will be near."

"She lisps," Gerardo said.

"She sounds like those Cubans at the party," Elena said. Elena had several times mentioned this "party" to which she and Gerardo had gone the night before, apparently thinking to annoy me and Carmen Arrellano in a single stroke. "Doesn't she, Gerardo. Those dreadful Cubans who came with Bebe Chicago. I don't mean the lisp, I mean the words."

"I'm only listening for the lisp," Gerardo said. "I wouldn't mention Bebe Chicago in front of Grace if I were you, she'll cut off your clothes allowance."

I said nothing. Bebe Chicago was a West Indian homosexual

who after some years at the London School of Economics and a few more organizing Caribbean "liberation fronts" out of Mexico had turned up in Boca Grande to see what he could promote. His name was François Parmentier but everyone called him Bebe Chicago. I have no idea why. He was said to have connections with the *guerrilleros*. I heard about him frequently, from both Victor and Tuck Bradley. People like Bebe Chicago come and go in Boca Grande, and the main mark they leave is to have provided inadvertent employment for the many other people required to follow them around and tap their telephones.

"Grace thinks Bebe Chicago and I are using you," Gerardo said.

"Delicious," Elena said. "Do it."

"Actually that's not the dynamic." Gerardo smiled at me and Elena. "Actually I'm using Bebe Chicago. Listen to this girl. I like the lisp and the pinafore together. Very nice."

"All you think about is sex," Elena said.

"You wish that were true," Gerardo said. "But it's not."

"She bores me," Carmen Arrellano said sullenly. Carmen had been arranged since dinner in a corner of the room where she could gaze at herself in a mirror. "It bores me."

"Of course it bores you," Gerardo said. "You don't like sex. You can't dress for it, there are never any photographers. Or is that what bores you?"

"The *radio*," Carmen said sullenly.

"I didn't dream you were listening," Elena said. "I thought you were devising a new makeup. Have you ever thought of bleaching your eyebrows?"

"I said this is boring me," Carmen said to Gerardo.

Gerardo held up a hand to silence her and moved closer to the radio.

"This was really a terribly amusing party you missed last night," Elena said to Carmen.

Carmen picked up a magazine.

"Steel band," Elena said. Actually Elena had not found the "party" amusing at all. Actually Elena had complained before she stopped speaking to me that Gerardo's friends did not dance but sat around a filthy room watching a Cuban film about sugar production. Elena smiled at Carmen. "Lots of

Dominicans and these frightful Cubans. We danced until five this morning. Are you still bored?"

"Carmen is always bored," Gerardo said. "Excuse me. *Camilla* is always bored. I want to hear this lisp."

"We shall reply to repression with liberation. We shall reply to the terrorism of the dictatorship with the terrorism of the revolution."

Elena continued to smile benignly at Carmen.

Carmen dropped her magazine on the floor and stood up.

"We're tiring your mother," Carmen announced to Gerardo. "And your amusing aunt."

"I should say," Elena said. "It's nearly nine."

"I'll take you home when this is over," Gerardo said. "Meanwhile you might listen."

"Pinched little parrot talking about capitalism," Carmen said. "Who cares about capitalism."

"That's very interesting, Carmen." Gerardo was turning the radio dials to keep the relay from fading. "It's very interesting because there's a body of thought that capitalism is precisely what ruined your character."

There was a silence.

Elena giggled.

"Also yours," Gerardo said to Elena. "Not that I agree entirely."

I was relieved when the relay faded out.

I was equally tired of listening to Gerardo and Elena and Carmen Arrellano and the little girl on the tape.

I recall that none of the four had my sympathy that night.

6

THE NIGHT CHARLOTTE first heard the tape she apparently tried to transcribe it word for word, so that she could explain to Leonard and Warren what Marin had in mind. She got only as far as the part where Marin discussed what she called the revolutionary character of her organization. "*Now I would like to discuss the revolutionary character of our organization,*" Marin definitely said on the tape. "*The fact that our organization is revolutionary in character is due above all to the fact that all our activity is defined as revolutionary.*"

Charlotte read this sentence several times. She wondered if she had misheard Marin, or missed an important clause. The tape was still running and Marin could still be heard, talking about "expropriation" and "firepower" and "revolutionary justice" and about how the Transamerica Building was one of many symbols of imperialist *latifundismo* in San Francisco, but Charlotte was still fixed on that one sentence. *The fact that our organization is revolutionary in character is due above all to the fact that all our activity is defined as revolutionary.* She could parse the sentence but she could make no sense of it, could find no way to rephrase it so that Leonard and Warren would understand.

As it turned out she did not need to explain the sentence to Leonard because when he arrived from the airport at midnight he said that the sentence was not original with Marin but had been lifted from a handbook by a Brazilian guerrilla theorist named Marighella.

"I've got just one thing to say about the operation," Leonard said.

Charlotte waited.

"I know where they got their rhetoric but I'd like to know where they got their hardware."

As it turned out Charlotte did not need to explain the sentence to Warren either because when he called from New York at two that morning he had already heard the tape and, like Leonard, he had just one thing to say about the operation.

"Fuck Marin," he said.

I think Warren Bogart would have had my sympathy that night.

7

WHEN I MARRIED Edgar Strasser-Mendana I received, from an aunt in Denver who had been taken as a bride to a United Fruit station in Cuba, twenty-four Haviland dessert plates in the "Windsor Rose" pattern and a letter of instructions for living in the tropics. I was to allow no nightsoil on my kitchen garden, boil water for douches as well as for drinking, preserve my husband's books with a thin creosote solution, schedule regular hours for sketching or writing and regard the playing of bridge as an avoidance of reality to be indulged only at biweekly intervals and never with depressive acquaintances. In this regime I could perhaps escape what the letter called the fever and disquiet of the latitudes. That I had been living in these same latitudes unmarried for some years made no difference to my aunt: she appeared to locate the marriage bed as the true tropic of fever and disquiet.

So in many ways did Charlotte.

As it happens I understand this position, having observed it for years in societies quite distant from San Francisco and Denver, but some women do not. Some women lie easily in whatever beds they make. They marry or do not marry with equanimity. They divorce or do not. They can leave a bed and forget it. They sleep dreamlessly, get up and scramble eggs.

Not Charlotte.

Never Charlotte.

I think I have never known anyone who regarded the sexual connection as quite so unamusing a contract. So dark and febrile and outside the range of the normal did all aspects of this contract seem to Charlotte that she was for example incapable of walking normally across a room in the presence of two men with whom she had slept. Her legs seemed to lock unnaturally into her pelvic bones. Her body went stiff, as if convulsed by the question of who had access to it and who did not. Whenever I saw her with both Victor and Gerardo it struck me that her every movement was freighted with this question. Who had prior claim. Whose call on her was most insistent. To whom did she owe what. If Gerardo's hand brushed hers in front of

Victor her face would flush, her eyes drop. If she needed a bottle of wine opened on those dismal valiant occasions when she put on her gray chiffon dress and tried to "entertain" she could never just hand the corkscrew to Gerardo. Nor could she hand the corkscrew to Victor. Instead she would evade the question by opening the wine herself, usually breaking the cork. I recall once telling Charlotte about a village on the Orinoco where female children were ritually cut on the inner thigh by their first sexual partners, the point being to scar the female with the male's totem. Charlotte saw nothing extraordinary in this. "I mean that's pretty much what happens everywhere, isn't it," she said. "Somebody cuts you? Where it doesn't show?"

I keep those cuts that don't show in mind when I think about Charlotte Douglas's passage from the house on California Street to the Boca Grande airport. Charlotte Amelia Douglas. Charlotte Amelia Bogart. Born Charlotte Amelia Havemeyer. Charlotte. I am not even certain she was talking figuratively.

In the first week after the release of Marin's tape these events occurred.

Charlotte received a call from a young woman in New York who said that Warren would arrive in San Francisco on a midnight plane. Warren did not.

Charlotte received a call from a spiritualist in the Netherlands who said that he perceived the aura of a girl in a pinafore selling tripe in the Belleville section of Paris. He would discuss his vision in detail upon receipt of a first-class airplane ticket to San Francisco, round-trip and refundable.

Leonard received a call from the sister of a convict at San Quentin who said that her brother had reason to know that Marin was working as an aide in a state mental hospital. He would name the state upon receipt of an unconditional parole.

The young woman in New York called back to say that Warren had missed the midnight plane but would arrive in San Francisco the next afternoon. Warren did not.

A pair of FBI men came for coffee every morning.

An apartment-court manager on the outskirts of Detroit told NBC that he had seen Marin and "two jumped-up coloreds" loading carbines into the trunk of a 1957 Pontiac at dawn in the Livonia Mall parking lot. By the time he appeared on CBS he described Marin's companions as "possibly black or Indian" and the car as a 1957 Pontiac "or some later-model General Motors vehicle." In the *Detroit Free Press* the story was headlined "A SEARCH FOR A NERVOUS INDIAN."

Marin was said to be in Havana.

Marin was said to be in Hanoi.

Warren left two messages on the answering service that he would definitely arrive in San Francisco via TWA the following morning at 10:35 A.M. He did not.

"What have we here," Leonard said when he finally walked into the room Charlotte had taken in the Fairmont Hotel. Leonard had addressed a bar luncheon on constitutional law at the Fairmont and a telephone had been brought to the dais and it was Warren calling from New York. Charlotte had watched Leonard take the call from Warren and then she had left the dais and gone to the desk and asked for a room and telephoned Leonard to meet her upstairs when he finished lunch. The room was cold and the radiator jammed off and the big windows overlooking the Pacific Union Club would not close. Yet for an hour and ten minutes Charlotte had been sitting barefoot in the gray afternoon light wearing only the handmade navy-blue silk underwear she had just bought in a shop in the lobby. She had been trying not to remember about Marin or Warren. She had been trying to remember a carnal mood.

"No. Don't tell me," Leonard said. "Let me guess. You decided the way to avoid seeing Warren was to move to the Fairmont."

"I don't want to talk about Warren," Charlotte said.

"I got him a ride out."

"Don't talk about him," Charlotte said. "Come here."

"I know perfectly well what you're doing. Even if you don't."

"Don't talk about it. Don't laugh. I just want it."

"You don't want it at all."

Charlotte sat on the edge of the bed and pulled the spread around herself. "I did."

"You're transparent, Charlotte. To everyone but yourself."

Charlotte gazed out the window. "Somebody died," she said after a while. "Somebody died at the Pacific Union Club. While you were talking. Downstairs."

"How do you know."

"The fire department came. The resuscitator squad. And then an ambulance. And they lowered the flag."

Leonard sat on a chair facing the bed. "I know exactly what you're trying to do."

"Look. You can see the flag. Half mast. What do you mean, you got him a ride out?"

"Never mind Warren. It's a lousy idea, Charlotte, trying to have a baby."

"Who said anything about a baby? I say I want to fuck, you say I don't. You say you got Warren a ride out, I say how, you say never mind Warren. I say somebody died at the Pacific Union Club, you start talking about having a baby. I don't know what you're talking about."

Leonard kept his eyes on Charlotte but she did not meet them.

"Quite honestly I don't."

"Quite honestly I don't think you do. Quite honestly I always know what you're thinking before you do. What you're thinking now is this: you get yourself pregnant, Warren can't get to you. ABC. QED. Don't ask me why. Where did you get that underwear."

Charlotte said nothing.

"Has it ever occurred to you that your primary erogenous zone is your underwear?"

Charlotte had pulled the bedspread closer and smoked a cigarette without speaking and there had not seemed any point in staying in the cold room after that. In the elevator it occurred to her that he had been trying to make her laugh with him but that was another mood she could not remember. In fact she did want a baby.

"He apparently called the office and gave Suzy a lot of shit before he got me here." Leonard nodded at the Fairmont doorman. "'Your friend *Warren*,' Suzy calls him."

"I don't want him to come out here."

"It's not up to you, Charlotte. Come out of your trance. He wants to come out."

"Then why hasn't he."

"You know as well as I do *why hasn't he*, Charlotte, he hasn't been able to promote an airplane ticket, that's *why hasn't he*."

"He didn't say that."

"Of course he didn't say that. Wake up."

Charlotte concentrated on trying to tie her scarf in the wind.

"So as soon as the Q-A was over I made a call and got him a ride out on Bashti Levant's plane."

"I can't—" Charlotte broke off.

"You can't what."

Charlotte shrugged.

"You can't what, Charlotte."

"I can't see Warren on a small plane with Bashti Levant for five hours." She had just seized on this but it was true. Bashti Levant was in the music business. Bashti Levant had "labels," and three-piece suits and large yellow teeth and obscure Balkan proclivities. "They won't like each other."

"No. They won't. They will cordially dislike each other and they will entirely entertain each other. That's not what you were going to say. You can't what."

Charlotte gave up on the scarf. "I can't deal with Warren right now."

"What's to 'deal with'? You were married to him, now you're married to me. You think you're the only two people in the world who used to fuck and don't any more?"

"Not at all." Another thing Charlotte could not deal with was Leonard's essentially rational view of the sexual connection. "There's also you and me."

"Not bad. You're waking up." Leonard seemed pleased. "Here's a taxi."

"I think I'll walk."

"Then walk," Leonard said as he got into the taxi.

Charlotte walked as far as Grace Cathedral and stood for a while just inside the nave in a particular pool of yellow light Marin had liked as a child. When the light shifted on the window and there was no more yellow Charlotte left the cathedral. She intended walking back to the Fairmont to get a taxi but there was one idling outside the cathedral, and Leonard was waiting in it, just as he had been waiting in a taxi outside the courthouse the morning she divorced Warren.

"She had a straw hat one Easter." Charlotte had taken Leonard's hand in the taxi but neither of them spoke until the house on California Street was in sight. "And a flowered lawn dress."

"Don't think you have to get yourself pregnant just to prove he doesn't have you any more, Charlotte."

"We took her to lunch at the Carlyle, I remember she was cold."

"Don't make the mistake of thinking you can just run it back through the projector, Charlotte."

"Warren gave her his coat."

Upstairs in the house on California Street Charlotte took off her skirt and sweater and laid them on a chair. She took off the pieces of handmade navy-blue underwear and let them drop to the floor. At the bottom of a drawer she found a faded flannel nightgown and she pulled on the nightgown and she lay on the bed and watched the last light leave the windows.

"And we drank a lot of Ramos Fizzes. And in the middle of lunch Warren said he had an appointment downtown. And when the check came I didn't have any money. I didn't even have two dollars for a taxi, Marin and I walked home." She turned to Leonard. "She was three. Everybody admired her hat. I think I was never so happy on a Sunday. Why are you bringing him out."

"He's her father, isn't he."

"I can't handle it."

Leonard sat on the edge of the bed and picked up the handmade pieces of navy-blue silk from the floor. They were very plain. They had no lace or embroidery. They had only the rows of infinitesimal stitches. "Maybe I want to see if you can. Somebody in the Azores went blind making these."

"Why do you have to bring him out."

"Because he gave her his coat," Leonard said.

"Somebody in the Philippines," Charlotte said. "Not the Azores. The Philippines."

8

"THOSE WERE FOUR truly wonderful specimens you condemned me to fly out here with," Warren said when he walked into the house on California Street at nine-thirty the next morning.

Charlotte stood perfectly still. Warren looked as if he had not slept in several days. His eyes were bloodshot, his chin stubbled. He was wearing sneakers and a muffler Charlotte recognized as one she had knit for herself the winter they lived in an unheated apartment on East 93rd Street, and he was carrying not a suitcase but two shopping bags stuffed with what appeared to be dirty laundry. He was also carrying one red rose, which he handed to Charlotte without looking at her.

"Four authentic gargoyles," he said. "Some favor you did me. The four worst people in the world. Climbers. Vermin. Gargoyles. New York trash. Hogarth caricatures. 25,000 feet, no exit. Deliver me from favors. I need a drink."

"You repeated gargoyles," Leonard said. "Otherwise vintage."

"The FBI is due at ten," Charlotte said.

"What's that got to do with your getting me a drink. Me no get FBI joke."

"I haven't heard that since it was still 'me no get Indian joke,'" Leonard said. "Which I remember vividly from the night I introduced you to the Maharanee of wherever she was from."

"Lower Pelham," Warren said. "She was the Maharanee of Lower Pelham." He dropped the shopping bags on the floor in front of the fireplace. An aerosol can of shaving cream and a balled seersucker suit stuffed with dirty socks rolled out. "Get somebody to wash and iron that, Charlotte, all right? The suit just needs pressing."

"We don't have any washers and ironers on the place today." Charlotte retrieved the aerosol can before it hit the open fire. "Or any pressers."

"I can see you're in one of your interesting moods. Tell me what else you can't do for me today, Charlotte. You think you can give me a drink? Or can't you."

Charlotte filled a glass with ice and splashed bourbon into it. Her hands were shaking. The veins on her arms were standing out and she did not want Warren to see them. When she finally spoke her voice was neutral. "Who exactly was on this plane?"

"All friends of yours, I have no doubt. Which reminds me, you look like hell, your veins show." Warren took the glass and drained it. "This Levant creature, whoever he is."

"Bashti Levant controls three out of five pop records sold in America." Leonard seemed amused. "As you know perfectly well."

"Yeah, well, I had some fun at his expense, I don't mind telling you. I had a little fun with him and this fat castrato he had along to bray at his jokes. This pasty Palm Beach castrato. 'P.L.U.,' he kept saying. 'People Like Us.' I let him know what category that was, don't think I didn't. Fawning capon. French cuffs. Parasitical eunuch."

"You didn't like him," Leonard said.

"Palm Beach trash hanger-on. I let the women alone."

"The last Southern gentleman," Leonard said.

"Not that they deserved it. Two terrible women. Terrible voices, terrible brays. The castrato only brayed when the Levant creature snapped his fingers, but the women brayed all the time. 3,000 miles of braying. *Le island. Le weekend. Les monkey-gland injections. Le* New York trash." Warren held out his glass to Charlotte. "I believe one of them was married to the Levant creature. Whoever he is, I have no idea."

"That surprises me. Since Leonard just told you."

"That surprises you, does it." Warren rattled the ice in his glass. "You surprise easier than you used to. I suppose this creature is a client of Leonard's."

"As a matter of fact he is."

"Leonard's got all the luck. Arabs. Jews. Indians. Bashti Levant."

"Niggers," Leonard said. "You forgot niggers."

"How exactly did this creature come to your attention, Leonard? He rape an Arab? Or is that possible. Actually I believe that's a solecism. Raping an Arab."

"You've had that Arab in the wings, I can tell by your delivery." Leonard took Warren's glass and filled it. "I got involved with Bashti on a dope charge a few years ago. Involving certain of his artists."

"I don't believe what I'm hearing. Bashti's artists."

"There was a civil-liberties issue."

"Of course there was." Warren choked with laughter and slapped his knee. "I knew there was."

"There was," Charlotte said.

In the silence that followed she could hear her voice echo, harsh and ugly. She fixed her eyes on the ring Leonard had brought her from wherever he had gone to meet the man who financed the Tupamaros.

The square emerald ring.

The big square emerald from some capital she could not remember.

"Listen to that voice," Warren said. "Let's have that tone of voice again."

Leonard looked at Charlotte and shook his head slightly.

Charlotte picked up a cigarette and lit it.

"No wonder your daughter left home," Warren said.

The red rose Warren had given Charlotte fell from the table to the floor.

Charlotte said nothing.

"All I hold against your daughter is she didn't catch Bashti Levant with that pipe bomb. Bashti and certain of his artists. That's the only bone I want to pick with your daughter. Your daughter and mine."

"He doesn't mellow," Leonard said finally.

"What did you expect, Leonard? You expect I'd hit forty-five and start applauding the family of man?" Warren drained his second drink. "It's my birthday, Charlotte. You haven't wished me happy birthday."

"I'll tell you something I expected, I expected—" Charlotte broke off. She did not know what she had expected. She concentrated on the emerald.

Bogotá.

Quito.

She had no idea where Leonard had met the man who financed the Tupamaros.

"Today's not your birthday," she said finally. "Your birthday was last month."

"Your husband expected a humanist."

"Leonard," Leonard said.

"Pardon?"

"Her husband's name is Leonard."

"I stole that rose for you," Warren said. "Off the flight of the living dead."

Dwelling on the past leads to unsoundness and dementia, my aunt also advised.

And, *Don't cry over curdled milk, Grace, make cottage cheese of it.*

And to the same doubtful point: *Remember Lot's Wife, avoid the backward glance.*

"Wish me happy birthday," Warren said. "Have a drink on my forty-fifth birthday."

"Your birthday was October 23rd," Charlotte said.

"She doesn't drink before breakfast," Leonard said. "It's hard and fast with her, she never does."

"She did on my thirtieth," Warren said.

"*Which was on October 23rd nineteen-hundred and*—oh shit."

"Watch your language," Warren said.

Avoid the backward glance.

Until Marin disappeared Charlotte had arranged her days to do exactly that.

9

I KNOW WHY Charlotte liked talking to the FBI: the agents would let her talk about Marin. Their devotion to Marin seemed total. They were pilgrims pledged to the collection of relics from Marin's passion. During the days before Warren arrived in San Francisco the agents had taken Charlotte to see Marin's apartment on Haste Street in Berkeley. The agents had taken Charlotte to see the house on Grove Street in Berkeley where they had found the cache of .30-caliber Browning automatic rifles and the translucent pink orthodontal retainer Marin was supposed to wear to correct her bite. In both those places the gray morning light fell through dusty windows onto worn hardwood floors and Charlotte had remembered for the first time how sad she herself had been at Berkeley before Warren came to her door.

"Let's flop back to one of the theories you were espousing yesterday, Mrs. Douglas. When you—"

"Let's flop back to all of them," Warren said. Warren had been sitting in the same chair ever since he walked into the house and dropped his shopping bags. He had gotten up only to get himself drinks and once, perfunctorily, when the FBI men arrived and Leonard left. "I'm the felon's father," he had said to the FBI men. He seemed bent now in a fit of laughter. "I want to flop back to every one of these theories Mrs. Douglas has been espousing. In my absence. I've been out of touch, I didn't know Mrs. Douglas had theories. To espouse."

"When I what?" Charlotte said.

"Flip flop. We need ice, Charlotte."

"When you—" The FBI man glanced uneasily at Warren. "When you said yesterday that Marin 'might have been sad,' what exactly did you mean? Normal everyday blues? Or something more, uh, out of the mainstream?"

"Just your normal everyday mainstream power-to-the-people *latifundismo* Berkeley blues." Warren was still bent with laughter. "Just those old Amerikan blues. Spell that with a K."

"I don't know what I meant," Charlotte said.

"Some theory," Warren said. "Did you get the K? Did you spell it with a K?"

"To push on for a moment, Mrs. Douglas, the office raised one other question. Did your daughter ever mention a Russian, name of, uh, let's see."

The FBI man examined his notebook.

"Those old Amerikan blues didn't *come* up the river from New Orleans, they K-O-M-E up the river from New Orleans. Get it? Charlotte? Did he get the K?"

"He got it."

"Gurdjieff," the FBI man said. "Russian, name of Gurdjieff. Marin ever mention him?"

"In the first place he was an Armenian," Warren said. "Otherwise you're on top of the case."

"I'm not sure I get your meaning, Mr. Bogart."

"Not at all. You're doing fine."

"Excuse me. The Gurdjieff I'm thinking of is a Russian."

"Excuse me. The Gurdjieff you're thinking of is Bashti Levant."

"Warren. Please."

"Don't you think that's funny, Charlotte? 'Excuse me, the Gurdjieff you're thinking of is Bashti Levant'?"

"It's funny, Warren. Now—"

"You used to think I was funny."

"Let me try to put this on track." The FBI man cleared his throat. "Marin ever mention a Gurdjieff of *any* nationality? Ever mention reading about him?"

"No," Charlotte said.

"Marin can't read," Warren said. "She plays a good game of tennis, she's got a nice backhand, good strong hair and an IQ of about 103."

Charlotte closed her eyes.

"Charlotte. Face facts. Credit where credit is due, you raised her. She's boring."

"I'm not sure this is a productive tack," the FBI man said.

"Irving's not sure this is a productive tack." Warren rattled his ice. "Hear, hear, Charlotte. Listen to Irving."

"Bruno," the FBI man said. "The name is Bruno Furetta."

"Don't mind me, Irving, I've been drinking."

"I happen to know you're not all that drunk, Warren." Charlotte did not open her eyes. "I happen to know you're just amusing yourself. As usual."

"You get the picture."

Charlotte stood up. "And I want to tell you that *I am not*—"

"She's overwrought," Charlotte heard Warren say as she fled the room. "Let me give you some advice, Irving. Never mind the Armenians, *cherchez le tennis pro*."

10

"Boo hoo," Warren said when he came upstairs an hour later. "What happened to your sense of humor?"

Charlotte said nothing. Very deliberately she closed the book she had been trying to read since the day after the FBI first came to the house on California Street. The book was a detailed analysis of the three rose windows at Chartres, not illustrated, and every time Charlotte picked it up she began again on page one. She did not want Warren in the room. She did not want Warren to be in any room where she slept with Leonard, did not want him to see Leonard's Seconal and her hand cream together on the table by the bed, did not want to see him examining the neckties that Leonard had that morning tried, rejected, and left on the bed. In fact she did not want him to see the bed at all.

"We don't have anything in common any more." Warren picked up a yellow silk tie and knotted it around his collar. "You and me. Leonard won't miss this, he's jaundiced enough. You ever noticed? He's got bad color?"

"One thing we have in common is that we both agree that as far as having anything in common goes—" Charlotte broke off. She was watching a tube of KY jelly on the table by the bed. She did not see any way to move it into the drawer without attracting Warren's attention. "As far as having anything in common goes we don't have anything. In common."

"You sound like you had a stroke. You had a stroke?"

"I happen to have a headache."

"You mean I happen to give you a headache."

"I mean I want you to leave this room."

"Don't worry, I'll leave this room." Warren sat on the bed, picked up the tube of KY jelly and put it in the drawer. "I don't like this room."

Charlotte said nothing.

"I only flew out here to see how you were."

Still Charlotte said nothing.

"I don't like your room, I don't like your house, I don't like your life." Warren picked up a silver box from the table by the bed. The box held marijuana and played "Puff the Magic Dragon" when the lid was lifted. Warren lifted the lid and looked at Charlotte. "I bet the two of you talk about 'turning on.' See what I mean about your life?"

"Go away," Charlotte whispered.

"Excuse me. I mean your 'life-style.' You don't have a life, you have a 'life-style.' You still look good, though."

"Go away."

Warren looked at her for a while before he spoke.

"I want you to come to New Orleans with me."

Charlotte tried to concentrate on meeting Leonard for lunch. Very soon she would walk out of this room and down the stairs. She would walk out of this house and she would take a taxi to the Tadich Grill, alone.

"I said I want you to come to New Orleans with me, are you deaf? Or just rude."

She would go in the taxi alone to meet Leonard at the Tadich Grill.

"I want you to see Porter with me. Porter is dying. Porter wants to see you. Do this one thing for me."

Charlotte tried to keep her mind on whether to order sand dabs or oysters at the Tadich Grill. Porter was a distant cousin of Warren's. During the five years Charlotte and Warren were married Porter had invested $25,000 in an off-Broadway play that Warren never wrote, $30,000 in a political monthly that Warren never took beyond its dummy issue, and $2,653.84 in ransoming Warren's and her furniture and Marin's baby clothes from the Seven Santini Brothers Storage Company in Long Island City. Charlotte did not even like Porter.

Sand dabs.

No.

Oysters.

"If you won't do it for me you'll do it for Porter. Or you're a worse human being than even I think."

"I can't just leave. Can I."

"You're not leaving, you're paying a visit to Porter. Who is dying. Who loves you."

"I can't forgive Porter what he said to Leonard. At dinner out here. Two years ago. He behaved badly." In fact Charlotte could not even recall what Porter had said to Leonard, but whenever she talked to Warren she fell helplessly into both his diction and his rosary of other people's disloyalties. "I just can't forgive Porter that at all."

"Porter loves you."

"Leonard had to ask him to leave the house."

"What's that got to do with you."

There did not seem to Charlotte any ground on which this question could safely be met. She put it from her mind.

"I said what's that got to do with you."

Charlotte stood up, walked to the dressing room, and took a coat from the closet.

"Porter's dying, Charlotte."

Charlotte put the coat over her shoulders.

"Porter's dying and you're putting on your mink coat. You got Hadassah today? Mah-Jongg? You get the picture about your life?"

"It's not mink. It's sable. I have a lunch date."

"Say that again."

"I said: *I have a lunch date*. With Leonard."

"Don't let me keep you. Somebody who loves you is dying, your only child is lost, I'm asking you one last favor, and you've got a lunch date." Warren opened the lid of the silver box again. The mechanism began to play. "You getting it? You getting the picture? You're never going to see Marin again but never mind, you've got a lunch date? And maybe after your 'lunch date' you and your interesting husband can, what do you call it, 'get stoned'?"

"You *fuck*," Charlotte screamed.

Warren smiled.

Charlotte grabbed up a pair of scissors and clutched them, point out.

Charlotte's sable coat fell to the floor.

"You walk into the house four hours ago, you haven't said Marin's *name* except to make fun of her. You try to use Marin on me, you don't give a *fuck* about—"

Warren still smiled.

The music box still played "Puff the Magic Dragon."

Charlotte looked at her hand and opened it and the scissors fell to the floor. "About Marin," she said.

"Time and fevers," Warren said finally. His voice was tired. "Burn away."

"I don't know what you're saying."

"I'm not saying, babe. I'm quoting. 'And the grave proves the child ephemeral.' Who am I quoting?"

"Shakespeare. Milton. I don't know who you're quoting. Make that thing stop playing."

"Auden. W. H. Auden. You aren't any better read than you ever were, I'll give you that." Warren closed the box and picked up Charlotte's coat from the floor. "'But in my arms till break of day let the living creature lie.' Where's your lunch?"

"I can't go to lunch." She stood like a child and let Warren put the coat on her shoulders. "I can't go to lunch crying."

"Where was your lunch."

"Tadich's."

"Sure," Warren said. "Let's eat some fish."

Warren entertained Leonard at lunch with news of an automotive heir they both knew who was devoting his fortune to Micronesian independence; excused himself five times to make telephone calls; canceled the oysters Leonard had ordered for Charlotte because Pacific oysters would not compare with Gulf oysters; ordered oysters himself, drank three gin martinis and a German beer, fed Charlotte with his own fork because she was too thin not to eat, left the restaurant before Leonard ordered coffee and did not reappear that afternoon or evening. In the morning Charlotte told Leonard that she could not stay in the same house with Warren. Leonard moved Warren to a motel in the Marina, and paid for the room a week in advance. Charlotte stayed upstairs until they were gone. I understand what Warren Bogart could do to Charlotte Douglas because I met him, later, once in New Orleans: he had the look of a man who could drive a woman like Charlotte right off her head.

I have no idea what I mean by "a woman like Charlotte."

I suppose I mean only a woman so convinced of the danger that lies in the backward glance.

I might have said a woman so unstable, but I told you, Charlotte performed the tracheotomy, Charlotte dropped the clinic apron at the colonel's feet. I am less and less convinced that the word "unstable" has any useful meaning except insofar as it describes a chemical compound.

11

IN THE SECOND WEEK after the release of Marin's tape Leonard flew to Montreal to meet with leaders of a Greek liberation movement. A man who described himself as a disillusioned Scientologist called Charlotte to say that Marin was under the influence of a Clear in Shasta Lake. A masseuse at Elizabeth Arden called Charlotte to say that she had received definite word from Edgar Cayce via Mass Mind that Marin was with the Hunzas in the Himalayas. The partially decomposed body of a young woman was found in a shallow grave on the Bonneville Salt Flats but the young woman's dental work differed conclusively from Marin's.

Charlotte watched the rain blowing across California Street.

Leonard flew from Montreal to Chicago to speak at a Days of Rage memorial.

"You want to see bad teeth, get on down here," Warren said to Charlotte the first night he telephoned. He was calling not from the motel in the Marina but from the Polo Lounge of the Beverly Hills Hotel, where he had flown with Bashti Levant and one of his English bands. "The algae on the genetic pool. They drink Mai Tais. Get it?"

"I don't understand what you're doing there."

"I'm not screwing their women, if that's what you think. Not even with yours, Basil. 'Basil.' 'Ian.' 'Andrew.' English Jews. You over your homicidal mood?"

Charlotte said nothing.

"The women all had lobotomies at fourteen, but the teeth stop me. Will you see Porter on his deathbed or won't you?"

"What exactly is Porter dying of."

"Porter is dying of that long disease his life. Alexander Pope, lost on you. Never mind what Porter's dying of. Do it for me."

"I don't even believe Porter's dying. If Porter were dying I wouldn't think you'd be hanging around the Beverly Hills Hotel. With people you say you can't stand."

"I'm not 'hanging around,' Charlotte, I'm 'hanging out.' The phrase is 'hanging out.' You always did have a tin ear. Will you come to New Orleans or won't you."

"I won't."

"Why won't you?"

"Because if I went to New Orleans with you," Charlotte said, "I would end up murdering you. I would take a knife and murder you. In your sleep."

"I don't sleep anyway."

Charlotte said nothing.

"It doesn't matter to me what you do. Go, don't go. Come, don't come. Murder me, don't murder me. I'm only telling you what you have to do for your own peace of mind."

"I have had that shit," Charlotte whispered, and hung up.

"I would bet my life on your having some character," Warren said the second night he telephoned from the Beverly Hills Hotel. "Lucky for me I didn't."

Charlotte said nothing.

"Not that it matters. Not that it's worth anything. My life."

Charlotte said nothing.

"You're going to remember this, Charlotte. I tried to tell you what to do. You're going to lie awake and remember this for the rest of your miserable unfortunate life."

Charlotte said nothing.

Charlotte believed that there was something familiar about this telephone call but for a moment she could not put her finger on what it was. There had been something else she was supposed to lie awake and remember for the rest of her miserable unfortunate life.

Leaving him.

That was it.

She tried to put that other telephone call back out of her mind. It must have been after she left him, the other telephone call, because she had never exactly told him that she was leaving him. She had told him that she was going to her mother's funeral. This was true but not the whole truth. Her mother had just died and she was going to have some money to take care of herself and Marin and she did not want to give the money to Warren and she took Marin and flew out of Idlewild and never went back.

"You hear me, Charlotte?"

She had cried all the way to San Francisco and Marin had

been asleep on her lap and she remembered the landing and Marin's pale hair damp and sticky with sleep and tears.

"Charlotte? They ever mention sins of omission in those wonderful Okie schools you went to?"

For the rest of that week when the telephone rang between one and four A.M. Charlotte would hang up as soon as she heard Warren's voice. A few days later a copy of *Time* arrived with a photograph that showed Charlotte leaving the house on California Street with her hands over her face, and Charlotte wrote a letter to the editor pointing out that the description of her as a "reclusive socialite" was a contradiction in terms. Leonard returned from Chicago and asked Charlotte not to mail the letter.

"I just remembered I never told Warren I was leaving him," Charlotte said to Leonard.

"He's had fifteen years, I guess he's figured it out," Leonard said to Charlotte.

"I mean I just kissed him goodbye at Idlewild and said I'd be back in a week and I knew I wouldn't be."

"I know it."

"How could you know it."

"Because that's how you'll leave me."

"Fourteen years," Charlotte said. "Not fifteen. Fourteen."

Warren returned from Los Angeles and Leonard asked him to dinner but Warren did not arrive until eleven-thirty, accompanied by a 268-pound widow from Fort Worth he had met at Golden Gate Fields, the jockey who had that day ridden the woman's three-year-old filly to defeat, and a shy girl with long legs who was introduced to Leonard by Warren as the most brilliant mathematician at UCLA. Warren had met the most brilliant mathematician at UCLA at the pool of the Beverly Hills Hotel and had driven her Porsche north by way of Big Sur. She drank large quantities of apple juice and told Leonard that Marin could be located by sensitive programming of a Honeywell 782 solid-state computer. Charlotte had gone to bed with the book about the rose windows at Chartres and did not come downstairs. Charlotte had once taken Marin to see the glass at Chartres and Marin had cried because it was too beautiful.

Or so Charlotte said once.

Another time she told me that she herself had cried.

Still another time she told me that a British television crew had been filming inside the cathedral and she and Marin had been unable to see the glass at all because of the television lights.

I am now incapable of thinking about the glass at Chartres without seeing through every window the lights at the Tivoli Gardens.

12

"I've never been afraid of the dark."

"Actually I'm never depressed. Actually I don't believe in being depressed."

"By the way. Marin and I are inseparable."

Accept those as statements of how Charlotte wished it had been.

Charlotte also told me once that she and Warren Bogart were "inseparable."

Charlotte also told me once that she and Leonard Douglas were "inseparable."

Charlotte even told me once that she and her brother Dickie were "inseparable," and adduced as evidence the fact that he had once given her a Christmas present no one else would have thought to give her: twenty-eight acres in southern Nevada.

Of course it had not been exactly that way at all.

Of course there had been the usual days and weeks and even months when Charlotte had been separated from everyone she knew by a grayness so dense that the brightness of even her own child in the house was galling, insupportable, a reproach to be avoided at breakfast and on the stairs. During such periods Charlotte endured the usual intimations of erratic cell multiplication, dust and dry wind, sexual dysaesthesia, sloth, flatulence, root canal. During such periods Charlotte would rehearse cheerful dialogues she might need to have with Marin. For days at a time her answers to Marin's questions would therefore strike the child as weird and unsettling, cheerful but not quite responsive. "Do you think I'll get braces in fourth grade," Marin would ask. "You're going to love fourth grade," Charlotte would answer. During such periods Charlotte suffered the usual dread when forced to visit Marin's school and hear the doomed children celebrate all things bright and beautiful, all creatures great and small.

She would shut her ears.

She would watch Marin numbly, from the usual great distance.

She would hang on by the usual routines, fill in whole days by the usual numbers.

The problem was that Charlotte did not know that any of this was "usual."

Charlotte had no idea that anyone else had ever been afflicted by what she called the "separateness."

And because she did not she fought it, she denied it, she tried to forget it, and, during those first several weeks after Marin disappeared and obliterated all the numbers, spent many days without getting out of bed. I think I have never known anyone who led quite so unexamined a life.

13

CHARLOTTE DID NOT get out of bed the day after she went with Pete Wright to open the safe-deposit box.

"I'm not sure your daughter appreciates the legal bind she's put you in, Char."

Pete Wright was examining some stock certificates. Charlotte had known Pete Wright longer than she had known Leonard, he had roomed at Stanford with Dickie and he had handled her divorce from Warren and as Leonard's junior partner he had paid a Christmas call every year with a suitable present for Marin, but there in the safe-deposit vault of the Wells-Fargo Bank on Powell Street he had kept referring to Marin as "your daughter." Charlotte did not want to hear about the legal bind she was in and she did not want Pete Wright to call her Char. Only Dickie called her Char. There was something else about Pete Wright that bothered her but she did not want to think about that either.

"You're in a bit of a pickle here, Char."

"That's exactly what you said when I left Warren. And you took this enormous legal problem to Leonard and Leonard said I wasn't."

Charlotte took a gold pin of her grandmother's from the safe-deposit box.

Charlotte imagined the gold pin attached to the firing pin of a bomb.

Pete Wright had come to New York once when she was married to Warren.

"And I wasn't."

"You weren't what."

"I wasn't in a bit of a pickle."

"I have nothing but respect for Leonard as a lawyer, Charlotte, but as you know, Leonard leaves the estate work to me." Pete Wright took a deep breath. "Now. What we have here are stock certificates worth X dollars a quarter in dividends—"

"Eight-hundred and seven. $807 a quarter. I looked it up when you called me."

"What I'm saying, Charlotte, is that these particular certificates are in your and your daughter's names as joint tenants. Her signature—"

"I can forge it, can't I."

"Not legally, no."

"All right. I won't cash the checks. It's $807 a quarter, it's nothing."

The gold pin had a broken clasp. As Charlotte held the pin in her fingers she had an abrupt physical sense of eating chicken à la king and overdone biscuits at her grandmother's house in Hollister.

Pete Wright.

Pete Wright had been in New York once and had taken her to the Palm for dinner.

"What may seem 'nothing' to you, Charlotte—"

"I suppose you're about to tell me that $807 a quarter is the average annual income for a grape picker. Is that what you're about to tell me?"

"I'm about to overlook your hostility."

"Leonard leaves the estate work to you, you leave the grape pickers to Leonard. Is that fair?"

"We used to be friends, Charlotte, and I like to think—"

She could taste the soft bits of pimento in the chicken à la king.

She could smell the biscuits burning in the oven.

She could also smell citronella, and calamine lotion, and the sweetened milky emulsion in prescription bottles that contained aureomycin. She could taste the acrid goat cheese her father used to get from the man who ran his cattle on the ranch. Her father had died. She could feel crushed and browning in her hand the camellias her mother used to braid into her hair for birthday parties. Her mother had died. She had erased burned biscuits and citronella when Warren came to her door in Berkeley, and she seemed to have been busy since, but there in the safe-deposit vault of the Wells-Fargo Bank on Powell Street she was not so busy.

She had erased some other things too.

She had been too busy.

Charlotte closed her hand around the pin with the broken

clasp and tried not to think how it could be attached to the firing pin of a bomb.

She had gotten drunk at the Palm with Pete Wright.

"I gather by your silence you think Warren might oppose it."

"Oppose what," Charlotte said.

"Oppose declaring your daughter legally dead."

Charlotte looked at Pete Wright.

"It's a legality. It doesn't mean anything, but it would enable you to cash these particular dividend checks. Or sell this particular stock. Or whatever."

Charlotte picked up the certificates.

"As well as clarify the question of the ranch. Which I feel impelled to remind you is tied up in trust for her. A loose trust, granted, but—"

Charlotte tore the certificates in half.

Pete Wright gazed at the wall behind Charlotte and made a sucking noise with his teeth. "Warren's quite disturbed, I don't know if you realize that. He comes by the house, he drinks too much, he jumps all over Clarice about her hatha yoga class, he acts like—"

Her mother had died.

Warren had not come home the night she got drunk at the Palm with Pete Wright.

"You don't need to tell me what Warren acts like."

"I gather you and Warren have had some misunderstanding, the rights and wrongs of which are outside my purview, but—"

Her father had died.

Warren had called at four A.M. the night she got drunk at the Palm with Pete Wright and she had told him not to come home.

"—I must say I don't think you're solving anything by pretending there aren't certain complications to—"

People did die. People were loose in the world and left it, and she had been too busy to notice.

The morning after she got drunk at the Palm she and Warren had taken Marin to lunch at the Carlyle. Marin was cold.

"I'm trying to talk to you like a Dutch uncle," Pete Wright said.

Warren gave her his coat.

"I think I fucked you one Easter," Charlotte said.

For the next several days Charlotte wanted only to eat the food she had eaten in Hollister but she had lost the recipes her mother had written out and Charlotte did not know the number of any couple who would come to the house on California Street and do chicken à la king and burned biscuits. When I think of Charlotte Douglas apprehending death at the age of thirty-nine in the safe-deposit vault of a bank in San Francisco it occurs to me that there was some advantage in having a mother who died when I was eight, a father who died when I was ten, before I was busy.

14

CHARLOTTE DID NOT get out of bed the day after she met the woman named Enid Schrader.

"Mark spoke so very highly of you," the woman had said on the telephone. There had been in Enid Schrader's voice something Charlotte did not want to recognize: a forced gaiety, a haggard sprightliness, a separateness not unlike her own. "Of you and your beautiful home."

Mark Schrader was said to have been on the L–1011 with Marin. Mark Schrader had on his face, in the pictures Charlotte had seen of him, a pronounced scar from a harelip operation. It did not seem plausible to Charlotte that she could have met a boy with such a scar and forgotten him, nor did it seem plausible that anyone on the L–1011 with Marin had ever spoken highly of the house on California Street, but maybe the boy's mother was trying to tell her something. Maybe there was a code in that peculiar stilted diction. Maybe Enid Schrader knew where Marin was.

"I think we should meet," Charlotte said guardedly. "Could you have lunch at all? Today? The St. Francis Grill?"

"Delightful. Why."

"Why what?"

"Why the St. Francis Grill?"

"I just thought—" Charlotte did not know what she had just thought. She had rejected the house because it was watched. She had hit upon the St. Francis Grill as a place where all corners of the room could be seen. "Is there somewhere you'd rather go?"

"Not at all, I don't keep up with where the beautiful people eat. Not to worry about my recognizing you, I've seen pictures of you."

"I've seen pictures of you too."

"Before," the woman said. "I meant before. Pictures of you and your beautiful home."

Charlotte had met the woman at one-thirty and at two-thirty the code remained impenetrable. The woman did not seem interested in talking about her son, or about Marin. The woman seemed interested instead in talking about a friend who had a decorator's card.

"You'll adore Ruthie." The woman was drinking daiquiris and had refused lunch. "I'm getting you together soonest, that's definite, a promise. Meanwhile I'll borrow her card and we'll do the trade-only places. How's Tuesday?"

"How's Tuesday for what?" Charlotte said faintly.

"Monday's a no-no for me but if Tuesday's bad for you, let's say Wednesday. Earliest. Grab lunch where we find it."

"Listen." Charlotte glanced around the room before she spoke. "If there's something to see I think we should—I mean could we see it now?"

"But I haven't got Ruthie's card. I mean unless *you* have a card—" The woman looked up. "What's the matter?"

"I don't think I know what you're talking about."

"I'm talking about taking you shopping." The woman's eyes reddened and filled with tears. "Unless of course you're too busy. But of course you are. Too busy."

Charlotte touched the woman's hand.

The last woman Charlotte had known to talk about "shopping" was her mother.

The last time Charlotte had been asked to go "shopping" it had been by her mother.

"Your ex-husband isn't too busy. I heard him on the radio. He was blotto but he talked to me. I called in to chat, he wasn't too busy to chat. Although blotto. On the radio. Whatever his name is."

"Warren." Charlotte did not want to hear about Warren on the radio. Leonard had once said that Warren could arrive in a town where he knew no one and within twenty-four hours he would have had dinner at the country club, been offered a temporary chair in Southern politics at the nearest college, and been on the radio. Charlotte did not want to think about Warren on the radio and she did not want to think why Enid Schrader was crying and she did not want to think about her mother shopping. Her mother had been shopping the day she died, at Ransohoff's. "His name is Warren Bogart."

"Whatever. The little whore's father."

The woman gave one last cathartic sob.

Charlotte reached for the check.

"My treat," the woman cried, her voice again sprightly. "You do it next time."

All the next day Charlotte could not erase from her mind the first newspaper picture she had seen of Enid Schrader's son. "They'll ditch the harelip," Leonard had said when she showed him the picture. "The harelip's the fresh meat they'll throw on the trail, they can't afford him, Marin's not stupid."

"I wouldn't rely on that," Warren had said.

Another picture Charlotte could not erase from her mind was her mother alone at Ransohoff's.

I knew my mother was dead when I saw them carry out her bed to be burned, my father could not tell me. I knew my father was dead when the doorman at the Brown Palace would not let me go upstairs, he sent for a maid to tell me. She brought an éclair and cocoa. I waited for her on a red plush banquette. Unlike Charlotte I learned early to keep death in my line of sight, keep it under surveillance, keep it on cleared ground and away from any brush where it might coil unnoticed. The morning Edgar died I called Victor, signed the papers, walked out to Progreso as usual and ate lunch on the sea wall.

15

"I HAVE A lousy trip to Philadelphia, lousy flight back, I watch my own plane blow a tire on closed-circuit TV, I go to my office, I find Suzy in tears because Warren's camped in her one-room apartment, I come home and I find my wife hasn't gotten *dressed* in two days. I finish this call, Charlotte, I'm going to trot your ass over to Polly Orben's office, this isn't healthy." Leonard uncupped the receiver and spoke into it. "Try the other line, Suzy, see if you can keep your finger off the disconnect this time."

"Why don't you trot Suzy's ass over to Polly Orben's office," Charlotte said without turning around. She was watching the FBI man in the window of the apartment across the street. "Why don't you trot Warren's ass over to Polly Orben's office."

"Tell him we're going to trade off the felony and plead the two misdemeanors," Leonard said into the telephone.

"*Warren* and Polly Orben would be good," Charlotte said.

"And tell him I don't want any of that boom-boom shit at the hearing." Leonard hung up the telephone. "Speaking of Warren he says you won't see him. He says you misunderstand him."

"The *fuck* I misunderstand him."

"Felicitously put," Leonard said after a while. "In any case I told him to come by."

"Tell him I'm in Hollister. Tell him I'm in Hollister and about how there's no telephone on the ranch."

"There are eight telephones on the ranch. On three separate lines."

"He doesn't know that."

"For Christ's sake, Charlotte, *go* to Hollister if you don't want to see him. Go now. Go right now."

"I can't actually go to Hollister."

"Why can't you, besides the fact that it might entail getting dressed."

She could not go to Hollister because she was afraid Warren might find her there, alone at the ranch. She could not go to Hollister because if Warren found her there alone at the ranch something bad would happen. This seemed so obvious to Charlotte that she could not bring herself to say it. "I can't go to Hollister because you have people coming to the house for lunch tomorrow."

"Tell me who I have coming to the house for lunch tomorrow."

"Coming to the house for lunch tomorrow you have . . ." She could not think.

"Coming to the house for lunch tomorrow I have . . . the leaders of . . . two dissident factions within . . . the Haight-Divisadero Coalition. You got a whole lot you want to say to them?"

Charlotte picked up a brush and began attacking her hair in abrupt chops.

"On the subject of day-care versus guerrilla theater? Maybe we could get Dickie and Linda up from Hollister and get their thinking?"

"I don't know why you put all those telephones on the ranch anyway."

"I don't know, Charlotte. Communication?"

"Nobody in my family ever found it necessary to keep three different calls going on that ranch."

"Nobody in your family ever found it necessary to pay the taxes on that ranch, either. Tell me again why you can't go to Hollister."

The hair Charlotte pulled from her brush was dry and wiry and faded.

When Marin was small she had played a game with Charlotte's hair and called it gold.

"I feel so old," Charlotte said.

"Tell me why you can't go to Hollister."

"I keep remembering things."

"Most of us do. Tell me why you won't see Warren."

"You don't know what he wants."

"Of course I know what he wants. He wants you back. You think I make my living being dense?"

"Then *why did you ask*?"

Leonard lifted a mass of Charlotte's hair and let it drop through his fingers. "Because I was interested in whether you knew it. You don't look so old."

16

WHO CAN SAY why I crave the light in Boca Grande, who can say why my body grows cancers.

Who can say why Charlotte left Leonard Douglas.

Maybe she thought it was easier.

Maybe she believed herself loose in the world, maybe she was tired, maybe she had just remembered that people died. Maybe she thought that if she walked back into the Carlyle Hotel on Easter morning with Warren Bogart Marin would be there, in a flowered lawn dress.

"It's too late," she said to her gynecologist the morning he confirmed that she was carrying Leonard's child. "It didn't happen in time."

Somebody cuts you.

Where it doesn't show.

I have no way of knowing about the cuts that don't show.

I know only that during the fifth week after the release of Marin's tape Charlotte woke early every morning, dressed promptly, and immersed herself in the domestic maintenance of the house on California Street. She made inventories. She replaced worn sheets, chipped wine glasses, crazed plates. She paid an electrician time-and-a-half to rewire, on a Saturday, two crossed spots on the Jackson Pollock in the dining room. She was obsessed by errands, and she laid it to her pregnancy.

Leonard did not.

So entirely underwater did Charlotte live her life that she did not recognize her preoccupations as those of a woman about to abandon a temporary rental.

Leonard did.

17

PHOTOGRAPHS OF THE last evening Charlotte spent with Leonard Douglas appeared a year later in *Vogue*, Charlotte showed them to me.

There was Leonard, standing with an actor at the party in Beverly Hills, standing with his head bent, listening to the actor but looking somewhere else.

There was Charlotte, sitting with an actress at the party in Beverly Hills, Charlotte smiling, her eyes wide and glazed and in the end as impenetrable as Marin's.

She had not meant to go with Leonard to the party in Beverly Hills at all.

She had not even meant to go with Leonard to the airport.

But on the fifth day of the fifth week after the release of Marin's tape she had opened the door of the house on California Street and found Warren standing there.

"I guess you can give me a drink."

"Actually I'm just about to drive Leonard to the airport." She followed his gaze to the limousine idling at the curb. She had not until the moment intended going to the airport. "I mean I'm not exactly driving him to the airport but I'm driving *with* him to the airport."

"I guess there's room for me."

"Actually you don't want to drive to the airport, it could take hours." She had not in fact spoken to Warren since the nights he called from the Beverly Hills Hotel on Bashti Levant's bill. "This time of day. The traffic."

"I've got time."

"Hours. Literally."

"You're swimming upstream, Charlotte."

In the car Charlotte had sat on the jump seat and fixed her eyes on the driver's pigtail.

"While you were upstairs Warren was telling me about this ninety-two-year-old Trotskyist he drinks with in New York," Leonard said. "This Trotskyist lives at the Hotel Albert. Naturally."

"Charlotte knows Benny," Warren said. "You remember Benny, Charlotte."

Charlotte had not remembered Benny. Charlotte had not even thought that she was meant to remember Benny, whoever Benny was. Benny was only Warren's way of reminding her that he had a prior claim.

"This Trotskyist drinks Pisco Sours," Leonard said.

"Sazeracs," Warren said. "Not Pisco Sours. Sazeracs. Benny always asks about you, Charlotte. You ought to go see him, he's not going to live forever."

Charlotte kept her eyes on the driver's pigtail.

"Neither is Porter," Warren said. "In case you forgot."

"Neither is Charlotte," Leonard said. "You keep this up. Something I've never been able to understand is how you happen to know more Trotskyists than Trotsky did."

"You know more Arabs, it evens out. What am I going to tell Porter, Charlotte?"

"All of them ninety-two years old," Leonard said.

"I said what am I going to tell Porter, Charlotte."

"All of them sitting around the Hotel Albert drinking Pisco Sours," Leonard said.

"Sazeracs. What do you want me to tell Porter on his deathbed, Charlotte."

"Personally I want you to tell Porter about this ninety-two-year-old Trotskyist," Leonard said. "You're overplaying your hand, Warren. You're pushing her too hard while she's still got an ace. I'll lay you odds, she's going to see her ace. She's going to say she's coming with me."

"But I am." Charlotte looked at Leonard for the first time. "I am definitely coming with you. I always was."

"No," Leonard said. "You were not 'always' coming with me. You see, Warren? Bad hand. You didn't pace your play."

"But I always wanted to go with you," Charlotte said.

"Definitely you always wanted to go with him," Warren said. "You haven't met enough Arabs."

"He's going to Los Angeles and Miami," Charlotte said.

"Or enough Jews," Warren said.

Because Charlotte had gotten on the plane with no bag and because Leonard's presence was required at the party where the photographs were taken, a $250-a-ticket benefit in a tent behind someone's house in Beverly Hills, Charlotte was wearing, at the time she was photographed, a dress borrowed from the wife of the record executive who had organized the evening, a dress made entirely of colored ribbons.

"You shouldn't have told Warren to keep the car," she had said as she put on the dress. "He'll keep it all night. I look absurd."

"You wouldn't if you had a tambourine," Leonard said. "He'll keep it all week."

Charlotte sat down. She was very tired. She did not think she had ever been so tired. She did not see how she could finish tying the ribbons on the dress.

"Sometimes I wish," Leonard said after a while. He began tying the ribbons Charlotte had abandoned. "I don't know."

"Sometimes you wish what."

"Sometimes I wish you could just fuck him and get it over with."

"I don't want to."

"Charlotte. Shit. I know you don't *want* to."

A stage had been constructed over the swimming pool of the house in Beverly Hills and several entertainers auctioned their services, singing and dancing and placing surprise telephone calls to friends and relatives of high bidders. Leonard raised five hundred dollars by dancing the limbo under a pole held by the record executive's wife, a young woman with pale blond hair like Marin's and a Brahmin caste mark painted on her forehead, and, at Charlotte's table, an actress who had visited Hanoi spoke of the superior health and beauty of the children there.

"It's because they aren't raised by their mothers," the actress said. "They don't have any of that bourgeois personal crap laid on them."

Charlotte studied her wine glass and tried to think of something neutral to say to the actress. She wanted to get up but her chair was blocked by three men who seemed to be discussing the financing of a motion picture, or a war.

"No mama-papa-baby-nuclear-family bullshit," the actress said. "It's beautiful."

Charlotte concentrated on the details of the financing, the part to be played by the Canadians, the controls exerted by the Crédit Suisse.

"I know why you're crying," the actress said after a while.

Morocco would lend its army. Spain would not. Two-eight above the line.

"And I'm sorry, but that's exactly the kind of personal crap I never saw in Hanoi."

The flash bulb blazed.

Charlotte smiled.

The flash bulb dropped on the table.

"Did you know I spent a night once with Pete Wright," Charlotte said to Leonard as he led her from the table. "Did you know I did that and forgot it."

"You didn't forget it at all," Leonard said. "You told me the first night I met you."

"I am so tired. I am so tired of remembering things. Leonard. Tell me it's because I'm pregnant."

"I wish I could," Leonard said.

Leonard took Charlotte back to the Beverly Wilshire but she continued crying so Leonard, because he was due in Miami the next day to assist in the sale of four French Mirages from one Caribbean independency to another, called the record executive and borrowed a company Lear to fly Charlotte home. $216,000 was raised that night to benefit some one of Leonard's clients, Charlotte was unsure which until she saw the pictures in *Vogue*. She left the dress made entirely of colored ribbons on the floor of the suite at the Beverly Wilshire. I look at those pictures now and I see only Charlotte's smile.

18

"It's Charlotte," she said to her brother's wife from a pay phone on the highway outside Hollister. "I wondered if you and Dickie were going to be home."

"Richard and I play tennis every Saturday." There was a pause. "You want to use the pool, come on by, of course the heater's off."

"I thought I might see the children."

"They're at the gym."

There was a silence.

"Why exactly would I drive to Hollister to use your pool, Linda? I mean I get off a plane from Los Angeles and I sit in the airport all night and I rent a car and I'm out here on the highway and it's raining?"

Linda said nothing.

"Listen," Charlotte said finally. "Linda. Please ask me to dinner."

Before and during dinner Charlotte's brother drank steadily and did not mention Marin or Leonard or Warren. Linda sat at the table but refused to eat. She said that she had eaten macaroni and cheese with the children, who seemed to have come home from and returned to the gym before Charlotte's arrival.

"They're just wonderful normal kids," Linda said after dinner. "Aren't they, Richard. No matter what Warren says."

"What's Warren got to do with it," Charlotte said.

"How would I know whether they're wonderful normal kids." Dickie opened another bottle of bourbon. "Maybe Warren's right, maybe they're boring, how would I know. They're always at the goddamn gym."

"Most people would consider that a definite plus. I believe your sister needs an ashtray."

"What's Warren got to do with it," Charlotte repeated.

"Or eating goddamn Kraft Dinners with you at four o'clock."

"Richard and I don't smoke," Linda said.

"We don't fuck either," Dickie said.

Charlotte put out her cigarette in an empty nut dish.

"Warren paid us a little visit," Linda said. "Lasting eleven hours and a quart and a half of gin."

"Charlotte's not interested in that, Linda."

"Tanqueray gin."

"Linda. We enjoyed seeing him, Char."

"He had this very interesting friend with him. He'd just run into this friend, they hadn't seen each other since the Roosevelt Hotel in New Orleans. Where—"

"I'm warning you, Linda."

"Where this friend of Warren's tended bar. Which is what this friend still does, except at the Pacific Union Club."

"I warned you, Linda. If Charlotte's husband wants to bring a Negro to this house, this house is open. With bells on. All systems go."

"Charlotte's not married to Warren any more, Richard, you don't have to pretend you like him."

"*Goddamnit Linda*, he's better than the Jew, isn't he?"

Linda began plumping pillows.

Dickie avoided Charlotte's eyes.

"Actually Leonard's not a Jew," Charlotte said. "Actually it just amuses Warren to say that Leonard's a Jew. A private joke. If you follow."

"Warren's sense of humor is just a little bit twisted," Linda said. "If you ask me."

"I didn't mean that about Leonard, Char. Hey. Char. I think Leonard is—"

"Not that anybody ever does ask me," Linda said.

"—A very fine lawyer," Dickie said.

"Listen," Charlotte said finally. Linda was still plumping pillows with pointed energy. "Dickie. I've been remembering some things since Marin left."

"That's no good for you, Char, remembering. Remembering is shit. Forget her."

"I'm not talking about Marin, I'm talking about—"

"Forget goddamn Marin. Forget goddamn Warren. You did your best. Forget the other one too."

"He doesn't want to talk about Marin, Charlotte." Linda turned off a lamp. "He wants to believe your life is just pluperfect."

"You turn off another plu-fucking-perfect light, Linda, I'm walking out of here with Charlotte and don't wait up."

"Lucky Charlotte."

"I'm not talking about Marin," Charlotte said. "I'm talking about when we lived on the ranch."

"Don't sell the ranch, Char."

"I'm not. I'm talking about—do you remember how Nana would always burn the biscuits?"

"The ranch is the only home you've got, Char."

"Oh fine," Linda said. "Back to Tara. The Havemeyers are off to the races now. If you're looking for your car keys they're on the coffee table. Next to the ring from Massa Richard's glass."

"Remember the biscuits, Dickie? Halfway through dinner we'd smell them burning?"

"The only thing I remember your famous grandmother burning is every bedjacket I ever took her in the nursing home." Linda handed Charlotte her car keys. "Smoking in bed. Little holes in every one."

"You can't have forgotten the biscuits, Dickie."

"No good remembering, Char."

"Of course your sister wasn't here during that ordeal."

"Dickie," Charlotte said. "We used to laugh about it."

"You and me, Char." Dickie touched Charlotte's hair uncertainly and turned away. "Forget goddamn Marin. I say give her a Kraft Dinner and I say the hell with her."

Charlotte stayed that night in a motel off 101.

She tried to think about the biscuits but they kept fading out. She tried to think about the gold pin with the broken clasp but she kept seeing it on the bomb.

Her grandmother was dead and Marin was gone.

She had never gone shopping with her mother, she had never seen her father on Demerol, the ranch had eight telephones on three lines and Marin was gone.

It was Pete Wright who had told her that her father needed Demerol before he died.

The night she got drunk at the Palm.

She tried to think about Pete Wright in her bed that night but could not. She tried to think about Leonard in the bed of the house on California Street but she could see that bed only as it had been the day she picked up the scissors against Warren. She could see Warren sitting on that bed and she could also see Warren standing in front of her bed in New York the Easter morning after she got drunk at the Palm.

"Look at the slut on Easter morning."

She had screamed.

Marin had screamed.

She had picked up Marin and when Warren hit her again his hand glanced off Marin's temple.

She had picked up the kitchen knife.

She had thrown up.

She and Warren had taken Marin to the Carlyle and she had not had enough money to pay the bill. The beautiful *principessa*, the headwaiter had crooned over Marin. The beautiful *principessa*, the beautiful family. King of Crazy, Queen of Wrong. The headwaiter did not know that. The headwaiter would see to it that the bill was mailed. Charlotte lay on the motel bed and she thought about the beautiful *principessa* and about the beautiful family and about all the bills that had been mailed and never paid. She thought about all the unpaid bills and she thought about all the days and nights when she had promised Warren she would never leave.

There was another unpaid bill.

"You can't drink," Warren had said that Easter morning and held her shoulders as she threw up. "You can't drink at all, you never could." And then he washed her face and he took her to the Carlyle and she did not have enough money to pay the bill. Look at the slut on Easter morning. Marin had a straw hat one Easter, and a flowered lawn dress. Warren gave her his coat.

19

WHEN WARREN CAME that day to the door of the house on California Street Charlotte did not answer.

When Warren telephoned Charlotte hung up.

When Warren stood on the sidewalk outside the house on California Street at two A.M. and threw stones at the windows Charlotte closed the shutters.

When Warren left the note reading "THIS IS THE WORST BEHAVIOR YET" in the mailbox of the house on California Street Charlotte tore the note in half and avoided those rooms which fronted on the street.

When the two FBI men came to tell Charlotte that the boy with the harelip scar had been apprehended on an unrelated charge in Nogales, Arizona, and had hanged himself in his cell Charlotte left the room without speaking. That was on the second day of the sixth week after the release of Marin's tape.

On the morning of the third day of the sixth week after the release of Marin's tape Dickie called from Hollister to say that Warren was at the ranch.

"Acting crazy. Irrational. He told Linda that he talked to Leonard in Miami and Leonard said he could stay."

Charlotte said nothing.

"He yelled at Linda."

Charlotte said nothing.

"Obscenities."

Charlotte replaced the receiver and lay down on Marin's bed.

"You're aware Mark Schrader killed himself in Mexico," the reporter said on the telephone.

"Arizona," Charlotte said. She was still lying on Marin's bed. The sound of the man's voice hurt her ear and she held the receiver several inches away.

"About Mark and Marin—"

"Arizona. Not Mexico. He killed himself in Nogales, Arizona."

"Absolutely. My slip. Would you say that Marin was romantically involved with Mark?"

"Romantically involved," Charlotte repeated.

"Involved in a romantic way, yes."

The harelip's the fresh meat they'll throw on the trail, they can't afford him, Marin's not stupid.

I wouldn't rely on that.

"You see you're thinking of Nogales, Sonora," Charlotte said.

"Absolutely," the reporter said. "Very good. About Mark and—"

"You don't have to congratulate me. For knowing the difference between Arizona and Mexico."

"About Marin and—"

This is the worst behavior yet.

"Fuck Marin," Charlotte said.

"Because he was married to you," Leonard said when she called him in Miami. "That's why I told him he could stay at your fucking ranch. Because you kissed him goodbye at Idlewild and told him you'd be back in a week. Because he was Marin's father. And because I don't happen to believe it's Porter who is dying."

"*Is* Marin's father. *Is*."

"You didn't hear what I said. I said I don't happen to believe he's talking about anybody but himself."

There was a silence.

"I heard what you said," Charlotte said finally. "Tell me—"

"Tell you what."

"Tell me—"

"Tell you if you're not there when I get back I'll shoot myself?"

Charlotte said nothing.

"I won't. That's his game, not mine. I want you. I don't need you."

"If you think he's dying he's not," Charlotte said after a while. "If you're trying to say you think he's dying you're wrong."

Leonard said nothing.

"Something else you were wrong about," Charlotte said.

"You said I'd leave you the same way I left him. I'm not. I'm leaving you. I'm telling you."

The rain was light and the dark came early and the traffic moved. By the time she arrived at the turn-off to the Hollister ranch she was just ten months short of the Boca Grande airport. El Aeropuerto del Presidente General Luis Strasser-Mendana. My brother-in-law. Deceased.

THREE

I

SHE HAD BEEN going to one airport or another for four months, one could see it, looking at the visas on her passport. All those airports where Charlotte Douglas's passport had been stamped would have looked alike. Sometimes the sign on the tower would say "Bienvenidos" and sometimes the sign on the tower would say "Bienvenue," some places were wet and hot and others dry and hot, but at each of those airports the pastel concrete walls would rust and stain and the swamp off the runway would be littered with the fuselages of cannibalized Fairchild F–227's and the water would need boiling.

I knew why Charlotte went to the airport even if Victor did not.

I knew about airports.

People who go to the airport first invent some business to conduct there, a ticket to be adjusted, a query about cargo rates, a newspaper unavailable elsewhere. Then they convince themselves that the airport is cooler than the hotel, or has superior chicken salad. Then one day they see a plane, "their" plane, one plane of many but somehow marked, a mirage on the tarmac.

They pay the lunch check.

They buy the ticket, they glance at the clock above the counter.

Quite as if they were ordinary travelers.

Quite as if they traveled on ordinary timetables.

I supposed that one day Charlotte Douglas would be sitting in the Boca Grande airport and would see her plane and get on it, just as she had clearly gotten on her plane from New Orleans to Mérida and Mérida to Antigua and Antigua to Guadeloupe and Guadeloupe to Boca Grande, supposed that she would maintain that blind course south, but she never did.

2

LOOK AT THE VISAS. Trace back the course.

Before Boca Grande she had been on Guadeloupe.

A few tourists had been killed by terrorists on Guadeloupe that year and until the Air France crash Charlotte was the only guest at the hotel, which had been built just before the trouble and was very large with open terraces where the rain splashed. Her clothes mildewed. The untouched butter in the little crocks went rancid by noon and by dinner was dusted with the fine volcanic ash still falling from an eruption two years before. One of the killings had taken place on the dining terrace of the hotel, and there was a stubborn bloodstain on the concrete at which a busboy scrubbed desultorily every afternoon.

After the Paris–Lima flight hit the volcano there was another woman at the hotel, the wife of the Air France investigator, but she and Charlotte did not speak. The woman was very small and tanned and she played backgammon all day with the beach boys, cheating and winning. Charlotte rented a Peugeot to drive up the volcano but at the first turn she came upon a large black plastic tarpaulin on which lay fragments of metal and one teddy bear. As she drove back to the hotel it occurred to Charlotte that Marin could have been on that plane under a different name.

Marin could also have been on the Delta flight that crashed at Dulles.

Marin could have been on the Alitalia that exploded over the North Atlantic.

Marin was loose in the world and could leave it any time and Charlotte would have no way of knowing.

Before Guadeloupe Charlotte had been on Antigua.

Winds blew on Antigua and she rarely left the hotel. She was uncertain where the hotel even was, except that it was a long way from the airport: she recalled taxi rides through the cane and a small one-story hotel on the water. Her skin burned in the wind and in the odd glare off the opaque clouded sea and after the first week she did not go outside. In the evenings Charlotte and the other off-season guests, two Lesbians from

Toronto and for a while a man and a woman, Seventh-Day Adventists from Newport Beach, California, were served conch stew at a single table by the swimming pool. Perhaps because the man and the woman from Newport Beach were not married to each other or perhaps because as Seventh-Day Adventists they did not approve of drinking they would appear each night only when the plates were set on the table and vanish directly after the Key Lime pie. For the rest of the evening Charlotte would sit by the pool and look at the illustrated books the manager pressed on her, cheaply bound books with mildewed pages and titles like *The Funeral of King George VI* and *The Marriage of Princess Margaret*, and the Lesbians would get drunk on rum punches and dance to the Mabel Mercer records they had brought from Toronto. They had made a new life in Toronto and they were thinking about making another new life on Antigua but they were both Americans and they had both gone to Miss Porter's School in Farmington, Connecticut.

"Not together," the younger one said. "Not at the same time we didn't."

"We were both at Farmington," the older one said.

"At different times." The younger one took Charlotte's hand and studied it. "You have a beautiful life-line."

The older one wept.

Mabel Mercer sang "My Shining Hour."

Charlotte put down *The Marriage of Princess Margaret* and stared at the sea. She had the sense that she could swim from where she was to somewhere else, but she had no idea what lay out there, or in which direction she was staring. In any case she could not swim at night because she could not see the bottom. She remembered swimming at night with Marin on the reef off Waikiki and screaming when Marin's leg brushed hers.

Before Antigua Charlotte had been in Mérida.

Mérida was where she had taken the baby to die of complications, her baby, Leonard's baby, the baby she was carrying when she left California with Warren, the baby born prematurely, hydrocephalic, and devoid of viable liver function in the Ochsner Clinic in New Orleans. The doctors had said the baby would die in the hospital but it did not. It took a long time to die even in Mérida. She had taken the baby to Mérida because she thought it would die faster there but it did not. Toward the beginning of the two weeks she waited for the baby to die she moistened its lips with tap water and told it about the places they would see together.

They would of course see the Great Banyan at Calcutta.

They would see the stone slabs in the conservatory at Bangalore.

They would see the monkeys in the primeval garden at Singapore, they would see the Royal Palm Avenue at Peradeniya, due to reach its best appearance in the year 2050.

They would not see the cacti at San Marino. Marin had not minded the cacti at San Marino but Charlotte had. San Marino had given Charlotte bad dreams. Cacti. Fungi. Fat dry spikes. San Marino would give the baby bad dreams too.

"No San Marino," Charlotte promised the baby. "Quite frankly you wouldn't like it."

After a few days Charlotte exhausted her memory of botanical gardens around the world and began planning one for Mérida. She "named" everything around her. She asked the botanical names of all the plants outside the hotel in Mérida and listed them by genera and subgenera, made notations about color variation in seasonal blossoms, and engaged the manager of the hotel in an astonishing discussion of why he did not dedicate the parking lot to the cultivation of native flora; by the middle of the second week she had progressed from flora to fauna and was cataloguing the birds, the lizards, the insects that bred in the hotel plumbing and crawled from every drain in spite of daily flushings with Ortho-Muerte.

Typhoid was epidemic in the Yucatán that year but still the baby did not die.

By the end of the second week Charlotte was cataloguing the bacteria, the parasites, the sources of fever and intestinal infection: poinciana and poinsettia gave way to salmonella, another tropical flowering. The night in Mérida when the diarrhea finally came Charlotte held the small warm dehydrating creature in her arms all night. Toward midnight she weakened, tried to charter a plane to take her baby back to New Orleans or even to Miami, but no one answered the telephone at the airport, and when Charlotte went out there by taxi with the baby in her arms she found only the controller playing cards with a couple of Yucatair mechanics and they said there were no charters in Mérida that night.

3

LEONARD HAD NOT wanted her to see the baby but she had. Leonard had wanted her to leave the baby to die in the Ochsner Clinic but she would not.

There had been words about it.

There had been words between Leonard and Warren about it in the room at the Ochsner Clinic but she could barely remember the words.

There had been words in the room at the Ochsner Clinic and there had also been peonies. She could remember the peonies very clearly and she could remember the words only barely and mainly she remembered that she had not wanted the baby to die without her.

The baby did not die at the Mérida airport but an hour later, in the parking lot of the Coca-Cola bottling plant on the road back into town. The baby had gone into convulsions and projectile vomiting in the taxi and Charlotte had made the driver stop in the parking lot. She walked with the baby on the dark asphalt. She sang to the baby out on the edge of the asphalt where the rushes grew and a few trailers were parked. By the time the baby died the taxi had left but it was only a mile or two to the Centro Médico de Yucatán and Charlotte walked there with the baby in her arms, trusting at last, its vomit spent. The doctor did not speak English but marked the death certificate in English: *death by complications.*

"Complications of what," Charlotte said.

"Complications of dying," the doctor said. "Her name in Christ?"

The Louisiana birth certificate said *Douglas, Baby Girl.* The Mexican tourist card said *Douglas, Infanta.* Leonard said *it.* Charlotte said *baby.*

"Charlotte," Charlotte said. "Her name is Charlotte."

"Carlota," the doctor said, and made the sign of the Cross before he signed the certificate.

Carlota Douglas was buried in a short coffin which the doctor's brother-in-law would not close until Charlotte had inspected his work. He was very proud of the work he had done on the baby. He was very grateful to have the job and he wanted Charlotte to be pleased. He had wrapped the baby in a lavender nylon shawl and put a bow in her hair and tiny red shoes on her feet. Charlotte had looked once and then away. She had paid the doctor and his brother-in-law in American ten-dollar bills. Before she left Mérida she called Leonard in San Francisco and told him that the baby was dead.

"I'll come get you if you want," Leonard had said.

"Whatever you want," Charlotte had said.

"You have to say."

"They put shoes on her feet. Red shoes."

"It's over. Forget it. You never should have seen it. You never should have."

"Warren's not responsible. For my coming down here. If that's what you think."

"No," Leonard had said. "That's not what I think."

"I think I better call you back later," Charlotte had said, but she had not called Leonard back later.

She had not called Leonard back later and she had not called Warren at all.

In the evening before the plane left for Antigua she had gone back to the cemetery and tried to find the baby's grave but she could not. It was not a large cemetery but there seemed a large number of small fresh unmarked graves. She left the bougainvillea she had torn from the wall of the hotel on one of them.

FOUR

I

FEVERS RELAPSE HERE.

Bacteria proliferate.

Termites eat the presidential palace, rust eats my Oldsmobile.

Twice a year the sun is exactly vertical, and nothing casts a shadow.

The bite of one fly deposits an egg which in its pupal stage causes human flesh to suppurate.

The bite of another deposits a larval worm which three years later surfaces on and roams the human eyeball.

Everything here changes and nothing appears to. There is no perceptible wheeling of the stars in their courses, no seasonal wane in the length of the days or the temperature of air or earth or water, only the amniotic stillness in which transformations are constant. As elsewhere, certain phases in these transformations are called by certain names ("Oldsmobile," say, and "rust"), but the emotional field of such names tends to weaken as one leaves the temperate zones. At the equator the names are noticeably arbitrary. A banana palm is no more or less "alive" than its rot.

Is it.

I tried to tell Charlotte this but once again Charlotte did not quite see my point.

Charlotte did not take the equatorial view.

Of anything that had happened.

Charlotte did not even remember much of what had happened during the six months between leaving California with Warren and taking the baby to Mérida. She remembered certain days and nights very clearly but she did not remember their sequence. Someone had shuffled her memory. Certain cards were lost. She and Warren had been in the South. She knew that much. They had been in New Orleans a while in January and February, and then again when it was hot and raining and the baby was showing, she remembered that. She remembered arriving at the New Orleans airport. The airport must have been in January because the second time they arrived in New Orleans, the time it was hot and raining and the baby was showing and the girl was with them, they had not flown in but driven in, from Greenville. They had eaten some crab bisque once in Greenville. They had made that crab bisque in Greenville. She had bought the crabs and Warren had shown her how to make the bisque.

"You're ruining it," she had said. "You're putting in too much salt."

"You don't know anything about it."

"Taste it, it's brine."

"Taste it yourself," Warren had said, and pushed the wooden spoon in her face. The soup had gone up her nose and she had choked and he had hit her between the shoulder blades until she stopped. "I never cared for anybody like I cared for you but you never knew your ass about food."

Everyone else had liked that crab bisque but they had stayed too long in Greenville, they had stayed too long everywhere. After-three-days-guests-like-fish-begin-to-stink. She had heard that all over the South with Warren. After three weeks of hearing it from Howard Hollerith in Greenville she and Warren had moved from Howard Hollerith's place to a motel in town near the levee but Warren had kept on seeing Howard Hollerith's wife. And Howard Hollerith's girl too. The wife and the girl. "I want them to do it together," Warren said to Charlotte. The girl went to New Orleans with them.

But Greenville was May, June. She knew that Greenville was May or June because Birmingham was July.

The Mountain Brook Country Club in Birmingham was definitely July.

The New Orleans airport had been January.

Warren had been drunk and had twisted her arm behind her back at the Hertz counter.

"I don't have to be here," she had said. "I'm going home."

"Go home," Warren had said. "I'll send you home. I'll ask Porter for the fare, go into debt and send you home. How do you think you're going home without sending me into debt."

"The way I came," Charlotte said, and Warren had hit her.

"It's all right," Charlotte kept saying to the Hertz girl, and "No. Don't call. Please don't." The Hertz girl was calling the airport police and Warren was buying a postcard and mailing it to Leonard. The postcard showed a Confederate flag and a mule and the legend PUT YOUR *HEART* IN DIXIE OR GET YOUR *ASS* OUT. "It's all right," Charlotte said to the airport police. "It's nothing, it's personal, it's all right."

Delta had lost her bags but it did not seem to matter.

"You forgot your map," the Hertz girl said.

"Lower that white-trash voice," Warren said.

In the Hertz car they had driven from the airport to Porter's new house in Metairie and it began to appear that Leonard had been right again. Porter did not appear to be dying but Warren did. Porter told her that. Porter told her that while Warren was upstairs calling a girl he knew in Savannah and telling her to come down. Porter hoped that Charlotte would understand why she and Warren could not stay with him. Porter hoped that she would not think it inhospitable for him to have made a reservation for her and Warren at the Pontchartrain. By the way the reservation would be in her name because the last time Warren had stayed at the Pontchartrain there had been a little unpleasantness, Porter would not say what.

"Warren doesn't show his best side as a houseguest, Charlotte, you recognize that. If Warren has to leave us, I want to recall his many virtues only."

"What do you mean, leave us."

"About time he came home, stopped catting around New York. 'Dying Is But Going Home,' am I right? Ever hear that?"

"What are you talking about, dying."

"Used to see it on gravestones. 'Dying Is But Going Home.' 'The Angels Called Him,' that was popular too. At least around here it was popular. I don't know about out there."

"You said if Warren 'has to leave us,' Porter, what did you mean?"

"Don't bother yourself, Charlotte. I'm going to persuade Warren to let Ping Walker have a look, you remember Ping, Lady Duvall's boy? Lived up east a while? Came back down home around the time Lady married her fancy man?"

"I don't know any Ping Walker and I don't know any Lady Duvall and I don't see what they've got to do with Warren."

"Don't raise your voice, Charlotte, your husband out there allow you to converse like a fishwife? Ping is a specialist. I should say, a specialist. Very fine training. Tulane, Hopkins, Harvard. His father didn't pay for it, old Judge Duvall did."

"A specialist in what?"

"Bad blood," Warren said from the stairway, and both he and Porter laughed.

"Bad blood between Warren here and Lady's fancy man, if memory serves."

"Watch your mouth," Warren said.

"Porter said you were sick."

She was standing at the window in the room at the Pontchartrain watching the first light on the windows of the houses across the avenue. She did not have a bag, she did not have an aspirin, she did not have a toothbrush. The skirt she had put on the morning before in Hollister was wrinkled from the long drive to the San Francisco airport and the long flight to New Orleans and the long night watching Warren and Porter drink in Metairie. In a few hours she could go out and buy what she needed. She tried to concentrate on what she needed and did not think about what she was doing in a room at the Pontchartrain Hotel on St. Charles Avenue in New Orleans. In the empty house on California Street in San Francisco it would be three o'clock in the morning. The night light in Marin's bathroom would be burning just as she had left it. The crossed spots on the Pollock in the dining room would be burning just as she had left them. Leonard would have gone on by now from Miami to Havana via Mexico City. Leonard was in Havana and Marin was gone. Warren was either dying or not dying and Marin was gone.

"Porter said you were sick and he wasn't. At all."

"Porter's an ass, don't you be one." Warren lay on the bed and unbuttoned his shirt. "You got it wrong. As usual. Shut those curtains and come here."

We could have been doing this all our lives, Warren said.

We should be doing this all our lives, Warren said.

We should have done this all our lives, we should do this all our lives.

The verb form made a difference and she could not get it straight what Warren had said. She could not remember. She could remember the New Orleans airport and she could

remember the Mountain Brook Country Club in Birmingham but she could not remember too much in between. There must have been about five months in between, about twenty weeks, about 140 days, simple arithmetic told her how many days there must have been between the New Orleans airport and the Mountain Brook Country Club in Birmingham, but someone had shuffled them. Everywhere she had been with him he wanted the curtains shut in the daylight, she did remember that. She remembered darkened rooms with the light cracking through where the curtains were skimpy and all she could not remember was where those rooms were, or why she and Warren had been in them.

"You wanted to bring me home with you," she remembered saying in one of them. "Didn't you. You wanted to come home again."

"No," Warren had said. "I just wanted to fuck you again."

Sometimes those months in the South seemed so shattered that she suspected the Ochsner Clinic of having administered electroshock while she was under the anaesthesia for delivery. This suspicion was unfounded.

2

I SAID BEFORE he had the look of a man who could drive a woman like Charlotte right off her head.

His face had been coarsened by contempt.

His mind had been coarsened by self-pity.

As it happened he was quite often "right" to hold other people in contempt, and he was also "right" to regard himself with pity, but allow a dying woman a maxim or two.

I have noticed that it is never enough to be right.

I have noticed that it is necessary to be better.

His favorite hand was outrageousness; in a fluid world like Leonard Douglas's where no one could be outraged Warren Bogart was dimmed, confused, unable to operate. He could operate marginally in academe, and he maintained vague academic connections: a week at Yale, three days at Harvard, guest privileges at a number of Faculty Clubs where he never paid his bar bill. He could operate marginally on the Upper East Side of New York. He could operate very well in the South. Like many Southerners and like some Catholics and unlike Charlotte he was raised to believe not in "hard work" or "self-reliance" but in the infinite power of the personal appeal, the request for a favor, the intervention of one or another merciful Virgin. He had an inchoate but definite conviction that access to the mysteries of good fortune was arranged in the same way as access to the Boston Club, a New Orleans institution to which he did not belong but always had a guest card.

He belonged to nothing.

He was an outsider who lived by his ability to manipulate the inside.

His final hold on Charlotte was that he recognized in himself everything I have just told you about him, and said *mea culpa*.

As another outsider I recognized that hand too.

Outsider. *De afuera*.

We were both *de afuera*, Warren Bogart and I. At the time I met him we were also both dying of cancer, Warren Bogart

and I, which perhaps made us even more *de afuera* than usual, but that was a detail Charlotte had never made entirely clear.

Charlotte had trouble with the word.

Not the word "cancer."

The word "dying."

I met him only once, one evening in New Orleans four or five months after Charlotte first came to Boca Grande, one evening in the Garden District at the house of one of the fat brothers in white suits who factor our copra. I had flown to New Orleans that morning to receive cobalt and to renegotiate the copra contracts with Morgan Fayard; I was due to have dinner with Morgan and his wife and sister and to fly back to Boca Grande the next morning. I had not been invited to dinner to meet Warren Bogart, nor had Warren Bogart been invited at all. He was just there in Morgan and Lucy Fayard's living room when I arrived. He was a visible thorn in Lucy Fayard's plan for the evening. He seemed bent on embarrassing both Lucy and her sister-in-law Adele, as well as on humiliating the girl he had with him, but the central thrust of his visit seemed to be to see me. This girl he had with him was referred to as "Chrissie," or "Miss Bailey," or "our unexpected guest's little friend from Tupelo," depending on who referred to her, and she was thin and pale and spoke, when prodded, in sporadic and obscurely startling monologues. In fact she was not unlike Charlotte Douglas, give or take twenty years and the distinctions in cultural conditioning between Tupelo, Mississippi, and Hollister, California. Still I watched the two of them in the Fayards' living room for several minutes before I understood that this "Warren" who had arrived uninvited for drinks and would stay unasked through dinner and who studied my every reaction was the Warren who figured in what I had come to regard as Charlotte Douglas's hallucinations.

"Just so thoughtful of you to drop by, Warren." Lucy Fayard's voice carried clear and thin as glass. "Morgan and I long to have you for a whole evening one time soon. You and your friend. You're most definitely included, Miss Bailey."

The girl from Tupelo smiled wanly and tied on a scarf as if instructed to make her goodbyes.

"Here's-your-hat-what's-your-hurry." Warren Bogart held

out his glass to be filled. "Take that bandana off, Chrissie, don't mind your hostess. Mrs. Fayard's been learning West Texas manners."

"Just shush about that," Lucy Fayard said.

"Just don't start about that," Adele Fayard said.

"Lucy doesn't associate with West Texas trash," Morgan Fayard said. "I don't allow Adele to filthy this house with him. Grace doesn't know what we're talking about and it's rude to continue, in fact I forbid it."

As a matter of fact I knew precisely what they were talking about, because the last evening I had spent with the Fayards had been devoted exclusively to a heated discussion of this same "West Texas trash." It had appeared then that Adele Fayard was seeing a man from Midland of whom her brother did not approve. It appeared now that Lucy Fayard was seeing him as well, and that Morgan did not yet know it. Very soon now either Lucy or Adele would allude to one of Morgan's own indiscretions. All evenings with the Fayards were essentially Caribbean, volatile with conflicting pieties and intimations of sexual perfidy, and in that context were neither very difficult to understand nor, in the end, very engaging.

"That West Texas trash doesn't enter this house," Morgan Fayard said, ignoring his own injunction.

"My mistake then," Warren Bogart said. "I thought I met him here."

"I should say, your mistake," Lucy Fayard said.

"You are certainly set on making it difficult, Warren." Adele Fayard smiled. "Just as difficult as can be?"

"Set on making what difficult, Adele."

"You know perfectly well what's difficult, Warren."

"Difficult for you and your discourteous sister-in-law to continue to extend me your famous hospitality during my dying days? That about it, Adele? Or is it my mistake again."

"What dying days you talking about," Morgan Fayard said. "Nobody dying here."

"You're all dying. You're dying, your wife and sister are dying, your little children are dying, Chrissie here is dying, even Miss Tabor there is dying."

Warren Bogart watched me as he lit a cigar. I had not been introduced to him as Grace Tabor.

"But not one of you is dying as fast as I'm dying." Warren Bogart smiled. "Which I believe allows me certain privileges."

"Frankly he didn't behave any better when he wasn't dying," Adele Fayard said.

"Frankly it's not ennobling him one bit," Lucy Fayard said.

The girl from Tupelo laughed nervously.

"'*Sunset and evening star and one clear call for me!*'" Morgan Fayard cried suddenly. "'*And let there be no mourning at the bar when I put out to sea.*' Learned that at Charlottesville."

"Not any too well," Warren Bogart said.

"No mourning at the bar, Warren. Lesson there for all of us."

"It's 'moaning of' the bar, Morgan. Not 'mourning at' the bar. It's not a wake in one of those gin mills you frequent."

"I don't guess George Gordon Lord Byron is going to object."

"Wrong again, Morgan. You don't guess Alfred Lord Tennyson is going to object. You recite it, Chrissie. Stand up and recite. Recite that and 'Thanatopsis' both."

The girl looked at him pleadingly.

"Stand up," Warren Bogart said.

"I must say," Lucy Fayard said.

"Shut up, Lucy. I said stand up, Chrissie."

The girl from Tupelo stood up and gazed miserably at the floor.

"Speak up now, or I'll make you do 'Evangeline' too."

"'*Sunset and evening star—And one clear call for me—And may there be no—*'"

The girl's voice was low and wretched.

Warren Bogart picked up his drink and walked over to me.

"It is Miss Tabor, isn't it?"

"'*Twilight and evening bell—And after that the dark—*'"

The girl was speaking with her eyes shut. All three Fayards sat as if frozen.

"It was," I said finally.

"I believe you did research of some sort with my old friend Mr. McKay. In Peru."

"In Brazil." At the end of each line the girl would open her eyes and look at Warren Bogart's back as if he alone could save her. "If you're talking about Claude McKay it was Brazil."

"Somewhere down there, you may be right."

"I am right. I was there. What exactly are you doing to that child."

"Chrissie? Chrissie's brilliant, you should talk to her, she's very interested in anthropology, took some courses in it at Newcomb. Does some homework before she speaks. Mr. McKay would have been devoted to her. He had a place in Maryland, you probably know it, I used to drink with him there before he died." He glanced across the room at the girl, who had fallen silent. "Straighten those shoulders, Chrissie, don't slouch. 'Thanatopsis' now."

"'To him who in the love of nature holds—Communion with her visible forms—'"

The girl's voice was so low as to be inaudible.

"Would have been devoted to her," Warren Bogart repeated. "May he rest in peace. An American aristocrat, Claude McKay. One of the last. Gentleman. Well-born, well-bred."

The evening was hot. I was tired. When I am tired I remember what I was taught in Colorado. When I remember what I was taught in Colorado certain words set my teeth on edge. "Aristocrat" is one of those words. "Gentleman" is another. They remind me of that strain I dislike in Gerardo. As a child Gerardo once described the father of a classmate as "in trade" and I slapped his face.

"Last of a breed," Warren Bogart said, watching my face. "Used to speak about you. You should meet my good friend Miss Tabor, he'd say."

The last time I could recall seeing Claude McKay I had accused him of publishing my work under his name. I wondered when Warren Bogart would get around to Charlotte.

"I never thought I'd run into you here at Lucy's," he said.

I have never had patience with games.

"I expect you did," I said.

The girl from Tupelo had finished reciting. The room was silent. Warren Bogart was fingering his cigar and watching me warily.

"Warren," the girl said. "I finished. I'm through."

"Do 'Snowbound,'" Warren Bogart said. "There's nobody here wouldn't be improved by hearing 'Snowbound.'"

"I just won't allow this," Lucy Fayard said.

"I'd advise you to save that tone of voice for West Texas," Warren Bogart said.

"What's this he's saying about West Texas," Morgan Fayard said.

"Just nonsense, Bro." Adele Fayard stood up. "He's talking nonsense."

"I'm asking certain people in this room a question, Adele." Morgan Fayard pushed his sister back into her chair with the heel of his hand. "And I believe I'm owed the courtesy of a reply."

"What's the question, Bro?"

"God*damn* West Texas trash."

The girl from Tupelo began to cry.

Dinner was announced.

No one moved.

"This is a fucking circus. A freak show." Warren Bogart turned to me. "Doesn't this put you in mind of some third-rate traveling circus? Some Sells-Floto circus passing through that country you people run so well? Doesn't it?"

"No," I said. "It puts me in mind of the Mountain Brook Country Club in Birmingham, Alabama."

Warren Bogart looked at me and then away. "You're in over your head," he said finally, and that was all he said.

Trout was served in the dining room. Lemon mousse was served in the dining room. Coffee and praline cookies and pear brandy were served in the dining room. The dining room was hot and we could not seem to leave it. Lucy and Adele Fayard described their most recent Junior League project in compulsive detail. Lucy and Adele Fayard described dinner as we ate it. Lucy and Adele Fayard described a pet cobra they had seen drink Wild Turkey-and-water at a party the night before.

"I told Morgan," Lucy Fayard said, "'Look there, Morgan, I believe that cobra is taking some *drinks*.'"

"I said to Morgan," Adele Fayard said, "'Mark my words, Morgan, that cobra's going to have itself a *season* in New Orleans.'"

Morgan Fayard sulked. Warren Bogart remained in the living room with the girl from Tupelo. We could hear them at the piano. Warren Bogart seemed to be making the girl play, over and over again, the song that was always played in New Orleans at Mardi Gras. She played it badly.

"'*May the fish get legs and the cows lay*—' That's an A-flat, Chrissie, you missed the flat. Start over."

"*Dare* he sing that song," Morgan Fayard said.

Lucy Fayard raised her voice. "You're forgetting your duties, Morgan. Grace's glass is empty? You ever get ground artichokes down there, Grace? To put around game?"

"Not forgetting *my* duties," Morgan Fayard muttered. "Fine one to talk."

"'*May the fish get legs and the cows lay eggs—If ever I cease to love—May all dogs wag their*—' No. No, Chrissie. No."

"The *irony*," Morgan Fayard said. "You talking about *duties*."

"We should ship some down to you," Lucy Fayard said. "Ground artichokes. To put around game. Morgan. Grace's glass."

"Actually," I said, "I have to leave."

"See now what you've done, Morgan. Making us all suffer at this stuffy table instead of taking our coffee in the living room like civilized beings, no wonder Grace wants to leave."

"Not going out there to be insulted," Morgan Fayard said.

"'May the fish get legs and the cows lay eggs—If ever I cease to love—May all dogs wag their tails in front—'"

"Got no *right* to sing that song," Morgan Fayard said.

"He has too a right," Lucy Fayard said. "He's from here."

"Not from here at all. He's from—" Morgan Fayard spit the words out. "Plaquemines Parish. That's where he's from. Where he left a—"

"I don't guess Mardi Gras is your own personal property," Lucy Fayard said. "Just because your mother was Queen of Comus. Which Adele, incidentally, was not."

"—Where he no doubt left a promising future as assistant manager of a gasoline station, that's the kind of trash you—"

I stood up.

Something about the presence of Warren Bogart was causing the Fayards to outdo even themselves.

"You back on West Texas?" Lucy Fayard said. "Or you still on Warren."

"It's a tacky song anyway," Adele Fayard said. "Mardi Gras comes, I go out of town with the Jews. Do sit down, Grace."

"I won't tolerate this." Morgan Fayard slammed his fist on the table. "I will not tolerate having my little children exposed to this trash."

"Unless I'm very much mistaken your little children are at school in Virginia," Adele Fayard said. "Which makes your tolerance the slightest bit academic?"

"I been hearing certain things about you in the Quarter," I could hear Morgan Fayard saying as I left the dining room. "Sister."

"I understand you've been leaving your own visiting cards at a certain address in the Quarter," I could hear Adele Fayard saying as I walked through the living room. "Bro."

"'May the fish get legs and the cows lay eggs—If ever I cease to love—May the moon be turned to green cream cheese—If ever I cease to love—May the—'"

Warren Bogart looked up from the piano.

"Pretty little song, isn't it."

I said nothing.

"Tell Charlotte she was wrong," he said.

3

HERE AMONG THE three or four solvent families in Boca Grande we have specific traditional treatments for specific traditional complaints. Nausea is controlled locally by a few drops of 1:1000 solution of adrenalin in a little water, taken by mouth with sips of iced champagne. Neurasthenia is controlled locally by a half-grain of phenobarbitone three times a day and temporary removal to a hill station. In the absence of a hill Miami or Caracas will suffice. I have never known a treatment specific to the condition in which Charlotte Douglas arrived in Boca Grande, but after that one meeting with her first husband I began to see a certain interior logic in her inability to remember much about those last months she spent with him.

One thing she did remember was when and where she left him.

"I don't want to leave you ever," she remembered saying to him in Biloxi.

"How could I leave you," she remembered saying to him in Meridian.

She left him at ten minutes past eleven P.M. on the eighteenth of July in the bar of the Mountain Brook Country Club in Birmingham.

I'm dizzy and my head hurts, the girl had said.

I think she should see a doctor, Charlotte had said.

She doesn't need a doctor, Warren had said. She's drunk and she needs a sandwich.

Sometime in the next several minutes, at the very moment when Warren hit both the waiter and Minor Clark, Charlotte got up from the table and walked in the direction of the ladies' room and kept walking. She did not risk waiting to call a taxi. She just walked. She had been wearing a sweater in the bar but the night outside was hot and she dropped the sweater in a sand trap and kept walking. Once she was off the golf course she paused at each intersection to assess the size of the houses and the probable cost of their upkeep and then she walked in whichever direction the houses seemed smaller, the lawns less clipped. She had a fixed idea that she would not be safe until she had reached a part of town where people sat on their porches and on the fenders of parked cars and would be bored enough to take her side if Warren came after her. When it began to rain her feet slipped in her sandals and she took off her sandals and walked barefoot. She knew exactly what time it had been when she left the Mountain Brook Country Club because Minor Clark had said the girl did not need a sandwich, she needed a doctor, and Warren had ordered a sandwich and the waiter had said it was ten minutes past eleven and the kitchen was closed. So she had left the Mountain Brook Country Club at ten minutes past eleven and it was almost one before she came to a part of town so rundown she felt safe enough to stand in a lighted place and call a taxi.

The girl's name was Julia Erskine.

The girl was not whining as Warren said but crying because her head hurt. Charlotte believed that Julia Erskine's head hurt.

The girl said that her head hurt because she had fallen from a horse that morning while riding with Warren. Charlotte did not believe that Julia Erskine had fallen from a horse that morning while riding with Warren.

When the taxi came Charlotte went to the Birmingham airport. The first plane out was for New Orleans and Charlotte got on it. She was the only passenger. "You and I can watch the sunrise," the stewardess said. Charlotte did not feel safe until the plane was airborne and then she ordered a drink and sat with her head against the cold window and did not watch the sunrise but drank the bourbon very fast before the ice could dilute it. She had not eaten since lunch the day before at Minor and Suzanne Clark's, the lunch at Minor and Suzanne Clark's to which Julia Erskine and Warren had never come, and as the bourbon hit her stomach she was pleasantly astonished with herself.

She was pleasantly astonished that she could still do all these things.

Walk out.

Call a taxi.

Use her American Express card, get on a plane, order a drink.

While she was still being pleasantly astonished her water broke, and soaked the seat with amniotic fluid.

*

"You hurt that girl," Charlotte said to Warren when he brought the peonies to the Ochsner Clinic. Leonard was in the room. Charlotte did not know how Leonard happened to be in the room and she knew that she should not say anything about the girl in front of Leonard but it did not seem to matter any more what she said in front of anyone. "You hit her in the head. Didn't you."

"She's doped up," Leonard said. "Stay neutral."

"Don't talk about things you don't know about," Warren said to Charlotte. "What are you going to do about the baby?"

"Just the note I had in mind," Leonard said.

"How did you find me," Charlotte said.

"Never mind how I found you. I always find you. What about the baby."

"The baby is—you hit that girl in the head."

"You're on pills," Warren said. "You don't know what you're talking about."

"Don't let that stop you," Leonard said. "Pitch her another life decision."

"He doesn't want you to see the baby," Warren said. "Does he."

"No," Leonard said. "I don't. The topic is now closed. Now we're going to limit our remarks to areas in which Charlotte has no immediate interest. Sex. Politics. Religion. All right?"

"You don't know anything about Charlotte," Warren said. Charlotte could smell bay rum. Bay rum and cigar smoke. Warren. "You never did."

Charlotte tried to focus on the tight pink balls of peony blossom.

"He wants you to walk away," Warren said.

The tight pink balls seemed to swell as she watched them. The baby's head would swell if the baby lived but the baby could not live. They had told her so. The doctors. Leonard too. If Leonard had told her about the baby then Leonard had been in the room before, she had just forgotten.

"He wants you to walk away from here the same way you walked away from everything else in your life."

"You hit that girl in the head. You don't take care of anybody."

"I'm taking care of you right now. I'm telling you not to walk away."

"*I never did*," Charlotte said.

"'How could I leave you,'" Warren said. "The same way you left everybody. How-could-I-leave-you-*let-me-count-the ways*."

She closed her eyes against the obscene peonies.

"Never mind whether I take care of you," Warren said. "You can take care of me."

"Cut her loose," Leonard said.

"She doesn't want to be loose," Warren said.

The peonies were swelling behind her eyelids.

"It doesn't matter whether you take care of somebody or somebody takes care of you," Warren said. "It's the same thing in the end. It's all the same."

"You had your shot," Leonard said.

She kept her eyes closed and she heard their voices ugly and raised and by the time the voices were normal again the peonies had burst behind her eyelids and the warm drugs were pulling her back under and she knew what she was going to do. She was not going to do what they wanted her to do. She was not even sure what they wanted her to do but she was not going to do it.

"Tell her I said it's all the same," she heard Warren say to Leonard.

She was going to leave here alone with her baby.

"You want her to watch you die," she heard Leonard say to Warren.

She was going to let her baby die with her.

"Never mind what I want," she heard Warren say to Leonard. "Just tell her I said it's all the same. Tell her that for me."

4

WHEN I CONSIDER the pattern of their days and nights during those five months I see again that nothing outside that pattern happened at the Mountain Brook Country Club.

I wonder again why Charlotte left that night and not some other.

Charlotte could never tell me.

"But I had to leave," Charlotte would repeat, as if until ten minutes past eleven P.M. on the eighteenth of July there had been some imperative to her staying. "He'd been with this girl and he'd hurt her and he was acting crazy. After I left the Clarks took her to the hospital, she had a concussion. Mild."

Had not other such evenings occurred during those five months?

Charlotte said that she could not remember.

Bear in mind that I am talking here about a woman I believe to have been in shock.

Everywhere they went during those five months they ended up staying in a motel. Charlotte did remember the motels. They had stayed a while with Howard Hollerith in Greenville and they had stayed a while with Billy Daikin in Clarksdale and they had stayed a while with other people in other places but after a certain kind of evening they would always move to a motel. Usually Warren would not be present during the early part of this certain kind of evening. Usually Warren would be upriver or downriver or across the county with their host's wife or sister or recently divorced niece. Never daughter. Warren never went upriver or downriver or across the county with the daughter of a host.

Charlotte learned early to recognize the advent of such an evening.

For the day or two before such an evening Warren would announce his inability to sleep.

"I'm restless, I'm wired, I got the mean reds," he would say.

"Don't cross me," he would say.

"Don't mess with me," he would say.

For the day or two before such an evening their host would announce his inability to provide minor but key aspects of his normal hospitality.

"Wouldn't be surprised Warren's used up all those Peychaud bitters he can't take a drink without, what a shame, can't buy them up here."

"Damn that plumber, can't get here before Tuesday, daresay you'll be glad to get somewhere they've got the pipes in working order."

A familiar drift would emerge. Not only toilets but guestroom telephones would go out of order. Men would arrive to drain the swimming pool. Suggestions would be made for traveling before the rain set in, or the heat, or the projected work on the Interstate. Reminders would be made about promises to visit Charlie Ferris in Oxford, or Miss Anne Clary on the Gulf.

Doors would be closed.

Voices would be raised.

The evening itself would begin uneasily and end badly.

"Hope Warren has the courtesy to leave a little something for old Jennie, all the extra picking up she's done, you might remind him, Charlotte. Or isn't that the custom where you come from."

And: "Most interesting the way men where you come from allow their wives to traipse around as they please, must be very advanced thinkers in California."

And then: "The idea, your friend Warren going off and leaving you here alone, might not matter to you but it matters to me, a man insults a lady in my house he insults me. You wouldn't understand that, Mrs. Douglas, I'm certain it's all free and easy where your people come from."

And finally: "You say you're going to bed 'and fuck it,' Mrs. Douglas, I believe that is your name, just what am I meant to conclude? Am I meant to conclude there's a woman in my house who's certifiable? Or did my ears deceive me."

After Charlotte went to bed there would be silence for a few hours and then more raised voices, Warren's among them, and Charlotte would bury her head in one pillow and put another over her belly so the baby could not hear and the next day she and Warren would move to a motel.

"I don't like these people," she said to Warren after one such evening. "I don't like them and I don't want to be beholden to them."

"You're not beholden to anybody. You're too used to Arabs and Jews, you don't know how normal people behave."

"I can't help noticing Arabs and Jews are rather less insulting to their houseguests."

"Not to this houseguest they wouldn't be, babe." In the wreckage of these visits Warren seemed unfailingly cheerful. "You show me an Arab who'll put up with me, I'll show you an Arab doesn't get the picture."

In all those motels he wanted the curtains shut in the daytime.

In all those motels she would sit in the dark room a while and watch him sleep.

It seemed to her that toward the end of the five months they had spent more time in motels than toward the beginning of the five months but she could not be sure. Warren always paid for the rooms with crumpled bills fished from various of his pockets and she paid for meals, when they ate meals. She ate regularly, usually alone. She forced herself to eat, just as she forced herself to take her calcium and see an obstetrician in any town where they spent more than a day or two. There was no need for her to see an obstetrician that often but she wanted to have a number she could call in the middle of the night. An obstetrician would not question her reason for seeing him. An obstetrician was the logical doctor to see.

"You're sick," she had said the first time she saw Warren gray and sweating. He had swerved abruptly off the highway and stopped the car on the shoulder. "You're sick and you need a doctor."

"Not going running to any doctor." His breathing was harsh and shallow and he did not seem to have strength to turn off the ignition. "Not sick. Ran over a moccasin is all."

They sat in the idling car until his breathing evened out. He did not speak again but took her hand. When he finally put the car into gear and drove on she glanced back at the highway but of course there was no moccasin. It was after that day when she began to find an obstetrician in every town, began to get the questions done with early and the telephone number in hand. Some night in some town she was going to need to call a doctor and ask him for something and she wanted that doctor to take her call. She did not let her mind form the word "cancer" and she did not let her mind form the word "dying" but the word Demerol was always in her mind. She had not been there when her father died but Pete Wright had told her about the Demerol, the night they had dinner at the Palm.

5

SOMETIMES SHE WOULD leave the motel during the day. She would leave Warren sleeping and take the car and drive down the main street of whatever town it was and look for somewhere to spend an hour. She remembered sitting in the library in Demopolis, Alabama, every afternoon for most of a week. She had read back newspapers in the Demopolis library. She had followed the progress in the newspapers of a Greene County murder trial which had taken place some months before. They left Demopolis before she got to the verdict and when she asked the woman at the motel desk if she recalled how the trial came out the woman said curiosity killed the cat. She remembered having her nails manicured in a pine town above Mobile by a child who looked like Marin but was fifteen and married to a logger and running her mother's beauty shop in a trailer. She remembered drinking chocolate Cokes at the counter of the Trailways station in Pass Christian and reading an Associated Press story about the continuing search for Marin Bogart and she remembered leaving the paper on the counter and staring out at the dark glare off the Gulf. She remembered drinking chocolate Cokes at the counter of the Trailways station in a lot of towns. She remembered staring at the Gulf in a lot of towns. She remembered the Associated Press quoting Leonard as saying that she was "traveling with friends."

On those days when she did leave the motel she would usually come back toward sundown and find Warren gone, the bed unmade, the towels wet on the floor of the room, the curtains still closed and the air sweet and heavy with the smell of bay rum. Warren never put the top back on the bottle of bay rum. She remembered that. She would put the top back on the bottle of bay rum and call the maid and stand outside on the walkway while the room was made up. The air would be chilly and wet and then later in the spring it would be warm and wet. Toward eight or nine on those evenings Warren would telephone the motel and tell her where to meet him.

"Warren appears to have his mood upon him," someone would be saying wherever she met him.

"Warren is certainly himself tonight."

"Warren is incorrigible."

"Warren is without doubt the most incorrigible of anybody I know."

So self-absorbed was the texture of life in these rooms where Charlotte went to meet Warren that the facts that she had been married to him for some years and that they were the parents of a child whose photograph appeared somewhere in every post office and gas station in the county appeared not to have penetrated.

She was Warren's "friend from California."

She was "visiting with Warren."

Warren was "showing Mrs. Douglas the South."

"Why do you lie?" Charlotte said after one such evening. "Why do you pretend I'm just this pregnant acquaintance you happen to be showing around Biloxi?"

"I'm not lying. You're just here on a visit. You'll leave."

"That's not what you make me say in bed."

"Don't talk about what I make you say in bed. Don't talk about it, talk about it and you lose it, don't you know anything."

We could have been doing this all our lives, Warren had said.

We should be doing this all our lives, Warren had said.

We should have done this all our lives, we should do this all our lives.

"I don't want to leave you ever," Charlotte said.

"No," Warren said. "But you will."

After a while there were no more frosts at night and the wild carrot came out along all the roads and every night ended badly.

After a while there were no more tule fogs at dawn and all Charlotte wanted was one night that did not end badly.

After a while there was Howard Hollerith's girl.

"What do you suppose Marin did today," Charlotte said one night in the car when she thought Howard Hollerith's girl was asleep in the back seat.

"Played tennis," Warren said. "Marin played tennis today."

"Marin who?" Howard Hollerith's girl said.

"See what you're going to leave me to," Warren said to Charlotte.

In the coffee shop of a Holiday Inn outside New Orleans one morning in May or June Charlotte read another Associated Press story in which Leonard was again quoted as saying that Charlotte was "traveling with friends." This time Charlotte read the story several times and memorized the phrase. It occurred to her that possibly she had misunderstood the situation. Possibly Leonard and Warren and the Associated Press were right. She was simply traveling with friends, and Warren and Howard Hollerith's girl, asleep in the bed behind the second door past the ice machine, were simply the friends with whom she was traveling. Soothed by this construction Charlotte had another cup of coffee and worked the crossword in the *Picayune*.

6

THE LAST THING Charlotte remembered before the Mountain Brook Country Club in Birmingham was sitting and reading inside the cyclone fence around the swimming pool at a Howard Johnson's in Meridian. The Howard Johnson's was just off a curve on the Interstate between New York and New Orleans and all afternoon the big northern rigs would appear to hurtle toward the cyclone fence and then veer on south. The vibration made her teeth hurt. The shallow end of the pool was filled with prematurely thickened young girls celebrating a forthcoming marriage. They talked as if they were just a year or two out of high school but they were already matrons, careful not to splash one another's blown and lacquered hair. After a while the bridegroom-to-be arrived with a friend from his office. The bridegroom and his friend were both fleshy young men in short-sleeved white shirts and they placed two six-packs of beer on a damp metal table and they opened all the cans and started drinking the beer. It seemed to be a town in which everyone thickened early. Out of some deference or indifference to their own women the men ignored the shrieks from the pool and instead watched Charlotte as they drank the beer. "Somebody's gone and put a bun in that skinny little oven and I wouldn't mind it had been me," one of them said. "I never knew this Howard Johnson's was X-rated," the other one said. He held up one of the cans as if to offer it to Charlotte and the other one laughed. Charlotte felt old and awkward and dimly humiliated, a woman almost forty with a body that masqueraded as that of a young girl, a caricature of what they believed her to be. When she went back to the room Warren had the air-conditioning off and the windows closed and all the blankets and spreads from both beds piled over him. By Meridian he was having sweats and chills every day as he slept. By Meridian he did not sleep at night. By Meridian Howard Hollerith's girl was no longer with them. Charlotte supposed there had been a fight somewhere but she did not particularly remember it.

"I can't get it up," Warren said when she tried to wake him. "Baby, baby, I can't get it up."

"I don't want it," she said. "That's not what I want."

"Don't leave me. Don't leave me again."

"How could I leave you. Don't wake up."

How could I leave you.

The same way you left everybody.

"You like it too much," Warren said. "You like it more than anybody I ever knew. I know a girl in Birmingham likes it almost as much as you. We'll go do it with her. I want to see you with Julia."

"I didn't like that before."

"Did we do that before?"

"With Howard's girl. I didn't like it."

"You liked it all right."

We could have been doing this all our lives.

We should be doing this all our lives.

We should have done this all our lives, we should do this all our lives.

Talk about it and you lose it.

She was a woman almost forty whose fillings hurt when the highway vibrated. She was a woman almost forty waiting for the night she would call to get the Demerol. When Warren woke at sundown he took her to see a bike movie in a drive-in and drank a fifth of bourbon in the car and drove under the big pink arc lights with the rented car flat-out all the way to Birmingham. When the peonies swelled and broke behind her eyelids in the Ochsner Clinic they blazed like the big pink arc lights all the way to Birmingham. She could take care of somebody or somebody could take care of her and it was the same thing in the end.

Mérida.

Antigua.

Guadeloupe.

How could I leave you.

The same way you left everybody.

He wants you to walk away from here the same way you walked away from everything else in your life.

Tell her I said it's all the same.

El Aeropuerto del Presidente General Luis Strasser-Mendana, deceased.

Tell her that for me.

FIVE

I

OIL WELLS about to come in have a sound the attentive ear can detect.

As do earthquakes.

Volcanoes about to erupt transmit for days or weeks before their convulsion a signal called "the harmonic tremor."

Similarly I know for months before the fact when there is about to be a "transition" in Boca Grande. There is the occasional tank on the Avenida Centrale. Sentries with carbines appear on the roof of the presidential palace. For reasons I have never understood the postal rates begin to fluctuate mysteriously. There is a mounting mania for construction, for getting one's cut while the government lasts: dummy corporations multiply, phantom payrolls metastasize. No one has an office but everyone has a mail drop. A game is underway, the "winner" being the player who lands his marker in the Ministry of Defense, and the play has certain ritual moves: whoever wants the Ministry that year must first get the *guerrilleros* into the game. The *guerrilleros* seem always to believe that they are playing on their own, but they are actually a diversion, a disruptive element placed on the board only to be "quelled" by "stronger leadership." Guns and money begin to reach the *guerrilleros* via the usual channels. Mimeographed communiqués begin to appear, and twenty people are detained for questioning. A few are reported as prison suicides and a few more reported in exile but months later, again mysteriously, the same twenty are detained for questioning.

A mounting giddiness about the proximity of the *guerrilleros* sets the social tone of the city: many tea dances are planned, many adulterous liaisons initiated.

Many citizens adopt eccentric schedules to comply with the terms of their kidnapping insurance.

El Presidente, whoever is playing *El Presidente* at the moment, falls ill, and is urged to convalesce at Bariloche, in Argentina.

Gerardo arrives, and stays for the action.

These events in Boca Grande are inflexibly reported on the outside as signs of a popular uprising, but they are not. "NEW LEASE ON DEMOCRACY IN BOCA GRANDE" is one headline I recall from the *New York Times.* I believe Victor was the lessor of democracy in question.

I told Charlotte all along that I was hearing the harmonic tremor but Charlotte paid no attention.

Charlotte appeared to have used up all her attention.

2

I THINK NOW that in the beginning she stayed on in Boca Grande precisely because it seemed not to demand attentiveness. I recall having made, in the early days of my marriage to Edgar, somewhat the same mistake about Boca Grande, as well as about Edgar himself, but I revised my impressions to coincide with reality. Charlotte did the reverse. The city must have seemed to her at once familiar and distant, potentially "colorful" but in no way unmanageable, a place not unlike the matchbox model village that she and Dickie had once laid out along an irrigation ditch on the Hollister ranch: a place she could revise to suit herself as she had not been able to revise the other points on her recent itinerary. Here in Boca Grande there was the matchbox hotel in which one stayed, there was the matchbox hotel in which one did not stay. There was the "best" restaurant, there was the "second-best" restaurant, there were the districts in which nurses pushed baby carriages on Sunday afternoons and the districts in which nurses did not push baby carriages on Sunday afternoons.

There was no intimidating social life but only the Jockey Club, a place where a *norteamericana* in a good linen dress might well have expected to pass unnoticed.

There was no intimidating history but only the Museo de la República, a place where a *norteamericana* with a six-hundred-dollar handbag might well have expected to spend an undemanding hour studying cracked spinets and bronzed Winged Victories and other Strasser-Mendana family artifacts.

There were what seemed to Charlotte the "enchanting" children selling contraband Marlboro cigarettes outside the Caribe and there was what seemed to Charlotte the "amusing" accordionist playing "You're the Cream in My Coffee" in the Caribe lobby on Saturday nights and there were what must have seemed to Charlotte the toy soldiers with their toy carbines on the roof of the matchbox palace. The night Victor met Charlotte at the American Embassy Christmas party and took her for the first time to his apartment in the Residencia Vista del Palacio, Charlotte pulled back the curtains, gazed down at the palace, and pronounced its roof "ideal" for the fireworks which would officially open the mirage she was already calling the "Boca Grande Festival de Cine, First Annual." By the time Charlotte left Victor's apartment that night her festival was not only the First Annual but *Internacional.*

A few things about Boca Grande Charlotte did not perceive as toy.

She saw the American Embassy as "real" and she left her calling cards there in little lined envelopes embossed "Tiffany et Cie" and she never noticed the workmen who every morning scrubbed obscenities from the white limestone walls.

She saw the proximity of Caracas as "real" and she looked at a map every day to reassure herself on this point and she never knew that the four-lane Carretera del Libertador to Venezuela, marked so clearly on the maps, existed only on the maps, and possibly in the memory of whoever diverted the Alianza funding for the Carretera into the construction of the Residencia Vista del Palacio.

I believe this was Victor but it may have been Antonio.

It was certainly not Luis.

Luis was the Libertador to have been memorialized.

It occurs to me now that it could even have been Edgar but there remain some areas in which I, like Charlotte, prefer my own version.

As a matter of fact Charlotte saw everything about the actual geographical location of Boca Grande as "real," and crucial to her: in a certain dim way Charlotte believed that she had located herself at the very cervix of the world, the place through which a child lost to history must eventually pass. That Marin would turn up in Boca Grande Charlotte did not literally believe but never really doubted, at least until that day in September when Leonard told her where Marin actually was. Until that day when she learned for certain that Marin was not a victim of circumstance Charlotte believed without ever thinking it that she would be sitting at the Jockey Club one night and the waiter would tell her that a light-haired child who resembled her had come to the kitchen, applied for work as a waitress. Until that day when she learned for certain that Marin was not looking for her Charlotte believed instinctively that she would be buying the *Miami Herald* at the airport one morning and would hear a voice like her own on the tarmac.

Charlotte and Marin would share a room, order hot chocolate from room service, sit on the bed and catch up.

Charlotte and Marin would buy Marin a dress, get Marin a manicure, cure Marin's nerves with consommé and naps.

And when Marin was herself again Charlotte and Marin would drive to Caracas on the four-lane Carretera del Libertador, Charlotte and Marin would fly to Bogotá, Charlotte would show her only child the Andes.

Her only child.

Her oldest child.

The only child she ever dressed in flowered lawn for Easter.

One more thing in Boca Grande Charlotte saw as "real": the airport.

Of course the airport.

Perhaps because Charlotte believed in the airport and in the American Embassy and in the four-lane Carretera del Libertador to Venezuela she did not at first experience the weightless isolation which afflicts most visitors to Boca Grande. Perhaps because in those early days Charlotte had no letters to send or receive she did not notice that mail service was increasingly sporadic, that mailboxes all over the city were left to overflow and there was developing a currency market in stamps. Perhaps because for a while Charlotte had no calls to make or get she did not notice that the telephone lines were down more and more of the time, that calls to Miami were being routed through Quito and the American Embassy was resorting to ham radio to make routine contact with its consulate in Millonario.

She noticed that the lights at the Capilla del Mar resembled those at the Tivoli Gardens.

She did not notice that the pits in the porch railing at the Capilla del Mar resembled those made by carbine fire.

"Actually it doesn't involve me in the least," Charlotte told me. "I mean does it."

When I told Charlotte in March that there would come a day when it might be possible to interpret her presence in certain situations as "political."

"Actually I'm not 'political' in the least," Charlotte told me. "I mean my mind doesn't run that way."

When I told Charlotte in April that there would come a day when she should leave Boca Grande.

Meanwhile Charlotte would wait for Marin in this miniature capital where nothing need be real. Charlotte would remain as she waited an interested observer of everything she saw. Charlotte would remain a tourist, a traveler with good will and good credentials and no memory of how bougainvillea grew on a hotel wall in Mérida or how peonies could swell in a hospital room in New Orleans. Had Gerardo never come home Charlotte might have managed to maintain this fiction, although increasingly I doubt it.

Perhaps Gerardo does not play the motive role in this narrative I thought he did.

Perhaps only Charlotte Douglas and her husbands do.

Perhaps only Charlotte Douglas does, since it was Charlotte who chose to stay.

3

"YOU SMELL AMERICAN," was the first thing Gerardo ever said to Charlotte Douglas.

"I wonder if that could be because she *is*," Elena said.

"I wonder if *I* do," Ardis Bradley said.

I cannot now think how I happened to invite Charlotte for drinks that afternoon. It was Gerardo's second day home and he had asked to see only the family, and Tuck and Ardis Bradley, and Carmen Arrellano, who had been cultivating Antonio since Gerardo's last visit and on this particular afternoon was sulking in a hammock and ignoring her cousin, who happened to be passing the shrimp. As far as that went the only person Carmen Arrellano had acknowledged all afternoon was Antonio, and she had not exactly spoken to him. She had merely arched her back slightly whenever he passed the hammock where she lay.

But Charlotte.

I was not yet that close to Charlotte.

She had arrived in Boca Grande in November, Victor and I had met her at the Embassy in December, and when Gerardo came home it was late January, early February. I had not yet seen the pictures in *Vogue* of the last night she spent with her second husband. I had not yet met her first in New Orleans. I was just beginning cobalt, and was quite often tired, and impatient, and generally more absorbed with some gram-negative bacteria I was studying than with this woman I did not understand.

I suppose I might have invited Charlotte only to discomfit Victor.

Victor flatters himself that any woman he touches is rendered unfit for normal social encounter.

In fact I have no idea why I invited Charlotte.

I only remember Charlotte arriving late and the sun just falling and Gerardo watching her as she walked across the lawn with the last light behind her. I remember her dress, a thin batiste dress with pale wildflowers to her ankles. I remember her high-heeled sandals. I remember thinking that she looked at once absurdly frivolous and mildly "tragic," a word I do not use easily or with any great approval.

"Look at her *bébé* dress," Elena said. Elena was watching Gerardo. "Not that she is a *bébé*."

"So original actually," Ardis Bradley said. "If you like that."

But Gerardo only watched Charlotte Douglas.

I remember that the grass was wet and that Charlotte walked very slowly and that when she stumbled once on a sprinkler head she stopped and took off the high-heeled sandals and then walked on toward us, barefoot.

"Very *déjeuner sur l'herbe*," Elena said.

"California," Ardis Bradley said.

I remember that Charlotte only kissed me absently and dropped into a wicker chair and did not speak.

You smell American.

I wonder if that could be because she *is*.

I wonder if *I* do.

And still Charlotte said nothing at all.

"You haven't met my son," I remember saying in the silence. "Gerardo. Mrs. Douglas. Mrs. Douglas is staying at the Caribe."

But Gerardo said nothing, only touched Charlotte's hair, a touch so tentative that it was almost not a touch at all.

Almost not a touch.

But it was.

"Extraordinary," Elena said.

"I wonder what 'American' smells like exactly," Ardis Bradley said.

Charlotte stood up then and without taking her eyes from Gerardo she brushed back her hair where he had touched it. She did not seem to know what to do with her hands after that and she fingered the batiste of her skirt. She looked unsteady, ill, stricken by some fever she did not understand, and when I put out my hand to steady her she flinched and pulled away.

"I don't like the Caribe," was the second thing Gerardo ever said to Charlotte Douglas.

His voice was low but so conversational and so unexceptional that for the moment after he spoke I could see Ardis Bradley marshaling opinions on the Caribe, pro and con.

Not Elena.

Elena's only developed instinct is for the presence of the sexual current.

"I want you to take an apartment," was the third thing Gerardo ever said to Charlotte Douglas.

4

SEXUAL CURRENT.

The retreat into pastoral imagery to suggest this current has always seemed to me curious and decadent.

The dissolve through the goldenrod.

The romance of the rose.

Equally specious.

As usual I favor a mechanical view.

What Charlotte and Gerardo did that afternoon was reverse the entire neutron field on my lawn, exhausting and disturbing and altering not only the mood but possibly the cell structure (I am interested in this possibility) of everyone there. Charlotte never spoke at all to Gerardo, only turned away and engaged Tuck Bradley in one of those reflexive monologues she tended to initiate at the instant of distraction. It sometimes seemed to me that these monologues had for Charlotte the same protective function that ink has for a squid. This one touched on whether or not Tuck Bradley had ever been in the courtroom when Leonard did "one of his really dazzling redirects" (Tuck Bradley had not); what Tuck Bradley thought about the national lottery (Tuck Bradley saw both its "good points" and its "bad points"); what Tuck Bradley thought about assassination in the United States (Tuck Bradley thought it "deplorable"); and what "offbeat" hotels Tuck Bradley could recommend in Paris.

Tuck Bradley recommended the George V.

"What about London," Charlotte said, her voice suddenly weary. She did not turn to meet Gerardo's gaze.

"I would say . . ." Tuck Bradley tamped his pipe. "The Savoy."

Charlotte took a drink from a tray and I waited to see what she would do with it. Charlotte never exactly "drank" a drink. Sometimes she drained it like a child and sometimes she just played with the ice and quite often she dropped it. This time she set it on a tiled bench, quite carefully, without tasting it.

"Or Claridge's," Tuck Bradley said.

There was a silence.

"I want to jot all this down," Charlotte said vaguely, and then she turned away from Tuck Bradley.

Gerardo watched her as she ran across the lawn.

Victor watched her as she ran across the lawn.

Antonio crouched on the lawn by Carmen Arrellano's hammock and watched Gerardo and Victor.

"This is so absorbing but you can take me home now," Carmen Arrellano said to Antonio.

"*Norteamericana* cunt," Antonio said without moving.

"And I suppose another choice in Paris would be . . ." Tuck Bradley was still intent on his pipe. "The Plaza Athénée."

"She'll definitely want to jot that down," Elena said. "Possibly you could catch her and tell her. The Plaza Athénée. Are we going to get dinner? Is anyone going to *le* Jockey?"

"Did Charlotte Douglas say she was going to Paris?" Ardis Bradley said.

"'*Le* Jockey,'" Carmen Arrellano said to Antonio. "Listen to Elena. Your interesting sister-in-law thinks she's in Paris. I don't want dinner."

"I mean if she *is* going to Paris," Ardis Bradley said, "she's going to miss her husband."

I looked at Ardis Bradley.

She could not have had more than two drinks but she did not drink well.

No one else seemed to have heard what she said.

"*I* want dinner," Elena said. "And I also want to go to Paris."

"Go to Paris." Antonio rose from his crouch. Some chemical exchange in his brain seemed to have switched on another of his rages. I used to be interested in Antonio's cell metabolism. "Go to Paris, go to Geneva. Buy a parrot. Buy two parrots, give one to your friend the *norteamericana* cunt."

"The *norteamericana* cunt is not your sister-in-law's friend," Carmen Arrellano murmured from the depths of the hammock. "The *norteamericana* cunt is Victor's friend."

"Gerardo will drop you home now, Carmen." Victor spoke very clearly in a tired voice. His eyes were closed. "Won't you. Gerardo."

"No," Antonio said. "He won't."

"Antonio is going to drop Carmen home," Gerardo said. He was still gazing across the lawn. "Antonio is either going to drop Carmen home or Antonio is going to drop Carmen in Arizona. With Isabel and Dr. Schiff. Carmen's choice. Why is she here?"

"Who?" Victor said.

"Mrs. Douglas."

"More to the point, why are you here?" Victor did not open his eyes. "Why aren't you off bobsledding somewhere."

"I thought my country needed me," Gerardo said. He did not turn around. "*Patria*, Victor. Right or wrong. Where exactly is Mr. Douglas?"

The only sound was that of the DDT truck which grinds past this house early each evening to spray.

"Caracas," Ardis Bradley said.

This time everyone seemed to have heard what Ardis Bradley said.

"Or he was when he called Tuck."

Victor opened his eyes and stared at her.

"Wasn't it Caracas? Tuck?"

"I have no idea." Tuck Bradley stood up. "It's time, Ardis."

"I have always loathed that phrase. 'It's time, Ardis.' You told me Caracas."

"We'll get dinner, Ardis."

Ardis Bradley stood up unsteadily.

I watched the cloud of DDT settle over the spindly roses at the far end of the lawn.

It occurred to me that my attempt to grow roses and a lawn at the equator was a delusion worthy of Charlotte Douglas.

One of whose husbands appeared to be in Caracas.

Not a delusion at all.

"Is he coming here?" Victor said suddenly.

"I would rather hope not," Tuck Bradley said, and he smiled, and he took Ardis Bradley's arm and after they left no one spoke for a long time. I think no one bothered to get dinner that night except Charlotte, who was seen at the Jockey Club as usual and was reported to have eaten not only the *plato frío* and the spiny lobster but two orders of flan.

At the time this surprised me.

At the time I had no real idea of how oblivious Charlotte Douglas was to the disturbance she could cause in the neutron field of a room, or a lawn.

5

As a matter of fact Leonard Douglas did not come to Boca Grande that spring.

Leonard Douglas did not come to Boca Grande until early September, at a time when the airport was closed at least part of every day while the carriers negotiated with the *guerrilleros* and when visitors to the Caribe were routinely frisked before they could enter the dining room.

I have no idea whether he had even intended to come in the spring, or what he had called Tuck Bradley to say.

Or to ask.

Neither Ardis nor Tuck Bradley ever mentioned the call from Caracas again.

If he had called from Caracas to ask about Charlotte he never took the next step and called Charlotte herself: Victor had her calls monitored, both at the Caribe and at the apartment on the Avenida del Mar she rented the week after she met Gerardo, and, at least until the week the *guerrilleros* knocked out the central monitoring system, there was no record of a call from Leonard Douglas to Charlotte Douglas.

Nor, on the other hand, was there any record of a call from Leonard Douglas to Tuck Bradley, which made Victor depressed and suspicious about his Embassy surveillance team.

I believe he put the entire team under what he called "internal surveillance," but it turned out to be just another case of mechanical failure.

Most things at the Ministry did.

I recall thinking that Victor would not be entirely sorry to turn over the Ministry to whoever was trying to get it that year.

"You're aware Gerardo's still seeing the *norteamericana*," Victor said one morning in March.

I knew that he was disturbed because he had come to see me in my laboratory. Victor does not like to see me in my laboratory. His forehead sweats, his pupils contract. I have observed taboo systems in enough cultures to know precisely how Victor feels about me in my laboratory: Victor distrusts the scientific method, and my familiarity with it gives me a certain power over him.

In my laboratory I am therefore particularly taboo.

To Victor.

For some years I used this taboo to my advantage but I am no longer so sure that Victor was not right.

"I believe they're 'dating,' Victor." I did not look up from what I was doing. "I see her too. What about it."

"I'm not talking about you seeing her."

"I took her to Millonario. She killed a chicken. With her bare hands."

"I'm not talking about you seeing her and I'm not talking about any chickens seeing her. I'm talking about Gerardo seeing her. Observed at all hours. Entering and leaving. I don't like it."

"Why don't you have him deported," I said.

Victor took another tack.

"You're very sophisticated these days."

I said nothing.

"Very tolerant."

I said nothing.

"I suppose with your vast sophistication and tolerance you don't mind the fact that your son *also* spends time with the faggot. The West Indian faggot. Whatever his circus name is, I'm not familiar with it."

I transferred a piece of tissue from one solution to another.

Victor meant Bebe Chicago.

Victor was as familiar with Bebe Chicago's name as I was, probably more familiar, since Victor received a detailed report on Bebe Chicago every morning at nine o'clock.

With his coffee.

"I sometimes wonder if your son has leanings. That way."

"No need to worry about the *norteamericana*, then."

Victor drummed his fingers on a flask and watched me for a long time without speaking.

"The West Indian is financing the *guerrilleros*," he said suddenly. "I happen to know that."

"I know you 'happen to know that,' Victor. You told me

a year ago. When Gerardo and Elena were such a burden to you."

"It doesn't make any difference to you that this West Indian is financing the *guerrilleros*?"

"It doesn't make any difference to you either. If it did you'd arrest him."

"I don't arrest him because I don't want to embarrass your son."

I said nothing.

Victor would have arrested me if he thought he could carry it off.

"All right then," Victor said. "You tell me why I don't arrest him."

"You don't arrest him because you want to know who's financing *him*. That's why you don't arrest him."

Victor sat in silence drumming his fingers on the flask.

It was the usual unsolved equation of the harmonic tremor in Boca Grande.

If Bebe Chicago was running the *guerrilleros* then X must be running Bebe Chicago.

Who was X.

This time.

There you had it. The *guerrilleros* would stage their "expropriations" and leave their communiqués about the "People's Revolution" and everyone would know who was financing the *guerrilleros* but for a while no one would know for whose benefit the *guerrilleros* were being financed. In the end the *guerrilleros* would all be shot and the true players would be revealed.

Mirabile dictu.

People we knew.

I remembered Luis using the *guerrilleros* against Anastasio Mendana-Lopez and I also remember Victor using the *guerrilleros*, against Luis.

I only think that.

I never knew that. Empirically.

In this case of course it would turn out to be Antonio who was using the *guerrilleros*, against Victor, but no one understood this in March.

Except Gerardo.

Gerardo understood it in March.
Maybe Carmen Arrellano understood it in March too.
Charlotte never did understand it.
I don't know that either. Empirically.

"I suppose you *do* know who's running the West Indian?" Victor said after a while. He was still drumming his fingers on the flask, a barrage of little taps, a tattoo. "I suppose in your infinite wisdom you know who's running the West Indian and one day you might deign to tell me?"

"How would I know who's running the West Indian, Victor? I'm not the Minister of Defense. You might want to watch that flask you're banging around, it's cancer virus." It was not cancer virus but I liked to reinforce the taboo. "Live."

Victor stood up abruptly.

"Disgusting," he said finally. "Filthy. Crude. The thought of it makes me retch."

"Are you talking about the cancer virus or the *guerrilleros*?"

"I am talking," he whispered, his voice strangled, "about the kind of woman who would kill a chicken with her bare hands."

It occurred to me that morning that Charlotte Douglas was acquiring certain properties of taboo.

Which might have stood her in good stead.

Had Victor been in charge at the Estadio Nacional instead of waiting it out with *El Presidente* at Bariloche.

6

WHEN MARIN BOGART asked me without much interest what her mother had "done" in Boca Grande there was very little I could think to say.

Very little that Marin Bogart would have understood.

A lost child in a dirty room in Buffalo.

A child who claimed no interest in the past.

Or the future.

Or the present.

As far as I could see.

"She did some work in a clinic," I said.

"Charity," Marin Bogart said.

The indictment lay between us for a while.

"Cholera actually," I said.

Marin Bogart shrugged.

Cholera was something Marin Bogart had been protected against, along with diphtheria, pertussis, tetanus, tuberculosis, poliomyelitis, and undue dental decay.

Cholera was one more word Marin Bogart did not understand.

"And after that she worked in a birth control clinic."

"Classic," Marin Bogart said. "Absolutely classic."

"How exactly is it 'classic.'"

"Birth control is *the* most flagrant example of how the ruling class practices genocide."

"Maybe not *the* most flagrant," I said.

A lost daughter in a dirty room in Buffalo with dishes in the sink and an M–3 on the bed.

A daughter who never had much use for words but had finally learned to string them together so that they sounded almost like sentences.

A daughter who chose to believe that her mother had died on the wrong side of a "people's revolution."

"There was no 'right side,'" I said. "There was no issue. There were only—"

"That is a typically—"

"There were only personalities."

"—A typically bourgeois view of the revolutionary process."
She had Charlotte's eyes.
Maybe there is no motive role in this narrative.
Maybe it is just something that happened.
Then why is it in my mind when nothing else is.

7

WHAT HAD CHARLOTTE DOUGLAS "done" in Boca Grande.

I have no idea whether Marin Bogart was asking me that day what her mother had "done" with her life in Boca Grande or what her mother had "done" to get killed in Boca Grande.

In either case the answer is obscure.

The question of Charlotte Douglas has never been "settled" for me.

Never "decided."

I know how to make models of life itself, DNA, RNA, helices double and single and squared, but I try to make a model of Charlotte Douglas's "character" and I see only a shimmer.

Like the shimmer of the oil slick on the boulevards after rain in Progreso.

Let me try a less holistic approach to the model.

We had the cholera epidemic in April that year.

The cholera epidemic in which Charlotte volunteered to give inoculations, and did, for thirty-four hours without sleeping.

I gave inoculations with Charlotte, but only for a few hours the first morning, because I had no patience with the fact that almost no one in Boca Grande would cross the street to be inoculated. They were all *fatalistas* about cholera. Cholera was an opportunity for God to prove His love.

"Then let Him prove it," I said to Charlotte at the end of the first morning.

"We have to make it attractive," Charlotte said. "Obviously."

And she did.

She set out to make each inoculation seem to the inoculee not a hedge against the hereafter but an occasion of mild profit in the here and now. She left the clinic for an hour and she bought chocolates wrapped in pink tinfoil from the Caribe kitchen and she made a deal for whisky miniatures with an unemployed Braniff steward who had access to the airport catering trucks and, until the remaining vaccine was appropriated by a colonel named Rafael Higuera, she dispensed these favors with every 1.5 cc. shot of Lederle Cholera Strains Ogawa-Inaba.

"Why didn't she just lie down and open her legs for them," Antonio said to Gerardo in my living room. It was the evening of the day the vaccine had been appropriated and Antonio had already expressed his conviction that Higuera had performed a public service by preventing Charlotte from further contaminating the populace with her American vaccine. I have never known why Antonio was so particularly enraged by everything Charlotte did. I suppose she was a *norteamericana*, she was a woman, she was an unpredictable element. I suppose she was a version of me at whom he could vent his rage. "Ask the great lady why she didn't just do that. Higuera didn't go far *enough*."

"How far should he have gone," Gerardo said, and smiled slightly at me.

"She'd throw her apron on my feet once," Antonio said. "Just once."

"What would you do," Gerardo said.

"Drop her," Antonio said.

"Drop her," Gerardo said.

"Between the eyes."

"Seems extreme," Gerardo said.

"How can you be entertained by this?" I said to Gerardo.

"How can you not be?" Gerardo said to me.

During the week after the appropriation of the vaccine Charlotte spoke not at all to me, spoke only in a glazed and distracted way to Gerardo, and was known to have placed two telephone calls to Leonard Douglas, neither of them completed. At the end of the week she gave me her revised version of the appropriation of the vaccine, the version in which the army was lending its resources to the inoculation program, the version in which she had simply misunderstood Higuera, the version in which he had never offered to sell her the vaccine but had simply expressed concern as to whether she herself had been inoculated; once she had arrived at this version Charlotte never mentioned cholera again, although people continued dying from it for several weeks.

After the cholera epidemic she appeared for a while that May and June to retreat into unspecified gastrointestinal infection less often, and she perfected that frenetic public energy which made many people, particularly Elena, suspect her of a reliance on major amphetamines. Even after she had moved most of her things into the apartment on the Avenida del Mar, even after she had with her own hands whitewashed all the walls and filled the empty rooms with flowers and begun to have what she called her "evenings" there, she kept her room at the Caribe, and she would go there every day for breakfast and to spend most of the day.

She began her "writing" during these days she spent alone at the Caribe.

She remembered her "film festival," and she drew up endless lists of names: actors, directors, agents, former agents who were then studio executives, former studio executives who were then independent producers, and what I once heard her call "other movers and shakers." She had met many of these people with Leonard and she was certain that they would be delighted to lend their names and films, once she put it to them.

Which she intended to do as soon as she completed the lists.

She got the idea for her "boutique," and she planned her projected inventory: needlepoint canvases of her own design and Porthault linens, the market for which in Boca Grande would have seemed to be limited to Elena, Bianca, Isabel, and me. She had enlisted Gerardo's help in finding a storefront to rent and she was certain that the boutique would pick up the character of the entire neighborhood, once she got it in shape for the opening.

Which she intended to do as soon as Bebe Chicago got his Dominicans out of the storefront.

"Imagine cymbidiums," she said on the afternoon she showed me her storefront. "Masses of them. In hemp baskets. The illusion of the tropics. That's the effect to strive for."

As a matter of fact the illusion of the tropics seemed to me an odd effect to strive for in a city rotting on the equator, but the actual condition of the storefront was such that I could only nod. The room was cramped and grimy and the single window was blacked out. Outside the afternoon sun was blazing but inside there was only the light from two bare bulbs. In the room, besides Charlotte and me, there were several sleeping bags, a hot plate, an open and unflushed toilet, a cheap dinette chair in which Bebe Chicago sat talking on the telephone, and a table at which a man whom Charlotte had introduced as "Mr. Sanchez" seemed to be translating a United States Army arms manual into Spanish.

Charlotte appeared oblivious.

"Lighten, brighten, open it up. The perfect creamy white on the walls, maybe the *palest* robin's-egg on the ceiling. And lattice. Lots of lattice. Mr. Sanchez is doing the lattice for me." Charlotte smiled fondly at the man at the table. He did not smile back. "Aren't you."

"Mr. Sanchez" stared at Charlotte as if she were a moth he had never before observed and turned to Bebe Chicago. "Are we interested in the AR-16?" he said in Spanish.

"AR-15 only." Bebe Chicago hung up the telephone and smiled at me. "Gerardo's mama naturally speaks Spanish, *mon chéri*."

"Think of a lath-house crossed with a Givenchy perfume box," Charlotte said.

"Can I offer Gerardo's mama a *café-filtre*," Bebe Chicago said. He stood up with a magician's flourish and placed the dinette chair in front of me. "Can I offer Gerardo's mama this superb example of post-industrial craftsmanship."

I remained standing.

"Possibly gardenias," Charlotte said. "No. Cymbidiums."

Bebe Chicago smiled and sat in the chair himself.

"Then can I tell Gerardo's mama how much I admire her shoes," he said. "Can I at least tell her that."

"You can tell her what that Bren gun is doing behind the toilet," I said.

"That's not a Bren at all," Bebe Chicago said after only the slightest beat, his voice still silky. "That's a Kalashnikov. Russian. Out of Syria. The Chinese make one too, but it's inferior to the Russian. The Russian is the best. A really super weapon."

"Don't talk about guns," Charlotte said, and her voice was low and abrupt, and after that day she seemed to lose interest in her boutique.

During this period Charlotte also had her "research."

She had her "paperwork."

In other words she would sit alone in her room at the Caribe and she would try to read books and she would try to write letters. She tried to read a book about illiteracy in Latin America, but in lieu of finishing it she wrote a letter to *Prensa Latina* offering her services as author of a daily "literacy lesson." She tried to read Alberto Masferrer's *El Mínimum Vital* but she still had difficulty reading Spanish, and she had read a hundred pages of *El Mínimum Vital* before she learned from Gerardo that it was about the progressive tax. She borrowed from Ardis Bradley a volume that was obviously a CIA-sponsored "handbook" on Boca Grande, and she discovered in the introduction to this handbook an invitation to address her suggestions "for factual or interpretive or other changes" to a post-office box in Washington.

To this post-office box in Washington Charlotte addressed her suggestions for factual or interpretive or other changes on the subject of Boca Grande.

She never received an answer but first Kasindorf and then Riley and finally Tuck Bradley received word that she was in the country.

In case they had missed her.

Nor did Charlotte receive answers from most of the other officials and agencies and writers and editors to whom she addressed her suggestions for factual or interpretive or other changes on a wide range of subjects.

I believe mainly "other" changes.

The only bad time of these days Charlotte spent at the Caribe was about four o'clock.

At about four o'clock the shine of plausibility would seem to go off her projects.

At about four o'clock she would find herself sitting in the room at the Caribe remembering something.

She would sometimes call me up at four o'clock and tell me what she was remembering.

For example.

Those crossed spots on the Pollock in the dining room of the house on California Street.

Those crossed spots were too bright, or too exposed, she could not determine which.

Those spots had always been too bright, too exposed.

She should perhaps have them recessed in the ceiling.

What did I think.

At a certain point during each of these calls the possession would seem to fade from her voice, and by the time she hung up she would sound almost at peace. She would go downstairs then and sit by the pool and she would watch the peacocks hiding from the heat under the jacaranda trees and she would watch the blocks of ice being dragged across the concrete into the Caribe kitchen. She would imagine the various bacteria waiting in each block of ice. She counted bacteria instead of sheep. After a while a great lassitude would come over her and she would want to sleep, and sometimes she did sleep, there by the Caribe pool in the late afternoons, but at night in the apartment on the Avenida del Mar she did not sleep at all.

8

WE COULD HAVE been doing this all our lives.

We should do this all our lives.

Tell her I said it's all the same.

Tell her that for me.

Tell Charlotte she was wrong.

I never told Charlotte what Warren Bogart said.

I think she heard him say it every night.

She would get up some nights when Gerardo was asleep and she would pick up the half-filled glasses with which the strangers who came to her "evenings" had littered the empty rooms of the apartment on the Avenida del Mar and she would walk by herself to a theater downtown which showed dolorous Mexican movies all night, tales of betrayal and stolen babies and other sexual punishments. Other nights she would not leave the apartment but would only stand in the living room by the window and listen to the radio. Radio Boca Grande was allowed to broadcast only during restricted hours by that time but she could usually get Radio Jamaica and sometimes even Radio British Honduras and the Voice of the Caribbean from the Central American Mission in San José, Costa Rica. She thought she had New Orleans or Miami one night, dance music from some hotel or another in New Orleans or Miami, but it turned out to be only a pick-up from the Caribe. She recognized the accordionist.

Some nights when she could not even get Radio Jamaica she called San Francisco.

She did not call the number of the house on California Street in San Francisco.

She did not call the number of anyone she knew in San Francisco.

She called a number in San Francisco which gave, over and over again in a voice so monotonous as to seem to come from beyond the grave, the taped "road condition" report of the California Highway Patrol.

Interstate 80 Donner Pass was open.

U.S. 50 Echo Summit was closed.

State Route 88 Carson Pass was open.

State Route 89 Lassen Loop was closed, State Route 108 Sonora was closed, State Route 120 Tioga Pass was closed.

These calls were routed through Quito and Miami and took quite a long time to place.

By the end of May every road regularly reported upon by the California Highway Patrol was open.

According to Victor.

Who duly heard these calls and believed them coded.

"Quite frankly I don't think the California Highway Patrol is hooked up with the *guerrilleros*," I said to Victor.

"Then give me one reason for these calls."

"She's lonely, Victor." In fact "lonely" was never a word I would have used to characterize Charlotte Douglas but conversation with Victor requires broad strokes. "She's 'a woman alone.' As I believe you used to call her."

"She is no longer a woman alone. May I point out. On the occasion of all but one of these calls your son has been spending the night in this apartment. Where Bebe Chicago has been a frequent visitor."

"If I were you I'd listen to Bebe Chicago's calls and forget Charlotte's."

"Bebe Chicago's calls. Spare me any more of Bebe Chicago's calls." Victor mimicked a whispery falsetto. "'Ricardo? It's me. *C'est moi, chéri*. Bebe.'"

"Actually you aren't good at voices, Victor. What is it you want to know?"

"What I want to know, Grace, is what your son is doing while she makes these calls."

"Sleeping."

"'Sleeping'?"

"'Sleeping.' Yes."

Victor looked at me awhile, and then at his nails.

"Sleeping," he said finally. "What kind of man would be sleeping."

I was tired of Victor that spring.

I was also tired of whatever game Gerardo was playing with Bebe Chicago and the *guerrilleros* and the strangers he invited to Charlotte's "evenings" on the Avenida del Mar.

*

Charlotte's "evenings."

I would go sometimes.

There were always these strangers there, third-rate people Gerardo was using in his game, the object of which seemed to be to place his marker in Victor's office in as few moves as possible. His marker that year happened to be Antonio, but who it was mattered not at all to Gerardo. Gerardo plays only for the action. Part of the action in this case was the artful manipulation of what passed for the intelligentsia in Boca Grande, the point being to create an illusion of support for the *guerrilleros*, and it was the members of this "intelligentsia" who littered the apartment on the Avenida del Mar with half-filled glasses two or three nights a week. Of course Bebe Chicago was usually there, and a few "poets" who had published verses in anthologies with titles like *Fresh Wind in the Caribbean*, and the usual complement of translators and teachers and film critics who supported themselves stringing for newspapers and playing at politics. I recall one who read out loud at Charlotte's dinner table a paper he was writing called "The Singular Position of Intellectuals with Respect to the Crisis of the Underdeveloped World" and then read it again, over Charlotte's telephone, to a friend in Tenerife. I recall another who made marionettes to perform the plays of Arnold Wesker in schoolyards.

I have no idea what Charlotte thought of these people.

She told me she found them "terribly stimulating to listen to," but I never saw her "listen to" any one of them.

She had in the dining room of the apartment on the Avenida del Mar a large round table around which these people sat and talked about what they always called "the truly existential situation of the Central American," and Charlotte would sit at this table in her gray chiffon dress, but she seemed not to be there at all. She only stared at the kerosene lamp in the center of the table and watched moths batter themselves against the glass chimney. As the moths fell stunned to the table she would brush them toward her with a napkin, like someone dreaming. At the end of such an evening there would be moths drifted beneath her chair and moth wings caught in her gray chiffon skirt and no trace in her mind of what had been said. So dimly did Charlotte appear to perceive the nature of her evenings that she would sometimes invite Victor, and Victor would sit stiffly and finger his pistol and say that he did not quite comprehend why the situation of the Central American was so truly existential.

"What's to be done about it in any case," I recall Victor saying one night. "What does it mean."

Whenever I saw Victor at one of Charlotte's "evenings" I found myself rather liking him.

At least he was serious.

Unlike Gerardo.

"Don't worry about what it means," Gerardo said that night.

"'What does it mean,'" Bebe Chicago said. "A knotty question."

"I find it touching," the most offensive of the poets said. His name was Raúl Lara and he was working on a sequence of Mother-and-Child sonnets to present to the people of Cuba and all that evening he had been studying a mango, spitting on it, polishing it, holding it in different lights.

Raúl Lara held the mango now in front of Victor's eyes.

"A Strasser-Mendana. A man of action. Trapped in the quicksand of time and he asks us *what does it mean*. Give him Fanon. Give him Debray. Give him this fat mango."

Raúl Lara dropped the mango in Victor's lap.

With considerable dignity Victor stood up and placed the mango on the table in front of Charlotte.

The table fell silent.

Charlotte seemed to force herself to look away from the moths and at the mango. "Did someone need a fruit knife," she said finally.

"You weren't listening," Victor said gently.

"She never listens," Gerardo said.

"Why don't you listen," Victor said to Charlotte.

Charlotte smiled vaguely.

"Maybe she doesn't listen because she's afraid of what she'll hear," Raúl Lara said. "New ideas. Very threatening."

Charlotte looked directly at Raúl Lara for the first time that evening. She seemed tired. She seemed older. "I've heard some new ideas," she said after a while. "In my time."

Other than that Charlotte seemed to make no judgments at all on the people who came to the apartment on the Avenida del Mar, no judgments on them and no distinctions among them.

Among us.

I was there too.

We were voices. We were voices no different from the voices in Mexican movies. We were voices no different from the voices on Radio Jamaica or on the California Highway Patrol road reports. We were voices to fill the hours until it was time to go to the Caribe for breakfast.

Sometimes I forget that I was there too.

Charlotte's breakfasts at the Caribe.

Charlotte went to the Caribe for breakfast every morning for a while.

She went to the Caribe for breakfast because she worried about three children who every morning would crawl under the Caribe fence and leap screaming into the deep end of the pool. They did not seem to know how to swim. They would flounder and gasp to the side and leap in again. There was no lifeguard and the water was green with algae and Charlotte could never see the children beneath the surface of the water but every morning she would take her breakfast to the pool and try to insure that the children did not drown. She tried to distinguish their particular shrieks. She counted their heads compulsively. Because she believed that in the instant of a blink one of the heads would slip beneath the surface and stay there unseen she tried not to blink.

"There are no children registered at the hotel," the manager of the Caribe said when she mentioned the children in the pool. "So they aren't supposed to be there."

"But they are there."

"They aren't supposed to be there," the manager said, enunciating each word very carefully, "because there are no children registered at the hotel."

On the morning she could only see two of the three children for thirty straight seconds she screamed, and jumped into the pool with her clothes on. She choked and the murky water blinded her and when she came up all three children were standing on the edge of the pool fighting over her handbag. She watched them run away with the bag and she went upstairs and she stood for a long while in the lukewarm trickle from the shower and she thought about the pale wash of green Marin got in her hair every summer from the chlorine in pools.

California pools.

Swimming pools for children who knew how to swim.

She tried to stop thinking about swimming pools but could not.

"You don't seem to have heard of chlorine here," she said to me.

"We don't want to emphasize technology at the expense of traditional culture," I said.

I thought she was in a less literal mood than usual but apparently she was not.

"I see," she said.

"I wasn't serious," I said. "It was a joke. Irony."

"Is cheap," she said. Her expression did not change.

After that morning at the pool she stopped spending her days at the Caribe and volunteered as an advisor at the birth control clinic. She seemed to have entirely forgotten Colonel Higuera and the Lederle cholera vaccine, her previous essay into good works. She was a source of some exasperation at the birth control clinic, because she kept advising the women to request diaphragms they would never use instead of intrauterine devices they could not remove, but the job of "advisor" was largely academic anyway since only intrauterine devices were available. In any case Charlotte took her work very seriously and it seemed to lend a purpose to her days.

"Anyone can learn to use a diaphragm," she announced at my house one evening when I suggested that the diaphragm, however favored it might be in the practices of San Francisco gynecologists, was not generally considered the most practical means of birth control in underdeveloped countries. "I certainly did."

"You certainly did what?" Gerardo said.

"I certainly learned to use a diaphragm."

"Of course you did," Gerardo said. "What's that got to do with it? Grace wasn't talking about you."

"Grace was talking," Charlotte said, "about the difficulty of using diaphragms. And I said there wasn't any. Difficulty. Because I had no trouble whatsoever learning how."

Gerardo looked at me.

I think this was perhaps Gerardo's first exposure not to the *norteamericana* in Charlotte but to the westerner in Charlotte, the Hollister ranch child in Charlotte, the strain in Charlotte which insisted that the world was peopled with others exactly like herself.

"What is she saying," Gerardo said to me.

"Charlotte is an egalitarian," I said to Gerardo. "So am I. You are not."

"I am only saying," Charlotte said patiently, "that if I could learn to use a diaphragm then anyone could."

"Bullshit," Gerardo said.

Charlotte looked at Gerardo levelly for quite a long time.

There was a flicker of Warren Bogart on her face.

"Then don't you talk at me any more about what 'the people' can do," she said finally.

No irony.

However cheap.

I liked Charlotte very much that night but she still tended to take whatever Gerardo said precisely at face value. Gerardo only talked about "the people" that spring as a move in the particular game he was playing. As a matter of fact Charlotte tended to take what anyone said precisely at face value. When she showed me her next attempt at writing about Boca Grande, the next of those "Letters from Central America" which were the only one of her projects to survive the incident at the Caribe pool, the typed manuscript began: "A nation that refuses to emphasize technology at the expense of its traditional culture, Boca Grande is . . ."

Boca Grande is.

9

"YOU SHOULDN'T HAVE done that," I said to Victor the day Antonio's Bentley exploded in front of the Caribe, killing the chauffeur. Antonio had not even been using the Bentley. Carmen Arrellano had been using the Bentley, but at the instant of the explosion Carmen Arrellano had been having her legs waxed in the Caribe beauty shop. In short the job had been inept in the extreme, but this was not the aspect I wanted to stress with Victor. "You really shouldn't have."

"I didn't," Victor said. "I'm appalled you think I did. Appalled. Shocked. Hurt. It's an obscene accusation."

I said nothing.

"If you think I did it," Victor said after a while, "then you know *why* I did it. You're aware of what Antonio's trying to do."

I said nothing.

"I suppose your son told you," Victor said.

"Actually no."

"I suppose you prefer Antonio to me," Victor said.

"Not particularly."

Victor sat in silence for a while. He had come to visit in the middle of the afternoon. He never used to visit in the middle of the afternoon. Victor did not seem to know what to do with his afternoons that summer.

"Then why aren't you helping me," he said finally. "You know what Antonio's doing, you—"

"I don't know. I just suppose."

"—You *suppose* you know what Antonio's doing, why don't you discuss it with me? Why aren't you *with* me?"

"Because it doesn't make any difference to me," I said.

Victor sat slumped in a chair.

I have liked Victor on some occasions and pitied him on many. Edgar called him stupid. Luis laughed at him. Even Antonio was making a fool of him.

I took his ridiculous manicured hand.

"Because it's going to happen," I said. "Just let it happen. With grace."

"I can't do that," Victor said after a while.

I knew he couldn't do that.

Within the next two weeks three more explosions occurred in locations where Antonio might normally have been, killing six and injuring fourteen, and then there was the usual odd calm.

"'The outlook is not all bright.'" Charlotte was reading me the draft of an unfinished Letter from Central America. "'Nor is the outlook all black.' Paragraph. 'Nonetheless—'"

She broke off.

"That's where I seem to be blocked."

"I don't wonder," I said.

"What do you mean."

"'Nevertheless' *what*? I mean, Charlotte. If you say 'the outlook is not all bright' and then you say 'nor is the outlook all black,' then you can't start the next sentence with 'nevertheless.' It can't possibly mean anything."

"I didn't start the next sentence with 'nevertheless,'" Charlotte said. "I started it with 'nonetheless.'"

I said nothing.

"Anyway." Charlotte folded the pages of her unfinished Letter with a neat vertical crease as children fold their weekly themes. "It's not just a new sentence. It's a new paragraph."

It occurred to me that I had never before had so graphic an illustration of how the consciousness of the human organism is carried in its grammar.

Or the unconsciousness of the human organism.

If the organism under scrutiny is Charlotte.

"In any case," Charlotte said after a while. "It'll all fall together when I'm away."

"You're going away, then."

"Of course I'm going away. I mean I don't live here, do I."

"When?"

"I'm not quite sure when."

"Where?"

"I have to see someone."

I did not ask who.

"Or rather I want to see someone. My husband."

I did not ask which one.

"But I mean there's no immediate rush about it. Is there."

"I think there is, Charlotte." I was suddenly tired. "As a matter of fact I think it's imperative that you go very soon."

"No." She seemed abruptly agitated. "It is not imperative. At all. *He is not dying.*"

I sat without speaking awhile.

The tissue around Charlotte's eyes was reddening but she did not cry.

Tell Charlotte she was wrong.

"I didn't mean that it's imperative you go anywhere in particular," I said finally. "I don't care where you go. Go to Caracas, go to Managua. Just get out of here."

She put on her dark glasses and tried to smile.

"Just leave," I said.

"I don't believe I can quite manage this display of hospitality." There was in Charlotte's voice an inflection of which she seemed entirely unaware, an inflection I had heard before only in the Garden District of New Orleans. "Here's-your-hat-what's-your-hurry, seems about the size of it."

Here's-your-hat-what's-your-hurry.

Mrs. Fayard's been learning West Texas manners.

Tell Charlotte she was wrong.

"Charlotte." I felt as if I were talking to a child. "I've told you before, there is trouble here. There is going to be more trouble here. You are going to find yourself in the middle of this trouble which is not your business."

"I don't know anything about any trouble. So how could I possibly be in the middle of it."

"Because *Gerardo is.*"

She looked at me as if I had mentioned someone she had met a long time before and did not quite remember.

I think I fucked you one Easter.

I think I did that and forgot it.

I think she did forget it.

"In any case I'm not affected," she said after a while. "Because I'm simply not interested in any causes or issues."

"Neither is anyone here."

Charlotte said nothing.

"Charlotte." I tried again. "What do you think all those people were doing at your dining-room table?"

Charlotte looked at me.

"You were there too," she said finally.

That was July.

Boca Grande is.

10

I RECALL IT NOW as a year when we actually had "seasons." Definite "changes."

Changes not in the weather but in the caliber of the harmonic tremor.

I am not sure when everyone else realized that Antonio had diverted enough "secret" support from Victor's army to be finally immune from Victor but I know when I realized it. I realized it the evening Gerardo and Charlotte came back from Progreso and Charlotte began to cry at dinner.

"What upset her?" I said to Gerardo when Charlotte had left the table.

Gerardo was picking the meat from a crab and did not look at me.

"I suppose she didn't like Progreso," he said after a while. "I suppose she got tired. A day's outing. Very tiring."

"I said what upset her."

"I suppose she didn't find Progreso as peaceful as you claim to." Gerardo placed the crabmeat as he picked it on Charlotte's plate. "I suppose it's a special taste."

"I want to know what upset her out there."

"M–3's," Charlotte said from the doorway.

She had washed her face clean of makeup and she seemed entirely composed.

"I grew up with shotguns but I can't stand carbines." She sat down and picked up her napkin. "Why are you staring at me?"

There was a silence.

"Whose carbines?" I said.

Gerardo avoided my eyes. "Grace hasn't been out to Progreso lately, Charlotte. Grace hasn't seen—what did you call it? Did you call it 'the machinery'?"

"I called it the hardware," Charlotte said.

"She calls it the hardware," Gerardo said.

"I don't have cancer of the ear," I said. "Whose hardware is it?"

"Antonio's got some of the army with him. Of course." Gerardo shrugged. The only clear evidence I have of Gerardo's intelligence is that he has always known how to cut his losses, yield the position, supply the information. Gerardo differs in that respect from Victor. "Actually it wasn't the guns that upset Charlotte. It was Antonio. Antonio and Carmen. Antonio gave Carmen an M–3 and let her shoot up the place."

Charlotte picked up her fork and laid it down again.

"You have a rather bizarre idea of a day's outing," I said to Gerardo.

"Carmen wasn't using an M–3," Charlotte said. She leaned forward slightly and her face was entirely grave. "Antonio was. Carmen was using an M–16."

Gerardo looked away.

"And they weren't shooting up 'the place,' Gerardo. I mean what *is* 'the place.' 'The place' is some rusted Cats and five flamingoes. They were only shooting the crates."

Something about Charlotte's querulous precision seemed extreme, and unnatural.

"What crates?" I said.

Charlotte looked at me.

"The crates of vaccine," she said. "The Lederle vaccine."

Charlotte never changed her expression.

"Unopened crates of Lederle vaccine," she said. "Cholera. It ran on the street when they shot up the crates."

I looked at her for a long time.

"It ran on the street," she repeated. "If you call that a street."

I think I loved Charlotte in that moment as a parent loves the child who has just fallen from a bicycle, met a pervert, lost a prize, come up in any way against the hardness of the world.

I think I was also angry at her, again like a parent, furious that she hadn't known better, furious that she had been wrong.

Tell Charlotte she was wrong.

What had Charlotte been wrong about exactly.

Who was wrong here.

I looked away from her.

"Why are you doing this with Antonio?" I said to Gerardo.

"I'm not 'doing' it, it's done. It's in progress. Underway. Its own momentum now."

"I know that," I said. "I want to know why you did it."

"It was something to do," Gerardo said.

"I happen to know about M–16's because Marin had one

when she went to Utah," Charlotte said. Charlotte always referred to the day Marin hijacked the L–1011 and burned it on the Bonneville Salt Flats as "when Marin went to Utah," as if it had been a tour of National Parks. Charlotte was not looking at me any more. "Or so they told me."

"Get her out before it happens," I said to Gerardo.

"The M–16 is supposed to be the 'ideal' submachine gun," Charlotte said. "Leonard called it ideal. They didn't."

"Tell me when it's time," I said to Gerardo.

"You always hear it," Gerardo said. "Eat that crab, Charlotte. I picked that crab for you."

I always did hear it.

I heard it because I listened.

Charlotte heard even more than I heard but Charlotte seemed not to listen.

Charlotte seemed not to see.

Charlotte had stood out there in the bamboo at Progreso and let the sun burn her face and heard Antonio call her *norteamericana cunt* and heard Carmen Arrellano call her *la bonne bourgeoise* and heard the carbine fire shatter the vials of clear American vaccine and still she did not listen. Charlotte had watched the clear American vaccine shimmer on the boulevards of Progreso and still she did not see.

That was August.

Boca Grande is.

Boca Grande was.

Boca Grande shall be.

II

LAND OF CONTRASTS.

Economic fulcrum of the Americas.

By the day in early September when Leonard Douglas finally arrived in Boca Grande it was clear that Victor was only playing for time. His couriers shuttled between Boca Grande and Geneva carrying heavy pouches. Military passes had been canceled. All day long Radio Boca Grande broadcast a single message, delivered by two voices, one male, one female, each threatening terrorists and saboteurs with death. It was clear that Victor would be leaving soon to convalesce in Bariloche. *El Presidente* had in fact already left to convalesce in Bariloche, omitting even the traditional move in which he first spends a week confined to the palace with a respiratory infection complicated by extreme exhaustion. Ardis Bradley had discovered a pressing need to take her children to Boston for school interviews. Tuck Bradley had stayed on but had twenty seats reserved on every flight leaving Boca Grande for any destination. I had two.

One for me.

One for Charlotte.

In other words.

All the markers were on the board.

"I'm Charlotte Douglas's husband," Leonard Douglas said to me.

"I know you are," I said to Leonard Douglas.

I knew that he had arrived in Boca Grande on one of the two or three flights that had managed to land the day before. He had gone directly to the Caribe and after a while he and Charlotte had been observed walking on the Avenida del Mar. It had been assumed that they were walking to her apartment but instead they had turned onto Calle 11 and entered the birth control clinic.

Victor had told me that.

Tuck Bradley had also told me that.

Gerardo had told me that he had no interest in Charlotte Douglas's former life.

"I wouldn't call yesterday her 'former life' exactly," I had said to Gerardo.

Gerardo had told me that I had too literal a mind.

Charlotte had told me nothing at all.

I got Leonard Douglas a drink.

He sat in my living room and drank it.

"I met your husband once," he said finally.

"He's dead now."

"I know that."

I got him another drink.

He put it on the table untouched.

"In Bogotá," he said. "I met him in Bogotá."

"When was that?"

"Before he died."

"Not after, then."

The acerbity in my voice went unnoticed.

"We had some business."

Leonard Douglas seemed absorbed in some contemplation of either Bogotá or Edgar, I did not know which.

I recall being uneasy.

"Where's Charlotte?" I said abruptly. "Did Charlotte send you to see me?"

"No." Leonard Douglas picked up the drink and put it down again. "I liked him. Your husband. I think he liked me. He gave me an emerald. As I was leaving. He gave me an emerald to take to Charlotte."

The square emerald.

The big square emerald Charlotte wore in place of a wedding ring.

The big square emerald Leonard had brought her from wherever he was when he met the man who financed the Tupamaros.

Bogotá.

Quito.

Charlotte had no idea whether it was Bogotá or Quito.

It was Bogotá.

I had no idea.

I prided myself on listening and seeing and I had never even heard or seen that Edgar played the same games Gerardo played.

Leonard Douglas was watching me.

"Why did you tell me that," I said finally.

"I wanted you to know that I understand what's going on here."

"Why."

"Because," Leonard Douglas said, "I want you to get Charlotte out."

"It could be smooth," I said after a while. I did not believe that it would be smooth. "Sometimes it's smooth."

"It's not going to be smooth," Leonard Douglas said.

"How do you know."

"I don't want you to think I'm involved here."

"Nobody said you were."

"I want you to believe me." Leonard Douglas seemed to tense as he spoke. "I have no interest here."

"I believe you."

As a matter of fact I did believe him.

I also believed him about Edgar.

I still do.

It still disturbs me and I still believe him.

"It's not going to be smooth," he repeated. "I'm not involved but I hear things."

I said nothing.

"I hear there's more outside hardware than there's supposed to be. You know what I mean."

I did know what he meant.

He meant that someone had outplayed Gerardo and Antonio.

He meant that the *guerrilleros* were not going to just serve their purpose and get gunned down on the fourth day by an insurgent army under Antonio's command.

He meant that for a certain number of days or weeks no one at all could be certain of knowing the right people in Boca Grande.

"So get her out," he said finally.

"Why don't you take her out?"

"She won't go with me."

"Why not?"

Leonard Douglas sat for a while and ran his finger around the rim of his glass.

"She remembers everything," he said after a while.

And then: "You met Warren Bogart."

It was a question.

"Once. In New Orleans. He said he was dying."

"Yes. Well." Leonard Douglas looked suddenly exhausted. "He was right."

12

"WHO WAS THERE," Charlotte had said when Leonard told her that Warren Bogart was dead.

As he sat in my living room and told me what she had said he kept repeating the words as if he could not believe them: *who was there.*

He remembered that she said it at the corner of Avenida del Mar and Calle 11.

He had come to Boca Grande to tell her three things.

He had come to tell her that certain of his former clients had put him in touch with someone in the underground who had put him in touch with Marin.

He had come to tell her to get out of Boca Grande.

He had come to tell her that he had buried Warren Bogart a few days before in New Orleans.

He told her none of these things until they were out of the Caribe and walking on the Avenida del Mar where they could not be heard.

He told her that Marin was living with six other people in a semi-detached house in the industrial section of Buffalo and she said nothing at all. She began to cry and she kept on walking and she said nothing at all. He told her to get out of Boca Grande and she said nothing at all. She folded and refolded the piece of paper he had given her with the number of the post-office box in Buffalo and she said nothing at all. He told her that he had buried Warren Bogart and she walked until they reached the corner of Avenida del Mar and Calle 11 and as they turned the corner onto Calle 11 she said something. He remembered that he had just realized that she was walking not idly but toward a specific destination and then she said something.

She said *who was there.*

"I told you. He was alone. He'd been in and out of Ochsner for a month and this time he just walked out without anybody knowing and he was alone on the street. And he collapsed. And they took him to Long Memorial and they put him on life-support but he never woke up."

"Who was there."

"Charlotte. No one was there. He had a letter in his coat with the number on California Street. Your number and Porter's number. They tried to get Porter and they couldn't. Porter was in New York. They tried to get you and they got me. He was on the machine for the rest of the day and he died before I got there."

"Who was there," Charlotte repeated. "When he was buried. You said you buried him. *Who came.*"

"I got hold of Porter. Porter came."

She seemed to be waiting for something.

"A couple of people I didn't know."

She still seemed to be waiting for something.

"And six FBI."

She had stopped in front of a building on Calle 11 and still she seemed to be waiting.

"It was fine, Charlotte. He didn't want anyone there. The letter said so. The letter they found in his coat. All he wanted was nobody there and somebody singing 'Didn't I Ramble.'"

Charlotte said nothing.

The letter in Warren Bogart's coat also had a message for Charlotte and Marin but Leonard did not mention the message.

"He carried it in his coat. The letter." Leonard shook his head. "He did. Didn't he."

"He did what."

"He did ramble."

The message for Charlotte and Marin had read only "*you were both wrong but it's all the same in the end*" and Leonard did not mention the message.

"Not a letter really," he said. "A note. On the back of an envelope."

"This is where I work," Charlotte said. "I'm quite late now."

She looked directly at Leonard as she spoke and then she turned and walked inside and down a corridor and into an office. When he followed her into the office she was standing at the window smoking a cigarette and staring out at the blank wall of the adjoining building and she did not turn around.

"Would you go to the desk for me," she said after a while. She did not turn from the window. "Would you tell them I can't see anyone for a few minutes. Twenty minutes."

"I'll call." Leonard picked up the telephone and jiggled it. "How do you call?"

"You don't. The switchboard's out. Or something. Since the bomb."

He stared at her.

"You had a bomb here?"

"Or something."

"When was the bomb? Or something."

"I don't know. Yesterday. No, it was the day before, because I still had the curse, I was changing a Tampax when it went off. Would you please go to the desk?"

Leonard put the telephone down and watched Charlotte crush her cigarette on the ledge outside the window.

"I want you to come with me," he said after a while. "I never told you what to do but I'm telling you now. I want you to come with me to the airport. Now."

"Actually I can't." Charlotte said, and then she turned abruptly from the window. *"Didn't Marin come."*

"She couldn't have, Charlotte. I told you. The FBI were there. Naturally the FBI were there."

"Did you tell Marin."

"Yes."

"Did she want to come."

There was a silence.

"I don't know," Leonard said.

"Tell her she was wrong," Charlotte said. "Tell her that for me."

13

"AND WHAT ABOUT this fucking bomb," Leonard Douglas said to me.

He had finally drunk his second drink and then a third and a fourth. He was in no way drunk but he gave off the sense of a man who normally had one drink, maybe two when politesse required it, a man who prized control and had been pushed in a single week almost beyond it.

He had found Marin Bogart in an empty room in Buffalo.

He had buried Warren Bogart in an empty grave in New Orleans.

He had come to save Charlotte from an empty revolution in Boca Grande and Charlotte was not listening.

He had found his way to me and in my house there were flowers in the vases and ice cubes in the carafes and clean uniforms on the maids. In my house it did not seem so empty and I was listening.

"'A bomb or something,' she says. Don't miss the *or something*. I look around, I discover the back wing of the building blew up three days ago, I find four people died outright and the fifth's dying now, peritonitis, this fifth one got caught on the table, the doctor jumped and punctured this one's fucking—"

Leonard Douglas seemed to have rendered himself temporarily mute.

"Uterus," I said. "I heard there was a bomb. Before you came. I asked Charlotte about it. Charlotte said—"

I broke off. Charlotte had said that when the bomb went off she was in the bathroom and she had forgotten about her Tampax and had spotted blood all over the clinic without realizing it.

That was all she had said.

"She said it wasn't near her office," I said.

"Never mind where it *wasn't*. Because she goes charging in where it *was*, the ceiling's still falling, she gets three people out, she's a heroine, she's mad as hell, she's shouting '*Goddamn you all*' the whole time. *They* tell me that. *Charlotte* doesn't. All

Charlotte remembers about this bomb is it went off while she was changing her fucking Tampax."

"She bled." I did not know what else to say. "She remembers she bled all over the clinic."

Leonard Douglas looked at me a long while.

He loosened his tie and closed his eyes.

It was just sundown and I could hear the DDT truck outside.

"Yeah," he said finally. "She remembers she bled."

The DDT truck was gone before he spoke again.

"You didn't know about Bogotá, did you."

"No."

"I shouldn't have told you. It upset you."

"I should have known."

"She should have known too." Leonard Douglas stood up and picked up his jacket. He did not seem to be talking to me at all. "It wasn't the way she thought it was either. I wasn't the way she thought I was and Marin wasn't the way she thought Marin was and Warren wasn't the way she thought Warren was. She didn't know any of us."

"She remembers everything," I said. "You said she remembers everything."

"No," Leonard Douglas said. "She remembers she bled."

14

A FEW DAYS after Leonard Douglas left Boca Grande Charlotte told me that he had "passed through" but had left before she could "arrange an evening" for him.

"An 'evening,'" I remember saying. An evening for a man who had just found her child and buried her child's father. An evening for such a man in an equatorial city under martial law and rigid curfew. "What kind of 'evening' exactly did you have in mind?"

"An evening to meet everyone. Of course. I particularly wanted him to meet you."

"He did meet me," I said after a while. "He spent three hours here in this room. He told me about Marin. He told me about Warren."

She looked away before she spoke.

"I know he did," she said. "I don't want to talk about it."

Charlotte stood up then and walked out onto the terrace and across the lawn to where the roses grew. I remembered her walking across the lawn the night she met Gerardo and I remembered Elena and I remembered Ardis Bradley and I remembered Carmen Arrellano and I wished suddenly that Charlotte had gone to Paris.

You smell American.

I wonder what American smells like exactly.

Norteamericana cunt.

When Charlotte came back inside she did not look at me.

When Charlotte came back inside she was already talking and her voice was low.

Charlotte wondered if she had ever told me about the night Marin was born. Marin was born at Flower-Fifth Avenue Hospital in New York. Warren hit the head nurse on the maternity floor. The head nurse brought assault charges but later dropped them. Marin weighed six-eight at birth but only six-two by the time they took her home. Charlotte supposed that was normal. Warren was afraid to hold Marin in the taxi going home. Charlotte supposed he had been drinking. Instead of holding Marin he held his hands an inch or so above the soft spot on her head to protect it if the taxi bumped and he said over and over again that he did not want her to go to Smith and marry some eighth-rate ass from Sullivan and Cromwell.

"And I don't guess she ever will," Charlotte said finally. Her voice was devoid of expression. "I guess he got that wish."

There was a silence.

"Now you can see her," I said.

"No," Charlotte said. "I can't exactly."

"But you know how to reach her."

"She's always known how to reach me," Charlotte said. "If you want to look at it that way."

I said nothing.

"So in the first place it's not even Marin."

I think she meant that it was not the Marin she remembered.

There was nothing to say.

"Marin would have found Warren. Marin would have found me."

Tell Marin she was wrong. Tell her that for me.

Goddamn you all.

She remembers she bled.

15

ON THE AFTERNOON I went to the Caribe to tell Charlotte that she and I were leaving for New Orleans, that the last planes were getting out, that Tuck Bradley was closing the Embassy, Charlotte only shook her head.

"Not just yet," she said.

She was sitting in the lobby of the Caribe staring at a television screen which for days had shown only the emblem of La República de Boca Grande, with military music played over the emblem.

"Charlotte. Look at me. You plan to wait until they announce it on television?"

"I just want to see what happens."

"All that happens is that people get hurt. People get killed. You're maybe going to get killed if you stay here."

"Don't be operatic, Grace, I'm not staying here. I'm just not leaving tonight."

I said nothing.

"In the first place I don't like New Orleans. In the second place, take my word for it, it's going to be a very tedious flight with Tuck Bradley aboard. Carrying his flag."

"Charlotte. I'm going tonight."

"Of course you are. Remember to tell Tuck when you land, he's supposed to get off with the flag showing. Folded. Under his arm. But *showing*."

"I promised Leonard I'd take you out with me."

"*I* promised Leonard." Her voice was all gentle reproach and I never heard the steel in it until after she was dead. "I promised I'd see him very soon. There was no call for him to worry you. We talked about it."

She was still gazing at the television screen.

"In any case you're not to worry," she said without looking up. "I told Leonard what I was going to do."

I had asked Victor to make her leave and Victor had said he had no authority.

I had asked Gerardo to make her leave and Gerardo had said he would get her out.

I had asked Antonio to make her leave and Antonio had said *norteamericana cunt.*

Before I left for the airport that night Charlotte came to the house with presents for my trip: a travel-sized vial of Grès perfume, a gardenia for my dress, and all the latest magazines and papers. She was on her way to the Jockey Club for dinner.

16

IN FACT SHE HAD.

Told Leonard what she was going to do.

She was going to stay.

Not "stay" precisely.

"Not leave" is more like it.

"I walked away from places all my life and I'm not going to walk away from here," is exactly what she said to him.

She had said it to him at the clinic and she had said it to him at the Caribe and she had said it to him for the last time the night he left, while they waited for his flight to get clearance out.

I did not know the exact words until after she was dead.

I walked away from places all my life and I'm not going to walk away from here.

"You have to pick the places you don't walk away from," Leonard had said that night at the airport. The waiting room was empty and the runways were lit up with crossfire from the hardware that the *guerrilleros* were not supposed to have had. "This isn't one of those places. It's the wrong place, Charlotte."

"I think that's a song," Charlotte had said. "'The wrong place, the right face'? Is that how it goes?"

"Charlotte—"

"Sing it for me. No." She touched his lips with her fingers. "You have a terrible voice. Tell me about the terrific dinner we're going to have the next time we're in Paris."

"What about Marin."

"Get that big suite at the Plaza Athénée."

"Marin wants to see you."

"And get—she didn't say that. Did she."

Leonard said nothing.

Charlotte took Leonard's hand and she kissed each finger, very lightly, very precisely.

"I knew she didn't say that," she said then. "Another thing I knew, I knew you wouldn't lie to me. You lie for a living but you never lie to me."

"You don't get any real points for staying here, Charlotte."

"I can't seem to tell what you do get the real points for," Charlotte said. "So I guess I'll stick around here awhile."

And when his plane was cleared to leave she had walked out to the gate with him and he had said again *don't you want to see Marin* and she had said *I don't have to see Marin because I have Marin in my mind and Marin has me in her mind* and they closed the gate and that was the last time Leonard Douglas ever saw Charlotte alive.

The last time I ever saw Charlotte alive was the night two weeks later when I left for New Orleans.

When she pinned her gardenia on my dress.

When she dabbed her Grès perfume on my wrists.

Like a child helping her mother dress for a party.

17

I don't have to see Marin because I have Marin in my mind.
I don't have to see Marin because Marin has me in her mind.

In that dirty room in Buffalo those seemed increasingly ambiguous propositions.

"All right," I said finally to Marin Bogart. "You tell me. You tell *me* what you think your mother did in Boca Grande."

"I think she played tennis all day," Marin Bogart said.

"She didn't ever play tennis," I said.

"All day. Every day. I only remember her in a tennis dress."

"I never saw her in a tennis dress."

As a matter of fact Charlotte had told me that she and Marin once modeled matching tennis dresses in a fashion show at the Burlingame Country Club and that because she did not play tennis she had needed to ask Marin how to hold the racquet correctly.

"I'm quite sure your mother didn't play tennis," I said.

"She always wore a tennis dress," Marin Bogart said.

"More than once?"

"Always."

"Didn't you play tennis?"

"Tennis," Marin Bogart said, "is just one more mode of teaching an elitest strategy. If you subject it to a revolutionary analysis you'll see that. Not that I think you will."

We sat facing each other in the bleak room.

You were both wrong but it's all the same in the end.

We all remember what we need to remember.

Marin remembered Charlotte in a tennis dress and Charlotte remembered Marin in a straw hat for Easter. I remembered Edgar, I did not remember Edgar as the man who financed the Tupamaros. Charlotte remembered she bled. I remembered the light in Boca Grande. I sat in this room in Buffalo where I had no business being and I talked to this child who was not mine and I remembered the light in Boca Grande.

Another place I have no business being.

It seems to me now.

"Why did you bother agreeing to see me?" I said finally.

"My stepfather said he was putting you in touch with me because you had something important to tell me. I can see you don't."

I remember feeling ill and trying to control my dislike of Charlotte's child.

"I didn't understand your mother," I said finally.

"Try a class analysis."

I had not come ill to Buffalo to scream at Charlotte's child. "Your mother disturbed me," I said.

"She could certainly do that."

I tried again. "She had you in her mind. She always kept you in her mind."

"Not me," Marin Bogart said. "Some pretty baby. Not me."

"Could I have a glass of water," I said after a while.

"We don't have liquor."

"I didn't ask for liquor. Did I." I could hear the fury in my voice and could not stop. "I didn't ask for 'liquor' and I didn't ask for 'diet pills' and I didn't ask for Saran-Wrap and I didn't ask for white bread and I didn't ask for any of the other things I'm sure you make it a point not to have. I asked for a glass of water."

Marin Bogart watched me without expression for a moment and then stood up and turned to the sink full of dirty dishes.

"Did you like the Tivoli Gardens," I said suddenly.

"This water runs lukewarm. I better get you some ice, this is lukewarm water and I can at least get you some ice, can't I."

As she spoke she opened the refrigerator and took out an ice tray. Her movements were jerky and the tray was not frozen and the water splashed on the floor.

"I said did you like the Tivoli Gardens."

"God*damn* people around here, somebody took it out last night and never put it back, I mean *I* had to put it back this morning, I don't think—"

She was speaking very rapidly and for the first time something other than her eyes reminded me of Charlotte.

"—Anyone but me ever raises a finger around here, I honestly—"

"Tivoli," I said.

Marin Bogart turned suddenly, and she put the tray on the table, and her face was tight, and then she broke exactly as her mother must have broken the morning the FBI first came to the house on California Street.

SIX

I

IN THE END there was not much to tell Marin Bogart that she could understand and there was even less to tell Leonard Douglas that he could not have guessed.

It did not go smoothly at all.

Since I was in New Orleans I know only a few facts.

Since I do not entirely trust Gerardo's version of it I am certain of even fewer facts.

On the first day of what has come to be remembered as the October Violence the *guerrilleros* finally closed the airport altogether.

The final closing of the airport is what we usually call Day One.

I had flown out the night before, the evening of the day we usually call Day Minus One. I lost the gardenia in the crush at the airport.

The seat next to mine on the plane out was empty.

Charlotte was eating spiny lobster at the Jockey Club.

Day Minus One. Day One.

Day Two.

On Day Two the *guerrilleros* took over the radio stations.

On Day Three the *guerrilleros* neared the palace.

Those first three days went more or less as expected.

I have seen the troops on the palace roof waiting to pick off the *guerrilleros* before.

It was Day Four which did not go as planned. Day Four is supposed to end just after the heavy shooting at dawn, but this time it did not. The *guerrilleros* appeared not to know that they were on the board only to be gunned down at dawn of Day Four by the insurgent army under Antonio's "new leadership." The *guerrilleros* appeared to have more of everything than anyone except Leonard Douglas had supposed they had. Some say Kasindorf and Riley supplied the excess, some say other agencies. Some say Victor.

I think not Victor but have no empirical proof.

I also think (still) that Leonard Douglas was not involved but again this conclusion is not empirical.

In any case.

2

GERARDO HAD COUNTED on a smooth transition.

Gerardo had counted on dinner at the Jockey Club the evening of Day Four.

By Day Seven Gerardo wanted to get out himself.

"I couldn't possibly leave right now," Charlotte said when Gerardo told her about the helicopter in Millonario.

"You don't realize," Gerardo said.

"I realize," Charlotte said. "I do realize."

"Charlotte. You don't leave now, you're not going to leave at all, because Antonio wants Carmen Arrellano on that chopper and not you."

"Then take Carmen Arrellano. Carmen should get out, Carmen has connections here."

"So do you."

"No." Charlotte had seemed vague and distant. "I don't actually."

"Charlotte. *Remember Victor. Remember me.*"

And Charlotte had looked at Gerardo for a while and smiled as she sometimes smiled at strangers.

"I wasn't connected to you actually," Charlotte had said.

Gerardo had only stared at her.

"I mean I've got two or three people in my mind but I don't quite have you."

I trust Gerardo's version on this point.

I wasn't connected to you actually has the ring of Charlotte Douglas to me.

3

DAY EIGHT.

There had never been a Day Eight in Boca Grande before.

On Day Eight Charlotte appeared to have gone as usual to the clinic. She was reported to have stayed in her office all day but of course there would have been no callers for birth control devices on Day Eight. At five o'clock she closed the clinic and walked to the Caribe and apparently changed for dinner. At any rate she was wearing a clean linen dress when she left the Caribe at seven-thirty and began to walk in the direction of the Capilla del Mar.

Walking very deliberately.

Tying and retying a scarf which whipped in the hot night wind.

Seeming to concentrate on the scarf as if oblivious to the potholes in the sidewalk and the places where waste ran into the gutters.

At seven-forty-three exactly she reached the barricade on the sidewalk outside the Capilla del Mar and she stopped and she showed her passport.

Soy norteamericana, she said.

Soy una turista, she said.

The passport was knocked from her hand by the butt of a carbine.

"Don't you lay your fucking hands on me," she said in English.

Goddamn you all.

She was taken to the Escuela de los Niños Perdidos and detained overnight before she was transferred to the Estadio Nacional for interrogation. The moment and circumstances of her arrest are matters of record but the moment and circumstances of her death remain obscure. I do not even know which side killed her, who held the Estadio Nacional at the moment of death. I know that fire from either an AR-15 or an AR-16 entered her body just below the left shoulder-blade but I also know that all sides had both weapons.

Other than that I know only what Gerardo told me.

That she cried not for God but for Marin.

"She was shot in the back," I said to Gerardo.

"Maybe she wanted to have it that way," Gerardo said.

"She wouldn't have wanted to have it that way."

"Well," Gerardo said, "she did."

That Gerardo knew she cried for Marin suggests that Antonio was in charge of the Estadio Nacional at the moment of death but there are no real points in knowing one way or another.

As Leonard Douglas might say.

As Leonard Douglas did say, when I told him.

I no longer know where the real points are.

I am more like Charlotte than I thought I was.

On the day Antonio finally managed to take over Victor's office the October Violence ended. On the day after that Victor flew back from Bariloche, I flew back from New Orleans, and Charlotte Douglas's body was found, where it had been thrown, on the lawn of the American Embassy. Since all Embassy personnel had abandoned the building the point was lost on them.

Although not on me.

And possibly not even on Victor.

Norteamericana cunt.

4

ALL I CAN tell you directly about Charlotte Douglas's death is that I sent her body to San Francisco. I had the body put in a coffin and I went to the airport with the coffin and I waited there until I could see, for myself, the coffin loaded into the hold of the first Pan American flight to leave Boca Grande after the October Violence. I wanted to lay a flag on the coffin but there were no American flags in Boca Grande that week and in the end I bought a child's T-shirt in the gift shop at the airport. This T-shirt was printed like an American flag. I dropped this T-shirt on the coffin as it was loaded into the hold of the Boeing. I think this T-shirt did not have the correct number of stars or stripes but it did have the appearance of stars and stripes and it was red and it was white and it was blue. There were no real points in that either.

5

IN SUMMARY.

So you know the story.

Today we are clearing some coastal groves by slash-and-burn and a pall of smoke hangs over Boca Grande. The smoke colors everything. The smoke obscures the light. You will notice my use of the colonial pronoun, the overseer's "we." I mean it. I see now that I have no business in this place but I have been here too long to change. I mean "we." I wish that I could see the light today but I recognize the necessity for clearing groves. I also recognize the equivocal nature of even the most empirical evidence. Some evidence I did not know about until quite recently, when crates of mail uncollected during the October Violence that year were located and distributed. This evidence came to me long after I had talked to Leonard Douglas and been put in touch with Marin Bogart in Buffalo. This evidence came to me long after I had seen Marin Bogart in Buffalo. Here it is. Early on the evening of her arrest, from a box between the Caribe and the Capilla del Mar, Charlotte Douglas mailed me Marin's address. She also mailed me the big square emerald she wore in place of a wedding ring. I wrote to Marin and told her I have the emerald but have received no reply. I did not mention to Marin that the emerald was a memento from the man who financed the Tupamaros.

Marin has no interest in the past.

I still do, but understand it no better.

All I know now is that when I think of Charlotte Douglas walking in the hot night wind toward the lights at the Capilla del Mar I am less and less certain that this story has been one of delusion.

Unless the delusion was mine.

When I am tired I remember what I was taught in Colorado. On Day Minus One in Boca Grande Charlotte remembered to bring me a gardenia for my trip. Her mother taught her that. Marin and I are inseparable. She had a straw hat one Easter, and a flowered lawn dress. Tell Charlotte she was wrong. Tell Marin she was wrong. Tell her that for me. She remembers everything. She remembers she bled. The wind is up and I will die and rather soon and all I know empirically is *I am told*.

I am told, and so she said.

I heard later.

According to her passport. It was reported.

Apparently.

I have not been the witness I wanted to be.

THE WHITE ALBUM

For Earl McGrath,

and for Lois Wallace

I

THE WHITE ALBUM

The White Album

WE TELL OURSELVES stories in order to live. The princess is caged in the consulate. The man with the candy will lead the children into the sea. The naked woman on the ledge outside the window on the sixteenth floor is a victim of accidie, or the naked woman is an exhibitionist, and it would be "interesting" to know which. We tell ourselves that it makes some difference whether the naked woman is about to commit a mortal sin or is about to register a political protest or is about to be, the Aristophanic view, snatched back to the human condition by the fireman in priest's clothing just visible in the window behind her, the one smiling at the telephoto lens. We look for the sermon in the suicide, for the social or moral lesson in the murder of five. We interpret what we see, select the most workable of the multiple choices. We live entirely, especially if we are writers, by the imposition of a narrative line upon disparate images, by the "ideas" with which we have learned to freeze the shifting phantasmagoria which is our actual experience.

Or at least we do for a while. I am talking here about a time when I began to doubt the premises of all the stories I had ever told myself, a common condition but one I found troubling. I suppose this period began around 1966 and continued until 1971. During those five years I appeared, on the face of it, a competent enough member of some community or another, a signer of contracts and Air Travel cards, a citizen: I wrote a couple of times a month for one magazine or another, published two books, worked on several motion pictures; participated in the paranoia of the time, in the raising of a small child, and in the entertainment of large numbers of people passing through my house; made gingham curtains for spare bedrooms, remembered to ask agents if any reduction of points would be *pari passu* with the financing studio, put lentils to soak on Saturday night for lentil soup on Sunday, made quarterly F.I.C.A. payments and renewed my driver's license on time, missing on the written examination only the question about the financial responsibility of California drivers. It was a time of my life when I was frequently "named." I was named godmother to children. I was named lecturer and panelist, colloquist and conferee. I was even named, in 1968, a *Los Angeles Times* "Woman of the Year," along with Mrs. Ronald Reagan, the Olympic swimmer Debbie Meyer, and ten other California women who seemed to keep in touch and do good works. I did no good works but I tried to keep in touch. I was responsible. I recognized my name when I saw it. Once in a while I even answered letters addressed to me, not exactly upon receipt but eventually, particularly if the letters had come from strangers. "During my absence from the country these past eighteen months," such replies would begin.

This was an adequate enough performance, as improvisations go. The only problem was that my entire education, everything I had ever been told or had told myself, insisted that the production was never meant to be improvised: I was supposed to have a script, and had mislaid it. I was supposed to hear cues, and no longer did. I was meant to know the plot, but all I knew was what I saw: flash pictures in variable sequence, images with no "meaning" beyond their temporary arrangement, not a movie but a cutting-room experience. In what would probably be the middle of my life I wanted still to believe in the narrative and in the narrative's intelligibility, but to know that one could change the sense with every cut was to begin to perceive the experience as rather more electrical than ethical.

During this period I spent what were for me the usual proportions of time in Los Angeles and New York and Sacramento. I spent what seemed to many people I knew an eccentric amount of time in Honolulu, the particular aspect of which lent the illusion that I could at any minute order from room service a revisionist theory of my own history, garnished with a vanda orchid. I watched Robert Kennedy's funeral on a verandah at the Royal Hawaiian Hotel in Honolulu, and also the first reports from My Lai. I reread all of George Orwell on the Royal Hawaiian Beach, and I also read, in the papers that came one day late from the mainland, the story of Betty Lansdown Fouquet, a 26-year-old woman with faded blond hair who put her five-year-old daughter out to die on the center divider of Interstate 5 some miles south of the last Bakersfield exit. The child, whose fingers had to be pried loose from the Cyclone fence when she was rescued twelve hours later by the California Highway Patrol, reported that she had run after the car carrying her mother and stepfather and brother and sister for "a long time." Certain of these images did not fit into any narrative I knew.

Another flash cut:

> *"In June of this year patient experienced an attack of vertigo, nausea, and a feeling that she was going to pass out. A thorough medical evaluation elicited no positive findings and she was placed on Elavil, Mg 20, tid. . . . The Rorschach record is interpreted as describing a personality in process of deterioration with abundant signs of failing defenses and increasing inability of the ego to mediate the world of reality and to cope with normal stress. . . . Emotionally, patient has alienated herself almost entirely from the world of other human beings. Her fantasy life appears to have been virtually completely preempted by primitive, regressive libidinal preoccupations many of which are distorted and bizarre. . . . In a technical sense basic affective controls appear to be intact but it is equally clear that they are insecurely and tenuously maintained for the present by a variety of defense mechanisms including intellectualization, obsessive-compulsive devices, projection, reaction-formation, and somatization, all of which now seem inadequate to their task of controlling or containing an underlying psychotic process and are therefore in process of failure. The content of patient's responses is highly unconventional and frequently bizarre, filled with sexual and anatomical preoccupations, and basic reality contact is obviously and seriously impaired at times. In quality and level of sophistication patient's responses are characteristic of those of individuals of high average or superior intelligence but she is now functioning intellectually in impaired fashion at barely average level. Patient's thematic productions on the Thematic Apperception Test emphasize her fundamentally pessimistic, fatalistic, and depressive view of the world around her. It is as though she feels deeply that all human effort is foredoomed to failure, a conviction which seems to push her further into a dependent, passive withdrawal. In her view she lives in a*

world of people moved by strange, conflicted, poorly comprehended, and, above all, devious motivations which commit them inevitably to conflict and failure. . . ."

The patient to whom this psychiatric report refers is me. The tests mentioned—the Rorschach, the Thematic Apperception Test, the Sentence Completion Test and the Minnesota Multiphasic Personality Index—were administered privately, in the outpatient psychiatric clinic at St. John's Hospital in Santa Monica, in the summer of 1968, shortly after I suffered the "attack of vertigo and nausea" mentioned in the first sentence and shortly before I was named a *Los Angeles Times* "Woman of the Year." By way of comment I offer only that an attack of vertigo and nausea does not now seem to me an inappropriate response to the summer of 1968.

2

In the years I am talking about I was living in a large house in a part of Hollywood that had once been expensive and was now described by one of my acquaintances as a "senseless-killing neighborhood." This house on Franklin Avenue was rented, and paint peeled inside and out, and pipes broke and window sashes crumbled and the tennis court had not been rolled since 1933, but the rooms were many and high-ceilinged and, during the five years that I lived there, even the rather sinistral inertia of the neighborhood tended to suggest that I should live in the house indefinitely.

In fact I could not, because the owners were waiting only for a zoning change to tear the house down and build a high-rise apartment building, and for that matter it was precisely this anticipation of imminent but not exactly immediate destruction that lent the neighborhood its particular character. The house across the street had been built for one of the Talmadge sisters, had been the Japanese consulate in 1941, and was now, although boarded up, occupied by a number of unrelated adults who seemed to constitute some kind of therapy group. The house next door was owned by Synanon. I recall looking at a house around the corner with a rental sign on it: this house had once been the Canadian consulate, had 28 large rooms and two refrigerated fur closets, and could be rented, in the spirit of the neighborhood, only on a month-to-month basis, unfurnished. Since the inclination to rent an unfurnished 28-room house for a month or two is a distinctly special one, the neighborhood was peopled mainly by rock-and-roll bands, therapy groups, very old women wheeled down the street by practical nurses in soiled uniforms, and by my husband, my daughter and me.

Q. *And what else happened, if anything. . . .*
A. *He said that he thought that I could be a star, like, you know, a young Burt Lancaster, you know, that kind of stuff.*
Q. *Did he mention any particular name?*
A. *Yes, sir.*
Q. *What name did he mention?*
A. *He mentioned a lot of names. He said Burt Lancaster. He said Clint Eastwood. He said Fess Parker. He mentioned a lot of names. . . .*
Q. *Did you talk after you ate?*
A. *While we were eating, after we ate. Mr. Novarro told our fortunes with some cards and he read our palms.*
Q. *Did he tell you you were going to have a lot of good luck or bad luck or what happened?*
A. *He wasn't a good palm reader.*

These are excerpts from the testimony of Paul Robert Ferguson and Thomas Scott Ferguson, brothers, ages 22 and 17 respectively, during their trial for the murder of Ramon Novarro, age 69, at his house in Laurel Canyon, not too far from my house in Hollywood, on the night of October 30, 1968. I followed this trial quite closely, clipping reports from the newspapers and later borrowing a transcript from one of the defense attorneys. The younger of the brothers, "Tommy Scott" Ferguson, whose girl friend testified that she had stopped being in love with him "about two weeks after Grand Jury," said that he had been unaware of Mr. Novarro's career as a silent film actor until he was shown, at some point during the night of the murder, a photograph of his host as Ben-Hur. The older brother, Paul Ferguson, who began working carnivals when he was 12 and described himself at 22 as having had "a fast life and a good one," gave the jury, upon request, his definition of a hustler: "A hustler is someone who can talk—not just to men, to women, too. Who can cook. Can keep company. Wash a car. Lots of things make up a hustler. There are a lot of lonely people in this town, man." During the course of the trial each of the brothers accused the other of the murder. Both were convicted. I read the transcript several times, trying to bring the picture into some focus which did not suggest that I lived, as my psychiatric report had put it, "in a world of people moved by strange, conflicted, poorly comprehended and, above all, devious motivations"; I never met the Ferguson brothers.

I did meet one of the principals in another Los Angeles County murder trial during those years: Linda Kasabian, star witness for the prosecution in what was commonly known as the Manson Trial. I once asked Linda what she thought about the apparently chance sequence of events which had brought her first to the Spahn Movie Ranch and then to the Sybil Brand Institute for Women on charges, later dropped, of murdering Sharon Tate Polanski, Abigail Folger, Jay Sebring, Voytek Frykowski, Steven Parent, and Rosemary and Leno LaBianca. "Everything was to teach me something," Linda said. Linda did not believe that chance was without pattern. Linda operated on what I later recognized as dice theory, and so, during the years I am talking about, did I.

It will perhaps suggest the mood of those years if I tell you that during them I could not visit my mother-in-law without averting my eyes from a framed verse, a "house blessing," which hung in a hallway of her house in West Hartford, Connecticut.

God bless the corners of this house,
And be the lintel blest—
And bless the hearth and bless the board
And bless each place of rest—
And bless the crystal windowpane that lets the starlight in
And bless each door that opens wide, to stranger as to kin.

This verse had on me the effect of a physical chill, so insistently did it seem the kind of "ironic" detail the reporters would seize upon, the morning the bodies were found. In my neighborhood in California we did not bless the door that opened wide to stranger as to kin. Paul and Tommy Scott

Ferguson were the strangers at Ramon Novarro's door, up on Laurel Canyon. Charles Manson was the stranger at Rosemary and Leno LaBianca's door, over in Los Feliz. Some strangers at the door knocked, and invented a reason to come inside: a call, say, to the Triple A, about a car not in evidence. Others just opened the door and walked in, and I would come across them in the entrance hall. I recall asking one such stranger what he wanted. We looked at each other for what seemed a long time, and then he saw my husband on the stair landing. "Chicken Delight," he said finally, but we had ordered no Chicken Delight, nor was he carrying any. I took the license number of his panel truck. It seems to me now that during those years I was always writing down the license numbers of panel trucks, panel trucks circling the block, panel trucks parked across the street, panel trucks idling at the intersection. I put these license numbers in a dressing-table drawer where they could be found by the police when the time came.

That the time would come I never doubted, at least not in the inaccessible places of the mind where I seemed more and more to be living. So many encounters in those years were devoid of any logic save that of the dreamwork. In the big house on Franklin Avenue many people seemed to come and go without relation to what I did. I knew where the sheets and towels were kept but I did not always know who was sleeping in every bed. I had the keys but not the key. I remember taking a 25-mg. Compazine one Easter Sunday and making a large and elaborate lunch for a number of people, many of whom were still around on Monday. I remember walking barefoot all day on the worn hardwood floors of that house and I remember "Do You Wanna Dance" on the record player, "Do You Wanna Dance" and "Visions of Johanna" and a song called "Midnight Confessions." I remember a babysitter telling me that she saw death in my aura. I remember chatting with her about reasons why this might be so, paying her, opening all the French windows and going to sleep in the living room.

It was hard to surprise me in those years. It was hard to even get my attention. I was absorbed in my intellectualization, my obsessive-compulsive devices, my projection, my reaction-formation, my somatization, and in the transcript of the Ferguson trial. A musician I had met a few years before called from a Ramada Inn in Tuscaloosa to tell me how to save myself through Scientology. I had met him once in my life, had talked to him for maybe half an hour about brown rice and the charts, and now he was telling me from Alabama about E-meters, and how I might become a Clear. I received a telephone call from a stranger in Montreal who seemed to want to enlist me in a narcotics operation. "Is it cool to talk on this telephone?" he asked several times. "Big Brother isn't listening?"

I said that I doubted it, although increasingly I did not.

"Because what we're talking about, basically, is applying the Zen philosophy to money and business, dig? And if I say we are going to finance the underground, and if I mention major money, you know what I'm talking about because you know what's going down, right?"

Maybe he was not talking about narcotics. Maybe he was talking about turning a profit on M-1 rifles: I had stopped looking for the logic in such calls. Someone with whom I had gone to school in Sacramento and had last seen in 1952 turned up at my house in Hollywood in 1968 in the guise of a private detective from West Covina, one of very few licensed women private detectives in the State of California. "They call us Dickless Tracys," she said, idly but definitely fanning out the day's mail on the hall table. "I have a lot of very close friends in law enforcement," she said then. "You might want to meet them." We exchanged promises to keep in touch but never met again: a not atypical encounter of the period. The Sixties were over before it occurred to me that this visit might have been less than entirely social.

3

It was six, seven o'clock of an early spring evening in 1968 and I was sitting on the cold vinyl floor of a sound studio on Sunset Boulevard, watching a band called The Doors record a rhythm track. On the whole my attention was only minimally engaged by the preoccupations of rock-and-roll bands (I had already heard about acid as a transitional stage and also about the Maharishi and even about Universal Love, and after a while it all sounded like marmalade skies to me), but The Doors were different, The Doors interested me. The Doors seemed unconvinced that love was brotherhood and the Kama Sutra. The Doors' music insisted that love was sex and sex was death and therein lay salvation. The Doors were the Norman Mailers of the Top Forty, missionaries of apocalyptic sex. *Break on through*, their lyrics urged, and *Light my fire*, and:

Come on baby, gonna take a little ride
Goin' down by the ocean side
Gonna get real close
Get real tight
Baby gonna drown tonight—
Goin' down, down, down.

On this evening in 1968 they were gathered together in uneasy symbiosis to make their third album, and the studio was too cold and the lights were too bright and there were masses of wires and banks of the ominous blinking electronic circuitry with which musicians live so easily. There were three of the four Doors. There was a bass player borrowed from a band called Clear Light. There were the producer and the engineer and the road manager and a couple of girls and a Siberian husky named Nikki with one gray eye and one gold. There were paper bags half filled with hard-boiled eggs and chicken livers and cheeseburgers and empty bottles of apple juice and California rosé. There was everything and everybody The Doors needed to cut the rest of this third album except one thing, the fourth Door, the lead singer, Jim Morrison, a 24-year-old graduate of U.C.L.A. who wore black vinyl pants and no underwear and tended to suggest some range of the possible just beyond a suicide pact. It was Morrison who had described The Doors as "erotic politicians." It was Morrison who had defined the group's interests as "anything about revolt, disorder, chaos, about activity that appears to have no meaning." It was Morrison who got arrested in Miami in December of 1967 for giving an "indecent" performance. It was Morrison who wrote most of The Doors' lyrics, the peculiar character of which was to reflect either an ambiguous paranoia or a quite unambiguous insistence upon the love-death as the ultimate high. And it was Morrison who was missing. It was Ray Manzarek and Robby

Krieger and John Densmore who made The Doors sound the way they sounded, and maybe it was Manzarek and Krieger and Densmore who made seventeen out of twenty interviewees on *American Bandstand* prefer The Doors over all other bands, but it was Morrison who got up there in his black vinyl pants with no underwear and projected the idea, and it was Morrison they were waiting for now.

"Hey listen," the engineer said. "I was listening to an FM station on the way over here, they played three Doors songs, first they played 'Back Door Man' and then 'Love Me Two Times' and 'Light My Fire.'"

"I heard it," Densmore muttered. "I heard it."

"So what's wrong with somebody playing three of your songs?"

"This cat dedicates it to his family."

"Yeah? To his family?"

"To his family. Really crass."

Ray Manzarek was hunched over a Gibson keyboard. "You think *Morrison*'s going to come back?" he asked to no one in particular.

No one answered.

"So we can do some *vocals*?" Manzarek said.

The producer was working with the tape of the rhythm track they had just recorded. "I hope so," he said without looking up.

"Yeah," Manzarek said. "So do I."

My leg had gone to sleep, but I did not stand up; unspecific tensions seemed to be rendering everyone in the room catatonic. The producer played back the rhythm track. The engineer said that he wanted to do his deep-breathing exercises. Manzarek ate a hard-boiled egg. "Tennyson made a mantra out of his own name," he said to the engineer. "I don't know if he said 'Tennyson Tennyson Tennyson' or 'Alfred Alfred Alfred' or 'Alfred Lord Tennyson,' but anyway, he did it. Maybe he just said 'Lord Lord Lord.'"

"Groovy," the Clear Light bass player said. He was an amiable enthusiast, not at all a Door in spirit.

"I wonder what Blake said," Manzarek mused. "Too bad *Morrison*'s not here *Morrison* would know."

*

It was a long while later. Morrison arrived. He had on his black vinyl pants and he sat down on a leather couch in front of the four big blank speakers and he closed his eyes. The curious aspect of Morrison's arrival was this: no one acknowledged it. Robby Krieger continued working out a guitar passage. John Densmore tuned his drums. Manzarek sat at the control console and twirled a corkscrew and let a girl rub his shoulders. The girl did not look at Morrison, although he was in her direct line of sight. An hour or so passed, and still no one had spoken to Morrison. Then Morrison spoke to Manzarek. He spoke almost in a whisper, as if he were wresting the words from behind some disabling aphasia.

"It's an hour to West Covina," he said. "I was thinking maybe we should spend the night out there after we play."

Manzarek put down the corkscrew. "Why?" he said.

"Instead of coming back."

Manzarek shrugged. "We were planning to come back."

"Well, I was thinking, we could rehearse out there."

Manzarek said nothing.

"We could get in a rehearsal, there's a Holiday Inn next door."

"We could do that," Manzarek said. "Or we could rehearse Sunday, in town."

"I guess so." Morrison paused. "Will the place be ready to rehearse Sunday?"

Manzarek looked at him for a while. "No," he said then.

I counted the control knobs on the electronic console. There were seventy-six. I was unsure in whose favor the dialogue had been resolved, or if it had been resolved at all. Robby Krieger picked at his guitar, and said that he needed a fuzz box. The producer suggested that he borrow one from the Buffalo Springfield, who were recording in the next studio. Krieger shrugged. Morrison sat down again on the leather couch and leaned back. He lit a match. He studied the flame awhile and then very slowly, very deliberately, lowered it to the fly of his black vinyl pants. Manzarek watched him. The girl who was rubbing Manzarek's shoulders did not look at anyone. There was a sense that no one was going to leave the room, ever. It would be some weeks before The Doors finished recording this album. I did not see it through.

4

Someone once brought Janis Joplin to a party at the house on Franklin Avenue: she had just done a concert and she wanted brandy-and-Benedictine in a water tumbler. Music people never wanted ordinary drinks. They wanted sake, or champagne cocktails, or tequila neat. Spending time with music people was confusing, and required a more fluid and ultimately a more passive approach than I ever acquired. In the first place time was never of the essence: we would have dinner at nine unless we had it at eleven-thirty, or we could order in later. We would go down to U.S.C. to see the Living Theater if the limo came at the very moment when no one had just made a drink or a cigarette or an arrangement to meet Ultra Violet at the Montecito. In any case David Hockney was coming by. In any case Ultra Violet was not at the Montecito. In any case we would go down to U.S.C. and see the Living Theater tonight or we would see the Living Theater another night, in New York, or Prague. First we wanted sushi for twenty, steamed clams, vegetable vindaloo and many rum drinks with gardenias for our hair. First we wanted a table for twelve, fourteen at the most, although there might be six more, or eight more, or eleven more: there would never be one or two more, because music people did not travel in groups of "one" or "two." John and Michelle Phillips, on their way to the hospital for the birth of their daughter Chynna, had the limo detour into Hollywood in order to pick up a friend, Ann Marshall. This incident, which I often embroider in my mind to include an imaginary second detour, to the Luau for gardenias, exactly describes the music business to me.

5

Around five o'clock on the morning of October 28, 1967, in the desolate district between San Francisco Bay and the Oakland estuary that the Oakland police call Beat 101A, a 25-year-old black militant named Huey P. Newton was stopped and questioned by a white police officer named John Frey, Jr. An hour later Huey Newton was under arrest at Kaiser Hospital in Oakland, where he had gone for emergency treatment of a gunshot wound in his stomach, and a few weeks later he was indicted by the Alameda County Grand Jury on charges of murdering John Frey, wounding another officer, and kidnapping a bystander.

In the spring of 1968, when Huey Newton was awaiting trial, I went to see him in the Alameda County Jail. I suppose I went because I was interested in the alchemy of issues, for an issue is what Huey Newton had by then become. To understand how that had happened you must first consider Huey Newton, who he was. He came from an Oakland family, and for a while he went to Merritt College. In October of 1966 he and a friend named Bobby Seale organized what they called the Black Panther Party. They borrowed the name from the emblem used by the Freedom Party in Lowndes County, Alabama, and, from the beginning, they defined themselves as a revolutionary political group. The Oakland police knew the Panthers, and had a list of twenty or so Panther cars. I am telling you neither that Huey Newton killed John Frey nor that Huey Newton did not kill John Frey, for in the context of revolutionary politics Huey Newton's guilt or innocence was irrelevant. I am telling you only how Huey Newton happened to be in the Alameda County Jail, and why rallies were held in his name, demonstrations organized whenever he appeared in court. LET'S SPRING HUEY, the buttons read (fifty cents each), and here and there on the courthouse steps, among the Panthers with their berets and sunglasses, the chants would go up:

Get your M-
31.
'Cause baby we gonna
Have some fun.
BOOM BOOM. BOOM BOOM.

"Fight on, brother," a woman would add in the spirit of a good-natured amen. "Bang-bang."

Bullshit bullshit
Can't stand the game
White man's playing.
One way out, one way out.
BOOM BOOM. BOOM BOOM.

In the corridor downstairs in the Alameda County Courthouse there was a crush of lawyers and CBC correspondents and cameramen and people who wanted to "visit Huey."

"Eldridge doesn't mind if I go up," one of the latter said to one of the lawyers.

"If Eldridge doesn't mind, it's all right with me," the lawyer said. "If you've got press credentials."

"I've got kind of dubious credentials."

"I can't take you up then. *Eldridge* has got dubious credentials. One's bad enough. I've got a good working relationship up there, I don't want to blow it." The lawyer turned to a cameraman. "You guys rolling yet?"

On that particular day I was allowed to go up, and a *Los Angeles Times* man, and a radio newscaster. We all signed the police register and sat around a scarred pine table and waited for Huey Newton. "The only thing that's going to free Huey Newton," Rap Brown had said recently at a Panther rally in Oakland Auditorium, "is gunpowder." "Huey Newton laid down his life for us," Stokely Carmichael had said the same night. But of course Huey Newton had not yet laid down his life at all, was just here in the Alameda County Jail waiting to be tried, and I wondered if the direction these rallies were taking ever made him uneasy, ever made him suspect that in many ways he was more useful to the revolution behind bars than on the street. He seemed, when he finally came in, an extremely likable young man, engaging, direct, and I did not get the sense that he had intended to become a political martyr. He smiled at us all and waited for his lawyer, Charles Garry, to set up a tape recorder, and he chatted softly with Eldridge Cleaver, who was then the Black Panthers' Minister of Information. (Huey Newton was still the Minister of Defense.) Eldridge Cleaver wore a black sweater and one gold earring and spoke in an almost inaudible drawl and was allowed to see Huey Newton because he had those "dubious credentials," a press card from *Ramparts*. Actually his interest was in getting "statements" from Huey Newton, "messages" to take outside; in receiving a kind of prophecy to be interpreted as needed.

"We need a statement, Huey, about the ten-point program," Eldridge Cleaver said, "so I'll ask you a question, see, and you answer it . . ."

"How's Bobby," Huey Newton asked.

"He's got a hearing on his misdemeanors, see . . ."

"I thought he had a felony."

"Well, that's another thing, the felony, he's also got a couple of misdemeanors . . ."

Once Charles Garry had set up the tape recorder Huey Newton stopped chatting and started lecturing, almost without pause. He talked, running the words together because he had said them so many times before, about "the American capitalistic-materialistic system" and "so-called free enterprise" and "the fight for the liberation of black people throughout the world." Every now and then Eldridge Cleaver would signal Huey Newton and say something like, "There are a lot of people interested in the Executive Mandate Number Three you've issued to the Black Panther Party, Huey. Care to comment?"

And Huey Newton would comment. "Yes. Mandate Number Three is this demand from the Black Panther Party speaking for the black community. Within the Mandate we admonish the racist police force . . ." I kept wishing that he would talk about himself, hoping to break through the wall of rhetoric, but he seemed to be one of those autodidacts for whom all things specific and personal present themselves as mine fields to be avoided even at the cost of coherence, for whom safety lies in generalization. The newspaperman, the radio man, they tried:

Q. *Tell us something about yourself, Huey, I mean your life before the Panthers.*

A. *Before the Black Panther Party my life was very similar to that of most black people in this country.*

Q. *Well, your family, some incidents you remember, the influences that shaped you—*

A. *Living in America shaped me.*

Q. *Well, yes, but more specifically—*

A. *It reminds me of a quote from James Baldwin: "To be black and conscious in America is to be in a constant state of rage."*

"To be black and conscious in America is to be in a constant state of rage," Eldridge Cleaver wrote in large letters on a pad of paper, and then he added: *"Huey P. Newton quoting James Baldwin."* I could see it emblazoned above the speakers' platform at a rally, imprinted on the letterhead of an ad hoc committee still unborn. As a matter of fact almost everything Huey Newton said had the ring of being a "quotation," a "pronouncement" to be employed when the need arose. I had heard Huey P. Newton On Racism ("The Black Panther Party is against racism"), Huey P. Newton On Cultural Nationalism ("The Black Panther Party believes that the only culture worth holding onto is revolutionary culture"), Huey P. Newton On White Radicalism, On Police Occupation of the Ghetto, On The European Versus The African. "The European started to be sick when he denied his sexual nature," Huey Newton said, and Charles Garry interrupted then, bringing it back to first principles. "Isn't it true, though, Huey," he said, "that racism got its start for *economic* reasons?"

This weird interlocution seemed to take on a life of its own. The small room was hot and the fluorescent light hurt my eyes and I still did not know to what extent Huey Newton understood the nature of the role in which he was cast. As it happened I had always appreciated the logic of the Panther position, based as it was on the proposition that political power began at the end of the barrel of a gun (exactly what gun had even been specified, in an early memorandum from Huey P. Newton: "*Army .45; carbine; 12-gauge Magnum shotgun with 18" barrel, preferably the brand of High Standard; M-16; .357 Magnum pistols; P-38*"), and I could appreciate as well the particular beauty in Huey Newton as "issue." In the politics of revolution everyone was expendable, but I doubted that Huey Newton's political sophistication extended to seeing himself that way: the value of a Scottsboro case is easier to see if you are not yourself the Scottsboro boy. "Is there anything else you want to ask Huey?" Charles Garry asked. There did not seem to be. The lawyer adjusted his tape recorder. "I've had a request, Huey," he said, "from a high-school student, a reporter on his school paper, and he wanted a statement from you, and he's going to call me tonight. Care to give me a message for him?"

Huey Newton regarded the microphone. There was a moment in which he seemed not to remember the name of the play, and then he brightened. "I would like to point out," he said, his voice gaining volume as the memory disks clicked, *high school, student, youth, message to youth*, "that America is becoming a very young nation . . ."

> *I heard a moaning and a groaning, and I went over and it was—this Negro fellow was there. He had been shot in the stomach and at the time he didn't appear in any acute distress and so I said I'd see, and I asked him if he was a Kaiser, if he belonged to Kaiser, and he said, "Yes, yes. Get a doctor. Can't you see I'm bleeding? I've been shot. Now get someone out here." And I asked him if he had his Kaiser card and he got upset at this and he said, "Come on, get a doctor out here, I've been shot." I said, "I see this, but you're not in any acute distress." . . . So I told him we'd have to check to make sure he was a member. . . . And this kind of upset him more and he called me a few nasty names and said, "Now get a doctor out here right now, I've been shot and I'm bleeding." And he took his coat off and his shirt and he threw it on the desk there and he said, "Can't you see all this blood?" And I said, "I see it." And it wasn't that much, and so I said, "Well, you'll have to sign our admission sheet before you can be seen by a doctor." And he said, "I'm not signing anything." And I said, "You cannot be seen by a doctor unless you sign the admission sheet," and he said, "I don't have to sign anything" and a few more choice words . . .*

This is an excerpt from the testimony before the Alameda County Grand Jury of Corrine Leonard, the nurse in charge of the Kaiser Foundation Hospital emergency room in Oakland at 5:30 A.M. on October 28, 1967. The "Negro fellow" was of course Huey Newton, wounded that morning during the gunfire which killed John Frey. For a long time I kept a copy of this testimony pinned to my office wall, on the theory that it illustrated a collision of cultures, a classic instance of an historical outsider confronting the established order at its most petty and impenetrable level. This theory was shattered when I learned that Huey Newton was in fact an enrolled member of the Kaiser Foundation Health Plan, i.e., in Nurse Leonard's words, "a Kaiser."

6

One morning in 1968 I went to see Eldridge Cleaver in the San Francisco apartment he then shared with his wife, Kathleen. To be admitted to this apartment it was necessary to ring first and then stand in the middle of Oak Street, at a place which could be observed clearly from the Cleavers' apartment. After this scrutiny the visitor was, or was not, buzzed in. I was, and I climbed the stairs to find Kathleen Cleaver in the kitchen frying sausage and Eldridge Cleaver in the living room listening to a John Coltrane record and a number of other people all over the apartment, people everywhere, people standing in doorways and people moving around in one another's peripheral vision and people making and taking telephone calls. "When can you move on that?" I would hear in the background, and "You can't bribe me with a dinner, man, those *Guardian* dinners are all Old Left, like a wake." Most of these other people were members of the Black Panther Party, but one of them, in the living room, was Eldridge Cleaver's parole officer. It seems to me that I stayed about an hour. It seems to me that the three of us—Eldridge Cleaver, his parole officer and I—mainly discussed the commercial prospects of *Soul on Ice*, which, it happened, was being published that day. We discussed the advance ($5,000). We discussed the size of the first printing (10,000 copies). We discussed the advertising budget and we discussed the bookstores in which copies were or were not available. It was a not unusual discussion between writers, with the difference that one of the writers had his parole officer there and the other had stood out on Oak Street and been visually frisked before coming inside.

7

To Pack and Wear:

2 skirts
2 jerseys or leotards
1 pullover sweater
2 pair shoes
stockings

bra
nightgown, robe, slippers
cigarettes
bourbon
bag with:
  shampoo
  toothbrush and paste
  Basis soap
  razor, deodorant
  aspirin, prescriptions, Tampax
  face cream, powder, baby oil

To Carry:

mohair throw
typewriter
2 legal pads and pens
files
house key

This is a list which was taped inside my closet door in Hollywood during those years when I was reporting more or less steadily. The list enabled me to pack, without thinking, for any piece I was likely to do. Notice the deliberate anonymity of costume: in a skirt, a leotard, *and stockings*, I could pass on either side of the culture. Notice the mohair throw for trunk-line flights (i.e., no blankets) and for the motel room in which the air conditioning could not be turned off. Notice the bourbon for the same motel room. Notice the typewriter for the airport, coming home: the idea was to turn in the Hertz car, check in, find an empty bench, and start typing the day's notes.

It should be clear that this was a list made by someone who prized control, yearned after momentum, someone determined to play her role as if she had the script, heard her cues, knew the narrative. There is on this list one significant omission, one article I needed and never had: a watch. I needed a watch not during the day, when I could turn on the car radio or ask someone, but at night, in the motel. Quite often I would ask the desk for the time every half hour or so, until finally, embarrassed to ask again, I would call Los Angeles and ask my husband. In other words I had skirts, jerseys, leotards, pullover sweater, shoes, stockings, bra, nightgown, robe, slippers, cigarettes, bourbon, shampoo, toothbrush and paste, Basis soap, razor, deodorant, aspirin, prescriptions, Tampax, face cream, powder, baby oil, mohair throw, typewriter, legal pads, pens, files and a house key, but I didn't know what time it was. This may be a parable, either of my life as a reporter during this period or of the period itself.

8

Driving a Budget Rent-A-Car between Sacramento and San Francisco one rainy morning in November of 1968 I kept the radio on very loud. On this occasion I kept the radio on very loud not to find out what time it was but in an effort to erase six words from my mind, six words which had no significance for me but which seemed that year to signal the onset of anxiety or fright. The words, a line from Ezra Pound's "In a Station of the Metro," were these: *Petals on a wet black bough.* The radio played "Wichita Lineman" and "I Heard It on the Grapevine." *Petals on a wet black bough.* Somewhere between the Yolo Causeway and Vallejo it occurred to me that during the course of any given week I met too many people who spoke favorably about bombing power stations. Somewhere between the Yolo Causeway and Vallejo it also occurred to me that the fright on this particular morning was going to present itself as an inability to drive this Budget Rent-A-Car across the Carquinez Bridge. *The Wichita Lineman was still on the job.* I closed my eyes and drove across the Carquinez Bridge, because I had appointments, because I was working, because I had promised to watch the revolution being made at San Francisco State College and because there was no place in Vallejo to turn in a Budget Rent-A-Car and because nothing on my mind was in the script as I remembered it.

9

At San Francisco State College on that particular morning the wind was blowing the cold rain in squalls across the muddied lawns and against the lighted windows of empty classrooms. In the days before there had been fires set and classes invaded and finally a confrontation with the San Francisco Police Tactical Unit, and in the weeks to come the campus would become what many people on it were pleased to call "a battlefield." The police and the Mace and the noon arrests would become the routine of life on the campus, and every night the combatants would review their day on television: the waves of students advancing, the commotion at the edge of the frame, the riot sticks flashing, the instant of jerky camera that served to suggest at what risk the film was obtained; then a cut to the weather map. In the beginning there had been the necessary "issue," the suspension of a 22-year-old instructor who happened as well to be Minister of Education for the Black Panther Party, but that issue, like most, had soon ceased to be the point in the minds of even the most dense participants. Disorder was its own point.

I had never before been on a campus in disorder, had missed even Berkeley and Columbia, and I suppose I went to San Francisco State expecting something other than what I found there. In some not at all trivial sense, the set was wrong. The very architecture of California state colleges tends to deny radical notions, to reflect instead a modest and hopeful vision of progressive welfare bureaucracy, and as I walked across the campus that day and on later days the entire San Francisco State dilemma—the gradual politicization, the "issues" here and there, the obligatory "Fifteen Demands," the continual arousal of the police and the outraged citizenry—seemed increasingly off-key, an instance of the *enfants terribles* and the Board of Trustees unconsciously collaborating on a wishful fantasy (Revolution on Campus) and playing it out in time for the six o'clock news. "Adjet-prop committee meeting in the Redwood Room," read a scrawled note on the cafeteria door one morning; only someone who needed very badly to be alarmed could respond with force to a guerrilla band that not only announced its meetings on the enemy's bulletin board but seemed innocent of the spelling, and so the meaning, of the words it used. "Hitler Hayakawa," some of the faculty had begun calling S. I. Hayakawa, the semanticist who had become the college's third president in a year and had incurred considerable displeasure by trying to keep the campus open.

"*Eichmann*," Kay Boyle had screamed at him at a rally. In just such broad strokes was the picture being painted in the fall of 1968 on the pastel campus at San Francisco State.

The place simply never seemed serious. The headlines were dark that first day, the college had been closed "indefinitely," both Ronald Reagan and Jesse Unruh were threatening reprisals; still, the climate inside the Administration Building was that of a musical comedy about college life. "No *chance* we'll be open tomorrow," secretaries informed callers. "Go skiing, have a good time." Striking black militants dropped in to chat with the deans; striking white radicals exchanged gossip in the corridors. "No interviews, no press," announced a student strike leader who happened into a dean's office where I was sitting; in the next moment he was piqued because no one had told him that a Huntley-Brinkley camera crew was on campus. "We can still plug into that," the dean said soothingly. Everyone seemed joined in a rather festive camaraderie, a shared jargon, a shared sense of moment: the future was no longer arduous and indefinite but immediate and programmatic, aglow with the prospect of problems to be "addressed," plans to be "implemented." It was agreed all around that the confrontations could be "a very healthy development," that maybe it took a shutdown "to get something done." The mood, like the architecture, was 1948 functional, a model of pragmatic optimism.

Perhaps Evelyn Waugh could have gotten it down exactly right: Waugh was good at scenes of industrious self-delusion, scenes of people absorbed in odd games. Here at San Francisco State only the black militants could be construed as serious: they were at any rate picking the games, dictating the rules, and taking what they could from what seemed for everyone else just an amiable evasion of routine, of institutional anxiety, of the tedium of the academic calendar. Meanwhile the administrators could talk about programs. Meanwhile the white radicals could see themselves, on an investment of virtually nothing, as urban guerrillas. It was working out well for everyone, this game at San Francisco State, and its peculiar virtues had never been so clear to me as they became one afternoon when I sat in on a meeting of fifty or sixty SDS members. They had called a press conference for later that day, and now they were discussing "just what the format of the press conference should be."

"This has to be on our terms," someone warned. "Because they'll ask very leading questions, they'll ask *questions*."

"Make them submit any questions in writing," someone else suggested. "The Black Student Union does that very successfully, then they just don't answer anything they don't want to answer."

"That's it, don't fall into their trap."

"Something we should stress at this press conference is *who owns the media*."

"You don't think it's common knowledge that the papers represent corporate interests?" a realist among them interjected doubtfully.

"I don't think it's *understood*."

Two hours and several dozen hand votes later, the group had selected four members to tell the press who owned the media, had decided to appear *en masse* at an opposition press conference, and had debated various slogans for the next day's demonstration. "Let's see, first we have 'Hearst Tells It Like It Ain't', then 'Stop Press Distortion'—that's the one there was some political controversy about. . . ."

And, before they broke up, they had listened to a student who had driven up for the day from the College of San Mateo, a junior college down the peninsula from San Francisco. "I came up here today with some Third World students to tell you that we're with you, and we hope you'll be with *us* when we try to pull off a strike next week, because we're really into it, we carry our motorcycle helmets all the time, can't think, can't go to class."

He had paused. He was a nice-looking boy, and fired with his task. I considered the tender melancholy of life in San Mateo, which is one of the richest counties per capita in the United States of America, and I considered whether or not the Wichita Lineman and the petals on the wet black bough represented the aimlessness of the bourgeoisie, and I considered the illusion of aim to be gained by holding a press conference, the only problem with press conferences being that the press asked questions. "I'm here to tell you that at College of San Mateo we're living like *revolutionaries*," the boy said then.

10

We put "Lay Lady Lay" on the record player, and "Suzanne." We went down to Melrose Avenue to see the Flying Burritos. There was a jasmine vine grown over the verandah of the big house on Franklin Avenue, and in the evenings the smell of jasmine came in through all the open doors and windows. I made bouillabaisse for people who did not eat meat. I imagined that my own life was simple and sweet, and sometimes it was, but there were odd things going around town. There were rumors. There were stories. Everything was unmentionable but nothing was unimaginable. This mystical flirtation with the idea of "sin"—this sense that it was possible to go "too far," and that many people were doing it—was very much with us in Los Angeles in 1968 and 1969. A demented and seductive vortical tension was building in the community. The jitters were setting in. I recall a time when the dogs barked every night and the moon was always full. On August 9, 1969, I was sitting in the shallow end of my sister-in-law's swimming pool in Beverly Hills when she received a telephone call from a friend who had just heard about the murders at Sharon Tate Polanski's house on Cielo Drive. The phone rang many times during the next hour. These early reports were garbled and contradictory. One caller would say hoods, the next would say chains. There were twenty dead, no, twelve, ten, eighteen. Black masses were imagined, and bad trips blamed. I remember all of the day's misinformation very clearly, and I also remember this, and wish I did not: *I remember that no one was surprised.*

11

When I first met Linda Kasabian in the summer of 1970 she was wearing her hair parted neatly in the middle, no makeup, Elizabeth Arden "Blue Grass" perfume, and the unpressed blue uniform issued to inmates at the Sybil Brand Institute for Women in Los Angeles. She was at Sybil Brand in protective custody, waiting out the time until she could testify about the murders of Sharon Tate Polanski, Abigail Folger, Jay Sebring,

Voytek Frykowski, Steven Parent, and Rosemary and Leno LaBianca, and, with her lawyer, Gary Fleischman, I spent a number of evenings talking to her there. Of these evenings I remember mainly my dread at entering the prison, at leaving for even an hour the infinite possibilities I suddenly perceived in the summer twilight. I remember driving downtown on the Hollywood Freeway in Gary Fleischman's Cadillac convertible with the top down. I remember watching a rabbit graze on the grass by the gate as Gary Fleischman signed the prison register. Each of the half-dozen doors that locked behind us as we entered Sybil Brand was a little death, and I would emerge after the interview like Persephone from the underworld, euphoric, elated. Once home I would have two drinks and make myself a hamburger and eat it ravenously.

"Dig it," Gary Fleischman was always saying. One night when we were driving back to Hollywood from Sybil Brand in the Cadillac convertible with the top down he demanded that I tell him the population of India. I said that I did not know the population of India. "Take a guess," he prompted. I made a guess, absurdly low, and he was disgusted. He had asked the same question of his niece ("a college girl"), of Linda, and now of me, and none of us had known. It seemed to confirm some idea he had of women, their essential ineducability, their similarity under the skin. Gary Fleischman was someone of a type I met only rarely, a comic realist in a porkpie hat, a business traveler on the far frontiers of the period, a man who knew his way around the courthouse and Sybil Brand and remained cheerful, even jaunty, in the face of the awesome and impenetrable mystery at the center of what he called "the case." In fact we never talked about "the case," and referred to its central events only as "Cielo Drive" and "LaBianca." We talked instead about Linda's childhood pastimes and disappointments, her high-school romances and her concern for her children. This particular juxtaposition of the spoken and the unspeakable was eerie and unsettling, and made my notebook a litany of little ironies so obvious as to be of interest only to dedicated absurdists. An example: Linda dreamed of opening a combination restaurant-boutique and pet shop.

12

Certain organic disorders of the central nervous system are characterized by periodic remissions, the apparent complete recovery of the afflicted nerves. What happens appears to be this: as the lining of a nerve becomes inflamed and hardens into scar tissue, thereby blocking the passage of neural impulses, the nervous system gradually changes its circuitry, finds other, unaffected nerves to carry the same messages. During the years when I found it necessary to revise the circuitry of my mind I discovered that I was no longer interested in whether the woman on the ledge outside the window on the sixteenth floor jumped or did not jump, or in why. I was interested only in the picture of her in my mind: her hair incandescent in the floodlights, her bare toes curled inward on the stone ledge.

In this light all narrative was sentimental. In this light all connections were equally meaningful, and equally senseless. Try these: on the morning of John Kennedy's death in 1963 I was buying, at Ransohoff's in San Francisco, a short silk dress in which to be married. A few years later this dress of mine was ruined when, at a dinner party in Bel-Air, Roman Polanski accidentally spilled a glass of red wine on it. Sharon Tate was also a guest at this party, although she and Roman Polanski were not yet married. On July 27, 1970, I went to the Magnin-Hi Shop on the third floor of I. Magnin in Beverly Hills and picked out, at Linda Kasabian's request, the dress in which she began her testimony about the murders at Sharon Tate Polanski's house on Cielo Drive. "Size 9 Petite," her instructions read. "Mini but not extremely mini. In velvet if possible. Emerald green or gold. Or: A Mexican peasant-style dress, smocked or embroidered." She needed a dress that morning because the district attorney, Vincent Bugliosi, had expressed doubts about the dress she had planned to wear, a long white homespun shift. "Long is for evening," he had advised Linda. Long was for evening and white was for brides. At her own wedding in 1965 Linda Kasabian had worn a white brocade suit. Time passed, times changed. Everything was to teach us something. At 11:20 on that July morning in 1970 I delivered the dress in which she would testify to Gary Fleischman, who was waiting in front of his office on Rodeo Drive in Beverly Hills. He was wearing his porkpie hat and he was standing with Linda's second husband, Bob Kasabian, and their friend Charlie Melton, both of whom were wearing long white robes. Long was for Bob and Charlie, the dress in the I. Magnin box was for Linda. The three of them took the I. Magnin box and got into Gary Fleischman's Cadillac convertible with the top down and drove off in the sunlight toward the freeway downtown, waving back at me. I believe this to be an authentically senseless chain of correspondences, but in the jingle-jangle morning of that summer it made as much sense as anything else did.

13

I recall a conversation I had in 1970 with the manager of a motel in which I was staying near Pendleton, Oregon. I had been doing a piece for *Life* about the storage of VX and GB nerve gas at an Army arsenal in Umatilla County, and now I was done, and trying to check out of the motel. During the course of checking out I was asked this question by the manager, who was a Mormon: *If you can't believe you're going to heaven in your own body and on a first-name basis with all the members of your family, then what's the point of dying?* At that time I believed that my basic affective controls were no longer intact, but now I present this to you as a more cogent question than it might at first appear, a kind of koan of the period.

14

Once I had a rib broken, and during the few months that it was painful to turn in bed or raise my arms in a swimming pool I had, for the first time, a sharp apprehension of what it would be like to be old. Later I forgot. At some point during the years I am talking about here, after a series of periodic visual disturbances, three electroencephalograms, two complete sets of skull and neck X-rays, one five-hour glucose tolerance test, two electromyelograms, a battery of chemical tests and consultations with two ophthalmologists, one internist and three neurologists, I was told that the disorder was not really in my eyes, but in my central nervous system. I might or might not experience symptoms of neural damage all my life. These symptoms, which might or might not appear, might or might not involve my eyes. They might or might not involve my arms or legs, they might or might not be disabling. Their effects might be lessened by cortisone injections, or they might not. It could not be predicted. The condition had a name, the kind of name usually associated with telethons, but the name meant nothing and the neurologist did not like to use it. The name was multiple sclerosis, but the name had no meaning. This was, the neurologist said, an exclusionary diagnosis, and meant nothing.

I had, at this time, a sharp apprehension not of what it was like to be old but of what it was like to open the door to the stranger and find that the stranger did indeed have the knife. In a few lines of dialogue in a neurologist's office in Beverly Hills, the improbable had become the probable, the norm: things which happened only to other people could in fact happen to me. I could be struck by lightning, could dare to eat a peach and be poisoned by the cyanide in the stone. The startling fact was this: my body was offering a precise physiological equivalent to what had been going on in my mind. "Lead a simple life," the neurologist advised. "Not that it makes any difference we know about." In other words it was another story without a narrative.

15

Many people I know in Los Angeles believe that the Sixties ended abruptly on August 9, 1969, ended at the exact moment when word of the murders on Cielo Drive traveled like brushfire through the community, and in a sense this is true. The tension broke that day. The paranoia was fulfilled. In another sense the Sixties did not truly end for me until January of 1971, when I left the house on Franklin Avenue and moved to a house on the sea. This particular house on the sea had itself been very much a part of the Sixties, and for some months after we took possession I would come across souvenirs of that period in its history—a piece of Scientology literature beneath a drawer lining, a copy of *Stranger in a Strange Land* stuck deep on a closet shelf—but after a while we did some construction, and between the power saws and the sea wind the place got exorcised.

I have known, since then, very little about the movements of the people who seemed to me emblematic of those years. I know of course that Eldridge Cleaver went to Algeria and came home an entrepreneur. I know that Jim Morrison died in Paris. I know that Linda Kasabian fled in search of the pastoral to New Hampshire, where I once visited her; she also visited me in New York, and we took our children on the Staten Island Ferry to see the Statue of Liberty. I also know that in 1975 Paul Ferguson, while serving a life sentence for the murder of Ramon Novarro, won first prize in a PEN fiction contest and announced plans to "continue my writing." Writing had helped him, he said, to "reflect on experience and see what it means." Quite often I reflect on the big house in Hollywood, on "Midnight Confessions" and on Ramon Novarro and on the fact that Roman Polanski and I are godparents to the same child, but writing has not yet helped me to see what it means.

1968–1978

II

CALIFORNIA REPUBLIC

James Pike, American

IT IS A CURIOUS and arrogantly secular monument, Grace Episcopal Cathedral in San Francisco, and it imposes its tone on everything around it. It stands directly upon the symbolic nexus of all old California money and power, Nob Hill. Its big rose window glows at night and dominates certain views from the Mark Hopkins and the Fairmont, as well as from Randolph and Catherine Hearst's apartment on California Street. In a city dedicated to the illusion that all human endeavor tends mystically west, toward the Pacific, Grace Cathedral faces resolutely east, toward the Pacific Union Club. As a child I was advised by my grandmother that Grace was "unfinished," and always would be, which was its point. In the years after World War I my mother had put pennies for Grace in her mite box but Grace would never be finished. In the years after World War II I would put pennies for Grace in my mite box but Grace would never be finished. In 1964 James Albert Pike, who had come home from St. John the Divine in New York and *The Dean Pike Show* on ABC to be Bishop of California, raised three million dollars, installed images of Albert Einstein, Thurgood Marshall and John Glenn in the clerestory windows, and, in the name of God (James Albert Pike had by then streamlined the Trinity, eliminating the Son and the Holy Ghost), pronounced Grace "finished." This came to my attention as an odd and unsettling development, an extreme missing of the point—at least as I had understood the point in my childhood—and it engraved James Albert Pike on my consciousness more indelibly than any of his previous moves.

What was one to make of him. Five years after he finished Grace, James Albert Pike left the Episcopal Church altogether, detailing his pique in the pages of *Look*, and drove into the Jordanian desert in a white Ford Cortina rented from Avis. He went with his former student and bride of nine months, Diane. Later she would say that they wanted to experience the wilderness as Jesus had. They equipped themselves for this mission with an Avis map and two bottles of Coca-Cola. The young Mrs. Pike got out alive. Five days after James Albert Pike's body was retrieved from a canyon near the Dead Sea a Solemn Requiem Mass was offered for him at the cathedral his own hubris had finished in San Francisco. Outside on the Grace steps the cameras watched the Black Panthers demonstrating to free Bobby Seale. Inside the Grace nave Diane Kennedy Pike and her two predecessors, Jane Alvies Pike and Esther Yanovsky Pike, watched the cameras and one another.

That was 1969. For some years afterward I could make nothing at all of this peculiar and strikingly "now" story, so vast and atavistic was my irritation with the kind of man my grandmother would have called "just a damn old fool," the kind of man who would go into the desert with the sappy Diane and two bottles of Coca-Cola, but I see now that Diane and the Coca-Cola are precisely the details which lift the narrative into apologue. James Albert Pike has been on my mind quite a bit these past few weeks, ever since I read a biography of him by William Stringfellow and Anthony Towne, *The Death and Life of Bishop Pike*, an adoring but instructive volume from which there emerges the shadow of a great literary character, a literary character in the sense that Howard Hughes and Whittaker Chambers were literary characters, a character so ambiguous and driven and revealing of his time and place that his gravestone in the Protestant Cemetery in Jaffa might well have read only *JAMES PIKE, AMERICAN*.

Consider his beginnings. He was the only child of an ambitious mother and an ailing father who moved from Kentucky a few years before his birth in 1913 to homestead forty acres of mesquite in Oklahoma. There had been for a while a retreat to a one-room shack in Alamogordo, New Mexico, there had been always the will of the mother to improve the family's prospects. She taught school. She played piano with a dance band, she played piano in a silent-movie theater. She raised her baby James a Catholic and she entered him in the Better Babies Contest at the Oklahoma State Fair and he took first prize, two years running. "I thought you would like that," she told his biographers almost sixty years later. "He started out a winner."

He also started out dressing paper dolls in priests' vestments. The mother appears to have been a woman of extreme determination. Her husband died when James was two. Six years later the widow moved to Los Angeles, where she devoted herself to maintaining a world in which nothing "would change James' life or thwart him in any way," a mode of upbringing which would show in the son's face and manner all his life. "Needless to say this has all been a bit tedious for me to relive," he complained when the question of his first divorce and remarriage seemed to stand between him and election as Bishop of California; his biography is a panoply of surprised petulance in the face of other people's attempts to "thwart" him by bringing up an old marriage or divorce or some other "long-dead aspect of the past."

In Los Angeles there was Hollywood High, there was Mass every morning at Blessed Sacrament on Sunset Boulevard. After Hollywood High there was college with the Jesuits, at Santa Clara, at least until James repudiated the Catholic Church and convinced his mother that she should do the same. He was eighteen at the time, but it was characteristic of both mother and son to have taken this adolescent "repudiation" quite gravely: they give the sense of having had no anchor but each other, and to have reinvented their moorings every day. After Santa Clara, for the freshly invented agnostic, there was U.C.L.A., then U.S.C., and finally the leap east. Back East. Yale Law. A job in Washington with the Securities and Exchange Commission. "You have to understand that he was very lonely in Washington," his mother said after his death. "He really wanted to come home. I wish he had." And yet it must have seemed to such a western child that he had at last met the "real" world, the "great" world, the world to beat. The world in which, as the young man who started out a winner soon discovered and wrote to his mother, "practically every churchgoer you meet in our level of society is Episcopalian, and an R.C. or straight Protestant is as rare as hen's teeth."

One thinks of Gatsby, coming up against the East. One also thinks of Tom Buchanan, and his vast carelessness. (Some 25 years later, in Santa Barbara, when the Bishop of California's mistress swallowed 55 sleeping pills, he appears to have moved her from his apartment into her own before calling an ambulance, and to have obscured certain evidence before she died.) One even thinks of Dick Diver, who also started out a winner, and who tried to embrace the essence of the American continent in Nicole as James Albert Pike would now try to embrace it in the Episcopal Church. *"Practically every churchgoer you meet in our level of society is Episcopalian."*

It is an American Adventure of Barry Lyndon, this Westerner going east to seize his future, equipped with a mother's love and with what passed in the makeshift moorage from which he came as a passion for knowledge. As evidence of this passion his third wife, Diane, would repeat this curious story: he "had read both the dictionary and the phone book from cover to cover by the time he was five, and a whole set of the Encyclopaedia Britannica before he was ten." Diane also reports his enthusiasm for the Museum of Man in Paris, which seemed to him to offer, in the hour he spent there, "a complete education," the "entire history of the human race . . . in summary form."

In summary form. One gets a sense of the kind of mindless fervor that a wife less rapt than Diane might find unhinging. In the late thirties, as Communion was about to be served at the first Christmas Mass of James Albert Pike's new career as an Episcopalian, his first wife, Jane, another transplanted Californian, is reported to have jumped up and run screaming from the church. There would have been nothing in the phone book to cover that, or in the Britannica either. Later he invented an ecclesiastical annulment to cover his divorce from Jane, although no such annulment was actually granted. "In his mind," his biographers explain, "the marriage was not merely a mistake, but a nullity in the inception." In his mind. He needed to believe in the annulment because he wanted to be Bishop of California. "At heart he was a Californian," a friend said. "He had grown up with the idea that San Francisco was it . . . he was obsessed with the idea of being Bishop of California. Nothing in heaven or hell could have stopped him." In his mind. "Tom and Gatsby, Daisy and Jordan and I, were all Westerners," as Nick Carraway said, "and perhaps we possessed some deficiency in common which made us subtly unadaptable to Eastern life."

In his mind. I recall standing in St. Thomas Church in New York one Monday morning in 1964 debating whether or not to steal a book by James Albert Pike, a pastoral tract called *If You Marry Outside Your Faith.* I had only a twenty-dollar bill and could not afford to leave it in the box but I wanted to read the book more closely, because a few weeks before I had in fact married a Catholic, which was what Bishop Pike seemed to have in mind. I had not been brought up to think it made much difference what I married, as long as I steered clear of odd sects where they didn't drink at the wedding (my grandmother was an Episcopalian only by frontier chance; her siblings were Catholics but there was no Catholic priest around the year she needed christening), and I was struck dumb by Bishop Pike's position, which appeared to be that I had not only erred but had every moral right and obligation to erase this error by regarding my marriage as null, and any promises I had made as invalid. In other words the way to go was to forget it and start over.

In the end I did not steal *If You Marry Outside Your Faith*, and over the years I came to believe that I had doubtless misread it. After considering its source I am no longer so sure. "Jim never cleaned up after himself," a friend notes, recalling his habit of opening a shirt and letting the cardboards lie where they fell, and this *élan* seems to have applied to more than his laundry. Here was a man who moved through life believing that he was entitled to forget it and start over, to shed women when they became difficult and allegiances when they became tedious and simply *move on*, dismissing those who quibbled as petty and "judgmental" and generally threatened by his superior and more dynamic view of human possibility. That there was an ambivalence and a speciousness about this moral frontiersmanship has not gone unnoticed, but in the rush to call the life "only human" I suspect we are overlooking its real interest, which is as social history. The man was a Michelin to his time and place. At the peak of his career James Albert Pike carried his peace cross (he had put away his pectoral cross for the duration of the Vietnam war, which outlived him) through every charlatanic thicket in American life, from the Center for the Study of Democratic Institutions to the Aspen Institute of Humanistic Studies to Spiritual Frontiers, which was at the time the Ford Foundation of the spirit racket. James Albert Pike was everywhere at the right time. He was in Geneva for *Pacem in Terris*. He was in Baltimore for the trial of the Catonsville Nine, although he had to be briefed on the issue in the car from the airport. He was in the right room at the right time to reach his son, Jim Jr., an apparent suicide on Romilar, via séance. The man kept moving. If death was troubling then start over, and reinvent it as "The Other Side." If faith was troubling then leave the Church, and reinvent it as "The Foundation for Religious Transition."

This sense that the world can be reinvented smells of the Sixties in this country, those years when no one at all seemed to have any memory or mooring, and in a way the Sixties were the years for which James Albert Pike was born. When the man who started out a winner was lying dead in the desert his brother-in-law joined the search party, and prayed for the assistance of God, Jim Jr., and Edgar Cayce. I think I have never heard a more poignant trinity.

1976

Holy Water

SOME OF US who live in arid parts of the world think about water with a reverence others might find excessive. The water I will draw tomorrow from my tap in Malibu is today crossing the Mojave Desert from the Colorado River, and I like to think about exactly where that water is. The water I will drink tonight in a restaurant in Hollywood is by now well down the Los Angeles Aqueduct from the Owens River, and I also think about exactly where that water is: I particularly like to imagine it as it cascades down the 45-degree stone steps that aerate Owens water after its airless passage through the mountain pipes and siphons. As it happens my own reverence for water has always taken the form of this constant meditation upon where the water is, of an obsessive interest not in the politics of water but in the waterworks themselves, in the movement of water through aqueducts and siphons and pumps and forebays and afterbays and weirs and drains, in plumbing on the grand scale. I know the data on water projects I will never see. I know the difficulty Kaiser had closing the last two sluiceway gates on the Guri Dam in Venezuela. I keep watch on evaporation behind the Aswan in Egypt. I can put myself to sleep imagining the water dropping a thousand feet into the turbines at Churchill Falls in Labrador. If the Churchill Falls Project fails to materialize, I fall back on waterworks closer at hand—the tailrace at Hoover on the Colorado, the surge tank in the Tehachapi Mountains that receives California Aqueduct water pumped higher than water has ever been pumped before—and finally I replay a morning when I was seventeen years old and caught, in a military-surplus life raft, in the construction of the Nimbus Afterbay Dam on the American River near Sacramento. I remember that at the moment it happened I was trying to open a tin of anchovies with capers. I recall the raft spinning into the narrow chute through which the river had been temporarily diverted. I recall being deliriously happy.

I suppose it was partly the memory of that delirium that led me to visit, one summer morning in Sacramento, the Operations Control Center for the California State Water Project.

Actually so much water is moved around California by so many different agencies that maybe only the movers themselves know on any given day whose water is where, but to get a general picture it is necessary only to remember that Los Angeles moves some of it, San Francisco moves some of it, the Bureau of Reclamation's Central Valley Project moves some of it and the California State Water Project moves most of the rest of it, moves a vast amount of it, moves more water farther than has ever been moved anywhere. They collect this water up in the granite keeps of the Sierra Nevada and they store roughly a trillion gallons of it behind the Oroville Dam and every morning, down at the Project's headquarters in Sacramento, they decide how much of their water they want to move the next day. They make this morning decision according to supply and demand, which is simple in theory but rather more complicated in practice. In theory each of the Project's five field divisions—the Oroville, the Delta, the San Luis, the San Joaquin and the Southern divisions—places a call to headquarters before nine A.M. and tells the dispatchers how much water is needed by its local water contractors, who have in turn based their morning estimates on orders from growers and other big users. A schedule is made. The gates open and close according to schedule. The water flows south and the deliveries are made.

In practice this requires prodigious coordination, precision, and the best efforts of several human minds and that of a Univac 418. In practice it might be necessary to hold large flows of water for power production, or to flush out encroaching salinity in the Sacramento–San Joaquin Delta, the most ecologically sensitive point on the system. In practice a sudden rain might obviate the need for a delivery when that delivery is already on its way. In practice what is being delivered here is an enormous volume of water, not quarts of milk or spools of thread, and it takes two days to move such a delivery down through Oroville into the Delta, which is the great pooling place for California water and has been for some years alive with electronic sensors and telemetering equipment and men blocking channels and diverting flows and shoveling fish away from the pumps. It takes perhaps another six days to move this same water down the California Aqueduct from the Delta to the Tehachapi and put it over the hill to Southern California. "Putting some over the hill" is what they say around the Project

Operations Control Center when they want to indicate that they are pumping Aqueduct water from the floor of the San Joaquin Valley up and over the Tehachapi Mountains. "Pulling it down" is what they say when they want to indicate that they are lowering a water level somewhere in the system. They can put some over the hill by remote control from this room in Sacramento with its Univac and its big board and its flashing lights. They can pull down a pool in the San Joaquin by remote control from this room in Sacramento with its locked doors and its ringing alarms and its constant print-outs of data from sensors out there in the water itself. From this room in Sacramento the whole system takes on the aspect of a perfect three-billion-dollar hydraulic toy, and in certain ways it is. "LET'S START DRAINING QUAIL AT 12:00" was the 10:51 A.M. entry on the electronically recorded communications log the day I visited the Operations Control Center. "Quail" is a reservoir in Los Angeles County with a gross capacity of 1,636,018,000 gallons. "OK" was the response recorded in the log. I knew at that moment that I had missed the only vocation for which I had any instinctive affinity: I wanted to drain Quail myself.

Not many people I know carry their end of the conversation when I want to talk about water deliveries, even when I stress that these deliveries affect their lives, indirectly, every day. "Indirectly" is not quite enough for most people I know. This morning, however, several people I know were affected not "indirectly" but "directly" by the way the water moves. They had been in New Mexico shooting a picture, one sequence of which required a river deep enough to sink a truck, the kind with a cab and a trailer and fifty or sixty wheels. It so happened that no river near the New Mexico location was running that deep this year. The production was therefore moved today to Needles, California, where the Colorado River normally runs, depending upon releases from Davis Dam, eighteen to twenty-five feet deep. Now. Follow this closely: yesterday we had a freak tropical storm in Southern California, two inches of rain in a normally dry month, and because this rain flooded the fields and provided more irrigation than any grower could possibly want for several days, no water was ordered from Davis Dam.

No orders, no releases.

Supply and demand.

As a result the Colorado was running only seven feet deep past Needles today, Sam Peckinpah's desire for eighteen feet of water in which to sink a truck not being the kind of demand anyone at Davis Dam is geared to meet. The production closed down for the weekend. Shooting will resume Tuesday, providing some grower orders water and the agencies controlling the Colorado release it. Meanwhile many gaffers, best boys, cameramen, assistant directors, script supervisors, stunt drivers and maybe even Sam Peckinpah are waiting out the weekend in Needles, where it is often 110 degrees at five P.M. and hard to get dinner after eight. This is a California parable, but a true one.

I have always wanted a swimming pool, and never had one. When it became generally known a year or so ago that California was suffering severe drought, many people in water-rich parts of the country seemed obscurely gratified, and made frequent reference to Californians having to brick up their swimming pools. In fact a swimming pool requires, once it has been filled and the filter has begun its process of cleaning and recirculating the water, virtually no water, but the symbolic content of swimming pools has always been interesting: a pool is misapprehended as a trapping of affluence, real or pretended, and of a kind of hedonistic attention to the body. Actually a pool is, for many of us in the West, a symbol not of affluence but of order, of control over the uncontrollable. A pool is water, made available and useful, and is, as such, infinitely soothing to the western eye.

It is easy to forget that the only natural force over which we have any control out here is water, and that only recently. In my memory California summers were characterized by the coughing in the pipes that meant the well was dry, and California winters by all-night watches on rivers about to crest, by sandbagging, by dynamite on the levees and flooding on the first floor. Even now the place is not all that hospitable to extensive settlement. As I write a fire has been burning out of control for two weeks in the ranges behind the Big Sur coast. Flash floods last night wiped out all major roads into Imperial County. I noticed this morning a hairline crack in a living-room tile from last week's earthquake, a 4.4 I never felt. In the part of California where I now live aridity is the single most prominent feature of the climate, and I am not pleased to see, this year, cactus spreading wild to the sea. There will be days this winter when the humidity will drop to ten, seven, four. Tumbleweed will blow against my house and the sound of the rattlesnake will be duplicated a hundred times a day by dried bougainvillea drifting in my driveway. The apparent ease of California life is an illusion, and those who believe the illusion real live here in only the most temporary way. I know as well as the next person that there is considerable transcendent value in a river running wild and undammed, a river running free over granite, but I have also lived beneath such a river when it was running in flood, and gone without showers when it was running dry.

"The West begins," Bernard DeVoto wrote, "where the average annual rainfall drops below twenty inches." This is maybe the best definition of the West I have ever read, and it goes a long way toward explaining my own passion for seeing the water under control, but many people I know persist in looking for psychoanalytical implications in this passion. As a matter of fact I have explored, in an amateur way, the more obvious of these implications, and come up with nothing interesting. A certain external reality remains, and resists interpretation. The West begins where the average annual rainfall drops below twenty inches. Water is important to people who do not have it, and the same is true of control. Some fifteen years ago I tore a poem by Karl Shapiro from a magazine and pinned it on my kitchen wall. This fragment of paper is now on the wall of a sixth kitchen, and crumbles a little whenever I touch it, but I keep it there for the last stanza, which has for me the power of a prayer:

It is raining in California, a straight rain
Cleaning the heavy oranges on the bough,
Filling the gardens till the gardens flow,
Shining the olives, tiling the gleaming tile,
Waxing the dark camellia leaves more green,
Flooding the daylong valleys like the Nile.

I thought of those lines almost constantly on the morning in Sacramento when I went to visit the California State Water Project Operations Control Center. If I had wanted to drain Quail at 10:51 that morning, I wanted, by early afternoon, to do a great deal more. I wanted to open and close the Clifton Court Forebay intake gate. I wanted to produce some power down at the San Luis Dam. I wanted to pick a pool at random on the Aqueduct and pull it down and then refill it, watching for the hydraulic jump. I wanted to put some water over the hill and I wanted to shut down all flow from the Aqueduct into the Bureau of Reclamation's Cross Valley Canal, just to see how long it would take somebody over at Reclamation to call up and complain. I stayed as long as I could and watched the system work on the big board with the lighted checkpoints. The Delta salinity report was coming in on one of the teletypes behind me. The Delta tidal report was coming in on another. The earthquake board, which has been desensitized to sound its alarm (a beeping tone for Southern California, a high-pitched tone for the north) only for those earthquakes which register at least 3.0 on the Richter Scale, was silent. I had no further business in this room and yet I wanted to stay the day. I wanted to be the one, that day, who was shining the olives, filling the gardens, and flooding the daylong valleys like the Nile. I want it still.

1977

Many Mansions

THE NEW OFFICIAL residence for governors of California, unlandscaped, unfurnished, and unoccupied since the day construction stopped in 1975, stands on eleven acres of oaks and olives on a bluff overlooking the American River outside Sacramento. This is the twelve-thousand-square-foot house that Ronald and Nancy Reagan built. This is the sixteen-room house in which Jerry Brown declined to live. This is the vacant house which cost the State of California one-million-four, not including the property, which was purchased in 1969 and donated to the state by such friends of the Reagans as Leonard K. Firestone of Firestone Tire and Rubber and Taft Schreiber of the Music Corporation of America and Holmes Tuttle, the Los Angeles Ford dealer. All day at this empty house three maintenance men try to keep the bulletproof windows clean and the cobwebs swept and the wild grass green and the rattlesnakes down by the river and away from the thirty-five exterior wood and glass doors. All night at this empty house the lights stay on behind the eight-foot chain-link fence and the guard dogs lie at bay and the telephone, when it rings, startles by the fact that it works. "Governor's Residence," the guards answer, their voices laconic, matter-of-fact, quite as if there were some phantom governor to connect. Wild grass grows where the tennis court was to have been. Wild grass grows where the pool and sauna were to have been. The American is the river in which gold was discovered in 1848, and it once ran fast and full past here, but lately there have been upstream dams and dry years. Much of the bed is exposed. The far bank has been dredged and graded. That the river is running low is of no real account, however, since one of the many peculiarities of the new Governor's Residence is that it is so situated as to have no clear view of the river.

It is an altogether curious structure, this one-story one-million-four dream house of Ronald and Nancy Reagan's. Were the house on the market (which it will probably not be, since, at the time it was costing a million-four, local real estate agents seemed to agree on $300,000 as the top price ever paid for a house in Sacramento County), the words used to describe it would be "open" and "contemporary," although technically it is neither. "Flow" is a word that crops up quite a bit when one is walking through the place, and so is "resemble." The walls "resemble" local adobe, but they are not: they are the same concrete blocks, plastered and painted a rather stale yellowed cream, used in so many supermarkets and housing projects and Coca-Cola bottling plants. The door frames and the exposed beams "resemble" native redwood, but they are not: they are construction-grade lumber of indeterminate quality, stained brown. If anyone ever moves in, the concrete floors will be carpeted, wall to wall. If anyone ever moves in, the thirty-five exterior wood and glass doors, possibly the single distinctive feature in the house, will be, according to plan, "draped." The bathrooms are small and standard. The family bedrooms open directly onto the nonexistent swimming pool, with all its potential for noise and distraction. To one side of the fireplace in the formal living room there is what is known in the trade as a "wet bar," a cabinet for bottles and glasses with a sink and a long vinyl-topped counter. (This vinyl "resembles" slate.) In the entire house there are only enough bookshelves for a set of the World Book and some Books of the Month, plus maybe three Royal Doulton figurines and a back file of *Connoisseur*, but there is $90,000 worth of other teak cabinetry, including the "refreshment center" in the "recreation room." There is that most ubiquitous of all "luxury features," a bidet in the master bathroom. There is one of those kitchens which seem designed exclusively for defrosting by microwave and compacting trash. It is a house built for a family of snackers.

And yet, appliances notwithstanding, it is hard to see where the million-four went. The place has been called, by Jerry Brown, a "Taj Mahal." It has been called a "white elephant," a "resort," a "monument to the colossal ego of our former governor." It is not exactly any of these things. It is simply and rather astonishingly an enlarged version of a very common kind of California tract house, a monument not to colossal ego but to a weird absence of ego, a case study in the architecture of limited possibilities, insistently and malevolently "democratic," flattened out, mediocre and "open" and as devoid of privacy or personal eccentricity as the lobby area in a Ramada

Inn. It is the architecture of "background music," decorators, "good taste." I recall once interviewing Nancy Reagan, at a time when her husband was governor and the construction on this house had not yet begun. We drove down to the State Capitol Building that day, and Mrs. Reagan showed me how she had lightened and brightened offices there by replacing the old burnished leather on the walls with the kind of beige burlap then favored in new office buildings. I mention this because it was on my mind as I walked through the empty house on the American River outside Sacramento.

From 1903 until Ronald Reagan, who lived in a rented house in Sacramento while he was governor ($1,200 a month, payable by the state to a group of Reagan's friends), the governors of California lived in a large white Victorian Gothic house at 16th and H Streets in Sacramento. This extremely individual house, three stories and a cupola and the face of Columbia the Gem of the Ocean worked into the molding over every door, was built in 1877 by a Sacramento hardware merchant named Albert Gallatin. The state paid $32,500 for it in 1903 and my father was born in a house a block away in 1908. This part of town has since run to seed and small business, the kind of place where both Squeaky Fromme and Patricia Hearst could and probably did go about their business unnoticed, but the Governor's Mansion, unoccupied and open to the public as State Historical Landmark Number 823, remains Sacramento's premier example of eccentric domestic architecture.

As it happens I used to go there once in a while, when Earl Warren was governor and his daughter Nina was a year ahead of me at C. K. McClatchy Senior High School. Nina was always called "Honey Bear" in the papers and in *Life* Magazine but she was called "Nina" at C. K. McClatchy Senior High School and she was called "Nina" (or sometimes "Warren") at weekly meetings of the Mañana Club, a local institution to which we both belonged. I recall being initiated into the Mañana Club one night at the old Governor's Mansion, in a ceremony which involved being blindfolded and standing around Nina's bedroom in a state of high apprehension about secret rites which never materialized. It was the custom for the members to hurl mild insults at the initiates, and I remember being dumbfounded to hear Nina, by my fourteen-year-old lights the most glamorous and unapproachable fifteen-year-old in America, characterize me as "stuck on herself." There in the Governor's Mansion that night I learned for the first time that my face to the world was not necessarily the face in my mirror. "No smoking on the third floor," everyone kept saying. "Mrs. Warren *said*. No smoking on the third floor *or else*."

Firetrap or not, the old Governor's Mansion was at that time my favorite house in the world, and probably still is. The morning after I was shown the new "Residence" I visited the old "Mansion," took the public tour with a group of perhaps twenty people, none of whom seemed to find it as ideal as I did. "All those stairs," they murmured, as if stairs could no longer be tolerated by human physiology. "All those stairs," and "all that waste space." The old Governor's Mansion does have stairs and waste space, which is precisely why it remains the kind of house in which sixty adolescent girls might gather and never interrupt the real life of the household. The bedrooms are big and private and high-ceilinged and they do not open on the swimming pool and one can imagine reading in one of them, or writing a book, or closing the door and crying until dinner. The bathrooms are big and airy and they do not have bidets but they do have room for hampers, and dressing tables, and chairs on which to sit and read a story to a child in the bathtub. There are hallways wide and narrow, stairs front and back, sewing rooms, ironing rooms, secret rooms. On the gilt mirror in the library there is worked a bust of Shakespeare, a pretty fancy for a hardware merchant in a California farm town in 1877. In the kitchen there is no trash compactor and there is no "island" with the appliances built in but there are two pantries, and a nice old table with a marble top for rolling out pastry and making divinity fudge and chocolate leaves. The morning I took the tour our guide asked if anyone could think why the old table had a marble top. There were a dozen or so other women in the group, each of an age to have cooked unnumbered meals, but not one of them could think of a single use for a slab of marble in the kitchen. It occurred to me that we had finally evolved a society in which knowledge of a pastry marble, like a taste for stairs and closed doors, could be construed as "elitist," and as I left the Governor's Mansion I felt very like the heroine of Mary McCarthy's *Birds of America*, the one who located America's moral decline in the disappearance of the first course.

A guard sleeps at night in the old mansion, which has been condemned as a dwelling by the state fire marshal. It costs about $85,000 a year to keep guards at the new official residence. Meanwhile the current governor of California, Edmund G. Brown, Jr., sleeps on a mattress on the floor in the famous apartment for which he pays $275 a month out of his own $49,100 annual salary. This has considerable and potent symbolic value, as do the two empty houses themselves, most particularly the house the Reagans built on the river. It is a great point around the Capitol these days to have "never seen" the house on the river. The governor himself has "never seen" it. The governor's press secretary, Elisabeth Coleman, has "never seen" it. The governor's chief of staff, Gray Davis, admits to having seen it, but only once, when "Mary McGrory wanted to see it." This unseen house on the river is, Jerry Brown has said, "not my style."

As a matter of fact this is precisely the point about the house on the river—the house is not Jerry Brown's style, not Mary McGrory's style, *not our style*—and it is a point which presents a certain problem, since the house so clearly *is* the style not only of Jerry Brown's predecessor but of millions of Jerry Brown's constituents. Words are chosen carefully. Reasonable objections are framed. One hears about how the house is too far from the Capitol, too far from Legislature. One hears about the folly of running such a lavish establishment for an unmarried governor and one hears about the governor's temperamental austerity. One hears every possible reason for not living in the house except the one that counts: it is the kind of house that has a wet bar in the living room. It is the kind of house that has a refreshment center. It is the kind of house in which one does not live, but there is no way to say this without getting into touchy and evanescent and finally inadmissible questions of taste, and ultimately of class. I have seldom seen a house so evocative of the unspeakable.

1977

The Getty

THE PLACE MIGHT have been commissioned by The Magic Christian. Mysteriously and rather giddily splendid, hidden in a grove of sycamores just above the Pacific Coast Highway in Malibu, a commemoration of high culture so immediately productive of crowds and jammed traffic that it can now be approached by appointment only, the seventeen-million-dollar villa built by the late J. Paul Getty to house his antiquities and paintings and furniture manages to strike a peculiar nerve in almost everyone who sees it. From the beginning, the Getty was said to be vulgar. The Getty was said to be "Disney." The Getty was even said to be Jewish, if I did not misread the subtext in "like a Beverly Hills nouveau-riche dining room" (*Los Angeles Times*, January 6, 1974) and "gussied up like a Bel-Air dining room" (*New York Times*, May 28, 1974).

The Getty seems to stir up social discomforts at levels not easily plumbed. To mention this museum in the more enlightened of those very dining rooms it is said to resemble is to invite a kind of nervous derision, as if the place were a local hoax, a perverse and deliberate affront to the understated good taste and general class of everyone at the table. The Getty's intricately patterned marble floors and walls are "garish." The Getty's illusionistic portico murals are "back lot." The entire building, an informed improvisation on a villa buried by mud from Vesuvius in 79 A.D. and seen again only dimly during some eighteenth-century tunneling around Herculaneum, is ritually dismissed as "inauthentic," although what "authentic" could mean in this context is hard to say.

Something about the place embarrasses people. The collection itself is usually referred to as "that kind of thing," as in "not even the best of that kind of thing," or "absolutely top-drawer if you like that kind of thing," both of which translate "not our kind of thing." The Getty's damask-lined galleries of Renaissance and Baroque paintings are distinctly that kind of thing, there being little in the modern temperament that responds immediately to popes and libertine babies, and so are the Getty's rather unrelenting arrangements of French furniture. A Louis XV writing table tends to please the modern eye only if it has been demystified by a glass of field flowers and some silver-framed snapshots, as in a Horst photograph for *Vogue*. Even the Getty's famous antiquities are pretty much that kind of thing, evoking as they do not their own period but the eighteenth- and nineteenth-century rage for antiquities. The sight of a Greek head depresses many people, strikes an unliberated chord, reminds them of books in their grandmother's parlor and of all they were supposed to learn and never did. This note of "learning" pervades the entire Getty collection. Even the handful of Impressionists acquired by Getty were recently removed from the public galleries, put away as irrelevant. The Getty collection is in certain ways unremittingly reproachful, and quite inaccessible to generations trained in the conviction that a museum is meant to be fun, with Calder mobiles and Barcelona chairs.

In short the Getty is a monument to "fine art," in the old-fashioned didactic sense, which is part of the problem people have with it. The place resists contemporary notions about what art is or should be or ever was. A museum is now supposed to kindle the untrained imagination, but this museum does not. A museum is now supposed to set the natural child in each of us free, but this museum does not. This was art acquired to teach a lesson, and there is also a lesson in the building which houses it: the Getty tells us that the past was perhaps different from the way we like to perceive it. Ancient marbles were not always attractively faded and worn. Ancient marbles once appeared just as they appear here: as strident, opulent evidence of imperial power and acquisition. Ancient murals were not always bleached and mellowed and "tasteful." Ancient murals once looked as they do here: as if dreamed by a Mafia don. Ancient fountains once worked, and drowned out that very silence we have come to expect and want from the past. Ancient bronze once gleamed ostentatiously. The old world was once discomfitingly new, or even nouveau, as people like to say about the Getty. (I have never been sure what the word "nouveau" can possibly mean in America, implying as it does that the speaker is gazing down six hundred years of rolled lawns.) At a time when all our public conventions remain rooted in a kind of knocked-down romanticism, when the celebration of natural man's capacity for moving onward and upward has become a kind of official tic, the Getty presents us with an illustrated lesson in classical doubt. The Getty advises us that not much changes. The Getty tells us that we were never any better than we are and will never be any better than we were, and in so doing makes a profoundly unpopular political statement.

The Getty's founder may or may not have had some such statement in mind. In a way he seems to have wanted only to do something no one else could or would do. In his posthumous book, *As I See It*, he advises us that he never wanted "one of those concrete-bunker-type structures that are the fad among museum architects." He refused to pay for any "tinted-glass-and-stainless-steel monstrosity." He assures us that he was "neither shaken nor surprised" when his villa was finished and "certain critics sniffed." He had "calculated the risks." He knew that he was flouting the "doctrinaire and elitist" views he believed endemic in "many Art World (or should I say Artsy-Craftsy?) quarters."

Doctrinaire and elitist. Artsy-craftsy. On the surface the Getty would appear to have been a case of he-knew-what-he-liked-and-he-built-it, a tax dodge from the rather louche world of the international rich, and yet the use of that word "elitist" strikes an interesting note. The man who built himself the Getty never saw it, although it opened a year and a half before his death. He seems to have liked the planning of it. He personally approved every paint sample. He is said to have taken immense pleasure in every letter received from anyone who visited the museum and liked it (such letters were immediately forwarded to him by the museum staff), but the idea of the place seems to have been enough, and the idea was this: here was a museum built not for those elitist critics but for "the public." Here was a museum that would be forever supported by its founder alone, a museum that need never depend on any city or state or federal funding, a place forever "open to the public and free of all charges."

As a matter of fact large numbers of people who do not ordinarily visit museums like the Getty a great deal, just as its founder knew they would. There is one of those peculiar social secrets at work here. On the whole "the critics" distrust great wealth, but "the public" does not. On the whole "the critics" subscribe to the romantic view of man's possibilities, but "the public" does not. In the end the Getty stands above the Pacific Coast Highway as one of those odd monuments, a palpable contract between the very rich and the people who distrust them least.

1977

Bureaucrats

THE CLOSED DOOR upstairs at 120 South Spring Street in downtown Los Angeles is marked OPERATIONS CENTER. In the windowless room beyond the closed door a reverential hush prevails. From six A.M. until seven P.M. in this windowless room men sit at consoles watching a huge board flash colored lights. "There's the heart attack," someone will murmur, or "we're getting the gawk effect." 120 South Spring is the Los Angeles office of Caltrans, or the California Department of Transportation, and the Operations Center is where Caltrans engineers monitor what they call "the 42-Mile Loop." The 42-Mile Loop is simply the rough triangle formed by the intersections of the Santa Monica, the San Diego and the Harbor freeways, and 42 miles represents less than ten per cent of freeway mileage in Los Angeles County alone, but these particular 42 miles are regarded around 120 South Spring with a special veneration. The Loop is a "demonstration system," a phrase much favored by everyone at Caltrans, and is part of a "pilot project," another two words carrying totemic weight on South Spring.

The Loop has electronic sensors embedded every half-mile out there in the pavement itself, each sensor counting the crossing cars every twenty seconds. The Loop has its own mind, a Xerox Sigma V computer which prints out, all day and night, twenty-second readings on what is and is not moving in each of the Loop's eight lanes. It is the Xerox Sigma V that makes the big board flash red when traffic out there drops below fifteen miles an hour. It is the Xerox Sigma V that tells the Operations crew when they have an "incident" out there. An "incident" is the heart attack on the San Diego, the jackknifed truck on the Harbor, the Camaro just now tearing out the Cyclone fence on the Santa Monica. "Out there" is where incidents happen. The windowless room at 120 South Spring is where incidents get "verified." "Incident verification" is turning on the closed-circuit TV on the console and watching the traffic slow down to see (this is "the gawk effect") where the Camaro tore out the fence.

As a matter of fact there is a certain closed-circuit aspect to the entire mood of the Operations Center. "Verifying" the incident does not after all "prevent" the incident, which lends the enterprise a kind of tranced distance, and on the day recently when I visited 120 South Spring it took considerable effort to remember what I had come to talk about, which was that particular part of the Loop called the Santa Monica Freeway. The Santa Monica Freeway is 16.2 miles long, runs from the Pacific Ocean to downtown Los Angeles through what is referred to at Caltrans as "the East-West Corridor," carries more traffic every day than any other freeway in California, has what connoisseurs of freeways concede to be the most beautiful access ramps in the world, and appeared to have been transformed by Caltrans, during the several weeks before I went downtown to talk about it, into a 16.2-mile parking lot.

The problem seemed to be another Caltrans "demonstration," or "pilot," a foray into bureaucratic terrorism they were calling "The Diamond Lane" in their promotional literature and "The Project" among themselves. That the promotional literature consisted largely of schedules for buses (or "Diamond Lane Expresses") and invitations to join a car pool via computer ("Commuter Computer") made clear not only the putative point of The Project, which was to encourage travel by car pool and bus, but also the actual point, which was to eradicate a central Southern California illusion, that of individual mobility, without anyone really noticing. This had not exactly worked out. "FREEWAY FIASCO," the *Los Angeles Times* was headlining page-one stories. "THE DIAMOND LANE: ANOTHER BUST BY CALTRANS." "CALTRANS PILOT EFFORT ANOTHER IN LONG LIST OF FAILURES." "OFFICIAL DIAMOND LANE STANCE: LET THEM HOWL."

All "The Diamond Lane" theoretically involved was reserving the fast inside lanes on the Santa Monica for vehicles carrying three or more people, but in practice this meant that 25 per cent of the freeway was reserved for 3 per cent of the cars, and there were other odd wrinkles here and there suggesting that Caltrans had dedicated itself to making all movement around Los Angeles as arduous as possible. There was for example the matter of surface streets. A "surface street" is anything around

Los Angeles that is not a freeway ("going surface" from one part of town to another is generally regarded as idiosyncratic), and surface streets do not fall directly within the Caltrans domain, but now the engineer in charge of surface streets was accusing Caltrans of threatening and intimidating him. It appeared that Caltrans wanted him to create a "confused and congested situation" on his surface streets, so as to force drivers back to the freeway, where they would meet a still more confused and congested situation and decide to stay home, or take a bus. "We are beginning a process of deliberately making it harder for drivers to use freeways," a Caltrans director had in fact said at a transit conference some months before. "We are prepared to endure considerable public outcry in order to pry John Q. Public out of his car. . . . I would emphasize that this is a political decision, and one that can be reversed if the public gets sufficiently enraged to throw us rascals out."

Of course this political decision was in the name of the greater good, was in the interests of "environmental improvement" and "conservation of resources," but even there the figures had about them a certain Caltrans opacity. The Santa Monica normally carried 240,000 cars and trucks every day. These 240,000 cars and trucks normally carried 260,000 people. What Caltrans described as its ultimate goal on the Santa Monica was to carry the same 260,000 people, "but in 7,800 fewer, or 232,200 vehicles." The figure "232,200" had a visionary precision to it that did not automatically create confidence, especially since the only effect so far had been to disrupt traffic throughout the Los Angeles basin, triple the number of daily accidents on the Santa Monica, prompt the initiation of two lawsuits against Caltrans, and cause large numbers of Los Angeles County residents to behave, most uncharacteristically, as an ignited and conscious proletariat. Citizen guerrillas splashed paint and scattered nails in the Diamond Lanes. Diamond Lane maintenance crews expressed fear of hurled objects. Down at 120 South Spring the architects of the Diamond Lane had taken to regarding "the media" as the architects of their embarrassment, and Caltrans statements in the press had been cryptic and contradictory, reminiscent only of old communiqués out of Vietnam.

To understand what was going on it is perhaps necessary

to have participated in the freeway experience, which is the only secular communion Los Angeles has. Mere driving on the freeway is in no way the same as participating in it. Anyone can "drive" on the freeway, and many people with no vocation for it do, hesitating here and resisting there, losing the rhythm of the lane change, thinking about where they came from and where they are going. Actual participants think only about where they are. Actual participation requires a total surrender, a concentration so intense as to seem a kind of narcosis, a rapture-of-the-freeway. The mind goes clean. The rhythm takes over. A distortion of time occurs, the same distortion that characterizes the instant before an accident. It takes only a few seconds to get off the Santa Monica Freeway at National-Overland, which is a difficult exit requiring the driver to cross two new lanes of traffic streamed in from the San Diego Freeway, but those few seconds always seem to me the longest part of the trip. The moment is dangerous. The exhilaration is in doing it. "As you acquire the special skills involved," Reyner Banham observed in an extraordinary chapter about the freeways in his 1971 *Los Angeles: The Architecture of Four Ecologies*, "the freeways become a special way of being alive . . . the extreme concentration required in Los Angeles seems to bring on a state of heightened awareness that some locals find mystical."

Indeed some locals do, and some nonlocals too. Reducing the number of lone souls careering around the East-West Corridor in a state of mechanized rapture may or may not have seemed socially desirable, but what it was definitely not going to seem was easy. "We're only seeing an initial period of unfamiliarity," I was assured the day I visited Caltrans. I was talking to a woman named Eleanor Wood and she was thoroughly and professionally grounded in the diction of "planning" and it did not seem likely that I could interest her in considering the freeway as regional mystery. "Any time you try to rearrange people's daily habits, they're apt to react impetuously. All this project requires is a certain rearrangement of people's daily planning. That's really all we want."

It occurred to me that a certain rearrangement of people's daily planning might seem, in less rarefied air than is breathed at 120 South Spring, rather a great deal to want, but so impenetrable was the sense of higher social purpose there in the Operations Center that I did not express this reservation. Instead I changed the subject, mentioned an earlier "pilot project" on the Santa Monica: the big electronic message boards that Caltrans had installed a year or two before. The idea was that traffic information transmitted from the Santa Monica to the Xerox Sigma V could be translated, here in the Operations Center, into suggestions to the driver, and flashed right back out to the Santa Monica. This operation, in that it involved telling drivers electronically what they already knew empirically, had the rather spectral circularity that seemed to mark a great many Caltrans schemes, and I was interested in how Caltrans thought it worked.

"Actually the message boards were part of a larger pilot project," Mrs. Wood said. "An ongoing project in incident management. With the message boards we hoped to learn if motorists would modify their behavior according to what we told them on the boards."

I asked if the motorists had.

"Actually no," Mrs. Wood said finally. "They didn't react to the signs exactly as we'd hypothesized they would, no. *But.* If we'd *known* what the motorist would do . . . then we wouldn't have needed a pilot project in the first place, would we."

The circle seemed intact. Mrs. Wood and I smiled, and shook hands. I watched the big board until all lights turned green on the Santa Monica and then I left and drove home on it, all 16.2 miles of it. All the way I remembered that I was watched by the Xerox Sigma V. All the way the message boards gave me the number to call for CAR POOL INFO. As I left the freeway it occurred to me that they might have their own rapture down at 120 South Spring, and it could be called Perpetuating the Department. Today the California Highway Patrol reported that, during the first six weeks of the Diamond Lane, accidents on the Santa Monica, which normally range between 49 and 72 during a six-week period, totaled 204. Yesterday plans were announced to extend the Diamond Lane to other freeways at a cost of $42,500,000.

1976

Good Citizens

I WAS ONCE INVITED to a civil rights meeting at Sammy Davis, Jr.'s house, in the hills above the Sunset Strip. "Let me tell you how to get to Sammy's," said the woman to whom I was talking. "You turn left at the old Mocambo." I liked the ring of this line, summing up as it did a couple of generations of that peculiar vacant fervor which is Hollywood political action, but acquaintances to whom I repeated it seemed uneasy. Politics are not widely considered a legitimate source of amusement in Hollywood, where the borrowed rhetoric by which political ideas are reduced to choices between the good (equality is good) and the bad (genocide is bad) tends to make even the most casual political small talk resemble a rally. "Those who cannot remember the past are condemned to repeat it," someone said to me at dinner not long ago, and before we had finished our *fraises des bois* he had advised me as well that "no man is an island." As a matter of fact I hear that no man is an island once or twice a week, quite often from people who think they are quoting Ernest Hemingway. "What a sacrifice on the altar of nationalism," I heard an actor say about the death in a plane crash of the president of the Philippines. It is a way of talking that tends to preclude further discussion, which may well be its intention: the public life of liberal Hollywood comprises a kind of dictatorship of good intentions, a social contract in which actual and irreconcilable disagreement is as taboo as failure or bad teeth, a climate devoid of irony. "Those men are our unsung heroes," a quite charming and intelligent woman once said to me at a party in Beverly Hills. She was talking about the California State Legislature.

I remember spending an evening in 1968, a week or so before the California primary and Robert Kennedy's death, at Eugene's in Beverly Hills, one of the "clubs" opened by supporters of Eugene McCarthy. The Beverly Hills Eugene's, not unlike Senator McCarthy's campaign itself, had a certain *déjà vu* aspect to it, a glow of 1952 humanism: there were Ben Shahn posters on the walls, and the gesture toward a strobe light was nothing that might interfere with "good talk," and the music was not 1968 rock but the kind of jazz people used to have on their record players when everyone who believed in the Family of Man bought Scandinavian stainless-steel flatware and voted for Adlai Stevenson. There at Eugene's I heard the name "Erich Fromm" for the first time in a long time, and many other names cast out for the sympathetic magic they might work ("I saw the Senator in San Francisco, where I was with Mrs. Leonard Bernstein . . ."), and then the evening's main event: a debate between William Styron and the actor Ossie Davis. It was Mr. Davis' contention that in writing *The Confessions of Nat Turner* Mr. Styron had encouraged racism ("Nat Turner's love for a white maiden, I feel my country can become psychotic about this"), and it was Mr. Styron's contention that he had not. (David Wolper, who had bought the motion picture rights to *Nat Turner*, had already made his position clear: "How can anyone protest a book," he had asked in the trade press, "that has withstood the critical test of time since last October?") As the evening wore on, Mr. Styron said less and less, and Mr. Davis more and more ("So you might ask, why didn't *I* spend five years and write *Nat Turner?* I won't go into my reasons why, but . . ."), and James Baldwin sat between them, his eyes closed and his head thrown back in understandable but rather theatrical agony. Mr. Baldwin summed up: "If Bill's book does no more than what it's done tonight, it's a very important event." "Hear, hear," cried someone sitting on the floor, and there was general agreement that it had been a stimulating and significant evening.

Of course there was nothing crucial about that night at Eugene's in 1968, and of course you could tell me that there was certainly no harm and perhaps some good in it. But its curious vanity and irrelevance stay with me, if only because those qualities characterize so many of Hollywood's best intentions. Social problems present themselves to many of these people in terms of a scenario, in which, once certain key scenes are licked (the confrontation on the courthouse steps, the revelation that the opposition leader has an anti-Semitic past, the presentation of the bill of particulars to the President, a Henry Fonda cameo), the plot will proceed inexorably to an upbeat fade. Marlon Brando does not, in a well-plotted motion picture, picket San Quentin in vain: what we are talking about here is faith in a dramatic convention. Things "happen" in motion pictures. There is always a resolution, always a strong cause-effect dramatic line, and to perceive the world in those terms is to assume an ending for every social scenario. If Budd Schulberg goes into Watts and forms a Writers' Workshop, the "Twenty Young Writers" must emerge from it, because the scenario in question is the familiar one about how the ghetto teems with raw talent and vitality. If the poor people march on Washington and camp out, there to receive bundles of clothes gathered on the Fox lot by Barbra Streisand, then some good must come of it (the script here has a great many dramatic staples, not the least of them a sentimental notion of Washington as an open forum, *cf. Mr. Deeds Goes to Washington*), and doubts have no place in the story.

There are no bit players in Hollywood politics: everyone makes things "happen." As it happens I live in a house in Hollywood in which, during the late thirties and early fifties, a screenwriters' cell of the Communist Party often met. Some of the things that are in the house now were in it then: a vast Stalinist couch, the largest rag rug I have ever seen, cartons of *New Masses*. Some of the people who came to meetings in the house were blacklisted, some of them never worked again and some of them are now getting several hundred thousand dollars a picture; some of them are dead and some of them are bitter and most of them lead very private lives. Things did change, but in the end it was not they who made things change, and their enthusiasms and debates sometimes seem very close to me in this house. In a way the house suggests the particular vanity of perceiving social life as a problem to be solved by the good will of individuals, but I do not mention that to many of the people who visit me here.

2

Pretty Nancy Reagan, the wife then of the Governor of California, was standing in the dining room of her rented house on 45th Street in Sacramento, listening to a television newsman explain what he wanted to do. She was listening attentively. Nancy Reagan is a very attentive listener. The television crew wanted to watch her, the newsman said, while she was doing precisely what she would ordinarily be doing on a Tuesday morning at home. Since I was also there to watch her doing precisely what she would ordinarily be doing on a Tuesday morning at home, we seemed to be on the verge of exploring certain media frontiers: the television newsman and the two cameramen could watch Nancy Reagan being watched by me, or I could watch Nancy Reagan being watched by the three of them, or one of the cameramen could step back and do a *cinéma vérité* study of the rest of us watching and being watched by one another. I had the distinct sense that we were on the track of something revelatory, the truth about Nancy Reagan at 24 frames a second, but the television newsman opted to overlook the moment's peculiar essence. He suggested that we watch Nancy Reagan pick flowers in the garden. "That's something you might ordinarily do, isn't it?" he asked. "Indeed it is," Nancy Reagan said with spirit. Nancy Reagan says almost everything with spirit, perhaps because she was once an actress and has the beginning actress's habit of investing even the most casual lines with a good deal more dramatic emphasis than is ordinarily called for on a Tuesday morning on 45th Street in Sacramento. "Actually," she added then, as if about to disclose a delightful surprise, "actually, I really *do* need flowers."

She smiled at each of us, and each of us smiled back. We had all been smiling quite a bit that morning. "And then," the television newsman said thoughtfully, surveying the dining-room table, "even though you've got a beautiful arrangement right now, we could set up the pretense of your arranging, you know, the flowers."

We all smiled at one another again, and then Nancy Reagan walked resolutely into the garden, equipped with a decorative straw basket about six inches in diameter. "Uh, Mrs. Reagan," the newsman called after her. "May I ask what you're going to select for flowers?"

"Why, I don't know," she said, pausing with her basket on a garden step. The scene was evolving its own choreography.

"Do you think you could use rhododendrons?"

Nancy Reagan looked critically at a rhododendron bush. Then she turned to the newsman and smiled. "Did you know there's a Nancy Reagan rose now?"

"Uh, no," he said. "I didn't."

"It's awfully pretty, it's a kind of, of, a kind of coral color."

"Would the . . . the Nancy Reagan rose be something you might be likely to pick now?"

A silvery peal of laughter. "I could certainly *pick* it. But I won't be *using* it." A pause. "I *can* use the rhododendron."

"Fine," the newsman said. "Just fine. Now I'll ask a question, and if you could just be nipping a bud as you answer it . . ."

"Nipping a bud," Nancy Reagan repeated, taking her place in front of the rhododendron bush.

"Let's have a dry run," the cameraman said.

The newsman looked at him. "In other words, by a dry run, you mean you want her to fake nipping the bud."

"Fake the nip, yeah," the cameraman said. "Fake the nip."

3

Outside the Miramar Hotel in Santa Monica a hard subtropical rain had been falling for days. It scaled still more paint from the faded hotels and rooming houses that front the Pacific along Ocean Avenue. It streamed down the blank windows of unleased offices, loosened the soft coastal cliffs and heightened the most characteristic Santa Monica effect, that air of dispirited abandon which suggests that the place survives only as illustration of a boom gone bankrupt, evidence of some irreversible flaw in the laissez-faire small-business ethic. In any imaginative sense Santa Monica seemed an eccentric place for the United States Junior Chamber of Commerce to be holding a national congress, but there they were, a thousand delegates and wives, gathered in the Miramar Hotel for a relentless succession of keynote banquets and award luncheons and prayer breakfasts and outstanding-young-men forums. Now it was the President's Luncheon and everyone was listening to an animated singing group called The New Generation and I was watching the pretty young wife of one delegate pick sullenly at her lunch. "Let someone else eat this slop," she said suddenly, her voice cutting through not only the high generalities of the occasion but The New Generation's George M. Cohan medley as well. Her husband looked away, and she repeated it. To my left another delegate was urging me to ask every man in the room how the Jaycees had changed his life. I watched the girl down the table and asked the delegate how the Jaycees had changed his life. "It saved my marriage and it built my business," he whispered. "You could find a thousand inspirational stories right here at this President's Luncheon." Down the table the young wife was sobbing into a pink napkin. The New Generation marched into "Supercalifragilisticexpialidocious." In many ways the Jaycees' 32nd Annual Congress of America's Ten Outstanding Young Men was a curious and troubling way to spend a few days in the opening weeks of 1970.

I suppose I went to Santa Monica in search of the abstraction lately called "Middle America," went to find out how the Jaycees, with their Couéistic emphasis on improving one's world and one's self simultaneously, had weathered these past several years of cultural shock. In a very real way the Jaycees have exemplified, usually so ingenuously that it was popular to deride them, certain ideas shared by almost all of the people in America's small cities and towns and by at least some of the people in America's large cities, ideas shared in an unexamined way even by those who laughed at the Jaycees' boosterism and pancake breakfasts and safe-driving Road-e-os. There was the belief in business success as a transcendent ideal. There was the faith that if one transforms oneself from an "introvert" into an "extrovert," if one learns to "speak effectively" and "do a job," success and its concomitant, spiritual grace, follow naturally. There was the approach to international problems which construed the underdeveloped world as a temporarily depressed area in need mainly of People-to-People programs. ("Word of Operation Brotherhood swept through the teeming masses of Asia like a fresh wind from the sea," reads a Jaycee report on one such program in the late Fifties.) If only because these ideas, these last rattles of Social Darwinism, had in fact been held in common by a great many people who never bothered to articulate them, I wondered what the Jaycees were thinking now, wondered what their mood might be at a time when, as their national president put it one day at the Miramar, "so much of America seems to be looking at the negative."

At first I thought I had walked out of the rain into a time warp: the Sixties seemed not to have happened. All these Jaycees were, by definition, between 21 and 35 years old, but there was a disquieting tendency among them to have settled foursquare into middle age. There was the heavy jocularity, the baroque rhetoric of another generation entirely, a kind of poignant attempt to circumnavigate social conventions that had in fact broken down in the Twenties. Wives were lovely and forbearing. Getting together for drinks was having a cocktail reception. Rain was liquid sunshine and the choice of a table for dinner was making an executive decision. They knew that this was a brave new world and they said so. It was time to "put brotherhood into action," to "open our neighborhoods to those of all colors." It was time to "turn attention to the cities," to think about youth centers and clinics and the example set by a black policeman-preacher in Philadelphia who was organizing a decency rally patterned after Miami's. It was time to "decry apathy."

The word "apathy" cropped up again and again, an odd word to use in relation to the past few years, and it was a while before I realized what it meant. It was not simply a word remembered from the Fifties, when most of these men had frozen their vocabularies: it was a word meant to indicate that not enough of "our kind" were speaking out. It was a cry in the wilderness, and this resolute determination to meet 1950 head-on was a kind of refuge. Here were some people who had been led to believe that the future was always a rational extension of the past, that there would ever be world enough and time for "turning attention," for "problems" and "solutions." Of course they would not admit their inchoate fears that the world was not that way any more. Of course they would not join the "fashionable doubters." Of course they would ignore the "pessimistic pundits." Late one afternoon I sat in the Miramar lobby, watching the rain fall and the steam rise off the heated pool outside and listening to a couple of Jaycees discussing student unrest and whether the "solution" might not lie in on-campus Jaycee groups. I thought about this astonishing notion for a long time. It occurred to me finally that I was listening to a true underground, to the voice of all those who have felt themselves not merely shocked but personally betrayed by recent history. It was supposed to have been their time. It was not.

1968–1970

Notes Toward a Dreampolitik

ELDER ROBERT J. THEOBOLD, pastor of what was until October 12, 1968, the Friendly Bible Apostolic Church in Port Hueneme, California, is twenty-eight years old, born and bred in San Jose, a native Californian whose memory stream could encompass only the boom years; in other words a young man who until October 12, 1968, had lived his entire life in the nerve center of the most elaborately technological and media-oriented society in the United States, and so the world. His looks and to some extent his background are indistinguishable from those of a legion of computer operators and avionics technicians. Yet this is a young man who has remained immaculate of the constant messages with which a technological society bombards itself, for at the age of sixteen he was saved, received the Holy Spirit in a Pentecostal church. Brother Theobold, as the eighty-some members of his congregation call him, now gets messages only from the Lord, "forcible impressions" instructing him, for example, to leave San Jose and start a church in Port Hueneme, or, more recently, to lead his congregation on the 12th of October, 1968, from Port Hueneme to Murfreesboro, Tennessee, in order to avoid destruction by earthquake.

"We're leaving the 12th but I don't have any message that it's going to happen before the end of 1968," Brother Theobold told me one morning a few weeks before he and his congregation piled their belongings into campers and cars and left California for Tennessee. He was minding the children that morning, and his two-year-old walked around sucking on a plastic bottle while Brother Theobold talked to me and fingered the pages of a tooled-leather Bible. "This one minister I heard, he definitely said it would happen before the end of 1970, but as far as I'm concerned, the Lord has shown me that it's definitely coming but he hasn't shown me *when*."

I mentioned to Brother Theobold that most seismologists were predicting an imminent major earthquake on the San Andreas Fault, but he did not seem unduly interested: Brother Theobold's perception of the apocalypse neither began with nor depended upon the empirical. In a way the Pentecostal mind reveals itself most clearly in something like Brother Theobold's earthquake prophecy. Neither he nor the members of his congregation to whom I talked had ever been particularly concerned by reports in the newspapers that an earthquake was overdue. "Of course we'd *heard* of earthquakes," a soft-voiced woman named Sister Mosley told me. "Because the Bible mentions there'll be more and more toward the end of time." Nor was there any need to think twice about pulling up stakes and joining a caravan to a small town few of them had ever seen. I kept asking Brother Theobold how he had chosen Murfreesboro, and over and over he tried to tell me: he had "received a telephone call from a man there" or "God had directed this particular man to call on this particular day." The man did not seem to have made a direct entreaty to Brother Theobold to bring his flock to Tennessee, but there had been no question in Brother Theobold's mind that God's intention was exactly that. "From the natural point of view I didn't care to go to Murfreesboro at all," he said. "We just bought this place, it's the nicest place we ever had. But I put it up to the Lord, and the Lord said *put it up for sale*. Care for a Dr. Pepper?"

We might have been talking in different languages, Brother Theobold and I; it was as if I knew all the words but lacked the grammar, and so kept questioning him on points that seemed to him ineluctably clear. He seemed to be one of those people, so many of whom gravitate to Pentecostal sects, who move around the West and the South and the Border States forever felling trees in some interior wilderness, secret frontiersmen who walk around right in the ganglia of the fantastic electronic pulsing that is life in the United States and continue to receive information only through the most tenuous chains of rumor, hearsay, haphazard trickledown. In the social conventions by which we now live there is no category for people like Brother Theobold and his congregation, most of whom are young and white and nominally literate; they are neither the possessors nor the dispossessed. They participate in the national anxieties only through a glass darkly. They teach their daughters to eschew makeup and to cover their knees, and they believe in divine healing, and in speaking in tongues. Other people leave towns like Murfreesboro, and they move into them.

To an astonishing extent they keep themselves unviolated by common knowledge, by the ability to make routine assumptions; when Brother Theobold first visited Murfreesboro he was dumbfounded to learn that the courthouse there had been standing since the Civil War. "The *same building*," he repeated twice, and then he got out a snapshot as corroboration. In the interior wilderness no one is bloodied by history, and it is no coincidence that the Pentecostal churches have their strongest hold in places where Western civilization has its most superficial hold. There are more than twice as many Pentecostal as Episcopal churches in Los Angeles.

2

The scene is quite near the end of Roger Corman's 1966 *The Wild Angels*, which was the first and in many ways the classic exploitation bike movie. Here it is: the Angels, led by Peter Fonda, are about to bury one of their number. They have already torn up the chapel, beaten and gagged the preacher, and held a wake, during which the dead man's girl was raped on the altar and the corpse itself, propped up on a bench in full biker colors, dark goggles over the eyes and a marijuana cigarette between the lips, was made an object of necrophilia. Now they stand at the grave, and, uncertain how to mark the moment, Peter Fonda shrugs. "Nothing to say," he says.

What we have here is an obligatory bike-movie moment, the outlaw-hero embracing man's fate: I tell you about it only to suggest the particular mood of these pictures. Many of them are extraordinarily beautiful in their instinct for the real look of the American West, for the faded banners fluttering over abandoned gas stations and for the bleached streets of desert towns. These are the movies known to the trade as "programmers," and very few adults have ever seen one. Most of them are made for less than $200,000. They are shown in New York only occasionally. Yet for several years bike movies have constituted a kind of underground folk literature for adolescents, have located an audience and fabricated a myth to exactly express that audience's every inchoate resentment, every yearning for the extreme exhilaration of death. To die violently is "righteous," a flash. To keep on living, as Peter Fonda points out in *The Wild Angels*, is just to keep on paying rent. A successful bike movie is a perfect Rorschach of its audience.

I saw nine of them recently, saw the first one almost by accident and the rest of them with a notebook. I saw *Hell's Angels on Wheels* and *Hell's Angels '69*. I saw *Run Angel Run* and *The Glory Stompers* and *The Losers*. I saw *The Wild Angels*, I saw *Violent Angels*, I saw *The Savage Seven* and I saw *The Cycle Savages*. I was not even sure why I kept going. To have seen one bike movie is to have seen them all, so meticulously observed are the rituals of getting the bikers out of town and onto the highway, of "making a run," of terrorizing the innocent "citizens" and fencing with the Highway Patrol and, finally, meeting death in a blaze, usually quite a literal blaze, of romantic fatalism. There is always that instant in which the outlaw leader stands revealed as existential hero. There is always that "perverse" sequence in which the bikers batter at some psychic sound barrier, degrade the widow, violate the virgin, defile the rose and the cross alike, break on through to the other side and find, once there, "nothing to say." The brutal images glaze the eye. The senseless insouciance of all the characters in a world of routine stompings and casual death takes on a logic better left unplumbed.

I suppose I kept going to these movies because there on the screen was some news I was getting from *The New York Times*. I began to think I was seeing ideograms of the future. To watch a bike movie is finally to apprehend the extent to which the toleration of small irritations is no longer a trait much admired in America, the extent to which a nonexistent frustration threshold is seen not as psychopathic but as a "right." A biker is goaded on the job about the swastika on his jacket, so he picks up a wrench, threatens the foreman, and later describes the situation as one in which the foreman "got uptight." A biker runs an old man off the road: the old man was "in the way," and his subsequent death is construed as further "hassling." A nurse happens into a hospital room where a biker beats her unconscious and rapes her: that she later talks to the police is made to seem a betrayal, evidence only of some female hysteria, vindictiveness, sexual deprivation. Any girl who "acts dumb" deserves what she gets, and what she gets is beaten and turned out for the group. Anything less than instant service in a restaurant constitutes intolerable provocation, or "hassling": tear the place apart, leave the owner for dead, gangbang the waitress. Rev up the Harleys and ride.

To imagine the audience for whom these sentiments are tailored, maybe you need to have sat in a lot of drive-ins yourself, to have gone to school with boys who majored in shop and worked in gas stations and later held them up. Bike movies are made for all these children of vague "hill" stock who grow up absurd in the West and Southwest, children whose whole lives are an obscure grudge against a world they think they never made. These children are, increasingly, everywhere, and their style is that of an entire generation.

3

Palms, California, is a part of Los Angeles through which many people drive on their way from 20th Century-Fox to Metro-Goldwyn-Mayer, and vice versa. It is an area largely unnoticed by those who drive through it, an invisible prairie of stucco bungalows and two-story "units," and I mention it at all only because it is in Palms that a young woman named Dallas Beardsley lives. Dallas Beardsley has spent all of her twenty-two years on this invisible underside of the Los Angeles fabric, living with her mother in places like Palms and Inglewood and Westchester: she went to Airport Junior High School, out near Los Angeles International Airport, and to Westchester High School, where she did not go out with boys but did try out for cheerleader. She remembers not being chosen cheerleader as her "biggest discouragement." After that she decided to become an actress, and one morning in October of 1968 she bought the fifth page of *Daily Variety* for an advertisement which read in part: "There is no one like me in the world. I'm going to be a movie star."

It seemed an anachronistic ambition, wanting to be a movie star; girls were not supposed to want that in 1968. They were supposed to want only to perfect their *karma*, to give and get what were called good vibrations and to renounce personal ambition as an ego game. They were supposed to know that wanting things leads in general to grief, and that wanting to be a movie star leads in particular to U.C.L.A. Neuropsychiatric. Such are our conventions. But here was Dallas Beardsley, telling the world what she wanted for $50 down and $35 a month on an eight-month contract with *Variety. I'm going to be a movie star.*

I called Dallas, and one hot afternoon we drove around the Hollywood hills and talked. Dallas had long blond hair and a sundress and she was concerned about a run in her stocking and she did not hesitate when I asked what it meant to be a movie star. "It means being known all over the world," she said. "And bringing my family a bunch of presents on Christmas Day, you know, like carloads, and putting them by the tree. And it means happiness, and living by the ocean in a huge house." She paused. "But being *known*. It's important to me to be *known*." That morning she had seen an agent, and she was pleased because he had said that his decision not to handle her was "nothing personal." "The big agents are nice," she said. "They answer letters, they return your calls. It's the little ones who're nasty. But I understand, I really do." Dallas believes that all people, even agents, are "basically good inside," and that "when they hurt you, it's because they've been hurt themselves, and anyway maybe God means for you to be hurt, so some beautiful thing can happen later." Dallas attends the Unity Church in Culver City, the general thrust of which is that everything works out for the best, and she described herself as "pretty religious" and "politically less on the liberal side than most actors."

Her dedication to the future is undiluted. The jobs she takes to support herself—she has been a Kelly Girl, and worked in restaurants—do not intrude upon her ambitions. She does not go out to parties or on dates. "I work till six-thirty, then I have a dance lesson, then I rehearse at the workshop—when would I have time? Anyway I'm not interested in that." As I drove home that day through the somnolent back streets of Hollywood I had the distinct sense that everyone I knew had some fever which had not yet infected the invisible city. In the invisible city girls were still disappointed at not being chosen cheerleader. In the invisible city girls still got discovered at Schwab's and later met their true loves at the Mocambo or the Troc, still dreamed of big houses by the ocean and carloads of presents by the Christmas tree, still prayed to be known.

4

Another part of the invisible city.

"Speaking for myself," the young woman said, "in this seven months since I been on the program it's been real good. I was strictly a Gardena player, low-ball. I'd play in the nighttime after I got my children to bed, and of course I never got home before five A.M., and my problem was, I couldn't sleep then, I'd replay every hand, so the next day I'd be, you know, tired. Irritable. With the children."

Her tone was that of someone who had adapted her mode of public address from analgesic commercials, but she was not exactly selling a product. She was making a "confession" at a meeting of Gamblers Anonymous: nine o'clock on a winter evening in a neighborhood clubhouse in Gardena, California. Gardena is the draw-poker capital of Los Angeles County (no stud, no alcoholic beverages, clubs closed between five A.M. and nine A.M. and all day on Christmas Day), and the proximity of the poker clubs hung over this meeting like a paraphysical substance, almost as palpable as the American flag, the portraits of Washington and Lincoln, and the table laid by the Refreshments Committee. There it was, just around the corner, the action, and here in this overheated room were forty people, shifting uneasily on folding chairs and blinking against the cigarette smoke, who craved it. "I never made this Gardena meeting before," one of them said, "for one simple reason only, which is I break out in a cold sweat every time I pass Gardena on the freeway even, but I'm here tonight because every night I make a meeting is a night I don't place a bet, which with the help of God and you people is 1,223 nights now." Another: "I started out for a Canoga Park meeting and turned around on the freeway, that was last Wednesday, I ended up in Gardena and now I'm on the verge of divorce again." And a third: "I didn't lose no fortune, but I lost all the money I could get my hands on, it began in the Marine Corps, I met a lot of pigeons in Vietnam, I was making easy money and it was, you might say, this period in my life that, uh, led to my downfall." This last speaker was a young man who said that he had done OK in mechanical drawing at Van Nuys High School. He wore his hair in a sharp 1951 ducktail. He was, like Dallas Beardsley, twenty-two years old. Tell me the name of the elected representative from the invisible city.

1968–1970

III

WOMEN

The Women's Movement

TO MAKE AN OMELETTE you need not only those broken eggs but someone "oppressed" to break them: every revolutionist is presumed to understand that, and also every woman, which either does or does not make fifty-one per cent of the population of the United States a potentially revolutionary class. The creation of this revolutionary "class" was from the virtual beginning the "idea" of the women's movement, and the tendency for popular discussion of the movement to center for so long around day-care centers is yet another instance of that studied resistance to political ideas which characterizes our national life.

"The new feminism is not just the revival of a serious political movement for social equality," the feminist theorist Shulamith Firestone announced flatly in 1970. "It is the second wave of the most important revolution in history." This was scarcely a statement of purpose anyone could find cryptic, and it was scarcely the only statement of its kind in the literature of the movement. Nonetheless, in 1972, in a "special issue" on women, *Time* was still musing genially that the movement might well succeed in bringing about "fewer diapers and more Dante."

That was a very pretty image, the idle ladies sitting in the gazebo and murmuring *lasciate ogni speranza*, but it depended entirely upon the popular view of the movement as some kind of collective inchoate yearning for "fulfillment," or "self-expression," a yearning absolutely devoid of ideas and capable of engendering only the most *pro forma* benevolent interest. In fact there was an idea, and the idea was Marxist, and it was precisely to the extent that there was this Marxist idea that the curious historical anomaly known as the women's movement would have seemed to have any interest at all. Marxism in this country had ever been an eccentric and quixotic passion. One oppressed class after another had seemed finally to miss the point. The have-nots, it turned out, aspired mainly to having. The minorities seemed to promise more, but finally disappointed: it developed that they actually cared about the issues, that they tended to see the integration of the luncheonette and the seat in the front of the bus as real goals, and only rarely as ploys, counters in a larger game. They resisted that essential inductive leap from the immediate reform to the social ideal, and, just as disappointingly, they failed to perceive their common cause with other minorities, continued to exhibit a self-interest disconcerting in the extreme to organizers steeped in the rhetoric of "brotherhood."

And then, at that exact dispirited moment when there seemed no one at all willing to play the proletariat, along came the women's movement, and the invention of women as a "class." One could not help admiring the radical simplicity of this instant transfiguration. The notion that, in the absence of a cooperative proletariat, a revolutionary class might simply be invented, made up, "named" and so brought into existence, seemed at once so pragmatic and so visionary, so precisely Emersonian, that it took the breath away, exactly confirmed one's idea of where nineteenth-century transcendental instincts, crossed with a late reading of Engels and Marx, might lead. To read the theorists of the women's movement was to think not of Mary Wollstonecraft but of Margaret Fuller at her most high-minded, of rushing position papers off to mimeo and drinking tea from paper cups in lieu of eating lunch; of thin raincoats on bitter nights. If the family was the last fortress of capitalism, then let us abolish the family. If the necessity for conventional reproduction of the species seemed unfair to women, then let us transcend, via technology, "the very organization of nature," the oppression, as Shulamith Firestone saw it, "that goes back through recorded history to the animal kingdom itself." *I accept the universe*, Margaret Fuller had finally allowed: Shulamith Firestone did not.

It seemed very New England, this febrile and cerebral passion. The solemn *a priori* idealism in the guise of radical materialism somehow bespoke old-fashioned self-reliance and prudent sacrifice. The clumsy torrent of words became a principle, a renunciation of style as unserious. The rhetorical willingness to break eggs became, in practice, only a thrifty capacity for finding the sermon in every stone. Burn the literature, Ti-Grace Atkinson said in effect when it was suggested that, even come the revolution, there would still remain the whole body of "sexist" Western literature. But of course no books would be burned: the women of this movement were perfectly capable of crafting didactic revisions of whatever apparently intractable material came to hand. "As a parent you should become an interpreter of myths," advised Letty Cottin Pogrebin in the preview issue of *Ms.* "Portions of any fairy tale or children's story can be salvaged during a critique session with your child." Other literary analysts devised ways to salvage other books: Isabel Archer in *The Portrait of a Lady* need no longer be the victim of her own idealism. She could be, instead, the victim of a sexist society, a woman who had "internalized the conventional definition of wife." The narrator of Mary McCarthy's *The Company She Keeps* could be seen as "enslaved because she persists in looking for her identity in a man." Similarly, Miss McCarthy's *The Group* could serve to illustrate "what happens to women who have been educated at first-rate women's colleges—taught philosophy and history—and then are consigned to breast-feeding and gourmet cooking."

The idea that fiction has certain irreducible ambiguities seemed never to occur to these women, nor should it have, for fiction is in most ways hostile to ideology. They had invented a class; now they had only to make that class conscious. They seized as a political technique a kind of shared testimony at first called a "rap session," then called "consciousness-raising," and in any case a therapeutically oriented American reinterpretation, according to the British feminist Juliet Mitchell, of a Chinese revolutionary practice known as "speaking bitterness." They purged and regrouped and purged again, worried out one another's errors and deviations, the "elitism" here, the "careerism" there. It would have been merely sententious to call some of their thinking Stalinist: of course it was. It would have been pointless even to speak of whether one considered these women "right" or "wrong," meaningless to dwell upon the obvious, upon the coarsening of moral imagination to which such social idealism so often leads. To believe in "the greater good" is to operate, necessarily, in a certain ethical suspension. Ask anyone committed to Marxist analysis how many angels on the head of a pin, and you will be asked in return to never mind the angels, tell me who controls the production of pins.

To those of us who remain committed mainly to the exploration of moral distinctions and ambiguities, the feminist analysis may have seemed a particularly narrow and cracked determinism. Nonetheless it was serious, and for these high-strung idealists to find themselves out of the mimeo room and onto the Cavett show must have been in certain ways more unsettling to them than it ever was to the viewers. They were being heard, and yet not really. Attention was finally being paid, and yet that attention was mired in the trivial. Even the brightest movement women found themselves engaged in sullen public colloquies about the inequities of dishwashing and the intolerable humiliations of being observed by construction workers on Sixth Avenue. (This grievance was not atypic in that discussion of it seemed always to take on unexplored Ms. Scarlett overtones, suggestions of fragile cultivated flowers being "spoken to," and therefore violated, by uppity proles.) They totted up the pans scoured, the towels picked off the bathroom floor, the loads of laundry done in a lifetime. Cooking a meal could only be "dogwork," and to claim any pleasure from it was evidence of craven acquiescence in one's own forced labor. Small children could only be odious mechanisms for the spilling and digesting of food, for robbing women of their "freedom." It was a long way from Simone de Beauvoir's grave and awesome recognition of woman's role as "the Other" to the notion that the first step in changing that role was Alix Kates Shulman's marriage contract ("wife strips beds, husband remakes them"), a document reproduced in *Ms.*, but it was toward just such trivialization that the women's movement seemed to be heading.

Of course this litany of trivia was crucial to the movement in the beginning, a key technique in the politicizing of women who had perhaps been conditioned to obscure their resentments even from themselves. Mrs. Shulman's discovery that she had less time than her husband seemed to have was precisely the kind of chord the movement had hoped to strike in all women (the "click! of recognition," as Jane O'Reilly described it), but such discoveries could be of no use at all if one refused to perceive the larger point, failed to make that inductive leap from the personal to the political. Splitting up the week into hours during which the children were directed to address their "personal questions" to either one parent or another might or might not have improved the quality of Mr. and Mrs. Shulman's marriage, but the improvement of marriages would not a revolution make. It could be very useful to call housework, as Lenin did, "the most unproductive, the most barbarous and the most arduous work a woman can do," but it could be useful only as the first step in a political process, only in the "awakening" of a class to its position, useful only as a metaphor: to believe, during the late Sixties and early Seventies in the United States of America, that the words had literal meaning was not only to stall the movement in the personal but to seriously delude oneself.

More and more, as the literature of the movement began to reflect the thinking of women who did not really understand the movement's ideological base, one had the sense of this stall, this delusion, the sense that the drilling of the theorists had struck only some psychic hardpan dense with superstitions and little sophistries, wish fulfillment, self-loathing and bitter fancies. To read even desultorily in this literature was to recognize instantly a certain dolorous phantasm, an imagined Everywoman with whom the authors seemed to identify all too entirely. This ubiquitous construct was everyone's victim but her own. She was persecuted even by her gynecologist, who made her beg in vain for contraceptives. She particularly needed contraceptives because she was raped on every date, raped by her husband, and raped finally on the abortionist's table. During the fashion for shoes with pointed toes, she, like "many women," had her toes amputated. She was so intimidated by cosmetics advertising that she would sleep "huge portions" of her day in order to forestall wrinkling, and when awake she was enslaved by detergent commercials on television. She sent her child to a nursery school where the little girls huddled in a "doll corner," and were forcibly restrained from playing with building blocks. Should she work she was paid "three to ten times less" than an (always) unqualified man holding the same job, was prevented from attending business lunches because she would be "embarrassed" to appear in public with a man not her husband, and, when she traveled alone, faced a choice between humiliation in a restaurant and "eating a doughnut" in her hotel room.

The half-truths, repeated, authenticated themselves. The

bitter fancies assumed their own logic. To ask the obvious —why she did not get herself another gynecologist, another job, why she did not get out of bed and turn off the television set, or why, the most eccentric detail, she stayed in hotels where only doughnuts could be obtained from room service —was to join this argument at its own spooky level, a level which had only the most tenuous and unfortunate relationship to the actual condition of being a woman. That many women are victims of condescension and exploitation and sex-role stereotyping was scarcely news, but neither was it news that other women are not: nobody forces women to buy the package.

But of course something other than an objection to being "discriminated against" was at work here, something other than an aversion to being "stereotyped" in one's sex role. Increasingly it seemed that the aversion was to adult sexual life itself: how much cleaner to stay forever children. One is constantly struck, in the accounts of lesbian relationships which appear from time to time in movement literature, by the emphasis on the superior "tenderness" of the relationship, the "gentleness" of the sexual connection, as if the participants were wounded birds. The derogation of assertiveness as "machismo" has achieved such currency that one imagines several million women too delicate to deal at any level with an overtly heterosexual man. Just as one had gotten the unintended but inescapable suggestion, when told about the "terror and revulsion" experienced by women in the vicinity of construction sites, of creatures too "tender" for the abrasiveness of daily life, too fragile for the streets, so now one was getting, in the later literature of the movement, the impression of women too "sensitive" for the difficulties of adult life, women unequipped for reality and grasping at the movement as a rationale for denying that reality. The transient stab of dread and loss which accompanies menstruation simply never happens: we only thought it happened, because a male-chauvinist psychiatrist told us so. No woman need have bad dreams after an abortion: she has only been told she should. The power of sex is just an oppressive myth, no longer to be feared, because what the sexual connection really amounts to, we learn in one woman's account of a postmarital affair presented as liberated and liberating, is "wisecracking and laughing" and "lying together and then leaping up to play and sing the entire *Sesame Street Songbook*." All one's actual apprehension of what it is like to be a woman, the irreconcilable difference of it—that sense of living one's deepest life underwater, that dark involvement with blood and birth and death—could now be declared invalid, unnecessary, *one never felt it at all.*

One was only told it, and now one is to be reprogrammed, fixed up, rendered again as inviolate and unstained as the "modern" little girls in the Tampax advertisements. More and more we have been hearing the wishful voices of just such perpetual adolescents, the voices of women scarred not by their class position as women but by the failure of their childhood expectations and misapprehensions. "Nobody ever so much as mentioned" to Susan Edmiston "that when you say 'I do,' what you are doing is not, as you thought, vowing your eternal love, but rather subscribing to a whole system of rights, obligations and responsibilities that may well be anathema to your most cherished beliefs." To Ellen Peck "the birth of children too often means the dissolution of romance, the loss of freedom, the abandonment of ideals to economics." A young woman described on the cover of *New York* as "The Suburban Housewife Who Bought the Promises of Women's Lib and Came to the City to Live Them" tells us what promises she bought: "The chance to respond to the bright lights and civilization of the Big Apple, yes. The chance to compete, yes. But most of all, the chance to have some fun. Fun is what's been missing."

Eternal love, romance, fun. The Big Apple. These are relatively rare expectations in the arrangements of consenting adults, although not in those of children, and it wrenches the heart to read about these women in their brave new lives. An ex-wife and mother of three speaks of her plan to "play out my college girl's dream. I am going to New York to become this famous writer. Or this working writer. Failing that, I will get a job in publishing." She mentions a friend, another young woman who "had never had any other life than as a daughter or wife or mother" but who is "just discovering herself to be a gifted potter." The childlike resourcefulness—to get a job in publishing, to become a gifted potter!—bewilders the imagination. The astral discontent with actual lives, actual men, the denial of the real generative possibilities of adult sexual life, somehow touches beyond words. "It is the right of the oppressed to organize around their oppression *as they see and define it*," the movement theorists insist doggedly in an effort to solve the question of these women, to convince themselves that what is going on is still a political process, but the handwriting is already on the wall. These are converts who want not a revolution but "romance," who believe not in the oppression of women but in their own chances for a new life in exactly the mold of their old life. In certain ways they tell us sadder things about what the culture has done to them than the theorists ever did, and they also tell us, I suspect, that the movement is no longer a cause but a symptom.

1972

Doris Lessing

TO READ A GREAT deal of Doris Lessing over a short span of time is to feel that the original hound of heaven has commandeered the attic. She holds the mind's other guests in ardent contempt. She appears for meals only to dismiss as decadent the household's own preoccupations with writing well. For more than twenty years now she has been registering, in a torrent of fiction that increasingly seems conceived in a stubborn rage against the very idea of fiction, every tremor along her emotional fault system, every slippage in her self-education. *Look here*, she is forever demanding, a missionary devoid of any but the most didactic irony: *The Communist Party is not the answer. There is a life beyond vaginal orgasm. St. John of the Cross was not as dotty as certain Anglicans would have had you believe.* She comes hard to ideas, and, once she has collared one, worries it with Victorian doggedness.

That she is a writer of considerable native power, a "natural" writer in the Dreiserian mold, someone who can close her eyes and "give" a situation by the sheer force of her emotional energy, seems almost a stain on her conscience. She views her real gift for fiction much as she views her own biology, as another trick to entrap her. She does not want to "write well." Her leaden disregard for even the simplest rhythms of language, her arrogantly bad ear for dialogue—all of that is beside her own point. More and more, Mrs. Lessing writes exclusively in the service of immediate cosmic reform: she wants to write, as the writer Anna in *The Golden Notebook* wanted to write, only to "create a new way of looking at life."

Consider *Briefing for a Descent into Hell.* Here Mrs. Lessing gave us a novel exclusively of "ideas," not a novel about the play of ideas in the lives of certain characters but a novel in which the characters exist only as markers in the presentation of an idea. The situation in the novel was this: a well-dressed but disheveled man is found wandering, an amnesiac, on the embankment near the Waterloo Bridge in London. He is taken by the police to a psychiatric hospital where, in the face of total indifference on his part, attempts are made to identify him. He is Charles Watkins, a professor of classics at Cambridge. An authority in his field, an occasional lecturer on more general topics. Lately a stammerer. Lately prone to bad evenings during which he condemns not only his own but all academic disciplines as "pigswill." A fifty-year-old man who finally cracked, and in cracking personified Mrs. Lessing's conviction that "the millions who have cracked" were "making cracks where the light could shine through at last." For of course the "nonsense" that Charles Watkins talks in the hospital makes, to the reader although not to the doctors, unmistakable "sense."

So pronounced was Charles Watkins' acumen about the inner reality of those around him that much of the time *Briefing for a Descent into Hell* read like a selective case study from an R. D. Laing book. The reality Charles Watkins describes is familiar to anyone who has ever had a high fever, or been exhausted to the point of breaking, or is just on the whole only marginally engaged in the dailiness of life. He experiences the loss of ego, the apprehension of the cellular nature of all matter, the "oneness" of things that seems always to lie just past the edge of controlled conscious thought. He hallucinates, or "remembers," the nature of the universe. He "remembers"—or is on the verge of remembering, before electroshock obliterates the memory and returns him to "sanity"—something very like a "briefing" for life on earth.

The details of this briefing were filled in by Mrs. Lessing, only too relieved to abandon the strain of creating character and slip into her own rather more exhortative voice. Imagine an interplanetary conference, convened on Venus to discuss once again the problem of the self-destructive planet Earth. (The fancy that extraterrestrial life is by definition of a higher order than our own is one that soothes all children, and many writers.) The procedure is this: certain superior beings descend to Earth brainprinted with the task of arousing the planet to its folly. These emissaries have, once on Earth, no memory of their more enlightened life. They wake slowly to their mission. They recognize one another only vaguely, and do not remember why. We are to understand, of course, that Charles Watkins is among those who have made the Descent, whether literal or metaphorical, and is now, for just so long as he can resist therapy, awake. This is the initial revelation in the book, and it is also the only one.

Even given Mrs. Lessing's tendency to confront all ideas *tabula rasa*, we are dealing here with less than astonishing stuff. The idea that there is sanity in insanity, that truth lies on the far side of madness, informs not only a considerable spread of Western literature but also, so commonly is it now held, an entire generation's experiment with hallucinogens. Most of Mrs. Lessing's thoughts about the cultural definition of insanity reflect or run parallel to those of Laing, and yet the idea was already so prevalent that Laing cannot even be said to have popularized it: his innovation was only to have taken it out of the realm of instinctive knowledge and into the limited context of psychiatric therapy. Although Mrs. Lessing apparently thought the content of *Briefing for a Descent into Hell* so startling that she was impelled to add an explanatory afterword, a two-page parable about the ignorance of certain psychiatrists at large London teaching hospitals, she had herself dealt before with this very material. In *The Golden Notebook* Anna makes this note for a story: "A man whose 'sense of reality' has gone; and because of it, has a deeper sense of reality than 'normal' people." By the time Mrs. Lessing finished *The Four-Gated City* she had refined the proposition: Lynda Coldridge's deeper sense of reality is not the result but the definition of her madness. So laboriously is this notion developed in the closing three hundred pages of *The Four-Gated City* that one would have thought that Mrs. Lessing had more or less exhausted its literary possibilities.

But she was less and less interested in literary possibilities, which is where we strike the faultline. "If I saw it in terms of an artistic problem, then it'd be easy, wouldn't it," Anna tells her friend Molly, in *The Golden Notebook*, as explanation of her disinclination to write another book. "We could have ever such intelligent chats about the modern novel." This may seem a little on the easy side, even to the reader who is willing to overlook Anna's later assertion that she cannot write because "a Chinese peasant" is looking over her shoulder. ("Or one of Castro's guerrilla fighters. Or an Algerian fighting in the F.L.N.") *Madame Bovary* told us more about bourgeois life than several generations of Marxists have, but there does not seem much doubt that Flaubert saw it as an artistic problem.

That Mrs. Lessing does not suggests her particular dilemma. What we are witnessing here is a writer undergoing a profound and continuing cultural trauma, a woman of determinedly utopian and distinctly teleological bent assaulted at every turn by fresh evidence that the world is not exactly improving as promised. And, because such is the particular quality of her mind, she is compelled in the face of this evidence to look even more frenetically for the final cause, the unambiguous answer.

In the beginning her search was less frenzied. She came out of Southern Rhodesia imprinted ineradicably by precisely the kind of rigid agrarian world that most easily makes storytellers of its exiled children. What British Africa gave her, besides those images of a sky so empty and a society so inflexible as to make the slightest tremor in either worth remarking upon, was a way of perceiving the rest of her life: for a long time to come she could interpret all she saw in terms of "injustice," not merely the injustice of white man to black, of colonizer to colonized, but the more general injustices of class and particularly of sex. She grew up knowing not only what hard frontiers do to women but what women then do to the men who keep them there. She could hear in all her memories that "voice of the suffering female" passed on from mothers to daughters in a chain broken only at great cost.

Of these memories she wrote a first novel, *The Grass Is Singing*, entirely traditional in its conventions. Reality was *there*, waiting to be observed by an omniscient third person. *The Grass Is Singing* was neat in its construction, relatively scrupulous in its maintenance of tone, predicated upon a world of constants. Its characters moved through that world unconscious of knowledge shared by author and reader. The novel was, in brief, everything Mrs. Lessing was to reject as "false" and "evasive" by the time she wrote *The Golden Notebook*. "Why not write down, simply, what happened between Molly and her son today?" Anna demands of herself. "Why do I never write down, simply, what happens? Why don't I keep a diary? Obviously, my changing everything into fiction is simply a means of concealing something from myself. . . . I shall keep a diary."

It would be hard to imagine a character more unrelievedly self-conscious, or more insistently the author's surrogate, than Anna Gould in *The Golden Notebook*. The entire intention of the novel is to shatter the conventional distance of fiction, to deny all distinction between toad and garden, to "write down, simply, what happens." Call the writer Anna Gould or call her

Doris Lessing, *The Golden Notebook* is the diary of a writer in shock. There she is in London, 1950. A young woman determined to forge a life as a "free woman," as an "intellectual," she has come out of a simple society into what Robert Penn Warren once called the convulsion of the world, and she is finding some equivocation in the answers so clear to her in Africa. Her expectations give off a bright and dated valiance. Her disenchantments are all too familiar. The sheer will, the granitic ambitiousness of *The Golden Notebook* overrides everything else about it. Great raw hunks of undigested experience, unedited transcripts of what happened between Molly and her son today, overwhelming memories and rejections of those memories as sentimental, the fracturing of a sensibility beginning for the first time to doubt its perceptions: all of it runs out of the teller's mind and into the reader's with deliberate disregard for the nature of the words in between. The teller creates "characters" and "scenes" only to deny their validity. She berates herself for clinging to the "certainty" of her memories in the face of the general uncertainty. Mrs. Lessing looms through *The Golden Notebook* as a woman driven by doubts not only about what to tell but about the validity of telling it at all.

Yet she continued to write, and to write fiction. Not until the end of the five-volume *Children of Violence* series did one sense a weakening of that compulsion to remember, and a metastasis of that cognitive frenzy for answers. She had seen, by then, a great deal go, had seized a great many answers and lost them. Organized politics went early. Freudian determinism seemed incompatible. The Africa of her memory was another country. The voice she felt most deeply, that of women trying to define their relationships to one another and to men, first went shrill and then, appropriated by and reduced to a "movement," slipped below the range of her attention. She had been betrayed by all those answers and more, and yet, increasingly possessed, her only response has been to look for another. That she is scarcely alone in this possession is what lends her quest its great interest: the impulse to final solutions has been not only Mrs. Lessing's dilemma but the guiding delusion of her time. It is not an impulse I hold high, but there is something finally very moving about her tenacity.

1971

Georgia O'Keeffe

"WHERE I WAS BORN and where and how I have lived is unimportant," Georgia O'Keeffe told us in the book of paintings and words published in her ninetieth year on earth. She seemed to be advising us to forget the beautiful face in the Stieglitz photographs. She appeared to be dismissing the rather condescending romance that had attached to her by then, the romance of extreme good looks and advanced age and deliberate isolation. "It is what I have done with where I have been that should be of interest." I recall an August afternoon in Chicago in 1973 when I took my daughter, then seven, to see what Georgia O'Keeffe had done with where she had been. One of the vast O'Keeffe "Sky Above Clouds" canvases floated over the back stairs in the Chicago Art Institute that day, dominating what seemed to be several stories of empty light, and my daughter looked at it once, ran to the landing, and kept on looking. "Who drew it," she whispered after a while. I told her. "I need to talk to her," she said finally.

My daughter was making, that day in Chicago, an entirely unconscious but quite basic assumption about people and the work they do. She was assuming that the glory she saw in the work reflected a glory in its maker, that the painting was the painter as the poem is the poet, that every choice one made alone—every word chosen or rejected, every brush stroke laid or not laid down—betrayed one's character. *Style is character*. It seemed to me that afternoon that I had rarely seen so instinctive an application of this familiar principle, and I recall being pleased not only that my daughter responded to style as character but that it was Georgia O'Keeffe's particular style to which she responded: this was a hard woman who had imposed her 192 square feet of clouds on Chicago.

"Hardness" has not been in our century a quality much admired in women, nor in the past twenty years has it even been in official favor for men. When hardness surfaces in the very old we tend to transform it into "crustiness" or eccentricity, some tonic pepperiness to be indulged at a distance. On the evidence of her work and what she has said about it, Georgia O'Keeffe is neither "crusty" nor eccentric. She is simply hard, a straight shooter, a woman clean of received wisdom and open to what she sees. This is a woman who could early on dismiss most of her contemporaries as "dreamy," and would later single out one she liked as "a very poor painter." (And then add, apparently by way of softening the judgment: "I guess he wasn't a painter at all. He had no courage and I believe that to create one's own world in any of the arts takes courage.") This is a woman who in 1939 could advise her admirers that they were missing her point, that their appreciation of her famous flowers was merely sentimental. "When I paint a red hill," she observed coolly in the catalogue for an exhibition that year, "you say it is too bad that I don't always paint flowers. A flower touches almost everyone's heart. A red hill doesn't touch everyone's heart." This is a woman who could describe the genesis of one of her most well-known paintings—the "Cow's Skull: Red, White and Blue" owned by the Metropolitan—as an act of quite deliberate and derisive orneriness. "I thought of the city men I had been seeing in the East," she wrote. "They talked so often of writing the Great American Novel—the Great American Play—the Great American Poetry. . . . So as I was painting my cow's head on blue I thought to myself, 'I'll make it an American painting. They will not think it great with the red stripes down the sides—Red, White and Blue—but they will notice it.'"

The city men. The men. They. The words crop up again and again as this astonishingly aggressive woman tells us what was on her mind when she was making her astonishingly aggressive paintings. It was those city men who stood accused of sentimentalizing her flowers: "I made you take time to look at what I saw and when you took time to really notice my flower you hung all your associations with flowers on my flower and you write about my flower as if I think and see what you think and see—and I don't." *And I don't.* Imagine those words spoken, and the sound you hear is *don't tread on me.* "The men" believed it impossible to paint New York, so Georgia O'Keeffe painted New York. "The men" didn't think much of her bright color, so she made it brighter. The men yearned toward Europe so she went to Texas, and then New Mexico. The men talked about Cézanne, "long involved remarks about the 'plastic quality' of his form and color," and took one another's long involved remarks, in the view of this angelic rattlesnake in their midst, altogether too seriously. "I can paint one of those dismal-colored paintings like the men," the woman who regarded herself always as an outsider remembers thinking one day in 1922, and she did: a painting of a shed "all low-toned and dreary with the tree beside the door." She called this act of rancor "The Shanty" and hung it in her next show. "The men seemed to approve of it," she reported fifty-four years later, her contempt undimmed. "They seemed to think that maybe I was beginning to paint. That was my only low-toned dismal-colored painting."

Some women fight and others do not. Like so many successful guerrillas in the war between the sexes, Georgia O'Keeffe seems to have been equipped early with an immutable sense of who she was and a fairly clear understanding that she would be required to prove it. On the surface her upbringing was conventional. She was a child on the Wisconsin prairie who played with china dolls and painted watercolors with cloudy skies because sunlight was too hard to paint and, with her brother and sisters, listened every night to her mother read stories of the Wild West, of Texas, of Kit Carson and Billy the Kid. She told adults that she wanted to be an artist and was embarrassed when they asked what kind of artist she wanted to be: she had no idea "what kind." She had no idea what artists did. She had never seen a picture that interested her, other than a pen-and-ink Maid of Athens in one of her mother's books, some Mother Goose illustrations printed on cloth, a tablet cover that showed a little girl with pink roses, and the painting of Arabs on horseback that hung in her grandmother's parlor. At thirteen, in a Dominican convent, she was mortified when the sister corrected her drawing. At Chatham Episcopal Institute in Virginia she painted lilacs and sneaked time alone to walk out to where she could see the line of the Blue Ridge Mountains on the horizon. At the Art Institute in Chicago she was shocked by the presence of live models and wanted to abandon anatomy lessons. At the Art Students League in New York one of her fellow students advised her that, since he would be a great painter and she would end up teaching painting in a girls' school, any work of hers was less important than modeling for him. Another painted over her work to show her how the Impressionists did trees. She had not before heard how the Impressionists did trees and she did not much care.

At twenty-four she left all those opinions behind and went for the first time to live in Texas, where there were no trees to paint and no one to tell her how not to paint them. In Texas there was only the horizon she craved. In Texas she had her sister Claudia with her for a while, and in the late afternoons they would walk away from town and toward the horizon and watch the evening star come out. "That evening star fascinated me," she wrote. "It was in some way very exciting to me. My sister had a gun, and as we walked she would throw bottles into the air and shoot as many as she could before they hit the ground. I had nothing but to walk into nowhere and the wide sunset space with the star. Ten watercolors were made from that star." In a way one's interest is compelled as much by the sister Claudia with the gun as by the painter Georgia with the star, but only the painter left us this shining record. Ten watercolors were made from that star.

1976

IV

SOJOURNS

In the Islands

1969: I had better tell you where I am, and why. I am sitting in a high-ceilinged room in the Royal Hawaiian Hotel in Honolulu watching the long translucent curtains billow in the trade wind and trying to put my life back together. My husband is here, and our daughter, age three. She is blonde and barefoot, a child of paradise in a frangipani lei, and she does not understand why she cannot go to the beach. She cannot go to the beach because there has been an earthquake in the Aleutians, 7.5 on the Richter scale, and a tidal wave is expected. In two or three minutes the wave, if there is one, will hit Midway Island, and we are awaiting word from Midway. My husband watches the television screen. I watch the curtains, and imagine the swell of the water.

The bulletin, when it comes, is a distinct anticlimax: Midway reports no unusual wave action. My husband switches off the television set and stares out the window. I avoid his eyes, and brush the baby's hair. In the absence of a natural disaster we are left again to our own uneasy devices. We are here on this island in the middle of the Pacific in lieu of filing for divorce.

I tell you this not as aimless revelation but because I want you to know, as you read me, precisely who I am and where I am and what is on my mind. I want you to understand exactly what you are getting: you are getting a woman who for some time now has felt radically separated from most of the ideas that seem to interest other people. You are getting a woman who somewhere along the line misplaced whatever slight faith she ever had in the social contract, in the meliorative principle, in the whole grand pattern of human endeavor. Quite often during the past several years I have felt myself a sleepwalker, moving through the world unconscious of the moment's high issues, oblivious to its data, alert only to the stuff of bad dreams, the children burning in the locked car in the supermarket parking lot, the bike boys stripping down stolen cars on the captive cripple's ranch, the freeway sniper who feels "real bad" about picking off the family of five, the hustlers, the insane, the cunning Okie faces that turn up in military investigations, the sullen lurkers in doorways, the lost children, all the ignorant armies jostling in the night. Acquaintances read *The New York Times*, and try to tell me the news of the world. I listen to call-in shows.

You will perceive that such a view of the world presents difficulties. I have trouble making certain connections. I have trouble maintaining the basic notion that keeping promises matters in a world where everything I was taught seems beside the point. The point itself seems increasingly obscure. I came into adult life equipped with an essentially romantic ethic, holding always before me the examples of Axel Heyst in *Victory* and Milly Theale in *The Wings of the Dove* and Charlotte Rittenmayer in *The Wild Palms* and a few dozen others like them, believing as they did that salvation lay in extreme and doomed commitments, promises made and somehow kept outside the range of normal social experience. I still believe that, but I have trouble reconciling salvation with those ignorant armies camped in my mind. I could indulge here in a little idle generalization, could lay off my own state of profound emotional shock on the larger cultural breakdown, could talk fast about convulsions in the society and alienation and anomie and maybe even assassination, but that would be just one more stylish shell game. I am not the society in microcosm. I am a thirty-four-year-old woman with long straight hair and an old bikini bathing suit and bad nerves sitting on an island in the middle of the Pacific waiting for a tidal wave that will not come.

We spend, my husband and I and the baby, a restorative week in paradise. We are each the other's model of consideration, tact, restraint at the very edge of the precipice. He refrains from noticing when I am staring at nothing, and in turn I refrain from dwelling at length upon a newspaper story about a couple who apparently threw their infant and then themselves into the boiling crater of a live volcano on Maui. We also refrain from mentioning any kicked-down doors, hospitalized psychotics, any chronic anxieties or packed suitcases. We lie in the sun, drive out through the cane to Waimea Bay. We breakfast on the terrace, and gray-haired women smile benevolently at us. I smile back. Happy families are all alike on the terrace of the Royal Hawaiian Hotel in Honolulu. My husband comes in from Kalakaua Avenue one morning and tells me that he has seen a six-foot-two drag queen we know in Los Angeles. Our acquaintance was shopping, my husband reports, for a fish-net bikini and did not speak. We both laugh. I am reminded that we laugh at the same things, and read him this complaint from a very old copy of *Honolulu* Magazine I picked up in someone's office: "When President Johnson recently came to Honolulu, the morning paper's banner read something like 'PICKETS TO GREET PRESIDENT.' Would it not have been just as newsworthy to say 'WARM ALOHA TO GREET PRESIDENT'?" At the end of the week I tell my husband that I am going to try harder to make things matter. My husband says that he has heard that before, but the air is warm and the baby has another frangipani lei and there is no rancor in his voice. Maybe it can be all right, I say. Maybe, he says.

1970: Quite early every morning in Honolulu, on that stretch of Waikiki Beach which fronts the Royal Hawaiian Hotel, an employee of the hotel spends fifteen or twenty minutes raking the sand within a roped enclosure reserved for registered guests. Since this "private" beach differs from the "public" beach only by its raked sand, its rope, and its further remove from the water, it is at first difficult to see why anyone would sit there, but people do. They sit there all day long and in great numbers, facing the sea in even rows.

I had been an occasional visitor to Honolulu for several years before I entirely perceived that the roped beach was central to the essence of the Royal Hawaiian, that the point of sitting there was not at all exclusivity, as is commonly supposed on Waikiki, but inclusivity. Anyone behind the rope is presumed to be, by tacit definition, "our kind." Anyone behind the rope will watch over our children as we will watch over theirs, will not palm room keys or smoke dope or listen to Creedence Clearwater on a transistor when we are awaiting word from the Mainland on the prime rate. Anyone behind the rope, should we venture conversation, will "know people we know": the Royal's roped beach is an enclave of apparent strangers ever on the verge of discovering that their nieces roomed in Lagunita at Stanford the same year, or that their best friends lunched together during the last Crosby. The fact that anyone behind the rope would understand the word "Crosby" to signify a golf tournament at Pebble Beach suggests the extent to which the Royal Hawaiian is not merely a hotel but a social idea, one of the few extant clues to a certain kind of American life.

Of course great hotels have always been social ideas, flawless mirrors to the particular societies they service. Had there never been an Empire there would not have been a Raffles. To understand what the Royal is now you must first understand what it was, from 1927 through the Thirties, the distant and mildly exotic "pink palace" of the Pacific, the resort built by the Matson Line to rival and surpass such hotels as the Coronado, the Broadmoor, Del Monte. Standing then almost alone on Waikiki, the Royal made Honolulu a place to go, made all things "Hawaiian"—leis, ukuleles, luaus, coconut-leaf hats and the singing of "I Wanna Learn to Speak Hawaiian"—a decade's craze at country-club dances across the United States. During the fourteen years between the Royal's opening and Pearl Harbor people came in on the Matson Line's *Malolo* and *Lurline* and they brought with them not only steamer trunks but children and grandchildren and valets and nurses and silver Rolls-Royces and ultramarine-blue Packard roadsters. They "wintered" at the Royal, or "summered" there, or "spent several months." They came to the Royal to rest "after hunting in South Africa." They went home "by way of Banff and Lake Louise." In Honolulu there was polo, golf, bowling on the green. Every afternoon the Royal served tea on rattan tables. The maids wove leis for every guest. The chefs constructed, as table decoration, the United States Capitol Building in Hawaiian sugar.

The Royal's scrapbooks for those years survive as an index to America's industrial fortunes, large and small. Mellons and Du Ponts and Gettys and the man who had just patented the world's largest incubator (47,000-egg capacity) seem to differ not at all from one another, photographed at the Royal in 1928. Dorothy Spreckels strums a ukulele on the verandah. Walter P. Chrysler, Jr., arrives with his mother and father for a season at the Royal. A figure on the beach is described as "a Colorado Springs society woman," a young couple as "prominently identified with the young-married set in Akron." At the Royal they met not only one another but a larger world as well: Australian station owners, Ceylonese tea planters, Cuban sugar operators.

In the faded photographs one sees mostly mothers and daughters. The men, when they are present, display in the main an affecting awkwardness, an awareness that they have harsher roles, say as Mayor of Seattle or President of the Overland Motor Company, a resistance to the world of summering and wintering. In 1931 the son of President Hoover spent time at the Royal, was widely entertained, caught thirty-eight fish off the Kona coast of Hawaii, and had his picture taken on the Royal beach shaking hands with Duke Kahanamoku. This photograph appeared in *Town and Country*, which also reported in 1931 that "the diving boys in Honolulu harbor say that fishing has been good and there are no indications of hard times in the denominations of coins flipped to them as bait from incoming steamers."

Nor did the turnings of the Sixties effect much change at the Royal. What the place reflected in the Thirties it reflects still, in less flamboyant mutations: a kind of life lived always on the streets where the oldest trees grow. It is a life so secure in its traditional concerns that the cataclysms of the larger society disturb it only as surface storms disturb the sea's bottom, a long time later and in oblique ways. It is a life lived by millions of people in this country and largely forgotten by most of us. Sometimes I think I remember it only at the Royal Hawaiian. There in the warm early evenings, the women in turquoise-blue and buttercup-yellow chiffons seem, as they wait for cars under the pink porte-cochere, the natural inheritors of a style later seized upon by Patricia Nixon and her daughters. In the mornings, when the beach is just raked and the air damp and sweet from the dawn rain, I see the same women, now in printed silks and lined cashmere cardigans, eating papaya on the terrace just as they have done every few seasons since they were young girls, in the late Twenties, and came to the Royal with their mothers and sisters. Their husbands scan the San Francisco and Los Angeles papers with the practiced disinterest of men who believe their lives safe in municipal bonds. These papers arrive at the Royal one and sometimes two days late, which lends the events of the day a peculiar and unsettling distance. I recall overhearing a conversation at the Royal's newsstand on the morning after the California primary in June 1968, the morning Robert Kennedy lay dying in Good Samaritan Hospital in Los Angeles. "How'd the primary go?" a man buying cigarettes asked his wife. She studied the day-old headlines. "'Early Turnout Heavy,'" she said. Later in the morning I overheard this woman discussing the assassination: her husband had heard the news when he dropped by a brokerage office to get the day's New York closings.

To sit by the Royal pool and read *The New York Review of Books* is to feel oneself an asp, disguised in a voile beach robe, in the very bosom of the place. I put *The New York Review of Books* aside and talk to a pretty young woman who has honeymooned at the Royal, because honeymoons at the Royal are a custom in her family, with each of her three husbands. My daughter makes friends at the pool with another four-year-old, Jill, from Fairbanks, Alaska, and it is taken for granted by Jill's mother and aunt that the two children will meet again, year after year, in the immutable pleasant rhythms of a life that used to be, and at the Royal Hawaiian seems still to be. I sit in my voile beach robe and watch the children and wish, against all the evidence I know, that it might be so.

1970: To look down upon Honolulu from the high rain forest that divides windward Oahu from the leeward city is to see, in the center of an extinct volcano named Puowaina, a place so still and private that once seen it is forever in the mind. There are banyan trees in the crater, and rain trees, and 19,500 graves. Yellow primavera blazes on the hills above. Whole slopes seem clouded in mauve jacaranda. This is the place commonly called Punchbowl, the National Memorial Cemetery of the Pacific, and 13,000 of the dead in its crater were killed during World War II. Some of the rest died in Korea. For almost a decade now, in the outer sections just inside the rim of the crater, they have been digging graves for Americans killed in Vietnam, not many, a fraction of the total, one, two, three a week, most of them Island boys but some of them carried here by families who live thousands of miles across the Pacific, a gesture that touches by its very difficulty. Because the Vietnam dead are shipped first to Travis A.F.B. in California and then to the next of kin, those Mainland families burying their sons or husbands in Honolulu must bring the bodies back over the Pacific one last time. The superintendent of Punchbowl, Martin T. Corley, refers to such burials as his "ship-in Vietnams."

"A father or an uncle calls me from the Mainland and he says they're bringing their boy here, I don't ask why," Mr. Corley said when I talked to him not long ago. We were sitting in his office in the crater and on the wall hung the Bronze Star and Silver Star citations he had received in Europe in 1944, Martin T. Corley, a man in an aloha shirt who had gone from South Ozone Park in Queens to the Battle of the Bulge to a course in cemetery management at Fort Sam Houston and finally, twenty-some years later, to an office in an extinct volcano in the Pacific from which he could watch the quick and the dead in still another war.

I watched him leafing through a stack of what he called "transmittals," death forms from Vietnam. There in Martin T. Corley's office Vietnam seemed considerably less chimerical than it had seemed on the Mainland for some months, less last year's war, less successfully consigned to that limbo of benign neglect in which any mention of continuing casualties was made to seem a little counterproductive, a little démodé. There in the crater it seemed less easy to believe that weekly killed-in-action figures under 100 might by some sleight-of-hand add up to zero, a nonexistent war. There in sight of the automatic gravediggers what the figures added up to, for the first twelve weeks of 1970, was 1,078 dead. Martin T. Corley gets a transmittal on each of them. He holds these transmittal forms for fifteen or twenty days before throwing them away, just in case a family wants to bring its dead to Punchbowl. "See, we had a family bring a boy in from Oregon a few days ago," he said. "We've got a California coming in now. We figure they've got their reasons. We pick the plot, open the grave. These ship-in families, we don't see them until the hearse comes through the gate."

On a warm windy afternoon a few days later I stood with Mr. Corley on the soft grass up in Section K of the crater and waited for one such family to come through the gate. They had flown out from the Mainland with the body the night before, six of them, the mother and father and a sister and her husband and a couple of other relatives, and they would bury their boy in the afternoon sun and fly back a few hours later. We waited, and we watched, and then, on the road below, the six Air Force pallbearers snapped to attention. The bugler jumped up from beneath a banyan tree and took his place behind the honor guard. We could see the hearse then, winding up and around the circular road to Section K, the hearse and two cars, their headlights dim in the tropical sun. "Two of us from the office come to all the Vietnams," Mr. Corley said suddenly. "I mean in case the family breaks down or something."

All I can tell you about the next ten minutes is that they seemed a very long time. We watched the coffin being carried to the grave and we watched the pallbearers lift the flag, trying to hold it taut in the warm trade wind. The wind was blowing hard, toppling the vases of gladioli set by the grave, obliterating some of the chaplain's words. "If God is for us then who can be against us," the chaplain said, a red-headed young major in suntans, and then I did not hear any more for a while. I was standing behind the six canvas chairs where the family sat, standing there with Mr. Corley and an Air Force survival assistance officer, and I was looking beyond the chaplain to a scattering of graves so fresh they had no headstones, just plastic markers stuck in the ground. "We tenderly commit this body to the ground," the chaplain said then. The men in the honor guard raised their rifles. Three shots cracked out. The bugler played taps. The pallbearers folded the flag until only the blue field and a few stars showed, and one of them stepped forward to present the flag to the father. For the first time the father looked away from the coffin, looked away from the pallbearers and out across the expanse of graves. A slight man with his face trembling and his eyes wet, he stood facing Mr. Corley and me, and for a moment we looked directly at each other, but he was seeing not me, not Mr. Corley, not anyone.

It was not quite three o'clock. The father, transferring the flag from hand to hand as if it burned, said a few halting words to the pallbearers. I walked away from the grave then, down to my car, and waited for Mr. Corley to talk to the father. He wanted to tell the father that if he and his wife wanted to come back before their plane left, the grave would be covered by four o'clock. "Sometimes it makes them feel better to see it," Mr. Corley said when he caught up with me. "Sometimes they get on the plane and they worry, you know, it didn't get covered."

His voice trailed off. "We cover within thirty minutes," he said finally. "Fill, cover, get the marker on. That's one thing I remember from my training." We stood there a moment in the warm wind, then said goodbye. The pallbearers filed onto the Air Force bus. The bugler walked past, whistling "Raindrops Keep Fallin' on My Head." Just after four o'clock the father and mother came back and looked for a long while at the covered grave, then took a night flight back to the Mainland. Their son was one of 101 Americans killed that week in Vietnam.

1975: The 8:45 A.M. Pan American to Honolulu this morning was delayed half an hour before takeoff from Los Angeles. During this delay the stewardesses served orange juice and coffee and two children played tag in the aisles and, somewhere behind me, a man began screaming at a woman who seemed to be his wife. I say that the woman seemed to be his wife only because the tone of his invective sounded practiced, although the only words I heard clearly were these: "You are driving me to murder." After a moment I was aware of the door to the plane being opened a few rows behind me, and of the man rushing off. There were many Pan American employees rushing on and off then, and considerable confusion. I do not know whether the man reboarded the plane before takeoff or whether the woman came on to Honolulu alone, but I thought about it all the way across the Pacific. I thought about it while I was drinking a sherry-on-the-rocks and I thought about it during lunch and I was still thinking about it when the first of the Hawaiian Islands appeared off the left wing tip. It was not until we had passed Diamond Head and were coming in low over the reef for landing at Honolulu, however, that I realized what I most disliked about this incident: I disliked it because it had the aspect of a short story, one of those "little epiphany" stories in which the main character glimpses a crisis in a stranger's life —a woman weeping in a tearoom, often, or an accident seen from the window of a train, "tearooms" and "trains" still being fixtures of short stories although not of real life—and is moved to see his or her own life in a new light. I was not going to Honolulu because I wanted to see life reduced to a short story. I was going to Honolulu because I wanted to see life expanded to a novel, and I still do. I wanted room for flowers, and reef fish, and people who may or may not be driving one another to murder but in any case are not impelled, by the demands of narrative convention, to say so out loud on the 8:45 A.M. Pan American to Honolulu.

1977: I have never seen a postcard of Hawaii that featured Schofield Barracks. Schofield is off the track, off the tour, hard by the shadowy pools of the Wahiawa Reservoir, and to leave Honolulu and drive inland to Schofield is to sense a clouding of the atmosphere, a darkening of the color range. The translucent pastels of the famous coast give way to the opaque greens of interior Oahu. Crushed white coral gives way to red dirt, sugar dirt, deep red laterite soil that crumbles soft in the hand and films over grass and boots and hubcaps. Clouds mass over the Waianae Range. Cane fires smoke on the horizon and rain falls fitfully. BUY SOME COLLARD GREENS, reads a sign on a weathered frame grocery in Wahiawa, just across the two-lane bridge from the Schofield gate. MASSAGE PARLOR, CHECKS CASHED, 50TH STATE POOLROOM, HAPPY HOUR, CASH FOR CARS. Schofield Loan. Schofield Pawn. Schofield Sands Motor Lodge. Then, finally, Schofield itself, the Schofield we all know from James Jones's *From Here to Eternity*, The Schofield that is Home of the 25th "Tropic Lightning" Infantry Division, formerly the Hawaii Division, James Jones's own division, Robert E. Lee Prewitt's division, Maggio's and Warden's and Stark's and Dynamite Holmes's division, *Fit to Fight, Trained to Win, Ready to Go. All Wars Are Won in the End by the Infantryman. Through These Portals Pass the Finest Soldiers in the World*—25TH INFANTRY DIVISION SOLDIERS. TROPIC LIGHTNING REENLISTMENT. I have never driven into Schofield and seen those words without hearing the blues that end *From Here to Eternity:*

Got paid out on Monday
Not a dog soldier no more
They gimme all that money
So much my pockets is sore
More dough than I can use. Reenlistment Blues.
Ain't no time to lose. Reenlistment Blues.

Certain places seem to exist mainly because someone has written about them. Kilimanjaro belongs to Ernest Hemingway.

Oxford, Mississippi, belongs to William Faulkner, and one hot July week in Oxford I was moved to spend an afternoon walking the graveyard looking for his stone, a kind of courtesy call on the owner of the property. A place belongs forever to whoever claims it hardest, remembers it most obsessively, wrenches it from itself, shapes it, renders it, loves it so radically that he remakes it in his image, and not only Schofield Barracks but a great deal of Honolulu itself has always belonged for me to James Jones. The first time I ever saw Hotel Street in Honolulu was on a Saturday night in 1966 when all the bars and tattoo parlors were full of military police and girls looking for a dollar and nineteen-year-olds, on their way to or from Saigon, looking for a girl. I recall looking that night for the particular places that had figured in *From Here to Eternity*: the Black Cat, the Blue Anchor, the whorehouse Jones called the New Congress Hotel. I remember driving up Wilhemina Rise to look for Alma's house and I remember walking out of the Royal Hawaiian Hotel and expecting to see Prewitt and Maggio sitting on the curb and I remember walking the Waialae Country Club golf course, trying to figure exactly where Prewitt died. I think it was in the trap near the fifth green.

It is hard to see one of these places claimed by fiction without a sudden blurring, a slippage, a certain vertiginous occlusion of the imagined and the real, and this slippage was particularly acute the last time I arrived in Honolulu, on a June day when the author of *From Here to Eternity* had been dead just a few weeks. In New York the death of James Jones had been the occasion for many considerations and reconsiderations. Many mean guilts had been recalled and exorcised. Many lessons had been divined, in both the death and the life. In Honolulu the death of James Jones had been marked by the publication, in the *Honolulu Star-Bulletin*, of an excerpt from the author's *Viet Journal*, the epilogue, the part in which he talked about returning to Honolulu in 1973 and looking for the places he had remembered in *From Here to Eternity* but had last seen in 1942, when he was twenty-one years old and shipped out for Guadalcanal with the 25th Division. In 1973 the five pillboxes on Makapuu Head had seemed to James Jones exactly as he had left them in 1942. In 1973 the Royal Hawaiian Hotel had seemed to James Jones less formidably rich than he had left it in 1942, and it had occurred to him with considerable poignance that he was a man in his fifties who could walk into the Royal Hawaiian and buy whatever he wanted.

He had bought a beer and gone back to Paris. In June of 1977 he was dead and it was not possible to buy a copy of his great novel, his living novel, the novel in which he so loved Honolulu that he remade it in his image, in any of Honolulu's largest bookstores. "Is it a best-seller?" I was asked in one, and the golden child in charge of another suggested that I try the psychic-science shelf. In that instant I thought I grieved for James Jones, a man I never met, but I think I grieved for all of us: for Jones, for myself, for the sufferers of mean guilts and for their exorcists, for Robert E. Lee Prewitt, for the Royal Hawaiian Hotel and for this golden nitwit who believed eternity to be a psychic science.

I have never been sure whether the extreme gravity of *From Here to Eternity* is an exact reflection of the light at Schofield Barracks or whether I see the light as grave because I have read James Jones. "It had rained all morning and then suddenly cleared at noon, and the air, freshly washed today, was like dark crystal in the sharp clarity and sombre focus it gave to every image." It was in this sombre focus that James Jones rendered Schofield, and it was in this sombre focus that I last saw Schofield, one Monday during that June. It had rained in the morning and the smell of eucalyptus was sharp in the air and I had again that familiar sense of having left the bright coast and entered a darker country. The black outline of the Waianae Range seemed obscurely oppressive. A foursome on the post golf course seemed to have been playing since 1940, and to be doomed to continue. A soldier in fatigues appeared to be trimming a bougainvillea hedge, swinging at it with a scythe, but his movements were hypnotically slowed, and the scythe never quite touched the hedge. Around the tropical frame bungalows where the families of Schofield officers have always lived there was an occasional tricycle but no child, no wife, no sign of life but one: a Yorkshire terrier yapping on the lawn of a colonel's bungalow. As it happens I have spent time around Army posts in the role of an officer's child, have even played with lap dogs on the lawns of colonels' quarters, but I saw this Yorkshire with Prewitt's eyes, and I hated it.

I had driven out to Schofield in other seasons, but this trip was different. I was making this trip for the same reason I had walked the Oxford graveyard, a courtesy call on the owner. This trip I made appointments, spoke to people, asked questions and wrote down answers, had lunch with my hosts at the Aloha Lightning NCO Club and was shown the regimental trophies and studied the portraits of commanding officers in every corridor I walked down. Unlike the golden children in the Honolulu bookstores these men I met at Schofield, these men in green fatigues, all knew exactly who James Jones was and what he had written and even where he had slept and eaten and probably gotten drunk during the three years he spent at Schofield. They recalled the incidents and locations of *From Here to Eternity* in minute detail. They anticipated those places that I would of course want to see: D Quad, the old stockade, the stone quarry, Kolekole Pass. Some weeks before, there had been at the post theater a special screening of the movie *From Here to Eternity*, an event arranged by the Friends of the Tropic Lightning Historical Society, and everyone to whom I spoke at Schofield had turned out for this screening. Many of these men were careful to qualify their obvious attachment to James Jones's view of their life by pointing out that the Army had changed. Others did not mention the change. One, a young man who had re-upped once and now wanted out, mentioned that it had not changed at all. We were standing on the lawn in D Quad, Jones's quad, Robert E. Lee Prewitt's quad, and I was watching the idle movement around the square, a couple of soldiers dropping a basketball through a hoop, another cleaning an M-16, a desultory argument at the Dutch door of the supply room—when he volunteered a certain inchoate dissatisfaction with his six years in the 25th Division. "I read this book *From Here to Eternity*," he said, "and they still got the same little games around here."

I suppose everything had changed and nothing had. A mess hall was now called a "dining facility," but they still served chipped beef on toast and they still called it "S.O.S." A stockade was now called a "confinement facility," and the confinement facility for all military installations on Oahu was now at Pearl Harbor, but the old stockade at Schofield was now the headquarters for the military police, and during the time I was there the M.P.s brought in a handcuffed soldier, bare to the waist and shoeless. Investigators in aloha shirts chatted in the exercise yard. Office supplies were stored in some of the "close confinement" cells, but there were still the plain wooden bunks, "plate beds," beds for those occasions, it was explained to me by a major who had once been in charge of the Schofield stockade, "when a guy is completely berserk and starts ripping up his mattress." On the wall there were still the diagrams detailing the order in which belongings were to be arranged: WHITE TOWEL, SOAP WITH DISH, DEODORANT, TOOTHPASTE, TOOTHBRUSH, COMB, SHAVING CREAM, RAZOR.

In many ways I found it difficult to leave Schofield that day. I had fallen into the narcoleptic movements of the Army day. I had picked up the liquid speech patterns of the Army voice. I took a copy of the *Tropic Lightning News* back into Honolulu with me, and read it that night in my hotel room. During the month of May the Schofield military police had reported 32 arrests for driving under the influence of alcohol, 115 arrests for possession of marijuana, and the theft of a number of items, including one Sansui amplifier, one Sansui pre-amp and tuner, one Kenwood receiver and turntable, two Bose speakers and the tachometer from a 1969 Ford Mustang. One private, two spec fours and one sergeant were asked in the "Troop Talk" column to name their ideal, or favorite, post. One chose Fort Hood. Another chose Fort Sam Houston. None chose Schofield Barracks. In the letters column one correspondent advised a WAC who had objected to the shows at the NCO Club to stay home ("We once had it set up where you girls didn't have to see the entertainment, but the loverly libbers put an end to that"), and another advised "barracks rats" to stop limiting their lives to "erasing Army hatred by indulging in smoke or drink or listening to Peter Frampton at eighty decibels." I thought about barracks rats and I thought about Prewitt and Maggio and I thought about Army hatred and it seemed to me that night in Honolulu that only the details had changed, that James Jones had known a great simple truth: the Army was nothing more or less than life itself. I wish I could tell you that on the day in May when James Jones died someone had played a taps for him at Schofield Barracks, but I think this is not the way life goes.

1969–1977

In Hollywood

"YOU CAN TAKE HOLLYWOOD for granted like I did," Cecilia Brady tells the reader in *The Last Tycoon*, "or you can dismiss it with the contempt we reserve for what we don't understand. It can be understood, too, but only dimly and in flashes. Not half a dozen men have ever been able to keep the whole equation of pictures in their heads." To the extent that *The Last Tycoon* is "about" Hollywood it is about not Monroe Stahr but Cecilia Brady, as anyone who understands the equation of pictures even dimly or in flashes would apprehend immediately: the Monroe Stahrs come and go, but the Cecilia Bradys are the second generation, the survivors, the inheritors of a community as intricate, rigid, and deceptive in its mores as any devised on this continent. At midwinter in the survivors' big houses off Benedict Canyon the fireplaces blaze all day with scrub oak and eucalyptus, the French windows are opened wide to the subtropical sun, the rooms filled with white phalaenopsis and cymbidium orchids and needlepoint rugs and the requisite scent of Rigaud candles. Dinner guests pick with vermeil forks at broiled fish and limestone lettuce *vinaigrette*, decline dessert, adjourn to the screening room, and settle down to *The Heartbreak Kid* with a little seltzer in a Baccarat glass.

After the picture the women, a significant number of whom seem to have ascended through chronic shock into an elusive dottiness, discuss for a ritual half-hour the transpolar movements of acquaintances and the peace of spirit to be derived from exercise class, ballet class, the use of paper napkins at the beach. Quentin Bell's *Virginia Woolf* was an approved event this winter, as were the Chinese acrobats, the recent visits to Los Angeles of Bianca Jagger, and the opening in Beverly Hills of a branch Bonwit Teller. The men talk pictures, grosses, the deal, the morning line on the talent. "Face it," I heard someone say the other night of a director whose current picture had opened a few days before to tepid business. "Last week he was bankable."

Such evenings end before midnight. Such couples leave

together. Should there be marital unhappiness it will go unmentioned until one of the principals is seen lunching with a lawyer. Should there be illness it will go unadmitted until the onset of the terminal coma. Discretion is "good taste," and discretion is also good business, since there are enough imponderables in the business of Hollywood without handing the dice to players too distracted to concentrate on the action. This is a community whose notable excesses include virtually none of the flesh or spirit: heterosexual adultery is less easily tolerated than respectably settled homosexual marriages or well-managed liaisons between middle-aged women. "A nice lesbian relationship, the most common thing in the world," I recall Otto Preminger insisting when my husband and I expressed doubt that the heroine of the Preminger picture we were writing should have one. "Very easy to arrange, does not threaten the marriage."

Flirtations between men and women, like drinks after dinner, remain largely the luxury of character actors out from New York, one-shot writers, reviewers being courted by Industry people, and others who do not understand the *mise* of the local *scène.* In the houses of the inheritors the preservation of the community is paramount, and it is also Universal, Columbia, Fox, Metro, and Warner's. It is in this tropism toward survival that Hollywood sometimes presents the appearance of the last extant stable society.

One afternoon not long ago, at a studio where my husband was doing some work, the director of a picture in production collapsed of cardiac arrest. At six o'clock the director's condition was under discussion in the executives' steam room.

"I called the hospital," the head of production for the studio said. "I talked to his wife."

"Hear what Dick did," one of the other men in the steam room commanded. "Wasn't that a nice thing for Dick to do."

This story illustrates many elements of social reality in Hollywood, but few of the several non-Industry people to whom I have told it have understood it. For one thing it involves a "studio," and many people outside the Industry are gripped by the delusion that "studios" have nothing to do with the making of motion pictures in modern times. They have heard the phrase "independent production," and have fancied that the phrase means what the words mean. They have been told about "runaways," about "empty sound stages," about "death knell" after "death knell" sounding for the Industry.

In fact the Byzantine but very efficient economics of the business render such rhetoric even more meaningless than it sounds: the studios still put up almost all the money. The studios still control all effective distribution. In return for financing and distributing the average "independent" picture, the studio gets not only the largest share (at least half) of any profit made by the picture, but, more significantly, 100 per cent of what the picture brings in up to a point called the "break," or break-even, an arbitrary figure usually set at 2.7 or 2.8 times the actual, or "negative," cost of the picture.

Most significant of all, the "break-even" never represents the point at which the studio actually breaks even on any given production: that point occurs, except on paper, long before, since the studio has already received 10 to 25 per cent of the picture's budget as an "overhead" charge, has received additional rental and other fees for any services actually rendered the production company, and continues to receive, throughout the picture's release, a fee amounting to about a third of the picture's income as a "distribution" charge. In other words there is considerable income hidden in the risk itself, and the ideal picture from the studio's point of view is often said to be the picture that makes one dollar less than break-even. More perfect survival bookkeeping has been devised, but mainly in Chicago and Las Vegas.

Still, it is standard for anyone writing about Hollywood to slip out of the economic reality and into a catchier metaphor, usually paleontological, *vide* John Simon: "I shall not rehearse here the well-known facts of how the industry started dying from being too bulky, toothless, and dated—just like all those other saurians of a few aeons ago. . . ." So pervasive is this vocabulary of extinction (Simon forgot the mandatory allusion to the La Brea Tar Pits) that I am frequently assured by visitors that the studios are "morgues," that they are "shuttered up," that in "the new Hollywood" the "studio has no power." The studio has.

*

January in the last extant stable society. I know that it is January for an empirical fact only because wild mustard glazes the hills an acid yellow, and because there are poinsettias in front of all the bungalows down around Goldwyn and Technicolor, and because many people from Beverly Hills are at La Costa and Palm Springs and many people from New York are at the Beverly Hills Hotel.

"This whole town's dead," one such New York visitor tells me. "I dropped into the Polo Lounge last night, the place was a wasteland." He tells me this every January, and every January I tell him that people who live and work here do not frequent hotel bars either before or after dinner, but he seems to prefer his version. On reflection I can think of only three non-Industry people in New York whose version of Hollywood corresponds at any point with the reality of the place, and they are Johanna Mankiewicz Davis, Jill Schary Robinson and Jean Stein vanden Heuvel, the daughters respectively of the late screenwriter Herman Mankiewicz; the producer and former production chief of Metro, Dore Schary; and the founder of the Music Corporation of America and Universal Pictures, Jules Stein. "We don't go for strangers in Hollywood," Cecilia Brady said.

Days pass. Visitors arrive, scout the Polo Lounge, and leave, confirmed in their conviction that they have penetrated an artfully camouflaged disaster area. The morning mail contains a statement from 20th Century-Fox on a picture in which my husband and I are supposed to have "points," or a percentage. The picture cost $1,367,224.57. It has so far grossed $947,494.86. The statement might suggest to the casual subtracter that the picture is about $400,000 short of breaking even, but this is not the case: the statement reports that the picture is $1,389,112.72 short of breaking even. "$1,389,112.72 unrecovered" is, literally, the bottom line.

In lieu of contemplating why a venture that cost a million-three and has recovered almost a million remains a million-three in the red, I decide to get my hair cut, pick up the trades, learn that *The Poseidon Adventure* is grossing four million dollars a week, that Adolph "Papa" Zukor will celebrate his 100th birthday at a dinner sponsored by Paramount, and that James Aubrey, Ted Ashley and Freddie Fields rented a house together in

Acapulco over Christmas. At this moment in the action, James Aubrey is Metro-Goldwyn-Mayer. Ted Ashley is Warner Brothers. Freddie Fields is Creative Management Associates, First Artists and the Directors Company. The players will change but the game will stay the same. The bottom line seems clear on the survival of Adolph "Papa" Zukor, but not yet on that of James Aubrey, Ted Ashley and Freddie Fields.

"Listen, I got this truly beautiful story," the man who cuts my hair says to me. "Think about some new Dominique-Sanda-type unknown. *Comprenez* so far?"

So far *comprends.* The man who cuts my hair, like everyone else in the community, is looking for the action, the game, a few chips to lay down. Here in the grand casino no one needs capital. One needs only this truly beautiful story. Or maybe if no truly beautiful story comes to mind one needs $500 to go halves on a $1,000 option payment for someone else's truly beautiful but (face it) three-year-old property. (A book or a story is a "property" only until the deal; after that it is "the basic material," as in "I haven't read the basic material on *Gatsby.*") True, the casino is not now so wide open as it was in '69, summer and fall of '69 when every studio in town was narcotized by *Easy Rider*'s grosses and all that was needed to get a picture off the ground was the suggestion of a $750,000 budget, a low-cost NABET or even a nonunion crew, and this terrific 22-year-old kid director. As it turned out most of these pictures were shot as usual by IATSE rather than NABET crews and they cost as usual not seven-fifty but a million-two and many of them ended up unreleased, shelved. And so there was one very bad summer there, the hangover summer of 1970, when nobody could get past the gate without a commitment from Barbra Streisand.

That was the summer when all the terrific 22-year-old directors went back to shooting television commercials and all the creative 24-year-old producers used up the leases on their office space at Warner Brothers by sitting out there in the dull Burbank sunlight smoking dope before lunch and running one another's unreleased pictures after lunch. But that period is over and the game is back on, development money available, the deal dependent only upon the truly beautiful story and the right elements. The elements matter. "We like the *elements*," they say at studios when they are maybe going to make the deal. That is why the man who cuts my hair is telling me his story. A writer might be an element. I listen because in certain ways I am a captive but willing audience, not only to the hairdresser but at the grand casino.

The place makes everyone a gambler. Its spirit is speedy, obsessive, immaterial. The action itself is the art form, and is described in aesthetic terms: "A very imaginative deal," they say, or, "He writes the most creative deals in the business." There is in Hollywood, as in all cultures in which gambling is the central activity, a lowered sexual energy, an inability to devote more than token attention to the preoccupations of the society outside. The action is everything, more consuming than sex, more immediate than politics; more important always than the acquisition of money, which is never, for the gambler, the true point of the exercise.

I talk on the telephone to an agent, who tells me that he has on his desk a check made out to a client for $1,275,000, the client's share of first profits on a picture now in release. Last week, in someone's office, I was shown another such check, this one made out for $4,850,000. Every year there are a few such checks around town. An agent will speak of such a check as being "on my desk," or "on Guy McElwaine's desk," as if the exact physical location lent the piece of paper its credibility. One year they might be the *Midnight Cowboy* and *Butch Cassidy* checks, another year the *Love Story* and *Godfather* checks.

In a curious way these checks are not "real," not real money in the sense that a check for a thousand dollars can be real money; no one "needs" $4,850,000, nor is it really disposable income. It is instead the unexpected payoff on dice rolled a year or two before, and its reality is altered not only by the time lapse but by the fact that no one ever counted on the payoff. A four-million-dollar windfall has the aspect only of Monopoly money, but the actual pieces of paper which bear such figures have, in the community, a totemic significance. They are totems of the action. When I hear of these totems I think reflexively of Sergius O'Shaugnessy, who sometimes believed what he said and tried to take the cure in the very real sun of Desert D'Or with its cactus, its mountain, and the bright green foliage of its love and its money.

Since any survivor is believed capable in the community of conferring on others a ritual and lucky kinship, the birthday dinner for Adolph "Papa" Zukor turns out also to have a totemic significance. It is described by Robert Evans, head of production at Paramount, as "one of the memorable evenings in our Industry. . . . There's never been anyone who's reached one hundred before." Hit songs from old Paramount pictures are played throughout dinner. Jack Valenti speaks of the guest of honor as "the motion picture world's living proof that there is a connection between us and our past."

Zukor himself, who is described in *Who's Who* as a "motion picture mfr." and in *Daily Variety* as a "firm believer in the philosophy that today is the first day of the rest of your life," appears after dinner to express his belief in the future of motion pictures and his pleasure at Paramount's recent grosses. Many of those present have had occasion over the years to regard Adolph "Papa" Zukor with some rancor, but on this night there is among them a resigned warmth, a recognition that they will attend one another's funerals. This ceremonial healing of old and recent scars is a way of life among the survivors, as is the scarring itself. "Having some fun" is what the scarring is called. "Let's go see Nick, I think we'll have some fun," David O. Selznick remembered his father saying to him when the elder Selznick was on his way to tell Nick Schenk that he was going to take 50 per cent of the gross of *Ben-Hur* away from him.

The winter progresses. My husband and I fly to Tucson with our daughter for a few days of meetings on a script with a producer on location. We go out to dinner in Tucson: the sitter tells me that she has obtained, for her crippled son, an autographed picture of Paul Newman. I ask how old her son is. "Thirty-four," she says.

We came for two days, we stay for four. We rarely leave the Hilton Inn. For everyone on the picture this life on location will continue for twelve weeks. The producer and the director collect Navajo belts and speak every day to Los Angeles, New York, London. They are setting up other deals, other action. By the time this picture is released and reviewed they will be on location in other cities. A picture in release is gone. A picture in release tends to fade from the minds of the people who made

it. As the four-million-dollar check is only the totem of the action, the picture itself is in many ways only the action's by-product. "We can have some fun with this one," the producer says as we leave Tucson. "Having some fun" is also what the action itself is called.

I pass along these notes by way of suggesting that much of what is written about pictures and about picture people approaches reality only occasionally and accidentally. At one time the assurance with which many writers about film palmed off their misconceptions puzzled me a good deal. I used to wonder how Pauline Kael, say, could slip in and out of such airy subordinate clauses as "now that the studios are collapsing," or how she could so misread the labyrinthine propriety of Industry evenings as to characterize "Hollywood wives" as women "whose jaws get a hard set from the nights when they sit soberly at parties waiting to take their sloshed geniuses home." (This fancy, oddly enough, cropped up in a review of *Alex in Wonderland*, a Paul Mazursky picture which, whatever its faults, portrayed with meticulous accuracy that level of "young" Hollywood on which the average daily narcotic intake is one glass of a three-dollar Mondavi white and two marijuana cigarettes shared by six people.) These "sloshed" husbands and "collapsing" studios derive less from Hollywood life than from some weird West Side *Playhouse 90* about Hollywood life, presumably the same one Stanley Kauffmann runs on his mind's screen when he speaks of a director like John Huston as "corrupted by success."

What is there to be said about this particular cast of mind? Some people who write about film seem so temperamentally at odds with what both Fellini and Truffaut have called the "circus" aspect of making film that there is flatly no question of their ever apprehending the social or emotional reality of the process. In this connection I think particularly of Kauffmann, whose idea of a nasty disclosure about the circus is to reveal that the aerialist is up there to get our attention. I recall him advising his readers that Otto Preminger (the same Otto Preminger who cast Joseph Welch in *Anatomy of a Murder* and engaged Louis Nizer to write a script about the Rosenbergs) was a "commercial showman," and also letting them know that

he was wise to the "phoniness" in the chase sequence in *Bullitt:* "Such a chase through the normal streets of San Francisco would have ended in deaths much sooner than it does."

A curious thing about Kauffmann is that in both his dogged rightmindedness and his flatulent diction he is indistinguishable from many members of the Industry itself. He is a man who finds R. D. Laing "blazingly humane." Lewis Mumford is "civilized and civilizing" and someone to whom we owe a "long debt," Arthur Miller a "tragic agonist" hampered in his artistry only by "the shackles of our time." It is the vocabulary of the Jean Hersholt Humanitarian Award. Kauffmann divined in *Bullitt* not only its "phoniness" but a "possible propagandistic motive": "to show (particularly to the young) that law and order are not necessarily Dullsville." The "motive" in *Bullitt* was to show that several million people would pay three dollars apiece to watch Steve McQueen drive fast, but Kauffmann, like my acquaintance who reports from the Polo Lounge, seems to prefer his version. "People in the East pretend to be interested in how pictures are made," Scott Fitzgerald observed in his notes on Hollywood. "But if you actually tell them anything, you find . . . they never see the ventriloquist for the doll. Even the intellectuals, who ought to know better, like to hear about the pretensions, extravagances and vulgarities—tell them pictures have a private grammar, like politics or automobile production or society, and watch the blank look come into their faces."

Of course there is good reason for this blank look, for this almost queasy uneasiness with pictures. To recognize that the picture is but the by-product of the action is to make rather more arduous the task of maintaining one's self-image as (Kauffmann's own job definition) "a critic of new works." Making judgments on films is in many ways so peculiarly vaporous an occupation that the only question is why, beyond the obvious opportunities for a few lecture fees and a little careerism at a dispiritingly self-limiting level, anyone does it in the first place. A finished picture defies all attempts to analyze what makes it work or not work: the responsibility for its every frame is clouded not only in the accidents and compromises of production but in the clauses of its financing. *The Getaway* was Sam Peckinpah's picture, but Steve McQueen had the "cut," or final right to edit. *Up the Sandbox* was Irvin Kershner's picture, but Barbra Streisand had the cut. In a series of interviews with directors, Charles Thomas Samuels asked Carol Reed why he had used the same cutter on so many pictures. "I had no control," Reed said. Samuels asked Vittorio De Sica if he did not find a certain effect in one of his Sophia Loren films a bit artificial. "It was shot by the second unit," De Sica said. "I didn't direct it." In other words, Carlo Ponti wanted it.

Nor does calling film a "collaborative medium" exactly describe the situation. To read David O. Selznick's instructions to his directors, writers, actors and department heads in *Memo from David O. Selznick* is to come very close to the spirit of actually making a picture, a spirit not of collaboration but of armed conflict in which one antagonist has a contract assuring him nuclear capability. Some reviewers make a point of trying to understand whose picture it is by "looking at the script": to understand whose picture it is one needs to look not particularly at the script but at the deal memo.

About the best a writer on film can hope to do, then, is to bring an engaging or interesting intelligence to bear upon the subject, a king of *petit-point*-on-Kleenex effect which rarely stands much scrutiny. "Motives" are inferred where none existed; allegations spun out of thin speculation. Perhaps the difficulty of knowing who made which choices in a picture makes this airiness so expedient that it eventually infects any writer who makes a career of reviewing; perhaps the initial error is in making a career of it. Reviewing motion pictures, like reviewing new cars, may or may not be a useful consumer service (since people respond to a lighted screen in a dark room in the same secret and powerfully irrational way they respond to most sensory stimuli, I tend to think much of it beside the point, but never mind that); the review of pictures has been, as well, a traditional diversion for writers whose actual work is somewhere else. Some 400 mornings spent at press screenings in the late Thirties were, for Graham Greene, an "escape," a way of life "adopted quite voluntarily from a sense of fun." Perhaps it is only when one inflates this sense of fun into (Kauffmann again) "a continuing relation with an art" that one passes so headily beyond the reality principle.

*

February in the last extant stable society. A few days ago I went to lunch in Beverly Hills. At the next table were an agent and a director who should have been, at that moment, on his way to a location to begin a new picture. I knew what he was supposed to be doing because this picture had been talked about around town: six million dollars above the line. There was two million for one actor. There was a million and a quarter for another actor. The director was in for $800,000. The property had cost more than half a million; the first-draft screenplay $200,000, the second draft a little less. A third writer had been brought in, at $6,000 a week. Among the three writers were two Academy Awards and one New York Film Critics Award. The director had an Academy Award for his last picture but one.

And now the director was sitting at lunch in Beverly Hills and he wanted out. The script was not right. Only 38 pages worked, the director said. The financing was shaky. "They're in breach, we all recognize your right to pull out," the agent said carefully. The agent represented many of the principals, and did not want the director to pull out. On the other hand he also represented the director, and the director seemed unhappy. It was difficult to ascertain what anyone involved did want, except for the action to continue. "You pull out," the agent said, "it dies right here, not that I want to influence your decision." The director picked up the bottle of Margaux they were drinking and examined the label.

"Nice little red," the agent said.

"Very nice."

I left as the Sanka was being served. No decision had been reached. Many people have been talking these past few days about this aborted picture, always with a note of regret. It had been a very creative deal and they had run with it as far as they could run and they had had some fun and now the fun was over, as it also would have been had they made the picture.

1973

In Bed

THREE, FOUR, SOMETIMES FIVE times a month, I spend the day in bed with a migraine headache, insensible to the world around me. Almost every day of every month, between these attacks, I feel the sudden irrational irritation and flush of blood into the cerebral arteries which tell me that migraine is on its way, and I take certain drugs to avert its arrival. If I did not take the drugs, I would be able to function perhaps one day in four. The physiological error called migraine is, in brief, central to the given of my life. When I was 15, 16, even 25, I used to think that I could rid myself of this error by simply denying it, character over chemistry. "Do you have headaches *sometimes*? *frequently*? *never*?" the application forms would demand. "Check one." Wary of the trap, wanting whatever it was that the successful circumnavigation of that particular form could bring (a job, a scholarship, the respect of mankind and the grace of God), I would check one. "*Sometimes*," I would lie. That in fact I spent one or two days a week almost unconscious with pain seemed a shameful secret, evidence not merely of some chemical inferiority but of all my bad attitudes, unpleasant tempers, wrongthink.

For I had no brain tumor, no eyestrain, no high blood pressure, nothing wrong with me at all: I simply had migraine headaches, and migraine headaches were, as everyone who did not have them knew, imaginary. I fought migraine then, ignored the warnings it sent, went to school and later to work in spite of it, sat through lectures in Middle English and presentations to advertisers with involuntary tears running down the right side of my face, threw up in washrooms, stumbled home by instinct, emptied ice trays onto my bed and tried to freeze the pain in my right temple, wished only for a neurosurgeon who would do a lobotomy on house call, and cursed my imagination.

It was a long time before I began thinking mechanistically enough to accept migraine for what it was: something with which I would be living, the way some people live with diabetes. Migraine is something more than the fancy of a neurotic imagination. It is an essentially hereditary complex of symptoms, the most frequently noted but by no means the most unpleasant of which is a vascular headache of blinding severity, suffered by a surprising number of women, a fair number of men (Thomas Jefferson had migraine, and so did Ulysses S. Grant, the day he accepted Lee's surrender), and by some unfortunate children as young as two years old. (I had my first when I was eight. It came on during a fire drill at the Columbia School in Colorado Springs, Colorado. I was taken first home and then to the infirmary at Peterson Field, where my father was stationed. The Air Corps doctor prescribed an enema.) Almost anything can trigger a specific attack of migraine: stress, allergy, fatigue, an abrupt change in barometric pressure, a contretemps over a parking ticket. A flashing light. A fire drill. One inherits, of course, only the predisposition. In other words I spent yesterday in bed with a headache not merely because of my bad attitudes, unpleasant tempers and wrongthink, but because both my grandmothers had migraine, my father has migraine and my mother has migraine.

No one knows precisely what it is that is inherited. The chemistry of migraine, however, seems to have some connection with the nerve hormone named serotonin, which is naturally present in the brain. The amount of serotonin in the blood falls sharply at the onset of migraine, and one migraine drug, methysergide, or Sansert, seems to have some effect on serotonin. Methysergide is a derivative of lysergic acid (in fact Sandoz Pharmaceuticals first synthesized LSD-25 while looking for a migraine cure), and its use is hemmed about with so many contraindications and side effects that most doctors prescribe it only in the most incapacitating cases. Methysergide, when it is prescribed, is taken daily, as a preventive; another preventive which works for some people is old-fashioned ergotamine tartrate, which helps to constrict the swelling blood vessels during the "aura," the period which in most cases precedes the actual headache.

Once an attack is under way, however, no drug touches it. Migraine gives some people mild hallucinations, temporarily blinds others, shows up not only as a headache but as a gastrointestinal disturbance, a painful sensitivity to all sensory stimuli, an abrupt overpowering fatigue, a strokelike aphasia, and a crippling inability to make even the most routine connections. When I am in a migraine aura (for some people the aura lasts fifteen minutes, for others several hours), I will drive through red lights, lose the house keys, spill whatever I am holding, lose the ability to focus my eyes or frame coherent sentences, and generally give the appearance of being on drugs, or drunk. The actual headache, when it comes, brings with it chills, sweating, nausea, a debility that seems to stretch the very limits of endurance. That no one dies of migraine seems, to someone deep into an attack, an ambiguous blessing.

My husband also has migraine, which is unfortunate for him but fortunate for me: perhaps nothing so tends to prolong an attack as the accusing eye of someone who has never had a headache. "Why not take a couple of aspirin," the unafflicted will say from the doorway, or "I'd have a headache, too, spending a beautiful day like this inside with all the shades drawn." All of us who have migraine suffer not only from the attacks themselves but from this common conviction that we are perversely refusing to cure ourselves by taking a couple of aspirin, that we are making ourselves sick, that we "bring it on ourselves." And in the most immediate sense, the sense of why we have a headache this Tuesday and not last Thursday, of course we often do. There certainly is what doctors call a "migraine personality," and that personality tends to be ambitious, inward, intolerant of error, rather rigidly organized, perfectionist. "You don't look like a migraine personality," a doctor once said to me. "Your hair's messy. But I suppose you're a compulsive housekeeper." Actually my house is kept even more negligently than my hair, but the doctor was right nonetheless: perfectionism can also take the form of spending most of a week writing and rewriting and not writing a single paragraph.

But not all perfectionists have migraine, and not all migrainous people have migraine personalities. We do not escape heredity. I have tried in most of the available ways to escape my own migrainous heredity (at one point I learned to give myself two daily injections of histamine with a hypodermic needle, even though the needle so frightened me that I had to close my eyes when I did it), but I still have migraine. And I have learned now to live with it, learned when to expect it, how to outwit it, even how to regard it, when it does come, as more friend than lodger. We have reached a certain understanding, my migraine and I. It never comes when I am in real trouble. Tell me that my house is burned down, my husband has left me, that there is gunfighting in the streets and panic in the banks, and I will not respond by getting a headache. It comes instead when I am fighting not an open guerrilla war with my own life, during weeks of small household confusions, lost laundry, unhappy help, canceled appointments, on days when the telephone rings too much and I get no work done and the wind is coming up. On days like that my friend comes uninvited.

And once it comes, now that I am wise in its ways, I no longer fight it. I lie down and let it happen. At first every small apprehension is magnified, every anxiety a pounding terror. Then the pain comes, and I concentrate only on that. Right there is the usefulness of migraine, there in that imposed yoga, the concentration on the pain. For when the pain recedes, ten or twelve hours later, everything goes with it, all the hidden resentments, all the vain anxieties. The migraine has acted as a circuit breaker, and the fuses have emerged intact. There is a pleasant convalescent euphoria. I open the windows and feel the air, eat gratefully, sleep well. I notice the particular nature of a flower in a glass on the stair landing. I count my blessings.

1968

On the Road

Where are we heading, they asked in all the television and radio studios. They asked it in New York and Los Angeles and they asked it in Boston and Washington and they asked it in Dallas and Houston and Chicago and San Francisco. Sometimes they made eye contact as they asked it. Sometimes they closed their eyes as they asked it. Quite often they wondered not just where we were heading but where we were heading "as Americans," or "as concerned Americans," or "as American women," or, on one occasion, "as the American guy and the American woman." I never learned the answer, nor did the answer matter, for one of the eerie and liberating aspects of broadcast discourse is that nothing one says will alter in the slightest either the form or the length of the conversation. Our voices in the studios were those of manic actors assigned to do three-minute, four-minute, seven-minute improvs. Our faces on the monitors were those of concerned Americans. On my way to one of those studios in Boston I had seen the magnolias bursting white down Marlborough Street. On my way to another in Dallas I had watched the highway lights blazing and dimming pink against the big dawn sky. Outside one studio in Houston the afternoon heat was sinking into the deep primeval green of the place and outside the next, that night in Chicago, snow fell and glittered in the lights along the lake. Outside all these studios America lay in all its exhilaratingly volatile weather and eccentricity and specificity, but inside the studios we shed the specific and rocketed on to the general, for they were The Interviewers and I was The Author and the single question we seemed able to address together was *where are we heading*.

8:30 A.M. to 9:30 A.M.: LIVE on WFSB TV/THIS MORNING.
10 A.M. to 10:30 A.M.: LIVE on WINF AM/THE WORLD TODAY.
10:45 A.M. to 11:45 A.M.: PRESS INTERVIEW with HARTFORD COURANT.
12 noon to 1:30 P.M.: AUTOGRAPHING at BARNES AND NOBLE.

2 P.M. to 2:30 P.M.: TAPE at WDRC AM/FM.
3 P.M. to 3:30 P.M.: PRESS INTERVIEW with THE HILL INK.
7:30 P.M. to 9 P.M.: TAPE at WHNB TV/WHAT ABOUT WOMEN.

From 12 noon to 1:30 P.M., that first day in Hartford, I talked to a man who had cut a picture of me from a magazine in 1970 and had come round to Barnes and Noble to see what I looked like in 1977. From 2 P.M. to 2:30 P.M., that first day in Hartford, I listened to the receptionists at WDRC AM/FM talk about the new records and I watched snow drop from the pine boughs in the cemetery across the street. The name of the cemetery was Mt. St. Benedict and my husband's father had been buried there. "Any Steely Dan come in?" the receptionists kept asking. From 8:30 A.M. until 9 P.M., that first day in Hartford, I neglected to mention the name of the book I was supposed to be promoting. It was my fourth book but I had never before done what is called in the trade a book tour. I was not sure what I was doing or why I was doing it. I had left California equipped with two "good" suits, a box of unanswered mail, Elizabeth Hardwick's *Seduction and Betrayal*, Edmund Wilson's *To the Finland Station*, six Judy Blume books and my eleven-year-old daughter. The Judy Blume books were along to divert my daughter. My daughter was along to divert me. Three days into the tour I sent home the box of unanswered mail to make room for a packet of Simon and Schuster press releases describing me in favorable terms. Four days into the tour I sent home *Seduction and Betrayal* and *To the Finland Station* to make room for a thousand-watt hair blower. By the time I reached Boston, ten days into the tour, I knew that I had never before heard and would possibly never again hear America singing at precisely this pitch: ethereal, speedy, and angel choir on Dexamyl.

Where were we heading. The set for this discussion was always the same: a cozy oasis of wicker and ferns in the wilderness of cables and cameras and Styrofoam coffee cups that was the actual studio. On wicker settees across the nation I expressed my conviction that we were heading "into an era" of whatever the clock seemed to demand. In green rooms across the nation I listened to other people talk about where we were heading, and also about their vocations, avocations, and secret interests. I discussed L-dopa and bio-rhythm with a woman whose father invented prayer breakfasts. I exchanged makeup tips with a former Mouseketeer. I stopped reading newspapers and started relying on bulletins from limo drivers, from Mouseketeers, from the callers-in on call-in shows and from the closed-circuit screens in airports that flashed random stories off the wire ("CARTER URGES BARBITURATE BAN" is one that got my attention at La Guardia) between advertisements for *Shenandoah.* I gravitated to the random. I swung with the non-sequential.

I began to see America as my own, a child's map over which my child and I could skim and light at will. We spoke not of cities but of airports. If rain fell at Logan we could find sun at Dulles. Bags lost at O'Hare could be found at Dallas/Fort Worth. In the first-class cabins of the planes on which we traveled we were often, my child and I, the only female passengers, and I apprehended for the first time those particular illusions of mobility which power American business. Time was money. Motion was progress. Decisions were snap and the ministrations of other people were constant. Room service, for example, assumed paramount importance. We needed, my eleven-year-old and I, instant but erratically timed infusions of consommé, oatmeal, crab salad and asparagus vinaigrette. We needed Perrier water and tea to drink when we were working. We needed bourbon on the rocks and Shirley Temples to drink when we were not. A kind of irritable panic came over us when room service went off, and also when no one answered in the housekeeping department. In short we had fallen into the peculiar hormonal momentum of business travel, and I had begun to understand the habituation many men and a few women have to planes and telephones and schedules. I had begun to regard my own schedule—a sheaf of thick cream-colored pages printed with the words "SIMON & SCHUSTER/A DIVISION OF GULF & WESTERN CORPORATION"—with a reverence approaching the mystical. We wanted 24-hour room service. We wanted direct-dial telephones. We wanted to stay on the road forever.

*

We saw air as our element. In Houston the air was warm and rich and suggestive of fossil fuel and we pretended we owned a house in River Oaks. In Chicago the air was brilliant and thin and we pretended we owned the 27th floor of the Ritz. In New York the air was charged and crackling and shorting out with opinions, and we pretended we had some. Everyone in New York had opinions. Opinions were demanded in return. The absence of opinion was construed as opinion. Even my daughter was developing opinions. "Had an interesting talk with Carl Bernstein," she noted in the log she had been assigned to keep for her fifth-grade teacher in Malibu, California. Many of these New York opinions seemed intended as tonic revisions, bold corrections to opinions in vogue during the previous week, but since I had just dropped from the sky it was difficult for me to distinguish those opinions which were "bold" and "revisionist" from those which were merely "weary" and "rote." At the time I left New York many people were expressing a bold belief in "joy"—joy in children, joy in wedlock, joy in the dailiness of life—but joy was trickling down fast to show-business personalities. Mike Nichols, for example, was expressing his joy in the pages of *Newsweek*, and also his weariness with "lapidary bleakness." Lapidary bleakness was definitely rote.

We were rethinking the Sixties that week, or Morris Dickstein was.

We were taking another look at the Fifties that week, or Hilton Kramer was.

I agreed passionately. I disagreed passionately. I called room service on one phone and listened attentively on the other to people who seemed convinced that the "texture" of their lives had been agreeably or adversely affected by conversion to the politics of joy, by regression to lapidary bleakness, by the Sixties, by the Fifties, by the recent change in administrations and by the sale of *The Thorn Birds* to paper for one-million-nine.

I lost track of information.

I was blitzed by opinion.

I began to see opinions arcing in the air, intersecting flight patterns. The Eastern shuttle was cleared for landing and so was lapidary bleakness. John Leonard and joy were on converging vectors. I began to see the country itself as a projection on air, a kind of hologram, an invisible grid of image and opinion and electronic impulse. There were opinions in the air and there were planes in the air and there were even people in the air: one afternoon in New York my husband saw a man jump from a window and fall to the sidewalk outside the Yale Club. I mentioned this to a *Daily News* photographer who was taking my picture. "You have to catch a jumper in the act to make the paper," he advised me. He had caught two in the act but only the first had made the paper. The second was a better picture but coincided with the crash of a DC-10 at Orly. "They're all over town," the photographer said. "Jumpers. A lot of them aren't even jumpers. They're window washers. Who fall."

What does that say about us as a nation, I was asked the next day when I mentioned the jumpers and window washers on the air. *Where are we headed.* On the 27th floor of the Ritz in Chicago my daughter and I sat frozen at the breakfast table until the window washers glided safely out of sight. At a call-in station in Los Angeles I was told by the guard that there would be a delay because they had a jumper on the line. "I say let him jump," the guard said to me. I imagined a sky dense with jumpers and fallers and DC-10s. I held my daughter's hand at takeoff and landing and watched for antennae on the drive into town. The big antennae with the pulsing red lights had been for a month our landmarks. The big antennae with the pulsing red lights had in fact been for a month our destinations. "Out I-10 to the antenna" was the kind of direction we had come to understand, for we were on the road, on the grid, on the air and also in it. *Where were we heading.* I don't know where you're heading, I said in the studio attached to the last of these antennae, my eyes fixed on still another of the neon FLEETWOOD MAC signs that flickered that spring in radio stations from coast to coast, but I'm heading home.

1977

On the Mall

THEY FLOAT ON THE landscape like pyramids to the boom years, all those Plazas and Malls and Esplanades. All those Squares and Fairs. All those Towns and Dales, all those Villages, all those Forests and Parks and Lands. Stonestown. Hillsdale. Valley Fair, Mayfair, Northgate, Southgate, Eastgate, Westgate. Gulfgate. They are toy garden cities in which no one lives but everyone consumes, profound equalizers, the perfect fusion of the profit motive and the egalitarian ideal, and to hear their names is to recall words and phrases no longer quite current. Baby Boom. Consumer Explosion. Leisure Revolution. Do-It-Yourself Revolution. Backyard Revolution. Suburbia. "The Shopping Center," the Urban Land Institute could pronounce in 1957, "is today's extraordinary retail business evolvement. . . . The automobile accounts for suburbia, and suburbia accounts for the shopping center."

It was a peculiar and visionary time, those years after World War II to which all the Malls and Towns and Dales stand as climate-controlled monuments. Even the word "automobile," as in "the automobile accounts for suburbia and suburbia accounts for the shopping center," no longer carries the particular freight it once did: as a child in the late Forties in California I recall reading and believing that the "freedom of movement" afforded by the automobile was "America's fifth freedom." The trend was up. The solution was in sight. The frontier had been reinvented, and its shape was the subdivision, that new free land on which all settlers could recast their lives *tabula rasa*. For one perishable moment there the American idea seemed about to achieve itself, via F.H.A. housing and the acquisition of major appliances, and a certain enigmatic glamour attached to the architects of this newfound land. They made something of nothing. They gambled and sometimes lost. They staked the past to seize the future. I have difficulty now imagining a childhood in which a man named Jere Strizek, the developer of Town and Country Village outside Sacramento (143,000 square feet gross floor area, 68 stores, 1000 parking spaces, the Urban Land Institute's "prototype for centers using heavy timber and tile construction for informality"), could materialize as a role model, but I had such a childhood, just after World War II, in Sacramento. I never met or even saw Jere Strizek, but at the age of 12 I imagined him a kind of frontiersman, a romantic and revolutionary spirit, and in the indigenous grain he was.

I suppose James B. Douglas and David D. Bohannon were too.

I first heard of James B. Douglas and David D. Bohannon not when I was 12 but a dozen years later, when I was living in New York, working for *Vogue*, and taking, by correspondence, a University of California Extension course in shopping-center theory. This did not seem to me eccentric at the time. I remember sitting on the cool floor in Irving Penn's studio and reading, in *The Community Builders Handbook*, advice from James B. Douglas on shopping-center financing. I recall staying late in my pale-blue office on the twentieth floor of the Graybar Building to memorize David D. Bohannon's parking ratios. My "real" life was to sit in this office and describe life as it was lived in Djakarta and Caneel Bay and in the great châteaux of the Loire Valley, but my dream life was to put together a Class-A regional shopping center with three full-line department stores as major tenants.

That I was perhaps the only person I knew in New York, let alone on the Condé Nast floors of the Graybar Building, to have memorized the distinctions among "A," "B," and "C" shopping centers did not occur to me (the defining distinction, as long as I have your attention, is that an "A," or "regional," center has as its major tenant a full-line department store which carries major appliances; a "B," or "community," center has as its major tenant a junior department store which does not carry major appliances; and a "C," or "neighborhood," center has as its major tenant only a supermarket): my interest in shopping centers was in no way casual. I did want to build them. I wanted to build them because I had fallen into the habit of writing fiction, and I had it in my head that a couple of good centers might support this habit less taxingly than a pale-blue office at *Vogue*. I had even devised an original scheme by which I planned to gain enough capital and credibility to enter the shopping-center game: I would lease warehouses in, say, Queens, and offer Manhattan delicatessens the opportunity to sell competitively by buying cooperatively, from my trucks. I see a few wrinkles in this scheme now (the words "concrete overcoat" come to mind), but I did not then. In fact I planned to run it out of the pale-blue office.

James B. Douglas and David D. Bohannon. In 1950 James B. Douglas had opened Northgate, in Seattle, the first regional center to combine a pedestrian mall with an underground truck tunnel. In 1954 David D. Bohannon had opened Hillsdale, a forty-acre regional center on the peninsula south of San Francisco. That is the only solid bio I have on James B. Douglas and David D. Bohannon to this day, but many of their opinions are engraved on my memory. David D. Bohannon believed in preserving the integrity of the shopping center by not cutting up the site with any dedicated roads. David D. Bohannon believed that architectural setbacks in a center looked "pretty on paper" but caused "customer resistance." James B. Douglas advised that a small-loan office could prosper in a center only if it were placed away from foot traffic, since people who want small loans do not want to be observed getting them. I do not now recall whether it was James B. Douglas or David D. Bohannon or someone else altogether who passed along this hint on how to paint the lines around the parking spaces (actually this is called "striping the lot," and the spaces are "stalls"): make each space a foot wider than it need be—ten feet, say, instead of nine—when the center first opens and business is slow. By this single stroke the developer achieves a couple of important objectives, the appearance of a popular center and the illusion of easy parking, and no one will really notice when business picks up and the spaces shrink.

Nor do I recall who first solved what was once a crucial center dilemma: the placement of the major tenant vis-à-vis the parking lot. The dilemma was that the major tenant—the draw, the raison d'être for the financing, the Sears, the Macy's, the May Company—wanted its customer to walk directly from car to store. The smaller tenants, on the other hand, wanted that same customer to *pass their stores* on the way from the car to, say, Macy's. The solution to this conflict of interests was actually very simple: *two major tenants*, one at each end of a mall. This is called "anchoring the mall," and represents seminal work in shopping-center theory. One thing you will note about shopping-center theory is that you could have thought of it yourself, and a course in it will go a long way toward dispelling the notion that business proceeds from mysteries too recondite for you and me.

A few aspects of shopping-center theory do in fact remain impenetrable to me. I have no idea why the Community Builders' Council ranks "Restaurant" as deserving a Number One (or "Hot Spot") location but exiles "Chinese Restaurant" to a Number Three, out there with "Power and Light Office" and "Christian Science Reading Room." Nor do I know why the Council approves of enlivening a mall with "small animals" but specifically, vehemently, and with no further explanation, excludes "monkeys." If I had a center I would have monkeys, and Chinese restaurants, and Mylar kites and bands of small girls playing tambourine.

A few years ago at a party I met a woman from Detroit who told me that the Joyce Carol Oates novel with which she identified most closely was *Wonderland*.

I asked her why.

"Because," she said, "my husband has a branch there."

I did not understand.

"In Wonderland the center," the woman said patiently. "My husband has a branch in Wonderland."

I have never visited Wonderland but imagine it to have bands of small girls playing tambourine.

A few facts about shopping centers.

The "biggest" center in the United States is generally agreed to be Woodfield, outside Chicago, a "super" regional or "leviathan" two-million-square-foot center with four major tenants.

The "first" shopping center in the United States is generally agreed to be Country Club Plaza in Kansas City, built in the twenties. There were some other early centers, notably Edward H. Bouton's 1907 Roland Park in Baltimore, Hugh Prather's 1931 Highland Park Shopping Village in Dallas, and Hugh Potter's 1937 River Oaks in Houston, but the developer of Country Club Plaza, the late J. C. Nichols, is referred to with ritual frequency in the literature of shopping centers, usually as "pioneering J. C. Nichols," "trailblazing J. C. Nichols," or "J. C. Nichols, father of the center as we know it."

Those are some facts I know about shopping centers because I still want to be Jere Strizek or James B. Douglas or David D. Bohannon. Here are some facts I know about shopping centers because I never will be Jere Strizek or James B. Douglas or David D. Bohannon: a good center in which to spend the day if you wake feeling low in Honolulu, Hawaii, is Ala Moana, major tenants Liberty House and Sears. A good center in which to spend the day if you wake feeling low in Oxnard, California, is The Esplanade, major tenants the May Company and Sears. A good center in which to spend the day if you wake feeling low in Biloxi, Mississippi, is Edgewater Plaza, major tenant Godchaux's. Ala Moana in Honolulu is larger than The Esplanade in Oxnard, and The Esplanade in Oxnard is larger than Edgewater Plaza in Biloxi. Ala Moana has carp pools. The Esplanade and Edgewater Plaza do not.

These marginal distinctions to one side, Ala Moana, The Esplanade, and Edgewater Plaza are the same place, which is precisely their role not only as equalizers but in the sedation of anxiety. In each of them one moves for a while in an aqueous suspension not only of light but of judgment, not only of judgment but of "personality." One meets no acquaintances at The Esplanade. One gets no telephone calls at Edgewater Plaza. "It's a hard place to run in to for a pair of stockings," a friend complained to me recently of Ala Moana, and I knew that she was not yet ready to surrender her ego to the idea of the center. The last time I went to Ala Moana it was to buy *The New York Times*. Because *The New York Times* was not in, I sat on the mall for a while and ate caramel corn. In the end I bought not *The New York Times* at all but two straw hats at Liberty House, four bottles of nail enamel at Woolworth's, and a toaster, on sale at Sears. In the literature of shopping centers these would be described as impulse purchases, but the impulse here was obscure. I do not wear hats, nor do I like caramel corn. I do not use nail enamel. Yet flying back across the Pacific I regretted only the toaster.

1975

In Bogotá

ON THE COLOMBIAN coast it was hot, fevered, eleven degrees off the equator with evening trades that did not relieve but blew hot and dusty. The sky was white, the casino idle. I had never meant to leave the coast but after a week of it I began to think exclusively of Bogotá, floating on the Andes an hour away by air. In Bogotá it would be cool. In Bogotá one could get *The New York Times* only two days late and the *Miami Herald* only one day late and also emeralds, and bottled water. In Bogotá there would be fresh roses in the bathrooms at the Hotel Tequendama and hot water twenty-four hours a day and numbers to be dialed for chicken sandwiches from room service and Xerox *rápido* and long-distance operators who could get Los Angeles in ten minutes. In my room in Cartagena I would wake to the bleached coastal morning and find myself repeating certain words and phrases under my breath, an incantation: *Bogotá, Bacatá.* El Dorado. Emeralds. Hot water. Madeira consommé in cool dining rooms. *Santa Fé de Bogotá del Nuevo Reino de Granada de las Indias del Mar Océano.* The Avianca flight to Bogotá left Cartagena every morning at ten-forty, but such was the slowed motion of the coast that it took me another four days to get on it.

Maybe that is the one true way to see Bogotá, to have it float in the mind until the need for it is visceral, for the whole history of the place has been to seem a mirage, a delusion on the high savannah, its gold and its emeralds unattainable, inaccessible, its isolation so splendid and unthinkable that the very existence of a city astonishes. There on the very spine of the Andes gardeners espalier roses on embassy walls. Swarms of little girls in proper navy-blue school blazers line up to enter the faded tent of a tatty traveling circus: the elephant, the strong man, the tattooed man from Maracaibo. I arrived in Bogotá on a day in 1973 when the streets seemed bathed in mist and thin brilliant light and in the amplified pop voice of Nelson Ned, a Brazilian dwarf whose records played in every *disco* storefront. Outside the sixteenth-century Church of San Francisco, where the Spanish viceroys took office when the country was Nueva Granada and where Simón Bolívar assumed the presidency of the doomed republic called Gran Colombia, small children and old women hawked Cuban cigars and cartons of American cigarettes and newspapers with the headline "JACKIE Y ARI." I lit a candle for my daughter and bought a paper to read about Jackie and Ari, how the princess *de los norteamericanos* ruled the king of the Greek sea by demanding of him pink champagne every night and *medialunas* every morning, a story a child might invent. Later, in the Gold Museum of the Banco de la República, I looked at the gold the Spaniards opened the Americas to get, the vision of El Dorado which was to animate a century and is believed to have begun here, outside Bogotá, at Lake Guatavita. "Many golden offerings were cast into the lake," wrote the anthropologist Olivia Vlahos of the nights when the Chibcha Indians lit bonfires on the Andes and confirmed their rulers at Guatavita.

> *Many more were heaped on a raft. . . . Then into the firelight stepped the ruler-to-be, his nakedness coated with a sticky resin. Onto the resin his priests applied gold dust and more gold dust until he gleamed like a golden statue. He stepped onto the raft, which was cut loose to drift into the middle of the lake. Suddenly he dived into the black water. When he emerged, the gold was gone, washed clean from his body. And he was king.*

Until the Spaniards heard the story, and came to find El Dorado for themselves. "One thing you must understand," a young Colombian said to me at dinner that night. We were at Eduardo's out in the Chico district and the piano player was playing "Love Is Blue" and we were drinking an indifferent bottle of Château Léoville-Poyferré which cost $20 American. "Spain sent all its highest aristocracy to South America." In fact I had heard variations on this hallucination before, on the coast: when Colombians spoke about the past I often had the sense of being in a place where history tended to sink, even as it happened, into the traceless solitude of autosuggestion. The princess was drinking pink champagne. High in the mountains the men were made of gold. Spain sent its highest aristocracy to South America. They were all stories a child might invent.

Many years later, as he faced the firing squad, Colonel Aureliano Buendia was to remember that distant afternoon when his father took him to discover ice.

—The opening line of *One Hundred Years of Solitude*, by the Colombian novelist Gabriel García Marquez.

At the big movie theaters in Bogotá in the spring of 1973 *The Professionals* was playing, and *It's A Mad Mad Mad Mad World*, two American pictures released in, respectively, 1967 and 1964. The English-language racks of paperback stands were packed with Edmund Wilson's *The Cold War and the Income Tax*, the 1964 Signet edition. This slight but definite dislocation of time fixed on the mind the awesome isolation of the place, as did dislocations of other kinds. On the fourth floor of the glossy new Bogotá Hilton one could lunch in an orchid-filled gallery that overlooked the indoor swimming pool, and also overlooked a shantytown of packing-crate and tin-can shacks where a small boy, his body hideously scarred and his face obscured by a knitted mask, played listlessly with a yo-yo. In the lobby of the Hotel Tequendama two Braniff stewardesses in turquoise-blue Pucci pantsuits flirted desultorily with a German waiting for the airport limousine; a third ignored the German and stood before a relief map on which buttons could be pressed to light up the major cities of Colombia. Santa Marta, on the coast; Barranquilla, Cartagena. Medellín, on the Central Cordillera. Cali, on the Cauca River, San Agustín on the Magdalena. Leticia, on the Amazon.

I watched her press the buttons one by one, transfixed by the vast darkness each tiny bulb illumined. The light for Bogotá blinked twice and went out. The girl in the Pucci pantsuit traced the Andes with her index finger. *Alto arrecife de la aurora humana*, the Chilean poet Pablo Neruda called the Andes. *High reef of the human dawn.* It cost the *conquistador* Gonzalo Jiménez de Quesada two years and the health of most of his men to reach Bogotá from the coast. It cost me $26.

"I knew they were your bags," the man at the airport said, producing them triumphantly from a moraine of baggage and cartons and rubble from the construction that seemed all over

Bogotá a chronic condition. "They smelled American." *Parece una turista norteamericana*, I read about myself in *El Espectador* a few mornings later. She resembles an American tourist. In fact I was aware of being an American in Colombia in a way I had not been in other places. I kept running into Americans, compatriots for whom the emotional center of Bogotá was the massive concrete embassy on Carrera 10, members of a phantom colony called "the American presence" which politesse prevented them from naming out loud. Several times I met a young American who ran an "information" office, which he urged me to visit; he had extremely formal manners, appeared for the most desultory evening in black tie, and was, according to the Colombian I asked, CIA. I recall talking at a party to a USIS man who spoke in a low mellifluous voice of fevers he had known, fevers in Sierra Leone, fevers in Monrovia, fevers on the Colombian coast. Our host interrupted this litany, demanded to know why the ambassador had not come to the party. "Little situation in Cali," the USIS man said, and smiled professionally. He seemed very concerned that no breach of American manners be inferred, and so, absurdly, did I. We had nothing in common except the eagles on our passports, but those eagles made us, in some way I did not entirely understand, co-conspirators, two strangers heavy with responsibility for seeing that the eagle should not offend. We would prefer the sweet local Roman-Cola to the Coca-Cola the Colombians liked. We would think of Standard Oil as Esso Colombiano. We would not speak of fever except to one another. Later I met an American actor who had spent two weeks taking cold showers in Bogotá before he discovered that the hot and cold taps in the room assigned him were simply reversed: he had never asked, he said, because he did not want to be considered an arrogant *gringo*.

In *El Tiempo* that morning I had read that General Gustavo Rojas Pinilla, who took over Colombia in a military coup in 1953 and closed down the press before he was overthrown in 1957, was launching a new bid for power on a Peronist platform, and I had thought that perhaps people at the party would be talking about that, but they were not. Why had the American film industry not made films about the Vietnam War, was what the Colombian stringer for the Caribbean newspaper wanted to talk about. The young Colombian filmmakers looked at him incredulously. "What would be the point," one finally shrugged. "They run that war on television."

The filmmakers had lived in New York, spoke of Rip Torn, Norman Mailer, Ricky Leacock, Super 8. One had come to the party in a stovepipe preacher's hat; another in a violet macramé shawl to the knees. The girl with them, a famous beauty from the coast, wore a flamingo-pink sequinned midriff, and her pale red hair was fluffed around her head in an electric halo. She watched the *cumbia* dancers and fondled a baby ocelot and remained impassive both to the possibility of General Gustavo Rojas Pinilla's comeback and to the question of why the American film industry had not made films about the Vietnam War. Later, outside the gate, the filmmakers lit thick marijuana cigarettes in view of the uniformed *policia* and asked if I knew Paul Morrissey's and Andy Warhol's address in Rome. The girl from the coast cradled her ocelot against the wind.

Of the time I spent in Bogotá I remember mainly images, indelible but difficult to connect. I remember the walls on the second floor of the Museo Nacional, white and cool and lined with portraits of the presidents of Colombia, a great many presidents. I remember the emeralds in shop windows, lying casually in trays, all of them oddly pale at the center, somehow watered, cold at the very heart where one expects the fire. I asked the price of one: "Twenty-thousand American," the woman said. She was reading a booklet called *Horóscopo: Sagitario* and did not look up. I remember walking across Plaza Bolívar, the great square from which all Colombian power emanates, at mid-afternoon when men in dark European suits stood talking on the steps of the Capitol and the mountains floated all around, their perspective made fluid by sun and shadow; I remember the way the mountains dwarfed a deserted Ferris wheel in the Parque Nacional in late afternoon.

In fact the mountains loom behind every image I remember, and perhaps are themselves the connection. Some afternoons I would drive out along their talus slopes through the Chico district, out Carrera 7 where the grounds of the great houses were immaculately clipped and the gates bore brass plaques with the names of European embassies and American foundations and Argentinian neurologists. I recall stopping in El Chico to make a telephone call one day, from a small shopping center off Carrera 7; the shopping center adjoined a church where a funeral mass had just taken place. The mourners were leaving the church, talking on the street, the women, most of them, in black pantsuits and violet-tinted glasses and pleated silk dresses and Givenchy coats that had not been bought in Bogotá. In El Chico it did not seem so far to Paris or New York, but there remained the mountains, and beyond the mountains that dense world described by Gabriel García Marquez as so recent that many things lacked names.

And even just a little farther, out where Carrera 7 became the Carretera Central del Norte, the rutted road that plunged through the mountains to Tunja and eventually to Caracas, it was in many ways a perpetual frontier, vertiginous in its extremes. Rickety buses hurtled dizzyingly down the center of the road, swerving now and then to pick up a laborer, to avoid a pothole or a pack of children. Back from the road stretched large *haciendas*, their immense main houses barely visible in the folds of the slopes, their stone walls splashed occasionally with red paint, crude representations of the hammer and sickle and admonitions to vote *comunista*. One day when I was out there a cloud burst, and because my rented car with 110,000 miles on it had no windshield wipers, I stopped by the side of the road. Rain streamed over the MESA ARIZONA WESTWOOD WARRIORS and GO TIDE decals on the car windows. Gullies formed on the road. Up in the high gravel quarries men worked on, picking with shovels at the Andes for twelve and a half pesos a load.

Through another of our cities without a center, as
hideous
as Los Angeles, and with as many cars
per head, and past the 20-foot neon sign
for Coppertone *on a church, past the population*
earning $700 per capita
in jerry skyscraper living-slabs, and on to the White
House
of El Presidente Leoni, his small men with 18-
inch repeating pistols, firing 45 bullets a minute,
the two armed guards petrified beside us, while we had
champagne,

and someone bugging the President: "Where are the
girls?"
And the enclosed leader, quite a fellow, saying,
"I don't know where yours are, but I know where to
find mine." . . .
This house, this pioneer democracy, built
on foundations, not of rock, but blood as hard as rock.
—Robert Lowell, "Caracas"

There is one more image I remember, and it comes in two parts. First there was the mine. Tunneled into a mountain in Zipaquirá, fifty kilometers north of Bogotá, is a salt mine. This single mine produces, each year, enough salt for all of South America, and has done so since before Europeans knew the continent existed: salt, not gold, was the economic basis of the Chibcha Empire, and Zipaquirá one of its capitals. The mine is vast, its air oppressive. I happened to be inside the mine because inside the mine there is, carved into the mountain 450 feet below the surface, a cathedral in which 10,000 people can hear mass at the same time. Fourteen massive stone pilasters support the vault. Recessed fluorescent tubes illuminate the Stations of the Cross, the dense air absorbing and dimming the light unsteadily. One could think of Chibcha sacrifices here, of the *conquistador* priests struggling to superimpose the European mass on the screams of the slaughtered children.

But one would be wrong. The building of this enigmatic excavation in the salt mountain was undertaken not by the Chibcha but by the Banco de la República, in 1954. In 1954 General Gustavo Rojas Pinilla and his colonels were running Colombia, and the country was wrenched by *La Violencia*, the fifteen years of anarchy that followed the assassination of Jorge Gaitán in Bogotá in 1948. In 1954 people were fleeing the terrorized countryside to squat in shacks in the comparative safety of Bogotá. In 1954 Colombia still had few public works projects, no transportation to speak of: Bogotá would not be connected by rail with the Caribbean until 1961. As I stood in the dim mountain reading the Banco de la República's dedicatory plaque, 1954 seemed to me an extraordinary year to have hit on the notion of building a cathedral of salt, but the Colombians to whom I mentioned it only shrugged.

*

The second part of the image. I had come up from the mine and was having lunch on the side of the salt mountain, in the chilly dining room of the Hostería del Libertador. There were heavy draperies that gave off a faint muskiness when touched. There were white brocade tablecloths, carefully darned. For every stalk of blanched asparagus served, there appeared another battery of silverplated flatware and platters and *vinaigrette* sauceboats, and also another battery of "waiters": little boys, twelve or thirteen years old, dressed in tailcoats and white gloves and taught to serve as if this small inn on an Andean precipice were Vienna under the Hapsburgs.

I sat there for a long time. All around us the wind was sweeping the clouds off the Andes and across the savannah. Four-hundred and fifty feet beneath us was the cathedral built of salt in the year 1954. *This house, this pioneer democracy, built on foundations, not of rock, but blood as hard as rock.* One of the little boys in white gloves picked up an empty wine bottle from a table, fitted it precisely into a wine holder, and marched toward the kitchen holding it stiffly before him, glancing covertly at the *mâitre d'hôtel* for approval. It seemed to me later that I had never before seen and would perhaps never again see the residuum of European custom so movingly and pointlessly observed.

1974

At the Dam

SINCE THE AFTERNOON IN 1967 when I first saw Hoover Dam, its image has never been entirely absent from my inner eye. I will be talking to someone in Los Angeles, say, or New York, and suddenly the dam will materialize, its pristine concave face gleaming white against the harsh rusts and taupes and mauves of that rock canyon hundreds or thousands of miles from where I am. I will be driving down Sunset Boulevard, or about to enter a freeway, and abruptly those power transmission towers will appear before me, canted vertiginously over the tailrace. Sometimes I am confronted by the intakes and sometimes by the shadow of the heavy cable that spans the canyon and sometimes by the ominous outlets to unused spillways, black in the lunar clarity of the desert light. Quite often I hear the turbines. Frequently I wonder what is happening at the dam this instant, at this precise intersection of time and space, how much water is being released to fill downstream orders and what lights are flashing and which generators are in full use and which just spinning free.

I used to wonder what it was about the dam that made me think of it at times and in places where I once thought of the Mindanao Trench, or of the stars wheeling in their courses, or of the words *As it was in the beginning, is now and ever shall be, world without end, amen*. Dams, after all, are commonplace: we have all seen one. This particular dam had existed as an idea in the world's mind for almost forty years before I saw it. Hoover Dam, showpiece of the Boulder Canyon project, the several million tons of concrete that made the Southwest plausible, the *fait accompli* that was to convey, in the innocent time of its construction, the notion that mankind's brightest promise lay in American engineering.

Of course the dam derives some of its emotional effect from precisely that aspect, that sense of being a monument to a faith since misplaced. "They died to make the desert bloom," reads a plaque dedicated to the 96 men who died building this first of the great high dams, and in context the worn phrase touches, suggests all of that trust in harnessing resources, in the meliorative power of the dynamo, so central to the early Thirties. Boulder City, built in 1931 as the construction town for the dam, retains the ambience of a model city, a new town, a toy triangular grid of green lawns and trim bungalows, all fanning out from the Reclamation building. The bronze sculptures at the dam itself evoke muscular citizens of a tomorrow that never came, sheaves of wheat clutched heavenward, thunderbolts defied. Winged Victories guard the flagpole. The flag whips in the canyon wind. An empty Pepsi-Cola can clatters across the terrazzo. The place is perfectly frozen in time.

But history does not explain it all, does not entirely suggest what makes the dam so affecting. Nor, even, does energy, the massive involvement with power and pressure and the transparent sexual overtones to that involvement. Once when I revisited the dam I walked through it with a man from the Bureau of Reclamation. For a while we trailed behind a guided tour, and then we went on, went into parts of the dam where visitors do not generally go. Once in a while he would explain something, usually in that recondite language having to do with "peaking power," with "outages" and "dewatering," but on the whole we spent the afternoon in a world so alien, so complete and so beautiful unto itself that it was scarcely necessary to speak at all. We saw almost no one. Cranes moved above us as if under their own volition. Generators roared. Transformers hummed. The gratings on which we stood vibrated. We watched a hundred-ton steel shaft plunging down to that place where the water was. And finally we got down to that place where the water was, where the water sucked out of Lake Mead roared through thirty-foot penstocks and then into thirteen-foot penstocks and finally into the turbines themselves. "Touch it," the Reclamation man said, and I did, and for a long time I just stood there with my hands on the turbine. It was a peculiar moment, but so explicit as to suggest nothing beyond itself.

There was something beyond all that, something beyond energy, beyond history, something I could not fix in my mind. When I came up from the dam that day the wind was blowing harder, through the canyon and all across the Mojave. Later, toward Henderson and Las Vegas, there would be dust blowing, blowing past the Country-Western Casino FRI & SAT

NITES and blowing past the Shrine of Our Lady of Safe Journey STOP & PRAY, but out at the dam there was no dust, only the rock and the dam and a little greasewood and a few garbage cans, their tops chained, banging against a fence. I walked across the marble star map that traces a sidereal revolution of the equinox and fixes forever, the Reclamation man had told me, for all time and for all people who can read the stars, the date the dam was dedicated. The star map was, he had said, for when we were all gone and the dam was left. I had not thought much of it when he said it, but I thought of it then, with the wind whining and the sun dropping behind a mesa with the finality of a sunset in space. Of course that was the image I had seen always, seen it without quite realizing what I saw, a dynamo finally free of man, splendid at last in its absolute isolation, transmitting power and releasing water to a world where no one is.

1970

V

ON THE MORNING AFTER THE SIXTIES

On the Morning After the Sixties

I AM TALKING HERE about being a child of my time. When I think about the Sixties now I think about an afternoon not of the Sixties at all, an afternoon early in my sophomore year at Berkeley, a bright autumn Saturday in 1953. I was lying on a leather couch in a fraternity house (there had been a lunch for the alumni, my date had gone on to the game, I do not now recall why I had stayed behind), lying there alone reading a book by Lionel Trilling and listening to a middle-aged man pick out on a piano in need of tuning the melodic line to "Blue Room." All that afternoon he sat at the piano and all that afternoon he played "Blue Room" and he never got it right. I can hear and see it still, the wrong note in "We will thrive on / Keep alive on," the sunlight falling through the big windows, the man picking up his drink and beginning again and telling me, without ever saying a word, something I had not known before about bad marriages and wasted time and looking backward. That such an afternoon would now seem implausible in every detail—the idea of having had a "date" for a football lunch now seems to me so exotic as to be almost czarist—suggests the extent to which the narrative on which many of us grew up no longer applies.

The distance we have come from the world in which I went to college was on my mind quite a bit during those seasons when not only Berkeley but dozens of other campuses were periodically shut down, incipient battlegrounds, their borders sealed. To think of Berkeley as it was in the Fifties was not to think of barricades and reconstituted classes. "Reconstitution" would have sounded to us then like Newspeak, and barricades are never personal. We were all very personal then, sometimes relentlessly so, and, at that point where we either act or do not act, most of us are still. I suppose I am talking about just that: the ambiguity of belonging to a generation distrustful of political highs, the historical irrelevancy of growing up convinced that the heart of darkness lay not in some error of social organization but in man's own blood. If man was bound to err, then any social organization was bound to be in error. It was a premise which still seems to me accurate enough, but one which robbed us early of a certain capacity for surprise.

At Berkeley in the Fifties no one was surprised by anything at all, a *donnée* which tended to render discourse less than spirited, and debate nonexistent. The world was by definition imperfect, and so of course was the university. There was some talk even then about IBM cards, but on balance the notion that free education for tens of thousands of people might involve automation did not seem unreasonable. We took it for granted that the Board of Regents would sometimes act wrongly. We simply avoided those students rumored to be FBI informers. We were that generation called "silent," but we were silent neither, as some thought, because we shared the period's official optimism nor, as others thought, because we feared its official repression. We were silent because the exhilaration of social action seemed to many of us just one more way of escaping the personal, of masking for a while that dread of the meaningless which was man's fate.

To have assumed that particular fate so early was the peculiarity of my generation. I think now that we were the last generation to identify with adults. That most of us have found adulthood just as morally ambiguous as we expected it to be falls perhaps into the category of prophecies self-fulfilled: I am simply not sure. I am telling you only how it was. The mood of Berkeley in those years was one of mild but chronic "depression," against which I remember certain small things that seemed to me somehow explications, dazzling in their clarity, of the world I was about to enter: I remember a woman picking daffodils in the rain one day when I was walking in the hills. I remember a teacher who drank too much one night and revealed his fright and bitterness. I remember my real joy at discovering for the first time how language worked, at discovering, for example, that the central line of *Heart of Darkness* was a postscript. All such images were personal, and the personal was all that most of us expected to find. We would make a separate peace. We would do graduate work in Middle English, we would go abroad. We would make some money and live on a ranch. We would survive outside history, in a kind of *idée fixe* referred to always, during the years I spent at Berkeley, as "some little town with a decent beach."

about "improving your rating" and "being more of an asset to your department," about "really knowing your business." Dick Haddock's business for all these twenty-six years has been that of a professional lifeguard for the Los Angeles County Department of Beaches, and his office is a $190,000 lookout on Zuma Beach in northern Malibu.

It was Thanksgiving morning, 1975. A Santa Ana wind was just dying after blowing in off the Mojave for three weeks and setting 69,000 acres of Los Angeles County on fire. Squadrons of planes had been dropping chemicals on the fires to no effect. Querulous interviews with burned-out householders had become a fixed element of the six o'clock news. Smoke from the fires had that week stretched a hundred miles out over the Pacific and darkened the days and lit the nights and by Thanksgiving morning there was the sense all over Southern California of living in some grave solar dislocation. It was one of those weeks when Los Angeles seemed most perilously and breathtakingly itself, a cartoon of natural disaster, and it was a peculiar week in which to spend the day with Dick Haddock and the rest of the Zuma headquarters crew.

Actually I had wanted to meet the lifeguards ever since I moved to Malibu. I would drive past Zuma some cold winter mornings and see a few of them making their mandatory daily half-mile swims in open ocean. I would drive past Zuma some late foggy nights and see others moving around behind the lookout's lighted windows, the only other souls awake in all of northern Malibu. It seemed to me a curious, almost beatified career choice, electing to save those in peril upon the sea forty hours a week, and as the soot drifted down around the Zuma lookout on that Thanksgiving morning the laconic routines and paramilitary rankings of these civil servants in red trunks took on a devotionary and dreamlike inevitability. There was the "captain," John McFarlane, a man who had already taken his daily half-mile run and his daily half-mile swim and was putting on his glasses to catch up on paperwork. Had the water been below 56 degrees he would have been allowed to swim in a wet suit, but the water was not below 56 degrees and so he had swum as usual in his red trunks. The water was 58 degrees. John McFarlane is 48. There was the "lieutenant,"

Dick Haddock, telling me about how each of the Department's 125 permanent lifeguards (there are also 600 part-time or "recurrent" lifeguards) learns crowd control at the Los Angeles County Sheriff's Academy, learns emergency driving techniques at the California Highway Patrol Academy, learns medical procedures at the U.S.C. Medical Center, and, besides running the daily half-mile and swimming the daily half-mile, does a monthly 500-meter paddle and a monthly pier jump. A "pier jump" is just what it sounds like, and its purpose is to gain practice around pilings in heavy surf.

There was as well the man out on patrol.

There were as well the "call-car personnel," two trained divers and cliff-climbers "ready to roll at any time" in what was always referred to as "a Code 3 vehicle with red light and siren," two men not rolling this Thanksgiving morning but sitting around the lookout, listening to the Los Angeles Rams beat the Detroit Lions on the radio, watching the gray horizon and waiting for a call.

No call came. The radios and the telephones crackled occasionally with reports from the other "operations" supervised by the Zuma crew: the "rescue-boat operation" at Paradise Cove, the "beach operations" at Leo Carrillo, Nicholas, Point Dume, Corral, Malibu Surfrider, Malibu Lagoon, Las Tunas, Topanga North and Topanga South. Those happen to be the names of some Malibu public beaches but in the Zuma lookout that day the names took on the sound of battle stations during a doubtful cease-fire. All quiet at Leo. Situation normal at Surfrider.

The lifeguards seemed most comfortable when they were talking about "operations" and "situations," as in "a phone-watch situation" or "a riptide situation." They also talked easily about "functions," as in "the function of maintaining a secure position on the beach." Like other men at war they had charts, forms, logs, counts kept current to within twelve hours: *1405 surf rescues off Zuma between 12:01 A.M. January 1, 1975 and 11:59 P.M. Thanksgiving Eve 1975*. As well as: *36,120 prevention rescues, 872 first aids, 176 beach emergency calls, 12 resuscitations, 8 boat distress calls, 107 boat warnings, 438 lost-and-found children*, and *0 deaths*. Zero. No body count. When he had occasion to use the word "body" Dick Haddock would hesitate and glance away.

On the whole the lifeguards favored a diction as flat and finally poetic as that of Houston Control. Everything that morning was "real fine." The headquarters crew was "feeling good." The day was "looking good." Malibu surf was "two feet and shape is poor." Earlier that morning there had been a hundred or so surfers in the water, a hundred or so of those bleached children of indeterminate age and sex who bob off Zuma and appear to exist exclusively on packaged beef jerky, but by ten they had all pocketed their Thanksgiving jerky and moved on to some better break. "It heats up, we could use some more personnel," Dick Haddock said about noon, assessing the empty guard towers. "That happened, we might move on a decision to open Towers One and Eleven, I'd call and say we need two recurrents at Zuma, plus I might put an extra man at Leo."

It did not heat up. Instead it began to rain, and on the radio the morning N.F.L. game gave way to the afternoon N.F.L. game, and after a while I drove with one of the call-car men to Paradise Cove, where the rescue-boat crew needed a diver. They did not need a diver to bring up a body, or a murder weapon, or a crate of stolen ammo, or any of the things Department divers sometimes get their names in the paper for bringing up. They needed a diver, with scuba gear and a wet suit, because they had been removing the propeller from the rescue boat and had dropped a metal part the size of a dime in twenty feet of water. I had the distinct impression that they particularly needed a diver in a wet suit because nobody on the boat crew wanted to go back in the water in his trunks to replace the propeller, but there seemed to be some tacit agreement that the lost part was to be considered the point of the dive.

"I guess you know it's fifty-eight down there," the diver said.

"Don't need to tell me how cold it is," the boat lieutenant said. His name was Leonard McKinley and he had "gone permanent" in 1942 and he was of an age to refer to Zuma as a "bathing" beach. "After you find that little thing you could put the propeller back on for us, you wanted. As long as you're in the water anyway? In your suit?"

"I had a feeling you'd say that."

Leonard McKinley and I stood on the boat and watched the diver disappear. In the morning soot from the fires had coated the surface but now the wind was up and the soot was clouding the water. Kelp fronds undulated on the surface. The boat rocked. The radio sputtered with reports of a yacht named *Ursula* in distress.

"One of the other boats is going for it," Leonard McKinley said. "We're not. Some days we just sit here like firemen. Other days, a day with rips, I been out ten hours straight. You get your big rips in the summer, swells coming up from Mexico. A Santa Ana, you get your capsized boats, we got one the other day, it was overdue out of Santa Monica, they were about drowned when we picked them up."

I tried to keep my eyes on the green-glass water but could not. I had been sick on boats in the Catalina Channel and in the Gulf of California and even in San Francisco Bay, and now I seemed to be getting sick on a boat still moored at the end of the Paradise Cove pier. The radio reported the *Ursula* under tow to Marina del Rey. I concentrated on the pilings.

"He gets the propeller on," Leonard McKinley said, "you want to go out?"

I said I thought not.

"You come back another day," Leonard McKinley said, and I said that I would, and although I have not gone back there is no day when I do not think of Leonard McKinley and Dick Haddock and what they are doing, what situations they face, what operations, what green-glass water. The water today is 56 degrees.

3

Amado Vazquez is a Mexican national who has lived in Los Angeles County as a resident alien since 1947. Like many Mexicans who have lived for a long time around Los Angeles he speaks of Mexico as "over there," remains more comfortable in Spanish than in English, and transmits, in his every movement, a kind of "different" propriety, a correctness, a cultural reserve. He is in no sense a Chicano. He is rather what California-born Mexicans sometimes call "Mexican-from-Mexico," pronounced as one word and used to suggest precisely that difference, that rectitude, that personal conservatism. He was born in Ahualulco, Jalisco. He was trained as a barber at the age of ten.

Since the age of twenty-seven, when he came north to visit his brother and find new work for himself, he has married, fathered two children, and become, to the limited number of people who know and understand the rather special work he found for himself in California, a kind of legend. Amado Vazquez was, at the time I first met him, head grower at Arthur Freed Orchids, a commercial nursery in Malibu founded by the late motion-picture producer Arthur Freed, and he is one of a handful of truly great orchid breeders in the world.

In the beginning I met Amado Vazquez not because I knew about orchids but because I liked greenhouses. All I knew about orchids was that back in a canyon near my house someone was growing them *in greenhouses.* All I knew about Amado Vazquez was that he was the man who would let me spend time alone in these greenhouses. To understand how extraordinary this seemed to me you would need to have craved the particular light and silence of greenhouses as I did: all my life I had been trying to spend time in one greenhouse or another, and all my life the person in charge of one greenhouse or another had been trying to hustle me out. When I was nine I would deliberately miss the school bus in order to walk home, because by walking I could pass a greenhouse. I recall being told at that particular greenhouse that the purchase of a nickel pansy did not entitle me to "spend the day," and at another that my breathing was "using up the air."

And yet back in this canyon near my house twenty-five years later were what seemed to me the most beautiful greenhouses in the world—the most aqueous filtered light, the softest tropical air, the most silent clouds of flowers—and the person in charge, Amado Vazquez, seemed willing to take only the most benign notice of my presence. He seemed to assume that I had my own reasons for being there. He would speak only to offer a nut he had just cracked, or a flower cut from a plant he was pruning. Occasionally Arthur Freed's brother Hugo, who was then running the business, would come into the greenhouse with real customers, serious men in dark suits who appeared to have just flown in from Taipei or Durban and who spoke in hushed voices, as if they had come to inspect medieval enamels, or uncut diamonds.

But then the buyers from Taipei or Durban would go into

the office to make their deal and the silence in the greenhouse would again be total. The temperature was always 72 degrees. The humidity was always 60 per cent. Great arcs of white phalaenopsis trembled overhead. I learned the names of the crosses by studying labels there in the greenhouse, the exotic names whose value I did not then understand. *Amabilis* × *Rimestadiana* = *Elisabethae. Aphrodite* × *Rimestadiana* = *Gilles Gratiot. Amabilis* × *Gilles Gratiot* = *Katherine Siegwart* and *Katherine Siegwart* × *Elisabethae* = *Doris. Doris* after Doris Duke. *Doris* which first flowered at Duke Farms in 1940. At least once each visit I would remember the nickel pansy and find Amado Vazquez and show him a plant I wanted to buy, but he would only smile and shake his head. "For breeding," he would say, or "not for sale today." And then he would lift the spray of flowers and show me some point I would not have noticed, some marginal difference in the substance of the petal or the shape of the blossom. "Very beautiful," he would say. "Very nice you like it." What he would not say was that these plants he was letting me handle, these plants "for breeding" or "not for sale today," were stud plants, and that the value of such a plant at Arthur Freed could range from ten thousand to more than three-quarters of a million dollars.

I suppose the day I realized this was the day I stopped using the Arthur Freed greenhouses as a place to eat my lunch, but I made a point of going up one day in 1976 to see Amado Vazquez and to talk to Marvin Saltzman, who took over the business in 1973 and is married to Arthur Freed's daughter Barbara. (As in *Phal. Barbara Freed Saltzman* "Jean McPherson," *Phal. Barbara Freed Saltzman* "Zuma Canyon," and *Phal. Barbara Freed Saltzman* "Malibu Queen," three plants "not for sale today" at Arthur Freed.) It was peculiar talking to Marvin Saltzman because I had never before been in the office at Arthur Freed, never seen the walls lined with dulled silver awards, never seen the genealogical charts on the famous Freed hybrids, never known anything at all about the actual business of orchids.

"Frankly it's an expensive business to get into," Marvin Saltzman said. He was turning the pages of *Sander's List*, the standard orchid studbook, published every several years and showing the parentage of every hybrid registered with the

Royal Horticultural Society, and he seemed oblivious to the primeval silence of the greenhouse beyond the office window. He had shown me how Amado Vazquez places the pollen from one plant into the ovary of a flower on another. He had explained that the best times to do this are at full moon and high tide, because phalaenopsis plants are more fertile then. He had explained that a phalaenopsis is more fertile at full moon because in nature it must be pollinated by a night-flying moth, and over sixty-five million years of evolution its period of highest fertility began to coincide with its period of highest visibility. He had explained that a phalaenopsis is more fertile at high tide because the moisture content of every plant responds to tidal movement. It was all an old story to Marvin Saltzman. I could not take my eyes from the window.

"You bring back five-thousand seedlings from the jungle and you wait three years for them to flower," Marvin Saltzman said. "You find two you like and you throw out the other four-thousand-nine-hundred-ninety-eight and you try to breed the two. Maybe the pollenization takes, eighty-five per cent of the time it doesn't. Say you're lucky, it takes, you'll still wait another four years before you see a flower. Meanwhile you've got a big capital investment. An Arthur Freed could take $400,000 a year from M.G.M. and put $100,000 of it into getting this place started, but not many people could. You see a lot of what we call backyard nurseries—people who have fifty or a hundred plants, maybe they have two they think are exceptional, they decide to breed them—but you talk about major nurseries, there are maybe only ten in the United States, another ten in Europe. That's about it. Twenty."

Twenty is also about how many head growers there are, which is part of what lends Amado Vazquez his legendary aspect, and after a while I left the office and went out to see him in the greenhouse. There in the greenhouse everything was operating as usual to approximate that particular level of a Malaysian rain forest—not on the ground but perhaps a hundred feet up—where epiphytic orchids grow wild. In the rain forest these orchids get broken by wind and rain. They get pollinated randomly and rarely by insects. Their seedlings are crushed by screaming monkeys and tree boas and the orchids live unseen and die young. There in the greenhouse nothing would break the orchids and they would be pollinated at full moon and high tide by Amado Vazquez, and their seedlings would be tended in a sterile box with sterile gloves and sterile tools by Amado Vazquez's wife, Maria, and the orchids would not seem to die at all. "We don't know how long they'll live," Marvin Saltzman told me. "They haven't been bred under protected conditions that long. The botanists estimate a hundred and fifty, two hundred years, but we don't know. All we know is that a plant a hundred years old will show no signs of senility."

It was very peaceful there in the greenhouse with Amado Vazquez and the plants that would outlive us both. "We grew in osmunda then," he said suddenly. Osmunda is a potting medium. Amado Vazquez talks exclusively in terms of how the orchids grow. He had been talking about the years when he first came to this country and got a job with his brother tending a private orchid collection in San Marino, and he had fallen silent. "I didn't know orchids then, now they're like my children. You wait for the first bloom like you wait for a baby to come. Sometimes you wait four years and it opens and it isn't what you expected, maybe your heart wants to break, but you love it. You never say, 'that one was prettier.' You just love them. My whole life is orchids."

And in fact it was. Amado Vazquez's wife, Maria (as in *Phal. Maria Vasquez* "Malibu," the spelling of Vazquez being mysteriously altered by everyone at Arthur Freed except the Vazquezes themselves), worked in the laboratory at Arthur Freed. His son, George (as in *Phal. George Vasquez* "Malibu"), was the sales manager at Arthur Freed. His daughter, Linda (as in *Phal. Linda Mia* "Innocence"), worked at Arthur Freed before her marriage. Amado Vazquez will often get up in the night to check a heater, adjust a light, hold a seed pod in his hand and try to sense if morning will be time enough to sow the seeds in the sterile flask. When Amado and Maria Vazquez go to Central or South America, they go to look for orchids. When Amado and Maria Vazquez went for the first time to Europe a few years ago, they looked for orchids. "I asked all over Madrid for orchids," Amado Vazquez recalled. "Finally they tell me about this one place. I go there, I knock. The woman finally lets me in. She agrees to let me see the orchids. She takes me into a house and . . ."

Amado Vazquez broke off, laughing.

"She has three orchids," he finally managed to say. "Three. One of them dead. All three from Oregon."

We were standing in a sea of orchids, an extravagance of orchids, and he had given me an armful of blossoms from his own cattleyas to take to my child, more blossoms maybe than in all of Madrid. It seemed to me that day that I had never talked to anyone so direct and unembarrassed about the things he loved. He had told me earlier that he had never become a United States citizen because he had an image in his mind which he knew to be false but could not shake: the image was that of standing before a judge and stamping on the flag of Mexico. "And I love my country," he had said. Amado Vazquez loved his country. Amado Vazquez loved his family. Amado Vazquez loved orchids. "You want to know how I feel about the plants," he said as I was leaving. "I'll tell you. I will die in orchids."

4

In the part of Malibu where I lived from January of 1971 until quite recently we all knew one another's cars, and watched for them on the highway and at the Trancas Market and at the Point Dume Gulf station. We exchanged information at the Trancas Market. We left packages and messages for one another at the Gulf station. We called one another in times of wind and fire and rain, we knew when one another's septic tanks needed pumping, we watched for ambulances on the highway and helicopters on the beach and worried about one another's dogs and horses and children and corral gates and Coastal Commission permits. An accident on the highway was likely to involve someone we knew. A rattlesnake in my driveway meant its mate in yours. A stranger's campfire on your beach meant fire on both our slopes.

In fact this was a way of life I had not expected to find in Malibu. When I first moved in 1971 from Hollywood to a house on the Pacific Coast Highway I had accepted the conventional notion that Malibu meant the easy life, had worried that we would be cut off from "the real world," by which I believe I meant daily exposure to the Sunset Strip. By the time we left Malibu, seven years later, I had come to see the spirit of the place as one of shared isolation and adversity, and I think now that I never loved the house on the Pacific Coast Highway more than on those many days when it was impossible to leave it, when fire or flood had in fact closed the highway. We moved to this house on the highway in the year of our daughter's fifth birthday. In the year of her twelfth it rained until the highway collapsed, and one of her friends drowned at Zuma Beach, a casualty of Quaaludes.

One morning during the fire season of 1978, some months after we had sold the house on the Pacific Coast Highway, a brush fire caught in Agoura, in the San Fernando Valley. Within two hours a Santa Ana wind had pushed this fire across 25,000 acres and thirteen miles to the coast, where it jumped the Pacific Coast Highway as a half-mile fire storm generating winds of 100 miles per hour and temperatures up to 2500 degrees Fahrenheit. Refugees huddled on Zuma Beach. Horses caught fire and were shot on the beach, birds exploded in the air. Houses did not explode but imploded, as in a nuclear strike. By the time this fire storm had passed 197 houses had vanished into ash, many of them houses which belonged or had belonged to people we knew. A few days after the highway reopened I drove out to Malibu to see Amado Vazquez, who had, some months before, bought from the Freed estate all the stock at Arthur Freed Orchids, and had been in the process of moving it a half-mile down the canyon to his own new nursery, Zuma Canyon Orchids. I found him in the main greenhouse at what had been Arthur Freed Orchids. The place was now a range not of orchids but of shattered glass and melted metal and the imploded shards of the thousands of chemical beakers that had held the Freed seedlings, the new crosses. "I lost three years," Amado Vazquez said, and for an instant I thought we would both cry. "You want today to see flowers," he said then, "we go down to the other place." I did not want that day to see flowers. After I said goodbye to Amado Vazquez my husband and daughter and I went to look at the house on the Pacific Coast Highway in which we had lived for seven years. The fire had come to within 125 feet of the property, then stopped or turned or been beaten back, it was hard to tell which. In any case it was no longer our house.

1976–1978

CHRONOLOGY

NOTE ON THE TEXTS

NOTES

INDEX

Chronology

1934–36 Born December 5, 1934, at Mercy General Hospital in Sacramento, California, the first of two children of Eduene Jerrett and Frank Reese Didion, who married on January 1. Mother, twenty-four, worked as an assistant city librarian. Father, twenty-six, is an insurance salesman, prone to drink and dread. He often drives to Nevada to shoot craps. The family shares a house on Highland Avenue in Sacramento with Didion's maternal grandparents. She is a fifth-generation Californian: her great-great-great-grandfather on her father's side, Matthew Kilgore, left Ohio for Sacramento in 1855, and on her mother's side her great-great-great-grandmother, Nancy Hardin Cornwall, came west from Arkansas in 1846.

1937–46 In November 1937, father joins the National Guard. Brother Jim is born in December 1939; the following year, the family moves into a home of their own at 2211 U Street. Mother gives her a Big Five tablet so she can "amuse [her]self"; she begins to visit the public library's Ella K. McClatchy branch. On December 7, 1941, Japanese bombers attack Pearl Harbor, in Hawaii, and the United States enters World War II. Father is sent by the Army Air Corps to Fort Lewis in Tacoma, Washington, then to Duke University in Durham, North Carolina, and finally to Peterson Field in Colorado Springs. The family travels to accompany him. In Colorado Springs, suffers her first migraine; she is eight years old. Learns from an issue of *Vogue* about the magazine's Prix de Paris essay contest for college seniors; her mother says she "could win when I got old enough." In late 1943, the family returns to Sacramento after father is reassigned to Detroit. Attends the Arden School in Sacramento.

1947–48 Reads Ernest Hemingway's *A Farewell to Arms* and retypes the first paragraph to get inside the language and see what makes it work. At her eighth-grade graduation in June 1948, delivers a speech on California heritage. "They who came to California," she declares, "were not the self-satisfied, happy and content people, but the adventurous, the restless, and the daring. They were different even from those who settled in other western states." Family moves to Walnut Avenue in Sacramento, and father buys land for development. That summer, on a family vacation, walks into the Pacific, wanting "to know what it would feel like"; back home, she is fascinated by Sacramento's river culture. In the fall, begins freshman year at C.K. McClatchy Senior High School.

1949–52 Becomes a member of the Mañana Society, a sorority sponsored by the Sacramento school district to promote civic and cultural values; her initiation takes place in the Governor's Mansion, where her friend Nina Warren's father, Earl—later chief justice of the United States Supreme Court—is in his second term as chief executive. An indifferent student, she enjoys acting, both in school productions and at a local repertory house. Reads *Moby-Dick* and *An American Tragedy*, and the work of Henry James. The family moves into a "big dark Victorian" three-bedroom house at 500 Hawthorn Street. In 1950, she learns to drive in an Army jeep her father has bought for her and takes friends to Lake Tahoe on weekend trips. Becomes a member of the Student Council and the Press Club and works on the school newspaper, *The Prospector*, and the yearbook. Takes an after-school job with the society page of *The Sacramento Union*. In April 1952, is rejected by Stanford University, her college of choice. Takes classes at Sacramento Junior College in the fall.

1953 Begins at the University of California at Berkeley in the spring, pledging Delta (Tri-Delt) and living in the sorority house on Warring Street. Among her sorority sisters is Barbara Brown, daughter of future California governor Edmund Gerald (Pat) Brown, Sr. Joins staff of student newspaper *The Daily Californian* her first semester. Coedits a special fashion edition with friend Peggy LaViolette; attempts to interview poet W. H. Auden for the paper but, as she later recalls, "was so absolutely terrified that I couldn't think of any questions." Father is sent to Letterman Army Hospital at the Presidio in San Francisco for observation and treatment of drinking and emotional withdrawal. Visits him on weekends with her mother; they have lunch and watch pickup baseball games.

1954 Leaving sorority life, moves into a house at 2520 Ridge Road, which she shares with three other undergraduate women. In the fall is admitted to Mark Schorer's sought-after creative writing workshop, for which she writes short stories. ("He gave me a sense of what writing was about, what it was for," she later remembers.)

1955 Takes a literature class with Schorer. Is selected by *Mademoiselle* magazine to participate in their summer guest editor program, becoming guest editor in fiction. (Prior participants include Sylvia Plath, who was managing guest editor in 1953.) Arrives in Manhattan in May, staying at the Barbizon Hotel for Women; others in her cohort include Gael Greene and Janet Burroway. On June 14, interviews Jean Stafford for the magazine. Returns to Sacramento by train in July, visiting Boston, Quebec, and Chicago en route. Takes a job for the rest of the summer at *The Sacramento Union*, composing wedding notices. Turns down offer to become society editor. In August, her Stafford piece comes out, her first publication in a national venue. Studies Henry James in a class taught by Henry Nash Smith, who praises her "truly remarkable abilities as a critic." Enters the Prix de Paris writing competition, administered by *Vogue*.

1956–58 Becomes editor of *The Occident*, the UC Berkeley student literary magazine, and publishes her first short story, "Sunset," there. Makes the second round of the Prix de Paris competition, and submits a profile of California residential architect William Wilson Wurster as her final contest entry; on May 15, 1956, is awarded first prize. Choosing a $1,000 cash prize over a two-week trip to Paris, she is also offered a job at *Vogue* in New York for $45 a week. Over the summer, travels from Sacramento to Berkeley each week to complete a Milton course required for graduation. In the fall, moves to New York, where she lives on East 79th Street. At first, writes only promotional copy, on a schedule that allows her to submit to other magazines. Rents a third-floor walkup at 1215 Park Avenue for $130 a month. Meets Noel Parmentel and becomes involved with him; he becomes her guide to literary New York. Learns concision from editor Allene Talmey, who edits her captions with a ruthless efficiency. Begins working on a novel, at first titled *Harvest Home* and then *In the Night Season*, which will eventually be published as *Run River*. In 1958, Parmentel introduces her to John Gregory Dunne, soon to be a writer at *Time*.

1959–62 In the summer of 1959, gives notice at *Vogue* to become college editor at *Mademoiselle*, but decides to stay after *Vogue* editor Jessica Daves offers a new job as feature associate, writing articles at a higher salary. On November 1, begins writing the "People Are Talking About" column, contributing unsigned pieces to the magazine. Continues to freelance for other publications, including *Mademoiselle*, and begins an association with the *National Review*, writing book and film reviews. In the evenings works on her novel, hanging its pages on her living room wall. Publishes her first signed piece in *Vogue* in June 1961, "Jealousy: Is It a Curable Illness?" Moves to 41 East 75th Street. Breaks up with Parmentel and becomes involved with Dunne. Submits pages of the novel as a partial manuscript; a dozen publishers turn it down. At Parmentel's instigation, submits to Ivan Obolensky, who offers an advance of $1,000 but insists she change the title to *Run River*. The money allows her to take a two-month leave from *Vogue* to complete the book. In June 1962, she flies to California; votes for Joe Shell over Richard M. Nixon in the Republican gubernatorial primary because Nixon is insufficiently conservative.

1963 *Run River* is published on April 26. Reviews are brief and mixed, and sales are disappointing. Dunne grows increasingly dissatisfied at *Time*, where, by order of top editors—who support United States military efforts—he has been told to sanitize reports from Vietnam. In the fall, he and Didion become engaged.

1964 Marries Dunne on January 30 at the mission church at San Juan Bautista. Back in New York, begins to write a film column for *Vogue*, but feels overwhelmed by the city. Her anxiety becomes debilitating; as she describes the episode in her 1967 essay "Goodbye to All That," it is hard to leave the house. In April, decides with Dunne to leave New York for Los Angeles on a temporary basis—six or seven months. In June, they rent the Hardin Gatehouse, a four-bedroom home on two acres at 5500 Palos Verdes Drive South, on the Palos Verdes Peninsula in Portuguese Bend. Rent is $500 a month. Aided by Dunne's brother Dominick, a producer, they meet with television executives hoping to write scripts, and sell a story idea to the anthology series *Chrysler Theatre* for $1,000. *Vogue* cancels her film column; she writes short stories, publishing "Coming Home" in *The Saturday Evening Post* on July 11. With Dunne, proposes a film treatment of his project *Show Me a Hero* to agents at William Morris; attends screenings and reads screenplays. Supports Barry Goldwater in the 1964 presidential election, won in a landslide by Lyndon Baines Johnson.

1965 Travels to Mexico for *The Saturday Evening Post*, where John Wayne is working on *The Sons of Katie Elder*. The resulting piece, "John Wayne: A Love Story," offers a template to which she will return, framing her reporting through a personal, even autobiographical, lens. On August 11, Marquette Frye, a twenty-one-year-old African American man, is stopped in the South Los Angeles community of Watts by California Highway Patrol officer Lee Minikus. An altercation ensues, triggering the Watts Riots, which cause 34 deaths and more than 1,000 injuries before they end on August 16. "For days," Didion will write in her 1967 essay "Los Angeles Notebook," "one could drive the Harbor Freeway and see the city on fire, just as we had always known it would be in the end."

1966 Meets Blake Watson, a physician at St. John's Hospital in Santa Monica, who facilitates the private adoption of a baby girl, born on March 3. Didion and Dunne name her Quintana Roo, after the Mexican state on the Yucatan Peninsula. They bring the child home on March 6, cancelling a planned trip to Saigon for *The Saturday Evening Post* after realizing that they cannot take a baby to a war. On May 1, they are evicted from their house in Portuguese Bend and take up temporary residence at 155 Fifth Anita Drive in West Los Angeles, home of Sara Mankiewicz, widow of screenwriter

Herman J. Mankiewicz. Six days later, Didion publishes her most ambitious piece of early journalism, "Some Dreamers of the Golden Dream"—originally titled "How Can I Tell Them There's Nothing Left?" —in *The Saturday Evening Post.* In June, Quintana is christened in Brentwood, at St. Martin of Tours Catholic Church. The couple meets Henry Robbins, an editor at Farrar, Straus & Giroux, who will be influential in both of their careers. Leaving Quintana with her grandparents in Sacramento, they travel to the Central Valley town of Delano to report on Cesar Chavez and the National Farm Workers' strike against grape growers for *The Saturday Evening Post.* In August, they visit Hawaii, the subject of Didion's "Letter from Paradise, 21 19′ N., 157 52′ W." Back in Los Angeles, they move into a crumbling mansion at 7406 Franklin Avenue in Hollywood, at a rent of $400 a month.

1967 On January 14, the Human Be-In takes place at the Polo Fields in San Francisco's Golden Gate Park; more than 20,000 people come to hear Timothy Leary, Allen Ginsberg, Gary Snyder, and bands including the Grateful Dead, Jefferson Airplane, and Big Brother and the Holding Company. The event is widely regarded as introducing the hippie movement to the national consciousness. Didion meets Paul Hawken, a Haight-Ashbury insider who offers her access to the community. She travels to the Bay Area in the spring and summer, staying in Berkeley. On June 3, she publishes her first of more than twenty "Points West" columns in *The Saturday Evening Post*, alternating with Dunne. On July 12, she signs a two-book deal with Henry Robbins for a nonfiction book about "the LSD life in California" and a novel called *Maria Talking* (later published as *Play It As It Lays*). The contract stipulates an advance of $6,000 per title. "Slouching Towards Bethlehem," gathering her impressions of Haight-Ashbury life, appears as the *Post*'s cover story on September 23. Decides she can't expand the essay and instead begins to gather and revise pieces for a collection of her previously published nonfiction.

1968 In the spring, visits California First Lady Nancy Reagan in Sacramento for *The Saturday Evening Post*; the resulting story, "Pretty Nancy," is the first of many she will write about the Reagans. On April 4, the Reverend Martin Luther King, Jr., is shot and killed in Memphis, Tennessee. *Slouching Towards Bethlehem* is published on May 10; Dan Wakefield in *The New York Times*, among many laudatory reviewers, calls it "a rich display of some of the best prose written today in this country." *Time* sends Julian Wasser to photograph Didion; the ensuing sessions, which feature her smoking, with her Corvette Stingray, become the first iconic images of her. On June 5, Senator Robert F. Kennedy is shot in the kitchen of the Ambassador Hotel on Wilshire Boulevard after winning the California Democratic presidential primary; he dies the following day. Didion checks herself into the outpatient psychiatric clinic at St. John's Hospital for vertigo, nausea, and extreme alienation; this, she will later write in "The White Album," "does not now seem to me an inappropriate response to the summer of 1968." In August, Richard M. Nixon is nominated as the Republican candidate for president at the party's convention in Miami Beach. Three weeks later, amidst a police riot against student protesters in Chicago, Vice President Hubert H. Humphrey is nominated by the Democrats. In November, Nixon wins the presidency. Didion, Dunne, and Dunne's brother Dominick acquire the rights to James Mills's 1966 novel *The Panic in Needle Park*, with the couple attached as screenwriters. Didion is named as one of the *Los Angeles Times*'s Women of the Year.

1969 Publishes "The Revolution Game," her final piece in *The Saturday Evening Post*, on January 25; the magazine suspends publication in February. On August 9, while swimming in her sister-in-law's Beverly Hills pool, learns of the killings of actress Sharon Tate, hairdresser Jay Sebring, and three others at Tate's Benedict Canyon home. "There were twenty dead, no, twelve, ten, eighteen," she will write of the rumors that swirled through the community. "Black masses were imagined, and bad trips blamed." The next night, supermarket executive Leno LaBianca and his wife Rosemary are murdered in their house at 3301 Waverly Drive. The killers, who won't be arrested until December, are members of the Manson Family, a loose tribe of outcasts, led by a charismatic ex-convict named Charles Manson, who have hung around the countercultural fringes of the entertainment industry since 1968. On November 14, finishes a draft of her second novel, *Play It As It Lays.* She is offered a column by *Life* magazine. Her first piece, written from Hawaii (where she has gone with her family) and later collected in *The White Album* under the title "In the Islands," causes a stir for its revelation that she and Dunne are "on this island in the middle of the Pacific in lieu of filing for divorce."

1970 In January, preproduction begins on *The Panic in Needle Park*, with Dominick Dunne producing and Jerry Schatzberg directing, starring Al Pacino and Kitty Winn. *Play It As It Lays* is published on July 27 to rapturous reviews. It furthers Didion's investigation into fragmentation and narrative breakdown, operating as a series of vignettes separated by white space, like cinematic jump cuts, to tell the story of Maria Wyeth, an actress recovering from a breakdown as she unravels in late 1960s Los Angeles. That summer, she meets Linda Kasabian, a participant in the Tate-LaBianca murders who has chosen to cooperate with prosecuting attorneys in return for a promise of immunity. The *Los Angeles Times* reports in August that Didion is writing a book about her, but the project rapidly unravels. Accompanied by Dunne, spends a month traveling in the South to research a piece for *Life*. Although the article is never finished, the notes will be published in 2017 as part of *South and West.* In October, filming of *The Panic in Needle Park* begins, after six weeks of rehearsal, in Manhattan; shooting wraps on December 22.

1971–72 In January 1971, *Play It As It Lays* is nominated for a National Book Award. Moves with Dunne to 33428 Pacific Coast Highway in Malibu; they hire Harrison Ford, then a carpenter and contractor, to handle renovations. In May, *The Panic in Needle Park* premieres at Cannes. Reviews are mixed, but Kitty Winn is named Best Actress of the Festival. The film cements Didion and Dunne's place at the center of the Hollywood intelligentsia. They are offered projects: a remake of *Tender Is the Night*, a sequel to *The Graduate.* They ultimately settle on an adaptation of *Play It As It Lays*, directed by Frank Perry and produced by Dominick Dunne. It comes out October 19, 1972, starring Tuesday Weld as Maria; she is nominated for a Golden Globe. Didion is diagnosed with multiple sclerosis, the cause of her temporary blindness years before.

1973 In the spring, Henry Robbins is made editor-in-chief of Farrar, Straus & Giroux and offers Didion a $60,000 advance for her next essay collection. Not long afterward, he has a heart attack; he leaves FSG to become executive editor at Simon & Schuster. Didion wants him to remain her editor, offering to return the first half of her advance. Meets Robert Silvers, editor of *The New York Review of Books*, and writes her first piece for him ("Hollywood: Having Fun," published on March 22). During the summer, with Dunne, attends the Cartagena Film Festival in Colombia. From Cartagena, they travel to Bogotá, then back to Los Angeles, stopping to refuel in Panama. The trip inspires her essay "In Bogotá" and her novel *A Book of Common Prayer*, the first of many works on the subject of Latin America and its relationship to the United States. In the fall, begins working with Dunne on *Rainbow Road*, a screenplay loosely adapting *A Star Is Born* (1937/1954) for the rock era; they spend three weeks on the road with rock bands, including Led Zeppelin and Uriah Heep. Dunne envisions James Taylor and Carly Simon in the leading roles.

1974 In May, receives a $210,000 combined advance for her next novel (*A Book of Common Prayer*) and essay collection (*The White Album*), Henry Robbins at Simon & Schuster outbidding others in an auction arranged by her agent, Lois Wallace. In August, with Dunne, submits the third and final draft of *Rainbow Road*, in which Barbra Streisand has taken an interest; they withdraw from the project, receiving $125,000 and 10 percent of future grosses. Other writers will later revise their screenplay, which is retitled *A Star Is Born*.

1975–76 Spends a month at UC Berkeley in the spring of 1975 as a Regents' Lecturer, teaching a class and working on *A Book of Common Prayer*. On April 20, while she is at Berkeley, Saigon falls to the Viet Cong and the People's Army of Vietnam. Three weeks later, delivers a talk titled "Why I Write" to a standing-room-only crowd: "I write entirely to find out what I'm thinking, what I'm looking at, what I see and what it means. What I want and what I fear." On September 18, heiress turned Symbionese Liberation Army revolutionary Patricia Hearst is arrested in San Francisco; *Rolling Stone* editor Jann Wenner asks Didion to cover her trial. After briefly attending the trial, however, she backs away from Hearst as subject, writing about her only in a 1982 essay, "Girl of the Golden West." (She will later publish fourteen pages of her *Rolling Stone* notes in *South and West.*) On December 8, 1976, *A Star Is Born* comes out, to lackluster reviews.

1977–78 *A Book of Common Prayer*—Didion's third novel, set in the fictional Latin American country of Boca Grande —is published on March 1, 1977. She takes eleven-year-old Quintana with her on a national book tour. Dunne publishes his novel *True Confessions*, which becomes a New York Times best seller. They visit London in November; the following July, they move from Malibu to 202 Chadbourne Avenue in Brentwood Park, the family's last address in Los Angeles. Three months later, the Agoura fire jumps the Pacific Coast Highway and burns to within 125 feet of their former Malibu property.

1979–80 Didion's second essay collection, *The White Album*, is published on June 19, 1979; it gathers and extends the nonfiction she has published since *Slouching Towards Bethlehem*, and is widely and glowingly reviewed. ("Essentially," Jerzy Kozinski writes in the *Los Angeles Times*, "*The White Album* is about our American mythologies, both private and collective, and realities both private and collective. Joan Didion is once again our quintessential essayist.") On July 31, Henry Robbins dies of a heart attack on a platform of the Union Square subway station in Manhattan. He is fifty-one years old. In an October *Nation* article titled "Joan Didion: Only Disconnect," Barbara Grizzuti Harrison questions Didion's increasingly high reputation and mocks her style, describing her as "neurasthenic Cher." In June 1980, reviews V. S. Naipaul's recent work in *The New York Review of Books*, whose editor, Robert Silvers, encourages her to write more overtly about politics.

1981–83 With Dunne, works on a screen adaptation of his novel *True Confessions.* Directed by Ulu Grosbard and starring Robert De Niro and Robert Duvall, the film premieres at the Venice Film Festival in September 1981 to considerable acclaim. On June 15, 1982, the couple travels to El Salvador, where they spend just under two weeks; in mid-July, she sends her first report on the trip to *The New York Review of Books.* On October 30, Dominick Dunne's daughter Dominique is strangled by her boyfriend. She dies on November 4. The same day, *The New York Review of Books* publishes the first of three installments of *Salvador.* It is released in book form in March 1983.

1984 *Democracy*, Didion's fourth novel, is published by Simon & Schuster on April 1. A metafiction of sorts, the novel is narrated by a character named Joan Didion, who seems to be reporting on the narrative rather than creating it. Writing in *The New York Times*, Mary McCarthy praises the book's "technical mastery and on-target social observation" but criticizes its "knowingness" and "depthlessness."

1985–86 In November 1985, reads from her work at Bennington College in Vermont, where Quintana is a sophomore, and speaks at a PEN writers' conference in New York. Spends time in Miami the following spring, researching her next book.

1987–88 Publishes *Miami*, her fourth book of nonfiction, on October 1, 1987. The book connects the politics of the 1960s with those of the 1980s—the Kennedy assassination to the Iran-Contra scandal. Dunne learns he is "a candidate for a catastrophic cardiovascular event" and undergoes an angiogram and an angioplasty. He views this new lease on life as a chance to change things up and pushes for the couple to move to New York. In early 1988, they sell their house in Brentwood Park and buy an apartment at 30 East 71st Street in Manhattan. Didion begins to write the "Letter from Los Angeles" for *The New Yorker* and continues to write about politics for *The New York Review of Books.* (Many of these pieces will be collected in her third book of essays, *After Henry.*) During the summer of 1988, she covers the Jesse Jackson campaign and the Democratic Convention in Atlanta.

1989–91 On April 19, 1989, a twenty-eight-year-old woman named Trisha Meili is raped and beaten while jogging in Central Park, and five young men of color are arrested and charged. Didion's account, published in the January 17, 1991, issue of *The New York Review of Books* under the title "Sentimental Journeys," is a ruthless dissection of this constructed narrative. "It is precisely in this conflation of victim and city, this confusion of personal woe with public distress," she writes, "that the crime's 'story' would be found." On December 25, 1990, Dunne faints at Honolulu International Airport. Back in New York, he has open-heart surgery to insert a plastic valve. The couple continues to write scripts, beginning a project based on the life and death of anchorwoman Jessica Savitch. It will eventually be released as *Up Close & Personal*, with Robert Redford and Michelle Pfeiffer. In early 1991, tries to get out of her Simon & Schuster contract, but the company refuses to let her go. Later in the year, participates in a celebrity ad campaign for the Gap; is photographed by Annie Leibovitz with Quintana, wearing matching black turtlenecks. Donates her papers to the Bancroft Library at UC Berkeley.

1992–93 On May 1, 1992, third collection of essays, *After Henry*, is published. The title is an homage to Henry Robbins. The book gathers twelve pieces, including "Sentimental Journeys" and "Girl of the Golden West." Several pieces deal with presidential politics, signaling a new direction, one she will explore throughout the decade. Supports Jerry Brown for president, although she does not register to vote. In July, covers the Democratic National Convention at Madison Square Garden in New York. In December, Frank Reese Didion dies in Monterey at eighty-four. In March 1993, addresses the Charter Day ceremony at the University of California, Berkeley.

1994–98 In June 1994, O.J. Simpson is arrested for murdering his wife, Nicole, and Ronald Goldman after a slow-speed police chase. His trial, which extends into the following year, captivates the nation. Dunne covers it for *The New York Review of Books*. In March 1996, *Up Close & Personal* is released, the last script by Didion and Dunne to be produced. On August 27, Didion's fifth novel, *The Last Thing He Wanted*, is published. Registers to vote to support President Bill Clinton's re-election. In January 1997, Dominick Dunne's ex-wife Lenny dies at sixty-four. In 1998, reports on Clinton's impeachment for *The New York Review of Books*. In October, Quintana is contacted by her birth sister, and meets her biological family for the first time.

1999–2000 Contributes essays on religion in American political life to *The New York Review of Books*, and a profile of Martha Stewart to *The New Yorker*.

2001 On May 15, Eduene Jerrett Didion dies in California, two weeks before her ninety-first birthday. "The preceding afternoon," her daughter writes, "I had talked to her on the telephone from New York and she had hung up midsentence, a way of saying goodbye so characteristic of her . . . that it did not occur to me until morning, when my brother called, that in this one last instance she had been just too frail to keep the connection." On September 11, two hijacked airliners hit the World Trade Center towers in lower Manhattan, destroying them. Another strikes the Pentagon, and a fourth crashes in a field in Pennsylvania, after a passenger revolt. The same day, *Political Fictions*, Didion's fourth book of essays, is published. It collects her political writing from the previous decade and zeroes in on what has become a key theme: that public life is a matter of narrative rather than policy. This represents not just a degradation of the discourse but also another way that "we tell ourselves stories in order to live."

2002 On November 13, gives the Robert B. Silvers Lecture at the New York Public Library; published in *The New York Review of Books* the following January as "Fixed Opinions, or The Hinge of History" and in book form in May as *Fixed Ideas: America Since 9.11*, it argues that the Bush administration has used the events of 9/11 "to stake new ground in old domestic wars."

2003 In June, Dunne has a pacemaker installed, but his health continues to fail. On July 26, Quintana marries Gerry Michael, a Manhattan bartender, in a ceremony at New York's Cathedral of Saint John the Divine. On September 23, publishes *Where I Was From*, her long-anticipated California book, in which she takes apart the myths—the narratives—on which she was raised. "Actually," she will later tell an interviewer, "I started that book several years before my mother and father died. I was unable to get very far with it. Once my mother and father died, I immediately picked it up again after twenty years, and I realized that it had been impossible to write while my mother and father were alive because I didn't want to present a version of California that they would not recognize." On Christmas Day, Quintana is taken to Beth Israel North Hospital in Manhattan. She is admitted to the ICU and diagnosed with pneumonia in both lungs and septic shock. She is put in an induced coma. On December 30, after visiting her at the hospital, Dunne suffers a heart attack and dies. "*Life changes fast*," his wife will write. ". . . *Life changes in the instant. . . . You sit down to dinner and life as you know it ends*." He is seventy-one.

2004 On January 22, Quintana is released from the hospital. Three days later, she is admitted to Columbia-Presbyterian Hospital in Manhattan with pulmonary embolisms. On March 23, a memorial service for Dunne is held at the Cathedral of Saint John the Divine. Speakers include his wife, daughter, and brother, as well as Calvin Trillin and Susanna Moore. On March 25, Quintana collapses at Los Angeles International Airport and undergoes emergency neurosurgery at UCLA Medical Center in Westwood. Didion flies to California, staying at the Beverly Wilshire Hotel. On April 30, Quintana is transferred to the Rusk Institute at New York University Hospital. She remains there until July. In October, Didion begins to write *The Year of Magical Thinking*, a memoir of her season of grief. She finishes the manuscript at the end of the year.

2005 Writes on "The Case of Teresa Schiavo" for *The New York Review of Books* of June 9. On August 26, Quintana dies of acute pancreatitis at New York–Presbyterian/Weill Cornell Medical Center. On October 11, *The Year of Magical Thinking* is published, and, despite her loss, Didion embarks on a national tour. Following *Where I Was From*, the book cements a new role for her as memoirist, excavating personal narratives as well as public ones. It sells more than 200,000 copies in hardcover, the biggest numbers of her career. In

October, producer Scott Rudin approaches her about developing the memoir as a play. On November 16, *The Year of Magical Thinking* receives the National Book Award for nonfiction.

2006–7 In January, Didion agrees to the stage adaptation of *The Year of Magical Thinking*, and meets with Rudin and director David Hare. In the spring, Vanessa Redgrave agrees to portray Didion. In the fall, writes a lengthy takedown of Dick Cheney; it appears as the cover story of *The New York Review of Books* on October 5. On March 29, 2007, *The Year of Magical Thinking* premieres at the Booth Theatre on Broadway for a limited run of 144 performances. The play—a one-woman show—diverges from, and expands upon, the book by engaging with Quintana in more detail, functioning as a bridge between the memoir and *Blue Nights*. In an interview, Didion calls the process one of "maintaining movement. And also maintaining a version of things that I could live with. That was very strong with the play. Because as I said in *Blue Nights*, watching that play on 45th Street at night was one moment during the day when Quintana did not necessarily die." In November, she is honored for Distinguished Service to American Letters at the National Book Awards.

2008–10 Reads from her work at Dartmouth College in October 2008 and meets with students. The next year, on August 26, Dominick Dunne dies of bladder cancer at the age of eighty-three.

2011 In the spring, receives an honorary Doctor of Letters from Yale University. On November 4, her memoir *Blue Nights* is published; the book addresses her own aging, as well as her daughter's life and death. "I hadn't dealt with Quintana," she will tell an interviewer. "I had dealt with her to some extent in the play, but the play had, from my point of view, a whole other way of preserving myself, at a distance. Yet, part of the point is that you never work it out."

2012–16 Cancels a planned trip to California after fracturing a kneecap, but is able to travel to Hartford on June 28, 2012, to speak at the Mark Twain House and Museum. On July 3, 2013, is awarded the National Humanities Medal at the White House, by President Barack

Obama. In January 2015 appears in an advertising campaign for the designer Céline, wearing a black pullover and oversized dark glasses.

2017 On March 7, publishes *South and West*, a book of nonfiction gathering material from two early, unfinished pieces: her journey through the South in 1970 and her notes on Patty Hearst for *Rolling Stone*. The book occasions a number of wide-ranging career retrospectives. On October 11, Netflix releases the documentary *Joan Didion: The Center Will Not Hold*, directed by her nephew, Griffin Dunne, the son of Dominick and Lenny.

2018–20 An adaptation of her novel *The Last Thing He Wanted* begins filming in June 2018. Directed by Dee Rees and starring Anne Hathaway and Ben Affleck, it premieres on Netflix on February 21, 2020.

2021 Knopf publishes *Let Me Tell You What I Mean* on January 26, gathering a dozen previously uncollected essays on subjects including the underground press, San Simeon, Martha Stewart, and "Why I Write." Dies at home in Manhattan from complications of Parkinson's disease, on December 23.

Note on the Texts

This volume contains five works by Joan Didion originally published from 1963 to 1979: the novels *Run River* (1963), *Play It As It Lays* (1970), and *A Book of Common Prayer* (1977), and the essay collections *Slouching Towards Bethlehem* (1968) and *The White Album* (1979). All of these works have appeared in numerous printings and editions since their initial publication, both in the United States and in Great Britain, but Didion has not sought to correct or revise them, and the texts included here have been taken from first printings.

Run River. In the fall of 1956, as a recent graduate of the University of California at Berkeley, Didion moved to New York to take a job at *Vogue*. She wrote the first half of *Run River*—her first novel, initially titled *Harvest Home*—in the evenings over a period of years, after her workdays at *Vogue* were done. Having completed about 150 pages, she began to make inquiries of publishers; a dozen by her later count rejected the novel before her friend Noel Parmentel persuaded Ivan Obolensky to take an interest. With a contract and an advance from Obolensky in hand, in 1961 she took a two-month leave of absence from her magazine work and finished the second half of the book both in New York and in California, retitling the whole *In the Night Season.*

The novel Didion submitted to her publisher was substantially revised before it appeared in print, and the process was contentious. Most prominently, Obolensky insisted on a new title that Didion "hated," *Run River.* He also "pressed" her, as she later recalled, "to straighten out the chronology, so it became a simple novel with a flashback, which wasn't my intention at all . . . I had wanted *Run River* to be very complicated chronologically, to somehow have the past and the present operating simultaneously, but I wasn't accomplished enough to do that with any clarity. Everybody who read it said it wasn't working. So I straightened it out . . . I just wasn't good enough." Obolensky himself later complained that "there was very little [Didion] would change," though he had hired a freelance editor, Carol Houck Smith, to work with her. Parmentel reviewed the manuscript at various points, Didion reportedly yielding to his judgment more often than not.

Ivan Obolensky published *Run River* on April 26, 1963. The novel has since appeared in many new printings and editions, but Didion is not known to have been responsible for subsequent alterations to the text, including the addition of a comma to the title of the first British edition, *Run, River*, published by Jonathan Cape in London in 1964. The text of *Run River* in the present volume is that of the 1963 Ivan Obolensky first printing.

Slouching Towards Bethlehem. On July 12, 1967, Henry Robbins at Farrar, Straus & Giroux offered Didion a $12,000 advance for two largely unwritten books. One, a novel, would appear just over three years later as *Play It As It Lays.* The other, as Robbins envisioned it, would be "a nonfiction book, tentatively titled *Slouching Towards Bethlehem* and dealing with the LSD life in California"; it would extend the article of the same title on which she was then at work for *The Saturday Evening Post.*

Didion quickly rejected the idea of a book-length "Slouching Towards Bethlehem" and worried at first that Robbins's alternative proposal, a collection of her nonfiction, "would either prove that I contradicted myself every month or that I always said the same thing every month, and I don't know which would be worse." By early August, however, she was gathering and arranging her articles and essays for the new book. The earliest of these had appeared in 1961; others she had yet to write. Most she revised substantially, altering titles, adding or cutting paragraphs, and rewriting sentences. In "Los Angeles Notebook," she combined sections of previously published pieces with new material.

The following is a list of the original magazine items from which her finished book was assembled:

Some Dreamers of the Golden Dream. *Saturday Evening Post*, May 7, 1966 (as "How Can I Tell Them There's Nothing Left?").
John Wayne: A Love Song. *Saturday Evening Post*, August 14, 1965.
Where the Kissing Never Stops. *New York Times Magazine*, February 27, 1966 (as "Just Folks at a School for Non-Violence").
Comrade Laski, C.P.U.S.A. (M.-L.). *Saturday Evening Post*, November 18, 1967.
7000 Romaine, Los Angeles 38. *Saturday Evening Post*, September 23, 1967 (as "The Howard Hughes Underground").
California Dreaming. *Saturday Evening Post*, October 21, 1967.
Marrying Absurd. *Saturday Evening Post*, December 16, 1967.
Slouching Towards Bethlehem. *Saturday Evening Post*, September 23, 1967.
On Keeping a Notebook. *Holiday*, December 1966.
On Self-Respect. *Vogue*, August 1961 (as "Self-Respect: Its Source, Its Power").
I Can't Get That Monster out of My Mind. *The American Scholar*, Autumn 1964.

On Morality. *The American Scholar*, Autumn 1965 (as "The Insidious Ethic of Conscience").

On Going Home. *Saturday Evening Post*, June 3, 1967 (as "Going Home").

Notes from a Native Daughter. *Holiday*, October 1965.

Letter from Paradise, 21° 19′ N., 157° 52′ W. *Saturday Evening Post*, December 17, 1966 (as "Hawaii: Taps at Pearl Harbor").

Rock of Ages. *Saturday Evening Post*, July 1, 1967.

The Seacoast of Despair. *Saturday Evening Post*, July 29, 1967.

Guaymas, Sonora. *Vogue*, March 1968 (as "Guaymas, Mexico, 'Graham Greene Might Have Written It'").

Los Angeles Notebook. *Saturday Evening Post*, August 26, 1967 (as "The Santa Ana"); *Saturday Evening Post*, January 30, 1965 (as "Bosses Make Lousy Lovers").

Goodbye to All That. *Saturday Evening Post*, January 14, 1967 (as "Farewell to the Enchanted City").

Slouching Towards Bethlehem was published by Farrar, Straus & Giroux on May 10, 1968. The text in the present volume is that of the first printing.

Play It As It Lays. Didion started what she referred to as "the actual physical writing" of her second novel, *Play It As It Lays*, in January 1969, though she had been making notes for it "over several years," changing its title from *Maria Talking* to *Play It As It Lays* in August 1967. On November 14, 1969, she shared a draft—"quite rough, with places marked 'chapters to come'"—with her husband John Gregory Dunne and her editor Henry Robbins. Dunne, then in Hawaii, wrote her with his reactions on November 18, and soon thereafter the three of them discussed the novel in New York. All agreeing on what it needed, she completed a final draft over the next couple of weeks. Farrar, Straus & Giroux published *Play It As It Lays* on July 27, 1970. The text in the present volume is that of the first printing.

A Book of Common Prayer. Describing the beginnings of her "just finished" third novel, *A Book of Common Prayer*, on May 20, 1975, in a lecture at the University of California at Berkeley titled "Why I Write," Didion recalled a brief, early morning stop at the Panama City airport en route to Bogotá in the summer of 1973. Her vivid impression of the moment and the scene "remained superimposed on everything I saw until the day I finished," she explained; it prompted the questions and provided the mood around which her work coalesced.

Didion arrived at Berkeley, where she spent most of the spring of 1975, with about a third of the novel drafted and with her notebooks;

a researcher, Tina Moore, had helped her investigate what she later described as "rules for living in the tropics." She gave copies of her manuscript in progress to John Gregory Dunne and to Henry Robbins around the time of her Berkeley lecture, which both attended, and then continued to revise the novel into the following year, partly in response to their comments. Robbins wrote her in praise of her finished draft on March 24, 1976.

Simon & Schuster published *A Book of Common Prayer* on March 1, 1977; Robbins had recently become executive editor of the firm, and Didion chose to follow him there. The text of *A Book of Common Prayer* in the present volume is that of the March 1977 Simon & Schuster first printing.

The White Album. Didion's second essay collection, *The White Album*, gathered items she had published in magazines and newspapers from 1968 to 1977. In most cases she made substantial revisions to the texts contained in these original periodicals, and in a few cases she expanded them significantly; only three of the title essay's fifteen sections are known to have previously appeared in print, for example.

The following is a list of the original magazine and newspaper pieces from which *The White Album* was assembled:

The White Album. *Saturday Evening Post*, March 9, 1968 (as "Waiting for Morrison"); *Saturday Evening Post*, May 4, 1968 (as "Black Panther"); *Saturday Evening Post*, January 25, 1969 (as "The Revolution Game").

James Pike, American. *Esquire*, November 1976 (as "The Late Great Bishop of California").

Holy Water. *Esquire*, December 1977.

Many Mansions. *Esquire*, January 1977 (as "House of the Unspeakable").

The Getty. *Esquire*, March 1977 (as "Getty's Little House on the Highway").

Bureaucrats. *Esquire*, August 1976 (as "The Diamond Lane Showdown").

Good Citizens. *Saturday Evening Post*, July 27, 1968 (as "Dreampolitik"); *Saturday Evening Post*, June 1, 1968 (as "Pretty Nancy"); *Life*, January 30, 1970 (as "1950 Was More Than 20 Years Ago").

Notes Toward a Dreampolitik. *Saturday Evening Post*, November 16, 1968 (as "Brother Theobald's Earthquake"); *Life*, May 8, 1970 (as "Nine Bike Movies in Seven *Vroom!* Days"); *Saturday Evening Post*, December 14, 1968 (as "I'm Going to Be a Movie Star"); *Saturday Evening Post*, February 10, 1968 (as "Getting Serenity").

The Women's Movement: *New York Times Book Review*, July 30, 1972.
Doris Lessing. *New York Times Book Review*, March 14, 1971 (as "Briefing for a Descent into Hell").
Georgia O'Keeffe. *Los Angeles Times Book Review*, December 5, 1976 (as "An Unsentimental Journey Through Georgia O'Keeffe").
In the Islands. *Life*, December 5, 1969 (as "A Problem of Making Connections"); *Life*, April 24, 1970 (as "Scrapbook of a Pink Palace in the Sand"); *Life*, April 10, 1970 (as "Ten Long Minutes in the Punchbowl"); *Esquire*, October 1977 (as "Good-bye, Gentleman-Ranker").
In Hollywood. *New York Review of Books*, March 22, 1973 (as "Hollywood: Having Fun").
In Bed. *Saturday Evening Post*, June 29, 1968 (as "Migraine").
On the Road. *Esquire*, August 1977 (as "O My America").
On the Mall. *Esquire*, December 1975 (as "The Shopping Center").
In Bogotá. *Travel & Leisure*, August 1974 (as "Bogotá").
At the Dam. *Life*, March 13, 1970 (as "A Piece of Work for Now and Doomsday").
On the Morning After the Sixties. *Life*, June 5, 1970 (as "A Generation Not for Barricades").
Quiet Days in Malibu. *Esquire*, April 1976 (as "Watching the Sea at Zuma HQ"); *Esquire*, June 1976 (as "The Man in a Greenhouse of Orchids").

Simon & Schuster published *The White Album* on June 19, 1979. Earlier that month, on June 4, the book's title essay appeared for the first time in its entirety in *New West*, as "The White Album: A Chronicle of Survival in the Sixties." The text of *The White Album* in the present volume is that of the Simon & Schuster first printing.

This volume presents the texts of the original printings chosen for inclusion here, but it does not attempt to reproduce features of their design and layout. The texts are presented without change, except for the correction of typographical errors. Spelling, punctuation, and capitalization are often expressive features and they are not altered, even when inconsistent or irregular. The following is a list of errors corrected, cited by page and line number: 31.23–24, inadmissable; 50.3, Katherine; 63.10, monogramed; 67.23, loss.'"; 146.9, The would; 165.10, had virus; 228.12, twenty-four-old; 237.4, barbituates; 257.19, Ghandian,; 264.3, Ghandi; 302.20, he says; 329.30, Minelli; 341.4, Western; 361.25, eightteen; 396.29 (and *passim*), crap; 550.6, five-inches; 559.6, be-beneath; 596.26, Marighela; 631.18, ninety-two-years; 633.15, all, Leonard; 679.19, game The; 753.10, *Bert*; 764.25, *Army. 45;*; 788.18, place; 794.12, wall,; 811.27, now; 848.5, greal; 862.18, Mankiewicz,; 871.24, the the; 905.16, seemd; 905.37, in Taipei.

Notes

In the notes below, the reference numbers denote page and line of this volume (the line count includes chapter headings but not blank lines). Biblical quotations are keyed to the King James Version, and references to Shakespeare to *The Riverside Shakespeare*, ed. G. Blakemore Evans (Boston: Houghton Mifflin, 1974). For further information about Didion's life and works, and references to other studies, see Tracy Daugherty, *The Last Love Song: A Biography of Joan Didion* (New York: St. Martin's Press, 2015); Sharon Felton, ed., *The Critical Response to Joan Didion* (Westport, Conn.: Greenwood Publishing, 1993); Ellen G. Friedman, ed., *Joan Didion: Essays & Conversations* (Princeton, NJ: Ontario Review Press, 1984); Mark Royden Winchell, *Joan Didion* (Boston: Twayne, 1980).

RUN RIVER

3.1–6 "All night . . . LOWELL] From "Man and Wife" by Robert Lowell (1917–1977), first collected in *Life Studies* (1959).

9.7–8 Columbus Iselin or Mad Dog Coll] Iselin (1851–1933) was a financier and philanthropist prominent in Gilded Age New York, and Vincent "Mad Dog" Coll (1908–1932) a New York mobster and hitman.

9.34 the Senator] Italianate hotel across the street from the California State Capitol in Sacramento that served as an unofficial hub for state political life from its opening in 1924.

11.10 Ivar Kreuger] Swedish industrialist (1880–1932) known as "the Match King."

13.23 T-Bird] Ford Thunderbird, a luxury car model introduced in 1955.

16.35–36 *we will . . . but kisses.*] From "Blue Room," song from the 1926 musical *The Girl Friend* by Richard Rodgers (1902–1979) and Lorenz Hart (1895–1943).

18.36 *Willows whiten, aspen quiver*] From "The Lady of Shalott" by Alfred, Lord Tennyson (1809–1892), first published in 1833.

21.31 *Holiday* magazine] American travel magazine published from 1946 to 1977.

25.22 *Pity her simplicity . . . Thee.*] See "Gentle Jesus, Meek and Mild," a hymn by Charles Wesley (1707–1788).

25.33 chemin de fer] A version of the casino card game baccarat.

25.34 neither the C.I.D. . . . Sureté] Neither the Criminal Investigation Division of the United States Army nor the French National Police.

34.24–25 Jean Harlow] Harlow (1911–1937), a Hollywood movie star of the 1930s, was sometimes described as "the Blonde Bombshell."

37.4 *Of Thee I Sing*] Broadway musical with score and lyrics by George and Ira Gershwin and book by George S. Kaufman and Morrie Ryskind. It opened in 1931, and the following year became the first musical to win the Pulitzer Prize for Drama.

38.2 Luchow's.] Restaurant located in the East Village from 1882 to 1983.

38.23 Sutter Club] Exclusive Sacramento social club founded in 1889.

39.4–5 *Progress and Poverty* . . . Henry George] 1879 best seller that argues in favor of a land value tax as the solution to poverty. Its author, Henry George (1839–1897), was an American economist and political philosopher.

39.31–32 Culbert Olson's California] Olson (1876–1962), a Democratic politician, served as governor of California from 1939 to 1943.

39.39–40 Dr. Townsend . . . Sheridan Downey."] Francis Townsend (1867–1960) had proposed the "Townsend Plan," an old-age pension scheme, in 1933; Downey (1884–1961), elected U.S. senator from California in 1938, published *Why I Believe in the Townsend Plan* in 1936.

40.3 Ham and Eggs.] A movement promoting old-age pension reform, on the ballot in California in 1938 and 1939.

40.6 "We Are Climbing Jacob's Ladder,"] A traditional African American spiritual.

40.34 a Mother Hubbard] A loose-fitting, long-sleeved, high-necked dress.

40.35–36 Aimee Semple McPherson] McPherson (1890–1944), a Canadian American Pentecostal evangelist, has been described as "the first modern celebrity preacher."

43.13 Russ Building] Neo-Gothic office building, completed in 1927 and until 1964 the tallest structure in San Francisco.

45.18 Harry Bridges] Australian-born labor leader (1901–1990) who founded the International Longshore and Warehouse Union (ILWU) in 1937.

45.30 Eumenides] In Greek mythology, the Eumenides, Erinyes, or Furies were the deities of vengeance.

46.4 *In Dubious Battle*] 1936 novel by John Steinbeck (1902–1968) about a California fruit-picker's strike.

46.7 Upton Sinclair and EPIC] Sinclair (1878–1968), a prolific author whose muckraking novel *The Jungle* (1906) helped precipitate the passage of the Pure Food and Drug Act, moved to California in the 1920s and ran as a Socialist for Congress and for California governor. In 1934, he won the Democratic gubernatorial nomination. His platform, End Poverty in California, or EPIC, offered programs and policies intended to help mitigate poverty and unemployment at the height of the Depression, and influenced the federal Works Progress Administration. As a candidate, Sinclair was targeted by attacks from Hollywood (the studios made propaganda films to undermine his candidacy), as well as the *Los Angeles Times* and the *San Francisco Examiner*. He lost the general election to Republican Frank Merriam by more than 350,000 votes.

48.34 Madame Chaing Kai-shek] Soong Mei-ling (1897–2003), First Lady of the Republic of China from 1948 to 1975.

49.34 Native Sons of the Golden West] Fraternal organization founded in San Francisco in 1875, to celebrate the legacy of the Gold Rush; its membership was limited to native-born Californians.

50.3–4 Katharine Cornell . . . Flush] Cornell (1893–1974) played English poet Elizabeth Barrett (1806–1861) in *The Barretts of Wimpole Street*, which opened on Broadway in 1931 and was revived in 1935 and 1945.

50.39 *The Anatomy of Melancholy*] A 1621 treatise on melancholia by Robert Burton (1577–1640), an English cleric and scholar, widely considered one of the masterpieces of English literature.

62.7–8 Dr. Grantly Dick-Read.] British obstetrician (1890–1959) and author of *Natural Childbirth* (1933).

63.5 the Lunts] Alfred Lunt (1892–1977) and his wife Lynne Fontanne (1887–1983), who acted together in more than twenty plays.

66.10 Giant Orange] Chain of California roadside juice stands, founded in 1926 by Frank E. Pohl (1880–1961).

70.9–10 *By the rivers of Babylon . . . down*] See Psalms 137.1.

72.18–20 *A Farewell* . . . Lieutenant Henry.] Frederic Henry, protagonist of Ernest Hemingway's 1929 novel *A Farewell to Arms*.

78.26–27 *For a thousand years . . . watch in the night*] See Psalms 90:4.

82.1 John Sutter] Swiss pioneer (1803–1880) who in 1839 established the colony Nueva Helvetia, later known as Sutter's Fort, in the Mexican province of Alta California, near what is now downtown Sacramento.

82.5–6 Donner-Reed crossing] In the winter of 1846–47, a wagon train on the way to California from Missouri became snowbound in the Sierra Nevada; only forty-eight of the party's original eighty-seven members survived to be rescued, some having resorted to cannibalism.

83.20–21 Alice Lee Grosjean . . . Long Administration] Huey Long (1893–1935), governor of Louisiana from 1928 to 1932, appointed his private secretary and rumored girlfriend Grosjean (1905–1994) to the position of secretary of state in 1930; she subsequently served as supervisor of accounts.

83.33 V-Mail."] Short for Victory Mail, a Second World War mail system in which letters were transmitted on microfilm and printed on arrival.

86.15–16 the International Workers of the World] Labor union, founded in Chicago on 1905 by, among others, William (Big Bill) Haywood, Mary Harris Jones (Mother Jones), and Eugene V. Debs. Its members were known as "Wobblies."

86.18–22 Tom Mooney's . . . Preparedness Day Parade bombing] Mooney (1882–1942), a labor activist, was convicted and sentenced to death for a bombing in San Francisco on July 22, 1916, during a parade marking preparations for America's entry into World War I. His sentence commuted at the request of President Woodrow Wilson, he spent twenty-two years in prison and in 1939 was pardoned by California governor Cuthbert Olson.

86.25 1913 Wheatland Riot] Confrontation on August 3, 1913, between fieldworkers, affiliated with the IWW, and hops farmer Ralph H. Durst (1865–1938) in California's Central Valley. Four people were killed, including two pickers, Deputy Sheriff Eugene Riordan, and Yuba County district attorney Edward Manwell.

89.11 "I Spoke to Jefferson at Guadalcanal,"] Song from the 1944 film *Follow the Boys*, with music by Lou Singer (1912–1966) and lyrics by Hy Zaret (1919–2007).

92.9 zoot-suiters] The zoot suit, a loose-fitting men's suit style popular in the jitterbug scene, was deemed "unpatriotic" by the War Production Board in 1942 for its excessive use of wool. In the Zoot Suit Riots of June 1943, white soldiers and civilians in Los Angeles fought with Mexican American and other nonwhite "zoot suiters."

92.22 *roman de la rose.*] See *Le Roman de la Rose*, a thirteenth-century French poem about courtly love.

94.11 OPA.] The Office of Price Administration, which regulated supplies and prices of sugar and other goods during the Second World War.

97.28 Harold Ickes] Ickes (1874–1952) served as secretary of the interior from 1933 to 1946 and directed the Public Works Administration.

103.23 Charles Addams] American cartoonist (1912–1988) known for his macabre characters.

114.3 Elizabeth Taylor in *National Velvet*] Taylor (1932–2011), then twelve years old, starred in the equestrian film *National Velvet* in 1944.

116.2 *Oklahoma!*] 1943 musical by Richard Rodgers (1902–1979) and Oscar Hammerstein II (1895–1960), adapted for film in 1955.

120.13 Lucky Lager] American beer, introduced in 1934 by the General Brewing Company of San Francisco. Throughout the 1950s, it was among the most popular beers in the American West.

128.24 Bruce Barton and Albert Lasker] Barton (1886–1967) and Lasker (1880–1952) were both advertising executives.

128.32 "Irium."] A neologism for sodium lauryl sulfate, created to sell Pepsodent toothpaste.

131.5–7 *Give me land . . . Don't fence me in*] From "Don't Fence Me In," a 1934 popular song by Cole Porter (1891–1964) and Robert Fletcher (1885–1972).

132.22 John C. Frémont] American explorer and soldier (1813–1890) who on January 13, 1847, accepted the surrender of Mexican governor Pio Pico and signed the Treaty of Cahuenga, effectively ending the Mexican-American War. He briefly served as military governor of California and was the first United States senator from California.

134.2–3 Will Semple Green] California pioneer and publisher (1832–1905) who arrived in San Francisco during the Gold Rush, and founded the town of Colusa. In 1863, he established the Sacramento Valley Irrigation Company.

135.26 *Winterset*] 1935 verse drama by Maxwell Anderson (1888–1959); it ran for 195 performances on Broadway.

136.2 the Tenney Committee] Officially known as the California Senate Fact-finding Subcommittee on Un-American Activities, the Tenney Committee, chaired by Republican state senator Jack Tenney from 1941 to 1949, investigated alleged communists in the state.

151.4 Lloyd Warner?] See *The Status System of a Modern Community* (1942) by American anthropologist W. Lloyd Warner (1898–1970).

152.13 Jinx Falkenburg] American actress (1919–2003) who with her husband Tex McCrary (1910–2003) hosted talk shows, first on radio and beginning in 1947 on television.

153.33–34 Kukla, Fran, and Ollie.] Television show that aired from 1947 to 1957 featuring comedian Fran Allison (1907–1989) and puppets Kukla and Ollie.

157.7 Ernie Heckscher] Heckscher (1916–1996) led the Ernie Heckscher Orchestra, a society dance band based in San Francisco's Fairmont Hotel beginning in 1948.

161.22 Henry Kaiser] American industrialist and shipbuilder (1882–1967) who later established the Kaiser Foundation and Kaiser Permanente health care.

161.34 Crocker or Spreckels] Wealthy San Francisco families. Charles Crocker (1822–1888) was in charge of construction of the Central Pacific Railroad, and Claus Spreckels (1828–1908) completed the San Francisco and San Joaqin Valley Railway.

162.19 the *Lurline*] One of four ocean liners built by the Matson Line for travel between San Francisco and Honolulu. The ship made its first voyage in 1932.

164.1-2 *Above thy deep . . . go by.*] From "O Little Town of Bethlehem," a Christmas carol written in 1868 by Phillips Brooks (1835–1893).

189.17 Calavo trust] The California Avocado Growers Exchange, an agricultural cooperative, became "Calavo Growers of California" in 1927.

194.36 Duke Snider] Professional baseball player (1926–2011) who played for the Dodgers from 1947 to 1962.

195.13 Idlewild] Original name of John F. Kennedy International Airport in Jamaica, Queens.

212.6–7 *Drive far away . . . peace bestow.*] From the ninth-century hymn "Veni Creator Spiritus," as translated in the 1840s by Edward Caswell (1814–1878).

SLOUCHING TOWARDS BETHLEHEM

225.29 *Double Indemnity*] Crime novel by James M. Cain (1892–1977) first serialized in *Liberty* magazine in 1936 and adapted for the screen in 1944, about an unhappy wife who lures an insurance salesman into helping her to kill her husband for the money on the policy.

239.37 Stan Laurel's death] Laurel, of the comic duo Laurel and Hardy, died at seventy-four on February 23, 1965.

243.19–20 *War of the Wildcats*] 1943 American Western film starring John Wayne and Martha Scott and directed by Albert S. Rogell.

245.4–6 *Out where . . . West begins.*] See "Out Where the West Begins," a poem by Arthur Chapman (1873–1935) first published in 1917.

245.19 Henry Hathaway] Hathaway (1898–1985), a director of films including *The Sons of Katie Elder* (1965) and *True Grit* (1969), specialized in Westerns.

245.21 Hal Wallis] Wallis (1898–1986) produced films including *Little Caesar* (1931), *Casablanca* (1942), and *Barefoot in the Park* (1967).

245.34 Mack Gray] American actor (1905–1981).

247.9 Merle Oberon Pagliai] Actress Merle Oberon (1911–1979), nominated for an Academy Award for her performance in *The Dark Angel* (1935), lived in Mexico after her marriage to industrialist Bruno Pagliai in 1957.

248.2 Mike Mazurki] American actor and professional wrestler (1907–1990).

248.19 Hedda Hopper] Hopper (1885–1966) wrote a Hollywood gossip column from 1938 until her death in 1966.

248.30 William S. Hart] Hart (1864–1946) starred in many silent-era Westerns.

249.4 the Ringo Kid] Wayne's character in the 1939 John Ford Western *Stagecoach.*

251.27–28 "The Red River Valley" . . . *The High and the Mighty*] "The Red River Valley," a nineteenth-century cowboy song, was first recorded in the 1920s and has subsequently been performed by Woody Guthrie, Bing Crosby, Connie Francis, and others. Dimitri Tiomkin (1894–1979) composed the theme music for *The High and the Mighty*, a 1954 aviation adventure in which Wayne starred, and Ned Washington (1901–1976) wrote the lyrics; they received an Academy Award nomination for the title song.

254.11 *The Bostonians*] 1886 novel by Henry James (1843–1916) about the romance between the conservative Basil Ransom and the younger, progressive suffragette Verena Tarrant.

254.20 "House of the Rising Sun"] Traditional folk song, dating from the beginning of the twentieth century, about a New Orleans house of prostitution.

255.5–6 Child ballads . . . Mary Hamilton?"] A group of traditional ballads collected by Francis James Child (1825–1896) and published in five volumes as *The English and Scottish Popular Ballads* (1882–98). "Mary Hamilton," a sixteenth-century Scottish ballad recorded by Baez in 1960, is Child #173.

256.3 the Rima . . . deer.] Heroine of the novel *Green Mansions: A Romance of the Tropical Forest* (1904) by W. H. Hudson (1841–1922).

257.4–5 Vietnam Day Committee . . . Hell's Angels] On October 15, 1965, an antiwar march organized by the Vietnam Day Committee in Berkeley was met at the Oakland-Berkeley line by police and also by members of the Hell's Angels motorcycle gang, who attacked the marchers for being un-American. With another march scheduled for November 20, poet Allen Ginsberg (1926–1997) visited Angel leader Sonny Barger (born 1938) to broker a peace, leading the Hell's Angels to announce that they would neither attend the march nor oppose the marchers.

257.17 A.E.C.] The United States Atomic Energy Commission.

257.18 Canada-to-Cuba march] The Quebec-Washington-Guantánamo Walk for Peace, sponsored by the Committee for Nonviolent Action, departed from Quebec City on May 26, 1963.

259.26–27 Adam Powell . . . King] Unlike activists Bayard Rustin (1912–1987), James Farmer (1920–1999), and Martin Luther King Jr. (1929–1968), Adam Clayton Powell Jr. (1908–1972) served in the House of Representatives, to which he was elected from Harlem in 1945.

265.18 Gus Hall] Labor leader (1910–2000) and chairman of the Communist Party USA from 1951 to 1991. He was a four-time party nominee for President of the United States.

265.20 H. Rap Brown] Brown (b. 1943) served as chairman of the Student Nonviolent Coordinating Committee (SNCC) in 1967 and 1968.

269.27 *The Big Sleep*] 1939 crime novel by Raymond Chandler (1888–1959), the first to feature his detective hero Philip Marlowe.

272.2–3 Shoeless Joe Jackson . . . *are fallen.*] Jackson (1887–1951), a star player for the Chicago White Sox, was banned from baseball in 1920 for alleged involvement in the Black Sox scandal, in which eight Chicago players conspired to lose the 1919 World Series to the Cincinnati Reds. Harding (1865–1923), the twenty-ninth president of the United States, died halfway through his term of office; his administration was beset by scandals, most significantly the Teapot Dome scandal.

272.4–5 Charles Lindbergh . . . *and damned.*] Lindbergh (1902–1974), who made the first solo, nonstop transatlantic airplane flight (from New York to Paris) in 1927, suffered the kidnapping and murder of his baby son in 1932. Scott (1895–1940) and Zelda Fitzgerald (1900–1948), who married in 1920 and became Jazz Age celebrities, both died young. Monroe (1926–1962), a movie star, died of a barbiturate overdose at age thirty-six.

272.21–31 Lionel Trilling . . . great literary way."] See Trilling's essay "The Function of the Little Magazine," collected in *The Liberal Imagination: Essays on Literature and Society* (1950).

274.31 Bishop James Pike] Pike (1913–1969) served as Episcopal bishop of California from 1958 to 1966; see Didion's essay "James Pike, American" on pages 781–86 of the present volume.

274.37–275.1 Bennett Cerf . . . Paul Hoffman] Cerf (1898–1971) cofounded Random House in 1927; Hoffman (1891–1974), an automobile industry executive, led the agency implementing the Marshall Plan from 1948 to 1950, the Ford Foundation from 1950 to 1953, and the United Nations Development Program from 1966 to 1972.

276.23 Couéism] A psychotherapeutic method based on optimistic autosuggestion, introduced by French psychologist Emile Coué (1857–1926).

280.4 baby Crosbys.] On May 4, 1958, Dennis Crosby (1934–1991), son of actor and singer Bing Crosby (1903–1977), married showgirl Pat Sheehan (1931–2006) at a Las Vegas wedding chapel, in between her performances at the Tropicana hotel. Sheehan had previously dated the father, and news of the wedding was widely reported.

280.9 *Miami Syndicate.*"] No film of this title is known to have been made. Didion may be remembering *The Miami Story* (1954), in which Miami officials enlist a former gangster to fight the city's largest crime syndicate.

280.26 Lohengrin.] 1850 opera by Richard Wagner (1813–1883).

288.8 Officer Krupke] A beat cop who confronts street gangs in the 1957 Broadway musical *West Side Story.*

290.9 STP] "Serenity, Tranquility, and Peace," an amphetamine.

292.6 VISTA] Volunteers in Service to America, a federal antipoverty program established in 1964.

292.18 Diggers] San Francisco–based street theater group founded by, among others, Peter Berg (1937–2011), Emmett Grogan (1942–1978), and Peter Coyote (b. 1941). The group grew out of the San Francisco Mime Troupe and took its name from the original English Diggers of the seventeenth century, a utopian anarchist collective.

293.2 cybernated] Controlled by a computer or electronic system.

293.29 mikes] Micrograms.

294.10–13 *Paranoia strikes deep . . .* sings] Lyrics from the 1966 song "For What It's Worth," written and sung by Stephen Stills (b. 1945) and the folk-rock band Buffalo Springfield. The song was inspired by the Sunset Strip riots of late 1966, in which demonstrators gathered to protest the imposition of a curfew on music clubs in West Hollywood.

294.25–26 Big Brother and the Holding Company] Rock band formed in San Francisco in 1965. Its classic lineup included Janis Joplin (1943–1970), James Gurley (1939–2009), Sam Andrew (1941–2015), Peter Albin (b. 1944), and Dave Getz (b. 1940). The band played a central role in the San Francisco psychedelic rock scene, along with groups such as the Grateful Dead and Jefferson Airplane.

295.4 the Avalon Ballroom] San Francisco music venue founded by Chet Helms (1942–2005) of Family Dog Productions; it was open from 1966 to 1969 and hosted many of the major groups of the era, including The Doors, the Grateful Dead, and the Paul Butterfield Blues Band.

298.16 *Quicksilver Messenger Service*] American rock band formed in 1965 in San Francisco. Its members included Dino Valenti (1937–1994), John Cipollina (1943–1989), Greg Elmore (b. 1946), David Freiberg (b. 1938), and Gary Duncan (1946–2019).

298.17 Herb Caen's column] Caen (1916–1997) wrote a daily column for the *San Francisco Chronicle* from 1938 until his retirement in 1990, interrupted only by his service during the Second World War and an eight-year position at the *San Francisco Examiner* during the 1950s.

301.1–4 *No milk today . . . dreams*] From "No Milk Today," a 1966 song written by Graham Gouldman (born 1946), and performed by the British pop group Herman's Hermits.

301.38 nothin'-says-lovin'-like-something-from-the-oven] From a Pillsbury Company advertising jingle introduced in 1957.

302.1 the Feminine Mystique] A phrase coined by Betty Friedan (1921–2006) in her 1963 book of the same title to describe an ideal of femininity to which postwar women were pressured to conform.

302.21 Job's Daughters] A Masonic-affiliated girls' organization.

304.1 Jook Savages] California artist collective, including psychedelic poster designer Rick Griffin (1944–1991), that relocated from Southern California to San Francisco in 1966.

304.21 Mr. O] Augustus Owsley Stanley III (1935–2011), also known as Owsley or Bear, became the sound engineer for the Grateful Dead in 1965; the same year, he began making LSD, and is said to have produced and distributed more than five million doses during the peak years of the counterculture.

304.24–25 *San Francisco Oracle*] Underground newspaper, founded by Allen Cohen (1940–2004) and based in Haight-Ashbury, that published from 1966 to 1968.

304.37 Laura Huxley's *You Are Not the Target.*] 1963 self-help book offering "recipes" for living.

305.36 Swami A.C. Bhaktivedanta] A. C. Bhaktivedanta Swami Prabhupada (1896–1977), an Indian spiritualist and teacher who founded the International Society for Krishna Consciousness (more commonly recognized as the Hare Krishna movement) in New York in 1966.

309.10–11 San Francisco Mime Troupe] Political street theater group founded in 1959 and active in the 1960s countercultural scene centered in the city's Haight-Ashbury district.

309.14 Hunter's Point riots] Civil disturbances that erupted in the Hunters Point neighborhood of San Francisco on September 27, 1966, after Matthew Johnson, an African American teenager, was shot and killed by white San Francisco police officer Alvin Johnson.

309.23–24 the way *Life* . . . Cuba] *Life* published "Inside Castro's Cuba," a photo-essay by Henri Cartier-Bresson (1908–2004), on March 15, 1963.

317.35–37 Bettina Aptheker . . . Stauffer] Aptheker (b. 1944) was active in the Free Speech Movement at the University of California at Berkeley while an undergraduate there in 1964. Benjamin Sonnenberg may refer to playwright and later literary magazine publisher Ben Sonnenberg (1936–2010) or to his father, Benjamin Sr. (1901–1978), a public relations executive. Staufer (1909–1991), a Swiss bandleader who escaped Nazi Germany for Acapulco, Mexico, married actress Hedy Lamarr (1914–2000) in 1951 and in 1956 opened an Acapulco resort.

318.9–10 "The Eighty-Yard Run."] Short story by Irwin Shaw (1913–1984), first published in *Esquire* in January 1941.

318.17–18 "You're the least . . . Jessica Mitford] See Mitford's "Maine Chance Diary," first published in *McCall's* in March 1966 as "The American Way of Aging."

321.2–3 Les Paul and Mary Ford . . . "How High the Moon"] A 1951 hit song for the husband-and-wife duo Les Paul (1915–2009) and Mary Ford

(1924–1977), "How High the Moon" was originally written for the 1940 Broadway revue *Two for the Show*.

321.24 Baby Pignatari] Brazilian entrepreneur and playboy Francisco Pignatari (1916–1977).

323.12 Raskolnikov] The protagonist of Fyodor Dostoevsky's 1867 novel *Crime and Punishment*, who believes his intelligence will allow him to commit murder and avoid punishment.

324.5 Rhett Butler told Scarlett O'Hara] Principal characters in the 1936 novel *Gone with the Wind* by Margaret Mitchell (1900–1949), adapted for film in 1939.

324.33 *Appointment in Samarra*] 1934 debut novel by John O'Hara (1905–1970).

324.35 *The Great Gatsby*] 1925 novel by F. Scott Fitzgerald (1896–1940).

325.24 Chinese Gordon] Charles George Gordon (1833–1855), a British army officer nicknamed "Chinese Gordon" for his leadership during the Taiping Rebellion; he gained further notoriety for his role in the siege of Khartoum in 1884–85.

326.38–39 Francesca . . . Annie Sullivan] Francesca da Rimini (1255–c. 1285) to her lover Paolo Malatesta (c. 1246–1285), contemporaries of Dante Alighieri who appear in his *Inferno*, and author and activist Keller (1880–1968) to her teacher and companion Sullivan (1866–1936), their relationship recounted in Keller's *The Story of My Life* (1903).

328.34 the Garden of Allah] Los Angeles hotel renowned as the residence of writers and celebrities including F. Scott Fitzgerald, Robert Benchley, and Frank Sinatra.

328.35 Thalberg Building] The administration building at the Metro-Goldwyn-Mayer studio in Culver City, dedicated in 1938 and named for production chief Irving Thalberg (1899–1936).

328.37 the Algonquin] Manhattan hotel that served as the meeting place during the 1920s of the Algonquin Round Table, a group of wits and writers including Robert Benchley (1889–1945), Alexander Woollcott (1887–1943), Dorothy Parker (1893–1967), and *New Yorker* editor Harold Ross (1892–1951).

329.2–3 Graybar Building] Manhattan headquarters until 1973 of Conde Nast publications including *Vanity Fair* and *Vogue*.

329.28 *Cahiers du Cinéma*] Influential French film magazine founded in Paris in 1951.

329.30–31 Vincente Minnelli . . . Nicholas Ray] Minnelli (1903–1986) is most often remembered for his movie musicals, including *Meet Me in St. Louis* (1944) and *Gigi* (1958), for which he won an Academy Award for Best

Director. Ray (1911–1979), who directed *In a Lonely Place* (1950) and *Rebel Without a Cause* (1955) among other films, was notably lauded by filmmakers of the French New Wave.

333.13–14 Charles Jackson short story] Jackson (1903–1968), most widely known for his novel *The Lost Weekend* (1944), published two collections of stories, *The Sunnier Side: Twelve Acadian Tales* (1950) and *Earthly Creatures* (1953).

335.4 The Jayhawkers] A group originally composed of thirty-six young men who left Illinois for California in 1849 as part of the Gold Rush.

336.31–33 Klaus Fuchs . . . Alfred Rosenberg] Fuchs (1911–1988), a German physicist who had worked at Los Alamos Laboratory, was convicted in 1950 of giving nuclear secrets to the Soviet Union. Members of the Nauvoo Legion, a Mormon militia, attacked an emigrant wagon train at Mountain Meadows, Utah, in September 1857, killing approximately 120 civilians. Rosenberg (1893–1946), a Nazi ideologue and government official, was sentenced to death at Nuremberg for crimes against humanity and later executed.

337.3 *The Deer Park*] Satirical novel (1955) by Norman Mailer (1923–2007).

337.11–16 "We must . . . our coercion."] See Trilling's essay "Manners, Morals, and the Novel," collected in *The Liberal Imagination* (1950).

340.15 *Long Day's Journey into Night*] 1956 play by Eugene O'Neill (1888–1953).

349.20–30 a W. S. Merwin poem . . . *the wide rivers.*] See Merwin's "After Some Years," first published in *Harper's* in June 1957.

351.6–13 "You look up . . . another road] See the opening paragraph of Warren's novel *All the King's Men* (1946), describing the fictional Highway 58 on the way to Mason City.

355.31–34 *Margaret, are you grieving . . . mourn for*] From "Spring and Fall," an 1880 poem by Gerard Manley Hopkins (1844–1889).

356.16–17 Doris Duke and Henry Kaiser] Duke (1912–1993), an heiress and philanthropist, built a mansion near Honolulu during the 1930s that she called Shangri-La; industrialist Kaiser (1882–1967) moved to Hawaii in 1955.

356.35 pikake] Hawaiian name for the fragrant climbing shrub *Jasminum sambac.*

361.27 taxi-dance places] Establishments at which male patrons paid for dances with their female partners, who worked on commission.

361.28–29 Lili St. Cyr and Tempest Storm] Stage names of striptease artists Willis Marie Van Schaack (1918–1999) and Annie Blanche Banks (b. 1928).

362.6–7 "King of the Road"] 1965 song written and recorded by Roger Miller (1936–1992). It reached number one on the U.S. country chart.

362.20 Webley Edwards] Edwards (1902–1977), a radio producer and correspondent, was the first announcer to report the attack on Pearl Harbor, which drew the United States into World War II.

364.23 Walter Dillingham] Born in Honolulu, Dillingham (1875–1963) founded the Hawaiian Dredging Company, inherited the presidency of the Oahu Railway and Land Company, and at various times served as director of many major Hawaiian companies.

364.37 a Nisei.] A second-generation Japanese immigrant.

365.3 I.L.W.U.] International Longshore and Warehouse Union.

365.9 Chinn Ho] Ho (1904–1987), an entrepreneur, had served as head of the Honolulu Stock Exchange, and advocated for Asian economic interests in Hawaii.

366.37 Tantalus.] Mount Tantalus, a peak overlooking Honolulu.

367.7–8 James Michener rhetoric] See Michener's 1959 novel *Hawaii.*

368.20–21 the Birdman and Mickey Cohen] Robert Stroud (1890–1963), an inmate at Alcatraz Federal Penitentiary from 1942 to 1959, was known as "the Birdman" for his ornithological research prior to his incarceration there; his story was fictionalized in the film *Birdman of Alcatraz* in 1962. Cohen (1913–1976), a Los Angeles gangster, was sent briefly to Alcatraz in 1961.

371.14–15 *où sont les croquet wickets d'antan*] Where are the croquet wickets of yesteryear (a play on the famous refrain of François Villon's "Ballade," c. 1461).

371.15–18 Edith Wharton . . . discretion."] Wharton spent her summers at Newport as a child and purchased a house there, Land's End, in 1893; James's essay "The Sense of Newport" was collected in 1907 in *The American Scene.*

372.10 *la cuesta encantada*] The enchanted hill.

372.21 Big Jim Fair] James Graham Fair (1831–1894), a wealthy mining engineer whose daughter Theresa Fair Oelrichs (1871–1926) commissioned Rosecliff.

372.22–23 Old Man Berwind] Edward Julius Berwind (1848–1936), coal baron for whom The Elms was built.

373.34 Brook Farm] Utopian community in West Roxbury, Massachusetts, established in 1841 and closed by 1847.

374.30 Graham Greene] Greene (1904–1991) wrote about Mexico in his travel narrative *The Lawless Roads* (1939) and in his novel *The Power and the Glory* (1940).

376.29–32 "On nights like that . . . can happen."] From "Red Wind," a 1938 novella by Raymond Chandler (1888–1959).

378.23–24 The city burning . . . *The Day of the Locust*] In West's 1939 novel, set designer Tod Hackett dreams of painting an enormous image called "The Burning of Los Angeles."

379.18 *The Man in the Gray Flannel Suit*] Best-selling 1955 novel by Sloan Wilson (1920–2003), often noted for its depiction of corporate conformity and discontent.

379.20–21 Hefner's . . . another area."] Hugh Hefner (1926–2017) founded *Playboy* magazine in 1953.

382.2–7 *How many . . . by candlelight.*] An English nursery rhyme.

382.23–25 a song on all the jukeboxes . . . used to be me,"] From "When the World Was Young," an English adaptation by Johnny Mercer (1909–1976) of the French "Chevalier de Paris"; it was first recorded by Peggy Lee (1920–2002) in 1953.

384.30 Hattie Carnegie] American fashion designer and entrepreneur (1886–1956).

386.15 Lester Lanin] Lanin (1907–2004), a bandleader, played at society events and expensive hotels.

386.26 Estoril] Resort town on the Portuguese Riviera.

388.37 Lowestoft] English porcelain manufacturer in operation from 1757 to 1802.

390.7 some Veblenesque gorge] In his *Theory of the Leisure Class* (1899), Norwegian-American sociologist Thorstein Veblen (1857–1929) introduced the phrase "conspicuous consumption."

PLAY IT AS IT LAYS

396.24 a Flying A] A gasoline station; the Tidewater Oil Company marketed its products under the Flying A brand from 1932 to 1966.

397.18–20 *cross the ocean . . . wet with rain*] From "You Belong to Me," a 1952 song written by Chilton Price (1913–2010), Pee Wee King (1914–2000), and Redd Stewart (1923–2003), first recorded by Joni James (b. 1930) and popularized by Jo Stafford (1917–2008).

397.33 Margaret Sullavan] Stage and film actress (1909–1960) nominated for an Academy Award for her performance in *Three Comrades* (1938).

408.5 La Costa] Upscale resort and spa in Carlsbad, California, opened in 1965.

409.29 Cedars."] Cedars-Sinai Medical Center, located in the Beverly Grove neighborhood of Los Angeles.

413.4 Baker] Small town in the Mojave Desert, about ninety miles southwest of Las Vegas, Nevada.

415.27 the Marmont] The Chateau Marmont, a Los Angeles hotel modeled on the Château d'Amboise in the Loire Valley, opened in 1929.

419.15 *Gaslight*] 1944 film directed by George Cukor (1899–1983), and starring Charles Boyer (1899–1978), Ingrid Bergman (1915–1982), and Joseph Cotton (1905–1994). The story of a woman married to a man who keeps manipulating her to question her sanity, it is the source of the term "gaslighting."

424.6 Chasen's] Beverly Hills restaurant noted for its celebrity clientele, open from 1936 to 1995.

437.19 Fremont Street] Major street in downtown Las Vegas, Nevada, on which several early casinos such as Binion's Horseshoe, Golden Nugget, and The Mint were located.

437.25 *How High the Moon* . . . Mary Ford] See note 321.2–3.

440.10 Methylphenidate hydrochloride] Central nervous system stimulant used to treat attention deficit disorder and narcolepsy.

444.6–7 *I Get a Kick Out of You*] Song written by Cole Porter (1891–1964) and originally performed by Ethel Merman (1908–1984) in the Broadway musical *Anything Goes* (1934).

448.10 Paula Raymond] American movie and television actress (1924–2003).

451.6–7 McCarran] McCarran International Airport, the main airport serving Las Vegas, Nevada.

456.6 St. John's] A Santa Monica hospital, now known as Providence St. John's Health Center.

459.11–13 Philip Dunne . . . Sidney Howard] Dunne (1908–1992) wrote Academy Award–nominated screenplays for *How Green Was My Valley* (1941) and *David and Bathsheba* (1951); in 1947 he testified in front of the House Un-American Activities Committee to protest the committee's methods. Howard (1891–1939), a playwright and screenwriter, received the 1925 Pulitzer Prize in Drama for *They Knew What They Wanted* (1924).

462.6 Schwab's] Schwab's Pharmacy, a Hollywood drugstore open from 1932 to 1983 and popular among actors and other film industry insiders.

462.8 Tujunga Wash] Thirteen-mile-long flood channel in Los Angeles County. In 1969, flooding in the Wash led to the loss of several homes.

465.29 Laszlo] Skincare regimen prescribed by the exclusive Ernö László Institute, established in 1927.

473.3 Ocho Rios] Resort town on the north coast of Jamaica.

473.13 D & C] Dilation and curettage, a surgical procedure sometimes performed after an abortion or miscarriage.

484.5 Abe Lipsey] Beverly Hills furrier (1903–1998) who catered to celebrities.

486.3 the *auteur* principle] Film theory, developed in the 1950s by the critics of *Cahiers du cinéma*, arguing that the director is the de facto "author" of a film.

495.11 *Midnight Hour*] "In the Midnight Hour," 1965 hit song by the American soul singer Wilson Pickett (1941–2006), cowritten by Pickett and guitarist Steve Cropper (born 1941).

503.10 Lurex] A trademarked metallic yarn.

505.32–33 *the only man . . . preacher man*] See "Son of a Preacher Man" (1968), a song written and composed by John Hurley (1941–1986) and Ronnie Wilkins (b. 1941) and first released by Dusty Springfield (1939–1999).

505.34–35 *rode a painted wheel . . . wheel spin.*] See "Spinning Wheel" (1968), a Blood, Sweat & Tears song written by David Clayton-Thomas (b. 1941).

510.7 Merck."] Pharmaceutical-grade cocaine produced by the German firm Merck since the 1860s.

512.25 *Dark Passage*] 1946 noir novel by David Goodis (1917–1967), filmed the following year by director Delmar Daves (1904–1977) in an adaptation starring Humphrey Bogart (1899–1957) and Lauren Bacall (1924–2014).

533.36–37 *King of the Road*] See note 362.6–7.

A BOOK OF COMMON PRAYER

541.18 paregorina] Brand name of a Spanish antidiarrheal medicine produced by Laboratorio Gálvez beginning in 1923.

541.30 anthropos] Greek: man, human being.

541.30–31 Kroeber . . . Lévi-Strauss] Alfred L. Kroeber (1876–1960), American anthropologist and longtime professor at the University of California at Berkeley, and Claude Lévi-Strauss (1908–2009), French anthropologist who taught at the University of São Paulo from 1935 to 1939.

551.6 framboesia] Also known as yaws, an infectious tropical disease characterized by raspberry-colored skin lesions.

551.19 "Mountain Greenery."] Song from the Broadway revue *Garrick Gaieties* (1925) by Richard Rodgers (1902–1979) and Lorenz Hart (1895–1943).

560.38–39 Valerian Rybar] Yugoslav-born interior designer (1919–1990) known for his opulent taste, wealthy clients, and extravagant parties.

566.28 Jacqueline de Ribes] French fashion designer (b. 1929).

575.12–13 *Sand-strewn caverns . . . asleep.*] From "The Forsaken Merman" by Matthew Arnold (1822–1888), first collected in *The Strayed Reveller, and Other Poems* (1849).

578.35 PSUC brigades and POUM militia] Rival Republican factions during the Spanish Civil War, the Partit Socialista Unificat de Catalunya and the Partido Obrero de Unificación Marxista.

579.26 an OAS] The Organization of American States, a "League of Nations of the Americas" founded in 1948.

590.38 Bohemian Grove] A private campground in Monte Rio, California, belonging to the exclusive, all-male Bohemian Club of San Francisco and the site of an annual summer gathering of prominent businessmen and politicians.

596.16 *latifundismo*] System of large landed estates in Central and South America.

596.25–26 a handbook . . . named Marighella.] See *Minimanual do Guerrilheiro Urbano* (1969) by Carlos Marighella (1911–1969), first translated into English in 1970 as *Minimanual of the Urban Guerrilla* (1969).

603.16 Hogarth] William Hogarth (1697–1764), English painter and satirist, known for his *Rake's Progress* series of moralist illustrations.

605.11 the Tupamaros] A Uruguayan Marxist guerilla organization, the Movimento de Liberación Nacional-Tupamaros, active in the late 1960s and early 1970s.

608.11 Gurdjieff] George Gurdjieff (1866–1949), Armenian mystic and philosopher.

611.1–2 "Puff the Magic Dragon"] Song written by Peter Yarrow (b. 1938) and Leonard Lipton (b. 1940) and released by Peter, Paul and Mary in 1963; it was subsequently associated with marijuana smoking.

613.2–9 'And the grave . . . living creature lie.'] From "Lullaby" (1937) by W. H. Auden (1907–1973).

614.5–6 a Clear] Within Scientology, the religion established by science fiction writer L. Ron Hubbard (1911–1986) in 1952, a "clear" is an individual who has attained an elevated spiritual state.

614.6–7 Elizabeth Arden] A cosmetics firm founded by Canadian American businesswoman Florence Nightingale Graham (1878–1966).

614.8 Edgar Cayce] American psychic (1877–1945) and founder in 1931 of the Association for Research and Enlightenment.

614.9 the Hunzas] Pakistani ethnic group to whom exceptional longevity has been attributed.

614.14–15 Days of Rage] Four days of often violent anti–Vietnam War demonstrations in Chicago in October 1969, organized by the Weather Underground faction of Students for a Democratic Society.

614.30 that long disease . . . Alexander Pope] See Pope's "Epistle to Dr. Arbuthnot," first published in 1735.

659.7–9 '*Sunset and evening star . . . out to sea!*'] From "Crossing the Bar," 1889 poem by Alfred Tennyson (1809–1892).

659.19 'Thanatopsis'] 1817 poem by William Cullen Bryant (1794–1878).

659.26 'Evangeline'] 1847 epic poem by Henry Wadsworth Longfellow (1807–1882).

660.38 'Snowbound'] "Snow-Bound: A Winter Idyl" (1866), by American poet John Greenleaf Whittier (1807–1892).

662.2–4 the song . . . *and the cows lay*—] "If Ever I Cease to Love," an 1871 British comic song with words and music by George Leybourne (1842–1884), popular during Mardi Gras since 1872.

662.32 Comus] The Mistick Krewe of Comus, a New Orleans secret society founded in 1856 to celebrate Mardi Gras.

681.31 "You're the Cream in My Coffee"] Song from the 1928 Broadway musical *Hold Everything!*

686.11 *déjeuner sur l'herbe*] Luncheon on the grass: an allusion to Édouard Manet's 1863 painting in which two women, one nude and the other scantily dressed, picnic in the woods with two clothed men.

690.35 *plato frío*] Cold dish.

701.2 *Prensa Latina*] The official Cuban state news agency, established in 1959.

701.4 Alberto Masferrer's *El Mínimum Vital*] Masferrer (1868–1932), a Salvadoran journalist, argues in this 1929 essay that all individuals have the right to a "vital minimum" or basic standard of living, including adequate food, water, clothing, shelter, employment, education, healthcare, and access to justice.

705.23 Arnold Wesker] English dramatist (1932–2016) and one of Britain's "angry young men" whose plays often depicted the everyday lives of working-class characters.

706.22 Fanon . . . Debray] Frantz Fanon (1925–1961), Martinican philosopher concerned with the negative effects of colonialism and the consequences of decolonization, and Régis Debray (b. 1940), French philosopher who studied radical social and political movements in Latin America.

THE WHITE ALBUM

746.1–2 Earl McGrath . . . Lois Wallace] McGrath (1931–2016) was a record executive and gallery owner, and Wallace (1940–2014) Didion's literary agent.

750.35 the first reports from My Lai.] The massacre of South Vietnamese civilians by U.S. troops on March 16, 1968, at My Lai, began to be reported in the American press in November 1969.

752.31–32 the Talmadge sisters] Norma Talmadge (1894–1957), Constance Talmadge (1898–1973), and Natalie Talmadge (1896–1969), silent movie stars whose careers faltered with the transition to talking pictures.

752.35 Synanon.] Established in 1958 as a drug rehabilitation program, Synanon became increasingly cultlike over the course of the 1960s and ultimately disbanded as the Church of Synanon.

753.16 *Fess Parker*] American movie and television actor (1924–2010) who starred in the series *Daniel Boone* from 1964 to 1970.

753.19 *Mr. Novarro*] Ramon Novarro (1899–1968), a Mexican-born actor of the silent film era most widely known for his lead role in *Ben-Hur* (1925).

755.30–32 "Do You Wanna Dance" . . . "Midnight Confessions."] The Beach Boys recorded "Do You Want to Dance," a 1958 hit by Bobby Freeman (1940–2017), as "Do You Wanna Dance?" in 1965; Bob Dylan (b. 1941) performed "Visions of Johanna" on his 1966 album *Blonde on Blonde*; "Midnight Confessions," written by Lou Josie (b. 1938), was a hit for The Grass Roots in 1968 after a version by The Ever-Green Blues failed to chart.

760.11 the Living Theater] Experimental theater troupe founded in New York in 1947 by Julian Beck (1925–1985) and Judith Malina (1926–2015).

760.13 Ultra Violet] Professional name of Isabelle Collin Dufresne (1935–2014), an artist and actress who worked for Salvador Dalí and became a central figure in Andy Warhol's Factory during the 1960s.

760.14 David Hockney] British painter, photographer, and collagist (b. 1937) who played a key role in the pop art movement of the 1960s and in works such as "A Bigger Splash" (1967) popularized a particular sunstruck image of Southern California.

760.23–25 John and Michelle . . . Chynna] John Phillips (1935–2001) and his wife Michelle Phillips (born 1944) were members of the Mamas & the Papas, a folk-rock group active from 1965 to 1968; their daughter Chynna was born on February 12, 1968.

762.19 Stokely Carmichael] Carmichael (1941–1998), who later took the name Kwame Ture, was a civil rights activist and former president of the Student Nonviolent Coordinating Committee who helped shape the Black Power movement.

763.34–36 *a quote from James Baldwin . . . rage."*] From a symposium presented over WBAI radio and published in *Cross Currents* (1961) as "The Negro in American Culture": "to be a Negro in this country and to be relatively conscious, is to be in a rage almost all the time."

764.31–32 a Scottsboro case . . . Scottsboro boy] The Scottsboro Boys were nine young African American men, wrongly accused and convicted of raping two white women in Alabama in 1931. The case became a cause célèbre and was appealed twice to the United States Supreme Court.

770.1 "*Eichmann*," Kay Boyle had screamed] See *The Long Walk at San Francisco State* (1970) by Kay Boyle (1902–1992).

770.6 Jesse Unruh] Unruh (1922–1987), a Democratic politician, served as speaker of the California State Assembly from September 1961 to January 1969.

770.15 Huntley-Brinkley] The nightly national television news team of Chet Huntley (1911–1974) and David Brinkley (1920–2003), whose broadcast aired on NBC from 1956 to 1970.

770.26 Evelyn Waugh] British satirist and author (1903–1966); his novels include *Scoop* (1938), *Brideshead Revisited* (1945), and *The Loved One* (1948).

770.39 SDS] Students for a Democratic Society, a student activist organization founded in 1960.

772.3 Flying Burritos] The Flying Burrito Brothers, a Los Angeles–based country-rock band founded in 1968 by Gram Parsons (1946–1973) and Chris Hillman (b. 1944).

776.36 *Stranger in a Strange Land*] 1961 science-fiction novel by Robert A. Heinlein (1907–1988).

781.8 Randolph and Catherine Hearst] Son (1915–2000) and daughter-in-law (1907–1999) of publishing magnate William Randolph Hearst (1863–1951), and parents of Patricia Hearst (b. 1954).

781.17 mite box] A small box distributed to receive charitable offerings.

782.20–21 Whittaker Chambers] Writer and editor (1901–1961) who in 1948 testified before the House Un-American Activities Committee, naming members of the Communist Party.

783.37–39 Dick Diver . . . Nicole] The principal characters in F. Scott Fitzgerald's novel *Tender Is the Night* (1934).

784.1 Barry Lyndon] Central character of *The Luck of Barry Lyndon* (1844), a novel by William Makepeace Thackeray (1811–1863) adapted for film as *Barry Lyndon* in 1975.

785.37 *Pacem in Terris.*] "Peace on Earth," an encyclical letter of Pope John XXIII issued on April 11, 1963.

785.37–38 the trial of the Catonsville Nine] On October 5–9, 1968, nine Catholic activists who had burned draft records from the Catonsville, Maryland, Selective Service office in an antiwar protest on May 17 were tried in federal court in Baltimore. Daniel Berrigan (1921–2016), one of the defendants, later published a verse play about the trial, *The Trial of the Catonsville Nine* (1970).

787.8 Owens River] A river in eastern California; its water rights were acquired by the city of Los Angeles in the first decade of the twentieth century and water was diverted by way of the Los Angeles Aqueduct, completed in 1913.

790.3–4 Sam Peckinpah's . . . truck] Director Sam Peckinpah (1925–1984) included the scene in his 1978 action film *Convoy.*

791.16–17 "The West begins . . . twenty inches."] See "The West: A Plundered Province" by historian Bernard DeVoto (1897–1955), first published in *Harper's* in August 1934.

791.28–38 a poem by Karl Shapiro . . . *the Nile.*] The final stanza of Shapiro's "California Winter," first published in *The New Yorker* on January 26, 1957.

795.22 Squeaky Fromme and Patricia Hearst] Lynette "Squeaky" Fromme (b. 1948), a member of the Manson Family, was sentenced to life in prison after attempting to assassinate President Gerald Ford on September 5, 1975, in Sacramento; Hearst (b. 1954), an heiress turned revolutionary, was arrested in San Francisco on September 18, 1975, and charged with bank robbery; she was sentenced to thirty-five years in prison the following year.

797.1 *Birds of America*] 1971 novel by American writer and critic Mary McCarthy (1912–1989) that addresses the social and political upheavals of the 1960s.

797.17 Mary McGrory] American newspaper columnist (1918–2004), principally associated with the *Washington Star*; she won the 1975 Pulitzer Prize for Commentary.

798.2–3 The Magic Christian] A luxury cruise ship in Terry Southern's 1959 satirical novel *The Magic Christian* and Joseph McGrath's 1969 film of the same title; Didion may refer to the protagonist of both works, Guy Grand, a billionaire who goes out of his way to push the bounds of the acceptable.

799.4 Horst] Horst P. Horst (1906–1999), a German American fashion photographer who worked for *Vogue* from 1931 to 1991.

807.5 the old Mocambo] Nightclub and celebrity hot spot located at 8588 Sunset Boulevard in West Hollywood, open from 1941 to 1958.

807.16 *fraises des bois*] Wild strawberries, *Fragaria vesca.*

807.33 Eugene McCarthy] McCarthy (1916–2005), a senator from Minnesota, ran an insurgent, antiwar campaign for the Democratic presidential nomination in 1968; his strong showing in the New Hampshire primary forced incumbent President Lyndon Baines Johnson to withdraw from the race.

807.35–36 Ben Shahn posters] Shahn (1898–1969), a painter and graphic artist, contributed a poster to the McCarthy campaign featuring a red, white, and blue dove and the word "PEACE."

808.5 Erich Fromm] Psychologist and sociologist (1900–1980) whose books included *Escape from Freedom* (1941) and *The Art of Loving* (1956).

808.9–11 a debate . . . encouraged racism.] On May 28, 1968, James Baldwin (1924–1987) moderated a debate between white writer William Styron (1925–2006) and black actor Ossie Davis (1917–2005) about Styron's controversial 1967 novel *The Confessions of Nat Turner*; Davis ultimately succeeded in his effort to halt a movie based on the novel.

808.39–40 Marlon Brando . . . San Quentin] Brando (1924–2004) was active in an international campaign to commute the death sentence of author and convicted kidnapper Caryl Chessman (1921–1960), and rallied crowds at San Quentin on May 2, 1960, the day of Chessman's execution.

809.4–5 Budd Schulberg . . . Writers' Workshop] Schulberg (1914–2009), known for his Hollywood novel *What Makes Sammy Run?* (1941) and for his 1954 *On the Waterfront* screenplay, organized a Writers' Workshop in Watts in September 1965, after six days of rioting there in August; writers who came out of the Workshop include Quincy Troupe (b. 1939) and Wanda Coleman (1946–2013), as well as the poetry performance group the Watts Prophets.

809.13 *Mr. Deeds Goes to Washington*] A conflation of the titles of two films directed by Frank Capra (1897–1991), *Mr. Deeds Goes to Town* (1936) and *Mr. Smith Goes to Washington* (1939).

812.10 Couéistic] See note 276.23.

819.32 a Kelly Girl] A temporary employee hired through Kelly Services, Inc., or its predecessors, or more generically any temporary employee.

820.3–4 the Troc] The Cafe Trocadero, a West Hollywood nightclub favored by celebrities and film stars and open from 1934 to 1947.

825.1 *The Women's Movement*] Before it appeared in *The White Album*, this essay was published on July 30, 1972, in *The New York Times Book Review*, which listed the following books as "the basis of Joan Didion's reflections on the women's movement": *The Second Sex* by Simone de Beauvoir; *Sexual Politics* by Kate Millett; *The Female Eunuch* by Germaine Greer; *The Prisoner of Sex* by Norman Mailer; *Feminism: The Essential Historical Writings*, edited by Miriam Schneir; *The Silenced Majority* by Kirsten Amundsen; *Rebirth of Feminism* by Judith Hole and Ellen Levine; *Woman in a Sexist Society*, edited by Vivian Gornick and Barbara K. Moran; *Woman's Estate* by Juliet Mitchell; *A Young Woman's Guide to Liberation* by Karen De Crow; *The Dialectic of Sex: The Case for Feminist Revolution* by Shulamith Firestone; *Born Female* by Caroline Bird;

Open Secrets by Barbaralee Diamonstein; *Notes from the Second Year: Women's Liberation, Major Writings of the Radical Feminists*, ed. Shulamith Firestone and Anne Koedt; and *Notes from the Third Year: Women's Liberation, Major Writings of the Radical Feminists*, ed. Shulamith Firestone and Anne Koedt.

825.14–15 Shulamith Firestone] Pioneering second-wave feminist (1945–2012) who cofounded the group New York Radical Women in 1967.

826.22 Mary Wollstonecraft . . . Fuller] Wollstonecraft (1759–1797) was the author of *A Vindication of the Rights of Woman* (1792) and Fuller (1810–1850) of *Woman in the Nineteenth Century* (1845).

828.15 Ms. Scarlett overtones] See note 324.5.

828.36 the "click! . . . Jane O'Reilly] See O'Reilly's essay "The Housewife's Moment of Truth," first published in *Ms.* on December 20, 1971.

829.4–5 Lenin . . . a woman can do,"] See Lenin's essay "The Tasks of the Working Women's Movement in the Soviet Republic," first published in 1919.

830.38–831.2 one woman's account . . . *Sesame Street Songbook*."] See "Notes of a Recycled Housewife" by Jennifer Skolnik (b. 1940), published in the May 22, 1972, issue of *New York* magazine.

831.13–18 "Nobody ever so much . . . cherished beliefs."] See "How to Write Your Own Marriage Contract" by Susan Edmiston (b. 1940), in the December 20, 1971, issue of *New York* magazine.

831.20–27 A young woman . . . missing."] See note 830.38–831.2.

834.14 R. D. Laing] Scottish psychiatrist (1927–1989) associated with the antipsychiatry movement and known for his radical approach to mental illness.

837.4–5 Robert Penn Warren . . . convulsion of the world] See the final sentence of Warren's novel *All the King's Men* (1946).

838.2–4 "Where I was . . . book of paintings and words] See O'Keeffe's 1976 autobiography *Georgia O'Keeffe*.

838.6 Stieglitz] Alfred Stieglitz (1864–1946), O'Keeffe's husband.

839.5–9 one she liked . . . courage."] Alon Bement (1876–1954), with whom O'Keeffe studied.

846.11–13 *Victory* . . . *The Wild Palms*] Joseph Conrad (1857–1924) published his novel *Victory* in 1915; Henry James (1843–1916) his novel *The Wings of the Dove* in 1902; and William Faulkner (1897–1962) his novel *The Wild Palms* in 1939, the last of these reissued as *If I Forget Thee, Jerusalem* in 1990.

848.18 *Malolo*] Sister ship to the *Lurline*, built by the Matson Line for travel between Los Angeles, San Francisco, and Honolulu; it made its first voyage in 1927.

848.35 Dorothy Spreckels] Spreckels (1913–2000) was the daughter of San Francisco sugar magnate Adolph B. Spreckels (1857–1924).

848.36 Walter P. Chrysler, Jr.] Chrysler Jr. (1909–1988), an art collector, was the son of automobile manufacturer Walter Chrysler (1875–1940), who founded the Chrysler Corporation in 1925.

849.11 Duke Kahanamoku] Hawaiian swimmer (1890–1968) who won medals at the 1912, 1920, and 1924 Summer Olympics and who is widely regarded as the progenitor of modern surfing.

854.21–22 *From Here to Eternity*] 1951 debut novel by James Jones (1921–1977), set at a United States Army installation in Hawaii, the Schofield Barracks, in the lead-up to the attack on Pearl Harbor.

859.1 *In Hollywood*] Before it was collected in *The White Album*, this essay appeared in the March 22, 1973, issue of *The New York Review of Books*, which listed *Memo from David O. Selznick*, edited by Rudy Behlmer, and *Figures of Light: Film Criticism and Comment* by Stanley Kauffmann as books under review.

859.3 *The Last Tycoon*] Unfinished fifth novel by F. Scott Fitzgerald (1896–1940); left incomplete upon Fitzgerald's death, it was edited for publication by Fitzgerald's friend, the critic Edmund Wilson (1895–1972), and published in 1941.

859.22 *The Heartbreak Kid*] 1972 romantic comedy directed by Elaine May (b. 1932), with a screenplay by Neil Simon (1927–2018).

859.29 Quentin Bell's *Virginia Woolf*] Bell's *Virginia Woolf: A Biography* was published in two volumes in June and October 1972.

860.14–15 the Preminger picture we were writing] Didion and her husband John Gregory Dunne worked on the screenplay of Preminger's *Such Good Friends* (1971), ultimately completed by Elaine May credited pseudonymously to Esther Dale.

862.37 *The Poseidon Adventure*] 1972 adventure movie produced by Irwin Allen (1916–1991) and directed by Ronald Neame (1911–2010), based on the 1969 Paul Gallico (1897–1976) novel of the same title, about an ocean liner capsized by a tidal wave. The cast included Gene Hackman (b. 1930), Shelley Winters (1920–2006), Leslie Nielsen (1926–2010), and Ernest Borgnine (1917–2012).

862.38 Adolph "Papa" Zukor] American film pioneer (1873–1976) and founder of Paramount Pictures.

863.9–10 Dominique-Sanda-type] French actress (b. 1948) who made her film debut in *Une femme douce* (1968).

863.22 *Easy Rider*'s grosses] Produced for under $400,000, the independent film *Easy Rider* (1969) went on to gross over $60,000,000.

863.24–26 NABET . . . IATSE] The National Association of Broadcast Employees and Technicians, and the International Alliance of Theatrical Stage Employees.

864.38 Sergius O'Shaugnessy] Protagonist of the Hollywood novel *The Deer Park* (1955) by Norman Mailer (1923–2007).

865.8 Jack Valenti] Valenti (1921–2007) served as president of the Motion Picture Association of America from 1966 until 2004.

865.23 David O. Selznick] As an independent producer with Selznick International Pictures, Selznick (1902–1965) won back-to-back Academy Awards for Best Picture for *Gone With the Wind* (1939) and *Rebecca* (1940).

866.11 Pauline Kael] Film critic (1919–2001) who wrote for *The New Yorker* from 1967 to 1991.

866.24 *Playhouse 90*] Prestigious CBS anthology drama series produced from 1956 to 1961.

866.37 Joseph Welch] Welch (1890–1960), an attorney, was famous for confronting Senator Joseph McCarthy (1908–1957) of Wisconsin during the Army-McCarthy Hearings on June 9, 1954: "Have you no sense of decency, sir? At long last, have you left no sense of decency?" The incident is widely regarded as signaling the beginning of the end of the McCarthy era.

866.38 Louis Nizer] Prominent trial lawyer (1902–1994) and author of *The Implosion Conspiracy* (1972), an account of the trial of Julius and Ethel Rosenberg for espionage in 1951.

867.7 Lewis Mumford] Mumford (1895–1990), a historian and critic, won the National Book Award in Nonfiction for *The City in History* (1961).

868.6–8 Sophia Loren . . . Carlo Ponti] Ponti (1912–2007), producer of more than 100 films, including *La Strada* (1954), *Blowup* (1966), and *Zabriskie Point* (1970), was married to Sophia Loren (b. 1934) from 1957 until his death in 2007.

868.35–36 Graham Greene . . . sense of fun."] See Greene's essay "Memories of a Film Critic," first published in the 1958 *International Film Annual.*

875.21–22 Elizabeth Hardwick's . . . *Finland Station*] Hardwick's *Seduction and Betrayal* (1974) is a collection of criticism about women writers and female characters; Wilson's *To the Finland Station* (1940), a history of revolutionary socialism from the French Revolution to 1917.

877.9–10 Carl Bernstein] Bernstein (b. 1944) and his *Washington Post* colleague Bob Woodward (b. 1943) reported on the Watergate scandal beginning in June 1972 and in 1974 published *All the President's Men.*

877.20–2 Mike Nichols . . . bleakness."] In "Annie Takes Broadway" (*Newsweek*, May 2, 1977), Nichols (1931–2014) compares his musical *Annie* with other recent musical theater: "because of the nature of the world lately, either the music is small and bitty because there's no strong feeling, or if there is strong feeling it's anger or regret. I'm tired of lapidary bleakness."

877.23–24 rethinking the Sixties . . . Morris Dickstein] See Dickstein's *Gates of Eden: American Culture in the Sixties* (1977).

877.25–26 another look at the Fifties . . . Hilton Kramer] See Kramer's essay "Trashing the Fifties"—a response to Dickstein's *Gates of Eden*—published in *The New York Times Book Review* on April 10, 1977.

877.33 the sale of *The Thorn Birds* to paper] Avon Publishing purchased the paperback reprint rights to *The Thorn Birds*, a romance novel by Australian writer Collen McCullough (1937–2015), for the then-record sum of $1.9 million; the novel appeared in hardcover in April.

877.38 John Leonard] American cultural critic (1939–2008) who wrote a column for *The New York Times*, "Private Lives," from 1977 to 1980.

880.13 Irving Penn's studio] Penn (1917–2009), a fashion and portrait photographer who worked extensively for *Vogue*.

885.9 *medialunas*] Croissants.

885.16 Chibcha Indians] Indigenous society of more than 500,000 who lived in the valleys near what is now Bogotá, Colombia, destroyed by the arrival of the Spanish in the sixteenth century. Their economy was built on trade and agriculture, and gold was extensively used.

886.32–33 *Alto arrecife* . . . Pablo Neruda] See section VI of Neruda's 1947 poem "Alturas de Macchu Picchu."

887.36 Peronist] Populist and authoritarian in the manner of Juan Perón (1895–1974), president of Argentina from 1946 to 1955 and from 1973 until his death the following year.

888.5–6 Rip Torn, Norman Mailer, Ricky Leacock, Super 8.] Actor Rip Torn (1931–2019) and novelist Norman Mailer (1923–2007) famously brawled on camera during the filming of Mailer's *Maidstone* (1970). Leacock (1921–2011), a British documentary filmmaker, pioneered the use of handheld cameras and relatively inexpensive Super 8 film, introduced in 1965.

888.11 *cumbia*] Folkloric dance tradition of Colombia and Panama.

897.9 Lionel Trilling] American literary critic (1905–1975) known for his essay collection *The Liberal Imagination* (1950).

897.11 "Blue Room"] See note 16.35–36.

898.33–34 the central line of *Heart of Darkness* . . . postscript.] In Joseph Conrad's 1899 novella *Heart of Darkness*, narrator Charles Marlow quotes from a report written by Mr. Kurtz, the ivory trader, for the International Society for the Suppression of Savage Customs, to which Kurtz has added a postscript, "Exterminate all the brutes!"

Index

This book is set in 10 point ITC Galliard, a face designed for digital composition by Matthew Carter and based on the sixteenth-century face Granjon. The paper is acid-free lightweight opaque that will not turn yellow or brittle with age. The binding is sewn, which allows the book to open easily and lie flat. The binding board is covered in Brillianta, a woven rayon cloth made by Van Heek–Scholco Textielfabrieken, Holland.

Composition by Dianna Logan, Clearmont, MO.

Printing by Sheridan, Grand Rapids, MI.

Binding by Dekker Bookbinding, Wyoming, MI.

Designed by Bruce Campbell.